Also available

THE MAMMOTH BOOK OF
20TH CENTURY SCIENCE FICTION

VOLUME ONE

EDITED BY DAVID G. HARTWELL

ROBINSON
London

Constable & Robinson Ltd
3 The Lanchesters
162 Fulham Palace Road
London W6 9ER
www.constablerobinson.com

First published in the USA as part of *The Science Fiction Century*
by Tor Books, 1997

This edition first published in the UK by Robinson,
an imprint of Constable & Robinson Ltd, 2003

A copy of the British Library Cataloguing in
Publication data is available from the British Library

ISBN 1-84119-513-8

Printed and bound in the EU

10 9 8 7 6 5 4 3 2

Contents

Copyright Acknowledgments

Acknowledgments

*To Maron Waxman, Susan Ann Protter, Les Pockell, and
Kathryn Cramer, without whom this book would never
have been completed.*

I would like to acknowledge the significant presence of John W.
Campbell, Isaac Asimov, Robert A. Heinlein, and Arthur C. Clarke,
and all the other science fiction writers who are not reprinted in this
book. I used their work to support my argument for the consideration
of science fiction as a worthwhile literature in *The World Treasury of
Science Fiction*. I used many of them again to illuminate and uphold the
value of the hard SF tradition in *The Ascent of Wonder*. In this book, I
chose the work of other major writers, some of them less familiar, some
of them equally famous, so as not to allow my argument to get lost in
the particular aesthetic of SF that is so dominant in their work. But
their presence is here anyway, anyhow, even in the absence of
representative examples of their work.

Rooted as they are in the facts of contemporary life, the phantasies of even a second-rate writer of modern Science Fiction are incomparably richer, bolder, and stranger than the Utopian or Millennial imaginings of the past.

– ALDOUS HUXLEY

Science fiction is no more written for scientists than ghost stories are written for ghosts. Most frequently, the scientific dressing clothes fantasy. As fantasies are as meaningful as science, the phantasms of technology now fittingly embody our hopes and anxieties.

– BRIAN W. ALDISS

Introduction

Science fiction is a literature for people who value knowledge and who desire to understand how things work in the world and in the universe. In science fiction, knowledge is power and power is technology and technology is good and useful in improving the human condition. It is, by extension, a literature of empowerment. The lesson of the genre megatext – that body of genre literature that in aggregate embodies the standard plots, tropes, images, specialized diction, and clichés – is that one can solve problems through the application of knowledge of science and technology. By further extension, the SF megatext is an allegory of faith in science. Everyone knows there are science fiction addicts – I am one – and this is why: it expresses, represents and confirms faith in science and reason.

The literary history of the twentieth century in the US is significantly different to that of the UK in regard to science fiction. The tradition of H. G. Wells remained stronger, for longer, in the UK, and although many of the works in the Wells tradition (the Scientific Romance tradition delineated by Brian Stableford in his fine book, *Scientific Romance in Britain, 1890–1950*) prior to 1950 are remembered today only by literary historians, it was not until the late 1940s, after the Second World War, that American SF became the primary model for the genre outside of its own national boundaries. And as many critics have noted, there were and remained characteristic differences between American Science Fiction and British Scientific Romance even into and during the decades of international American dominance of the genre.

This has meant, among other things that the British tradition, while not acceptable to the Modernists from the beginning, was still a literary tradition that might aspire to high art, although it usually had other intentions.

This is clear in the resolution of the famous literary argument between H. G. Wells and Henry James at the start of the twentieth century. James, who was often referred to as Master by the modernist writers of the day, carried the literary high ground and Wells declared that he was not an artist but a journalist. Wells did not so much desire to dominate literature as to dominate reality, so he ceded the territory of literary art to James and the Modernists.

At the time of the first edition of *The Science Fiction Century*, I thought everybody knew about this and I was wrong. Brian Aldiss and John Clute remarked at a conference shortly after the original publication that there was no apparent evidence for my assertion that SF was generally anti-Modernist. I promised them both that I would get around to writing up some of the evidence, and this revised introduction is my first attempt to do so. On the face of it, I never intended my statement to hold entirely for British SF, which has a different, although still strained, relationship with Modernism than the US branch of the genre. And of course the New Wave of the 1960s stood for the injection of modernist literary techniques and the abandonment of genre attitudes. The influence of the New Wave has been dominant in the UK ever since, as it has not in the US.

The idea that modernist poetry is nonsense goes back a long way in SF. As early as the 1920s, at the very beginning of the fashion for Modernism in the USA, H. P. Lovecraft, a virulent anti-Modernist whose influence on SF writers in the 1930s and beyond is unquestionable, wrote a long parody of T. S. Eliot's *The Waste Land*, called 'Waste Paper', and never reconciled himself to the new attitudes of fashionable literature. This response extends at least into the 1980s – Lester del Rey and I had more than one discussion in which he maintained stoutly that contemporary poetry had died in the 1930s, with the triumph of modernist free verse. Del Rey remained an anti-Modernist to the end. So was John W. Campbell. So was Isaac Asimov. So is Orson Scott Card.

And from the 1920s to the late 1940s, one of the main voices raised outside the SF field in America against Modernism was that of the editor of the important little magazine, *Wings*, Stanton A. Coblentz, a minor poet and, coincidentally, a significant SF writer of the period. He is now more often remembered by graduate students and literary historians of twentieth-century American literature as the loser who led the vocal opposition than he is remembered as an SF writer or by SF readers. Coblentz was still mentioned in American literature graduate school courses at Columbia University in the late 1960s when I studied there.

Some of the attitudes of the field toward Modernism in the 1950s are apparent in the fiction. For example in the fantasy story 'Stickney and the Critics' by Mildred Clingerman (F&SF, Feb. 1953), the dead poet Stickney (and it is not unlikely that Clingerman is alluding to the modernist poet Trumball Stickney) has critics that interpret deep metaphors into his poetry, when in fact it is has literal correspondences. While of course this is an attack on modernist criticism, not necessarily the writing itself, the clear implication is that the writing would be nonsense if it didn't have those literal referents. So I see the story, which was anthologized by Judith Merril, among others, as clearly anti-Modernist.

However, there have been notable defenders of Modernism in the American SF field, Alfred Bester and James Blish it seems to me were among the most prominent from the 1940s until the 1960s advent of the New Wave. Bester left college in the late 1930s and famously bored some of the New York SF writers of the early 1940s with talk of the virtues of James Joyce. James Blish was an authentic Joyce scholar (he gave papers at academic conferences) but there is no noticeable influence of this in his science fiction or fantasy until perhaps, arguably, his late novel, *The Day After Judgment*. Bester got a job outside SF for almost a decade in the early 1940s and again for nearly fifteen years in the late 1950s, and James Blish moved to England in the mid-60s. This would have been more comfortable for these writers because the American SF scene was not in general hospitable to Modernism or modernist techniques until the 1970s.

The Milford Writing Workshops of the 1950s were an early injection of modernist ideas about writing into SF, and in my opinion were the seeds that germinated to form the American New Wave. In any case, by the middle of the 1960s the idea that an individual style was of value in SF, as well as in mainstream writing had caught hold, and since Modernism had lost most of its force and authority in high literary circles, over the next decade Modernism became merely a repository of techniques and attitudes which might be appropriated piecemeal by a science fiction writer. In particular the modernist idea that fiction is properly about the inner life of a character in relatively ordinary circumstances took hold for the first time in SF, and by the

1980s had become a common mode in the field, though certainly not universal.

However, a substantial body of SF even today is not devoted to the illumination of character but to the external circumstances of the story. Much SF is about what actions a character takes and what happens in strange and unusual circumstances, not primarily about how someone feels about it.

Nevertheless, the genre has been strengthened and enriched immeasurably in my opinion by the proliferation of possibilities in literary treatment, and by the aesthetic conflicts and arguments which have ensued. For instance, the Humanist versus Cyberpunk arguments of the middle 1980s (see Michael Swanwick's essay, 'A Users Guide to the Postmoderns' for coverage of that in medias res.).

Gregory Benford, a writer who has prominently appropriated chunks of modernist technique and attitude in the service of his SF, wrote in response,

> I believe you're fundamentally right about classical SF opposing modernism, but with the caution that one must not mistake fuddy-duddy reactionism for theoretical difference. Many, like Lester del Rey, opposed modernism because they opposed the entire literary culture, or didn't know any better. Their critiques were not profound, but visceral.
>
> Further, the customary choice of 'plain writing' because the landscapes of SF are already strange enough works only in a limited sense. The reaction of real people in such stories can have all the signatures of modernist modes, particularly in the rejection of a consensus epistemology. In Bester's narrative gyres we are swept along by people who themselves find their worlds wrenching. Conveying this requires more than the flat, clear prose of a Clarke or Niven – who nonetheless are stylists, too.

I quite agree with the second of Benford's paragraphs, but wish to say that Although Del Rey's critique could be mistaken for shallowness, I believe it was not. Lester del Rey was an articulate and intelligent polemicist who hung out with contemporary poets in New York City in the 1930s and '40s, (in somewhat the same circles as Theodore Sturgeon did) and did know about Modernism, although his particular critique was generally and globally anti-literary in later years, a part I believe of his decision circa 1970 to become a marketer to the non-literary popular culture of the mass market. His Del Rey

Books period is not continuous with his earlier personality or intellectual stance.

Orson Scott Card went through a graduate school programme in English Literature and has chosen to reject Modernism and its high art/low art distinctions by name, yet does not reject the entire literary culture – only that portion of it that maintains that SF is inherently second rate, if I understand him correctly.

Furthermore, a large portion of the discourse about Modernism has been encoded in the SF versus the mainstream arguments that have persisted since the late 1930s, in which Modernism has rarely been mentioned by name.

Having now written at some length about this subject, I return to the object of this anthology, and these stories that show much of what was present in the fiction from the beginning to the end of the century just gone. I would like to point out that *The Science Fiction Century* was conceived as a companion volume to an earlier large anthology, *The World Treasury of Science Fiction*, and the two were originally to be sold together. The writers and stories in the *World Treasury* were a kind of penumbra to this book, in which the selection of writers and stories was, in addition to other purposes, meant to complement the earlier compilation. This is why there is so little overlap in writers between the two huge books. Together, they form a representative selection of world SF in the twentieth century. Since the *World Treasury* is now out of print, and *The Science Fiction* Century is being re-published as two Mammoth volumes by Constable & Robinson, I tell you this to explain why some obvious representative stories by masters of SF are not in evidence here. You hold in your hands only one part of a much larger possible selection formed in the mind of this editor; a selection from a glorious and terrible century, filled with wonder for those with eyes to see.

David G. Hartwell,
Pleasantville, N.Y., 2003

Beam Us Home

JAMES TIPTREE, JR.

James Tiptree, Jr. was the pseudonym of Alice B. Sheldon (1915–87), an ex-employee of the CIA who became a psychologist and then, secretly, an SF writer. Unlike the pseudonymous Cordwainer Smith, a writer who remained silent and mysterious, Tiptree was vociferous, opinionated, passionate, and involved in the SF field. Thus it was a substantial shock to the social system of science fiction in the late 1970s when the Tiptree pseudonym was penetrated, when in the midst of a rising tide of feminist consciousness he was discovered to be a feminist she.

Tiptree made her essential impact with a continuing stream of powerful short stories. Many of her best stories appeared in her first four collections (*Ten Thousand Light Years from Home* [1973], *Warm Worlds and Otherwise* [1975], *Star Songs of an Old Primate* [1978], and *Out of the Everywhere and Other Extraordinary Visions* [1981]). Her two novels, *Up the Walls of the World* (1978) and *Brightness Falls from the Air* (1985), are underappreciated. Perhaps the shock of her suicide in 1987 has made it difficult for many readers to gain perspective on her later, darker stories.

The closest parallel to her work in impact, in attitude, in attention to craft and art, is Theodore Sturgeon's writing of the 1950s. Also like him, when she erred it was in the direction of too much sentiment. She was obsessed with the theme and the imagery of the alien biologically and emotionally. Yet at least one of her stories, "The Girl Who Was Plugged In" (1973, one of her several award-winners), is acknowledged by William Gibson as one of the sources of cyberpunk.

Tiptree continually challenged the idea of the coldness of the universe, portraying that coldness as a negative aspect of human character rather than an affect existing somehow in external reality – until her last stories. *Crown of Stars* (1988) gathers most of her final tales, suicide-filled and full of the idea of honorable death. She was a deeply moral writer, even when embracing death.

In the 1990s, friends and especially a younger generation of women SF writers have created an award in her memory, the annual James Tiptree, Jr., Award "for genderbending science fiction." A collection of her nonfiction pieces and a biography have been announced as forthcoming. This story, one of Tiptree's earliest, refers to the influence of a certain television show popular among the young in the 1960s, *Star Trek* (though the name is never mentioned in the text). Joanna Russ, the feminist critic and a correspondent of Tiptree's, sometimes tells this story aloud, and then weeps.

Hobie's parents might have seen the first signs if they had been watching about eight-thirty on Friday nights. But Hobie was the youngest of five active bright-normal kids. Who was to notice one more uproar around the TV?

A couple of years later, Hobie's Friday-night battles shifted to 10 p.m. and then his sisters got their own set. Hobie was growing fast then. In public he featured chiefly as a tanned streak on the tennis courts and a ninety-ninth percentile series of math grades. To his parents, Hobie featured as the one without problems. This was hard to avoid in a family that included a diabetic, a girl with an IQ of 185 and another with controllable petit mal, and a would-be ski star who spent most of his time in a cast. Hobie's own IQ was in the fortunate 140s, the range where you're superior enough to lead, but not too superior to be followed. He seemed perfectly satisfied with his communications with his parents, but he didn't use them much.

Not that he was in any way neglected when the need arose. The time he got staph in a corneal scratch, for instance, his parents did a great job of supporting him through the pain bit and the hospital bit and so on. But they couldn't know all the little incidents. Like the night when Hobie called so fiercely for Dr. McCoy that a young intern named McCoy went in and joked for half an hour with the feverish boy in his dark room.

To the end, his parents probably never understood that there was anything to understand about Hobie. And what was to see? His tennis and his model rocket collection made him look almost too normal for the small honors school he went to first.

Then his family moved to an executive bedroom suburb where the school system had a bigger budget than Monaco and a soccer team loaded with National Merit Science finalists. Here Hobie blended right in with the scenery. One more healthy, friendly, polite kid with bright gray eyes under a blond bowl-cut and very fast with any sort of ball game.

The brightest eyes around him were reading *The Double Helix* to find out how to make it in research, or marking up the Dun & Bradstreet flyers. If Hobie stood out at all, it was only that he didn't seem to be worried about making it in research or any other way, particularly. But that fitted in, too. Those days a lot of boys were standing around looking as if they couldn't believe what went on, as if they were waiting for – who knows? – a better world, their glands, something. Hobie's faintly aghast expression was not unique. Events like the installation of an armed patrol around the school enclave were bound to have a disturbing effect on the more sensitive kids.

People got the idea that Hobie was sensitive in some indefinite way. His usual manner was open but quiet, tolerant of a put-on that didn't end.

His adviser did fret over his failure to settle on a major field in time for the oncoming threat of college. First his math interest seemed to evaporate after the special calculus course, although he never blew an exam. Then he switched to the precollege anthropology panel the school was trying. Here he made good grades and acted very motivated, until the semester when the visiting research team began pounding on sampling techniques and statistical significance. Hobie had no trouble with things like Chi square, of course. But after making his A in the final he gave them his sweet, unbelieving smile and faded. His adviser found him spending a lot of hours polishing a six-inch telescope lens in the school shop.

So Hobie was tagged as some kind of an underachiever, but nobody knew what kind because of those grades. And something about that smile bothered them; it seemed to stop sound.

The girls liked him, though, and he went through the usual phases rather fast. There was the week he and various birds went to thirty-five drive-in movies. And the month he went around humming "Mrs. Robinson" in a meaningful way. And the warm, comfortable summer when he and his then-girl and two other couples went up to Stratford, Ontario, with sleeping bags to see the Czech multimedia thing.

Girls regarded him as different, although he never knew why. "You look at me like it's always good-bye," one of them told him. Actually, he treated girls with an odd detached gentleness, as though he knew a secret that might make them all disappear. Some of them hung around because of his quick brown hands or his really great looks, some because they hoped to share the secret. In this they were disappointed. Hobie talked and he listened carefully, but it wasn't the mutual talk-talk-talk of total catharsis that most couples went through. But how could Hobie know that?

Like most of his peer group, Hobie stayed away from heavies and agreed that pot was preferable to getting juiced. His friends never crowded him too much after the beach party where he spooked everybody by talking excitedly for hours to people who weren't there. They decided he might have a vulnerable ego-structure.

The official high school view was that Hobie had no real problems. In this they were supported by a test battery profile that could have qualified him as the ideal normal control. Certainly there was nothing to get hold of in his routine interviews with the high school psychologist.

Hobie came in after lunch, a time when Dr. Morehouse knew he was not at his most intuitive. They went through the usual openers, Hobie sitting easily, patient and interested, with an air of listening to some sound back of the acoustical ceiling tiles.

"I meet a number of young people involved in discovering who they really are. Searching for their own identities," Morehouse offered. He was idly trueing up a stack of typing headed *Sex Differences in the Adolescent Identity Crisis*.

"Do you?" Hobie asked politely.

Morehouse frowned at himself and belched disarmingly.

"Sometimes I wonder who *I* am," he smiled.

"Do you?" inquired Hobie.

"Don't you?"

"No" said Hobie.

Morehouse reached for the hostility that should have been there, found it wasn't. Not passive aggression. What? His intuition awoke briefly. He looked into Hobie's light hazel eyes and suddenly found himself slipping toward some very large uninhabited dimension. A real pubescent preschiz, he wondered hopefully? No again, he decided, and found himself thinking, What if a person is sure of his identity but it isn't his identity? He often wondered that; perhaps it could be worked up into a creative insight.

"Maybe it's the other way around," Hobie was saying before the pause grew awkward.

"How do you mean?"

"Well, maybe you're all wondering who you are," Hobie's lips quirked; it was clear he was just making conversation.

"I asked for that," Morehouse chuckled. They chatted about sibling rivalry and psychological statistics and wound up in plenty of time for Morehouse's next boy, who turned out to be a satisfying High Anx. Morehouse forgot about the empty place he had slid into. He often did that too.

It was a girl who got part of it out of Hobie, at three in the morning. "Dog" she was called then, although her name was Jane. A tender, bouncy little bird who cocked her head to listen up at him in a way Hobie liked. Dog would listen with the same soft intensity to the supermarket clerk and the pediatrician later on, but neither of them knew that.

They had been talking about the state of the world, which was then quite prosperous and peaceful. That is to say, about seventy million people were starving to death, a number of advanced nations were maintaining themselves on police terror tactics, four or five borders were being fought over, Hobie's family's maid had just been cut up by the suburban peacekeeper squad, and the school had added a charged wire and two dogs to its patrol. But none of the big nations were waving fissionables, and the U.S.-Sino-Soviet detente was a twenty-year reality.

Dog was holding Hobie's head over the side of her car because he had been the one who found the maid crawling on her handbones among the azaleas.

"If you feel like that, why don't you do something?" Dog asked him between spasms. "Do you want some Slurp? It's all we've got."

"Do what?" Hobie quavered.

"Politics?" guessed Dog. She really didn't know. The Protest Decade was long over, along with the New Politics and Ralph Nader. There was a school legend about a senior who had come back from Miami with a busted collarbone. Sometime after that the kids had discovered that flowers weren't really very powerful, and that movement organizers had their own bag. Why go on the street when you could really do more in one of the good jobs available Inside? So Dog could offer only a vague image of Hobie running for something, a sincere face on TV.

"You could join the Young Statesmen."

"Not to interfere," gasped Hobie. He wiped his mouth. Then he pulled himself together and tried some of the Slurp. In the dashlight his seventeen-year-old sideburns struck Dog as tremendously mature and beautiful.

"Oh, it's not so bad," said Hobie. "I mean, it's not *unusually* bad. It's just a stage. This world is going through a primitive stage. There's a lot of stages. It takes a long time. They're just very very backward, that's all."

"They," said Dog, listening to every word.

"I mean," he said.

"You're alienated," she told him. "Rinse your mouth out with that. You don't relate to people."

"I think you're people," he said, rinsing. He'd heard this before. "I relate to you," he said. He leaned out to spit. Then he twisted his head to look up at the sky and stayed that way a while, like an animal's head sticking out of a crate. Dog could feel him trembling the car.

"Are you going to barf again?" she asked.

"No."

But then suddenly he did, roaringly. She clutched at his shoulders while he heaved. After a while he sagged down, his head lolling limply out at one arm.

"It's such a mess," she heard him whispering. "It's such a s—ting miserable mess mess mess MESS MESS – "

He was pounding his hand on the car side.

"I'll hose it," said Dog, but then she saw he didn't mean the car.

"Why does it have to go on and on?" he croaked. "Why don't they just stop it? I can't bear it much longer, please, please, I can't – "

Dog was scared now.

"Honey, it's not that bad. Hobie honey, it's not that bad," she told him, patting at him, pressing her soft front against his back.

Suddenly he came back into the car on top of her, spent.

"It's unbearable," he muttered.

"What's unbearable?" she snapped, mad at him for scaring her. "What's unbearable for you and not for me? I mean, I know it's a mess, but why is it so bad for *you?* I have to live here too."

"It's your world," he told her absently, lost in some private desolation.

Dog yawned.

"I better drive you home now," she said.

He had nothing more to say and sat quietly. When Dog glanced at his profile, she decided he looked calm. Almost stupid, in fact; his mouth hung open a little. She didn't recognize the expression, because she had never seen people looking out of cattle cars.

Hobie's class graduated that June. His grades were well up, and everybody understood that he was acting a little unrelated because of the traumatic business with the maid. He got a lot of sympathy.

It was after the graduation exercises that Hobie surprised his parents for the first and last time. They had been congratulating themselves on having steered their fifth offspring safely through the college crisis and into a high-status Eastern. Hobie announced that he had applied for the United States Air Force Academy.

This was a bomb, because Hobie had never shown the slightest interest in things military. Just the opposite, really. Hobie's parents took it for granted that the educated classes viewed the military with tolerant distaste. Why did their son want this? Was it another of his unstable motivational orientations?

But Hobie persisted. He didn't have any reasons, he had just thought carefully and felt that this was for him. Finally they recalled that early model rocket collection; his father decided he was serious, and began sorting out the generals his research firm did business with. In September Hobie disappeared into Colorado Springs. He reappeared for Christmas in the form of an exotically hairless, erect and polite stranger in uniform.

During the next four years, Hobie the person became effectively invisible behind a growing pile of excellent evaluation reports. There seemed to be no doubt that he was working very hard, and his motivation gave no sign of flagging. Like any cadet, he bitched about many of the Academy's little ways and told some funny stories. But he never seemed discouraged. When he elected to spend his summers in special aviation skills training, his parents realized that Hobie had found himself.

Enlightenment – of a sort – came in his senior year when he told them he had applied for and been accepted into the new astronaut training program. The U.S. space program was just then starting up again after the revulsion caused by the tragic loss of the manned satellite lab ten years before.

"I bet that's what he had in mind all along," Hobie's father chuckled. "He didn't want to say so before he made it." They were all relieved. A son in the space program was a lot easier to live with, statuswise.

When she heard the news, Dog, who was now married and called herself Jane, sent him a card with a picture of the Man in the Moon. Another girl, more percipient, sent him a card showing some stars.

But Hobie never made it to the space program.

It was the summer when several not-very-serious events happened all together. The British devalued their wobbly pound again, just when it was found that far too many dollars were going out of the States. North and South Korea moved a step closer to reunion, which generated a call for strengthening the U.S. contribution to the remains of SEATO. Next there was an expensive, though luckily nonlethal, fire at Kennedy, and the Egyptians announced a new Soviet aid pact. And in August it was discovered that the Guévarrista rebels in Venezuela were getting some very unpleasant-looking hardware from their Arab allies.

Contrary to the old saying that nations never learn from history, the U.S. showed that it had learned from its long agony in Vietnam. What it had learned was not to waste time messing around with popular elections and military advisory and training programs, but to ball right in. Hard.

When the dust cleared, the space program and astronaut training were dead on the pad and a third of Hobie's graduating class was staging through Caracas. Technically, he had volunteered.

He found this out from the task force medico.

"Look at it this way, lieutenant. By entering the Academy, you volunteered for the Air Force, right?"

"Yes. But I opted for the astronaut program. The Air Force is the only way you can get in. And I've been accepted."

"But the astronaut program has been suspended. Temporarily, of course. Meanwhile the Air Force – for which you volunteered – has an active requirement for your training. You can't expect them just to let you sit around until the program resumes, can you? Moreover you have been given the very best option available. Good God, man, the Volunteer Airpeace Corps is considered a superelite. You should see the fugal depressions we have to cope with among men who have been rejected for the VAC."

"Mercenaries," said Hobie. "Regressive."

"Try 'professional,' it's a better word. Now – about those headaches."

The headaches eased up some when Hobie was assigned to long-range sensor recon support. He enjoyed the work of flying, and the long, calm, lonely sensor missions were soothing. They were also quite safe. The Guévarristas had no air strength to waste on recon planes and the U.A.R. SAM sites were not yet operational. Hobie flew the pattern, and waited zombielike for the weather, and flew again. Mostly he waited, because the fighting was developing in a steamy jungle province where clear sensing was a sometimes thing. It was poorly mapped. The ground troops could never be sure about the little brown square men who gave them so much trouble; on one side of an unknown line they were Guévarristas who should be obliterated, and on the other side they were legitimate national troops warning the blancos away. Hobie's recon tapes were urgently needed, and for several weeks he was left alone.

Then he began to get pulled up to a forward strip for one-day chopper duty when their tactical duty roster was disrupted by gee-gee. But this was relatively peaceful too, being mostly defoliant spray missions. Hobie, in fact, put in several months without seeing, hearing, smelling, or feeling the war at all. He would have been grateful for this if he had realized it. As it was he seemed to be trying not to realize anything much. He spoke very little, did his work, and moved like a man whose head might fall off if he jostled anything.

Naturally he was one of the last to hear the rumors about gee-gee when they filtered back to the coastal base, where Hobie was quartered with the long-range stuff. Gee-gee's proper name was Guairas Grippe. It was developing into a severe problem in the combat zone. More and more replacements and relief crews were being called forward for temporary tactical duty. On Hobie's next trip in, he couldn't help but notice that people were acting pretty haggard, and the roster was all scrawled up with changes. When they were on course, he asked about it.

"Are you kidding?" his gunner grunted.

"No. What is it?"

"B.W."

"What?"

"Bacteriological weapon, skyhead. They keep promising us vaccines. Stuck in their zippers – look out, there's a ground burst."

They held Hobie up front for another mission, and another after that, and then they told him that a sector quarantine was now in force.

The official notice said that movement of personnel between sectors would be reduced to a minimum as a temporary measure to control the spread of respiratory ailments. Translation: you could go from the support zone to the front, but you couldn't go back.

Hobie was moved into a crowded billet and assigned to Casualty and Supply. Shortly he discovered that there was a translation for respiratory ailments too. Gee-gee turned out to be a multiform misery of groin rash, sore throat, fever, and unending trots. It didn't seem to become really acute; it just cycled along. Hobie was one of those who were only lightly affected, which was lucky because the hospital beds were full. So were the hospital aisles. Evacuation of all casualties had been temporarily suspended until a controlled corridor could be arranged.

The Gués did not, it seemed, get gee-gee. The ground troops were definitely sure of that. Nobody knew how it was spread. Rumor said it was bats one week, and then the next week they were putting stuff in the water. Poisoned arrows, roaches, women, disintegrating canisters, all had their advocates. However it was done, it was clear that the U.A.R. technological aid had included more than hardware. The official notice about a forthcoming vaccine yellowed on the board.

Ground fighting was veering closer to Hobie's strip. He heard mortars now and then, and one night the Gués ran in a rocket launcher and nearly got the fuel dump before they were chased back.

"All they got to do is wait," said the gunner. "We're dead."

"Geegee doesn't kill you," said C/S control. "You just wish it did."

"They say."

The strip was extended, and three attack bombers came in. Hobie looked them over. He had trained on AX92's all one summer; he could fly them in his sleep. It would be nice to be alone.

He was pushing the C/S chopper most of the daylight hours now. He had gotten used to being shot at and to being sick. Everybody was sick, except a couple of replacement crews who were sent in two weeks apart, looking startlingly healthy. They said they had been immunized with a new antitoxin. Their big news was that gee-gee could be cured outside the zone.

"We're getting reinfected," the gunner said. "That figures. They want us out of here."

That week there was a big drive on bats, but it didn't help. The next week the first batch of replacements were running fevers. Their shots hadn't worked and neither did the stuff they gave the second batch.

After that, no more men came in except a couple of volunteer medicos. The billets and the planes and the mess were beginning to stink. That dysentery couldn't be controlled after you got weak.

What they did get was supplies. Every day or so another ton of stuff would drift down. Most of it was dragged to one side and left to rot. They were swimming in food. The staggering cooks pushed steak and lobster at men who shivered and went out to retch. The hospital even had ample space now, because it turned out that gee-gee really did kill you in the end. By that time, you were glad to go. A cemetery developed at the far side of the strip, among the skeletons of the defoliated trees.

On the last morning Hobie was sent out to pick up a forward scout team. He was one of the few left with enough stamina for long missions. The three-man team was far into Gué territory, but Hobie didn't care. All he was thinking about was his bowels. So far he had not fouled himself or his plane. When he was down by their signal, he bolted out to squat under the chopper's tail. The grunts climbed in, yelling at him.

They had a prisoner with them. The Gué was naked and astonishingly broad. He walked springily; his arms were lashed with wire and a shirt was tied over his head. This was the first Gué Hobie had been close to. As he got in he saw how the Gué's firm brown flesh glistened and bulged around the wire. He wished he could see his face. The gunner said the Gué was a Sirionó, and this was important because the Sirionós were not known to be with the Gués. They were a very primitive nomadic tribe.

When Hobie began to fly home, he realized he was getting sicker. It became a fight to hold onto consciousness and keep on course. Luckily nobody shot at them. At one point he became aware of a lot of screaming going on behind him, but couldn't pay attention. Finally he came over the strip and horsed the chopper down. He let his head down on his arms.

"You okay?" asked the gunner.

"Yeah," said Hobie, hearing them getting out. They were moving something heavy. Finally he got up and followed them. The floor was wet. That wasn't unusual. He got down and stood staring in, the floor a foot under his nose. The wet stuff was blood. It was sprayed around, with one big puddle. In the puddle was something soft and fleshy-looking.

Hobie turned his head. The ladder was wet. He held up one hand and looked at the red. His other hand too. Holding them out stiffly, he turned and began to walk away across the strip.

Control, who still hoped to get an evening flight out of him, saw him fall and called the hospital. The two replacement parameds were still in pretty good shape. They came out and picked him up.

When Hobie came to, one of the parameds was tying his hands down to the bed so he couldn't tear the IV out again.

"We're going to die here," Hobie told him.

The paramed looked noncommittal. He was a thin dark boy with a big Adam's apple.

"'But I shall dine at journey's end with Landor and with Donne,'" said Hobie. His voice was light and facile.

"Yeats," said the paramed. "Want some water?"

Hobie's eyes flickered. The paramed gave him some water.

"I really believed it, you know," Hobie said chattily. "I had it all figured out." He smiled, something he hadn't done for a long time.

"Landor and Donne?" asked the medic. He unhooked the empty IV bottle and hung up a new one.

"Oh, it was pathetic, I guess," Hobie said. "It started out . . . I believed they were real, you know? Kirk, Spock, McCoy, all of them. And the ship. To this day, I swear . . . one of them talked to me once; I mean, he really did . . . I had it all figured out; they had me left behind as an observer." Hobie giggled.

"They were coming back for me. It was secret. All I had to do was sort of fit in and observe. Like a report. One day they would come back and haul me up in that beam thing; maybe you know about that? And there I'd be back in real time where human beings were, where they were human. I wasn't really stuck here in the past. On a backward planet."

The paramed nodded.

"Oh, I mean, I didn't really *believe* it; I knew it was just a show. But I did believe it, too. It was like *there*, in the background, underneath, no matter what was going on. They were coming for me. All I had to do was observe. And not to interfere. You know? Prime directive . . . Of course after I grew up, I realized they weren't; I mean, I realized consciously. So I was going to go to them. Somehow, somewhere. Out there . . . Now I know. It really isn't so. None of it. Never. There's nothing . . . Now I know I'll die here."

"Oh now," said the paramed. He got up and started to take things away. His fingers were shaky.

"It's clean there," said Hobie in a petulant voice. "None of this shit. Clean and friendly. They don't torture people," he explained, thrashing his head. "They don't kill – " He slept. The paramed went away.

Somebody started to yell monotonously.

Hobie opened his eyes. He was burning up.

The yelling went on, became screaming. It was dusk. Footsteps went by, headed for the screaming. Hobie saw they had put him in a bed by the door.

Without his doing much about it, the screaming seemed to be lifting him out of the bed, propelling him through the door. Air. He kept getting close-ups of his hands clutching things. Bushes, shadows. Something scratched him.

After a while the screaming was a long way behind him. Maybe it was only in his ears. He shook his head, felt himself go down onto boards. He thought he was in the cemetery.

"No," he said. "Please. Please no." He got himself up, balanced, blundered on, seeking coolness.

The side of the plane felt cool. He plastered his hot body against it, patting it affectionately. It seemed to be quite dark now. Why was he inside with no lights? He tried the panel, the lights worked perfectly. Vaguely he noticed some yelling starting outside again. It ignited the screaming in his head. The screaming got very loud – loud – LOUD – and appeared to be moving him, which was good.

He came to above the overcast and climbing. The oxy-support tube was hitting him in the nose. He grabbed for the mask, but it wasn't there. Automatically, he had leveled off. Now he rolled and looked around.

Below him was a great lilac sea of cloud, with two mountains sticking through it, their western tips on fire. As he looked, they dimmed. He shivered, found he was wearing only sodden shorts. How had he got here? Somebody had screamed intolerably and he had run.

He flew along calmly, checking his board. No trouble except the fuel. Nobody serviced the AX92's any more. Without thinking about it, he began to climb again. His hands were a yard away and he was shivering but he felt clear. He reached up and found his headphones were in place; he must have put them on along with the rest of the drill. He clicked on. Voices rattled and roared at him. He switched off. Then he took off the headpiece and dropped it on the floor.

He looked around: 18,000, heading 88-05. He was over the Atlantic. In front of him the sky was darkening fast. A pinpoint glimmer ten o'clock high. Sirius, probably.

He thought about Sirius, trying to recall his charts. Then he thought about turning and going back down. Without paying much attention, he noticed he was crying with his mouth open.

Carefully he began feeding his torches and swinging the nose of his pod around and up. He brought it neatly to a point on Sirius. Up. Up. Behind him a great pale swing of contrail fell away above the lilac shadow, growing, towering to the tiny plane that climbed at its tip. Up. Up. The contrail cut off as the plane burst into the high cold dry.

As it did so, Hobie's ears skewered and he screamed wildly. The pain quit; his drums had burst. Up! Now he was gasping for air, strangling. The great torches drove him up, up, over the curve of the world. He was hanging on the star. Up! The fuel gauges were knocking. Any second they would quit and he and the bird would be a falling stone. "Beam us up, Scotty!" he howled at Sirius, laughing, coughing – coughing to death, as the torches faltered –

– And was still coughing as he sprawled on the shining resiliency under the arcing grids. He gagged, rolled, finally focused on a personage leaning toward him out of a complex chair. The personage had round eyes, a slitted nose, and the start of a quizzical smile.

Hobie's head swiveled slowly. It was not the bridge of the *Enterprise*. There were no viewscreens, only a View. And Lieutenant Uhura would have had trouble with the freeform flashing objects suspended in front of what appeared to be a girl wearing spots. The spots, Hobie made out, were fur.

Somebody who was not Bones McCoy was doing something to Hobie's stomach. Hobie got up a hand and touched the man's gleaming back. Under the mesh it was firm and warm. The man looked up, grinned; Hobie looked back at the captain.

"Do not have fear," a voice was saying. It seemed to be coming out of a globe by the captain's console. "We will tell you where you are."

"I know where I am," Hobie whispered. He drew a deep, sobbing breath.

"I'm HOME!" he yelled. Then he passed out.

The Music Master of Babylon

EDGAR PANGBORN

Edgar Pangborn (1909–76) attended Harvard and The New England Conservatory of Music and then published his first novel, a mystery (*A-100,* under the pseudonym Bruce Harrison). Two decades later, he turned to writing science fiction and wrote several SF novels and a number of stories from the 1950s through the 1970s. Damon Knight, describing Pangborn's first story, "Angel's Egg," and his novels *West of the Sun* (1953) and *A Mirror for Observers* (1954), says, "The style is leisurely and reflective: the mood is one of blended sorrow and delight . . . It is as if [Pangborn's] eye sees only certain moral and emotional colors . . . we can only assume that he has blinded himself in half the spectrum in order to see more radiantly in the rest. Certainly nothing is lacking in these stories for want of skill. It may well be that this is the only song Pangborn was made to sing: and a mournfully beautiful one it is – very like the thing that Stapledon was always talking about but never managed to convey: the regretful, ironic, sorrowful, deeply joyous – and purblind – love of the world and all in it."

Davy (1964) is generally considered his masterpiece. Critics generally find it hard to articulate the virtues of this novel that Robert A. Heinlein compared to *Huckleberry Finn.* Perhaps this is in part because there was little discourse about gay fiction until recently. *Dictionary of Literary Biography* (volume 8), for instance, says it "reads like a collaboration between Mark Twain, Dylan Thomas, and André Gide." There is more warmth than illumination in such statements. It is an intensely sensual book. His later works include two collections of stories, *Good Neighbors and Other Strangers* (1972) and *Still I Persist in Wondering* (1978).

This story is from his 1950s advent, the mournfully beautiful period that so impressed Knight and others.

_____

For twenty-five years no one came.

In the seventy-sixth year of his life Brian Van Anda was still trying not to remember a happy boyhood. To do so was irrelevant and dangerous, although every instinct of his old age tempted him to reject the present and live in the lost times. He would recall stubbornly that the present year, for example, was 2096 according to the Christian calendar, that he had been born in 2020, seven years after the close of the civil war, fifty years before the last war, twenty-five years before the departure of the First Interstellar. The First and Second Interstellar would be still on the move, he supposed. It had been understood, obvious, long ago, that after radio contact faded out the world would not hear of them again for many lifetimes, if ever. They would be on the move, farther and farther away from a planet no longer capable of understanding such matters.

Brian sometimes recalled his place of birth, New Boston, the fine planned city far inland from the old metropolis which a rising sea had reclaimed after the earthquake of 1994. Such things, places and dates, were factual props, useful when Brian wanted to impose an external order on the vagueness of his immediate existence. He tried to make sure they became no more than that, to shut away the colors, the poignant sounds, the parks and the playgrounds of New Boston, the known faces (many of them loved), and the later years when he had experienced a curious intoxication called fame.

It was not necessarily better or wiser to reject these memories, but it was safer, and nowadays Brian was often sufficiently tired, sufficiently conscious of his growing weakness and lonely unimportance, to crave safety as a meadow mouse craves a burrow.

He tied his canoe to the massive window which for many years had been a port and a doorway. Lounging there with a suspended sense of time, he hardly knew he was listening. In a way, all the twenty-five years had been a listening. He watched Earth's patient star sink toward the rim of the forest on the Palisades. At this hour it was sometimes possible, if the sun-crimsoned water lay still, to cease grieving at the greater stillness.

There must be scattered human life elsewhere, he knew – probably a great deal of it. After twenty-five years alone, that also often seemed irrelevant. At other times than mild evenings – on hushed noons or in the mornings always so empty of human commotion – Brian might lapse into anger, fight the calm by yelling, resent the swift dying of his own echoes. Such moods were brief. A kind of humor remained in him, not to be ruined by any sorrow.

He remembered how, ten months or possibly ten years ago, he had encountered a box turtle in a forest clearing, and had shouted at it: "They went that-away!" The turtle's rigidly comic face, fixed in a caricature of startled disapproval, had seemed to point up some truth or other. Brian had hunkered down on the moss and laughed uproariously until he observed that some of the laughter was weeping.

Today had been rather good. He had killed a deer on the Palisades, and with bow and arrow, not spending a bullet – irreplaceable toy of civilization.

Not that he needed to practice such economy. He could live, he supposed, another ten years at the outside. His rifles were in good condition, his hoarded ammunition would easily outlast him. So would the stock of canned and dried food stuffed away in his living quarters. But there was satisfaction in primitive effort, and no compulsion to analyze the why of it.

The stored food was more important than the ammunition; a time was coming soon enough when he would no longer have the strength for hunting. He would lose the inclination to depart from his fortress for trips to the mainland. He would yield to such timidity or laziness for days, then weeks. Sometime, after such an interlude, he might find himself too feeble to risk climbing the cliff wall into the forest. He would then have the good sense, he hoped, to destroy the canoe, thus making of his weakness a necessity.

There were books. There was the Hall of Music on the next floor above the water, probably safe from its lessening encroachment. To secure fresh water he need only keep track of the tides, for the Hudson had cleaned itself and now rolled down sweet from the lonely uncorrupted hills. His decline could be comfortable. He had provided for it and planned it.

Yet now, gazing across the sleepy water, seeing a broad-winged hawk circle in freedom above the forest, Brian was aware of the old thought moving in him: *If I could hear voices – just once, if I could hear human voices . . .*

The Museum of Human History, with the Hall of Music on what Brian thought of as the second floor, should also outlast his requirements. In the flooded lower floor and basement the work of slow destruction must be going on: Here and there the unhurried waters

could find their way to steel and make rust of it; the waterproofing of
the concrete was nearly a hundred years old. But it ought to be good
for another century or two.

Nowadays the ocean was mild. There were moderate tides, winds no
longer destructive. For the last six years there had been no more of the
heavy storms out of the south; in the same period Brian had noted a
rise in the water level of a mere nine inches. The windowsill, his port,
stood six inches above high-tide mark this year. Perhaps Earth was
settling into a new amiable mood. The climate had become delightful,
about like what Brian remembered from a visit to southern Virginia in
his childhood.

The last earthquake had come in 2082 – a large one, Brian guessed,
but its center could not have been close to the rock of Manhattan. The
Museum had only shivered and shrugged – it had survived much
worse than that, half a dozen times since 1994. Long after the tremor,
a tall wave had thundered in from the south. Its force, like that of
others, had mostly been dissipated against the barrier of tumbled rock
and steel at the southern end of the submerged island – an undersea
dam, man-made though not man-intended – and when it reached the
Museum it did no more than smash the southern windows in the Hall
of Music, which earlier waves had not been able to reach; then it
passed on up the river enfeebled.

The windows of the lower floor had all been broken long before
that. After the earthquake of '82 Brian had spent a month in boarding
up all the openings on the south side of the Hall of Music – after all, it
was home – with lumber painfully ferried over from mainland ruins.
By that year he was sixty-two years old and not moving with the ease
of youth. He deliberately left cracks and knotholes. Sunlight sifted
through in narrow beams, like the bars of dusty gold Brian could
remember in a hayloft at his uncle's farm in Vermont.

That hawk above the Palisades soared nearer over the river and
receded. Caught in the evening light, he was himself a little sun, dying
and returning.

The Museum had been finished in 2003. Manhattan, strangely
enough, had never taken a bomb, although in the civil war two of the
type called "small clean fission" had fallen on the Brooklyn and New
Jersey sides – so Brian recalled from the jolly history books which had
informed his adolescence that war was definitely a thing of the past. By
the time of the next last war, in 2070, the sea, gorged on melting ice
caps, had removed Manhattan Island from current history.

Everything left standing above the waters south of the Museum had been knocked flat by the tornadoes of 2057 and 2064. A few blobs of empty rock still demonstrated where Central Park and Mount Morris Park had been: not significant. Where Long Island once rose, there was a troubled area of shoals and small islands, probably a useful barrier of protection for the receding shore of Connecticut. Men had yielded their great city inch by inch, then foot by foot; a full mile in 2047, saying: "The flood years have passed their peak, and a return to normal is expected." Brian sometimes felt a twinge of sympathy for the Neanderthal experts who must have told each other to expect a return to normal at the very time when the Cro-Magnons were drifting in.

In 2057 the Island of Manhattan had to be yielded. New York City, half-new, half-ancient, sprawled stubborn and enormous upstream, on both sides of a river not done with its anger. Yet the Museum stood. Aided by sunken rubble of other buildings of its kind, aided also by men because they still had time to move it, the museum stood, and might for a long time yet – weather permitting.

The hawk floated out of sight above the Palisades into the field of the low sun.

The Museum of Human History covered an acre of ground north of 125th Street, rising a modest fifteen stories, its foundation secure in that layer of rock which mimics eternity. It deserved its name; here men had brought samples of everything man-made, literally everything known in the course of human creation since prehistory. Within human limits it was definitive.

No one had felt anything unnatural in the refusal of the Directors of the Museum to move the collection after the building weathered the storm of 2057. Instead, ordinary people donated money so that a mighty abutment could be built around the ground floor and a new entrance designed on the north side of the second. The abutment survived the greater tornado of 2064 without damage, although during those seven years the sea had risen another eight feet in its old ever-new game of making monkeys out of the wise. (It was left for Brian Van Anda, alone, in 2079, to see the waters slide quietly over the abutment, opening the lower regions for the use of fishes and the more secret water-dwellers who like shelter and privacy. In the '90s, Brian suspected the presence of an octopus or two in the vast vague territory that had once been parking lot, heating plant, storage space, air-raid shelter, etc. He couldn't prove it; it just seemed like a decent, comfortable place for an octopus.) In 2070 plans were under consideration for building a new causeway to the Museum from the still expanding city in the north. In 2070, also, the last war began and ended.

When Brian Van Anda came down the river late in 2071, a refugee from certain unfamiliar types of savagery, the Museum was empty of the living. He spent many days in exhaustive exploration of the building. He did this systematically, toiling at last up to the Directors' meeting room on the top floor. There he observed how they must have been holding a conference at the very time when a new gas was tried out over New York in a final effort to persuade the Western Federation that the end justifies the means. (Too bad, Brian sometimes thought, that he would never know exactly what had become of the Asian Empire. In the little splinter state called the Soviet of North America, from which Brian had fled in '71, the official doctrine was that the Asian Empire had won the war and the saviors of humanity would be flying in any day now. Brian had inadvertently doubted this out loud and then stolen a boat and gotten away safely under cover of night.)

Up in the meeting room, Brian had seen how that up-to-date neurotoxin had been no respecter of persons. An easy death, however, by the look of it. He observed also how some things endure. The Museum, for instance: virtually unharmed.

Brian often recalled those moments in the meeting room as a sort of island in time. They were like the first day of falling in love, the first hour of discovering that he could play Beethoven. And a little like the curiously cherished, more than life-size half-hour back there in Newburg, in that ghastly year 2071, when he had briefly met and spoken with an incredibly old man, Abraham Brown. Brown had been President of the Western Federation at the time of the civil war. Later, retired from the uproar of public affairs, he had devoted himself to philosophy, unofficial teaching. In 2071, with the world he had loved in almost total ruin around him, Brown had spoken pleasantly to Brian Van Anda of small things – of chrysanthemums that would soon be blooming in the front yard of the house where he lived with friends, of a piano recital by Van Anda back in 2067 which the old man still remembered with warm enthusiasm.

Only a month later more hell was loose and Brian himself in flight.

Yes, the Museum Directors had died easily. Brooding in the evening sunlight, Brian reflected that now, all these years later, the innocent bodies would be perfectly decent. No vermin in the Museum. The doorways and the floors were tight, the upper windows unbroken.

One of the white-haired men had had a Ming vase on his desk. He had not dropped out of his chair, but looked as if he had fallen asleep in front of the vase with his head on his arms. Brian had left the vase untouched, but had taken one other thing, moved by some stirring of his own never-certain philosophy and knowing that he would not return to this room, ever.

One of the Directors had been opening a wall cabinet when he fell; the key lay near his fingers. Their discussion had not been concerned only with war, perhaps not at all with war. After all, there were other topics. The Ming vase must have had a part in it. Brian wished he could know what the old man had meant to take from the cabinet. Sometimes he dreamed of conversations with that man, in which the Director told him the truth of this and other matters, but what was certainty in sleep was in the morning gone like childhood.

For himself Brian had taken a little image of rock-hard clay, blackened, two-faced, male and female. Prehistoric, or at any rate wholly savage, unsophisticated, meaningful like the blameless motion of an animal in sunlight. Brian had said: "With your permission, gentlemen." He had closed the cabinet and then, softly, the outer door.

"I'm old, too," Brian said to the red evening. He searched for the hawk and could no longer find it in the deepening sky. "Old, a little foolish – talk aloud to myself. I'll have some Mozart before supper."

He transferred the fresh venison from the canoe to a small raft hitched inside the window. He had selected only choice pieces, as much as he could cook and eat in the few days before it spoiled, leaving the rest for the wolves or any other forest scavengers which might need it. There was a rope strung from the window to the marble steps leading to the next floor of the Museum, which was home.

It had not been possible to save much from the submerged area, for its treasure was mostly heavy statuary. Through the still water, as he pulled the raft along the rope, the Moses of Michelangelo gazed up at him in tranquillity. Other faces watched him; most of them watched infinity. There were white hands that occasionally borrowed motion from ripples made by the raft. "I got a deer, Moses," said Brian Van Anda, smiling down in companionship, losing track of time . . . "Good night, Moses." He carried his juicy burden up the stairway.

Brian's living quarters had once been a cloakroom for Museum attendants. Four close walls gave it a feel of security. A ventilating shaft now served as a chimney for the wood stove Brian had salvaged from a mainland farmhouse. The door could be tightly locked. There were no windows. You do not want windows in a cave.

Outside was the Hall of Music, a full acre, an entire floor of the Museum, containing an example of every musical instrument that was known or could be reconstructed in the twenty-first century. The library of scores and recordings lacked nothing – except electricity to make the recordings speak. A few might still be made to sound on a hand-cranked phonograph, but Brian had not bothered with that toy for years; the springs were probably rusted.

Brian sometimes took out orchestra and chamber music scores to read at random. Once, reading them, his mind had been able to furnish ensembles, orchestras, choirs of a sort, but lately the ability had weakened. He remembered a day, possibly a year ago, when his memory refused to give him the sound of oboe and clarinet in unison. He had wandered, peevish, distressed, unreasonably alarmed, among the racks and cases of woodwinds and brasses and violins. He tried to sound a clarinet; the reed was still good in the dust proof case, but he had no lip. He had never mastered any instrument except the pianoforte.

He recalled – it might have been that same day – opening a chest of double basses. There was a three-stringer in the group, old, probably from the early nineteenth century, a trifle fatter than its more modern companions. Brian touched its middle string in an idle caress, not intending to make it sound, but it had done so. When in use, it would have been tuned to D; time had slackened the heavy murmur to A or something near it. That had throbbed in the silent room with finality, a sound such as a programmatic composer, say Tchaikovsky, might have used as a tonal symbol for the breaking of a heart. It stayed in the air as other instruments whispered a dim response. "All right, gentlemen," Brian said, "that was your A . . ."

Out in the main part of the hall, a place of honor was given to what may have been the oldest of the instruments, a seven-note marimba of phonolitic schist discovered in Indo-China in the twentieth century and thought to be at least 5,000 years of age. The xylophone-type rack was modern. Brian for twenty-five years had obeyed a compulsion to keep it free of cobwebs. Sometimes he touched the singing stones, not for amusement but because there was comfort in it. They answered to the light tap of a fingernail. Beside them on a little table of its own he had placed the Stone Age god of two faces.

On the west side of the Hall of Music, a rather long walk from Brian's cave, was a small auditorium. Lectures, recitals, chamber music concerts had been given there in the old days. The pleasant room held a twelve-foot concert grand, made in 2043, probably the finest of the many pianos in the Hall of Music, a summit of technical achievement. Brian had done his best to preserve this beautiful artifact, prayerfully tuning it three times a year, robbing other pianos in the Museum to provide a reserve supply of strings, oiled and sealed against rust. When not in use his great piano was covered by stitched-together sheets. To remove the cover was a somber ritual. Before touching the keys, Brian washed his hands with needless fanatical care.

Some years ago he had developed the habit of locking the auditorium doors before he played. Yet even then he preferred not to glance toward the vista of empty seats, not much caring whether this inhibition derived from a Stone Age fear of finding someone there or from a flat civilized understanding that no one could be. It never occurred to him to lock the one door he used, when he was absent from the auditorium. The key remained on the inside; if he went in merely to tune the piano or to inspect the place, he never turned it.

The habit of locking it when he played might have started (he could not remember) back in the year 2076, when so many bodies had floated down from the north on the ebb tides. Full horror had somehow been lacking in the sight of all that floating death. Perhaps it was because Brian had earlier had his fill of horrors, or perhaps in 2076 he already felt so divorced from his own kind that what happened to them was like the photograph of a war in a distant country. Some had bobbed and floated quite near the Museum. Most of them had the gaping obvious wounds of primitive warfare, but some were oddly discolored – a new pestilence? So there was (or had been) more trouble up there in what was (or had been) the short-lived Soviet of North America, a self-styled "nation" that took in east central New York and most of New England. So . . . Yes, that was probably the year when he had started locking the doors between his private concerts and an empty world.

He dumped the venison in his cave. He scrubbed his hands, showing high blue veins now, but still tough, still knowing. Mozart, he thought, and walked, not with much pleasure of anticipation but more like one externally driven, through the enormous hall that was so full and yet so empty and growing dim with evening, with dust, with age, with loneliness. Music should not be silent.

When the piano was uncovered, Brian delayed. He exercised his hands unnecessarily. He fussed with the candelabrum on the wall, lighting three candles, then blowing out two for economy. He admitted presently that he did not want the emotional clarity of Mozart at all, not now. The darkness of 2070 was too close, closer than he had felt it for a long time. It would never have occurred to Mozart, Brian thought, that a world could die. Beethoven could have entertained the idea soberly enough, and Chopin probably; even Brahms. Mozart, Haydn, Bach would surely have dismissed it as somebody's bad dream, in poor taste. Andrew Carr, who lived and died in the latter half of the twentieth century, had endured the idea deep in his bloodstream from the beginning of his childhood.

The date of Hiroshima was 1945; Carr was born in 1951. The wealth of his music was written between 1969, when he was eighteen, and 1984, when he died among the smells of an Egyptian jail from injuries received in a street brawl.

"If not Mozart," said Brian Van Anda to his idle hands, "there is always the Project."

To play Carr's last sonata as it should be played – as Carr was supposed to have said he couldn't play it himself: Brian had been thinking of that as the Project for many years. It had begun teasing his mind long before the war, at the time of his triumphs in a civilized world which had been warmly appreciative of the polished interpretive artist (once he got the breaks) although no more awake than in any other age to the creative sort. Back there in the undestroyed society, Brian had proposed to program that sonata in the company of works that were older but no greater, and to play it – well, beyond his best, so that even music critics would begin to see its importance in history.

He had never done it, had never felt the necessary assurance that he had entered into the sonata and learned the depth of it. Now, when there was none to hear or care, unless the harmless brown spiders in the corners of the auditorium had a taste for music, there was still the Project. *I* hear, Brian thought. *I* care, and with myself for audience I wish to hear it once as it ought to be, a final statement for a world that was (I think) too good to die.

Technically, of course, he had it. The athletic demands Carr made on the performer were tremendous, but, given technique, there was nothing impossible about them. Anyone capable of concert work could at least play the notes at the required tempi. And any reasonably shrewd pianist could keep track of the dynamics, saving strength for the shattering finale. Brian had heard the sonata played by others two or three times in the old days – competently. Competency was not enough.

For example, what about the third movement, the mad scherzo, and the five tiny interludes of quiet scattered through its plunging fury?

They were not alike. Related, but each one demanded a new climate of heart and mind – tenderness, regret, simple relaxation. Flowers on a flood – no. Window lights in a storm – no. The innocence of a child in a bombed city – no, not really. Something of all those. Much more, too, defying words.

What of the second movement, the largo, where in a way the pattern was reversed, the midnight introspection interrupted by moments of anger, or longing, or despair like the despair of an angel beating his wings against a prison of glass?

It was a work in which something of Carr's life, Carr's temperament, had to come into you, whether you dared welcome it or not; otherwise your playing was no more than reproduction of notes on a page. Carr's life was not for the contemplation of the timid.

The details were superficially well-known; the biographies were like musical notation, meaningless without interpretation and insight. Carr was a drunken roarer, a young devil-god with such a consuming hunger for life that he choked to death on it. His friends hated him for the way he drained their lives, loving them to distraction and the next moment having no time for them because he loved his work more. His enemies must have had times of helplessly admiring him if only because of a translucent honesty that made him more and less than human. A rugged Australian, not tall but built like a hero, a face all forehead and jaw and glowing hyperthyroid eyes. He wept only when he was angry, the biographic storytellers said. In one minute of talk he might shift from gutter obscenity to some extreme of altruistic tenderness, and from that perhaps to a philosophic comment of cold intelligence. He passed his childhood on a sheep farm, ran away on a freighter at thirteen, was flung out of two respectable conservatories for drunkenness and "public lewdness," then studied like a slave in London with single-minded desperation, as if he knew the time was short. He was married twice and twice divorced. He killed a man in a silly brawl on the New Orleans docks, and wrote his First Symphony while he was in jail for that. He died of stab wounds from a broken bottle in a Cairo jail, and was recognized by the critics. It all had relevancy; relevant or not, if the sonata was in your mind, so was the life.

You had to remember also that Andrew Carr was the last of civilization's great composers. No one in the twenty-first century approached him – they ignored his explorations and carved cherry-stones. He belonged to no school, unless you wanted to imagine a school of music beginning with Bach, taking in perhaps a dozen along the way, and ending with Carr himself. His work was a summary as well as an advance along the mainstream into the unknown; in the light of the year 2070, it was also a completion.

Brian was certain he could play the first movement of the sonata as he wished to. Technically it was not revolutionary, and remained rather close to the ancient sonata form. Carr had even written in a double bar for a repeat of the entire opening statement, something that had made his cerebral contemporaries sneer with great satisfaction; it never occurred to them that Carr was inviting the performer to use his head.

The bright – sorrowful second movement, unfashionably long, with its strange pauses, unforeseen recapitulations, outbursts of savage change – that was where Brian's troubles began. ("Reminiscent of Franck," said the hunters for comparisons whom we have always with us.) It did not help Brian to be old, remembering the inner storms of forty years ago and more.

His single candle fluttered. For once Brian had forgotten to lock the door into the Hall of Music. This troubled him, but he did not rise from the piano chair. He chided himself instead for the foolish neuroses of aloneness – what could it matter? Let it go. He shut his eyes. The sonata had long ago been memorized; printed copies were safe in the library. He played the opening of the first movement as far as the double bar, opened his eyes to the friendly black-and-white of clean keys, and played the repetition with new lights, new emphasis. Better than usual, he thought –

Yes. Good . . . Now that naïve-appearing modulation into A major, which only Carr would have wanted just there in that sudden obvious way, like the opening of a door on shining fields. On toward the climax – I *am playing* it, *I think* – through the intricate revelations of development and recapitulation. And the conclusion, lingering, half-humorous, not unlike a Beethoven *I'm-not-gone-yet* ending, but with a questioning that was all Andrew Carr. After that –

"No more tonight," said Brian aloud. "Some night, though . . . Not competent right now, my friend." He replaced the cover of the piano and blew out the candle. He had brought no torch, long use having taught his feet every inch of the small journey. It was quite dark. The never-opened western windows of the auditorium were dirty, most of the dirt on the outside, crusted windblown salt.

In this partial darkness something was wrong.

At first Brian found no source for the faint light, dim orange with a hint of motion. He peered into the gloom of the auditorium, fixing his eyes on the oblong of blacker shadow that was the doorway into the

Hall of Music. The windows, of course! – he had almost forgotten there were any. The light, hardly deserving the name of light, was coming through them. But sunset was surely past. He had been here a long time, delaying and brooding before he played. Sunset should not flicker.

So there was some kind of fire on the mainland. There had been no thunderstorm. How should fire start, over there where no one ever came?

He stumbled a few times, swearing petulantly, locating the doorway again and groping through it into the Hall of Music. The windows out here were just as dirty; no use trying to see through them. There must have been a time when he had looked through them, enjoyed looking through them. He stood shivering in the marble silence, trying to remember.

Time was a gradual, continual dying. Time was the growth of dirt and ocean salt, sealing in, covering over. He stumbled for his cloak-room cave, hurrying now, and lit two candles. He left one by the cold stove and used the other to light his way down the stairs to his raft; once down there, he blew it out, afraid. The room a candle makes in the darkness is a vulnerable room. Having no walls, it closes in a blind-ness. He pulled the raft by the guide-rope, gently, for fear of noise.

He found his canoe tied as he had left it. He poked his white head slowly beyond the sill, staring west.

Merely a bonfire gleaming, reddening the blackness of the cliff.

Brian knew the spot, a ledge almost at water level, at one end of it the troublesome path he usually followed in climbing to the forest at the top of the Palisades. Usable driftwood was often there, the supply renewed by the high tides.

"No." Brian said. "Oh no! . . ."

Unable to accept or believe, or not believe, he drew his head in, resting his forehead on the coldness of the sill, waiting for dizziness to pass, reason to return.

It might have been a long time, a kind of blackout. Now he was again in command of his actions and even rather calm, once more leaning out over the sill. The fire still shone and was therefore not a disordered dream of old age. It was dying to a dull rose of embers.

He wondered about the time. Clocks and watches had stopped long ago; Brian had ceased to want them. A sliver of moon was hanging over the water to the east. He ought to be able to remember the phases, deduce the approximate time from that. But his mind was too tired or distraught to give him the data. Maybe it was somewhere around midnight.

He climbed on the sill and lifted the canoe over it to the motionless water inside. Useless, he decided, as soon as the grunting effort was finished. That fire had been lit before daylight passed; whoever lit it would have seen the canoe, might even have been watching Brian himself come home from his hunting. The canoe's disappearance in the night would only rouse further curiosity. But Brian was too exhausted to lift it back.

And why assume that the maker of the bonfire was necessarily hostile? Might be good company . . . He pulled his raft through the darkness, secured it at the stairway, and groped back to his cave.

He locked the door. The venison was waiting; the sight made him ravenous. He lit a small fire in the stove, one that he hoped would not still be sending smoke from the ventilator shaft when morning came. He cooked the meat crudely and wolfed it down, all enjoyment gone at the first mouthful. He was shocked to discover the dirtiness of his white beard. He hadn't given himself a real bath in – weeks, was it? He searched for scissors and spent an absentminded while in trimming the beard back to shortness. He ought to take some soap – valuable stuff – down to Moses' room, and wash.

Clothes, too. People probably still wore clothes. He had worn none for years, except for sandals. He used a carrying satchel for trips to the mainland. He had enjoyed the freedom at first, and especially the discovery that in his rugged fifties he did not need clothes even for the soft winters, except perhaps a light covering when he slept. Later, total nakedness had become so natural it required no thought at all. But the owner of that bonfire could have inherited or retained the pruderies of the lost culture.

He checked his rifles. The .22 automatic, an Army model from the 2040's, was the best – any amount of death in that. The tiny bullets carried a paralytic poison: graze a man's finger and he was almost painlessly dead in three minutes. Effective range, with telescopic sights, three kilometers; weight, a scant five pounds. Brian sat a long time cuddling that triumph of military science, listening for sounds that never came. Would it be two o'clock? He wished he could have seen the Time Satellite, renamed in his mind the Midnight Star, but when he was down there at his port, he had not once looked up at the night sky. Delicate and beautiful, bearing its everlasting freight of men who must have been dead now for twenty-five years and who would be dead a very long time – well, it was better than a clock, if you happened to look at the midnight sky at the right time of the month when the man-made star caught the moonlight. But he had missed it tonight. Three o'clock? . . .

At some time during the long dark he put the rifle away on the floor. With studied, self-conscious contempt for his own weakness, he unlocked the door and strode out noisily into the Hall of Music, with a fresh-lit candle. This same bravado, he knew, might dissolve at the first alien noise. While it lasted, it was invigorating.

The windows were still black with night. As if the candle flame had found its own way, Brian was standing by the ancient marimba in the main hall, the gleam slanting carelessly away from his gaunt hand. And nearby sat the Stone Age god.

It startled him. He remembered clearly how he himself had placed it there, obeying a half-humorous whim. The image and the singing stones were both magnificently older than history, so why shouldn't they live together? Whenever he dusted the marimba, he dusted the image respectfully, and its table. It would not have needed much urging from the impulses of a lonely mind to make him place offerings before it – winking first, of course, to indicate that rituals suitable to a pair of aging gentlemen did not have to be sensible in order to be good.

The clay face remembering eternity was not deformed by the episode of civilization. Chipped places were simple honorable scars. The two faces stared mildly from the single head, uncommunicative, serene.

A wooden hammer of modern make rested on the marimba. Softly Brian tapped a few of the stones. He struck the shrillest one harder, waking many slow-dying overtones, and laid the hammer down, listening until the last murmur perished and a drop of wax hurt his thumb. He returned to his cave and blew out the candle, never thinking of the door, or if he thought, not caring.

Face down, he rolled his head and clenched his fingers into his pallet, seeking in pain, finding at last the relief of stormy childish weeping in the dark.

Then he slept.

They looked timid. The evidence of it was in their tense squatting pose, not in what the feeble light allowed Brian to see of their faces, which were blank as rock. Hunkered down just inside the doorway of the dim cloakroom cave, a morning grayness from the Hall of Music behind them, they were ready for flight, and Brian's intelligence warned his body to stay motionless. Readiness for flight could also be readiness for attack. He studied them through slit eyelids, knowing he was in deep shadow.

They were very young, sixteen or seventeen, firm-muscled, the boy slim but heavy in the shoulders, the girl a fully developed woman. They were dressed alike: loincloths of some coarse dull fabric, and moccasins that were probably deerhide. Their hair grew nearly to the shoulders and was cut off carelessly, but they were evidently in the habit of combing it. They appeared to be clean. Their complexion, so far as Brian could guess it in the meager light, was brown, like a heavy tan. With no immediate awareness of emotion, he decided they were beautiful, and then within his own poised and perilous silence Brian reminded himself that the young are always beautiful.

The woman muttered softly: "He wake."

A twitch of the man's head was probably meant to warn her to be quiet. He clutched the shaft of a javelin with a metal blade which had once belonged to a breadknife. The blade was polished, shining, lashed to a peeled stick. The javelin trailed, ready for use at a flick of the young man's arm. Brian sighed deliberately. "Good morning."

The man, or boy, said: "Good morning, sa."

"Where do you come from?"

"Millstone." The man spoke automatically, but then his facial rigidity dissolved into astonishment and some kind of distress. He glanced at his companion, who giggled uneasily.

"The old man pretends to not know," she said, and smiled, and seemed to be waiting for the young man's permission to go on speaking. He did not give it, but she continued: "Sa, the old ones of Millstone are dead." She thrust her hand out and down, flat, a picture of finality, adding with nervous haste: "As the Old Man knows. He who told us to call him Jonas, she who told us to call her Abigail, dead. They are still-without-moving the full six days, then we do the burial as they told us. As the Old Man knows."

"But I don't know!" said Brian, and sat up on his pallet too quickly, startling them. But their motion was backward, a readying for flight. "Millstone? Where is Millstone?"

They looked wholly bewildered and dismayed. They stood up with animal grace, stepping backward out of the cave, the girl whispering in the man's ear. Brian caught two words: " – is angry."

He jumped up. "Don't go! Please don't go!" He followed them out of the cave, slowly now, aware that he might be an object of terror in the half-dark, aware of his gaunt, graceless age, and nakedness, and dirty hacked-off beard. Almost involuntarily he adopted something of the flat stilted quality of their speech. "I will not hurt you. Do not go."

They halted. The girl smiled dubiously. The man said: "We need old ones. They die. He who told us to call him Jonas said, many days in the boat, not with the sun-path, he said, across the sun-path, he said, keeping land on the left hand. We need old ones, to speak the – to speak . . . The Old Man is angry?"

"No. I am not angry. I am never angry." Brian's mind groped, certain of nothing. No one came, for twenty-five years.

Millstone?

There was red-gold on the dirty eastern windows of the Hall of Music, a light becoming softness as it slanted down, touching the long rows of cases, the warm brown of an antique spinet, the clean gold of a twentieth century harp, the gray of singing stones five thousand years old and a two-faced god much older than that. "Millstone." Brian pointed in inquiry, southwest.

The girl nodded, pleased and not at all surprised that he should know, watching him now with a squirrel's stiff curiosity. Hadn't there been a Millstone River in or near Princeton, once upon a time? Brian thought he remembered that it emptied into the Raritan Canal. There was some moderately high ground there. Islands now, no doubt. Perhaps they would tell him. "There were old people in Millstone," he said, trying for peaceful dignity, "and they died. So now you need old ones to take their place."

The girl nodded vigorously many times. Her glance at the young man was shy, possessive, maybe amused. "He who told us to call him Jonas said no marriage without the words of Abraham."

"Abr – " Brian checked himself. If this was religion, it would not do to speak the name Abraham with a rising inflection. "I have been for a long time – " He checked himself again: A man old, ugly, and strange enough to be sacred should never stoop to explain anything.

They were standing by the seven-stone marimba. His hand dropped, his thumbnail clicking against the deepest stone and waking a murmur. The children drew back, alarmed. Brian smiled. "Don't be afraid." He tapped the other stones lightly. "It is only music. It will not hurt you." They were patient and respectful, waiting for more light. He said carefully: "He who told you to call him Jonas – he taught you all the things you know?"

"All things," the boy said, and the girl nodded three or four times, so that the soft brownness of her hair tumbled about her face, and she pushed it back in a small human motion as old as the clay image.

"Do you know how old you are?"

They looked blank. Then the girl said: "Oh – summers!" She held up her two hands with spread fingers, then one hand. "Three fives." She chuckled, and sobered quickly. "As the Old Man knows."

"I am very old," said Brian. "I know many things, but sometimes I wish to forget, and sometimes I wish to hear what others know, even though I may know it myself."

They looked uncomprehending and greatly impressed. Brian felt a smile on his face and wondered why it should be there. They were nice children. Born ten years after the death of a world; twenty, perhaps. *I think I am seventy-six, but what if I dropped a decade somewhere and never noticed the damned thing . . . ?*" He who told you to call him Jonas – he taught you all you know of Abraham?"

At the sound of the name, both made swift circular motions, first at the forehead, then at the breast. "He taught us all things," the young man said. "He, and she who told us to call her Abigail. The hours to rise, to pray, to wash, to eat. The laws for hunting, and I know the Abraham-words for that: Sol-Amra, I take this for my need."

Brian felt lost again, and looked down to the clay faces of the image for counsel, and found none. "They who told you to call them Jonas and Abigail, they were the only ones who lived with you? – the only old ones?"

Again that look of bewilderment and disappointment. "The only ones, sa, the young man said. "As the Old Man knows."

I could never persuade them that, being old, I know very nearly nothing . . .

Brian straightened to his full great height. The young people were not tall. Though stiff and worn with age, Brian knew he was still over-powering. Once, among men, he had gently enjoyed being more than life-size. As a shield for loneliness and fright within, he now adopted a phony sternness. "I wish to examine you for your own good, my children, about Millstone and your knowledge of Abraham. How many others live at Millstone, tell me."

"Two fives, sa," said the boy promptly, "and I the one who may be called Jonason and this girl who may be called Paula. Two fives and two. We are the biggest. The others are only children, but the one who may be called Jimi has killed his deer; he sees after them now while we go across the sun-path."

Under Brian's questioning, more of the story came, haltingly, obscured by the young man's conviction that the Old Man already knew everything. Sometime, probably in the middle 2080's, Jonas and Abigail (whoever they were) had come on a group of twelve wild children who were keeping alive somehow in a ruined town where their elders had all died. Jonas and Abigail had brought them all to an island they called Millstone. Jonas and Abigail came originally from "up across the sun-path" – the boy seemed to mean north – and they were very old, which might mean, Brian guessed, anything between thirty and ninety. In teaching the children primitive means of survival, Jonas and Abigail had brought off a brilliant success: Jonason and Paula were well-fed, shining with health and the strength of wildness, and clean. Their speech, limited and odd though it was, had not been learned from the ignorant. Its pronunciation faintly suggested New England, so far as it had any local accent. "Did they teach you reading and writing?" Brian asked, and made writing motions on the flat of his palm, which the two watched in vague alarm.

The boy asked: "What is that?"

"Never mind." *I could quarrel with some of your theories, Mister-whom-I-may-call-Jonas.* But maybe, he thought, there had been no books, no writing materials, no way to get them. What's the minimum of technology required to keep the human spirit alive? . . . "Well – well, tell me what they taught you of Abraham. I wish to hear how well you remember."

Both made again the circular motion at forehead and breast, and the young man said with the stiffness of recitation: "Abraham was the Son of Heaven who died that we might live." The girl, her obligation discharged with the religious gesture, tapped the marimba shyly, fascinated, and drew her finger back, smiling up at Brian in apology for naughtiness. "He taught the laws, the everlasting truth of all time," the boy gabbled, "and was slain on the wheel at Nuber by the infidels; therefore since he died for us, we look up across the sun-path when we pray to Abraham Brown who will come again." The boy Jonason sighed and relaxed.

Abraham – Brown? But –

But I knew him. I met him. Nuber? Newburg, temporary capital of the Soviet of – oh, damn that . . . Met him, 2071 – the concert of mine he remembered . . . The wheel? The wheel? "And when did Abraham die, boy?"

"Oh – " Jonason moved fingers helplessly, embarrassed. Dates would be no part of the doctrine. "Long ago. A – a – " He glanced up hopefully. "A thousand years? I think – he who told us to call him Jonas did not teach us that."

"I see. Never mind. You speak well, boy." *Oh, my good Doctor, ex-President – after all! Artist, statesman, student of ethics, agnostic philosopher – all that long life you preached charity and skepticism, courage without the need of faith, the positive uses of the suspended judgment. All so clear, simple, obvious – needing only that little bit more of patience and courage which your human hearers were not ready to give. You must have known they were not, but did you know this would happen?*

Jonas and Abigail – some visionary pair, Brian supposed, full of this theory and that, maybe gone a bit foolish under the horrors of those years. Unthinking admirers of Brown, or perhaps not even that, perhaps just brewing their own syncretism because they thought a religion was needed, and using Brown's name – why? Because it was easy to remember? They probably felt some pride of creation in the job; possibly belief even grew in their own minds as they found the children accepting it and building a ritual life around it.

It was impossible, Brian thought, that Jonas and Abigail could have met the living Abraham Brown. Brown accepted mysteries because he faced the limitations of human intelligence; he had only contempt for the needless making of mysteries. He was without arrogance. No one could have talked five minutes with him without hearing a tranquil: "I don't know."

The *wheel* at Nuber? – but Brian realized he would never learn how Brown actually died. *I hope you suffered no more than most prophets.*

He was pulled from the pit of abstraction by the girl's awed question: "What is that?"

She was pointing to the clay image in its dusty sunlight. Brian was almost deaf to his own words until they were past recovering: "Oh, that – that is very old. Very old and very sacred." She nodded, round-eyed, and stepped back a pace or two. "And that was all they taught you of Abraham Brown?"

Astonished, the boy asked: "Is it not enough?"

There is always the Project. "Why, perhaps – "

"We know all the prayers, Old Man."

"Yes, yes, I'm sure you do."

"The Old Man will come with us." It was not a question.

"Eh?" *There is always the Project* . . . "Come with you?"

"We look for old ones." There was a new note in the young man's fine firm voice, and it was impatience. "We traveled many days, up across the sun-path. We want you to speak the Abraham-words for marriage. The old ones said we must not mate as the animals do without the words. "We want – "

"Marry, of course," Brian grumbled. *Poor old Jonas and Abigail, faithful to your century, such as it was!* Brian felt tired and confused, and rubbed a great long-fingered hand across his face so that the words might have come out blurred and dull. "Naturally, kids. Beget. Replenish the earth. I'm damned tired. I don't know any special hocus-pocus – I mean, any Abraham-words – for marriage. Just go ahead and breed. Try again – "

"But the Old Ones said – "

"Wait!" Brian cried. "Wait! Let me think . . . Did he – he who told you to call him Jonas – did he teach you anything about the world as it was in the old days, before you were born?"

"Before – the Old Man makes fun of us."

"No, no." Since he now had to fight down a certain physical fear as well as confusion, Brian spoke more harshly than he intended: "Answer my question! What do you know of the old days? I was a young man once, do you understand that? – as young as you. What do you know about the world I lived in?"

The young man laughed. There was new-born suspicion in him as well as anger, stiffening his shoulders, narrowing his innocent gray eyes. "There was always the world," he said, "ever since God made it a thousand years ago."

"Was there? . . . I was a musician. Do you know what a musician is?"

The young man shook his head lightly, watching Brian, too alertly, watching his hands, aware of him in a new way, no longer humble. Paula sensed the tension and did not like it. She said worriedly, politely: "We forget some of the things they taught us, sa. They were Old Ones. Most of the days they were away from us in places where we were not to go, praying. Old Ones are always praying."

"I will hear this Old Man pray," said Jonason. The butt of the javelin rested against Jonason's foot, the blade swaying from side to side, a waiting snake's head. A misstep, a wrong word – any trifle, Brian knew, could make them decide he was evil and not sacred. Their religion would inevitably require a devil.

He thought also: *It would merely be one of the ways of dying, not the worst.*

"You shall hear me make music," he said sternly, "and you shall be content with that. Come this way!" In fluctuating despair, he was wondering if any good might come of anger. "Come this way! You shall hear a world you never knew." Naked and ugly, he stalked across the Hall of Music, not looking behind him, though he sensed every glint of light from that bread-knife javelin. "This way!" he shouted. "Come in here!" He flung open the door of the auditorium and strode up on the platform. "Sit down!" he roared at them. "Sit down over there and be quiet, be quiet!"

He thought they did – he could not look at them. He knew he was muttering between his noisy outbursts as he twitched the cover off the piano and raised the lid, muttering bits and fragments from the old times and the new: "They went thataway . . . Oh, Mr. Van Anda, it just simply goes right through me – I can't express it. Madam, such was my intention, or as Brahms is supposed to have said on a slightly different subject, any ass knows that . . . Brio, Rubato, and Schmalz went to sea in a – Jonason, Paula, this is a pianoforte; it will not hurt you. Sit there, be quiet, and I pray you listen . . ."

He found calm. *Now, if ever, when there is living proof that human nature, some sort of human nature, is continuing – now if ever, the Project –*

With the sudden authority that was natural to Andrew Carr, Andrew Carr took over. In the stupendous opening chords of the introduction, Brian very nearly forgot his audience. Not quite. The children had sat down out there in the dusty region where none but ghosts had lingered for twenty-five years, but the piano's first sound brought them to their feet. Brian played through the first four bars, piling the chords like mountains, then held the last one with the pedal and waved his right hand at Jonason and Paula in a furious downward motion.

He thought they understood. He thought he saw them sit down again. But he could pay them no more attention, for the sonata was coming alive under his fingers, waking, growing, rejoicing.

He did not forget the children. They were important, too important, terrifying at the fringe of awareness. But he could not look toward them any more, and presently he shut his eyes.

He had never played like this in the flood of his prime, in the old days, before audiences that loved him. Never.

His eyes were still closed, holding him secure in a world that was not all darkness, when he ended the first movement, paused very briefly, and moved on with complete assurance to explore the depth and height of the second. This was true statement. This was Andrew Carr; he lived, even if after this late morning he might never live again.

And now the third, the storm and the wrath, the interludes of calm, the anger, denials, affirmations . . .

Without hesitation, without awareness of self, of age or pain or danger or loss, Brian was entering on the broad reaches of the last movement when he glanced out into the auditorium and understood the children were gone.

Too big. It had frightened them away. He could visualize them, stealing out with backward looks of panic, and remembering apparently to close the exit door. To them it was incomprehensible thunder.

Children – savages – to see or hear or comprehend the beautiful, you must first desire it. he could not think much about them now, when Andrew Carr was still with him. He played on with the same assurance, the same sense of victory. Children and savages, so let them go, with leave and goodwill.

Some external sound troubled him, something that must have begun under cover of these rising, pealing octave passages – storm waves, each higher than the last, until even the superhuman swimmer must be exhausted. It was some indefinable alien noise, a humming. Wind perhaps. Brian shook his head in irritation, not interrupting the work of his hands. It couldn't matter – everything was here, in the labors his hands still had to perform. The waves were growing more quiet, subsiding, and he must play the curious arpeggios he had never quite understood – but for this interpretation he understood them. Rip them out of the piano like showers of sparks, like distant lightning moving farther and farther away across a world that could never be at rest.

The final section at last. Why, it was a variation – and why had he never quite recognized it? – on a theme of Brahms, from the German Requiem. Quite plain, simple – Brahms would have approved. *Blessed are the dead* . . . Something more remained to be said, and Brian searched for it through the mighty unfolding of the finale. No hurrying, no crashing impatience any more, but a moving through time without fear of time, through radiance and darkness with no fear of either. *That they may rest from their labors, and their works do follow after them.*

Brian stood up, swaying and out of breath. So the music was over, and the children were gone, but a jangling, humming confusion was filling the Hall of Music out there – hardly a wind – distant but entering with some violence even here, now that the piano was silent. He moved stiffly out of the small auditorium, more or less knowing what he would find.

The noise became immense, the unchecked overtones of the marimba fuming and quivering as the smooth, high ceiling of the Hall of Music caught them and flung them about against the answering strings of pianos and harps and violins, the sulky membranes of drums, the nervous brass of cymbals.

The girl was playing it. Brian laughed once, softly, in the shadows, and was not heard. She had hit on a primeval rhythm natural for children or savages and needed nothing else, banging it out on one stone and another, wanting no rest or variation.

The boy was dancing, slapping his feet and pounding his chest, thrusting out his javelin in time to the clamor, edging up to his companion, grimacing, drawing back in order to return. Neither one was laughing, or close to laughter. Their faces were savage-solemn, grim with the excitement and healthy lust. All as spontaneous as the drumming of partridges. It was a long time before they saw Brian in the shadows.

Reaction was swift. The girl dropped the hammer. The boy froze, his javelin raised, then jerked his head at Paula, who snatched at some-thing – only moments later did Brian understand she had taken the clay image before she fled.

Jonason covered her retreat, stepping backward, his face blank and dangerous with fear. So swiftly, so easily, by grace of great civilized music and a few wrong words, had a sacred Old One become a Bad Old One.

They were gone, down the stairway, leaving the echo of Brian's voice crying: "Don't go! Please don't go!"

Brian followed them. Unwillingly. He was slow to reach the bottom of the stairway; there he looked across the shut-in water to his raft, which they had used and left at the windowsill port. Brian had never been a good swimmer, and would not attempt it now, but clutched the rope and hitched himself hand over hand to the windowsill, collapsing awhile until he found strength to scramble into his canoe and grope for the paddle.

The children's canoe was already far off. Heading up the river, the boy paddling with deep powerful strokes. Up the river, of course. They had to find the right kind of Old Ones. Up across the sun-path.

Brian dug his blade in the quiet water. For a time his rugged, ancient muscles were willing. There was sap in them yet. Perhaps he was gaining. He shouted hugely: "Bring back my two-faced god! And what about my music? You? Did you like it? Speak up!"

They must have heard his voice booming at them. At least the girl looked back, once. The boy, intent on his paddling, did not. Brian roared: "Bring back my little god!"

He was not gaining on them. After all they had a mission. They had to find an Old One with the right Abraham-words. Brian thought: *Damn it, hasn't MY world some rights? We'll see about this!*

He lifted his paddle like a spear, and flung it, knowing even as his shoulder winced with the backlash of the thrust that his action was at the outer limit of absurdity. The children were so far away that even an arrow from a bow might not have reached them. The paddle splashed in the water. Not far away. A small infinity.

It swung about, adjusting to the current, the heavy end pointing downstream, obeying the river and the ebb tide. It nuzzled companionably against a gray-faced chunk of driftwood, diverting it, so that presently the chunk floated into Brian's reach. He flung it back toward the paddle, hoping it might fall on the other side and send the paddle near him, but it fell short. In his unexpectedly painless extremity Brian was not surprised, but merely watched the gray face floating and bobbing along beside him out of reach, and his irritation became partly friendliness. The driftwood fragment suggested the face of a music critic he had once met – New Boston, was it? Denver? London? – no matter.

"Why," he said aloud, detachedly observing the passage of his canoe beyond the broad morning shadow of the Museum, "why, I seem to have killed myself."

"Mr. Van Anda has abundantly demonstrated a mastery of the instrument and of the" – *Oh, go play solfeggio on your linotype!* – "literature of both classic and contemporary repertory. While we cannot endorse the perhaps overemotional quality of his Bach, and there might easily be two views of his handling of the passage in double thirds which – "

"I can't swim it, you know," said Brian. "Not against the ebb, that's for sure."

" – so that on the whole one feels he has earned himself a not discreditable place among – " Gaining on the canoe, passing it, the gray-faced chip moved on benignly twittering toward the open sea, where the canoe must follow. With a final remnant of strength Brian inched forward to the bow and gathered the full force of his lungs to shout up the river to the children: "Go in peace!"

They could not have heard him. They were too far away, and a new morning wind was blowing, fresh and sweet, out of the northwest.

Hot Planet

HAL CLEMENT

Hal Clement (the pen name of Harry Clement Stubbs [1922–]) is a retired science teacher who has published science fiction since 1942, and whose work has become a paradigm for that branch of science fiction that delights in careful extrapolation from a scientific principle or idea. *Science Fiction Writers* (1996) says, "Clement and his classic fiction are mentioned whenever the discussion of science in the genre comes up . . . their distinguishing characteristic is that a problematic condition in physical reality, or simply a condition of difference such as an increase or decrease in heat or gravity, must be elaborated upon, explained, and taken through certain plot changes so that the reader can simply understand the problem or the difference. This is a literature of total mimesis, in which the facts of the universe are mimed." It is commonly referred to as hard science fiction (think of hard rock or the hard sciences – physics, chemistry, astronomy).

Clement's mastery of the astronomy, physics, and chemistry in stories set in space and on other worlds became famous with the publication of the *Astounding* serial, "Heavy Planet" (later published as *Mission of Gravity,* 1954), but especially with the immediately subsequent publication of a nonfiction article in the same magazine, detailing the process by which he had figured out the physics, astronomy, and biochemistry of the world of Mesklin. With the publication of *Mission of Gravity,* Clement in effect redefined the game of hard SF as an exercise in interrelating the sciences to achieve a created world that would plausibly withstand rigorous examination from many angles. Of such conceptual break-throughs are scientific revolutions accomplished, and this was a revolution in science fiction, a slow and subtle one that took more than a decade to take hold. Gradually Clement gained a worldwide reputation as a quintessential hard SF writer whose works in later years more or less defined the term.

"Hot Planet" builds a consistent and detailed world for its alien characters to operate in, a world radically distanced from our own by its physical nature but also clearly, through our knowledge of science, connected to it: it is plausible. The story has the beauty of science at its heart, the awe-inspiring vistas of universal truth made manifest. Clement's work is presently the most influential model for hard science fiction writers.

The wind which had nearly turned the *Albireo's* landing into a disaster instead of a mathematical exercise was still playing tunes about the fins and landing legs as Schlossberg made his way down to Deck Five.

The noise didn't bother him particularly, though the endless seismic tremors made him dislike the ladders. But just now he was able to ignore both. He was curious – though not hopeful.

"Is there anything at all obvious on the last sets of tapes, Joe?"

Mardikian, the geophysicist, shrugged. "Just what you'd expect . . . on a planet which has at least one quake in each fifty-mile-square area every five minutes. You know yourself we had a nice seismic program set up, but when we touched down we found we couldn't carry it out. We've done our best with the natural tremors – incidentally stealing most of the record tapes the other projects would have used. We have a lot of nice information for the computers back home; but it will take all of them to make any sense out of it."

Schlossberg nodded; the words had not been necessary. His astronomical program had been one of those sabotaged by the transfer of tapes to the seismic survey.

"I just hoped," he said. "We each have an idea why Mercury developed an atmosphere during the last few decades, but I guess the high school kids on Earth will know whether it's right before we do. I'm resigned to living in a chess-type universe – few and simple rules, but infinite combinations of them. But it would be nice to know an answer sometime."

"So it would. As a matter of fact, I need to know a couple right now. From you. How close to finished are the other programs – or what's left of them?"

"I'm all set," replied Schlossberg. "I have a couple of instruments still monitoring the sun just in case, but everything in the revised program is on tape."

"Good. Tom, any use asking you?"

The biologist grimaced. "I've been shown two hundred and sixteen different samples of rock and dust. I have examined in detail twelve crystal growths which looked vaguely like vegetation. Nothing was alive or contained living things by any standards I could conscientiously set."

Mardikian's gesture might have meant sympathy.

"Camille?"

"I may as well stop now as any time. I'll never be through. Tape didn't make much difference to me, but I wish I knew what weight of specimens I could take home."

"Eileen?" Mardikian's glance at the stratigrapher took the place of the actual question.

"Cam speaks for me, except that I could have used any more tape you could have spared. What I have is gone."

"All right, that leaves me, the tape-thief. The last spools are in the seismographs now, and will start running out in seventeen hours. The tractors will start out on their last rounds in sixteen, and should be back in roughly a week. Will, does that give you enough to figure the weights we rockhounds can have on the return trip?"

The *Albireo*'s captain nodded. "Close enough. There really hasn't been much question since it became evident we'd find nothing for the mass tanks here. I'll have a really precise check in an hour, but I can tell right now that you have about one and a half metric tons to split up among the three of you.

"Ideal departure time is three hundred ten hours away, as you all know. We can stay here until then, or go into a parking-and-survey orbit at almost any time before then. You have all the survey you need, I should think, from the other time. But suit yourselves."

"I'd just as soon be space-sick as seasick," remarked Camille Burkett. "I still hate to think that the entire planet is as shivery as the spot we picked."

Willard Rowson smiled. "You researchers told me where to land after ten days in orbit mapping this rockball. I set you just where you asked. If you'd found even five tons of juice we could use in the reaction tanks I could still take you to another one – if you could agree which one. I hate to say, 'Don't blame me,' but I can't think of anything else that fits."

"So we sit until the last of the tractors is back with the precious seismo tapes, playing battleship while our back teeth are being shaken out by earthquakes – excuse the word. What a thrill! Glorious adventure!" Zaino, the communications specialist who had been out of a job almost constantly since the landing, spoke sourly. The captain was the only one who saw fit to answer.

"If you want adventure, you made a mistake exploring space. The only space adventures I've heard of are secondhand stories built on guesswork; the people who really had them weren't around to tell about it. Unless Dr. Marini discovers a set of Mercurian monsters at the last minute and they invade the ship or cut off one of the tractors, I'm afraid you'll have to do without adventures." Zaino grimaced.

"That sounds funny coming from a spaceman, Captain. I didn't really mean adventure, though; all I want is something to do besides betting whether the next quake will come in one minute or five. I haven't even had to fix a suit-radio since we touched down. How about my going out with one of the tractors on this last trip, at least?"

"It's all right with me," replied Rowson, "but Dr. Mardikian runs the professional part of this operation. I require that Spurr, Trackman, Hargedon and Aiello go as drivers, since without them even a minor mechanical problem would be more than an adventure. As I recall it, Dr. Harmon, Dr. Schlossberg, Dr. Marini and Dr. Mardikian are scheduled to go; but if any one of them is willing to let you take his or her place, I certainly don't mind."

The radioman looked around hopefully. The geologists and the biologist shook their heads negatively, firmly and unanimously; but the astronomer pondered for a moment. Zaino watched tensely.

"It may be all right," Schlossberg said at last. "What I want to get is a set of wind, gas pressure, gas temperature and gas composition measures around the route. I didn't expect to be more meteorologist than astronomer when we left Earth, and didn't have exactly the right equipment. Hargedon and Aiello helped me improvise some, and this is the first chance to use it on Darkside. If you can learn what has to be done with it before starting time, though, you are welcome to my place."

The communicator got to his feet fast enough to leave the deck in Mercury's feeble gravity.

"Lead me to it, Doc. I guess I can learn to read a homemade weathervane!"

"Is that merely bragging, or a challenge?" drawled a voice which had not previously joined the discussion. Zaino flushed a bit.

"Sorry, Luigi," he said hastily. "I didn't mean it just that way. But I still think I can run the stuff."

"Likely enough," Aiello replied. "Remember though, it wasn't made just for talking into." Schlossberg, now on his feet, cut in quickly.

"Come on, Arnie. We'll have to suit up to see the equipment; it's outside."

He shepherded the radioman to the batch at one side of the deck and shooed him down toward the engine and air lock levels. Both were silent for some moments; but safely out of earshot of Deck Five the younger man looked up and spoke.

"You needn't push, Doc. I wasn't going to make anything of it. Luigi was right, and I asked for it." The astronomer slowed a bit in his descent.

"I wasn't really worried," he replied, "but we have several months yet before we can get away from each other, and I don't like talk that could set up grudges. Matter of fact, I'm even a little uneasy about having the girls along, though I'm no misogynist."

"Girls? They're not – "

"There goes your foot again. Even Harmon is about ten years older than you, I suppose. But they're girls to me. What's more important, they no doubt think of themselves as girls."

"Even Dr. Burkett? That is – I mean – "

"Even Dr. Burkett. Here, get into your suit. And maybe you'd better take out the mike. It'll be enough if you can listen for the next hour or two." Zaino made no answer, suspecting with some justice that anything he said would be wrong.

Each made final checks on the other's suit; then they descended one more level to the airlock. This occupied part of the same deck as the fusion plants, below the wings and reaction mass tanks but above the main engine. Its outer door was just barely big enough to admit a space-suited person. Even with the low air pressure carried by space-ships, a large door area meant large total force on jamb, hinges and locks. It opened onto a small balcony from which a ladder led to the ground. The two men paused on the balcony to look over the landscape.

This hadn't changed noticeably since the last time either had been out, though there might have been some small difference in the volcanic cones a couple of miles away to the northeast. The furrows down the sides of these, which looked as though they had been cut by water but were actually bone-dry ash slides, were always undergoing alteration as gas from below kept blowing fresh scoria fragments out of the craters.

The spines – steep, jagged fragments of rock which thrust upward from the plain beyond and to both sides of the cones – seemed dead as ever.

The level surface between the *Albireo* and the cones was more inter-esting. Mardikian and Schlossberg believed it to be a lava sheet dating from early in Mercury's history, when more volatile substances still existed in the surface rocks to cut down their viscosity when molten. They supposed that much – perhaps most – of the surface around the "twilight" belt had been flooded by this very liquid lava, which had cooled to a smoother surface than most Earthly lava flows.

How long it had stayed cool they didn't guess. But both men felt sure that Mercury must have periodic upheavals as heat accumulated inside it – heat coming not from radioactivity but from tidal energy. Mercury's orbit is highly eccentric. At perihelion, tidal force tries to pull it apart along the planet-to-sun line, while at aphelion the tidal force is less and the little world's own gravity tries to bring it back to a spherical shape. The real change in form is not great, but a large force working through even a small amount of distance can mean a good deal of energy.

If the energy can't leak out – and Mercury's rocks conduct heat no better than those of Earth – the temperature must rise.

Sooner or later, the men argued, deeply buried rock must fuse to magma. Its liquefaction would let the bulk of the planet give farther under tidal stress, so heat would be generated even faster. Eventually a girdle of magma would have to form far below the crust all around the twilight strip, where the tidal strain would be greatest. Sooner or later this would melt its way to the surface, giving the zone a period of intense volcanic activity and, incidentally, giving the planet a temporary atmosphere.

The idea was reasonable. It had, the astronomer admitted, been suggested long before to account for supposed vulcanism on the moon. It justified the careful examination that Schlossberg and Zaino gave the plain before they descended the ladder; for it made reasonable the occasional changes which were observed to occur in the pattern of cracks weaving over its surface.

No one was certain just how permanent the local surface was – though no one could really justify feeling safer on board the *Albireo* than outside on the lava. If anything really drastic happened, the ship would be no protection.

The sun, hanging just above the horizon slightly to the watcher's right, cast long shadows which made the cracks stand out clearly; as far as either man could see, nothing had changed recently. They

descended the ladder carefully – even the best designed space suits are
somewhat vulnerable – and made their way to the spot where the
tractors were parked.

A sheet-metal fence a dozen feet high and four times as long
provided shade, which was more than a luxury this close to the sun.
The tractors were parked in this shadow, and beside and between
them were piles of equipment and specimens. The apparatus
Schlossberg had devised was beside the tractor at the north end of the
line, just inside the shaded area.

It was still just inside the shade when they finished, four hours later.
Hargedon had joined them during the final hour and helped pack the
equipment in the tractor he was to drive. Zaino had had no trouble in
learning to make the observations Schlossberg wanted, and the youngster was almost unbearably cocky. Schlossberg hoped, as they returned
to the *Albireo,* that no one would murder the communications expert in
the next twelve hours. There would be nothing to worry about after
the trip started; Hargedon was quite able to keep anyone in his place
without being nasty about it. If Zaino had been going with Aiello or
Harmon – but he wasn't, and it was pointless to dream up trouble.

And no trouble developed all by itself.

Zaino was not only still alive but still reasonably popular when the first
of the tractors set out, carrying Eileen Harmon and Eric Trackman,
the *Albireo's* nuclear engineer.

It started more than an hour before the others, since the stratigrapher's drilling program, "done" or not, took extra time. The tractor
hummed off to the south, since both Darkside routes required a long
detour to pass the chasm to the west. Routes had been worked out
from the stereo-photos taken during the orbital survey. Even Darkside
had been covered fairly well with Uniquantum film under Venus light.

The Harmon-Trackman vehicle was well out of sight when
Mardikian and Aiello started out on one of the Brightside routes, and
a few minutes later Marini set out on the other with the space-suit
technician, Mary Spurr, driving.

Both vehicles disappeared quickly into a valley to the northeast,
between the ash cones and a thousand-foot spine which rose just south
of them. All the tractors were in good radio contact; Zaino made sure
of that before he abandoned the radio watch to Rowson, suited up and
joined Hargedon at the remaining one. They climbed in, and
Hargedon set it in motion.

At about the same time, the first tractor came into view again, now traveling north on the farther side of the chasm. Hargedon took this as evidence that the route thus far was unchanged, and kicked in highest speed.

The cabin was pretty cramped, even though some of the equipment had been attached outside. The men could not expect much comfort for the next week.

Hargedon was used to the trips, however. He disapproved on principle of people who complained about minor inconveniences such as having to sleep in space suits; fortunately, Zaino's interest and excitement overrode any thought he might have had about discomfort.

This lasted through the time they spent doubling the vast crack in Mercury's crust, driving on a little to the north of the ship on the other side and then turning west toward the dark hemisphere. The route was identical to that of Harmon's machine for some time, though no trace of its passage showed on the hard surface. Then Hargedon angled off toward the southwest. He had driven this run often enough to know it well even without the markers which had been set out with the seismographs. The photographic maps were also aboard. With them, even Zaino had no trouble keeping track of their progress while they remained in sunlight.

However, the sun sank as they traveled west. In two hours its lower rim would have been on the horizon, had they been able to see the horizon; as it was, more of the "sea level" lava plain was in shadow than not even near the ship, and their route now lay in semidarkness.

The light came from peaks projecting into the sunlight, from scattered skylight which was growing rapidly fainter and from the brighter celestial objects such as Earth. Even with the tractor's lights it was getting harder to spot crevasses and seismometer markers. Zaino quickly found the fun wearing off . . . though his pride made him cover this fact as best he could.

If Hargedon saw this, he said nothing. He set Zaino to picking up every other instrument, as any partner would have, making no allowance for the work the youngster was doing for Schlossberg. This might, of course, have had the purpose of keeping the radioman too busy to think about discomfort. Or it might merely have been Hargedon's idea of normal procedure.

Whatever the cause, Zaino got little chance to use the radio once they had driven into the darkness. He managed only one or two brief talks with those left at the ship.

The talks might have helped his morale, since they certainly must have given the impression that nothing was going on in the ship while at least he had something to do in the tractor. However, this state of affairs did not last. Before the vehicle was four hours out of sight of the *Albireo*, a broadcast by Camille Burkett reached them.

The mineralogist's voice contained at least as much professional enthusiasm as alarm, but everyone listening must have thought promptly of the dubious stability of Mercury's crust. The call was intended for her fellow geologists Mardikian and Harmon. But it interested Zaino at least as much.

"Joe! Eileen! There's a column of what looks like black smoke rising over Northeast Spur. It can't be a real fire, of course; I can't see its point of origin, but if it's the convection current it seems to me the source must be pretty hot. It's the closest thing to a genuine volcano I've seen since we arrived; it's certainly not another of those ash mounds. I should think you'd still be close enough to make it out, Joe. Can you see anything?"

The reply from Mardikian's tractor was inaudible to Zaino and Hargedon, but Burkett's answer made its general tenor plain.

"I hadn't thought of that. Yes, I'd say it was pretty close to the Brightside route. It wouldn't be practical for you to stop your run now to come back to see. You couldn't do much about it anyway. I could go out to have a look and then report to you. If the way back is blocked there'll be plenty of time to work out another." Hargedon and Zaino passed questioning glances at each other during the shorter pause that followed.

"I know there aren't," the voice then went on, responding to the words they could not hear, "but it's only two or three miles, I'd say. Two to the spur and not much farther to where I could see the other side. Enough of the way is in shade so I could make it in a suit easily enough. I can't see calling back either of the Darkside tractors. Their work is just as important as the rest – anyway, Eileen is probably out of range. She hasn't answered yet."

Another pause.

"That's true. Still, it would mean sacrificing that set of seismic records – no, wait. We could go out later for those. And Mel could take his own weather measures on the later trip. There's plenty of time!"

Pause, longer this time.

"You're right, of course. I just wanted to get an early look at this volcano, if it is one. We'll let the others finish their runs, and when you get back you can check the thing from the other side yourself. If it is blocking your way there's time to find an alternate route. We could be doing that from the maps in the meantime, just in case."

Zaino looked again at his companion.

"Isn't that just my luck!" he exclaimed. "I jump at the first chance to get away from being bored to death. The minute I'm safely away, the only interesting thing of the whole operation happens – back at the ship!"

"Who asked to come on this trip?"

"Oh, I'm not blaming anyone but myself. If I'd stayed back there the volcano would have popped out here somewhere, or else waited until we were gone."

"If it is a volcano. Dr. Burkett didn't seem quite sure."

"No, and I'll bet a nickel she's suiting up right now to go out and see. I hope she comes back with something while we're still near enough to hear about it."

Hargedon shrugged. "I suppose it was also just your luck that sent you on a Darkside trip? You know the radio stuff. You knew we couldn't reach as far this way with the radios. Didn't you think of that in advance?"

"I didn't think of it, any more than you would have. It was bad luck, but I'm not grousing about it. Let's get on with this job." Hargedon nodded with approval, and possibly with some surprise, and the tractor hummed on its way.

The darkness deepened around the patches of lava shown by the driving lights; the sky darkened toward a midnight hue, with stars showing ever brighter through it; and radio reception from the *Albireo* began to get spotty. Gas density at the ion layer was high enough so that recombination of molecules with their radiation-freed electrons was rapid. Only occasional streamers of ionized gas reached far over Darkside. As these thinned out, so did radio reception. Camille Burkett's next broadcast came through very poorly.

There was enough in it, however, to seize the attention of the two men in the tractor.

She was saying: "real all right, and dangerous. It's the . . . thing I ever saw . . . kinds of lava from what looks like . . . same vent. There's high viscosity stuff building a spatter cone to end all spatter cones, and some very thin fluid from somewhere at the bottom. The flow has already blocked the valley used by the Brightside routes and is coming along it. A new return route will have to be found for the tractors that . . . was spreading fast when I saw it. I can't tell how much will come. But unless it stops there's nothing at all to keep the flow away from the ship. It isn't coming fast, but it's coming. I'd advise all tractors to turn back. Captain Rowson reminds me that only one takeoff is possible. If we leave this site, we're committed to leaving Mercury. Arnie and Ren, do you hear me?"

Zaino responded at once. "We got most of it, Doctor. Do you really think the ship is in danger?"

"I don't know. I can only say that *if* this flow continues the ship will have to leave, because this area will sooner or later be covered. I can't guess how likely . . . check further to get some sort of estimate. It's different from any Earthly lava source – maybe you heard – should try to get Eileen and Eric back, too. I can't raise them. I suppose they're well out from under the ion layer by now. Maybe you're close enough to them to catch them with diffracted waves. Try, anyway. Whether you can raise them or not you'd better start back yourself."

Hargedon cut in at this point. "What does Dr. Mardikian say about that? We still have most of the seismometers on this route to visit."

"I think Captain Rowson has the deciding word here, but if it helps your decision Dr. Mardikian has already started back. He hasn't finished his route, either. So hop back here, Ren. And Arnie, put that technical skill you haven't had to use yet to work raising Eileen and Eric."

"What I can do, I will," replied Zaino, "but you'd better tape a recall message and keep it going out on – let's see – band F."

"All right. I'll be ready to check the volcano as soon as you get back. How long?"

"Seven hours – maybe six and a half," replied Hargedon. "We have to be careful."

"Very well. Stay outside when you arrive; I'll want to go right out in the tractor to get a closer look." She cut off.

"And *that* came through clearly enough!" remarked Hargedon as he swung the tractor around. "I've been awake for fourteen hours, driving off and on for ten of them; I'm about to drive for another six; and then I'm to stand by for more."

"Would you like me to do some of the driving?" asked Zaino.

"I guess you'll have to, whether I like it or not," was the rather lukewarm reply. "I'll keep on for a while, though – until we're back in better light. You get at your radio job."

Zaino tried. Hour after hour he juggled from one band to another. Once he had Hargedon stop while he went out to attach a makeshift antenna which, he hoped, would change his output from broadcast to some sort of beam; after this he kept probing the sky with the "beam," first listening to the *Albireo's* broadcast in an effort to find projecting wisps of ionosphere and then, whenever he thought he had one, switching on his transmitter and driving his own message at it.

Not once did he complain about lack of equipment or remark how much better he could do once he was back at the ship.

Hargedon's silence began to carry an undercurrent of approval not usual in people who spent much time with Zaino. The technician made no further reference to the suggestion of switching drivers. They came in sight of the *Albireo* and doubled the chasm with Hargedon still at the wheel, Zaino still at his radio and both of them still uncertain whether any of the calls had gotten through.

Both had to admit, even before they could see the ship, that Burkett had had a right to be impressed.

The smoke column showed starkly against the sky, blowing back over the tractor and blocking the sunlight which would otherwise have glared into the driver's eyes. Fine particles fell from it in a steady shower; looking back, the men could see tracks left by their vehicle in the deposit which had already fallen.

As they approached the ship the dark pillar grew denser and narrower, while the particles raining from it became coarser. In some places the ash was drifting into fairly deep piles, giving Hargedon some anxiety about possible concealed cracks. The last part of the trip, along the edge of the great chasm and around its end, was really dangerous; cracks running from its sides were definitely spreading. The two men reached the *Albireo* later than Hargedon had promised, and found Burkett waiting impatiently with a pile of apparatus beside her.

She didn't wait for them to get out before starting to organize.

"There isn't much here. We'll take off just enough of what you're carrying to make room for this. No – wait. I'll have to check some of your equipment; I'm going to need one of Milt Schlossberg's gadgets, I think, so leave that on. We'll take – "

"Excuse me, Doctor," cut in Hargedon. "Our suits need servicing, or at least mine will if you want me to drive you. Perhaps Arnie can help you load for a while, if you don't think it's too important for him to get at the radio – "

"Of course. Excuse me. I should have had someone out here to help me with this. You two go on in. Ren, please get back as soon as you can. I can do the work here; none of this stuff is very heavy."

Zaino hesitated as he swung out of the cab. True, there wasn't too much to be moved, and it wasn't very heavy in Mercury's gravity, and he really should be at the radio; but the thirty-nine-year-old mineralogist was a middle-aged lady by his standards, and shouldn't be allowed to carry heavy packages . . .

"Get along, Arnie!" the middle-aged lady interrupted this train of thought. "Eric and Eileen are getting farther away and harder to reach every second you dawdle!"

He got, though he couldn't help looking northeast as he went rather than where he was going.

The towering menace in that direction would have claimed anyone's attention. The pillar of sable ash was rising straighter, as though the wind were having less effect on it. An equally black cone had risen into sight beyond Northeast Spur – a cone that must have grown to some two thousand feet in roughly ten hours. It had far steeper sides than the cinder mounds near it; it couldn't be made of the same loose ash. Perhaps it consisted of half-melted particles which were fusing together as they fell – that might be what Burkett had meant by "spatter-cone." Still, if that were the case, the material fountaining from the cone's top should be lighting the plain with its incandescence rather than casting an inky shadow for its entire height.

Well, that was a problem for the geologists; Zaino climbed aboard and settled to his task.

The trouble was that he could do very little more here than he could in the tractor. He could have improvised longer-wave transmitting coils whose radiations would have diffracted a little more effectively beyond the horizon, but the receiver on the missing vehicle would not have detected them. He had more power at his disposal, but could only beam it into empty space with his better antennae. He had better equipment for locating any projecting wisps of charged gas which might reflect his waves, but he was already located under a solid roof of the stuff – the *Albireo* was technically on Brightside. Bouncing his beam from this layer still didn't give him the range he needed, as he had found both by calculation and trial.

What he really needed was a relay satellite. The target was simply too far around Mercury's sharp curve by now for anything less.

Zaino's final gesture was to set his transmission beam on the lowest frequency the tractor would pick up, aim it as close to the vehicle's direction as he could calculate from map and itinerary and set the recorded return message going. He told Rowson as much.

"Can't think of anything else?" the captain asked. "Well, neither can I, but of course it's not my field. I'd give a year's pay if I could. How long before they should be back in range?"

"About four days. A hundred hours, give or take a few. They'll be heading back anyway by that time."

"Of course. Well, keep trying."

"I am – or rather, the equipment is. I don't see what else I can do unless a really bright idea should suddenly sprout. Is there anywhere else I could be useful? I'm as likely to have ideas working as just sitting."

"We can keep you busy, all right. But how about taking a transmitter up one of those mountains? That would get your wave farther."

"Not as far as it's going already. I'm bouncing it off the ion layer, which is higher than any mountain we've seen on Mercury even if it's nowhere near as high as Earth's."

"Hmph. All right."

"I could help Ren and Dr. Burkett. I could hang on outside the tractor – "

"They've already gone. You'd better call them, though, and keep a log of what they do."

"All right." Zaino turned back to his board and with no trouble raised the tractor carrying Hargedon and the mineralogist. The latter had been trying to call the *Albireo* and had some acid comments about radio operators who slept on the job.

"There's only one of me, and I've been trying to get the Darkside team," he pointed out. "Have you found anything new about this lava flood?"

"Flow, not flood," corrected the professional automatically. "We're not in sight of it yet. We've just rounded the corner that takes us out of your sight. It's over a mile yet, and a couple of more corners, before we get to the spot where I left it. Of course, it will be closer than that by now. It was spreading at perhaps a hundred yards an hour then. That's one figure we must refine . . . Of course, I'll try to get samples, too. I wish there were some way to get samples of the central cone. The whole thing is the queerest volcano I've ever heard of. Have you gotten Eileen started back?"

"Not as far as I can tell. As with your cone samples, there are practical difficulties," replied Zaino. "I haven't quit yet, though."

"I should think not. If some of us were paid by the idea we'd be pretty poor, but the perspiration part of genius is open to all of us."

"You mean I should charge a bonus for getting this call through?" retorted the operator.

Whatever Burkett's reply to this might have been was never learned; her attention was diverted at that point.

"We've just come in sight of the flow. It's about five hundred yards ahead. We'll get as close as seems safe, and I'll try to make sure whether it's really lava or just mud."

"Mud? Is that possible? I thought there wasn't – couldn't be – any water on this planet!"

"It is, and there probably isn't. The liquid phase of mud doesn't have to be water, even though it usually is on Earth. Here, for example, it might conceivably be sulfur."

"But if it's just mud, it wouldn't hurt the ship, would it?"

"Probably not."

"Then why all this fuss about getting the tractors back in a hurry?"

The voice which answered reminded him of another lady in his past, who had kept him after school for drawing pictures in math class.

"Because in my judgment the flow is far more likely to be lava than mud, and if I must be wrong I'd rather my error were one that left us alive. I have no time at the moment to explain the basis of my judgment. I will be reporting our activities quite steadily from now on, and would prefer that you not interrupt unless a serious emergency demands it, or you get a call from Eileen.

"We are about three hundred yards away now. The front is moving about as fast as before, which suggests that the flow is coming only along this valley. It's only three or four feet high, so viscosity is very low or density very high. Probably the former, considering where we are. It's as black as the smoke column."

"Not glowing?" cut in Zaino thoughtlessly.

"*Black*, I said. Temperature will be easier to measure when we get closer. The front is nearly straight across the valley, with just a few lobes projecting ten or twelve yards and one notch where a small spine is being surrounded. By the way, I trust you're taping all this?" Again Zaino was reminded of the afternoon after school.

"Yes, Ma'am," he replied. "On my one and only monitor tape."

"Very well. We're stopping near the middle of the valley one hundred yards from the front. I am getting out, and will walk as close as I can with a sampler and a radiometer. I assume that the radio equipment will continue to relay my suit broadcast back to you." Zaino cringed a little, certain as he was that the tractor's electronic apparatus was in perfect order.

It struck him that Dr. Burkett was being more snappish than usual. It never crossed his mind that the woman might be afraid.

"Ren, don't get any closer with the tractor unless I call. I'll get a set of temperature readings as soon as I'm close enough. Then I'll try to get a sample. Then I'll come back with that to the tractor, leave it and the radiometer and get the markers to set out."

"Couldn't I be putting out the markers while you get the sample, Doctor?"

"You could, but I'd rather you stayed at the wheel." Hargedon made no answer, and Burkett resumed her description for the record.

"I'm walking toward the front, a good deal faster than it's flowing toward me. I am now about twenty yards away, and am going to take a set of radiation-temperature measures. A brief pause. "Readings coming. Nine sixty. Nine eighty. Nine ninety – that's from the bottom edge near the spine that's being surrounded. Nine eighty-five – " The voice droned on until about two dozen readings had been taped. Then, "I'm going closer now. The sampler is just a ladle on a twelve-foot handle we improvised, so I'll have to get that close. The stuff is moving slowly; there should be no trouble. I'm in reach now. The lava is very liquid; there's no trouble getting the sampler in – or out again – it's not very dense, either. I'm heading back toward the tractor now. No, Ren, don't come to meet me."

There was a minute of silence, while Zaino pictured the space-suited figure with its awkwardly long burden, walking away from the creeping menace to the relative safety of the tractor. "It's frozen solid already; we needn't worry about spilling. The temperature is about – five eighty. Give me the markers, please."

Another pause, shorter this time. Zaino wondered how much of that could be laid to a faster walk without the ladle and how much to the lessening distance between flow and tractor. "I'm tossing the first marker close to the edge – it's landed less than a foot from the lava. They're all on a light cord at ten-foot intervals; I'm paying out the cord as I go back to the tractor. Now we'll stand by and time the arrival at each marker as well as we can."

"How close are you to the main cone?" asked Zaino.

"Not close enough to see its base, I'm afraid. Or to get a sample of it, which is worse. We – goodness, what was that?"

Zaino had just time to ask, "What was what?" when he found out.

For a moment, he thought that the *Albireo* had been flung bodily into the air. Then he decided that the great metal pillar had merely fallen over. Finally he realized that the ship was still erect, but the ground under it had just tried to leave.

Everyone in the group had become so used to the almost perpetual ground tremors that they had ceased to notice them; but this one demanded attention. Rowson, using language which suggested that his career might not have been completely free of adventure after all, flashed through the communication level on his way down to the power section. Schlossberg and Babineau followed, the medic pausing to ask Zaino if he were all right. The radioman merely nodded affirmatively; his attention was already back at his job. Burkett was speaking a good deal faster than before.

"Never mind if the sample isn't lashed tight yet – if it falls off there'll be plenty more. There isn't time! Arnie, get in touch with Dr. Mardikian and Dr. Marini. Tell them that this volcano is explosive, that all estimates of what the flow may do are off until we can make more measures, and in any case the whole situation is unpredictable. Everyone should get back as soon as possible. Remember, we decided that those big craters Eileen checked were not meteor pits. I don't know whether this thing will let go in the next hour, the next year, or at all. Maybe what's happening now will act as a safety valve – but let's get out. Ren, that flow is speeding up and getting higher, and the ash rain is getting a lot worse. Can you see to drive?"

She fell silent. Zaino, in spite of her orders, left his set long enough to leap to the nearest port for a look at the volcano.

He never regretted it.

Across the riven plain, whose cracks were now nearly hidden under the new ash, the black cone towered above the nearer elevations. It was visibly taller than it had been only a few hours before. The fountain from its top was thicker, now jetting straight up as though wind no longer meant a thing to the fiercely driven column of gas and dust. The darkness was not so complete; patches of red and yellow incandescence showed briefly in the pillar, and glowing sparks rather than black cinders rained back on the steep slopes. Far above, a ring of smoke rolled and spread about the column, forming an ever-broadening blanket of opaque cloud above a landscape which had never before been shaded from the sun. Streamers of lightning leaped between cloud and pillar, pillar and mountain, even cloud and ground. Any thunder there might have been was drowned in the howl of the escaping gas, a roar which seemed to combine every possible note from the shrillest possible whistle to a bass felt by the chest rather than heard by the ears. Rowson's language had become inaudible almost before he had disappeared down the hatch.

For long moments the radioman watched the spreading cloud, and wondered whether the *Albireo* could escape being struck by the flickering, ceaseless lightning. Far above the widening ring of cloud the smoke fountain drove, spreading slowly in the thinning atmosphere and beyond it. Zaino had had enough space experience to tell at a glance whether a smoke or dust cloud was in air or not. This wasn't, at least at the upper extremity . . .

And then, quite calmly, he turned back to his desk, aimed the antenna straight up, and called Eileen Harmon. She answered promptly.

The stratigrapher listened without interruption to his report and the order to return. She conferred briefly with her companion, replied, "We'll be back in twelve hours," and signed off. And that was that.

Zaino settled back with a sigh, and wondered whether it would be tactful to remind Rowson of his offer of a year's pay.

All four vehicles were now homeward bound; all one had to worry about was whether any of them would make it. Hargedon and Burkett were fighting their way through an ever-increasing ash rain a scant two miles away – ash which not only cut visibility but threatened to block the way with drifts too deep to negotiate. The wind, now blowing fiercely toward the volcano, blasted the gritty stuff against their front window as though it would erode through; and the lava flow, moving far faster than the gentle ooze they had never quite measured, surged – and glowed-grimly behind.

A hundred miles or more to the east, the tractors containing Mardikian, Marini and their drivers headed southwest along the alternate route their maps had suggested; but Mardikian, some three hours in the lead, reported that he could see four other smoke columns in that general direction.

Mercury seemed to be entering a new phase. The maps might well be out of date.

Harmon and Trackman were having no trouble at the moment, but they would have to pass the great chasm. This had been shooting out daughter cracks when Zaino and Hargedon passed it hours before. No one could say what it might be like now, and no one was going out to make sure.

"We can see you!" Burkett's voice came through suddenly. "Half a mile to go, and we're way ahead of the flow."

"But it's coming?" Rawson asked tensely. He had returned from the power level at Zaino's phoned report of success.

"It's coming."

"How fast? When will it get here? Do you know whether the ship can stand contact with it?"

"I don't know the speed exactly. There may be two hours, maybe five or six. The ship can't take it. Even the temperature measures I got were above the softening point of the alloys, and it's hotter and much deeper now. Anyway, if the others aren't back before the flow reaches the ship they won't get through. The tractor wheels would char away, and I doubt that the bodies would float. You certainly can't wade through the stuff in a space suit, either."

"And you think there can't be more than five or six hours before the flow arrives?"

"I'd say that was a very optimistic guess. I'll stop and get a better speed estimate if you want, but won't swear to it."

Rowson thought for a moment.

"No," he said finally, "don't bother. Get back here as soon as you can. We need the tractor and human muscles more than we need even expert guesses." He turned to the operator.

"Zaino, tell all the tractors there'll be no answer from the ship for a while, because no one will be aboard. Then suit up and come outside." He was gone.

Ten minutes later, six human beings and a tractor were assembled in the flamelit near-darkness outside the ship. The cloud had spread to the horizon, and the sun was gone. Burkett and Hargedon had arrived, but Rowson wasted no time on congratulations.

"We have work to do. It will be easy enough to keep the lava from the ship, since there seems to be a foot or more of ash on the ground and a touch of main drive would push it into a ringwall around us; but that's not the main problem. We have to keep it from reaching the chasm anywhere south of us, since that's the way the others will be coming. If they're cut off, they're dead. It will be brute work. We'll use the tractor any way we can think of. Unfortunately it has no plow atttachment, and I can't think of anything aboard which could be turned into one. You have shovels, such as they are. The ash is light, especially here, but there's a mile and a half of dam to be built. I don't see how it can possibly be done . . . but it's going to be."

"Come on, Arnie! You're young and strong," came the voice of the mineralogist. "You should be able to lift as much of this stuff as I can. I understand you were lucky enough to get hold of Eileen – have you asked for the bonus yet? – but your work isn't done."

"It wasn't luck," Zaino retorted. Burkett, in spite of her voice, seemed much less of a schoolmistress when encased in a space suit and carrying a shovel, so he was able to talk back to her. "I was simply alert enough to make use of existing conditions, which I had to observe for myself in spite of all the scientists around. I'm charging the achievement to my regular salary. I saw – "

He stopped suddenly, both with tongue and shovel. Then, "Captain!"

"What is it?"

"The only reason we're starting this wall here is to keep well ahead of the flow so we can work as long as possible, isn't it?"

"Yes, I suppose so. I never thought of trying anywhere else. The valley would mean a much shorter dam, but if the flow isn't through it by now it would be before we could get there – oh! Wait a minute!"

"Yes, sir. You can put the main switch anywhere in a D.C. circuit. Where are the seismology stores we never had to use?"

Four minutes later the tractor set out from the *Albireo*, carrying Rowson and Zaino. Six minutes after that it stopped at the base of the ash cone which formed the north side of the valley from which the lava was coming. They parked a quarter of the way around the cone's base from the emerging flood and started to climb on foot, both carrying burdens.

Forty-seven minutes later they returned empty-handed to the vehicle, to find that it had been engulfed by the spreading liquid.

With noticeable haste they floundered through the loose ash a few yards above the base until they had outdistanced the glowing menace, descended and started back across the plain to where they knew the ship to be, though she was invisible through the falling detritus. Once they had to detour around a crack. Once they encountered one which widened toward the chasm on their right, and they knew a detour would be impossible. Leaping it seemed impossible, too, but they did it. Thirty seconds after this, forty minutes after finding the tractor destroyed, the landscape was bathed in a magnesium-white glare as the two one-and-a-half kiloton charges planted just inside the crater rim let go.

"Should we go back and see if it worked?" asked Zaino.

"What's the use? The only other charges we had were in the tractor. Thank goodness they were nuclear instead of H.E. If it didn't work we'd have more trouble to get back than we're having now."

"If it didn't work, is there any point in going back?"

"Stop quibbling and keep walking. Dr. Burkett, are you listening?"

"Yes, Captain."

"We're fresh out of tractors, but if you want to try it on foot you might start a set of flow measures on the lava. Arnie wants to know whether our landslide slid properly."

However, the two were able to tell for themselves before getting back to the *Albireo*.

The flow didn't stop all at once, of course; but with the valley feeding it blocked off by a pile of volcanic ash four hundred feet high on one side, nearly fifty on the other and more than a quarter of a mile long, its enthusiasm quickly subsided. It was thin, fluid stuff, as Burkett had noted; but as it spread it cooled, and as it cooled it thickened.

Six hours after the blast it had stopped with its nearest lobe almost a mile from the ship, less than two feet thick at the edge.

When Mardikian's tractor arrived, Burkett was happily trying to analyze samples of the flow, and less happily speculating on how long it would be before the entire area would be blown off the planet. When Marini's and Harmon's vehicles arrived, almost together, the specimens had been loaded and everything stowed for acceleration. Sixty seconds after the last person was aboard, the *Albireo* left Mercury's surface at two gravities.

The haste, it turned out, wasn't really necessary. She had been in parking orbit nearly forty-five hours before the first of the giant volcanoes reached its climax, and the one beside their former site was not the first. It was the fourth.

"And that seems to be that," said Camille Burkett rather tritely as they drifted a hundred miles above the little world's surface. "Just a belt of white-hot calderas all around the planet. Pretty, if you like symmetry."

"I like being able to see it from this distance," replied Zaino, floating weightless beside her. "By the way, how much bonus should I ask for getting that idea of putting the seismic charges to use after all?"

"I wouldn't mention it. Any one of us might have thought of that. We all knew about them."

"Anyone *might* have. Let's speculate on how long it would have been before anyone *did*."

"It's still not like the other idea, which involved your own specialty. I still don't see what made you suppose that the gas pillar from the volcano would be heavily charged enough to reflect your radio beam. How did that idea strike you?"

Zaino thought back, and smiled a little as the picture of lightning blazing around pillar, cloud and mountain rose before his eyes.

"You're not quite right," he said. "I was worried about it for a while, but it didn't actually strike me."

It fell rather flat; Camille Burkett, Ph.D., had to have it explained to her.

The Hounds of Tindalos

FRANK BELKNAP LONG

Frank Belknap Long (1903–92) as a young man was the closest friend and associate of H. P. Lovecraft. Long was a poet and fiction writer who became adept at the new SF genre in the 1920s and continued to publish widely for decades. His first book (of poetry) appeared in 1924, and he remained actively writing through the 1980s.

Weird science fiction, which borders on the supernatural, was characteristic of the Lovecraft "Circle" that included Long, Donald and Howard Wandrei, Clark Ashton Smith, Robert E. Howard, Robert Bloch, Fritz Leiber, and others, and centered around the pulp magazine *Weird Tales* in the 1920s and '30s. Lovecraft was a rationalist, but the affect of the fiction was fear and wonder.

Long's reputation in later years, after the 1960s, was dominated by the impact of his early horror fiction, and he suffered as well as benefitted from the adulation of the followers of Lovecraft, who cared little for his non-Lovecraftian writings. He wrote a number of women's gothic romances under his wife's name when he found it difficult to sell his own books.

His early stories are clearly influenced by Lovecraft, and of them the most famous is this one, which decades later would be one of the models for Stephen King's "The Mist." It is a paradigm of the alien creatures from another dimension story in genre science fiction.

1

"I'm glad you came," said Chalmers. He was sitting by the window and his face was very pale. Two tall candles guttered at his elbow and cast a sickly amber light over his long nose and slightly receding chin. Chalmers would have nothing modern about his apartment. He had the soul of a mediaeval ascetic, and he preferred illuminated manuscripts to automobiles, and leering stone gargoyles to radios and adding-machines.

As I crossed the room to the settee he had cleared for me I glanced at his desk and was surprised to discover that he had been studying the mathematical formulae of a celebrated contemporary physicist, and that he had covered many sheets of thin yellow paper with curious geometric designs.

"Einstein and John Dee are strange bedfellows," I said as my gaze wandered from his mathematical charts to the sixty or seventy quaint books that comprised his strange little library. Plotinus and Emanuel Moscopulus, St. Thomas Aquinas and Frenicle de Bessy stood elbow to elbow in the somber ebony bookcase, and chairs, table and desk were littered with pamphlets about mediaeval sorcery and witchcraft and black magic, and all of the valiant glamorous things that the modern world has repudiated.

Chalmers smiled engagingly, and passed me a Russian cigarette on a curiously carved tray. "We are just discovering now," he said, "that the old alchemists and sorcerers were two-thirds *right,* and that your modern biologist and materialist is nine-tenths *wrong.*"

"You have always scoffed at modern science," I said, a little impatiently.

"Only at scientific dogmatism," he replied. "I have always been a rebel, a champion of originality and lost causes; that is why I have chosen to repudiate the conclusions of contemporary biologists."

"And Einstein?" I asked.

"A priest of transcendental mathematics!" he murmured reverently. "A profound mystic and explorer of the great *suspected.*"

"Then you do not entirely despise science."

"Of course not," he affirmed. "I merely distrust the scientific positivism of the past fifty years, the positivism of Haeckel and Darwin and of Mr. Bertrand Russell. I believe that biology has failed pitifully to explain the mystery of man's origin and destiny."

"Give them time," I retorted.

Chalmers' eyes glowed. "My friend," he murmured, "your pun is sublime. Give them *time*. That is precisely what I would do. But your modern biologist scoffs at time. He has the key but he refuses to use it. What do we know of time, really? Einstein believes that it is relative, that it can be interpreted in terms of space, of *curved* space. But must we stop there? When mathematics fails us can we not advance by – insight?"

"You are treading on dangerous ground," I replied. "That is a pitfall that your true investigator avoids. That is why modern science has advanced so slowly. It accepts nothing that it cannot demonstrate. But you – "

"I would take hashish, opium, all manner of drugs. I would emulate the sages of the East. And then perhaps I would apprehend – "

"What?"

"The fourth dimension."

"Theosophical rubbish!"

"Perhaps. But I believe that drugs expand human consciousness. William James agreed with me. And I have discovered a new one."

"A new drug?"

"It was used centuries ago by Chinese alchemists, but it is virtually unknown in the West. Its occult properties are amazing. With its aid and the aid of my mathematical knowledge I believe that I can go *back through time*."

"I do not understand."

"Time is merely our imperfect perception of a new dimension of space. Time and motion are both illusions. Everything that has existed from the beginning of the world *exists now*. Events that occurred centuries ago on this planet continue to exist in another dimension of space. Events that will occur centuries from now *exist already*. We cannot perceive their existence because we cannot enter the dimension of space that contains them. Human beings as we know them are merely fractions, infinitesimally small fractions of one enormous whole. Every human being is linked with *all* the life that has preceded him on this planet. All of his ancestors are parts of him. Only time separates him from his forebears, and time is an illusion and does not exist."

"I think I understand," I murmured.

"It will be sufficient for my purpose if you can form a vague idea of what I wish to achieve. I wish to strip from my eyes the veils of illusion that time has thrown over them, and see the *beginning and the end*."

"And you think this new drug will help you?"

"I am sure that it will. And I want you to help me. I intend to take the drug immediately. I cannot wait. I must *see*." His eyes glittered strangely. "I am going back, back through time."

He rose and strode to the mantel. When he faced me again he was holding a small square box in the palm of his hand. "I have here five pellets of the drug Liao. It was used by the Chinese philosopher Lao Tze, and while under its influence he visioned Tao. Tao is the most mysterious force in the world; it surrounds and pervades all things; it contains the visible universe and everything that we call reality. He who apprehends the mysteries of Tao sees clearly all that was and will be."

"Rubbish!" I retorted.

"Tao resembles a great animal, recumbent, motionless, containing in its enormous body all the worlds of our universe, the past, the present and the future. We see portions of this great monster through a slit, which we call time. With the aid of this drug I shall enlarge the slit. I shall behold the great figure of life, the great recumbent beast in its entirety."

"And what do you wish me to do?"

"Watch, my friend. Watch and take notes. And if I go back too far you must recall me to reality. You can recall me by shaking me violently. If I appear to be suffering acute physical pain you must recall me at once."

"Chalmers," I said, "I wish you wouldn't make this experiment. You are taking dreadful risks. I don't believe that there is any fourth dimension and I emphatically do not believe in Tao. And I don't approve of your experimenting with unknown drugs."

"I know the properties of this drug," he replied. "I know precisely how it affects the human animal and I know its dangers. The risk does not reside in the drug itself. My only fear is that I may become lost in time. You see, I shall assist the drug. Before I swallow this pellet I shall give my undivided attention to the geometric and algebraic symbols that I have traced on this paper." He raised the mathematical chart that rested on his knee. "I shall prepare my mind for an excursion into time. I shall approach the fourth dimension with my conscious mind before I take the drug which will enable me to exercise occult powers of perception. Before I enter the dream world of the Eastern mystics I shall acquire all of the mathematical help that modern science can offer. This mathematical knowledge, this conscious approach to an actual apprehension of the fourth dimension of time, will supplement the work of the drug. The drug will open up stupendous new vistas – the mathematical preparation will enable me to grasp them intellect-

ually. I have often grasped the fourth dimension in dreams, emotionally, intuitively, but I have never been able to recall, in waking life, the
occult splendors that were momentarily revealed to me.

"But with your aid, I believe that I can recall them. You will take
down everything that I say while I am under the influence of the drug.
No matter how strange or incoherent my speech may become you will
omit nothing. When I awake I may be able to supply the key to whatever is mysterious or incredible. I am not sure that I shall succeed, but
if I do succeed" – his eyes were strangely luminous – "*time will exist for
me no longer!*"

He sat down abruptly. "I shall make the experiment at once. Please
stand over there by the window and watch. Have you a fountain pen?"

I nodded gloomily and removed a pale green Waterman from my
upper vest pocket.

"And a pad, Frank?"

I groaned and produced a memorandum book. "I emphatically
disapprove of this experiment," I muttered. "You're taking a frightful
risk."

"Don't be an asinine old woman!" he admonished. "Nothing that
you can say will induce me to stop now. I entreat you to remain silent
while I study these charts."

He raised the charts and studied them intently. I watched the clock
on the mantel as it ticked out the seconds, and a curious dread
clutched at my heart so that I choked.

Suddenly the clock stopped ticking, and exactly at that moment
Chalmers swallowed the drug.

I rose quickly and moved toward him, but his eyes implored me not
to interfere. "The clock has stopped," he murmured. "The forces that
control it approve of my experiment. *Time* stopped, and I swallowed
the drug. I pray God that I shall not lose my way."

He closed his eyes and leaned back on the sofa. All of the blood had
left his face and he was breathing heavily. It was clear that the drug
was acting with extraordinary rapidity.

"It is beginning to get dark," he murmured. "Write that. It is beginning to get dark and the familiar objects in the room are fading out. I
can discern them vaguely through my eyelids, but they are fading
swiftly."

I shook my pen to make the ink come and wrote rapidly in short-
hand as he continued to dictate.

"I am leaving the room. The walls are vanishing and I can no longer
see any of the familiar objects. Your face, though, is still visible to me.

I hope that you are writing. I think that I am about to make a great leap – a leap through space. Or perhaps it is through time that I shall make the leap. I cannot tell. Everything is dark, indistinct."

He sat for a while silent, with his head sunk upon his breast. Then suddenly he stiffened and his eyelids fluttered open. "God in heaven!" he cried. "I *see*!"

He was straining forward in his chair, staring at the opposite wall. But I knew that he was looking beyond the wall and that the objects in the room no longer existed for him. "Chalmers," I cried, "Chalmers, shall I wake you?"

"Do not!" he shrieked. "I see *everything*. All of the billions of lives that preceded me on this planet are before me at this moment. I see men of all ages, all races, all colors. They are fighting, killing, building, dancing, singing. They are sitting about rude fires on lonely gray deserts, and flying through the air in monoplanes. They are riding the seas in bark canoes and enormous steamships; they are painting bison and mammoths on the walls of dismal caves and covering huge canvases with queer futuristic designs. I watch the migrations from Atlantis. I watch the migrations from Lemuria. I see the elder races – a strange horde of black dwarfs overwhelming Asia, and the Neandertalers with lowered heads and bent knees ranging obscenely across Europe. I watch the Achaeans streaming into the Greek islands, and the crude beginnings of Hellenic culture. I am in Athens and Pericles is young. I am standing on the soil of Italy. I assist in the rape of the Sabines; I march with the Imperial Legions. I tremble with awe and wonder as the enormous standards go by and the ground shakes with the tread of the victorious *bastati*. A thousand naked slaves grovel before me as I pass in a litter of gold and ivory drawn by night-black oxen from Thebes, and the flower-girls scream *'Ave Caesar'* as I nod and smile. I am myself a slave on a Moorish galley. I watch the erection of a great cathedral. Stone by stone it rises, and through months and years I stand and watch each stone as it falls into place. I am burned on a cross head downward in the thyme-scented gardens of Nero, and I watch with amusement and scorn the torturers at work in the chambers of the Inquisition.

"I walk in the holiest sanctuaries; I enter the temples of Venus. I kneel in adoration before the Magna Mater, and I throw coins on the bare knees of the sacred courtesans who sit with veiled faces in the groves of Babylon. I creep into an Elizabethan theater and with the stinking rabble about me I applaud *The Merchant of Venice*. I walk with Dante through the narrow streets of Florence. I meet the young

Beatrice, and the hem of her garment brushes my sandals as I stare enraptured. I am a priest of Isis, and my magic astounds the nations. Simon Magus kneels before me, imploring my assistance, and Pharaoh trembles when I approach. In India I talk with the Masters and run screaming from their presence, for their revelations are as salt on wounds that bleed.

"I perceive everything *simultaneously*. I perceive everything from all sides; I am a part of all the teeming billions about me. I exist in all men and all men exist in me. I perceive the whole of human history in a single instant, the past and the present.

"By simply *straining* I can see farther and farther back. Now I am going back through strange curves and angles. Angles and curves multiply about me. I perceive great segments of time through *curves*. There is *curved time*, and *angular time*. The beings that exist in angular time cannot enter curved time. It is very strange.

"I am going back and back. Man has disappeared from the earth. Gigantic reptiles crouch beneath enormous palms and swim through the loathly black waters of dismal lakes. Now the reptiles have disappeared. No animals remain upon the land, but beneath the waters, plainly visible to me, dark forms move slowly over the rotting vegetation.

"The forms are becoming simpler and simpler. Now they are single cells. All about me there are angles – strange angles that have no counterparts on the earth. I am desperately afraid.

"There is an abyss of being which man has never fathomed."

I stared. Chalmers had risen to his feet and he was gesticulating helplessly with his arms. "I am passing through unearthly angles; I am approaching – oh, the burning horror of it."

"Chalmers!" I cried. "Do you wish me to interfere?"

He brought his right hand quickly before his face, as though to shut out a vision unspeakable. "Not yet!" he cried; "I will go on. I will see – what – lies – beyond – "

A cold sweat streamed from his forehead and his shoulders jerked spasmodically. "Beyond life there are" – his face grew ashen with terror – "*things* that I cannot distinguish. They move slowly through angles. They have no bodies, and they move slowly through outrageous angles."

It was then that I became aware of the odor in the room. It was a pungent, indescribable odor, so nauseous that I could scarcely endure it. I stepped quickly to the window and threw it open. When I returned to Chalmers and looked into his eyes I nearly fainted.

"I think they have scented me!" he shrieked. "They are slowly turning toward me."

He was trembling horribly. For a moment he clawed at the air with his hands. Then his legs gave way beneath him and he fell forward on his face, slobbering and moaning.

I watched him in silence as he dragged himself across the floor. He was no longer a man. His teeth were bared and saliva dripped from the corners of his mouth.

"Chalmers," I cried. "Chalmers, stop it! Stop it, do you hear?"

As if in reply to my appeal he commenced to utter hoarse convulsive sounds which resembled nothing so much as the barking of a dog, and began a sort of hideous writhing in a circle about the room. I bent and seized him by the shoulders. Violently, desperately, I shook him. He turned his head and snapped at my wrist. I was sick with horror, but I dared not release him for fear that he would destroy himself in a paroxysm of rage.

"Chalmers," I muttered, "you must stop that. There is nothing in this room that can harm you. Do you understand?"

I continued to shake and admonish him, and gradually the madness died out of his face. Shivering convulsively, he crumpled into a grotesque heap on the Chinese rug.

I carried him to the sofa and deposited him upon it. His features were twisted in pain, and I knew that he was still struggling dumbly to escape from abominable memories.

"Whisky," he muttered. "You'll find a flask in the cabinet by the window – upper left-hand drawer."

When I handed him the flask his fingers tightened about it until the knuckles showed blue. "They nearly got me," he gasped. He drained the stimulant in immoderate gulps, and gradually the color crept back into his face.

"That drug was the very devil!" I murmured.

"It wasn't the drug," he moaned.

His eyes no longer glared insanely, but he still wore the look of a lost soul.

"They scented me in time," he moaned. "I went too far."

"What were *they* like?" I said, to humor him.

He leaned forward and gripped my arm. He was shivering horribly. "No words in our language can describe them!" He spoke in a hoarse whisper. "They are symbolized vaguely in the myth of the Fall, and in an obscene form which is occasionally found engraved on ancient tablets. The Greeks had a name for them, which veiled their essential foulness. The tree, the snake and the apple – these are the vague symbols of a most awful mystery."

His voice had risen to a scream. "Frank, Frank, a terrible and unspeakable *deed* was done in the beginning. Before time, the *deed*, and from the deed – "

He had risen and was hysterically pacing the room. "The seeds of the deed move through angles in dim recesses of time. They are hungry and athirst!"

"Chalmers," I pleaded to quiet him. "We are living in the third decade of the Twentieth Century."

"They are lean and athirst!" he shrieked. *"The Hounds of Tindalos!"*

"Chalmers, shall I phone for a physician?"

"A physician cannot help me now. They are horrors of the soul, and yet" – he hid his face in his hands and groaned – "they are real, Frank. I saw them for a ghastly moment. For a moment I stood on the *other side*. I stood on the pale gray shores beyond time and space. In an awful light that was not light, in a silence that shrieked, I saw *them*.

"All the evil in the universe was concentrated in their lean, hungry bodies. Or had they bodies? I saw them only for a moment; I cannot be certain. *But I heard them breathe.* Indescribably for a moment I felt their breath upon my face. They turned toward me and I fled screaming. In a single moment I fled screaming through time. I fled down quintillions of years.

"But they scented me. Men awake in them cosmic hungers. We have escaped, momentarily, from the foulness that rings them round. They thirst for that in us which is clean, which emerged from the deed without stain. There is a part of us which did not partake in the deed, and that they hate. But do not imagine that they are literally, prosaically evil. They are beyond good and evil as we know it. They are that which in the beginning fell away from cleanliness. Through the deed they became bodies of death, receptacles of all foulness. But they are not evil in *our* sense because in the spheres through which they move there is no thought, no morals, no right or wrong as we understand it. There is merely the pure and the foul. The foul expresses itself through angles; the pure through curves. Man, the pure part of him, is descended from a curve. Do not laugh. I mean that literally."

I rose and searched for my hat. "I'm dreadfully sorry for you, Chalmers," I said, as I walked toward the door. "But I don't intend to stay and listen to such gibberish. I'll send my physician to see you. He's an elderly, kindly chap and he won't be offended if you tell him to go to the devil. But I hope you'll respect his advice. A week's rest in a good sanitarium should benefit you immeasurably."

I heard him laughing as I descended the stairs, but his laughter was so utterly mirthless that it moved me to tears.

2

When Chalmers phoned the following morning my first impulse was to hang up the receiver immediately. His request was so unusual and his voice was so wildly hysterical that I feared any further association with him would result in the impairment of my own sanity. But I could not doubt the genuineness of his misery, and when he broke down completely and I heard him sobbing over the wire I decided to comply with his request.

"Very well," I said. "I will come over immediately and bring the plaster."

En route to Chalmers' home I stopped at a hardware store and purchased twenty pounds of plaster of Paris. When I entered my friend's room he was crouching by the window watching the opposite wall out of eyes that were feverish with fright. When he saw me he rose and seized the parcel containing the plaster with an avidity that amazed and horrified me. He had extruded all of the furniture and the room presented a desolate appearance.

"It is just conceivable that we can thwart them!" he exclaimed, "But we must work rapidly. Frank, there is a stepladder in the hall. Bring it here immediately. And then fetch a pail of water."

"What for?" I murmured.

He turned sharply and there was a flush on his face. "To mix the plaster, you fool!" he cried. "To mix the plaster that will save our bodies and souls from a contamination unmentionable. To mix the plaster that will save the world from – Frank, *they must be kept out!*"

"Who?" I murmured.

"The Hounds of Tindalos!" he muttered. "They can only reach us through angles. We must eliminate all angles from this room. I shall plaster up all of the corners, all of the crevices. We must make this room resemble the interior of a sphere."

I knew that it would have been useless to argue with him. I fetched the stepladder, Chalmers mixed the plaster, and for three hours we labored. We filled in the four corners of the wall and the intersections of the floor and wall and the wall and ceiling, and we rounded the sharp angles of the window-seat.

"I shall remain in this room until they return in time," he affirmed when our task was completed. "When they discover that the scent leads through curves they will return. They will return ravenous and snarling and unsatisfied to the foulness that was in the beginning, before time, beyond space."

He nodded graciously and lit a cigarette. "It was good of you to help," he said.

"Will you not see a physician, Chalmers?" I pleaded.

"Perhaps – tomorrow," he murmured. "But now I must watch and wait."

"Wait for what?" I urged.

Chalmers smiled wanly. "I know that you think me insane," he said. "You have a shrewd but prosaic mind, and you cannot conceive of an entity that does not depend for its existence on force and matter. But did it ever occur to you, my friend, that force and matter are merely the barriers to perception imposed by time and space? When one knows, as I do, that time and space are identical and that they are both deceptive because they are merely imperfect manifestations of a higher reality, one no longer seeks in the visible world for an explanation of the mystery and terror of being."

I rose and walked toward the door.

"Forgive me," he cried. "I did not mean to offend you. You have a superlative intellect, but I – I have a *superhuman* one. It is only natural that I should be aware of your limitations."

"Phone if you need me," I said, and descended the stairs two steps at a time. "I'll send my physician over at once," I muttered, to myself. "He's a hopeless maniac, and heaven knows what will happen if someone doesn't take charge of him immediately."

3

The following is a condensation of two announcements which appeared in the Partridgeville Gazette *for July 3, 1928*:

Earthquake Shakes Financial District

At 2 o'clock this morning an earth tremor of unusual severity broke several plate-glass windows in Central Square and completely disorganized the electric and street railway systems. The tremor was felt in the outlying districts and the steeple of the First Baptist Church on Angell Hill (designed by Christopher Wren in 1717) was entirely demolished. Firemen are now attempting to put out a blaze which threatens to destroy the Partridgeville Glue Works. An investigation is promised by the mayor and an immediate attempt will be made to fix responsibility for this disastrous occurrence.

OCCULT WRITER MURDERED BY UNKNOWN GUEST

Horrible Crime in Central Square

Mystery Surrounds Death of Halpin Chalmers

At 9 a.m. today the body of Halpin Chalmers, author and journalist, was found in an empty room above the jewelry store of Smithwick and Isaacs, 24 Central Square. The coroner's investigation revealed that the room had been rented furnished to Mr. Chalmers on May 1, and that he had himself disposed of the furniture a fortnight ago. Chalmers was the author of several recondite books on occult themes, and a member of the Bibliographic Guild. He formerly resided in Brooklyn, New York.

At 7 a.m. Mr. L. E. Hancock, who occupies the apartment opposite Chalmers' room in the Smithwick and Isaacs establishment, smelt a peculiar odor when he opened his door to take in his cat and the morning edition of the *Partridgeville Gazette*. The odor he describes as extremely acrid and nauseous, and he affirms that it was so strong in the vicinity of Chalmers' room that he was obliged to hold his nose when he approached that section of the hall.

He was about to return to his own apartment when it occurred to him that Chalmers might have accidentally forgotten to turn off the gas in his kitchenette. Becoming considerably alarmed at the thought, he decided to investigate, and when repeated tappings on Chalmers' door brought no response he notified the superintendent. The latter opened the door by means of a pass key, and the two men quickly made their way into Chalmers' room. The room was utterly destitute of furniture, and Hancock asserts that when he first glanced at the floor his heart went cold within him, and that the superintendent, without saying a word, walked to the open window and stared at the building opposite for fully five minutes.

Chalmers lay stretched upon his back in the center of the room. He was starkly nude, and his chest and arms were covered with a peculiar bluish pus or ichor. His head lay grotesquely upon his chest. It had been completely severed from his body, and the features were twisted and torn and horribly mangled. Nowhere was there a trace of blood.

The room presented a most astonishing appearance. The intersections of the walls, ceiling and floor had been thickly smeared with plaster of Paris, but at intervals fragments had cracked and fallen off, and someone had grouped these upon the floor about the murdered man so as to form a perfect triangle.

Beside the body were several sheets of charred yellow paper. These bore fantastic geometric designs and symbols and several hastily scrawled sentences. The sentences were almost illegible and so absurd in content that they furnished no possible clue to the perpetrator of the crime. "I am waiting and watching," Chalmers wrote. "I sit by the window and watch walls and ceiling. I do not believe they can reach me, but I must beware of the Doels. Perhaps *they* can help them break through. The satyrs will help, and they can advance through the scarlet circles. The Greeks knew a way of preventing that. It is a great pity that we have forgotten so much."

On another sheet of paper, the most badly charred of the seven or eight fragments found by Detective Sergeant Douglas (of the Partridgeville Reserve), was scrawled the following:

"Good God, the plaster is falling! A terrific shock has loosened the plaster and it is falling. An earthquake perhaps! I never could have anticipated this. It is growing dark in the room. I must phone Frank. But can he get here in time? I will try. I will recite the Einstein formula. I will – God, they are breaking through! They are breaking through! Smoke is pouring from the corners of the wall. Their tongues – ahhhhh – "

In the opinion of Detective Sergeant Douglas, Chalmers was poisoned by some obscure chemical. He has sent specimens of the strange blue slime found on Chalmers' body to the Partridgeville Chemical Laboratories; and he expects the report will shed new light on one of the most mysterious crimes of recent years. That Chalmers entertained a guest on the evening preceding the earthquake is certain, for his neighbor distinctly heard a low murmur of conversation in the former's room as he passed it on his way to the stairs. Suspicion points strongly to this unknown visitor and the police are diligently endeavoring to discover his identity.

4

Report of James Morton, chemist and bacteriologist:

My dear Mr. Douglas:

The fluid sent to me for analysis is the most peculiar that I have ever examined. It resembles living protoplasm, but it lacks the peculiar substances known as enzymes. Enzymes catalyze the chemical reactions occurring in living cells, and when the cell dies they cause it to disintegrate by hydrolyzation. Without enzymes protoplasm should possess enduring vitality, i.e., immortality. Enzymes are the negative components, so to speak, of unicellular organism, which is the basis of all life. That living matter can exist without enzymes biologists emphatically deny. And yet the substance that you have sent me is alive and it lacks these "indispensable" bodies. Good God, sir, do you realize what astounding new vistas this opens up?

5

Excerpt from The Secret Watchers *by the late Halpin Chalmers:*

What if, parallel to the life we know, there is another life that does not die, which lacks the elements that destroy *our* life? Perhaps in another dimension there is a *different* force from that which generates our life. Perhaps this force emits energy, or something similar to energy, which passes from the unknown dimension where *it* is and creates a new form of cell life in our dimension. No one knows that such new cell life does exist in our dimension. Ah, but I have seen *its* manifestations. I have *talked* with them. In my room at night I have talked with the Doels. And in dreams I have seen their maker. I have stood on the dim shore beyond time and matter and seen *it*. *It* moves through strange curves and outrageous angles. Some day I shall travel in time and meet *it* face to face.

The Angel of Violence

ADAM WISNIEWSKI-SNERG
(Translated by Tomasz Mirkowicz)

Adam Snerg (1937–95) lived in Warsaw, Poland. He published his first
story in 1968 and his first novel, *Robot* in 1973. *Robot* takes place inside
a bomb shelter below a large city torn out of the Earth by an alien spaceship and carried through space to an unknown destination as a scientists'
sample collected for later study. It is an ambitious investigation into the
nature of time, evolution, free will, and the theory of relativity. Polish SF
fans voted it the best Polish SF book published since World War Two,
quite an honor in Stanislaw Lem's native country.

He published three later novels that were fantastic but not science
fiction, and then in 1990 published an original and highly controversial
non-fiction work presenting his own theory of the space-time continuum.
At the time of his death by his own hand in August, 1995, he had been
working on another non-fiction book, a more accessible version of his
theory.

"The Angel of Violence" is one of his six uncollected short stories and
the first of his works to be translated into English, in a translation commissioned for this book.

On the thirteenth floor of the Cybernetics Institute Lucy interrupted
the guide's patter to tell her that several of the tourists were missing.
They had lagged behind the group and probably lost their way in the
maze of corridors and rooms of the vast building, the chief attraction
of the tour around the recently excavated ancient city. The guide did

not seem in the least put out. Instead of worrying about her missing charges or explaining the exhibits on display to the remaining tourists, she continued to praise the sound and light show her agency organized every night in the ruins of a nearby nuclear power plant.

Lucy got lost on the sixteenth floor. She had lingered a moment too long by the main computer, staring dumbly at the old cabinets housing the giant electronic brain. The guide had said that its makers, medieval craftsmen once known as "programmers," were assured a permanent place in the annals of history. And yet "the moving beauty of this price-less treasure" – the guide's exact words – did not move Lucy in the least. She decided to ask the woman for some pointers on appreciating ancient artifacts. But when she went out into the corridor, it was empty.

She couldn't hear the other tourists and had no idea which way they had gone. She started looking for them, wandering in and out of ancient labs filled with primitive, twenty-first-century equipment.

Time had not been kind to the priceless exhibits. Their plastic parts were full of holes made by second-generation borers, and their metal parts, the paint removed long ago by colonies of industrious, once unknown microorganisms, were corroded and covered with rust peeling away in large flakes.

The group was nowhere in sight. After another fifteen minutes Lucy gave up her search and, feeling oppressed by the somber atmosphere of the ancient building, decided to forgo the rest of the tour. She resolved to take the elevator to the ground floor and find her way to the antique bus waiting in front of the Institute.

She had her first misadventure in the elevator: it stopped between floors. Lucy pressed the alarm button. After a brief silence a male voice spoke to her from a speaker set above the buttons.

"Do you want to be the queen?" it asked.

"Do I want to be *what*?"

"The king's wife, the first lady of the realm."

"The king's wife?"

"Yes."

"You must be joking!"

"No, I'm not. You can become the queen."

"How?"

"No problem. It so happens we are looking for the right candidate. The former queen had to go. The tourists are already downstairs, waiting for you."

"Where?"

"Press the sixth floor button. Then go to room 628."

The unusual offer had taken her by surprise, but Lucy quickly guessed what it was all about: some kind of show put on by the tourist agency in the ruins of the freshly excavated city. It sounded intriguing. She liked surprises. Why shouldn't she play a part in some medieval drama? She had heard of picturesque castles built on the forbidden peaks of nuclear power plants by tyrants armed with tridents who forced their subjects to watch television. Maybe she wasn't confusing different historical periods, but she was overjoyed at the prospect of participating in the show, the more so since she'd be viewing everything from the queen's throne.

Although she pressed the right button, the elevator passed the sixth floor and continued to descend; it passed the ground floor and finally stopped on the sixth underground level. Lucy hadn't even known there were any underground levels in the building.

She walked down a wide, clean corridor until she reached room 628. She opened the door and walked in.

The first things she saw were the bare legs of a woman standing behind a metal screen suspended from the ceiling.

"Excuse me," Lucy said, "I was told some kind of show is being staged here."

The woman hidden by the screen gave a jump and moved a little closer. But the screen, hanging in front of an open doorway leading to the next room, continued to cover her, so all Lucy saw were the woman's legs.

"Do you know where the tourists are waiting?"

The legs were very shapely. But when they walked out from behind the screen and with one bare foot kicked the door shut, Lucy stopped admiring their proportions. She could hardly believe her eyes.

The legs weren't attached to a body! Lucy screamed with horror and ran into the next room. Inside, she saw many more pairs of moving legs. Although no people were present, the whole room was filled with animated motion.

A sign on the wall said: "PROSTHETIC WORKS – LOWER LIMBS." A slowly moving conveyor belt passed along a row of machines. Each machine was operated by a pair of synthetic hands steered efficiently by invisible plastic tendons. Imitating human hands to perfection, they were assembling artificial legs. At the end of the assembly line the legs jumped off the conveyor belt. The last machine joined them into matching pairs and sent them off to an obstacle course. After completing it, the legs marched obediently to the next section, where a mechanical fitter equipped them with arms.

Each hasp joining the legs together, its ends inserted into their thighs, had the shape of an inverted U. The fitter attached the arms to the top of the hasp. A dozen of such limbomats were already working on the assembly line or molding parts from which the limbs were made; others were repairing defective machines or building new ones.

Lucy noticed one limbomat standing by a high-tension console and suddenly felt the muscles of her legs and arms tense as if she were a weightlifter readying to set a world record. When she caught sight of the video cameras and antennas attached to the walls, she began to understand what had happened.

She knew that the twenty-first century scientists who had abandoned the building during an earthquake had left all the machinery running, supplied with energy from a local source. The room she was in was an old workshop that had originally produced prototypes of artificial limbs for the handicapped. Cut off for centuries from the rest of the world, the Institute's main computer had carried on production, resourcefully modifying and improving the artificial limbs. It was a case of perfect symbiosis: the computer created more and more advanced limbomats, steering their artificial nervous systems by remote control, while they – replacing the human technicians – maintained and expanded his electronic brain.

When Lucy had walked into the view of the computer's video cameras, she had immediately caught its attention. After years of controlling artificial limbs the computer wanted to test its power over real ones. A live human being was just what it needed.

Lucy wanted to flee, but as soon as the computer registered her presence, her muscles turned rigid as if numbed by electric shock. For several minutes her whole body jerked convulsively, until finally, after a violent battle over its control between two command centers – her own brain and the electronic brain of the computer – her body began to carry out the machine's orders.

Propelled by regular impulses, she passed the conveyor belt and came to a large door which opened by itself, revealing an unusual sight.

All the tourists who had strayed from the group were standing in the middle of an enormous chamber. They smiled at the terrified girl. After her initial shock she smiled back at them. She wondered whether the computer had really forced her to walk in here; maybe she had just imagined it. Anyway, now she was back among people she knew; she was so relieved, she could have hugged them.

She took a few steps in their direction, then once again looked at them, and froze.

The very moment she had sighed with relief, happy her misadventures were over, one of the men raised the heavy ax he was holding and with one blow split in two the skull of the tourist standing next to him. As the man toppled to the floor, a stiff cable with a sharp hook at the end shot out from the side of the chamber. It embedded itself in the body and began pulling it toward the wall, to a pile of similarly massacred corpses, leaving an ugly red stain on the shiny marble floor.

Lucy screamed with horror, but her scream was cut short by a painful constriction of her throat. The strange power was again taking control of her body. Plastic limbs ripped off her clothes. She stumbled toward the exit. She would have fallen, but her leg muscles held her up, artificially tensed by the computer's will.

Naked, her back toward the silent group, she waited for a deadly blow. The brutal murder she had witnessed kept replaying itself in her mind. She was overcome by a sense of unreality, just like a few minutes ago, when she walked into the workshop and saw the moving legs.

Instead of an ax blow, she felt the touch of another of the limbed monsters. It was pulling over her head a long dress richly decorated with golden lace. Although her heart was pounding with fear, outwardly she seemed as calm as if she were getting ready for a party. She could move her head freely. All of a sudden she realized there was something odd about the tourists and, in spite of her fear, looked at them more closely.

They were all smiling and standing as still as statues, not saying a word. And they were all dressed in costumes from early antiquity and armed with equally ancient weapons: axes, tridents, swords, spears, even clubs studded with iron nails.

A minute later another incident made her blood curdle. As she watched, a woman lifted her spear and threw it with incredible strength. It pierced the chest of a young man, its tip coming out his back. When he fell the woman walked over to him, surefooted, and pulled her weapon out of his bloodied chest. The dying man continued to smile even when the hook embedded itself in his side and started dragging him off toward the wall.

What happened over the next twenty minutes in the huge silent chamber was as mysterious as the computer's method of controlling the nervous systems of living organisms. Tensing the tourists' muscles, it forced them to participate in what seemed like a cross between an exotic ritual dance and the drill of ancient recruits.

During this macabre extravaganza the hook pulled away two more corpses. The limbomats left the chamber, closing the door behind them. Before leaving, they attached something heavy to Lucy's back. Forced by a series of impulses, she began walking toward the group of tourists. Suddenly she was made to stop and turn around. Looking at the wall, she saw a large white computer set in a deep recess.

Then she saw a second computer, a black one, set in a recess in the opposite wall.

Just as she began to grasp what was happening, a thin wisp of smoke shot out from the black computer. There was a crackle of short-circuiting cables and the overhead lights went out. The stench of burning insulation filled the air. Both computer screens were still alight in the dark, and so was every other square of the marble floor: it became clear to the terror-stricken tourists that they were standing on a huge chessboard and were the unwilling participants in a game of chess played by two computers.

A limbomat with a burning torch in one hand rushed into the chamber. Two others opened a fuse box and began repairing the damage. The tourists remained in their spots on the chessboard. One of the pieces, a man dressed in white, made a move. The white computer clearly didn't need the overhead lights and, having summoned the repair crew, continued the game.

Each side of the huge chessboard measured eight yards. In the light of the torch the white squares became somewhat dimmer but remained visible. The insulation must have caught fire when the cable was overloaded by the sudden surge in electricity needed by one of the players to solve an exceptionally difficult problem. Now Lucy knew why the limbomats had dressed some tourists in white and some in black costumes. She noted that she herself was wearing a white dress and was standing outside the chessboard, though near its edge, on the side of the black computer. At first this seemed a good sign: she was beyond the battlefield and hadn't yet participated in the game that obviously had been going on for some time.

Did this mean that she was in no danger?

There were twenty people on the chessboard. The corpses of twelve more, eliminated from the game, were piled by the wall. The tourists wore hats and helmets in the shapes of the pieces they represented in the game. Miserable, they twisted their necks looking around. So far they had been convinced that they'd either be killed by a sudden blow or have to deal one themselves at a random moment picked by the main computer; now they realized their fate depended on the situation on the chessboard. If the two computers involved in the game decided on a draw or if one checkmated the other, this would save the lives of the remaining tourists; otherwise only the two kings were certain to survive.

The white computer had foreseen many of the moves a long time ago. That's why, when Lucy entered the elevator, it invited her to be the queen. As soon as she thought of this, the man in front of her walked off the chessboard, while she, obeying the impulses in her legs, quickly took his place.

The man, a white pawn, had reached the eighth line and so could be replaced by any figure of the white computer's choice. The pawn's promotion, when Lucy took his place, seemed as innocent as a change of guards.

As soon as she stepped on the chessboard, she lifted her hands to the mysterious weight on her back; with one hand she detached a crossbow and a quiver of bolts and with the other a golden crown, which she placed on her head. The crossbow's string was drawn. Lucy notched a bolt and aimed it at the black king.

In response to the white computer's "check" the black player shielded his king with a knight. Lucy turned to the middle of the chessboard. A sudden impulse made her release the bolt. She heard the twang of the bowstring but, having quickly closed her eyes, did not see the bolt hit its target. She opened them at the sound of a deadweight dropping to the floor. A black bishop's helmet rolled toward her feet. The bolt had pierced the heart of the felled figure. Lucy recognized the woman who had earlier thrown her spear at the young man. After the shot, Lucy's muscles forced her to leave her square. She walked, sure-footed, to the spot where her victim had stood.

The black computer wasted no time in responding to its opponent's move: one of its pawns decapitated with his sword a white knight. The role of knight was played by an old boxing coach armed with a trident; the pawn was his pupil, a young, superbly built heavyweight. The blow was delivered with such force that the old man's weapon flew out of his hand and with a loud *clunk!* hit the white computer.

Several crooked lines appeared on its screen; the image wavered and split. As this was happening, Lucy was forced to walk to a new spot. The next moment the screen returned to normal and Lucy felt her legs tense again; she marched back to her former position.

She knew she was the white queen. At an earlier stage of the game the white player had lost or, more likely, sacrificed this piece to improve his overall position. Now, after the foreseen promotion of the pawn and the exchange of several pieces, neither player had a visible lead or more pieces than his opponent – a situation typical of most games played by champions. Even if she had known chess well enough to tell whether the white computer had a positional advantage, she would have been unable to do so at this macabre moment when, in the glow of the burning torch, the hook pulled two more bodies toward the wall.

A red light began blinking on top of the black computer, and it pointed its video camera's snout at Lucy. The white computer rewound a few feet of its videotape and played the last segment to show the accident it had suffered. It even made Lucy stomp her foot, but the black computer – as if refusing to accept the white player's arguments – repeated its angry signals.

It was clear that the black chess player, citing the accepted rules, was protesting his opponent's decision to take back the move he had made with his queen, while the white player was trying to explain he had been temporarily indisposed.

A limbomat controlled by the judge – the main computer – rushed up to the white computer and, brandishing a heavy hammer, forced the machine to obey the rules. Lucy received a command to return to the spot in question. She did so. Walking to it, she saw a man who, when they were sightseeing the city, had always lagged behind, lost in thought, until finally one of the other tourists, as a joke, had discreetly pinned to his back a scrap of paper with the words: TOUR'S END. Lucy had talked with this man, a composer, the day before and had enjoyed their conversation.

Now he marched past her, a black rook-shaped helmet on his head, and stopped three squares away, ready to defend the black queen, played by Lucy's friend.

The black queen had not yet removed her weapon from her back. She was waiting for the white computer's move. Lucy could see her imploring gaze. She herself felt she was going to faint, but she rested her crossbow against the floor and began turning its handle to draw the bowstring. Her heart was pounding; she realized the white computer had decided on an exchange of queens in order to force the black rook – by making it kill Lucy – to move to a less advantageous spot.

She felt as if she were shooting at her own mirror image when her bolt hit the other queen in the belly.

She didn't look at the composer's face when the hook started to pull away her friend's body. She didn't want to see the smile the machine forced him to wear. Wishing to shorten her own agony, she stretched her neck toward the black rook's descending ax. It dropped past her head and chopped off her arm and then rose once more, glinting in the light of the torch – and fell again.

She heard waves beating softly against the shore and, instead of pain in her arm, felt a gentle breeze caress her naked skin. Only the golden crown was still exerting pressure on her temples, so she lifted her hand to push it back. She could move her limbs freely. When she opened her eyes, she was sure she was dreaming.

First she saw the sky. There were a few small clouds, but otherwise it was clear blue, stretching to the horizon. When she raised herself a little, she saw the sea. She was lying under a red umbrella, dressed in a swimming suit. The sparse clouds were hanging low over the beach. The gentle breeze rippled the water. A number of people were sunbathing on the sand.

For a moment she stared into the distance, and then she noticed cables running from her forehead to the plastic box standing by her bag. Suddenly she regained her awareness of time and place. She took the heavy ring off her head, wound the cable around it, and placed it on the blanket. She knew now who she was and where she was. Although this wasn't the first cassette she had seen, she still had trouble believing that what had happened to her a moment ago was just a nightmarish illusion. The magnetic dream produced by the local videofate company had seemed incredibly real.

She walked out from under the umbrella into the sun. She was still thinking of what she'd been through when she heard her husband's voice:

"Why don't we go swimming before lunch?"

"Where were you?"

"Talking to the engineer of this beach. In exchange for the Martian's ear I gave him, he told me about the secret report he just received. The news is really alarming."

"What's happening?"

"The seventh squadron of shuffling dishes is swimming our way. They are expected to invade this shore tomorrow." He laughed. "The locals are preparing nets, clubs, impregnating agents, and glow paints for painting their tentacles. Maybe here, in Borneo, where everybody's already got a flying saucer, an attack by tentacled sea monsters is exactly what is needed to alleviate the boredom. And it should create a boom in the souvenir trade. How did you like *The Angel of Violence*?"

"What?"

He bent over the machine, took out the cassette, and showed her the colorful label with the words THE ANGEL OF VIOLENCE printed across the drawing of a white computer.

"It was a nightmare!" she cried. "How could you get me something so awful?"

"You wanted to see a horror videofate."

"You should have warned me what it was about!"

"That wouldn't have done you any good. The moment you turn on the machine you lose all consciousness of your real past. It becomes replaced by a fictitious one, created to fit the plot on tape."

"Do all horror videofates end with the viewer's simulated death?"

"Yes, with no exception. If the viewing is interrupted, he or she dies in a sudden accident. Time flies with incredible speed in a videofate; in one day you go through a whole life."

A child left alone under the next umbrella suddenly began crying and jumping around on one foot. From the radio tack stuck to the heel of its other foot emerged an announcer's voice:

"We have just received news from Singapore concerning the anthropoid apes living in a nature preserve on one of the islands off the coast of Borneo. The leader of the gorillas, who have reached a very high level of intelligence, called a press conference and proudly announced that scientists from his pack will soon construct their first atom bomb. The gorillas, of course, do not intend to use this medieval weapon against the chimpanzees inhabiting the neighboring preserve, although the gorilla leader did say its detonation would be a definite solution to their differences. He also said the gorillas feel their security among all of the island's inhabitants."

Lucy pulled the talking tack out of the child's foot, still thinking of the videofate. She could not get used to the sudden change of environment, the more so since she was now twenty years older than in the film.

"Where is that island?" she asked her husband.

"There." He pointed toward the horizon.

For several minutes they stared in silence.

"Time for lunch," Lucy's husband finally said. "I want to go for a last swim before we leave the beach. You coming?"

The water was clear and warm. On the way back to their spot on the sand they passed a group of people playing volleyball. Suddenly Lucy screamed and covered her face with her hands. A move made by one of the players who jumped to hit the ball had terrified her. The strangers stopped playing and stood there, waiting.

They smiled at her, but this was no help; she felt she was back on the chessboard and a deadly blow would split her skull any moment.

"Why did these machines force people to kill their friends?" she asked her husband when they reached their blanket.

"You mean in *The Angel of Violence*?"

"Yes."

"Simple. They were programmed by two chess players and were checking the merits of their respective game plans."

"On people?"

He looked at her serious face. "Is that what's bothering you? Look, it was just a story, some improbable rubbish made up by the scriptwriters of horror videofates."

"Wait . . . Didn't multimillion medieval armies murder each other freely? They weren't made-up criminals, were they?"

He laughed loudly. "Of course not! You silly thing, you really don't know? Soldiers killed willingly and died gladly. And they weren't criminals because in those days all bad people locked away in prisons. Just think! If things were otherwise, if good people did not kill of their own free will, then in order to explain the mechanism of war we'd have to accept as fact a version of history very much like the plot of *The Angel of Violence*. And because the idea of two invisible players hunched over the chessboard of the world is too fanciful to contemplate, we would be forced to assume that medieval kings had at their disposal fantastic machines allowing them to control remotely the muscles of millions and that they used these machines to make peace loving people kill each other."

"But it does sound fantastic, doesn't it? Bad people locked away in prisons, and good people – " She didn't finish. As she spoke the beach became dissected by long black shadows cast by standing tourists. It seemed as if a blindingly brilliant sun had torn asunder the darkness of night. The glow of the most nightmarish dawn imaginable illuminated the sky behind Lucy's back.

In the blink of an eye the whole shore was drenched with heat. A crimson flash, ten times brighter than the sun, scorched the lush vegetation, engulfing it in flames and reducing to ash; human bodies were transformed into pillars of fire.

A fraction of a second earlier Lucy had turned toward the source of light. The cloud of an atomic explosion, gigantic in size, mushroomed over the island of the apes. Its top reached high into the atmosphere. She knew that in a few seconds the coast would be hit by a thundering shock wave and everything, including her, would be swept off the surface of the earth.

But she wasn't there to see this.

She discovered that she was lying inside a glass cubicle. Her naked body was submerged in a transparent liquid. In the sudden silence a pleasant female voice spoke into her ear:

"We apologize for interrupting your videofate. Is your number nine hundred forty billion five million seventy-one?"

On a small console at the end of the glass container she saw the silver number 940,005,000,071.

"Yes," she said.

"How old are you?"

The age indicator had golden numerals. "Nineteen."

"Then everything's in order," the pleasant voice said. "After waiting your turn for a hundred and twenty years you have obtained the right to twenty-four hours of authentic life. Your place will be free in an hour's time; that's why we had to wake you. Get ready! In fifteen minutes an express elevator will take your cabin two and a half miles up, to the roof of Europe. You will see the real sun, water, and trees. Once again we apologize for turning off your videofate. Enjoy yourself!"

All around, behind the glass walls of their cubicles, narrow as coffins, rested the sleeping forms of human beings. Only Lucy lay with her eyes open. For a dozen minutes or so she stared at the millions of naked bodies arranged symmetrically in lighted glass rows, converging in infinity.

The indicators on the console were behind a pane of glass. Lucy broke it with her elbow. She closed her eyes and yanked out all the cables, but when she opened her eyes and saw the world around her unchanged, she placed her wrist on the broken glass – to turn the picture off forever.

Nobody Bothers Gus

ALGIS BUDRYS

Algis Budrys (1931–) is the author of a number of SF novels including the highly regarded *Rogue Moon* (1960) and *Michelmas* (1977), the latest of which is *Hard Landing* (1993). Some of his short fiction, predominantly from the 1950s, is collected in *The Unexpected Dimension* (1960), *Budrys's Inferno* (1963), and *Blood and Burning* (1978).

James Bush in a laudatory essay on Budrys in his famous critical work, *More Issues at Hand* (1970), says, "His gifts go far beyond craftsmanship into that instinctual realm where dwell the genuine ear for the melos and the polyphony of the English language, and the fundamental insight into the human heart." Gene Wolfe, in *Science Fiction Writers,* says "Every age and every genre produce a few writers too good for them . . . Budrys is one of these. He is, in the best sense, too serious a writer for science fiction." And like Bush, Budrys is one of the best critics of science fiction, probably the best in the generation after Bush, Damon Knight, and Theodore Sturgeon, from the mid-'60s to the mid-'80s. A collection of his reviews and essays from *Galaxy* in the 1960s is *Benchmarks: Galaxy Bookshelf* (1985). Presently he is publishing and editing his own magazine of SF, *Tomorrow.*

Most SF writers sooner or later address the theme of human evolution and many attempt to portray what a superior human might be like. Budrys imagines he might be like Gus.

Two years earlier, Gus Kusevic had been driving slowly down the narrow back road into Boonesboro.

It was good country for slow driving, particularly in the late spring. There was nobody else on the road. The woods were just blooming into a deep, rich green as yet unburned by summer, and the afternoons were still cool and fresh. And, just before he reached the Boonesboro town line, he saw the locked and weathered cottage standing for sale on its quarter-acre lot.

He had pulled his roadcar up to a gentle stop, swung sideways in his seat, and looked at it.

It needed paint; the siding had gone from white to gray, and the trim was faded. There were shingles missing here and there from the roof, leaving squares of darkness on the sun-bleached rows of cedar, and inevitably, some of the windowpanes had cracked. But the frame hadn't slouched out of square, and the roof hadn't sagged. The chimney stood up straight.

He looked at the straggled clumps and windrowed hay that were all that remained of the shrubbery and the lawn. His broad, homely face bunched itself into a quiet smile along its well-worn seams. His hands itched for the feel of a spade.

He got out of the roadcar, walked across the road and up to the cottage door, and copied down the name of the real estate dealer listed on the card tacked to the door frame.

Now it was almost two years later, early in April, and Gus was top-dressing his lawn.

Earlier in the day he'd set up a screen beside the pile of topsoil behind his house, shoveled the soil through the screen, mixed it with broken peat moss, and carted it out to the lawn, where he left it in small piles. Now he was carefully raking it out over the young grass in a thin layer that covered only the roots, and let the blades peep through. He intended to be finished by the time the second half of the Giants-Kodiaks doubleheader came on. He particularly wanted to see it because Halsey was pitching for the Kodiaks, and he had something of an avuncular interest in Halsey.

He worked without waste motion or excess expenditure of energy. Once or twice he stopped and had a beer in the shade of the rose arbor he'd put up around the front door. Nevertheless, the sun was hot; by early afternoon, he had his shirt off.

Just before he would have been finished, a battered flivver settled down in front of the house. It parked with a flurry of its rotors, and a gangling man in a worn serge suit, with thin hair plastered across his tight scalp, climbed out and looked at Gus uncertainly.

Gus had glanced up briefly while the flivver was on its silent way down. He'd made out the barely-legible "Falmouth County Clerk's Office" lettered over the faded paint on its door, shrugged, and gone on with what he was doing.

Gus was a big man. His shoulders were heavy and broad; his chest was deep, grizzled with thick, iron-gray hair. His stomach had gotten a little heavier with the years, but the muscles were still there under the layer of flesh. His upper arms were thicker than a good many thighs, and his forearms were enormous.

His face was seamed by a network of folds and creases. His flat cheeks were marked out by two deep furrows that ran from the sides of his bent nose, merged with the creases bracketing his wide lips, and converged toward the blunt point of his jaw. His pale blue eyes twinkled above high cheekbones which were covered with wrinkles. His close-cropped hair was as white as cotton.

Only repeated and annoying exposure would give his body a tan, but his face was permanently browned. The pink of his body sunburn was broken in several places by white scar tissue. The thin line of a knife cut emerged from the tops of his pants and faded out across the right side of his stomach. The other significant area of scarring lay across the uneven knuckles of his heavy-fingered hands.

The clerk looked at the mailbox to make sure of the name, checking it against an envelope he was holding in one hand. He stopped and looked at Gus again, mysteriously nervous.

Gus abruptly realized that he probably didn't present a reassuring appearance. With all the screening and raking he'd been doing, there'd been a lot of dust in the air. Mixed with perspiration, it was all over his face, chest, arms, and back. Gus knew he didn't look very gentle even at his cleanest and best-dressed. At the moment, he couldn't blame the clerk for being skittish.

He tried to smile disarmingly.

The clerk ran his tongue over his lips, cleared his throat with a slight cough, and jerked his head toward the mail box. "Is that right? You Mr. Kusevic?"

Gus nodded. "That's right. What can I do for you?"

The clerk held up the envelope. "Got a notice here from the County Council," he muttered, but he was obviously much more taken up by his effort to equate Gus with the rose arbor, the neatly edged and carefully tended flower beds, the hedges, the flagstoned walk, the small goldfish pond under the willow tree, the white-painted cottage with its window boxes and bright shutters, and the curtains showing inside the sparkling windows.

Gus waited until the man was through with his obvious thoughts, but something deep inside him sighed quietly. He had gone through this moment of bewilderment with so many other people that he was quite accustomed to it, but that is not the same thing as being oblivious.

"Well, come on inside," he said after a decent interval. "It's pretty hot out here, and I've got some beer in the cooler."

The clerk hesitated again. "Well, all I've got to do it deliver this notice – " he said, still looking around. "Got the place fixed up real nice, don't you?"

Gus smiled. "It's my home. A man likes to live in a nice place. In a hurry?"

The clerk seemed to be troubled by something in what Gus had said. Then he looked up suddenly, obviously just realizing he'd been asked a direct question. "Huh?"

"You're not in any hurry, are you? Come on in; have a beer. Nobody's expected to be a ball of fire on a spring afternoon."

The clerk grinned uneasily. "No . . . nope, guess not." He brightened. "O.K.! Don't mind if I do."

Gus ushered him into the house, grinning with pleasure. Nobody's seen the inside of the place since he'd fixed it up; the clerk was the first visitor he'd had since moving in. There weren't even any delivery men; Boonesboro was so small you had to drive in for your own shopping. There wasn't any mail carrier service, of course – not that Gus ever received any mail.

He showed the clerk into the living room. "Have a seat. I'll be right back." He went quickly out to the kitchen, took some beer out of the cooler, loaded a tray with glasses, a bowl of chips and pretzels, and the beer, and carried it out.

The clerk was up, looking around the library that covered two of the living room walls.

Looking at his expression, Gus realized with genuine regret that the man wasn't the kind to doubt whether an obvious clod like Kusevic had read any of this stuff. A man like that could still be talked to, once the original misconceptions were knocked down. No, the clerk was too plainly mystified that a grown man would fool with books. Particularly a man like Gus; now, one of these kids that messed with college politics, that was something else. But a grown man oughtn't to act like that.

Gus saw it had been a mistake to expect anything of the clerk. He should have known better, whether he was hungry for company or not. He'd *always* been hungry for company, and it was time he realized, once and for all, that he just plain wasn't going to find any.

He set the tray down on the table, uncapped a beer quickly, and handed it to the man.

"Thanks," the clerk mumbled. He took a swallow, sighed loudly, and wiped his mouth with the back of his hand. He looked around the room again. "Cost you a lot to have all this put in?"

Gus shrugged. "Did most of it myself. Built the shelves and furniture; stuff like that. Some of the paintings I had to buy, and the books and records."

The clerk grunted. He seemed to be considerably ill at ease, probably because of the notice he'd brought, whatever it was. Gus found himself wondering what it could possibly be, but, now that he'd made the mistake of giving the man a beer, he had to wait politely until it was finished before he could ask.

He went over to the TV set. "Baseball fan?" he asked the clerk.

"Sure!"

"Giants-Kodiaks ought to be on." He switched the set on and pulled up a hassock, sitting on it so as not to get one of the chairs dirty. The clerk wandered over and stood looking at the screen, taking slow swallows of his beer.

The second game had started, and Halsey's familiar figure appeared on the screen as the set warmed up. The lithe young lefthander was throwing with his usual boneless motion, apparently not working hard at all, but the ball was whipping past the batters with a sizzle that the home plate microphone was picking up clearly.

Gus nodded toward Halsey. "He's quite a pitcher, isn't he?"

The clerk shrugged. "Guess so. Walker's their best man, though."

Gus sighed as he realized he'd forgotten himself again. The clerk wouldn't pay much attention to Halsey, naturally.

But he was getting a little irritated at the man, with his typical preconceptions of what was proper and what wasn't, of who had a right to grow roses and who didn't.

"Offhand," Gus said to the clerk, "could you tell me what Halsey's record was, last year?"

The clerk shrugged. "Couldn't tell you. Wasn't bad – I remember that much. 13–7, something like that."

Gus nodded to himself. "Uh-huh. How'd Walker do?"

"Walker! Why, man, Walker just won something like twenty-five games, that's all. And three no-hitters. How'd Walker do? Huh!"

Gus shook his head. "Walker's a good pitcher, all right – but he didn't pitch any no-hitters. And he only won eighteen games."

The clerk wrinkled his forehead. He opened his mouth to argue and then stopped. He looked like a sure-thing better who'd just realized that his memory had played him a trick.

"Say – I think you're right! Huh! Now what the Sam Hill made me think Walker was the guy? And you know something – I've been talking about him all winter, and nobody once called me wrong?" The clerk scratched his head. "Now, *somebody* pitched them games! Who the dickens was it?" He scowled in concentration.

Gus silently watched Halsey strike out his third batter in a row, and his face wrinkled into a slow smile. Halsey was still young; just hitting his stride. He threw himself into the game with all the energy and enjoyment a man felt when he realized he was at his peak, and that, out there on the mound in the sun, he was as good as any man who ever had gone before him in this profession.

Gus wondered how soon Halsey would see the trap he'd set for himself.

Because it wasn't a contest. Not for Halsey. For Christy Mathewson, it had been a contest. For Lefty Grove and Dizzy Dean, for Bob Feller and Slats Gould, it had been a contest. But for Halsey it was just a complicated form of solitaire that always came out right.

Pretty soon, Halsey'd realize that you can't handicap yourself at solitaire. If you knew where all the cards are; if you knew that unless you deliberately cheated against yourself, you couldn't help but win – what good was it? One of these days, Halsey'd realize there wasn't a game on Earth he couldn't beat; whether it was a physical contest, organized and formally recognized as a game, or whether it was the billion-triggered pinball machine called Society.

What then, Halsey? What then? And if you find out, please, in the name of whatever kind of brotherhood we share, let me know.

The clerk grunted. "Well, it don't matter, I guess. I can always look it up in the record book at home."

Yes, you can, Gus commented silently. But you won't notice what it says, and, if you do, you'll forget it and never realize you've forgotten.

The clerk finished his beer, set it down on the tray, and was free to remember what he'd come here for. He looked around the room again, as though the memory were a cue of some kind.

"Lots of books," he commented.

Gus nodded, watching Halsey walk out to the pitcher's mound again.

"Uh . . . you read 'em all?"

Gus shook his head.

"How about that one by the Miller fellow? I hear that's a pretty good one."

So. The clerk had a certain narrow interest in certain aspects of certain kinds of literature.

"I suppose it is," Gus answered truthfully. "I read the first three pages, once. And, having done so, he'd known how the rest of it was going to go, who would do what when, and he'd lost interest. The library had been a mistake, just one of a dozen similar experiments. If he'd wanted an academic familiarity with human literature, he could just as easily have picked it up by browsing through bookstores, rather than buying the books and doing substantially the same thing at home. He couldn't hope to extract any emotional empathies, no matter what he did.

Face it, though; rows of even useless books were better than bare wall. The trappings of culture were a bulwark of sorts, even though it was a learned culture and not a *felt* one, and meant no more to him than the culture of the Incas. Try as he might, he could never be an Inca. Nor even a Maya or an Aztec, or any kind of kin, except by the most tenuous of extensions.

But he had no culture of his own. There was the thing; the emptiness that nevertheless ached; the rootlessness, the complete absence of a place to stand and say: "This is my own."

Halsey struck out the first batter in the inning with three pitches. Then he put a slow floater precisely where the next man could get the best part of his bat on it, and did not even look up as the ball screamed out of the park. He struck out the next two men with a total of eight pitches.

Gus shook his head slowly. That was the first symptom; when you didn't bother to be subtle about your handicapping any more.

The clerk held out the envelope. "Here," he said brusquely, having finally shilly-shallied his resolution up to the point of doing it despite his obvious nervousness at Gus' probable reaction.

Gus opened the envelope and read the notice. Then, just as the clerk had been doing, he looked around the room. A dark expression must have flickered over his face, because the clerk became even more hesitant. "I . . . I want you to know I regret this. I guess all of us do."

Gus nodded hastily. "Sure, sure." He stood up and looked out the front window. He smiled crookedly, looking at the top-dressing spread carefully over the painstakingly rolled lawn, which was slowly taking form on the plot where he had plowed last year and picked out pebbles, seeded and watered, shoveled topsoil, laid out flower beds. . . ah, there was no use going into that now. The whole plot, cottage and all, was condemned, and that was that.

"They're . . . they're turnin' the road into a twelve-lane freight highway," the clerk explained.

Gus nodded absently.

The clerk moved closer and dropped his voice. "Look – I was told to tell you this. Not in writin'." He sidled even closer, and actually looked around before he spoke. He laid his hand confidentially on Gus' bare forearm.

"Any price you ask for," he muttered, "is gonna be O.K., as long as you don't get too greedy. The county isn't paying this bill. Not even the state, if you get what I mean."

Gus got what he meant. Twelve-lane highways aren't built by anything but national governments.

He got more than that. National governments don't work this way unless there's a good reason.

"Highway between Hollister and Farnham?" he asked.

The clerk paled. "Don't know for sure," he muttered.

Gus smiled thinly. Let the clerk wonder how he'd guessed. It couldn't be much of a secret, anyway – not after the grade was laid out and the purpose became self-evident. Besides, the clerk wouldn't wonder very long.

A streak of complete perversity shot through Gus. He recognized its source in his anger at losing the cottage, but there was no reason why he shouldn't allow himself to cut loose.

"What's your name?" he asked the clerk abruptly.

"Uh . . . Harry Danvers."

"Well, Harry, suppose I told you I could stop that highway, if I wanted to? Suppose I told you that no bulldozer could get near this place without breaking down, that no shovel could dig this ground, that sticks of dynamite just plain wouldn't explode if they tried to blast? Suppose I told you that if they put in the highway, it would turn soft as ice cream if I wanted it to, and run away like a river?"

"Huh?"

"Hand me your pen."

Danvers reached out mechanically and handed it to him. Gus put it between his palms and rolled it into a ball. He dropped it and caught it as it bounced up sharply from the soft, thick rug. He pulled it out between his fingers, and it returned to its cylindrical shape. He unscrewed the cap, flattened it out into a sheet between two fingers, scribbled on it, rolled it back into a cap, and, using his fingernail to draw out the ink which was now part of it, permanently inscribed Danvers' name just below the surface of the metal. Then he screwed the cap on again and handed the pen back to the country clerk. "Souvenir," he said.

The clerk looked down at it.

"Well?" Gus asked. "Aren't you curious about how I did it and what I am?"

The clerk shook his head. "Good trick. I guess you magician fellows must spend a lot of time practicing, huh? Can't say I could see myself spendin' that much working time on a hobby."

Gus nodded. "That's a good, sound, practical point of view," he said. Particularly when all of us automatically put out a field that damps curiosity, he thought. What point of view *could* you have?

He looked over the clerk's shoulder at the lawn, and one side of his mouth twisted sadly.

Only God can make a tree, he thought, looking at the shrubs and flower beds. Should we all, then, look for our challenge in landscape gardening? Should we become the gardeners of the rich humans in the expensive houses, driving up in our old, rusty trucks, oiling our lawn-mowers, kneeling on the humans' lawns with our clipping shears, coming to the kitchen door to ask for a drink of water on a hot summer day?

The highway. Yes, he could stop the highway. Or make it go around him. There was no way of stopping the curiosity damper, no more than there was a way of willing his heart to stop, but it could be stepped up. He could force his mind to labor near overload, and no one would ever even see the cottage, the lawn, the rose arbor, or the battered old man, drinking his beer. Or rather, seeing them, would pay them absolutely no attention.

But the first time he went into town, or when he died, the field would be off, and then what? The curiosity, then investigation, then, perhaps a fragment of theory here or there to be fitted to another somewhere else. And then what? Pogrom?

He shook his head. The humans couldn't win, and would lose monstrously. *That* was why he couldn't leave the humans a clue. He had no taste for slaughtering sheep, and he doubted if his fellows did.

His fellows. Gus stretched his mouth. The only one he could be sure of was Halsey. There had to be others, but there was no way of finding them. They provoked no reaction from the humans; they left no trail to follow. It was only if they showed themselves, like Halsey, that they could be seen. There was, unfortunately, no private telepathic party line among them.

He wondered if Halsey hoped someone would notice him and get in touch. He wondered if Halsey even suspected there were others like himself. He wondered if anyone had noticed *him*, when Gus Kusevic's name had been in the papers occasionally.

It's the dawn of my race, he thought. The first generation – or is it, and does it matter – and I wonder where the females are.

He turned back to the clerk. "I want what I paid for the place," he said. "No more."

The clerk's eyes widened slightly, then relaxed, and he shrugged. "Suit yourself. But if it was me, I'd soak the government good."

Yes, Gus thought, you doubtless would. But I don't want to, because you simply don't take candy from babies.

So the superman packed his bags and got out of the human's way. Gus choked a silent laugh. The damping field. The damping-field. The thrice-cursed, ever-benevolent, foolproof, autonomic, protective damping field.

Evolution had, unfortunately, not yet realized that there was such a thing as human society. It produced a being with a certain modification from the human stock, thereby arriving at practical psi. In order to protect this feeble new species, whose members were so terribly sparse, it gave them the perfect camouflage.

Result: When young Augustin Kusevic was enrolled in school, it was discovered that he had no birth certificate. No hospital recalled his birth. As a matter of brutal fact, his human parents sometimes forgot his existence for days at a time.

Result: When young Gussie Kusevic tried to enter high school, it was discovered that he had never entered grammar school. No matter that he could quote teachers' names, textbooks, or classroom numbers. No matter if he could produce report cards. They were misfiled, and the anguished interviews forgotten. No one doubted his existence – people remembered the fact of his being, and the fact of his having acted and being acted upon. But only as though they had read it in some infinitely boring book.

He had no friends, no girl, no past, no present, no love. He had no place to stand. Had there been such things as ghosts, he would have found his fellowship there.

By the time of his adolescence, he had discovered an absolute lack of involvement with the human race. He studied it, because it was the salient feature of his environment. He did not live with it. It said nothing to him that was of personal value; its motivations, morals, manners and morale did not find responsive reactions in him. And his, of course, made absolutely no impression on it.

The life of the peasant of ancient Babylon is of interest to only a few historical anthropologists, none of whom actually want to be Babylonian peasants.

Having solved the human social equation from his dispassionate viewpoint, and caring no more than the naturalist who finds that deer are extremely fond of green aspen leaves, he plunged into physical release. He discovered the thrill of picking fights and winning them; of *making* somebody pay attention to him by smashing his nose.

He might have become a permanent fixture on the Manhattan docks, if another longshoreman hadn't slashed him with a carton knife. The cultural demand on him had been plain. He'd had to kill the man.

That had been the end of unregulated personal combat. He discovered, not to his horror but to his disgust, that he could get away with murder. No investigation had been made; no search was attempted.

So that had been the end of that, but it had led him to the only possible evasion of the trap to which he had been born. Intellectual competition being meaningless, organized sports became the only answer. Simultaneously regulating his efforts and annotating them under a mound of journalistic record-keeping, they furnished the first official continuity his life had ever known. People still forgot his accomplishments, but when they turned to the records, his name was undeniably there. A dossier can be misfiled. School records can disappear. But something more than a damping field was required to shunt aside the mountain of news copy and statistics that drags, ball-like, at the ankle of even the mediocre athlete.

It seemed to Gus – and he thought of it a great deal – that this chain of progression was inevitable for any male of his kind. When, three years ago, he had discovered Halsey, his hypothesis was bolstered. But what good was Halsey to another male? To hold mutual consolation sessions with? He had no intention of ever contacting the man.

The clerk cleared his throat. Gus jerked his head around to look at him, startled. He'd forgotten him.

"Well, guess I'll be going. Remember, you've only got two months."

Gus gestured noncommittally. The man had delivered his message. Why didn't he acknowledge he'd served his purpose, and go?

Gus smiled ruefully. What purpose did homo *nondescriptus* serve, and where was he going? Halsey was already walking downhill along the well-marked trail. Were there others? If so, then they were in another rut, somewhere, and not even the tops of their heads showed. He and his kind could recognize each other only by an elaborate process of elimination; they had to watch for the people no one noticed.

He opened the door for the clerk, saw the road, and found his thoughts back with the highway.

The highway would run from Hollister, which was a railroad junction, to the Air Force Base at Farnham, where his calculations in sociomathematics had long ago predicted the first starship would be constructed and launched. The trucks would rumble up the highway, feeding the open maw with men and material.

He cleaned his lips. Up there in space, somewhere; somewhere outside the Solar System, was another race. The imprint of their visits here was plain. The humans would encounter them, and again he could predict the result; the humans would win.

Gus Kusevic could not go along to investigate the challenges that he doubted lay among the stars. Even with scrapbooks full of notices and clippings, he had barely made his career penetrate the public consciousness. Halsey, who had exuberantly broken every baseball record in the books, was known as a "pretty fair country pitcher."

What credentials could he present with his application to the Air Force? Who would remember them the next day if he had any? What would become of the records of his inoculations, his physical check-ups, his training courses? Who would remember to reserve a bunk for him, or stow supplies for him, or add his consumption to the total when the time came to allow for oxygen?

Stow away? Nothing easier. But, again; who would die so he could live within the tight lattice of shipboard economy? Which sheep would he slaughter, and to what useful purpose, in the last analysis?

"Well, so long," the clerk said.

"Good-bye," Gus said.

The clerk walked down the flagstones and out to his flivver.

I think, Gus said to himself, it would have been much better for us if Evolution had been a little less protective and a little more thoughtful. An occasional pogrom wouldn't have done us any harm. A ghetto at least keeps the courtship problem solved.

Our seed has been spilt on the ground.

Suddenly, Gus ran forward, pushed by something he didn't care to name. He looked up through the flivver's open door, and the clerk looked down apprehensively.

"Danvers, you're a sports fan," Gus said hastily, realizing his voice was too urgent; that he was startling the clerk with his intensity.

"That's right," the clerk answered, pushing himself nervously back along the seat.

"Who's heavyweight champion of the world?"

"Mike Frazier. Why?"

"Who'd he beat for the title? Who used to be champion?"

The clerk pursed his lips. "Huh! It's been years – gee, I don't know. I don't remember. I could look it up, I guess."

Gus exhaled slowly. He half-turned and looked back toward the cottage, the lawn, the flower beds, the walk, the arbor, and the fish pond under the willow tree. "Never mind," he said, and walked back into the house while the clerk wobbled his flivver into the air.

The TV set was blaring with sound. He checked the status of the game.

It had gone quickly. Halsey had pitched a one-hitter so far, and the Giants' pitcher had done almost as well. The score was tied at 1–1, the Giants were at bat, and it was the last out in the ninth inning. The camera boomed in on Halsey's face.

Halsey looked at the batter with complete disinterest in his eyes, wound up, and threw the home-run ball.

As Easy as ABC

RUDYARD KIPLING

Rudyard Kipling (1865–1936) is one of the major literary figures influencing the flowering of science fiction in the twentieth century. Kipling wrote two great SF stories, "With the Night Mail" and this one, a sequel set in the same imagined future. With them he became one of the progenitors of the genre. H. G. Wells was the great imaginative force behind Scientific Romance from 1895 to at least the 1920s, but Rudyard Kipling was the most popular English language writer of his day, and it was not Wellsian but Kiplingèsque storytelling and attitudes – and politics – that dominated American science fiction in the 1940s and '50s. While Robert A. Heinlein certainly borrowed techniques liberally from the fiction of H. G. Wells, the effect of his classic stories is markedly Kiplingesque. Poul Anderson and Gordon R. Dickson, to name only two others among many, also acknowledge a debt to Kipling.

Even though he wrote very little actual science fiction, fantastic elements abound in Kipling's fiction. The recent (1992) publication of a volume of *The Science Fiction of Rudyard Kipling*, laden with encomiums from such diverse SF writers as Jerry Pournelle, Gene Wolfe, and John Brunner, only confirms his enduring appeal and influence.

In his introduction to that volume John Brunner points out that Kipling uses the historic present tense, in his day an unusual usage in English, which became part of the arsenal of SF writers. He also points out, in his introduction to "As Easy as ABC," the crucial fact that Kipling was, politically, the ancestor of what we today call Libertarians. Brunner quotes Kipling's 1923 speech at St. Andrews to this effect: "At any price I can pay, let me own myself. And the price is worth paying if you keep what you have bought."

"As Easy as ABC" is if anything a companion piece to Forster's "The Machine Stops," a criticism of the Wellsian urban utopia, but with an attitude that leads toward, not away from, genre science fiction.

The ABC, that semi-elected, semi-nominated body of a few score persons, controls the Planet. Transportation is Civilization, our motto runs. Theoretically we do what we please, so long as we do not interfere with the traffic and all it implies. Practically, the ABC confirms or annuals all international arrangements, and, to judge from its last report, finds our tolerant, humorous, lazy little Planet only too ready to shift the whole burden of public administration on its shoulders.

"With the Night Mail," *Actions and Reactions*

Isn't it almost time that our Planet took some interest in the proceedings of the Aerial Board of Control? One knows that easy communications nowadays, and lack of privacy in the past, have killed all curiosity among mankind, but as the Board's Official Reporter I am bound to tell my tale.

At 9.30 a.m., 26 August, A.D. 2065, the Board, sitting in London, was informed by De Forest that the District of Northern Illinois had riotously cut itself out of all systems and would remain disconnected till the Board should take over and administer it direct.

Every Northern Illinois freight and passenger tower was, he reported, out of action; all District main, local, and guiding lights had been extinguished; all General Communications were dumb, and through traffic had been diverted. No reason had been given, but he gathered unofficially from the Mayor of Chicago that the District complained of "crowd-making and invasion of privacy."

As a matter of fact, it is of no importance whether Northern Illinois stay in or out of planetary circuit; as a matter of policy, any complaint of invasion of privacy needs immediate investigation, lest worse follow.

By 9.45 a.m. De Forest, Dragomiroff (Russia), Takahira (Japan), and Pirolo (Italy) were empowered to visit Illinois and "to take such steps as might be necessary for the resumption of traffic and *all that that implies.*" By 10 a.m. the Hall was empty, and the four Members and I were aboard what Pirolo insisted on calling "my leetle godchild" – that is to say, the new *Victor Pirolo*. Our Planet prefers to know Victor Pirolo as a gentle, grey-haired enthusiast who spends his time near Foggia, inventing or creating new breeds of Spanish-Italian olive-trees; but there is another side to his nature – the manufacture of quaint inventions, of which the *Victor Pirolo* is, perhaps, not the least surprising. She and a few score sister-craft of the same type embody his latest ideas. But she is not comfortable. An ABC boat does not take the air with the level-keeled lift of a liner, but shoots up rocket-fashion like the "aeroplane" of our ancestors, and makes her height at top-speed from the first. That is why I found myself sitting suddenly on the large lap of Eustace Arnott, who commands the ABC Fleet. One knows vaguely that there is such a thing as a Fleet somewhere on the planet, and that, theoretically, it exists for the purposes of what used to be known as "war." Only a week before, while visiting a glacier sanatorium behind Gothaven, I had seen some squadrons making false auroras far to the north while they maneuvered round the Pole; but, naturally, it had never occurred to me that the things could be used in earnest.

Said Arnott to De Forest as I staggered to a seat on the chart-room divan: "We're tremendously grateful to 'em in Illinois. We've never had a chance of exercising all the Fleet together. I've turned in a General Call, and I expect we'll have at least two hundred keels aloft this evening."

"Well aloft?" De Forest asked.

"Of course, sir. Out of sight till they're called for."

Arnott laughed as he lolled over the transparent chart-table where the map of the summer-blue Atlantic slid along, degree by degree, in exact answer to our progress. Our dial already showed 320 m.p.h. and we were two thousand feet above the uppermost traffic lines.

"Now, where is this Illinois District of yours?" said Dragomiroff. "One travels so much, one sees so little. Oh, I remember! It is in North America."

De Forest, whose business it is to know the out districts, told us that it lay at the foot of Lake Michigan, on a road to nowhere in particular, was about half an hour's run from end to end, and, except in one corner, as flat as the sea. Like most flat countries nowadays, it was heavily guarded against invasion of privacy by forced timber – fifty-foot spruce and tamarack, grown in five years. The population was close on two millions, largely migratory between Florida and California, with a backbone of small farms (they call a thousand acres a farm in Illinois) whose owners come into Chicago for amusements and society during the winter. They were, he said, noticeably kind, quiet folk, but a little exacting, as all flat countries must be, in their notions of privacy. There had, for instance, been no printed news-sheet in Illinois for twenty-seven years. Chicago argued that engines for printed news sooner or later developed into engines for invasion of privacy, which in turn might bring the old terror of Crowds and black-mail back to the Planet. So news-sheets were not.

"And that's Illinois," De Forest concluded. "You see, in the Old Days, she was in the forefront of what they used to call 'progress,' and Chicago – "

"Chicago?" said Takahira. "That's the little place where there is Salati's Statue of the Negro in Flames? A fine bit of old work."

"When did you see it?" asked De Forest quickly. "They only unveil it once a year."

"I know. At Thanksgiving. It was then," said Takahira, with a shudder. "And they sang MacDonough's Song, too."

"Whew!" De Forest whistled. "I did not know that! I wish you'd told me before. MacDonough's Song may have had its uses when it was composed, but it was an infernal legacy for any man to leave behind."

"It's protective instinct, my dear fellows," said Pirolo, rolling a cigarette. "The Planet, she has had her dose of popular government. She suffers from inherited agoraphobia. She has no – ah – use for crowds."

Dragomiroff leaned forward to give him a light. "Certainly," said the white-bearded Russian, "the Planet has taken all precautions against crowds for the past hundred years. What is our total population today? Six hundred million, we hope; five hundred, we think; but – but if next year's census shows more than four hundred and fifty, I myself will eat all the extra little babies. We have cut the birth-rate out – right out! For a long time we have said to Almighty God, 'Thank You, Sir, but we do not much like Your game of life, so we will not play.'"

"Anyhow," said Arnott defiantly, "men live a century apiece on the average now."

"Oh, that is quite well! I am rich – you are rich – we are all rich and happy because we are so few and we live so long. Only *I* think Almighty God He will remember what the Planet was like in the time of Crowds and the Plague. Perhaps He will send us nerves. Eh, Pirolo?"

The Italian blinked into space. "Perhaps," he said, "He has sent them already. Anyhow, you cannot argue with the Planet. She does not forget the Old Days, and – what can you do?"

"For sure we can't remake the world." De Forest glanced at the map flowing smoothly across the table from west to east. "We ought to be over our ground by nine tonight. There won't be much sleep after-wards."

On which hint we dispersed, and I slept till Takahira waked me for dinner. Our ancestors thought nine hours' sleep ample for their little lives. We, living thirty years longer, feel ourselves defrauded with less than eleven out of the twenty-four.

By ten o'clock we were over Lake Michigan. The west shore was lightless, except for a dull ground-glare at Chicago, and a single traffic-directing light – its leading beam pointing north – at Waukegan on our starboard bow. None of the Lake villages gave any sign of life; and inland, westward, so far as we could see, blackness lay unbroken on the level earth. We swooped down and skimmed low across the dark, throwing calls county by county. Now and again we picked up the faint glimmer of a house-light, or heard the rasp and rend of a cultivator being played across the fields, but Northern Illinois as a whole was one inky, apparently uninhabited, waste of high, forced woods. Only our illuminated map, with its little pointer switching from county to county, as we wheeled and twisted, gave us any idea of our position. Our calls, urgent, pleading, coaxing or commanding, through the General Communicator brought no answer. Illinois strictly maintained her own privacy in the timber which she grew for that purpose.

"Oh this is absurd!" said De Forest. "We're like an owl trying to work a wheat-field. Is this Bureau Creek? Let's land, Arnott, and get hold of some one."

We brushed over a belt of forced woodland – fifteen-year-old maple sixty feet high – grounded on a private meadow-dock, none too big, where we moored to our own grapnels, and hurried out through the warm dark night towards a light in a verandah. As we neared the garden gate I could have sworn we had stepped knee-deep in quicksand, for we could scarcely drag our feet against the prickling currents that clogged them. After five paces we stopped, wiping our foreheads, as hopelessly stuck on dry smooth turf as so many cows in a bog.

"Pest!" cried Pirolo angrily. "We are ground-circuited. And it is my own system of ground-circuits too! I know the pull."

"Good evening," said a girl's voice from the verandah. "Oh, I'm sorry! We've locked up. Wait a minute."

We heard the click of a switch, and almost fell forward as the currents round our knees were withdrawn.

The girl laughed, and laid aside her knitting. An old-fashioned Controller stood at her elbow, which she reversed from time to time, and we could hear the snort and clank of the obedient cultivator half a mile away, behind the guardian woods.

"Come in and sit down," she said. "I'm only playing a plough. Dad's gone to Chicago to – Ah! Then it was *your* call I heard just now!"

She had caught sight of Arnott's Board uniform, leaped to the switch, and turned it full on.

We were checked, gasping, waist-deep in current this time, three yards from the verandah.

"We only want to know what's the matter with Illinois," said De Forest placidly.

"Then hadn't you better go to Chicago and find out?" she answered. "There's nothing wrong here. We own ourselves."

"How can we go anywhere if you won't loose us?" De Forest went on, while Arnott scowled. Admirals of Fleets are still quite human when their dignity is touched.

"Stop a minute – you don't know how funny you look!" She put her hands on her hips and laughed mercilessly.

"Don't worry about that," said Arnott, and whistled. A voice answered from the *Victor Pirolo* in the meadow.

"Only a single-fuse ground-circuit!" Arnott called. "Sort it out gently, please."

We heard the ping of a breaking lamp; a fuse blew out somewhere in the verandah roof, frightening a nest full of birds. The ground-circuit was open. We stooped and rubbed our tingling ankles.

"How rude – how very rude of you!" the maiden cried.

"Sorry, but we haven't time to look funny," said Arnott. "We've got to go to Chicago; and if I were you, young lady, I'd go into the cellars for the next two hours, and take mother with me."

Off he strode, with us at his heels, muttering indignantly, till the humour of the thing struck and doubled him up with laughter at the foot of the gangway ladder.

"The Board hasn't shown what you might call a fat spark on this occasion, said De Forest, wiping his eyes. "I hope I didn't look as big a fool as you did, Arnott! Hullo! What on earth is that? Dad coming home from Chicago?"

There was a rattle and a rush, and a five-plough cultivator, blades in air like so many teeth, trundled itself at us round the edge of the timber, fuming and sparking furiously.

"Jump!" said Arnott, as we bundled ourselves through the none-too-wide door. "Never mind about shutting it. Up!"

The *Victor Pirolo* lifted like a bubble, and the vicious machine shot just underneath us, clawing high as it passed.

"There's a nice little spit-kitten for you!" said Arnott, dusting his knees. "We ask her a civil question. First she circuits us and then she plays a cultivator at us!"

"And then we fly," said Dragomiroff. "If I were forty years more young, I would go back and kiss her. Ho! Ho!"

"I," said Pirolo, "would smack her! My pet ship has been chased by a dirty plough; a – how do you say? – agricultural implement."

"Oh, that is Illinois all over," said De Forest. "They don't content themselves with talking about privacy. They arrange to have it. And now, where's your alleged fleet, Arnott? We must assert ourselves against this wench."

Arnott pointed to the black heavens.

"Waiting on – up there," said he. "Shall I give them the whole installation, sir?"

"Oh, I don't think the young lady is quite worth that," said De Forest. "Get over Chicago, and perhaps we'll see something."

In a few minutes we were hanging at two thousand feet over an oblong block of incandescence in the centre of the little town.

"That looks like the old City Hall. Yes, there's Salati's Statue in front of it," said Takahira. "But what on earth are they doing to the place? I thought they used it for a market nowadays! Drop a little, please."

We could hear the sputter and crackle of road-surfacing machines – the cheap Western type which fuse stone and rubbish into lava-like ribbed glass for their rough country roads. Three or four surfacers worked on each side of a square of ruins. The brick and stone wreckage crumbled, slid forward, and presently spread out into white-hot pools of sticky slag, which the levelling-rods smoothed more or less flat. Already a third of the big block had been so treated, and was cooling to dull red before our astonished eyes.

"It is the Old Market," said De Forest. "Well, there's nothing to prevent Illinois from making a road through a market. It doesn't inter-fere with traffic, that I can see."

"Hsh!" said Arnott, gripping me by the shoulder. "Listen! They're singing. Why on the earth are they singing?"

We dropped again till we could see the black fringe of people at the edge of that glowing square.

At first they only roared against the roar of the surfacers and levellers. Then the words came up clearly – the words of the Forbidden Song that all men knew, and none let pass their lips – poor Pat MacDonough's Song, made in the days of the Crowds and the Plague – every silly word of it loaded to sparking-point with the Planet's inherited memories of horror, panic, fear, and cruelty. And Chicago – innocent, contented little Chicago – was singing it aloud to the infernal tune that carried riot, pestilence and lunacy round our Planet a few generations ago!

> *Once there was The People – Terror gave it birth;*
> *Once there was The People, and it made a hell of earth!*

(Then the stamp and pause):

> *Earth arose and crushed it. Listen, oh, ye slain!*
> *Once there was The People – it shall never be again!*

The levellers thrust in savagely against the ruins as the song renewed itself again, again and again, louder than the crash of the melting walls.

De Forest frowned.

"I don't like that," he said. "They've broken back to the Old Days! They'll be killing somebody soon. I think we'd better divert 'em, Arnott."

"Ay, ay, sir." Arnott's hand went to his cap, and we heard the hull of the *Victor Pirolo* ring to the command: "Lamps! Both watches stand by! Lamps! Lamps! Lamps!"

"Keep still!" Takahira whispered to me. "Blinkers, please, quartermaster."

"It's all right – all right!" said Pirolo from behind, and to my horror slipped over my head some sort of rubber helmet that locked with a snap. I could feel thick colloid bosses before my eyes, but I stood in absolute darkness.

"To save the sight," he explained, and pushed me on to the chartroom divan. "You will see in a minute."

As he spoke I became aware of a thin thread of almost intolerable light, let down from heaven at an immense distance – one vertical hairsbreadth of frozen lightning.

"Those are our flanking ships," said Arnott at my elbow. "That one is over Galena. Look south – that other one's over Keithburg. Vincennes is behind us, and north yonder is Winthrop Woods. The Fleet's in position, sir" – this to De Forest. "As soon as you give the word."

"Ah no! No!" cried Dragomiroff at my side. I could feel the old man tremble. "I do not know all that you can do, but be kind! I ask you to be a little kind to them below! This is horrible – horrible!"

When a Woman kills a Chicken,
Dynasties and Empires sicken,

Takahira quoted. "It is too late to be gentle now."

"Then take off my helmet! Take off my helmet!" Dragomiroff began hysterically.

Pirolo must have put his arm round him.

"Hush," he said, "I am here. It is all right, Ivan, my dear fellow."

"I'll just send our little girl in Bureau County a warning," said Arnott. "She doesn't deserve it, but we'll allow her a minute or two to take mamma to the cellar."

In the utter hush that followed the growling spark after Arnott had linked up his Service Communicator with the invisible Fleet, we heard MacDonough's Song from the city beneath us grow fainter as we rose to position. Then I clapped my hand before my mask lenses for it was as though the floor of Heaven had been riddled and all the inconceivable blaze of suns in the making was poured through the manholes.

"You needn't count," said Arnott. I had had no thought of such a thing. "There are two hundred and fifty keels up there, five miles apart. Full power, please, for another twelve seconds."

The firmament, as far as eye could reach, stood on pillars of white fire. One fell on the glowing square at Chicago, and turned it black.

"Oh! Oh! Oh! Can men be allowed to do such things?" Dragomiroff cried, and fell across our knees.

"Glass of water, please," said Takahira to a helmeted shape that leaped forward. "He is a little faint."

The lights switched off, and the darkness stunned like an avalanche. We could hear Dragomiroff's teeth on the glass edge.

Pirolo was comforting him.

"All right, allra-ight," he repeated. "Come and lie down. Come below and take off your mask. I give you my word, old friend, it is all right. They are my siege-lights. Little Victor Pirolo's leetle lights. You know *me!* I do not hurt people."

"Pardon!" Dragomiroff moaned. "I have never seen Death. I have never seen the Board take action. Shall we go down and burn them alive, or is that already done?"

"Oh, hush," said Pirolo, and I think he rocked him in his arms.

"Do we repeat, sir?" Arnott asked De Forest.

"Give 'em a minute's break," De Forest replied. "They may need it."

We waited a minute, and then MacDonough's Song, broken but defiant, rose from undefeated Chicago.

"They seem fond of that tune," said De Forest. "I should let 'em have it, Arnott."

"Very good, sir," said Arnott, and felt his way to the Communicator keys.

No lights broke forth, but the hollow of the skies made herself the mouth for one note that touched the raw fibre of the brain. Men hear such sounds in delirium, advancing like tides from horizons beyond the ruled foreshores of space.

"That's our pitch-pipe," said Arnott. "We may be a bit ragged. I've never conducted two hundred and fifty performers before." He pulled out the couplers, and struck a full chord on the Service Communicators.

The beams of light leaped down again, and danced, solemnly and awfully, a stilt-dance, sweeping thirty or forty miles left and right at each stiff-legged kick, while the darkness delivered itself – there is no scale to measure against that utterance – of the tune to which they kept time. Certain notes – one learnt to expect them with terror – cut through one's marrow, but, after three minutes, thought and emotion passed in indescribable agony.

We saw, we heard, but I think we were in some sort swooning. The two hundred and fifty beams shifted, re-formed, straddled and split, narrowed, widened, rippled in ribbons, broke into a thousand white-hot parallel lines, melted and revolved in interwoven rings like old-fashioned engine-turning, flung up to the zenith, made as if to descend and renew the torment, halted at the last instant, twizzled insanely round the horizon, and vanished, to bring back for the hundredth time darkness more shattering than their instantly renewed light over all Illinois. Then the tune and lights ceased together, and we heard one single devastating wail that shook all the horizon as a rubbed wet finger shakes the rim of a bowl.

"Ah, that is my new siren," said Pirolo. "You can break an iceberg in half, if you find the proper pitch. They will whistle by squadrons now. It is the wind through pierced shutters in the bows."

I had collapsed beside Dragomiroff, broken and snivelling feebly, because I had been delivered before my time to all the terrors of Judgement Day, and the Archangels of the Resurrection were hailing me naked across the Universe to the sound of the music of the spheres.

Then I saw De Forest smacking Arnott's helmet with his open hand. The wailing died down in a long shriek as a black shadow swooped past us, and returned to her place above the lower clouds.

"I hate to interrupt a specialist when he's enjoying himself," said De

Forest. "But, as a matter of fact, all Illinois has been asking us to stop for these last fifteen seconds."

"What a pity." Arnott slipped off his mask. "I wanted you to hear us really hum. Our lower C can lift street-paving."

"It is Hell – Hell!" cried Dragomiroff, and sobbed aloud.

Arnott looked away as he answered:

"It's a few thousand volts ahead of the old shoot-'em-and-sink-'em game, but I should scarcely call it *that*. What shall I tell the Fleet, sir?"

"Tell 'em we're very pleased and impressed. I don't think they need wait on any longer. There isn't a spark left down there." De Forest pointed. "They'll be deaf and blind."

"Oh, I think not, sir. The demonstration lasted less than ten minutes."

"Marvellous!" Takahira sighed. "I should have said it was half a night. Now, shall we go down and pick up the pieces?"

"But first a small drink," said Pirolo. "The Board must not arrive weeping at its own works."

"I am an old fool – an old fool!" Dragomiroff began piteously. "I did not know what would happen. It is all new to me. We reason with them in Little Russia."

Chicago North landing-tower was unlighted, and Arnott worked his ship into the clips by her own lights. As soon as these broke out we heard groanings of horror and appeal from many people below.

"All right," shouted Arnott into the darkness. "We aren't beginning again!" We descended by the stairs, to find ourselves knee-deep in a grovelling crowd, some crying that they were blind, others beseeching us not to make anymore noises, but the greater part writhing face downward, their hands or their caps before their eyes.

It was Pirolo who came to our rescue. He climbed the side of a surfacing-machine, and there, gesticulating as though they could see, made oration to those afflicted people of Illinois.

"You stchewpids!" he began. "There is nothing to fuss for. Of course, your eyes will smart and be red tomorrow. You will look as if you and your wives had drunk too much, but in a little while you will see again as well as before. I tell you this, and I – *I* am Pirolo. Victor Pirolo!"

The crowd with one accord shuddered, for many legends attach to Victor Pirolo of Foggia, deep in the secrets of God.

"Pirolo?" An unsteady voice lifted itself. "Then tell us was there anything except light in those lights of yours just now?"

The question was repeated from every corner of the darkness.

Pirolo laughed.

"No!" he thundered. (Why have small men such large voices?) "I give you my word and the Board's word that there was nothing except light – just light! You stchewpids! Your birth rate is too low already as it is. Some day I must invent something to send it up, but send it down – never!"

"Is that true? – We thought – somebody said – "

One could feel the tension relax all round.

"You too big fools," Pirolo cried. "You could have sent us a call and we would have told you.

"Send you a call!" a deep voice shouted. "I wish you had been at our end of the wire."

"I'm glad I wasn't," said De Forest. "It was bad enough from behind the lamps. Never mind! It's over now. Is there any one here I can talk business with? I'm De Forest – for the Board."

"You might begin with me, for one – I'm Mayor," the bass voice replied.

A big man rose unsteadily from the street, and staggered towards us where we sat on the broad turf-edging, in front of the garden fences.

"I ought to be the first on my feet. Am I?" said he.

"Yes," said De Forest, and steadied him as he dropped down beside us.

"Hello, Andy. Is that you?" a voice called.

"Excuse me," said the Mayor; "that sounds like my Chief of Police, Bluthner!"

"Bluthner it is; and here's Mulligan and Keefe – on their feet."

"Bring 'em up please, Blut. We're supposed to be the Four in charge of this hamlet. What we says, goes. And, De Forest, what do you say?"

"Nothing – yet," De Forest answered, as we made room for the panting, reeling men. "You've cut out of system. Well?"

"Tell the steward to send down drinks, please," Arnott whispered to an orderly at his side.

"Good!" said the Mayor, smacking his dry lips. "Now I suppose we can take it, De Forest, that henceforward the Board will administer us direct?"

"Not if the Board can avoid it," De Forest laughed. "The ABC is responsible for the planetary traffic only."

"*And all that that implies.*" The big Four who ran Chicago chanted their Magna Charta like children at school.

"Well, get on," said De Forest wearily. "What is your silly trouble anyway?"

"Too much dam' Democracy," said the Mayor, laying his hand on De Forest's knee.

"So? I thought Illinois had had her dose of that."

"She has. That's why. Blut, what did you do with our prisoners last night?"

"Locked 'em in the water-tower to prevent the women killing 'em," the Chief of Police replied. "I'm too blind to move just yet, but – "

"Arnott, send some of your people, please, and fetch 'em along," said De Forest.

"They're triple-circuited," the Mayor called. "You'll have to blow out three fuses." He turned to De Forest, his large outline just visible in the paling darkness. "I hate to throw any more work on the Board. I'm an administrator myself, but we've had a little fuss with our Serviles. What? In a big city there's bound to be a few men and women who can't live without listening to themselves, and who prefer drinking out of pipes they don't own both ends of. They inhabit flats and hotels all the year round. They say it saves 'em trouble. Anyway, it gives em more time to make trouble for their neighbours. We call 'em Serviles locally. And they are apt to be tuberculous."

"Just so!" said the man called Mulligan. "Transportation is Civilization. Democracy is Disease. I've proved it by the blood-test, every time."

"Mulligan's our Health Officer, and a one-idea man," said the Mayor, laughing. "But it's true that most Serviles haven't much control. They *will* talk; and when people take to talking as a business, anything may arrive – mayn't it, De Forest?"

"Anything – except the facts of the case," said De Forest, laughing.

"I'll give you those in a minute," said the Mayor. "Our Serviles got to talking – first in their houses and then on the streets, telling men and women how to manage their own affairs. (You can't teach a Servile not to finger his neighbour's soul.) That's invasion of privacy, of course, but in Chicago we'll suffer anything sooner than make crowds. Nobody took much notice, and so I let 'em alone. My fault! I was warned there would be trouble, but there hasn't been a crowd or murder in Illinois for nineteen years."

"Twenty-two," said his Chief of Police.

"Likely. Anyway, we'd forgot such things. So, from talking in the houses and on the streets, our Serviles go to calling a meeting at the Old Market yonder." He nodded across the square where the wrecked buildings heaved up grey in the dawn-glimmer behind the square-cased statue of The Negro in Flames. "There's nothing to prevent any one calling meetings except that it's against human nature to stand in a crowd, besides being bad for the health. I ought to have known by the way our men and women attended that first meeting that trouble was brewing. There were as many as a thousand in the market-place, touching each other. Touching! Then the Serviles turned in all tongue-switches and talked, and we –

"What did they talk about?" said Takahira.

"First, how badly things were managed in the city. That pleased us Four – we were on the platform – because we hoped to catch one or two good men for City work. You know how rare executive capacity is. Even if we didn't it's – it's refreshing to find any one interested enough in our job to damn our eyes. You don't know what it means to work, year in, year out, without a spark of difference with a living soul."

"Oh, don't we!" said De Forest. "There are times on the Board when we'd give our positions if any one would kick us out and take hold of things themselves."

"But they won't," said the Mayor ruefully. "I assure you, sir, we Four have done things in Chicago, in the hope of rousing people, that would have discredited Nero. But what do they say? 'Very good, Andy. Have it your own way. Anything's better than a crowd. I'll go back to my land.' You *can't* do anything with folk who can go where they please, and don't want anything on God's earth except their own way. There isn't a kick or a kicker left on the Planet."

"Then I suppose that little shed yonder fell down by itself?" said De Forest. We could see the bare and still smoking ruins, and hear the slag-pools crackle as they hardened and set.

"Oh, that's only amusement. Tell you later. As I was saying, our Serviles held the meeting, and pretty soon we had to ground-circuit the platform to save 'em from being killed. And that didn't make our people any more pacific."

"How d'you mean?" I ventured to ask.

"If you've ever been ground-circuited," said the Mayor, "you'll know it don't improve any man's temper to be held up straining against nothing. No, sir! Eight or nine hundred folk kept pawing and buzzing like flies in treacle for two hours, while a pack of perfectly safe Serviles invades their mental and spiritual privacy, may be amusing to watch, but they are not pleasant to handle afterwards."

Pirolo chuckled.

"Our folk own themselves. They were of opinion things were going too far and too fiery. I warned the Serviles; but they're born house-dwellers. Unless a fact hits 'em on the head, they cannot see it. Would you believe me, they went on to talk of what they called 'popular government'? They did! They wanted us to go back to the old Voodoo-business of voting with papers and wooden boxes, and word-drunk people and printed formulas, and news-sheets! They said they practised it among themselves about what they'd have to eat in their flats and hotels. Yes, sir! They stood up behind Bluthner's doubled ground-circuits, and they said that, in this present year of grace, to self-owning men and women, on that very spot! Then they finished" – he lowered his voice cautiously – "by talking about 'The People.' And then Bluthner he had to sit up all night in charge of the circuits because he couldn't trust his men to keep 'em shut."

"It was trying 'em too high," the Chief of Police broke in. "But we couldn't hold the crowd ground-circuited for ever. I gathered in all the Serviles on charge of crowd-making, and put 'em in the water-tower, and then I let things cut loose. I had to! The District lit like a sparked gas-tank!"

"The news was out over seven degrees of country," the Mayor continued; "and when once it's a question of invasion of privacy, goodbye to right and reason in Illinois! They began turning out traffic-lights and locking up landing-towers on Thursday night. Friday, they stopped all traffic and asked for the Board to take over. Then they wanted to clean Chicago off the side of the Lake and rebuild elsewhere – just for a souvenir of 'The People' that the Serviles talked about. I suggested that they should slag the Old Market where the meeting was held, while I turned in a call to you all on the Board. That kept 'em quiet till you came along. And – and now *you* can take hold of the situation."

"Any chance of their quieting down?" De Forest asked.

"You can try," said the Mayor.

De Forest raised his voice in the face of the reviving crowd that had edged in towards us. Day was come.

"Don't you think this business can be arranged?" he began. But there was a roar of angry voices:

"We've finished with Crowds! We aren't going back to the Old Days! Take us over! Take the Serviles away! Administer direct or we'll kill 'em! Down with The People!"

An attempt was made to begin MacDonough's Song. It got no further than the first line, for the *Victor Pirolo* sent down a warning drone on one stopped horn. A wrecked side-wall of the Old Market tottered and fell inwards on the slag-pools. None spoke or moved till the last of the dust had settled down again, turning the steel case of Salati's Statue ashy grey.

"You see you'll just *have* to take us over," the Mayor whispered.

De Forest shrugged his shoulders.

"You talk as if executive capacity could be snatched out of the air like so much horse-power. Can't you manage yourselves on any terms?" he said.

"We can, if you say so. It will only cost those few lives to begin with."

The Mayor pointed across the square, where Arnott's men guided a stumbling group of ten or twelve men and women to the lake front and halted them under the Statue.

"Now I think," said Takahira under his breath, "there will be trouble."

The mass in front of us growled like beasts.

At that moment the sun rose clear, and revealed the blinking assembly to itself. As soon as it realized that it was a crowd we saw the shiver of horror and mutual repulsion shoot across it precisely as the steely flaws shot across the lake outside. Nothing was said, and, being half blind, of course it moved slowly. Yet in less than fifteen minutes most of that vast multitude – three thousand at the lowest count – melted away like frost on south eaves. The remnant stretched themselves on the grass, where a crowd feels and looks less like a crowd.

"These mean business," the Mayor whispered to Takahira. "There are a goodish few women there who've borne children. I don't like it."

The morning draught off the lake stirred the trees round us with promise of a hot day; the sun reflected itself dazzlingly on the canister-shaped covering of Salati's Statue; cocks crew in the gardens, and we could hear gatelatches clicking in the distance as people stumblingly resought their homes.

"I'm afraid there won't be any morning deliveries," said De Forest. "We rather upset things in the country last night."

"That makes no odds," the Mayor returned. "We're all provisioned for six months. We take no chances."

Nor, when you come to think of it, does any one else. It must be three-quarters of a generation since any house or city faced a food shortage. Yet is there house or city on the Planet today that has not half a year's provisions laid in? We are like the shipwrecked seamen in the old books, who, having once nearly starved to death, ever afterwards hide away bits of food and biscuit. Truly we trust no Crowds, nor system based on Crowds!

De Forest waited till the last footstep had died away. Meantime the prisoners at the base of the Statue shuffled, posed, and fidgeted, with the shamelessness of quite little children. None of them were more than six feet high, and many of them were as grey-haired as the ravaged, harassed heads of old pictures. They huddled together in actual touch, while the crowd, spaced at large intervals, looked at them with congested eyes.

Suddenly a man among them began to talk. The Mayor had not in the least exaggerated. It appeared that our Planet lay sunk in slavery beneath the heel of the Aerial Board of Control. The orator urged us to arise in our might, burst our prison doors and break our fetters (all his metaphors, by the way, were of the most medieval). Next he demanded that every matter of daily life, including most of the physical functions, should be submitted for decision at any time of the week, month, or year to, I gathered, anybody who happened to be passing by or residing within a certain radius, and that everybody should forthwith abandon his concerns to settle the matter, first by crowd-making, next by talking to the crowds made, and lastly by describing crosses on pieces of paper, which rubbish should later be counted with certain mystic ceremonies and oaths. Out of this amazing play, he assured us, would automatically arise a higher, nobler, and kinder world, based – he demonstrated this with the awful lucidity of the insane – based on the sanctity of the Crowd and the villainy of the single person. In conclusion, he called loudly upon God to testify to his personal merits and integrity. When the flow ceased, I turned bewildered to Takahira, who was nodding solemnly.

"Quite correct," said he. "It is all in the old books. He has left nothing out, not even the war-talk."

"But I don't see how this stuff can upset a child, much less a district," I replied.

"Ah, you are too young," said Dragomiroff. "For another thing, you are not a mamma. Please look at the mammas."

Ten or fifteen women who remained had separated themselves from the silent men, and were drawing in towards the prisoners. It reminded one of the stealthy encircling, before the rush in at the quarry, of wolves round musk-oxen in the North. The prisoners saw, and drew together more closely. The Mayor covered his face with his hands for an instant. De Forest, bareheaded, stepped forward between the prisoners and the slowly, stiffly moving line.

"That's all very interesting," he said to the dry-lipped orator. "But the point seems to be that you've been making crowds and invading privacy."

A woman stepped forward, and would have spoken, but there was a quick assenting murmur from the men, who realized that De Forest was trying to pull the situation down to ground-line.

"Yes! Yes!" they cried. "We cut out because they made crowds and invaded privacy! Stick to that! Keep on that switch! Lift the Serviles out of this! The Board's in charge! Hsh!"

"Yes, the Board's in charge," said De Forest. "I'll take formal evidence of crowd-making if you like, but the Members of the Board can testify to it. Will that do?"

The women had closed in another pace, with hands that clenched and unclenched at their sides.

"Good! Good enough!" the men cried. "We're content. Only take them away quickly."

"Come along up!" said De Forest to the captives. "Breakfast is quite ready."

It appeared, however, that they did not wish to go. They intended to remain in Chicago and make crowds. They pointed out that De Forest's proposal was gross invasion of privacy.

"My dear fellow," said Pirolo to the most voluble of the leaders, "you hurry, or your crowd that can't be wrong will kill you!"

"But that would be murder," answered the believer in crowds; and there was a roar of laughter from all sides that seemed to show the crisis had broken.

A woman stepped forward from the line of women, laughing, I protest, as merrily as any of the company. One hand, of course, shaded her eyes, the other was at her throat.

"Oh, they needn't be afraid of being killed!" she called.

"Not in the least," said De Forest. "But don't you think that, now the Board's in charge, you might go home while we get these people away?"

"I shall be home long before that. It – it has been rather a trying day."

She stood up to her full height, dwarfing even De Forest's six-foot-eight, and smiled, with eyes closed against the fierce light.

"Yes, rather," said De Forest. "I'm afraid you feel the glare a little. We'll have the ship down."

He motioned to the *Pirolo* to drop between us and the sun, and at the same time to loop-circuit the prisoners, who were a trifle unsteady. We saw them stiffen to the current where they stood. The woman's voice went on, sweet and deep and unshaken:

"I don't suppose you men realize how much this – this sort of thing

means to a woman. I've borne three. We women don't want our children given to Crowds. It must be an inherited instinct. Crowds make
trouble. They bring back the Old Days. Hate, fear, blackmail,
publicity, 'The People' – That! *That! That!"* She pointed to the Statue,
and the crowd growled once more.

"Yes, if they are allowed to go on," said De Forest. "But this little
affair – "

"It means so much to us women that this – this little affair should
never happen again. Of course, never's a big word, but one feels so
strongly that it is important to stop crowds at the very beginning.
Those creatures" – she pointed with her left hand at the prisoners
swaying like seaweed in a tideway as the circuit pulled them – "those
people have friends and wives and children in the city and elsewhere.
One doesn't want anything done to *them*, you know. It's terrible to
force a human being out of fifty or sixty years of good life. I'm only
forty myself. *I* know. But, at the same time, one feels that an example
should be made, because no price is too heavy to pay if – if these
people and *all that they imply* can be put an end to. Do you quite understand, or would you be kind enough to tell your men to take the casing
off the Statue? It's worth looking at."

"I understand perfectly. But I don't think anybody here wants to see
the Statue on an empty stomach. Excuse me one moment." De Forest
called up to the ship, "A flying loop ready on the port side, if you
please." Then to the woman he said with some crispness, "You might
leave us a little discretion in the matter."

"Oh, of course. Thank you for being so patient. I know my arguments are silly, but – " She half turned away and went on in a changed
voice, "Perhaps this will help you to decide."

She threw out her right arm with a knife in it. Before the blade could
be returned to her throat or her bosom it was twitched from her grip,
sparked as it flew out of the shadow of the ship above, and fell flashing
in the sunshine at the foot of the Statue fifty yards away. The outflung
arm was arrested, rigid as a bar for an instant, till the releasing circuit
permitted her to bring it slowly to her side. The other women shrank
back silent among the men.

Pirolo rubbed his hands, and Takahira nodded.

"That was clever of you, De Forest," said he.

"What a glorious pose!" Dragomiroff murmured, for the frightened
woman was on the edge of tears.

"Why did you stop me? I would have done it!" she cried.

"I have no doubt you would," said De Forest. "But we can't waste a life like yours on these people. I hope the arrest didn't sprain your wrist; it's so hard to regulate a flying loop. But I think you are quite right about those persons' women and children. We'll take them all away with us if you promise not to do anything stupid to yourself."

"I promise – I promise." She controlled herself with an effort. "But it is so important to us women. We know what it means; and I thought if you saw I was in earnest – "

"I saw you were, and you've gained your point. I shall take all your Serviles away with me at once. The Mayor will make lists of their friends and families in the city and the district, and he'll ship them after us this afternoon."

"Sure," said the Mayor, rising to his feet. "Keefe, if you can see, hadn't you better finish levelling off the Old Market? It don't look sightly the way it is now, and we shan't use it for crowds anymore."

"I think you had better wipe out that Statue as well, Mr Mayor," said De Forest. "I don't question its merits as a work of art, but I believe it's a shade morbid."

"Certainly, sir. Oh, Keefe! Slag the Negro before you go on to fuse the Market. I'll get to the Communicators and tell the District that the Board is in charge. Are you making any special appointments, sir?"

"None. We haven't men to waste on these backwoods. Carry on as before, but under the Board. Arnott, run your Serviles aboard, please. Ground ship and pass them through the bilge-doors. We'll wait till we've finished with this work of art."

The prisoners trailed past him, talking fluently, but unable to gesticulate in the drag of the current. Then the surfacers rolled up, two on each side of the Statue. With one accord the spectators looked elsewhere, but there was no need. Keefe turned on full power, and the thing simply melted within its case. All I saw was a surge of white-hot metal pouring over the plinth, a glimpse of Salati's inscription, "To the Eternal Memory of the Justice of the People," ere the stone base itself cracked and powdered into finest lime. The crowd cheered.

"Thank you," said De Forest; "but we want our breakfasts, and I expect you do too. Goodbye, Mr Mayor! Delighted to see you at any time, but I hope I shan't have to, officially, for the next thirty years. Goodbye, madam. Yes. We're all given to nerves nowadays. I suffer from them myself. Goodbye, gentlemen all! You're under the tyrannous heel of the Board from this moment, but if ever you feel like breaking your fetters you've only to let us know. This is no treat to us. Good luck!"

We embarked amid shouts, and did not check our lift till they had dwindled into whispers. Then De Forest flung himself on the chart-room divan and mopped his forehead.

"I don't mind men," he panted, "but women are the devil!"

"Still the devil," said Pirolo cheerfully. "That one would have suicided."

"I know it. That was why I signalled for the flying loop to be clapped on her. I owe you an apology for that, Arnott. I hadn't time to catch your eye, and you were busy with our caitiffs. By the way, who actually answered my signal? It was a smart piece of work."

"Ilroy," said Arnott; "but he overloaded the wave. It may be pretty gallery-work to knock a knife out of a lady's hand, but didn't you notice how she rubbed 'em? He scorched her fingers. Slovenly, I call it."

"Far be it from me to interfere with Fleet discipline, but don't be too hard on the boy. If that woman had killed herself they would have killed every Servile and everything related to a Servile throughout the district by nightfall."

"That was what she was playing for," Takahira said. "And with our Fleet gone we could have done nothing to hold them."

"I may be ass enough to walk into a ground-circuit," said Arnott, "but I don't dismiss my Fleet till I'm reasonably sure that trouble is over. They're in position still, and I intend to keep 'em there till the Serviles are shipped out of the district. That last little crowd meant murder, my friends."

"Nerves! All nerves!" said Pirolo. "You cannot argue with agora-phobia."

"And it is not as if they had seen much dead – or is it?" said Takahira.

"In all my ninety years I have never seen death." Dragomiroff spoke as one who would excuse himself. "Perhaps that was why – last night – "

Then it came out as we sat over breakfast, that, with the exception of Arnott and Pirolo, none of us had ever seen a corpse, or knew in what manner the spirit passes.

"We're a nice lot to flap about governing the Planet," De Forest laughed. "I confess, now it's all over, that my main fear was I mightn't be able to pull it off without losing a life."

"I thought of that too," said Arnott; "but there's no death reported, and I've enquired everywhere. What are we supposed to do with our passengers? I've fed 'em."

"We're between two switches," De Forest drawled. "If we drop them in any place that isn't under the Board, the natives will make their presence an excuse for cutting out, same as Illinois did, and forcing the Board to take over. If we drop them in any place under the Board's control they'll be killed as soon as our backs are turned."

"If you say so," said Pirolo thoughtfully, "I can guarantee that they will become extinct in process of time, quite happily. What is their birth-rate now?"

"Go down and ask 'em," said De Forest.

"I think they might become nervous and tear me to bits," the philosopher of Foggia replied.

"Not really? Well?"

"Open the bilge-doors," said Takahira with a downward jerk of the thumb.

"Scarcely – after all the trouble we've taken to save 'em," said De Forest.

"Try London," Arnott suggested. "You could turn Satan himself loose there, and they'd only ask him to dinner."

"Good man! You've given me an idea. Vincent! Oh, Vincent!" He threw the General Communicator open so that we could all hear, and in a few minutes the chartroom filled with the rich, fruity voice of Leopold Vincent, who has purveyed all London her choicest amusements for the last thirty years. We answered with expectant grins, as though we were actually in the stalls of, say, the Combination on a first night.

"We've picked up something in your line," De Forest began.

"That's good, dear man. If it's old enough. There's nothing to beat the old things for business purposes. Have you seen *London, Chatham, and Dover* at Earl's Court? No? I thought I missed you there. Im-mense! I've had the real steam locomotive engines built from the old designs and the iron rails cast specially by hand. Cloth cushions in the carriages, too! Im-mense! And paper railway tickets. And Polly Milton."

"Polly Milton back again!" said Arnott rapturously. "Book me two stalls for tomorrow night. What's she singing now, bless her?"

"The old songs. Nothing comes up to the old touch. Listen to this, dear men." Vincent carolled with flourishes:

> *Oh, cruel lamps of London,*
> *If tears your light could drown,*
> *Your victims' eyes would weep them,*
> *Oh, lights of London Town!*

"Then they weep."

"You see?" Pirolo waved his hands at us. "The old world always weeped when it saw crowds together. It did not know why, but it weeped. We know why, but we do not weep, except when we pay to be made to by fat, wicked old Vincent."

"Old, yourself!" Vincent laughed. "I'm a public benefactor, I keep the world soft and united."

"And I'm De Forest of the Board," said De Forest acidly, "trying to get a little business done. As I was saying, I've picked up a few people in Chicago."

"I cut out. Chicago is – "

"Do listen! They're perfectly unique."

"Do they build houses of baked mudblocks while you wait – eh? That's an old contact."

"They're an untouched primitive community, with all the old ideas."

"Sewing-machines and maypole-dances? Cooking on coal-gas stoves, lighting pipes with matches, and driving horses? Gerolstein tried that last year. An absolute blow-out!"

De Forest plugged him wrathfully, and poured out the story of our doings for the last twenty-four hours on the top-note.

"And they do it *all* in public," he concluded. "You can't stop 'em. The more public, the better they are pleased. They'll talk for hours – like you! Now you can come in again!"

"Do you really mean they know how to vote?" said Vincent. "Can they act it?"

"Act? It's their life to 'em! And you never saw such faces! Scarred like volcanoes. Envy, hatred, and malice in plain sight. Wonderfully flexible voices. They weep, too."

"Aloud? In public?"

"I guarantee. Not a spark of shame or reticence in the entire installation. It's the chance of your career."

"D'you say you've brought their voting props along – those papers and ballot-box things?"

"No, confound you! I'm not a luggage-lifter. Apply direct to the Mayor of Chicago. He'll forward you everything. Well?"

"Wait a minute. Did Chicago want to kill 'em? That 'ud look well on the Communicators."

"Yes! They were only rescued with difficulty from a howling mob – if you know what that is."

"But I don't," answered the Great Vincent simply.

"Well then, they'll tell you themselves. They can make speeches hours long."

"How many are there?"

"By the time we ship 'em all over they'll be perhaps a hundred, counting children. An old world in miniature. Can't you see it?"

"M-yes; but I've got to pay for it if it's a blow-out, dear man."

"They can sing the old war songs in the streets. They can get word-drunk, and make crowds, and invade privacy in the genuine old-fashioned way; and they'll do the voting trick as often as you ask 'em a question."

"Too good!" said Vincent.

"You unbelieving Jew! I've got a dozen head aboard here. I'll put you through direct. Sample 'em yourself."

He lifted the switch and we listened. Our passengers on the lower deck at once, but not less than five at a time, explained themselves to Vincent. They had been taken from the bosom of their families, stripped of their possessions, given food without finger-bowls, and cast into captivity in a noisome dungeon.

"But look here," said Arnott aghast; "they're saying what isn't true. My lower deck isn't noisome, and I saw to the finger-bowls myself."

"My people talk like that sometimes in Little Russia," said Dragomiroff. "We reason with them. We never kill. No!"

"But it's not true," Arnott insisted. "What can you do with people who don't tell facts? They're mad!"

"Hsh!" said Pirolo, his hand to his ear. "It is such a little time since all the Planet told lies."

We heard Vincent silkily sympathetic. Would they, he asked, repeat their assertions in public – before a vast public? only let Vincent give them a chance, and the Planet, they vowed, should ring with their wrongs. Their aim in life – two women and a man explained it together – was to reform the world. Oddly enough, this also had been Vincent's life-dream. He offered them an arena in which to explain, and by their living example to raise the Planet to loftier levels. He was eloquent on the moral uplift of a simple, old-world life presented in its entirety to a deboshed civilization.

Could they – would they – for three months certain, devote them-selves under his auspices, as missionaries, to the elevation of mankind at a place called Earl's Court, which he said, with some truth, was one of the intellectual centres of the Planet? They thanked him, and demanded (we could hear his chuckle of delight) time to discuss and to vote on the matter. The vote, solemnly managed by counting heads –

one head, one vote – was favourable. His offer, therefore, was accepted, and they moved a vote of thanks to him in two speeches – one by what they called the "proposer" and the other by the "seconder."

Vincent threw over to us, his voice shaking with gratitude:

"I've got 'em! Did you hear those speeches? That's Nature, dear men. Art can't teach *that*. And they voted as easily as lying. I've never had a troupe of natural liars before. Bless you, dear men! Remember, you're on my free lists for ever, anywhere – all of you. Oh, Gerolstein will be sick-sick!"

"Then you think they'll do?" said De Forest.

"Do? The Little Village'll go crazy! I'll knock up a series of old-world plays for em. Their voices will make you laugh and cry. My God, dear men, where do you suppose they picked up all their misery from, on this sweet earth? I'll have a pageant of the world's beginnings, and Mosenthal shall do the music. I'll – "

"Go and knock up a village for 'em by tonight. We'll meet you at No. 15 West Landing Tower," said De Forest. "Remember the rest will be coming along tomorrow."

"Let 'em all come!" said Vincent. "You don't know how hard it is nowadays even for me, to find something that really gets under the public's damned iridium-plated hide. But I've got it at last. Goodbye!"

"Well," said De Forest when we had finished laughing, "if any one understood corruption in London I might have played off Vincent against Gerolstein, and sold my captives at enormous prices. As it is, I shall have to be their legal adviser tonight when the contracts are signed. And they won't exactly press any commission on me, either."

"Meantime," said Takahira, "we cannot, of course, confine members of Leopold Vincent's last-engaged company. Chairs for the ladies, please, Arnott."

"Then I go to bed," said De Forest. "I can't face any more women!" And he vanished.

When our passengers were released and given another meal (finger-bowls came first this time) they told us what they thought of us and the Board; and, like Vincent, we all marvelled how they had contrived to extract and secrete so much bitter poison and unrest out of the good life God gives us. They raged, they stormed, they palpitated, flushed and exhausted their poor, torn nerves, panted themselves into silence, and renewed the senseless, shameless attacks.

"But can't you understand," said Pirolo pathetically to a shrieking woman, "that if we'd left you in Chicago you'd have been killed?"

"No, we shouldn't. You were bound to save us from being murdered."

"Then we should have had to kill a lot of other people."

"That doesn't matter. We were preaching the Truth. You can't stop us. We shall go on preaching in London; and *then* you'll see!"

"You can see now," said Pirolo, and opened a lower shutter.

We were closing on the Little Village, with her three million people spread out at ease inside her ring of girdling Main-Traffic lights – those eight fixed beams at Chatham, Tonbridge, Redhill, Dorking, Woking, St Albans, Chipping Ongar, and Southend.

Leopold Vincent's new company looked, with small pale faces, at the silence, the size, and the separated houses.

Then some began to weep aloud, shamelessly – always without shame.

Ginungagap

MICHAEL SWANWICK

Michael Swanwick (1950–) distinguished himself with a group of notable short stories in the early and mid-'80s. He has written both science fiction and fantasy, and, after reaching the height of his powers as a SF novelist in *Stations of the Tide* (1991), has turned increasingly toward fantasy in his two most recent novels, *The Iron Dragon's Daughter* (1993) and *Jack Faust* (1997).

"My father was an engineer . . . but I was lured away from engineering by science, and then lured away from science by literature," he says. *Science Fiction Writers* calls him "an author who produces thoughtful, speculative work in a complex, literary style without a strong, action-oriented plot." His early short fiction is collected in *Gravity's Angels* (1991).

Swanwick is also the author of two influential critical essays, one on science fiction, "User's Guide to the Postmoderns" (1985), and one on fantasy, "In The Tradition . . ." (1994). He remains one of the most significant genre writers of the '90s. "Ginungagap" was his first published story. It appeared in a special SF issue of the distinguished literary magazine *Triquarterly*. The title refers to the primordial chaos out of which the universe was born in Norse mythology.

Abigail checked out of Mother of Mercy and rode the translator web to Toledo Cylinder in Juno Industrial Park. Stars bloomed, dwindled, disappeared five times. It was a long trek, halfway around the sun.

Toledo was one of the older commercial cylinders, now given over almost entirely to bureaucrats, paper pushers, and free-lance-professionals. It was not Abigail's favorite place to visit, but she needed work and 3M had already bought out of her contract.

The job broker had dyed his chest hairs blond and his leg hairs red. They clashed wildly with his green *cache-sexe* and turquoise jewelry. His fingers played on a keyout, bringing up an endless flow of career trivia. "Cute trick you played," he said.

Abigail flexed her new arm negligently. It was a good job, but pinker than the rest of her. And weak, of course, but exercise would correct that. "Thanks," she said. She laid the arm underneath one breast and compared the colors. It matched the nipple perfectly. Definitely too pink. "Work outlook any good?"

"Naw," the broker said. A hummingbird flew past his ear, a nearly undetectable parting of the air. "I see here that you applied for the Proxima colony."

"They were full up," Abigail said. "No openings for a gravity bum, hey?"

"I didn't say that," the broker grumbled. "I'll find – Hello! What's this?" Abigail craned her neck, couldn't get a clear look at the screen. "There's a tag on your employment record."

"What's that mean?"

"Let me read." A honeysuckle flower fell on Abigail's hair and she brushed it off impatiently. The broker had an open-air office, framed by hedges and roofed over with a trellis. Sometimes Abigail found the older Belt cylinders a little too lavish for her taste.

"Mmp." The broker looked up. "Bell-Sandia wants to hire you. Indefinite term one-shot contract." He swung the keyout around so she could see. "Very nice terms, but that's normal for a high risk contract."

"High risk? From B-S, the Friendly Communications People? What kind of risk?"

The broker scrolled up new material. "There." He tapped the screen with a finger. "The language is involved, but what it boils down to is they're looking for a test passenger for a device they've got that uses black holes for interstellar travel."

"Couldn't work," Abigail said. "The tidal forces – "

"Spare me. Presumably they've found a way around that problem. The question is, are you interested or not?"

Abigail stared up through the trellis at a stream meandering across the curved land overhead. Children were wading in it. She counted to a hundred very slowly, trying to look as if she needed to think it over.

Abigail strapped herself into the translation harness and nodded to the technician outside the chamber. The tech touched her console and a light stasis field immobilized Abigail and the air about her while the chamber wall irised open. In a fluid bit of technological sleight of hand, the translator rechanneled her inertia and gifted her with a velocity almost, but not quite, that of the speed of light.

Stars bloomed about her and the sun dwindled. She breathed in deeply and – was in the receiver device. Relativity had cheated her of all but a fraction of the transit time. She shrugged out of harness and frog-kicked her way to the lip station's tug dock.

The tug pilot grinned at her as she entered, then turned his attention to his controls. He was young and wore streaks of brown makeup across his chest and thighs – only slightly darker than his skin. His mesh vest was almost in bad taste, but he wore it well and looked roguish rather than overdressed. Abigail found herself wishing she had more than a *cache-sexe* and nail polish on – some jewelry or makeup, perhaps. She felt drab in comparison.

The star-field wraparound held two inserts routed in by synchronous cameras. Alphanumerics flickered beneath them. One showed her immediate destination, the Bell-Sandia base *Arthur C. Clarke*. It consisted of five wheels, each set inside the other and rotating at slightly differing speeds. The base was done up in red-and-orange supergraphics. Considering its distance from the Belt factories, it was respectably sized.

Abigail latched herself into the passenger seat as the engines cut in. The second insert –

Ginungagap, the only known black hole in the sun's gravity field, was discovered in 2023, a small voice murmured. *Its presence explained the long-puzzling variations in the orbits of the outer planets. The* Arthur C. Clarke *was . . .*

"Is this necessary?" Abigail asked.

"Absolutely," the pilot said. "We abandoned the tourist program a year or so ago, but somehow the rules never caught up. They're very strict about the regs here." He winked at Abigail's dismayed expression. "Hold tight a minute while – " His voice faded as he tinkered with the controls.

. . . established forty years later and communications with the Proxima colony began shortly thereafter. Ginungagap . . .

The voice cut off. She grinned thanks. "Abigail Vanderhoek."

"Cheyney," the pilot said. "You're the gravity bum, right?"

"Yeah."

"I used to be a vacuum bum myself. But I got tired of it, and grabbed the first semipermanent contract that came along."

"I kind of went the other way."

"Probably what I should have done," Cheyney said amiably. "Still, it's a rough road. I picked up three scars along the way." He pointed them out: a thick slash across his abdomen, a red splotch beside one nipple, and a white crescent half obscured by his scalp. "I could've had them cleaned up, but the way I figure, life is just a process of picking up scars and experience. So I kept 'em."

If she had thought he was trying to impress her, Abigail would have slapped him down. But it was clearly just part of an ongoing self-dramatization, possibly justified, probably not. Abigail suspected that, tour trips to Earth excepted, the *Clarke* was as far down a gravity well as Cheyney had ever been. Still he did have an irresponsible, boyish appeal. "Take me past the net?" she asked.

Cheyney looped the tug around the communications net trailing the *Clarke*. Kilometers of steel lace passed beneath them. He pointed out a small dish antenna on the edge and a cluster of antennae on the back. "The loner on the edge transmits into Ginungagap," he said. "The others relay information to and from Mother."

"Mother?"

"That's the traditional name for the *Arthur* C. *Clarke*." He swung the tug about with a careless sweep of one arm, and launched into a long and scurrilous story about the origin of the nickname. Abigail laughed, and Cheyney pointed a finger. "There's Ginungagap."

Abigail peered intently. "Where? I don't see a thing." She glanced at the second wraparound insert, which displayed a magnified view of the black hole. It wasn't at all impressive: a red smear against black nothingness. In the star-field it was all but invisible.

"Disappointing, hey? But still dangerous. Even this far out, there's a lot of ionization from the accretion disk."

"Is that why there's a lip station?"

"Yeah. Particle concentration varies, but if the translator was right at the *Clarke,* we'd probably lose about a third of the passengers."

Cheyney dropped Abigail off at Mother's crew lock and looped the tug off and away. Abigail wondered where to go, what to do now.

"You're the gravity bum we're dumping down Ginungagap." The short, solid man was upon her before she saw him. His eyes were intense. His *cache-sexe* was a conservative orange. "I liked the stunt with the arm. It takes a lot of guts to do something like that." He pumped her arm. "I'm Paul Girard. Head of external security. In charge of your training. You play verbal Ping-Pong?"

"Why do you ask?" she countered automatically.

"Don't you know?"

"Should I?"

"Do you mean now or later?"

"Will the answer be different later?"

A smile creased Paul's solid face. "You'll do." He took her arm, led her along a sloping corridor. "There isn't much prep time. The dry run is scheduled in two weeks. Things will move pretty quickly after that. You want to start your training now?"

"Do I have a choice?" Abigail asked, amused.

Paul came to a dead stop. "Listen," he said. "Rule number one: don't play games with *me*. You understand? Because I always win. Not sometimes, not usually – always."

Abigail yanked her arm free. "You maneuvered me into that," she said angrily.

"Consider it part of your training." He stared directly into her eyes. "No matter how many gravity wells you've climbed down, you're still the product of a near-space culture – protected, trusting, willing to take things at face value. This is a dangerous attitude, and I want you to realize it. I want you to learn to look behind the mask of events. I want you to grow up. And you will."

Don't be so sure. A small smile quirked Paul's face as if he could read her thoughts. Aloud, Abigail said, "That sounds a little excessive for a trip to Proxima."

"Lesson number two," Paul said: "don't make easy assumptions. You're not going to Proxima." He led her outward-down the ramp to the next wheel, pausing briefly at the juncture to acclimatize to the slower rate of revolution. "You're going to visit spiders." He gestured. "The crew room is this way."

The crew room was vast and cavernous, twilight gloomy. Keyouts were set up along winding paths that wandered aimlessly through the work space. Puddles of light fell on each board and operator. Dark-loving foliage was set between the keyouts.

"This is the heart of the beast," Paul said. "The green keyouts handle all Proxima communications – pretty routine by now. But the blue . . ." His eyes glinting oddly, he pointed. Over the keyouts hung silvery screens with harsh, grainy images floating on their surfaces, black-and-white blobs that Abigail could not resolve into recognizable forms.

"Those," Paul said, "are the spiders. We're talking to them in real-time. Response delay is almost all due to machine translation."

In a sudden shift of perception, the blobs became arachnid forms. That mass of black fluttering across the screen was a spider leg and *that* was its thorax. Abigail felt an immediate, primal aversion, and then it was swept away by an all-encompassing wonder.

"Aliens?" she breathed.

"Aliens."

They actually looked no more like spiders than humans looked like apes. The eight legs had an extra joint each, and the mandible configuration was all wrong. But to an untrained eye they would do.

"But this is – How long have you – ? Why in God's name are you keeping this a secret?" An indefinable joy arose in Abigail. This opened a universe of possibilities, as if after a lifetime of being confined in a box someone had removed the lid.

"Industrial security," Paul said. "The gadget that'll send you through Ginungagap to *their* black hole is a spider invention. We're trading optical data for it, but the law won't protect our rights until we've demonstrated its use. We don't want the other corporations cutting in." He nodded toward the nearest black-and-white screen. "As you can see, they're weak on optics."

"I'd love to talk . . ." Abigail's voice trailed off as she realized how little-girl hopeful she sounded.

"I'll arrange an introduction."

There was a rustling to Abigail's side. She turned and saw a large black tomcat with white boots and belly emerge from the bushes. "This is the esteemed head of Alien Communications," Paul said sourly.

Abigail started to laugh, then choked in embarrassment as she realized that he was not speaking of the cat. "Julio Dominguez, section chief for translation," Paul said. "Abigail Vanderboek, gravity specialist."

The wizened old man smiled professorially. "I assume our resident gadfly has explained how the communications net works, has he not?"

"Well – " Abigail began.

Dominguez clucked his tongue. He wore a yellow *cache-sexe* and matching bow tie, just a little too garish for a man his age. "Quite simple, actually. Escape velocity from a black hole is greater than the speed of light. Therefore, within Ginungagap the speed of light is no longer the limit to the speed of communications."

He paused just long enough for Abigail to look baffled. "Which is just a stuffy way of saying that when we aim a stream of electrons into the boundary of the stationary limit, they emerge elsewhere – out of another black hole. And if we aim them *just so*" – his voice rose whimsically – "they'll emerge from the black hole of our choosing. The physics is simple. The finesse is in aiming the electrons."

The cat stalked up to Abigail, pushed its forehead against her leg, and mewed insistently. She bent over and picked it up. "But nothing can emerge from a black hole," she objected.

Dominguez chuckled. "Ah, but anything can fall in, hey? A positron can fall in. But a positron falling into Ginungagap in positive time is only an electron falling out in negative time. Which means that a positron falling into a black hole in negative time is actually an electron falling out in positive time – exactly the effect we want. Think of Ginungagap as being the physical manifestation of an equivalence sign in mathematics."

"Oh," Abigail said, feeling very firmly put in her place. White moths flittered along the path. The cat watched, fascinated, while she stroked its head.

"At any rate, the electrons do emerge, and once the data are in, the theory has to follow along meekly."

"Tell me about the spiders," Abigail said before he could continue. The moths were darting up, sideward, down, a chance ballet in three dimensions.

"The *aliens,*" Dominguez said, frowning at Paul, "are still a mystery to us. We exchange facts, descriptions, recipes for tools, but the important questions do not lend themselves to our clumsy mathematical codes. Do they know of love? Do they appreciate beauty? Do they believe in God, hey?"

"Do they want to eat us?" Paul threw in.

"Don't be ridiculous," Dominguez snapped. "Of course they don't."

The moths parted when they came to Abigail. Two went to either side; one flew over her shoulder. The cat batted at it with one paw. "The cat's name is Garble," Paul said. "The kids in Bio cloned him up."

Dominguex opened his mouth, closed it again.

Abigail scratched Garble under the chin. He arched his neck and purred all but noiselessly. "With your permission," Paul said. He stepped over to a keyout and waved its operator aside.

"Technically you're supposed to speak a convenience language, but if you keep it simple and non-idiomatic, there shouldn't be any difficulty." He touched the keyout. "Ritual greetings, spider." There was a blank pause. Then the spider moved, a hairy leg flickering across the screen.

"Hello, human."

"Introductions: Abigail Vanderhoek. She is our representative. She will ride the spinner." Another pause. More leg waving.

"Hello, Abigail Vanderhoek. Transition of vacuum garble resting garble commercial benefits garble still point in space."

"Tricky translation," Paul said. He signed to Abigail to take over.

Abigail hesitated, then said, "Will you come to visit us? The way we will visit you?"

"No, you see – " Dominguez began, but Paul waved him to silence.

"No, Abigail Vanderhoek. We are sulfur-based life."

"I do not understand."

"You can garble black hole through garble spinner because you arc carbon-based life. Carbon forms chains easily but sulfur combines in lattices or rosettes. Our garble simple form garble. Sometimes sulfur forms short chains."

"We'll explain later," Paul said. "Go on, you're doing fine."

Abigail hesitated again. What do you say to a spider, anyway? Finally, she asked, "Do you want to eat us?"

"Oh, Christ, get her off that thing," Dominguez said, reaching for the keyout.

Paul blocked his arm. "No," he said. "I want to hear this."

Several of the spider legs wove intricate patterns. "The question is false. Sulfur-based life derives no benefit from eating carbon-based life."

"You see," Dominguez said.

"But if it were possible," Abigail persisted. "If you *could* eat us and derive benefit. Would you?"

"Yes, Abigail Vanderhoek. With great pleasure."

Dominguez pushed her aside. "We're terribly sorry," he said to the alien. "This is a horrible, horrible misunderstanding. You!" he shouted to the operator. "Get back on and clear this mess up."

Paul was grinning wickedly. "Come," he said to Abigail. "We've accomplished enough here for one day."

As they started to walk away, Garble twisted in Abigail's arms and leaped free. He hit the floor on all fours and disappeared into the greenery. "Would they really eat us?" Abigail asked. Then amended it to, "Does that mean they're hostile?"

Paul shrugged. "Maybe they thought we'd be insulted if they *didn't* offer to eat us." He led her to her quarters. "Tomorrow we start training for real. In the meantime, you might make up a list of all the ways the spiders could hurt us if we set up transportation and they *are*

hostile. Then another list of all the reasons we shouldn't trust them."
He paused. "I've done it myself. You'll find that the lists get rather
extensive."

Abigail's quarters weren't flashy, but they fit her well. A full star field
was routed to the walls, floor, and ceiling, only partially obscured by a
trellis inner frame that supported fox-grape vines. Somebody had done
research into her tastes.

"Hi." The cheery greeting startled her. She whirled, saw that her
hammock was occupied.

Cheyney sat up, swung his legs over the edge of the hammock,
causing it to rock lightly. "Come on in." He touched an invisible
control and the star field blue-shifted down to a deep, erotic purple.

"Just what do you think you're doing here?" Abigail asked.

"I had a few hours free," Cheyney said, "so I thought I'd drop by
and seduce you."

"Well, Cheyney, I appreciate your honesty," Abigail said. "So I
won't say no."

"Thank you."

"I'll say maybe some other time. Now get lost. I'm tired."

"Okay." Cheyney hopped down, walked jauntily to the door. He
paused. "You said, 'Later,' right?"

"I said *maybe* later."

"Later. Gotcha." He winked and was gone.

Abigail threw herself into the hammock, red-shifted the star field
until the universe was a sparse smattering of dying embers.

Annoying creature! There was no hope for anything more than the
most superficial of relationships with him. She closed her eyes, smiled.
Fortunately, she wasn't currently in the market for a serious relationship.

She slept.

She was falling . . .

Abigail had landed the ship an easy walk from 3M's robot laboratory. The lab's geodesic dome echoed white clouds to the north, where
Nix Olympus peeked over the horizon. Otherwise all – land, sky, rocks
– was standard issue Martian orange. She had clambered to the
ground and shrugged on the supply backpack.

Resupplying 3M-RL stations was a gut contract, easy but dull. So
perhaps she was less cautious than usual going down the steep, rock-
strewn hillside, or perhaps the rock would have turned under her no

matter how carefully she placed her feet. Her ankle twisted and she lurched sideways, but the backpack had shifted her center of gravity too much for her to be able to recover.

Arms windmilling, she fell.

The rock slide carried her downhill in a panicky flurry of dust and motion, tearing her flesh and splintering her bones. But before she could feel pain, her suit shot her full of a nerve synthetic, translating sensation into colors – reds, russets, and browns, with staccato yellow spikes when a rock smashed into her ribs. So that she fell in a whirling rainbow of glorious light.

She came to rest in a burst of orange. The rocks were settling about her. A spume of dust drifted away, out toward the distant red horizon. A large, jagged slab of stone slid by, gently shearing off her backpack. Tools, supplies, airpacks flew up and softly rained down.

A spanner as long as her arm slammed down inches from Abigail's helmet. She flinched, and suddenly events became real. She kicked her legs and sand and dust fountained up. Drawing her feet under her body – the one ankle bright gold – she started to stand.

And was jerked to the ground by a sudden tug on one arm. Even as she turned her head, she became aware of a deep purple sensation in her left hand. It was pinioned to a rock not quite large enough to stake a claim to. There was no color in the fingers.

"Cute," she muttered. She tugged at the arm, pushed at the rock. Nothing budged.

Abigail nudged the radio switch with her chin. "Grounder to Lip Station," she said. She hesitated, feeling foolish, then said, "Mayday. Repeat, Mayday. Could you guys send a rescue party down for me?"

There was no reply. With a sick green feeling in the pit of her stomach, Abigail reached a gloved hand around the back of her helmet. She touched something jagged, a sensation of mottled rust, the broken remains of her radio.

"I think I'm in trouble." She said it aloud and listened to the sound of it. Flat, unemotional – probably true. But nothing to get panicky about.

She took quick stock of what she had to work with. One intact suit and helmet. One spanner. A worldful of rocks, many close at hand. Enough air for – she checked the helmet readout – almost an hour. Assuming the lip station ran its checks on schedule and was fast on the uptake, she had almost half the air she needed.

Most of the backpack's contents were scattered too far away to reach. One rectangular gaspack, however, had landed nearby. She reached for it but could not touch it, squinted but could not read the label on its nozzle. It was almost certainly liquid gas – either nitrogen or oxygen – for the robot lab. There was a slim chance it was the spare airpack. If it was, she might live to be rescued.

Abigail studied the landscape carefully, but there was nothing more. "Okay, then, it's an airpack." She reached as far as her tethered arm would allow. The gaspack remained a tantalizing centimeter out of reach.

For an instant she was stymied. Then, feeling like an idiot, she grabbed the spanner. She hooked it over the gaspack. Felt the gaspack move grudgingly. Slowly nudged it toward herself.

By the time Abigail could drop the spanner and draw in the gaspack, her good arm was blue with fatigue. Sweat running down her face, she juggled the gaspack to read its nozzle markings.

It was liquid oxygen – useless. She could hook it to her suit and feed in the contents, but the first breath would freeze her lungs. She released the gaspack and lay back, staring vacantly at the sky.

Up there was civilization: tens of thousands of human stations strung together by webs of communication and transportation. Messages flowed endlessly on laser cables. Translators borrowed and lent momentum, moving streams of travelers and cargo at almost (but not quite) the speed of light. A starship was being readied to carry a third load of colonists to Proxima. Up there, free from gravity's relentless clutch, people lived in luxury and ease. Here, however . . .

"I'm going to die." She said it softly and was filled with wondering awe. Because it was true. She was going to die.

Death was a black wall. It lay before her, extending to infinity in all directions, smooth and featureless and mysterious. She could almost reach out an arm and touch it. Soon she would come up against it and, if anything lay beyond, pass through. Soon, very soon, she would *know*.

She touched the seal to her helmet. It felt gray – smooth and inviting. Her fingers moved absently, tracing the seal about her neck. With sudden horror, Abigail realized that she was thinking about undoing it, releasing her air, throwing away the little time she had left . . .

She shuddered. With sudden resolve, she reached out and unsealed the shoulder seam of her captive arm.

The seal clamped down, automatically cutting off air loss. The flesh of her damaged arm was exposed to the raw Martian atmosphere. Abigail took up the gaspack and cradled it in the pit of her good arm. Awkwardly, she opened the nozzle with the spanner.

She sprayed the exposed arm with liquid oxygen for over a minute before she was certain it had frozen solid. Then she dropped the gaspack, picked up the spanner, and swung.

Her arm shattered into a thousand fragments.

She stood up.

Abigail awoke, tense and sweaty. She blue-shifted the walls up to normal light, and sat up. After a few minutes of clearing her head, she set the walls to cycle from red to blue in a rhythm matching her normal pulse. Eventually the womb-cycle lulled her back to sleep.

"Not even close," Paul said. He ran the tape backward, froze it on a still shot of the spider twisting two legs about each other. "That's the morpheme for 'extreme disgust,' remember. It's easy to pick out, and the language kids say that any statement with this gesture should be reversed in meaning. Irony, see? So when the spider says that the strong should protect the weak, it means – "

"How long have we been doing this?"

"Practically forever," Paul said cheerfully. "You want to call it a day?"

"Only if it won't hurt my standing."

"Hah! Very good." He switched off the keyout. "Nicely thought out. You're absolutely right; it would have. However, as reward for realizing this, you can take off early *without* it being noted on your record."

"Thank you," Abigail said sourly.

Like most large installations, the *Clarke* had a dozen or so smaller structures tagging along after it in minimum maintenance orbits. When Abigail discovered that these included a small wheel gymnasium, she had taken to putting in an hour's exercise after each training shift. Today she put in two.

The first hour she spent shadowboxing and practicing *savate* in heavy-gee to work up a sweat. The second hour she spent in the axis room, performing free-fall gymnastics. After the first workout, it made her feel light and nimble and good about her body.

She returned from the wheel gym sweaty and cheerful to find Cheyney in her hammock again. "Cheyney," she said, "this is not the first time I've had to kick you out of there. Or even the third, for that matter."

Cheyney held his palms up in mock protest. "Hey, no," he said. "Nothing like that today. I just came by to watch the raft debate with you."

Abigail felt pleasantly weary, decidedly uncerebral. "Paul said something about it, but . . ."

"Turn it on, then. You don't want to miss it." Cheyney touched her wall, and a cluster of images sprang to life at the far end of the room.

"Just what is a raft debate anyway?" Abigail asked, giving in gracefully. She hoisted herself onto the hammock, sat beside him. They rocked gently for a moment.

"There's this raft, see? It's adrift and powerless and there's only enough oxygen on board to keep one person alive until rescue. Only there are three on board – two humans and a spider."

"Do spiders breathe oxygen?"

"It doesn't matter. This is a hypothetical situation." Two thirds of the image area were taken up by Dominguez and Paul, quietly waiting for the debate to begin. The remainder showed a flat spider image.

"Okay, what then?"

"They argue over who gets to survive. Dominguez argues that he should, since he's human and human culture is superior to spider culture. The spider argues for itself and its culture." He put an arm around her waist. "You smell nice."

"Thank you." She ignored the arm. "What does Paul argue?"

"He's the devil's advocate. He argues that no one deserves to live and they should dump the oxygen."

"Paul would enjoy that role," Abigail said. Then, "What's the point to this debate?"

"It's an entertainment. There isn't supposed to be a point."

Abigail doubted it was that simple. The debate could reveal a good deal about the spiders and how they thought, once the language types were done with it. Conversely, the spiders would doubtless be studying the human responses. *This could be interesting,* she thought. Cheyney was stroking her side now, lightly but with great authority. She postponed reaction, not sure whether she liked it or not.

Louise Chang, a vaguely high-placed administrator, blossomed in the center of the image cluster. "Welcome," she said, and explained the rules of the debate. "The winner will be decided by acclaim," she said, "with half the vote being human and half alien. Please remember not to base your vote on racial chauvinism, but on the strengths of the arguments and how well they are presented." Cheyney's hand brushed casually across her nipples; they stiffened. The hand lingered. "The debate will begin with the gentleman representing the aliens presenting his thesis."

The image flickered as the spider waved several legs. "Thank you, Ms. Chairman. I argue that I should survive. My culture is superior because of our technological advancement. Three examples. Humans have used translation travel only briefly, yet we have used it for sixteens of garble. Our black hole technology is superior. And our garble has garble for the duration of our society."

"Thank you. The gentleman representing humanity?"

"Thank you, Ms. Chairman." Dominguez adjusted an armlet. Cheyney leaned back and let Abigail rest against him. Her head fit comfortably against his shoulder. "My argument is that technology is neither the sole nor the most important measure of a culture. By these standards dolphins would be considered brute animals. The aesthetic considerations – the arts, theology, and the tradition of philosophy – are of greater import. As I shall endeavor to prove."

"He's chosen the wrong tactic," Cheyney whispered in Abigail's ear. "That must have come across as pure garble to the spiders."

"Thank you. Mr. Girard?"

Paul's image expanded. He theatrically swigged from a small flask and hoisted it high in the air. "Alcohol! There's the greatest achievement of the human race!" Abigail snorted. Cheyney laughed out loud. "But I hold that neither Mr. Dominguez nor the distinguished spider deserves to live, because of the disregard both cultures have for sentient life." Abigail looked at Cheyney, who shrugged. "As I shall endeavor to prove." His image dwindled.

Chang said, "The arguments will now proceed, beginning with the distinguished alien."

The spider and then Dominguez ran through their arguments, and to Abigail they seemed markedly lackluster. She didn't give them her full attention, because Cheyney's hands were moving most interestingly across unexpected parts of her body. He might not be too bright, but he was certainly good at some things. She nuzzled her face into his neck, gave him a small peck, returned her attention to the debate.

Paul blossomed again. He juggled something in his palm, held his hand open to reveal three ball bearings. "When I was a kid I used to short out the school module and sneak up to the axis room to play marbles." Abigail smiled, remembering similar stunts she had played. "For the sake of those of us who are spiders, I'll explain that marbles is a game played in free-fall for the purpose of developing coordination and spatial perception. You make a six-armed star of marbles in the center . . ."

One of the bearings fell from his hand, bounced noisily, and disappeared as it rolled out of camera range. "Well, obviously it can't be played here. But the point is that when you shoot the marble just right, it hits the end of one arm and its kinetic energy is transferred from marble to marble along that arm. So that the shooter stops and the marble at the far end of the arm flies away." Cheyney was stroking her absently now, engrossed in the argument.

"Now, we plan to send a courier into Ginungagap and out the spiders' black hole. At least, that's what we say we're going to do.

"But what exits from a black hole is not necessarily the same as what went into its partner hole. We throw an electron into Ginungagap and another one pops out elsewhere. It's identical. It's a direct causal relationship. But it's like the marbles – they're identical to each other and have the same kinetic force. It's simply not the same electron."

Cheyney's hand was still, motionless. Abigail prodded him gently, touching his inner thigh. "Anyone who's interested can see the equations. Now, when we send messages, this doesn't matter. The message is important, not the medium. However, when we send a human being in . . . what emerges from the other hole will be cell for cell, gene for gene, atom for atom identical. *But it will not be the same person.*" He paused a beat, smiled.

"I submit, then, that this is murder. And further, that by conspiring to commit murder, both the spider and human races display absolute disregard for intelligent life. In short, no one on the raft deserves to live. And I rest my case."

"Mr. Girard!" Dominguez objected, even before his image was restored to full size. "The simplest mathematical proof is an identity: that A equals A. Are you trying to deny this?"

Paul held up the two ball bearings he had left. "These marbles are identical too. But they are not the same marble."

"We know the phenomenon you speak of," the spider said. "It is as if garble the black hole bulges out simultaneously. There is no violation of continuity. The two entities are the same. There is no death."

Abigail pulled Cheyney down, so that they were both lying on their sides, still able to watch the images. "So long as you happen to be the second marble and not the first," Paul said. Abigail tentatively licked Cheyney's ear.

"He's right," Cheyney murmured.

"No he's not," Abigail retorted. She bit his earlobe.

"You mean that?"

"Of course I mean that. He's confusing semantics with reality." She engrossed herself in a study of the back of his neck.

"Okay."

Abigail suddenly sensed that she was missing something. "Why do you ask?" She struggled into a sitting position. Cheyney followed.

"No particular reason." Cheyney's hands began touching her again. But Abigail was sure something had been slipped past her.

They caressed each other lightly while the debate dragged to an end. Not paying much attention, Abigail voted for Dominguez, and Cheyney voted for Paul. As a result of a nearly undivided spider vote, the spider won. "I told you Dominguez was taking the wrong approach," Cheyney said. He hopped off the hammock. "Look, I've got to see somebody about something. I'll be right back."

"You're not leaving *now?*" Abigail protested, dumbfounded. The door irised shut.

Angry and hurt, she leaped down, determined to follow him. She couldn't remember ever feeling so insulted.

Cheyney didn't try to be evasive; it apparently did not occur to him that she might follow. Abigail stalked him down a corridor, up an in-ramp, and to a door that irised open for him. She recognized that door.

Thoughtfully she squatted on her heels behind an untrimmed boxwood and waited. A minute later, Garble wandered by, saw her, and demanded attention. "Scat!" she hissed. He butted his head against her knee. "Then be quiet, at least." She scooped him up. His expression was smug.

The door irised open and Cheyney exited, whistling. Abigail waited until he was gone, stood, went to the door, and entered. Fish darted between long fronds under a transparent floor. It was an austere room, almost featureless. Abigail looked, but did not see a hammock.

"So Cheyney's working for you now," she said coldly. Paul looked up from a corner keyout.

"As a matter of fact, I've just signed him to permanent contract in the crew room. He's bright enough. A bit green. Ought to do well."

"Then you admit that you put him up to grilling me about your puerile argument in the debate?" Garble struggled in her arms. She juggled him into a more comfortable position. "And that you staged the argument for my benefit in the first place?"

"Ah," Paul said. "I knew the training was going somewhere. You've become very wary in an extremely short time."

"Don't evade the question."

"I needed your honest reaction," Paul said. "Not the answer you would have given me, knowing your chances of crossing Ginungagap rode on it."

Garble made an angry noise. "You tell him, Garble!" she said. "That goes double for me." She stepped out the door. "You lost the debate," she snapped.

Long after the door had irised shut, she could feel Paul's amused smile burning into her back.

Two days after she returned to kick Cheyney out of her hammock for the final time, Abigail was called to the crew room. "Dry run," Paul said. "Attendance is mandatory." And cut off.

The crew room was crowded with technicians, triple the number of keyouts. Small knots of them clustered before the screens, watching. Paul waved her to him.

"There," he motioned to one screen. "That's Clotho – the platform we built for the transmission device. It's a hundred kilometers off. I wanted more, but Dominguez overruled me. The device that'll unravel you and dump you down Ginungagap is that doohickey in the center." He tapped a keyout and the platform zoomed up to fill the screen. It was covered by a clear, transparent bubble. Inside, a space-suited figure was placing something into a machine that looked like nothing so much as a giant armor-clad clamshell. Abigail looked, blinked, looked again.

"That's Garble," she said indignantly.

"Complain to Dominguez. I wanted a baboon."

The clamshell device closed. The space-suited tech left in his tug, and alphanumerics flickered, indicating the device was in operation. As they watched, the spider-designed machinery immobilized Garble, transformed his molecules into one long continuous polymer chain, and spun it out an invisible opening at near light speed. The water in his body was separated out, piped away, and preserved. The electrolyte balances were recorded and simultaneously transmitted in a parallel stream of electrons. It would reach the spider receiver along with the lead end of the cat-polymer, to be used in the reconstruction.

Thirty seconds passed. Now Garble was only partially in Clotho. The polymer chain, invisible and incredibly long, was passing into Ginungagap. On the far side the spiders were beginning to knit it up.

If all was going well . . .

Ninety-two seconds after they flashed on, the alphanumerics stopped twinkling on the screen. Garble was gone from Clotho. The clamshell opened and the remote cameras showed it to be empty. A cheer arose.

Somebody boosted Dominguez atop a keyout. Intercom cameras swiveled to follow. He wavered fractionally, said "My friends," and launched into a speech. Abigail didn't listen.

Paul's hand fell on her shoulder. It was the first time he had touched her since their initial meeting. "He's only a scientist," he said. "He had no idea how close you are to that cat."

"Look, I *asked* to go. I knew the risks. But Garble's just an animal; he wasn't given the choice."

Paul groped for words. "In a way, this is what your training has been about – the reason you're going across instead of someone like Dominguez. He projects his own reactions onto other people. If – "

Then, seeing that she wasn't listening, he said, "Anyway, you'll have a cat to play with in a few hours. They're only keeping him long enough to test out the life support systems."

There was a festive air to the second gathering. The spiders reported that Garble had translated flawlessly. A brief visual display showed him stalking about Clotho's sister platform, irritable but apparently unharmed.

"There," somebody said. The screen indicated that the receiver net had taken in the running end of the cat's polymer chain. They waited a minute and a half and the operation was over.

It was like a conjuring trick: the clamshell closed on emptiness. Water was piped in. Then it opened and Garble floated over its center, quietly licking one paw.

Abigail smiled at the homeliness of it. "Welcome back, Garble," she said quietly. "I'll get the guys in Bio to brew up some cream for you."

Paul's eyes flicked in her direction. They lingered for no time at all, long enough to file away another datum for future use, and then his attention was elsewhere. She waited until his back was turned and stuck out her tongue at him.

The tub docked with Clotho and a technician floated in. She removed her helmet self-consciously, aware of her audience. One hand extended, she bobbed toward the cat, calling softly.

"Get that jerk on the line," Paul snapped. "I want her helmet back on. That's sloppy. That's real – "

And in that instant Garble sprang.

Garble was a black-and-white streak that flashed past the astonished tech, through the air lock, and into the open tug. The cat pounced on the pilot panel. Its forelegs hit the controls. The hatch slammed shut, and the tug's motors burst into life.

Crew room techs grabbed wildly at their keyouts. The tech on Clotho frantically tried to fit her helmet back on. And the tug took off, blasting away half the protective dome and all the platform's air.

The screens showed a dozen different scenes, lenses shifting from close to distant and back. "Cheyney," Paul said quietly. Dominguez was frozen, looking bewildered. "Take it out."

"It's coming right at us!" somebody shouted.

Cheyney's fingers flicked: rap-tap-rap.

A bright nuclear flower blossomed.

There was silence, dead and complete, in the crew room. *I'm missing something,* Abigail thought. *We just blew up 5 percent of our tug fleet to kill a cat.*

"*Pull* that transmitter!" Paul strode through the crew room, scattering orders. "Nothing goes out! You, you, and you" – he yanked techs away from their keyouts – "*off* those things. I want the whole goddamned net shut *down.*"

"Paul . . . ," an operator said.

"Keep on receiving." He didn't bother to look. "Whatever they want to send. Dump it all in storage and don't merge any of it with our data until we've gone over it."

Alone and useless in the center of the room, Dominguez stuttered, "What – what happened?"

"You blind idiot!" Paul turned on him viciously. "Your precious aliens have just made their first hostile move. The cat that came back was nothing like the one we sent. They made changes. They retransmitted it with instructions wet-wired into its brain."

"But why would they want to steal a tug?"

"We *don't know!*" Paul roared. "Get that through your head. We don't know their motives and we don't know how they think. But we would have known a lot more about their intentions than we wanted if I hadn't rigged that tug with an abort device."

"You didn't – " Dominguez began. He thought better of the statement.

" – have the authority to rig that device," Paul finished for him. "That's right. I didn't." His voice was heavy with sarcasm.

Dominguez seemed to shrivel. He stared bleakly, blankly, about him, then turned and left, slightly hunched over. Thoroughly discredited in front of the people who worked for him.

That was cold, Abigail thought. She marveled at Paul's cruelty. Not for an instant did she believe that the anger in his voice was real, that he was capable of losing control.

Which meant that in the midst of confusion and stress, Paul had found time to make a swift play for more power. To Abigail's newly suspicious eye, it looked like a successful one, too.

For five days Paul held the net shut by sheer willpower and force of personality. Information came in but did not go out. Bell-Sandia administration was not behind him; too much time and money had been sunk into Clotho to abandon the project. But Paul had the support of the tech crew, and he knew how to use it.

"Nothing as big as Bell-Sandia runs on popularity," Paul explained. "But I've got enough sympathy from above, and enough hesitation and official cowardice to keep this place shut down long enough to get a message across."

The incoming information flow fluctuated wildly, shifting from subject to subject. Data sequences were dropped halfway through and incomplete. Nonsense came in. The spiders were shifting through strategies in search of the key that would reopen the net.

"When they start repeating themselves," Paul said, "we can assume they understand the threat."

"But we *wouldn't* shut the net down permanently," Abigail pointed out.

Paul shrugged. "So it's a bluff."

They were sharing an after-shift drink in a fifth-level bar. Small red lizards scuttled about the rock wall behind the bartender. "And if your bluff doesn't work?" Abigail asked. "If it's all for nothing – what then?"

Paul's shoulders sagged, a minute shifting of tensions. "Then we trust in the goodwill of the spiders," he said. "We let them call the shots. And they will treat us benevolently or not, depending. In either case," his voice became dark, "I'll have played a lot of games and manipulated a lot of people for no reason at all." He took her hand. "If that happens, I'd like to apologize." His grip was tight, his knuckles pale.

That night Abigail dreamed she was falling.

Light rainbowed all about her, in a violent splintering of bone and tearing of flesh. She flung out an arm and it bounced on something warm and yielding.

"Abigail."

She twisted and tumbled and something smashed into her ribs. Bright spikes of yellow darted up.

"Abigail!" Someone was shaking her, speaking loudly into her face. The rocks and sky went gray, were overlaid by unresolved images. Her eyelids struggled apart, fell together, opened.

"Oh," she said.

Paul rocked back on his heels. Fish darted about in the water beneath him. "There now," he said. Blue-green lights shifted gently underwater, moving in long, slow arcs. "Dream over?"

Abigail shivered, clutched his arm, let go of it almost immediately. She nodded.

"Good. Tell me about it."

"I – " Abigail began. "Are you asking me as a human being or in your official capacity?"

"I don't make that distinction."

She stretched out a leg and scratched her big toe, to gain time to think. She really didn't have any appropriate thoughts. "Okay," she said, and told him the entire dream.

Paul listened intently, rubbed a thumb across his chin thoughtfully when she was done. "We hired you on the basis of that incident, you know," he said. "Coolness under stress. Weak body image. There were a lot of gravity bums to choose from. But I figured you were just a hair tougher, a little bit grittier."

"What are you trying to tell me? That I'm replaceable?"

Paul shrugged. "Everybody's replaceable. I just wanted to be sure you knew that you could back out if you want. It wouldn't wreck our project."

"I don't want to back out." Abigail chose her words carefully, spoke them slowly, to avoid giving vent to the anger she felt building up inside. "Look, I've been on the gravity circuit for ten years. I've been everywhere in the system there is to go. Did you know that there are less than two thousand people alive who've set foot on Mercury *and* Pluto? We've got a little club; we get together once a year." Seaweed shifted about her; reflections of the floor lights formed nebulous swimming shapes on the walls. "I've spent my entire life going around and around and around the sun, and never really getting anywhere. I want to travel, and there's nowhere left for me to go. So you offer me a way out and then ask if I want to back down. Like hell I do!"

"Why don't you believe that going through Ginungagap is death?" Paul asked quietly. She looked into his eyes, saw cool calculations going on behind them. It frightened her, almost. He was measuring her, passing judgment, warping events into long logical chains that did not take human factors into account. He was an alien presence.

"It's – common sense, is all. I'll be the same when I exit as when I go in. There'll be no difference, not an atom's worth, not a scintilla."

"The *substance* will be different. Every atom will be different. Not a single electron in your body will be the same one you have now."

"Well, how does that differ so much from normal life?" Abigail demanded. "All our bodies are in constant flux. Molecules come and go. Bit by bit, we're replaced. Does that make us different people from moment to moment? 'All that is body is as coursing vapors,' right?"

Paul's eyes narrowed. "Marcus Aurelius. Your quotation isn't complete, though. It goes on: 'All that is of the soul is dreams and vapors.'"

"What's that supposed to mean?"

"It means that the quotation doesn't say what you claimed it did. If you care to read it literally, it argues the opposite of what you're saying."

"Still, you can't have it both ways. Either the me that comes out of the spider black hole is the same as the one who went in, or I'm not the same person as I was an instant ago."

"I'd argue differently," Paul said. "But no matter. Let's go back to sleep."

He held out a hand, but Abigail felt no inclination to accept it. "Does this mean I've passed your test?"

Paul closed his eyes, stretched a little. "You're still reasonably afraid of dying, and you don't believe that you will," he said. "Yeah. You pass."

"Thanks a heap," Abigail said. They slept, not touching, for the rest of the night.

Three days later Abigail woke up, and Paul was gone. She touched the wall and spoke his name. A recording appeared. "Dominguez has been called up to Administration," it said. Paul appeared slightly distracted; he had not looked directly into the recorder and his image avoided Abigail's eyes. "I'm going to re-open the net before he returns. It's best we beat him to the punch." The recording clicked off.

Abigail routed an intercom call through to the crew room. A small chime notified him of her call, and he waved a hand in combined greeting and direction to remain silent. He was hunched over a keyout. The screen above it came to life.

"Ritual greetings, spider," he said.

"Hello, human. We wish to pursue our previous inquiry: the meaning of the term 'art' which was used by the human Dominguez six-sixteenths of the way through his major presentation."

"This is a difficult question. To understand a definition of art, you must first know the philosophy of aesthetics. This is a comprehensive field of knowledge comparable to the study of perception. In many ways it is related."

"What is the trade value of this field of knowledge?"

Dominguez appeared, looking upset. He opened his mouth, and

Paul touched a finger to his own lips, nodding his head toward the screen.

"Significant. Our society considers art and science as being of roughly equal value."

"We will consider what to offer in exchange."

"Good. We also have a question for you. Please wait while we select the phrasing." He cut the translation lines, turned to Dominguez. "Looks like your raft gambit paid off. Though I'm surprised they bit at that particular piece of bait."

Dominguez looked weary. "Did they mention the incident with the cat?"

"No, nor the communications blackout."

The old man sighed. "I always felt close to the aliens," he said. "Now they seem – cold, inhuman." He attempted a chuckle. "That was almost a pun, wasn't it?"

"In a human, we'd call it a professional attitude. Don't let it spoil your accomplishment," Paul said. "This could be as big as optics." He opened the communications line again. "Our question is now phrased." Abigail noted he had not told Dominguez of her presence.

"Please go ahead."

"Why did you alter our test animal?"

Much leg waving. "We improved the ratios garble centers of perception garble wetware garble making the animal twelve-sixteenths as intelligent as a human. We thought you would be pleased."

"We were not. Why did the test animal behave in a hostile manner toward us?"

The spider's legs jerked quickly and it disappeared from the screen. Like an echo, the machine said, "Please wait."

Abigail watched Dominguez throw Paul a puzzled look. In the background, a man with a leather sack looped over one shoulder was walking slowly along the twisty access path. His hand dipped into the sack, came out, sprinkled fireflies among the greenery. Dipped in, came out again. Even in the midst of crisis the trivia of day-to-day existence went on.

The spider reappeared, accompanied by two of its own kind. Their legs interlaced and retreated rapidly, a visual pantomime of an excited conversation. Finally one of their number addressed the screen.

"We have discussed the matter."

"So I see."

"It is our conclusion that the experience of translation through Ginungagap had a negative effect on the test animal. This was not anticipated. It is new knowledge. We know little of the psychology of carbon-based life."

"You're saying the test animal was driven mad?"

"Key word did not translate. We assume understanding. Steps must be taken to prevent a recurrence of this damage. Can you do this?"

Paul said nothing.

"Is this the reason why communications were interrupted?"

No reply.

"There is a cultural gap. Can you clarify?"

"Thank you for your cooperation," Paul said, and switched the screen off. "You can set your people to work," he told Dominguez. "No reason why they should answer the last few questions, though."

"Were they telling the truth?" Dominguez asked wonderingly.

"Probably not. But at least now they'll think twice before trying to jerk us around again." He winked at Abigail, and she switched off the intercom.

They re-ran the test using a baboon shipped out from the Belt Zoological Gardens. Abigail watched it arrive from the lip station, crated and snarling.

"They're a lot stronger than we are," Paul said. "Very agile. If the spiders want to try any more tricks, we couldn't offer them better bait."

The test went smooth as silk. The baboon was shot through Ginungagap, held by the spiders for several hours, and returned. Exhaustive testing showed no tampering with the animal.

Abigail asked how accurate the tests were. Paul hooked his hands behind his back. "We're returning the baboon to the Belt. We wouldn't do that if we had any doubts. But – " He raised an eyebrow, asking Abigail to finish the thought.

"But if they're really hostile, they won't underestimate us twice. They'll wait for a human to tamper with."

Paul nodded.

The night before Abigail's send-off they made love. It was a frenzied and desperate act, performed wordlessly and without tenderness. Afterward they lay together, Abigail idly playing with Paul's curls.

"Gail . . ." His head was hidden in her shoulder; she couldn't see his face. His voice was muffled.

"Mmmm?"

"Don't go."

She wanted to cry. Because as soon as he said it, she knew it was another test, the final one. And she also knew that Paul wanted her to fail it. That he honestly believed transversing Ginungagap would kill her, and that the woman who emerged from the spiders' black hole would not be herself.

His eyes were shut; she could tell by the creases in his forehead. He knew what her answer was. There was no way he could avoid knowing.

Abigail sensed that this was as close to a declaration of emotion as Paul was capable of. She felt how he despised himself for using his real emotions as yet another test, and how he could not even pretend to himself that there were circumstances under which he would *not* so test her. *This must be how it feels to think as he does,* she thought. *To constantly scrabble after every last implication, like eternally picking at a scab.*

"Oh, Paul," she said.

He wrenched about, turning his back to her. "Sometimes I wish" – his hands rose in front of his face like claws; they moved toward his eyes, closed into fists – "that for just ten goddamned minutes I could turn my mind off." His voice was bitter.

Abigail huddled against him, looped a hand over his side and onto his chest. "Hush," she said.

The tug backed away from Clotho, dwindling until it was one of a ring of bright sparks pacing the platform. Mother was a point source lost in the star field. Abigail shivered, pulled off her arm bands and shoved them into a storage sack. She reached for her *cache-sexe*, hesitated.

The hell with it, she thought. *It's nothing they haven't seen before.* She shucked it off, stood naked. Gooseflesh rose on the backs of her legs. She swam to the transmittal device, feeling awkward under the distant watching eyes.

Abigail groped into the clamshell. "Go," she said.

The metal closed about her seamlessly, encasing her in darkness. She floated in a lotus position, bobbing slightly.

A light, gripping field touched her, stilling her motion. On cue, hypnotic commands took hold in her brain. Her breathing became shallow; her heart slowed. She felt her body ease into stasis. The final command took hold.

Abigail weighed 50 keys. Even though the water in her body would not be transmitted, the polymer chain she was to be transformed into would be 275 kilometers long. It would take 15 minutes and 17 seconds to unravel at light speed, negligibly longer at translation speed. She would still be sitting in Clotho when the spiders began knitting her up.

It was possible that Garble had gone mad from a relatively swift transit. Paul doubted it, but he wasn't taking any chances. To protect Abigail's sanity, the meds had wet-wired a travel fantasy into her brain. It would blind her to external reality while she traveled.

She was an eagle. Great feathered wings extended out from her shoulders. Clotho was gone, leaving her alone in space. Her skin was red and leathery, her breasts hard and unyielding. Feathers covered her thighs, giving way at the knees to talons.

She moved her wings, bouncing lightly against the thin solar wind swirling down into Ginungagap. The vacuum felt like absolute freedom. She screamed a predator's exultant shrill. Nothing enclosed her; she was free of restrictions forever.

Below her lay Ginungagap, the primal chasm, an invisible challenge marked by a red smudge of glowing gases. It was inchoate madness, a gibbering, impersonal force that wanted to draw her in, to crush her in its embrace. Its hunger was fierce and insatiable.

Abigail held her place briefly, effortlessly. Then she folded her wings and dove.

A rain of X rays stung through her, the scattering of Ginungagap's accretion disk. They were molten iron passing through a ghost. Shrieking defiance, she attacked, scattering sparks in her wake.

Ginungagap grew, swelled until it swallowed up her vision. It was purest black, unseeable, unknowable, a thing of madness. It was Enemy.

A distant objective part of her knew that she was still in Clotho, the polymer chain being unraveled from her body, accelerated by a translator, passing through two black holes, and simultaneously being knit up by the spiders. It didn't matter.

She plunged into Ginungagap as effortlessly as if it were the film of a soap bubble.

In –

– And out.

It was like being reversed in a mirror, or watching an entertainment run backward. She was instantly flying out the way she came. The sky was a mottled mass of violet light.

The stars before her brightened from violet to blue. She craned her neck, looked back at Ginungagap, saw its disk-shaped nothingness recede, and screamed in frustration because it had escaped her. She spread her wings to slow her flight and –

– was sitting in a dark place. Her hand reached out, touched metal, recognized the inside of a clamshell device.

A hairline crack of light looped over her, widened. The clamshell opened.

Oceans of color bathed her face. Abigail straightened, and the act of doing so lifted her up gently. She stared through the transparent bubble at a phosphorescent foreverness of light.

My God, she thought. *The stars.*

The stars were thicker, more numerous than she was used to seeing them – large and bright and glittery rich. She was probably someplace significant, in a star cluster or the center of the galaxy; she couldn't guess. She felt irrationally happy to simply *be*; she took a deep breath, then laughed.

"Abigail Vanderhoek."

She turned to face the voice, and found that it came from a machine. Spiders crouched beside it, legs moving silently. Outside, in the hard vacuum, were more spiders.

"We regret any pain this may cause," the machine said.

Then the spiders rushed forward. She had no time to react. Sharp mandibles loomed before her, then dipped to her neck. Impossibly swift, they sliced through her throat, severed her spine. A sudden jerk and her head was separated from her body.

It happened in an instant. She felt brief pain, and the dissociation of actually *seeing* her decapitated body just beginning to react. And then she died.

A spark. A light. *I'm alive*, she thought. Consciousness returned like an ancient cathode tube warming up. Abigail stretched slowly, bobbing gently in the air, collecting her thoughts. She was in the sister-Clotho again – not in pain, her head and neck firmly on her shoulders. There were spiders in the platform, and a few floating outside.

"Abigail Vanderhoek," the machine said. "We are ready to begin negotiations."

Abigail said nothing.

After a moment, the machine said, "Are you damaged? Are your thoughts impaired?" A pause, then, "Was your mind not protected during transit?"

"Is that you waving the legs there? Outside the platform?"

"Yes. It is important that you talk with the other humans. You must convey our questions. They will not communicate with us."

"I have a few questions of my own," Abigail said. "I won't cooperate until you answer them."

"We will answer any questions provided you neither garble nor garble."

"What do you take me for?" Abigail asked. "Of course I won't."

Long hours later she spoke to Paul and Dominguez. At her request the spiders had withdrawn, leaving her alone. Dominguez looked drawn and haggard. "I swear we had no idea the spiders would attack you," Dominguez said. "We saw it on the screens. I was certain you'd been killed . . ." His voice trailed off.

"Well, I'm alive, no thanks to you guys. Just what *is* this crap about an explosive substance in my bones, anyway?"

"An explosive – I swear we know nothing of anything of the kind."

"A close relative to plastique," Paul said. "I had a small editing device attached to Clotho's translator. It altered roughly half the bone marrow in your sternum, pelvis, and femurs in transmission. I'd hoped the spiders wouldn't pick up on it so quickly."

"You actually did," Abigail marveled. "The spiders weren't lying; they decapitated me in self-defense. What the holy hell did you think you were *doing*?"

"Just a precaution," Paul said. "We wet-wired you to trigger the stuff on command. That way, we could have taken out the spider installation if they'd tried something funny."

"Um," Dominguez said, "this *is* being recorded. What I'd like to know, Ms. Vanderhoek, is how you escaped being destroyed."

"I didn't," Abigail said. "The spiders killed me. Fortunately, they anticipated the situation, and recorded the transmission. It was easy for them to recreate me – after they edited out the plastique."

Dominguez gave her an odd look. "You don't – feel anything particular about this?"

"Like what?"

"Well – " He turned to Paul helplessly.

"Like the real Abigail Vanderhoek died and you're simply a very realistic copy," Paul said.

"Look, we've been through this garbage before," Abigail began angrily. Paul smiled formally at Dominguez. It was hard to adjust to seeing the two in flat black-and-white. "She doesn't believe a word of it."

"If you guys can pull yourselves up out of your navels for a minute," Abigail said, "I've got a line on something the spiders have that you want. They claim they've sent probes through their black hole."

"Probes?" Paul stiffened. Abigail could sense the thoughts coursing through his skull, of defenses and military applications.

"Carbon-hydrogen chain probes. Organic probes. Self-constructing transmitters. They've got a carbon-based secondary technology."

"Nonsense," Dominguez said. "How could they convert back to coherent matter without a receiver?"

Abigail shrugged. "They claim to have found a loophole."

"How does it work?" Paul snapped.

"They wouldn't say. They seemed to think you'd pay well for it."

"That's very true," Paul said slowly. "Oh, yes."

The conference took almost as long as her session with the spiders had. Abigail was bone weary when Dominguez finally said, "That ties up the official minutes. We now stop recording." A line tracked across the screen, was gone. "If you want to speak to anyone off the record, now's your chance. Perhaps there is someone close to you . . ."

"Close? No." Abigail almost laughed. "I'll speak to Paul alone, though."

A spider floated by outside Clotho II. It was a golden, crablike being, its body slightly opalescent. It skittered along unseen threads strung between the open platforms of the spider star-city. "I'm listening," Paul said.

"You turned me into a *bomb*, you freak."

"So?"

"I could have been killed."

"Am I supposed to care?"

"You damn well ought to, considering the liberties you've taken with my fair white body."

"Let's get one thing understood," Paul said. "The woman I slept with, the woman I cared for, is dead. I have no feelings toward or obligations to you whatsoever."

"Paul," Abigail said. "*I'm not dead.* Believe me, I'd know if I were."

"How could I possibly trust what you think or feel? It could all be attitudes the spiders wet-wired into you. We know they have the technology."

"How do you know that *your* attitudes aren't wet-wired in? For that matter, how do you know anything is real? I mean, these are the most sophomoric philosophic ideas there are. But I'm the same woman I was a few hours ago. My memories, opinions, feelings – they're all the same as they were. There's absolutely no difference between me and the woman you slept with on the *Clarke*."

"I know." Paul's eyes were cold. "That's the horror of it." He snapped off the screen.

Abigail found herself staring at the lifeless machinery. *God, that hurt,* she thought. *It shouldn't, but it hurt.* She went to her quarters.

The spiders had done a respectable job of preparing for her. There were no green plants, but otherwise the room was the same as the one she'd had on the *Clarke*. They'd even been able to spin the platform, giving her an adequate down-orientation. She sat in her hammock, determined to think pleasanter thoughts. About the offer the spiders had made, for example. The one she hadn't told Paul and Dominguez about.

Banned by their chemistry from using black holes to travel, the spiders needed a representative to see to their interests among the stars. They had offered her the job.

Or perhaps the plural would be more appropriate – they had offered her the jobs. Because there were too many places to go for one woman to handle them all. They needed a dozen – in time, perhaps, a hundred – Abigail Vanderhoeks.

In exchange for licensing rights to her personality, the right to make as many duplicates of her as were needed, they were willing to give her the rights to the self-reconstructing black hole platforms.

It would make her a rich woman – a hundred rich women – back in human space. And it would open the universe. She hadn't committed herself yet, but there was no way she was going to turn down the offer. The chance to see a thousand stars? No, she would not pass it by.

When she got old, too, they could create another Abigail from their recording, burn her new memories into it, and destroy her old body.

I'm going to see the stars, she thought. *I'm going to live forever.* She couldn't understand why she didn't feel elated, wondered at the sudden rush of melancholy that ran through her like the precursor of tears.

Garble jumped into her lap, offered his belly to be scratched. The spiders had recorded him, too. They had been glad to restore him to his unaltered state when she made the request. She stroked his stomach and buried her face in his fur.

"Pretty little cat," she told him. "I thought you were dead."

Minister Without Portfolio

MILDRED CLINGERMAN

Mildred Clingerman (1918–97) wrote only a dozen or so SF and fantasy stories, but her works were a memorable feature of *The Magazine of Fantasy & Science Fiction* in the 1950s, and often reprinted. Her only book, *A Cupful of Space* (1961), collects all the stories. She was one of a notable group of women writers, including Judith Merril, Margaret St. Clair, and Shirley Jackson, who helped give *F & SF* a special aspect in that decade and beyond. I would describe that flavor, with the benefit of four decades of hindsight, as a *Twilight Zone* flavor.

In addition to genre science fiction and horror, *F & SF* published stories focused on an ordinary character (and this was unusual because genre science fiction had developed into a literature of extraordinary characters, usually exclusively men), often a woman, experiencing something extra-ordinary, something fantastic. The emotional point was often sentimental, as well as ironic.

This is the kind of plot Rod Serling appropriated, marketed, and made his own brand name, making television history in the process. Clingerman – along with Richard Matheson, Charles Beaumont and a few other men from *Fantasy & Science Fiction* who generally get almost all the credit – was one of the true originals.

This story, published in 1952, was her first. The central character is, to say the least, unusual in science fiction. She seems to have stepped out of a mid-century tale in *The Saturday Evening Post* into an SF story, and then to belong there.

Mrs. Chriswell's little roadster came to a shuddering halt. Here was the perfect spot. Only one sagging wire fence to step over and not a cow in sight. Mrs. Chriswell was terrified of cows, and if the truth were told, only a little less afraid of her daughter-in-law, Clara. It was all Clara's idea that her mother-in-law should now be lurking in meadows peering at birds. Clara had been delighted with the birdwatching idea, but frankly, Mrs. Chriswell was bored with birds. They *flew* so much. And as for their colours, it was useless for her to speculate. Mrs. Chriswell was one of those rare women who are quite, quite colour-blind.

"But, Clara," Mrs. Chriswell had pleaded, "what's the point if I can't tell what colour they are?"

"Well, but, darling," Clara had said crisply, "how much cleverer if you get to know them just from the distinctive markings!"

Mrs. Chriswell, sighing a little as she recalled the firm look of Clara's chin, manoeuvred herself and her burdens over the sagging wire fence. She successfully juggled the binoculars, the heavy bird book, and her purse, and thought how ghastly it was at sixty to be considered so useless that she must be provided with harmless occupations to keep her out of the way.

Since Mr. Chriswell's death she had moved in with her son and his wife to face a life of enforced idleness. The servants resented her presence in the kitchen, so cooking was out. Clara and the snooty nursemaid would brook no interference with the nursery routine, so Mrs. Chriswell had virtually nothing to do. Even her crocheted doilies disappeared magically soon after their presentation to Clara and the modern furniture.

Mrs. Chriswell shifted the heavy bird book and considered rebelling. The sun was hot and her load was heavy. As she toiled on across the field she thought she saw the glint of sun on water. She would sit and crochet in the shade nearby and remove the big straw cartwheel hat Clara termed "just the thing."

Arrived at the trees, Mrs. Chriswell dropped her burdens and flung the hat willy-nilly. Ugly, ridiculous thing. She glanced around for the water she thought she'd seen, but there was no sign of it. She leaned back against a tree trunk and sighed blissfully. A little breeze had sprung up and was cooling the damp tendrils on her forehead. She opened her big purse and scrambled through the muddle of contents for her crochet hook and the ball of thread attached to a half-finished doily. In her search she came across the snapshots of her grand-daughters – in colour, they were, but unfortunately Mrs. Chriswell saw them only in various shades of grey. The breeze was getting stronger now, very pleasant, but the dratted old cartwheel monstrosity was rolling merrily down the slight grade to the tangle of berry bushes a few yards away. Well, it would catch on the brambles. But it didn't. The wind flirted it right around the bushes, and the hat disappeared.

"Fiddle!" Mrs. Chriswell dared not face Clara without the hat. Still hanging on to the bulky purse, she got up to give chase. Rounding the tangle of bushes, she ran smack into a tall young man in uniform.

"Oh!" Mrs. Chriswell said. "Have you seen my hat?"

The young man smiled and pointed on down the hill. Mrs. Chriswell was surprised to see her hat being passed from hand to hand among three other tall young men in uniform. They were laughing at it, and she didn't much blame them. They were standing beside a low, silvery aircraft of some unusual design. Mrs. Chriswell studied it a moment, but, really, she knew nothing about such things . . . The sun glinted off it, and she realized this was what she had thought was water. The young man beside her touched her arm. She turned towards him and saw that he had put a rather lovely little metal hat on his head. He offered her one with grave courtesy. Mrs. Chriswell smiled up at him and nodded. The young man fitted the hat carefully, adjusting various little ornamental knobs on the top of it.

"Now we can talk," he said. "Do you hear well?"

"My dear boy," Mrs. Chriswell said, "of course I do. I'm not so old as that." She found a smooth stone and sat down to chat. This was much nicer than birdwatching, or even crochet.

The tall young man grinned and signalled excitedly to his companions. They too put on little metal hats and came bounding up the hill. Still laughing, they deposited the cartwheel in Mrs. Chriswell's lap. She patted the stone by way of invitation, and the youngest looking one of the four dropped down beside her.

"What is your name, Mother?" he asked.

"Ida Chriswell," she said. "What's yours?"

"My name is Jord," the boy said.

Mrs. Chriswell patted his hand. "That's a nice, unusual name." The boy grabbed Mrs. Chriswell's hand and rubbed it against the smoothness of his cheek.

"*You* are like my Mother's Mother," the boy explained, "whom I have not seen in too long." The other young men laughed, and the boy looked abashed and stealthily wiped with his hands at a tear that slid down his nose.

Mrs. Chriswell frowned warningly at the laughter and handed him her clean pocket handkerchief, scented with lavender. Jord turned it over and over in his hands, and then tentatively sniffed at it.

"It's all right," Mrs. Chriswell said. "Use it. I have another." But Jord only breathed more deeply of the faint perfume in its folds.

"This is only the thinnest thread of melody," he said, "but, Mother Ida, it is very like one note from the Harmony Hills of home!" He passed the handkerchief all around the circle, and the young men sniffed at it and smiled.

Mrs. Chriswell tried to remember if she had ever read of the Harmony Hills, but Mr. Chriswell had always told her she was lamentably weak in geography, and she supposed that this was one of her blank spots, like where on earth was Timbuktu? Or the Hellandgone people were always talking about? But it was rude not to make some comment. Wars shifted people about such a lot, and these boys must be homesick and weary of being strangers, longing to talk of home. She was proud of herself for realizing that they were strangers. But there was something . . . Hard to say, really. The way they had bounded up the hill? Mountain people, perhaps, to whom hills were mere springboards to heights beyond.

"Tell me about your hills," she said.

"Wait," Jord said. "I will show you." He glanced at his leader as if for approval. The young man who had fitted her hat nodded. Jord drew a fingernail across the breast of his uniform. Mrs. Chriswell was surprised to see a pocket opening where no pocket had been before. Really, the Air Force did amazing things with its uniforms, though, frankly, Mrs. Chriswell thought the cut of these a bit extreme.

Carefully, Jord was lifting out a packet of gossamer material. He gently pressed the centre of the packet and it blossomed out into voluminous clouds of featherweight threads, held loosely together in a wave like a giant spider web. To Mrs. Chriswell's eyes the mesh of threads was the colour of fog, and almost as insubstantial.

"Do not be afraid," Jord said softly, stepping closer to her. "Bend your head, close your eyes, and you shall hear the lovely Harmony Hills of home."

There was one quick-drawn breath of almost-fear, but before she shut her eyes Mrs. Chriswell saw the love in Jord's, and in that moment she knew how rarely she had seen this look, anywhere . . . anytime. If Jord had asked it of her, it was all right. She closed her eyes and bowed her head, and in that attitude of prayer she felt a soft weightlessness descend upon her. It was as if twilight had come down to drape itself on her shoulders. And then the music began. Behind the darkness of her eyes it rose in majesty and power, in colours she had never seen, never guessed. It blossomed like flowers – giant forests of them. Their scents were intoxicating and filled her with joy. She could not tell if the blending perfumes made the music, or if the music itself created the flowers and the perfumes that poured forth from them. She did not care. She wanted only to go on forever listening to all this colour. It seemed odd to be listening to colour, perhaps, but after all, she told herself, it would seem just as odd to me to *see* it.

She sat blinking at the circle of young men. The music was finished. Jord was putting away the gossamer threads in the secret pocket, and laughing aloud at her astonishment.

"Did you like it, Mother Ida?" He dropped down beside her again and patted her wrinkled face, still pink with excitement.

"Oh, Jord," she said, "how lovely . . . Tell me . . ."

But the leader was calling them all to order. "I'm sorry, Mother Ida, we must hurry about our business. Will you answer some questions? It is very important."

"Of course," Mrs. Chriswell said. She was still feeling a bit dazed. "If I can . . . If it's like the quizzes on the TV, though, I'm not very good at it."

The young man shook his head. "We," he said, "have been instructed to investigate and report on the true conditions of this . . . of the world." He pointed at the aircraft glittering in the sunlight. "We have travelled all around in that slow machine, and our observations have been accurate . . ." He hesitated, drew a deep breath and continued. ". . . and perhaps we shall be forced to give an unfavourable report, but this depends a great deal on the outcome of our talk with you. We are glad you stumbled upon us. We were about to set out on a foray to secure some individual for questioning. It is our last task." He smiled. "And Jord, here, will not be sorry. He is sick for home and loved ones." He sighed, and all the other young men echoed the sigh.

"Every night," Mrs. Chriswell said, "I pray for peace on earth. I cannot bear to think of boys like you fighting and dying, and the folks at home waiting and waiting She glanced all around at their listening faces. "And I'll tell you something else," she said, "I find I can't really hate anybody, even the enemy." Around the circle the young men nodded at each other. "Now ask me your questions." She fumbled in her purse for her crochet work and found it.

Beside her Jord exclaimed with pleasure at the sight of the half-finished doily. Mrs. Chriswell warmed to him even more.

The tall young man began his grave questioning. They were very simple questions, and Mrs. Chriswell answered them without hesitation. Did she believe in God? Did she believe in the dignity of man? Did she truly abhor war? Did she believe that man was capable of love for his neighbour? The questions went on and on, and Mrs. Chriswell crocheted while she gave her answers.

At last, when the young man had quite run out of questions, and Mrs. Chriswell had finished the doily, Jord broke the sun-lazy silence that had fallen upon them.

"May I have it, Mother?" He pointed to the doily. Mrs. Chriswell bestowed it upon him with great pleasure, and Jord, like a very small boy, stuffed it greedily into another secret pocket. He pointed at her stuffed purse.

"May I look, Mother?"

Mrs. Chriswell indulgently passed him her purse. He opened it and poured the litter of contents on the ground between them. The snapshots of Mrs. Chriswell's grandchildren stared up at him. Jord smiled at the pretty little-girl faces. He groped in the chest pocket and drew out snapshots of his own. "These," he told Mrs. Chriswell proudly, "are my little sisters. Are they not like these little girls of yours? Let us exchange, because soon I will be at home with them, and there will be no need for pictures. I would like to have yours."

Mrs. Chriswell would have given Jord the entire contents of the purse if he had asked for them. She took the snapshots he offered and looked with pleasure at the sweet-faced children. Jord still stirred at the pile of possessions from Mrs. Chriswell's purse. By the time she was ready to leave he had talked her out of three illustrated recipes torn from magazines, some swatches of material, and two pieces of peppermint candy.

The young man who was the leader helped her to remove the pretty little hat when Mrs. Chriswell indicated he should. She would have liked to keep it, but she didn't believe Clara would approve. She clapped the straw monstrosity on her head, kissed Jord's cheek, waved goodbye to the rest, and groped her way around the berry bushes. She had to grope because her eyes were tear-filled. They had saluted her so grandly as she left.

Clara's usually sedate household was in an uproar when Mrs. Chriswell returned. All the radios in the house were blaring. Even Clara sat huddled over the one in the library. Mrs. Chriswell heard a boy in the street crying "EXTRA! EXTRA!" and the upstairs maid almost knocked her down getting out the front door to buy one. Mrs. Chriswell, sleepy and somewhat sunburned, supposed it was something about the awful war.

She was just turning up the stairs to her room when the snooty nursemaid came rushing down to disappear kitchenwards with another newspaper in her hand. Good, the children were alone. She'd stop in to see them. Suddenly she heard the raised voices from the back of the house. The cook was yelling at somebody. "I tell you, I saw it! I took out some garbage and there it was, right over me!" Mrs. Chriswell lingered at the foot of the stairway puzzled by all the confusion. The housemaid came rushing in with the extra edition. Mrs. Chriswell quietly reached out and took it. "Thank you, Nadine," she said. The nursemaid was still staring at her as she climbed the stairs.

Edna and Evelyn were sitting on the nursery floor, a candy box between them, and shrieking at each other when their grandmother opened the door. They were cramming chocolates into their mouths between shrieks. Their faces and pinafores were smeared with the candy. Edna suddenly yanked Evelyn's hair, hard. "Pig!" she shouted. "You got three more than I did!"

"Children! Children! Not fighting?" Mrs. Chriswell was delighted. Here was something she could cope with. She led them firmly to the bathroom and washed their faces. "Change your frocks," she said, "and I'll tell you my adventure."

There were only hissing accusals and whispered countercharges behind her as she turned her back on the children to scan the newspaper. The headlines leapt up at her.

Mysterious broadcast interrupts programmes on all wave lengths
Unknown woman saves world, say men from space
One sane human found on earth
Cooking, needlework, home, religious interests sway space judges

Every column of the paper was crowded with the same unintelligible nonsense. Mrs. Chriswell folded it neatly, deposited it on the table, and turned to tie her grandaughters' sashes and tell her adventure.

". . . And then he gave me some lovely photographs. In colour, he said . . . Good little girls, just like Edna and Evelyn. Would you like to see them?"

Edna made a rude noise with her mouth pursed. Evelyn's face grew saintlike in retaliation. "Yes, show us," she said.

Mrs. Chriswell passed them the snapshots, and the children drew close together for the moment before Evelyn dropped the pictures as if they were blazing. She stared hard at her grandmother while Edna made a gagging noise.

"Green!" Edna gurgled. "Gaaa . . . green skins!"

"Grandmother!" Evelyn was tearful. "Those children are frog-coloured!"

Mrs. Chriswell bent over to pick up the pictures. "Now, now, children," she murmured absently. "We don't worry about the colour of people's skins. Red . . . yellow . . . black . . . we're all God's children. Asia or Africa, makes no difference . . ." But before she could finish her thought, the nursemaid loomed disapprovingly in the doorway. Mrs. Chriswell hurried out to her own room, while some tiny worry nagged at her mind. "Red, yellow, black, white," she murmured over and over, "and brown . . . but green . . . ?" Geography had always been her weak point. Green . . . Now where on earth . . . ?

Time in Advance

WILLIAM TENN

William Tenn is the pseudonym of Philip Klass (1920–), most of whose major SF work was published in the 1950s. He is legendary in the SF field as a wit and a satirist – and for his writing block, which has prevented him from finishing nearly any fiction from the early 1960s to the mid-'90s. His one novel, *Of Men and Monsters* (1968), was published along with five volumes of his short fiction containing most of his earlier work in that year, but he has had no books since.

In an essay introducing his first collection, *Of All Possible Worlds* (1955), he offered an eloquent defense of the genre and revealed a "passionate belief in science fiction as a means of literary expression that has particular validity and significance in this age." He recently retired from a long and distinguished career as a teacher of writing at Pennsylvania State University, where he was the mentor of, among others, David Morrell. *The Encyclopedia of Science Fiction* calls Tenn "one of the genre's very few genuinely comic, genuinely incisive writers of short fiction."

Dictionary of Literary Biography (volume 8) singles out "Time in Advance" as "one of Tenn's most thoughtful satires . . . its protagonist is one of Tenn's best-developed characters." It is a complex moral and psychological investigation. What if it were possible to serve your punishment before committing your crime? It seems to me one of the best stories from one of the best writers in the history of genre science fiction.

Twenty minutes after the convict ship landed at the New York Spaceport, reporters were allowed aboard. They came boiling up the main corridor, pushing against the heavily armed guards who were conducting them, the feature-story men and by-line columnists in the lead, the TV people with their portable but still-heavy equipment cursing along behind.

As they went, they passed little groups of spacemen in the black-and-red uniform of the Interstellar Prison Service walking rapidly in the opposite direction, on their way to enjoy five days of planetside leave before the ship roared away once more with a new cargo of convicts.

The impatient journalists barely glanced at these drab personalities who were spending their lives in a continuous shuttle from one end of the Galaxy to the other. After all, the life and adventures of an IPS man had been done thousands of times, done to death. The big story lay ahead.

In the very belly of the ship, the guards slid apart two enormous sliding doors – and quickly stepped aside to avoid being trampled. The reporters almost flung themselves against the iron bars that ran from floor to ceiling and completely shut off the great prison chamber. Their eager, darting stares were met with at most a few curious glances from the men in coarse gray suits who lay or sat in the tiers of bunks that rose in row after sternly functional row all the way down the cargo hold. Each man clutched – and some caressed – small package neatly wrapped in plain brown paper.

The chief guard ambled up on the other side of the bars, picking the morning's breakfast out of his front teeth. "Hi, boys," he said. "'Who're you looking for – as if I didn't know?"

One of the older, more famous columnists held the palm of his hand up warningly. "Look, Anderson: no games. The ship's been almost a half-hour late in landing and we were stalled for fifteen minutes at the gangplank. Now where the hell are they?"

Anderson watched the TV crews shoulder a place for themselves and their equipment right up to the barrier. He tugged a last bit of food out of one of his molars.

"Ghouls," he muttered. "A bunch of grave-happy, funeral-hungry ghouls." Then he hefted his club experimentally a couple of times and clattered it back and forth against the bars. "Crandall!" he bellowed. "Henck! Front and center!"

The cry was picked up by the guards strolling about, steadily, measuredly, club-twirlingly, inside the prison pen. "Crandall! Henck! Front and center!" It went ricocheting authoritatively up and down the tremendous curved walls. "Crandall! Henck! Front and center!"

Nicholas Crandall sat up cross-legged in his bunk on the fifth tier and grimaced. He had been dozing and now he rubbed a hand across his eyes to erase the sleep. There were three parallel scars across the back of his hand, old and brown and straight scars such as an animal's claws might rake out. There was also a curious zigzag scar just above his eyes that had a more reddish novelty. And there was a tiny, perfectly round hole in the middle of his left ear which, after coming fully awake, he scratched in annoyance.

"Reception committee," he grumbled. "Might have known. Same old goddam Earth as ever."

He flipped over on his stomach and reached down to pat the face of the little man snoring on the bunk immediately under him. "Otto," he called. "Blotto Otto – up and at 'em! They want us."

Henck immediately sat up in the same cross-legged fashion, even before his eyes had opened. His right hand went to his throat where there was a little network of zigzag scars of the same color and size as the one Crandall had on his forehead. The hand was missing an index and forefinger.

"Henck here, sir," he said thickly, then shook his head and stared up at Crandall. "Oh – Nick. what's up?"

"We've arrived, Blotto Otto," the taller man said from the bunk above. "We're on Earth and they're getting our discharges ready. In about half an hour, you'll be able to wrap that tongue of yours around as much brandy, beer, vodka and rotgut whiskey as you can pay for. No more prison-brew, no more raisin-jack from a tin can under the bed, Blotto Otto."

Henck grunted and flopped down on his back again. "In half an hour, but not now, so why did you have to go and wake me up? What do you take me for, some dewy, post-crime, petty-larceny kid, sweating out my discharge with my eyes open and my gut wriggling? Hey, Nick, I was dreaming of a new way to get Elsa, a brand-new, really ugly way."

"The screws are in an uproar," Crandall told him, still in a low, patient voice. "Hear them? They want us, you and me."

Henck sat up again, listened a moment, and nodded. "Why is it," he asked, "that only space-screws have voices like that?"

"It's a requirement of the service," Crandall assured him. "You've got to be at least a minimum height, have a minimum education and with a minimum nasty voice of just the right ear-splitting quality before you can get to be a space-screw. Otherwise, no matter how vicious a personality you have, you are just plain out of luck and have to stay behind on Earth and go on getting your kicks by running down slowpoke 'copters driven by old ladies."

A guard stopped below, banged angrily at one of the metal posts that supported their tier of bunks. "Crandall! Henck! You're still convicts, don't you forget that! If you don't front-and-center in a double-time hurry, I'll climb up there and work you over once more for old-time's sake!"

"Yes, *sir!* Coming, *sir!*" they said in immediate, mumbling unison and began climbing down from bunk to bunk, each still clutching the brown-paper package that contained the clothes they had once worn as free men and would shortly be allowed to wear again.

"Listen, Otto." Crandall leaned down as they climbed and brought his lips close to the little man's ear in the rapid-fire, extremely low-pitched prison whisper. "They're taking us to meet the television and news boys. We're going to be asked a lot of questions. One thing you want to be sure to keep your lip buttoned about – "

"Television and news? Why us? what do they want with us?"

"Because we're celebrities, knockhead! We've seen it through for the big rap and come out on the other side. How many men do you think have made it? But *listen,* will you? If they ask you who it is you're after, you just shut up and smile. You don't answer that question. Got that? You don't tell them whose murder you were sentenced for, no matter what they say. They can't make you. That's the law."

Henck paused a moment, one and a half bunks from the floor. "But, Nick, *Elsa* knows! I told her that day, just before I turned myself in. She knows I wouldn't take a murder rap for anyone but her!"

"She knows, she knows, of *course* she knows!" Crandall swore briefly and almost inaudibly. "But she can't *prove* it, you goddam human blotter! Once you say so in public, though, she's entitled to arm herself and shoot you down on sight – pleading self-defense. And till you say so, she can't; she's still your poor wife whom you've promised to love, honor and cherish. As far as the world is concerned – "

The guard reached up with his club and jolted them both angrily across the back. They dropped to the floor and cringed as he snarled over them: "Did I say you could have a talk-party? *Did I?* If we have any time left before you get your discharge, I'm taking you cuties into the guard-room for one last big going-over. Now pick them up and put them down!"

They scuttled in front of him obediently, like a pair of chickens before a snapping collie. At the barred gate near the end of the prison hold, he saluted and said: "Pre-criminals Nicholas Crandall and Otto Henck, sir."

Chief Guard Anderson wiped the salute back at him carelessly.

"These gentlemen want to ask you fellas a couple of questions. Won't hurt you to answer. That's all, O'Brien."

His voice was very jovial. He was wearing a big, gentle, half-moon smile. As the subordinate guard saluted and moved away, Crandall let his mind regurgitate memories of Anderson all through this month-long trip from Proxima Centaurus. Anderson nodding thoughtfully as that poor Minelli – Steve Minelli, hadn't that been his name? – was made to run through a gauntlet of club-swinging guards for going to the toilet without permission. Anderson chuckling just a moment before he'd kicked a gray-headed convict in the groin for talking on the chow-line. Anderson –

Well, the guy had guts, anyway, knowing that his ship carried two precriminals who had served out a murder sentence. But he probably also knew that they wouldn't waste the murder on him, however viciously he acted. A man doesn't volunteer for a hitch in hell just so he can knock off one of the devils.

"Do we have to answer these questions, sir?" Crandall asked cautiously, tentatively.

The chief guard's smile lost the tiniest bit of its curvature. "I said it wouldn't hurt you, didn't I? But other things might. They *still* might, Crandall. I'd like to do these gentlemen from the press a favor, so you be nice and cooperative, eh?" He gestured with his chin, ever so slightly, in the direction of the guardroom and hefted his club a bit.

"Yes, sir," Crandall said, while Henck nodded violently. "We'll be cooperative, sir.

Dammit, he thought, *if only I didn't have such a use for that murder! Let's keep remembering Stephanson, boy, no one but Stephanson! Not Anderson, not O'Brien, not anybody else: the name under discussion is Frederick Stoddard Stephanson!*

While the television men on the other side of the bars were fussing their equipment into position, the two convicts answered the preliminary, inevitable questions of the feature writers:

"How does it feel to be back?"

"Fine, just fine."

"What's the first thing you're going to do when you get your discharge?"

"Eat a good meal." (From Crandall.)

"Get roaring drunk." (From Henck.)

"Careful you don't wind up right behind bars again as a post-criminal." (From one of the feature writers.) A good-natured laugh in which all of them, the newsmen, Chief Guard Anderson, and Crandall and Henck, participated.

"How were you treated while you were prisoners?"

"Oh, pretty good." (From both of them, concurrent with a thoughtful glance at Anderson's club.)

"Either of you care to tell us who you're going to murder?"

(Silence.)

"Either of you changed your mind and decided not to commit the murder?"

(Crandall looked thoughtfully up, while Henck looked thoughtfully down.) Another general laugh, a bit more uneasy this time, Crandall and Henck not participating.

"All right, we're set. Look this way, please," the television announcer broke in. "And smile, men – let's have a really *big* smile."

Crandall and Henck dutifully emitted big smiles, which made three smiles, for Anderson had moved into the cheerful little group.

The two cameras shot out of the grasp of their technicians, one hovering over them, one moving restlessly before their faces, both controlled, at a distance, by thc little box of switches in the cameramen's hands. A red bulb in the nose of one of the cameras lit up.

"Here we are, ladies and gentlemen of the television audience," the announcer exuded in a lavish voice. "We are on board the convict ship *Jean Valjean*, which has just landed at the New York Spaceport. We are here to meet two men – two of the rare men who have managed to serve all of a voluntary sentence for murder and thus are legally entitled to commit one murder apiece.

"In just a few moments, they will be discharged after having served out seven full years on the convict planets – and they will be free to kill any man or woman in the Solar System with absolutely no fear of any kind of retribution. Take a good look at them, ladies and gentlemen of the television audience – it might be you they are after!"

After this cheering thought, the announcer let a moment or two elapse while the cameras let their lenses stare at the two men in prison gray. Then he stepped into range himself and addressed the smaller man.

"What is your name, sir?" he asked.

"Pre-criminal Otto Henck, 525514," Blotto Otto responded automatically, though not able to repress a bit of a start at the *sir*.

"How does it feel to be back?"

"Fine, just fine."

"What's the first thing you're going to do when you get your discharge?"

Henck hesitated, then said, "Eat a good meal," after a shy look at Crandall.

"How were you treated while you were a prisoner?"

"Oh, pretty good. As good as you could expect."

"As good as a criminal could expect, eh? Although you're not really a criminal yet, are you? You're a pre-criminal."

Henck smiled as if this were the first time he was hearing the term. "That's right, sir. I'm a pre-criminal."

"Want to tell the audience who the person is you're going to become a criminal for?"

Henck looked reproachfully at the announcer, who chuckled throatily – and alone.

"Or if you've changed your mind about him or her?" There was a pause. Then the announcer said a little nervously: "You've served seven years on danger-filled, alien planets, preparing them for human colonization. That's the maximum sentence the law allows, isn't it?"

"That's right, sir. With the pre-criminal discount for serving the sentence in advance, seven years is the most you can get for murder."

"Bet you're glad we're not back in the days of capital punishment, eh? That would make the whole thing impractical, wouldn't it? Now, Mr. Henck – or pre-criminal Henck, I guess I should still call you – suppose you tell the ladies and gentlemen of our television audience: what was the most horrifying experience you had while you were serving your sentence?"

"Well," Otto Henck considered carefully. "About the worst of the lot, I guess, was the time on Antares VIII, the second prison camp I was in, when the big wasps started to spawn. They got a wasp on Antares VIII, see, that's about a hundred times the size of – "

"Is that how you lost two fingers on your right hand?"

Henck brought his hand up and studied it for a moment. "No. The forefinger – I lost the forefinger on Rigel XII. We were building the first prison camp on the planet and I dug up a funny kind of red rock that had all sorts of little bumps on it. I poked it, kind of – you know, just to see how hard it was or something – and the tip of my finger disappeared. Pow – just like that. Later on, the whole finger got infected and the medics had to cut it off.

"It turned out I was lucky, though; some of the men – the convicts, I mean – ran into bigger rocks than the one I found. Those guys lost arms, legs – one guy even got swallowed whole. They weren't really rocks, see. They were alive – they were alive and hungry! Rigel XII was lousy with them. The middle finger – I lost the middle finger in a dumb kind of accident on board ship while we were being moved to – "

The announcer nodded intelligently, cleared his throat and said: "But those wasps, those giant wasps on Antares VIII – they were the worst?"

Blotto Otto blinked at him for a moment before he found the conversation again.

"Oh. They sure were! They were used to laying their eggs in a kind of monkey they have on Antares VIII, see? It was real rough on the monkey, but that's how the baby wasps got their food while they were growing up. Well, we get out there and it turns out that the wasps can't see any difference between those Antares monkeys and human beings. First thing you know, guys start collapsing all over the place and when they're taken to the dispensary for an X-ray, the medics see that they're completely crammed – "

"Thank you very much, Mr. Henck, but Herkimer's Wasp has already been seen by and described to our audience at least three times in the past on the Interstellar Travelogue, which is carried by this network, as you ladies and gentlemen no doubt remember, on Wednesday evening from seven to seven-thirty p.m. terrestrial standard time. And now, Mr. Crandall, let me ask you, sir: How does it feel to be back?"

Crandall stepped up and was put through almost exactly the same verbal paces as his fellow prisoner.

There was one major difference. The announcer asked him if he expected to find Earth much changed. Crandall started to shrug, then abruptly relaxed and grinned. He was careful to make the grin an extremely wide one, exposing a maximum of tooth and a minimum of mirth.

"There's one big change I can see already," he said. "The way those cameras float around and are controlled from a little switch-box in the cameraman's hand. That gimmick wasn't around the day I left. Whoever invented it must have been pretty clever."

"Oh, yes?" The announcer glanced briefly backward. "You mean the Stephanson Remote Control Switch? It was invented by Frederick Stoddard Stephanson about five years ago – Was it five years, Don?"

"Six years," said the cameraman. "Went on the market five years ago.

"It was *invented* six years ago, the announcer translated. "It went on the market *five* years ago."

Crandall nodded. "Well, this Frederick Stoddard Stephanson must be a clever man, a very clever man." And he grinned again into the cameras. *Look at my teeth,* he thought to himself. *I know you're watching, Freddy. Look at my teeth and shiver.*

The announcer seemed a bit disconcerted. "Yes," he said. "Exactly. Now, Mr. Crandall, what would you describe as the most horrifying experience in your entire . . ."

After the TV men had rolled up their equipment and departed, the two precriminals were subjected to a final barrage of questions from the feature writers and columnists in search of odd shreds of color.

"What about the women in your life?" "What books, what hobbies, what amusements filled your time?" "Did you find out that there are no atheists on convict planets?" "If you had the whole thing to do over again – "

As he answered, drably, courteously, Nicholas Crandall was thinking about Frederick Stoddard Stephanson seated in front of his luxurious wall-size television set.

Would Stephanson have clicked it off by now? Would he be sitting there, staring at the blank screen, pondering the plans of the man who had outlived odds estimated at ten thousand to one and returned after seven full, unbelievable years in the prison camps of four insane planets?

Would Stephanson be examining his blaster with sucked-in lips – the blaster that he might use only in an open-and-shut situation of self-defense? Otherwise, he would incur the full post-criminal sentence for murder, which, without the fifty per cent discount for punishment voluntarily undergone in advance of the crime, was as much as four-teen years in the many-pronged hell from which Crandall had just returned?

Or would Stephanson be sitting, slumped in an expensive bubblechair, glumly watching a still-active screen, frightened out of his wits but still unable to tear himself away from the well-organized program the network had no doubt built around the return of two – count 'em: *two!* – homicidal pre-criminals?

At the moment, in all probability, the screen was showing an inter-view with some Earthside official of the Interstellar Prison Service, an expansive public relations character who had learned to talk in sociology.

"Tell me, Mr. Public Relations," the announcer would ask (a different announcer, more serious, more intellectual), "how often do pre-criminals serve out a sentence for murder and return?"

"According to statistics – " a rustle of papers at this point and a penetrating glance downward – "according to statistics, we may expect a man who has served a full sentence for murder, with the 50 per cent pre-criminal discount, to return only once in 11.7 years on the average."

"You would say, then, wouldn't you, Mr. Public Relations, that the return of two such men on the same day is a rather unusual situation?"

"*Highly* unusual or you television fellas wouldn't be in such a fuss over it." A thick chuckle here, which the announcer dutifully echoes.

"And what, Mr. Public Relations, happens to the others who don't return?"

A large, well-fed hand gestures urbanely. "They get killed. Or they give up. Those are the only two alternatives. Seven years is a long time to spend on those convict planets. The work schedule isn't for sissies and neither are the life-forms they encounter – the big man-eating ones as well as the small virus-sized types.

"That's why prison guards get such high salaries and such long leaves. In a sense, you know, we haven't really abolished capital punishment; we've substituted a socially useful form of Russian Roulette for it. Any man who commits or pre-commits one of a group of particularly reprehensible crimes is sent off to a planet where his services will benefit humanity and where he's forced to take his chances on coming back in one piece, if at all. The more serious the crime, the longer the sentence and, therefore, the more remote the chances."

"I see. Now, Mr. Public Relations, you say they either get killed or they give up. Would you explain to the audience, if you please, just how they give up and what happens if they do?"

Here a sitting back in the chair, a locking of pudgy fingers over paunch. "You see, any pre-criminal may apply to his warden for immediate abrogation of sentence. It's just a matter of filling out the necessary forms. He's pulled off work detail right then and there and is sent home on the very next ship out of the place. The catch is this: Every bit of time he's served up to that point is canceled – he gets nothing for it.

"If he commits an actual crime after being freed, he has to serve the full sentence. If he wants to be committed as a pre-criminal again, he has to start serving the sentence, with the discount, from the beginning. Three out of every four pre-criminals apply for abrogation of sentence in their very first year. You get a bellyful fast in those places."

"I guess you certainly do," agrees the announcer. "What about the discount, Mr. Public Relations? Aren't there people who feel that's offering the pre-criminal too much inducement?"

The barest grimace of anger flows across the sleek face, to be succeeded by a warm, contemptuous smile. "Those are people, I'm afraid, who, however well-intentioned, are not well versed in the facts of modern criminology and penology. We don't want to discourage pre-criminals; we want to *encourage* them to turn themselves in.

"Remember what I said about three out of four applying for abrogation of sentence in their very first year? Now these are individuals who were sensible enough to try to get a discount on their sentence. Are they likely to be foolish enough to risk twice as much when they have found out conclusively they can't stand a bare twelve months of it? Not to mention what they have discovered about the value of human life, the necessity for social cooperation and the general desirability of civilized processes on those worlds where simple survival is practically a matter of a sweepstakes ticket.

"The man who doesn't apply for abrogation of sentence? Well, he has that much more time to let the desire to commit the crime go cold – and that much greater likelihood of getting killed with nothing to show for it. Therefore, so few pre-criminals in *any* of the categories return to tell the tale and do the deed that the social profit is absolutely enormous! Let me give you a few figures.

"Using the Lazarus Scale, it has been estimated that the decline in premeditated homicides alone, since the institution of the pre-criminal discount, has been forty-one per cent on Earth, thirty-three and a third per cent on Venus, twenty-seven per cent – "

Cold comfort, chillingly cold comfort, that would be to Stephanson, Nicholas Crandall reflected pleasurably, those forty-one per cents and thirty-three and a third per cents. Crandall's was the balancing statistic: the man who wanted to murder, and for good and sufficient cause, one Frederick Stoddard Stephanson. He was a leftover fraction on a page of reductions and cancellations – he had returned, astonishingly, unbelievably, after seven years to collect the merchandise for which he had paid in advance.

He and Henck. Two ridiculously long long-shots. Henck's wife Elsa – was she, too, sitting in a kind of bird-hypnotized-by-a-snake fashion before her television set, hoping dimly and desperately that some comment of the Interstellar Prison Service official would show her how to evade her fate, how to get out from under the ridiculously rare disaster that was about to happen to her?

Well, Elsa was Blotto Otto's affair. Let him enjoy it in his own way; he'd paid enough for the privilege. But Stephanson was Crandall's.

Oh, let the arrogant bean-pole sweat, he prayed. *Let me take my time and let him sweat!*

The newsman kept squeezing them for story angles until a loud-speaker in the overhead suddenly cleared its diaphragm and announced:

"Prisoners, prepare for discharge! You will proceed to the ship warden's office in groups of ten, as your name is called. Convict ship discipline will be maintained throughout. Arthur, Augluk, Crandall, Ferrara, Fu-Yen, Garfinkel, Gomez, Graham, Henck – "

A half hour later, they were walking down the main corridor of the ship in their civilian clothes. They showed their discharges to the guard at the gangplank, smiled still cringingly back at Anderson, who called from a porthole, "Hey, fellas, come back soon!" and trotted down the incline to the surface of a planet they had not seen for seven agonizing and horror-crowded years.

There were a few reporters and photographers still waiting for them, and one TV crew which had been left behind to let the world see how they looked at the moment of freedom.

Questions, more questions to answer, which they could afford to be brusque about, although brusqueness to any but fellow prisoners still came hard.

Fortunately, the newsmen got interested in another pre-criminal who was with them. Fu-Yen had completed the discounted sentence of two years for aggravated assault and battery. He had also lost both arms and one leg to a corrosive moss on Procyon III just before the end of his term and came limping down the gangplank on one real and one artificial leg, unable to grasp the hand-rails.

As he was being asked, with a good deal of interest, just how he intended to commit simple assault and battery, let alone the serious kind, with his present limited resources, Crandall nudged Henck and they climbed quickly into one of the many hovering gyrocabs. They told the driver to take them to a bar – any quiet bar – in the city.

Blotto Otto almost went to pieces under the impact of actual free choice. "I can't do it," he whispered. "Nick, there's just too damn much to drink!"

Crandall settled it by ordering for him. "Two double scotches," he told the waitress. "Nothing else."

When the scotch came, Blotto Otto stared at it with the kind of affectionate and wistful astonishment a man might show toward an adolescent son whom he saw last as a babe in arms. He put out a gingerly, trembling hand.

"Here's death to our enemies," Crandall said, and tossed his down. He watched Otto sip slowly and carefully, tasting each individual drop.

"You'd better take it easy," he warned. "Elsa might have no more trouble from you than bringing flowers every visiting day to the alcoholic ward."

"No fear," Blotto Otto growled into his empty glass. "I was weaned on this stuff. And, anyway, it's the last drink I have until I dump her. That's the way I've been figuring it, Nick: one drink to celebrate, then Elsa. I didn't go through those seven years to mess myself up at the payoff."

He set the glass down. "Seven years in one steaming hell after another. And before that, twelve years with Elsa. Twelve years with her pulling every dirty trick in the book on me, laughing in my face, telling me she was my wife and had me legally where she wanted me, that I was gonna support her the way she wanted to be supported and I was gonna like it. And if I dared to get off my knees and stand on my hind legs, *pow*, she found a way to get me arrested.

"The weeks I spent in the cooler, in the workhouse, until Elsa would tell the judge maybe I'd learned my lesson, she was willing to give me one more chance! And me begging for a divorce on my knees – hell, on my belly! – no children, she's able-bodied, she's young, and her laughing in my face. When she wanted me in the cooler, see, then she's crying in front of the judge; but when we're alone, she's always laughing her head off to see me squirm.

"I supported her, Nick. Honest, I gave her almost every cent I made, but that wasn't enough. She liked to see me squirm; she *told* me she did. Well, who's squirming now?" He grunted deep in his throat. "Marriage – it's for chumps!"

Crandall looked out of the open window he was sitting against, down through the dizzy, busy levels of Metropolitan New York.

"Maybe it is," he said thoughtfully. "I wouldn't know. My marriage was good while it lasted, five years of it. Then, all of a sudden, it wasn't good any more, just so much rancid butter."

"At least she gave you a divorce," said Henck. "She didn't take you."

"Oh, Polly wasn't the kind of girl to take anyone. A little mixed up, but maybe no more than I was. Pretty Polly, I called her; Big Nick, she called me. The starlight faded and so did I, I guess. I was still knocking myself out then trying to make a go out of the wholesale electronics business with Irv. Anyone could tell I wasn't cut out to be a million-aire. Maybe that was it. Anyway, Polly wanted out and I gave it to her. We parted friends. I wonder, every once in a while, what she's – "

There was a slight splashy noise, like a seal's flipper making a gesture in the water. Crandall's eyes came back to the table a moment after the green, melon-like ball had hit it. And, at the same instant, Henck's hand had swept the ball up and hurled it through the window. The long, green threads streamed out of the ball, but by then it was falling down the side of the enormous building and the threads found no living flesh to take root in.

From the corner of his eye, Crandall had seen a man bolt out of the bar. By the way people kept looking back and forth fearfully from their table to the open doorway, he deduced that the man had thrown it. Evidently Stephanson had thought it worthwhile to have Crandall followed and neutralized.

Blotto Otto saw no point in preening over his reflexes. The two of them had learned to move fast a long time ago – over a lot of dead bodies. "A Venusian dandelion bomb," he observed. "Well, at least the guy doesn't want to kill you, Nick. He just wants to cripple you."

"That would be Stephanson's style," Crandall agreed, as they paid their check and walked past the faces which were just now beginning to turn white. "He'd never do it himself. He'd hire a bully-boy. And he'd do the hiring through an intermediary just in case the bully-boy ever got caught and blabbed. But that still wouldn't be safe enough: he wouldn't want to risk a post-criminal murder charge.

"A dose of Venusian dandelion, he'd figure, and he wouldn't have to worry about me for the rest of my life. He might even come to visit me in the home for incurables – like the way he sent me a card every Christmas of my sentence. Always the same message: 'Still mad? Love, Freddy.'"

"Quite a guy, this Stephanson," Blotto Otto said, peering around the entrance carefully before stepping out of the bar and onto the fifteenth level walkway.

"Yeah, quite a guy. He's got the world by the tail and every once in a while, just for fun, he twists the tail. I learned how he operated when we were roommates way back in college, but do you think that did me any good? I ran into him just when that wholesale electronics business with Irv was really falling apart, about two years after I broke up with Polly.

"I was feeling blue and I wanted to talk to someone, so I told him all about how my partner was a penny-watcher and I was a big dreamer, and how between us we were turning a possible nice small business into a definite big bankruptcy. And then I got onto this remote-control switch I'd been fooling around with and how I wished I had time to develop it."

Blotto Otto kept glancing around uneasily, not from dread of another assassin, but out of the unexpected sensation of doing so much walking of his own free will. Several passersby turned around to have another stare at their out-of-fashion knee-length tunics.

"So there I was," Crandall went on. "I was a fool, I know, but take my word, Otto, you have no idea how persuasive and friendly a guy like Freddy Stephanson can be. He tells me he has this house in the country he isn't using right now and there's a complete electronics lab in the basement. It's all mine, if I want it, as long as I want it, starting next week; all I have to worry about is feeding myself. And he doesn't want any rent or anything – it's for old time's sake and because he wants to see me do something really big in the world.

"How smart could I be with a con-artist like that? It wasn't till two years later that I realized he must have had the electronics lab installed the same week I was asking Irv to buy me out of the business for a couple of hundred credits. After all, what would Stephanson, the owner of a brokerage firm, be doing with an electronics lab of his own? But who figures such things when an old roommate's so warm and friendly and interested in you?"

Otto sighed. "So he comes up to see you every few weeks. And then, about a month after you've got it all finished and working, he locks you out of the place and moves all your papers and stuff to another joint. And he tells you he'll have it patented long before you can get it all down on paper again, and anyhow it was his place – he can always claim he was subsidizing you. Then he laughs in your face, just like Elsa. Huh, Nick?"

Crandall bit his lip as he realized how thoroughly Otto Henck must have memorized the material. How many times had they gone over each other's planned revenge and the situations which had motivated it? How many times had they told and retold the same bitter stories to each other, elicited the same responses from each other, the same questions, the same agreements and even the very same disagreements?

Suddenly, he wanted to get away from the little man and enjoy the luxury of loneliness. He saw the sparkling roof of a hotel two levels down.

"Think I'll move into that. Ought to be thinking about a place to sleep tonight."

Otto nodded at his mood rather than at his statement. "Sure. I know just how you feel. But that's pretty plush, Nick: The Capricorn-Ritz. At least twelve credits a day."

"So what? I can live high for a week, if I want to. And with my background, I can always pick up a fast job as soon as I get low. I want something plush for tonight, Blotto Otto."

"Okay, okay. You got my address, huh, Nick? I'll be at my cousin's place."

"I have it, all right. Luck with Elsa, Otto."

"Thanks. Luck with Freddy. Uh – so long." The little man turned abruptly and entered a main street elevator. When the doors slid shut, Grandall found that he was feeling very uncomfortable. Henck had meant more to him than his own brother. Well, after all, he'd been with Henck day and night for a long time now. And he hadn't seen Dan for – how long was it? – almost nine years.

He reflected on how little he was attached to the world, if you excluded the rather negative desire of removing Stephanson from it. One thing he should get soon was a girl – almost any girl.

But, come to think of it, there was something he needed even more.

He walked swiftly to the nearest drugstore. It was a large one, part of a chain. And there, featured prominently in the window, was exactly what he wanted.

At the cigar counter, he said to the clerk: "It's pretty cheap. Do they work all right?"

The clerk drew himself up. "Before we put an item on sale, sir, it is tested thoroughly. We are the largest retail outlet in the Solar System – *that's* why it's so cheap."

"All right. Give me the medium-sized one. And two boxes of cartridges."

With the blaster in his possession, he felt much more secure. He had a good deal of confidence – based on years of escaping creatures with hair-trigger nervous systems – in his ability to duck and wriggle and jump to one side. But it would be nice to be able to fight back. And how did he know how soon Stephanson would try again?

He registered under a false name, a ruse he thought of at the last moment. That it wasn't worth much, as ruses went, he found out when the bellhop, after being tipped, said: "Thank you, Mr. Crandall. I hope you get your victim, sir."

So he was a celebrity. Probably everyone in the world knew exactly what he looked like. All of which might make it a bit more difficult to get at Stephanson.

While he was taking a bath, he asked the television set to check through Information's file on the man. Stephanson had been rich and moderately important seven years ago; with the Stephanson Switch –

how do you like that, the *Stephanson* Switch! – he must be even richer
now and much more important.

He was. The television set informed Crandall that in the last
calendar month, there were sixteen news items relating to Frederick
Stoddard Stephanson. Crandall considered, then asked for the most
recent.

That was datelined today. "Frederick Stephanson, the president of
the Stephanson Investment Trust and Stephanson Electronics
Corporation, left early this morning for his hunting lodge in Central
Tibet. He expects to remain there for at least – "

"That's enough!" Crandall called through the bathroom door.

Stephanson was scared! The arrogant bean-pole was frightened silly!
That was something; in fact, it was a large part of the return on those
seven years. Let him seethe in his own sweat for a while, until he found
the actual killing, when it did come at last, almost welcome.

Crandall asked the set for the fresh news and was immediately
treated to a bulletin about himself and how he had registered at the
Capricorn-Ritz under the name of Alexander Smathers. "But neither
is the correct name, ladies and gentlemen," the playback rolled out
unctuously. "Neither Nicholas Crandall nor Alexander Smathers is the
right name for this man. There is only one name for that man – and
that name is death! Yes, the grim reaper has taken up residence at the
Ritz-Capricorn Hotel tonight, and only he knows which one of us will
not see another sunrise. That man, that grim reaper, that deputy of
death, is the only one among us who knows – "

"Shut up!" Crandall yelled, exasperated. He had almost forgotten
the kind of punishment a free man was forced to endure.

The private phone circuit on the television screen lit up. He dried
himself, hurried into clothes and asked, "Who's calling?"

"Mrs. Nicholas Crandall," said the operator's voice.

He stared at the blank screen for a moment, absolutely thunderstruck. Polly! Where in the world had she come from? And how did
she know where he was? No, the last part was easy – he was a celebrity.

"Put her on," he said at last.

Polly's face filled the screen. Crandall studied her quizzically. She'd
aged a bit, but possibly it wasn't obvious at anything but this magni-
fication.

As if she realized it herself, Polly adjusted the controls of her set and
her face dwindled to life-size, the rest of her body as well as her
surroundings coming into the picture. She was evidently in the living
room of her home; it looked like a low-to-middle-income-range

furnished apartment. But she looked good – awfully good. There were such warm memories . . .

"Hi, Polly. What's this all about? You're the last person I expected to call me."

"Hello, Nick." She lifted her hand to her mouth and stared over its knuckles for some time at him. Then: "Nick. Please. Please don't play games with me."

He dropped into a chair. "Huh?"

She began to cry. 'Oh, Nick! *Don't!* Don't be that cruel! I know why you served that sentence – those seven years. The moment I heard your name today, I knew why you did it. But, Nick, it was only one man – just one man, Nick!"

"Just one man *what?*"

"It was just that one man I was unfaithful with. And I thought he loved me, Nick. I wouldn't have divorced you if I'd known what he was really like. But you know, Nick, don't you? You know how much he made me suffer. I've been punished enough. Don't kill me, Nick! Please don't kill me!"

"Listen, Polly," he began, completely confused. "Polly girl, for heaven's sake – "

"Nick!" she gulped hysterically. "Nick, it was over eleven years ago – ten, at least. Don't kill me for that, please, Nick, Nick, truly, I wasn't unfaithful to you for more than a year, two years at the most. Truly, Nick! And, Nick, it was only that one affair – the others didn't count. They were just, just casual things. They didn't matter at all, Nick! But don't kill me! Don't kill me!" She held both hands to her face and began rocking back and forth, moaning uncontrollably.

Crandall stared at her for a moment and moistened his lips. Then he said, "Whew!" and turned the set off. He leaned back in his chair. Again he said, "Whew!" and this time it hissed through his teeth.

Polly! Polly had been unfaithful during their marriage. For a year – no, two years! And – what had she said? – the others, the *others* had just been casual things!

The woman he had loved, the woman he suspected he had always loved, the woman he had given up with infinite regret and a deep sense of guilt when she had come to him and said that the business had taken the best part of him away from her, but that since it wasn't fair to ask him to give up something that obviously meant so much to him –

Pretty Polly. Polly girl. He'd never thought of another woman in all their time together. And if anyone, anyone at all, had ever suggested – had so much as *hinted* – he'd have used a monkey wrench on the meddler's face. He'd given her the divorce only because she'd asked for it, but he'd hoped that when the business got on its feet and Irv's bookkeeping end covered a wider stretch of it, they might get back together again. Then, of course, business grew worse, Irv's wife got sick and he put even less time in at the office and –

"I feel," he said to himself numbly, "as if I've just found out for certain that there is no Santa Claus. Not Polly, not all those good years! One affair! And the others were just casual things!"

The telephone circuit went off again. "Who is it?" he snarled.

"Mr. Edward Ballaskia."

"What's he want?" Not *Polly, not Pretty Polly!*

An extremely fat man came on the screen. He looked to right and left cautiously. "I must ask you, Mr. Crandall, if you are positive that this line isn't tapped."

"What the hell do you want?" Crandall found himself wishing that the fat man were here in person. He'd love to sail into sombody right now.

Mr. Edward Ballaskia shook his head disapprovingly, his jowls jiggling slowly behind the rest of his face. "Well, then, sir, if you won't give me your assurances, I am forced to take a chance. I am calling, Mr. Crandall, to ask you to forgive your enemies, to turn the other cheek. I am asking you to remember faith, hope and charity – and that the greatest of these is charity. In other words, sir, open your heart to him or her you intended to kill, understand the weaknesses which caused them to give offenses – and forgive them."

"Why should I?" Crandall demanded.

"Because it is to your profit to do so, sir. Not merely morally profitable – although let us not overlook the life of the spirit – but financially profitable. *Financially* profitable Mr. Crandall."

"Would you kindly tell me what you are talking about?"

The fat man leaned forward and smiled confidentially. "If you can forgive the person who caused you to go off and suffer seven long, seven *miserable* years of acute discomfort Mr. Crandall, I am prepared to make you a most attractive offer. You are entitled to commit one murder. I desire to have one murder committed. I am very wealthy. You, I judge – and please take no umbrage, sir – are very poor.

"I can make you comfortable for the rest of your life, extremely comfortable, Mr. Crandall, if only you will put aside your thoughts, your unworthy thoughts, of anger and personal vengeance. I have a business competitor, you see, who has been – "

Crandall turned him off. "Go serve your own seven years," he venomously told the blank screen. Then, suddenly, it was funny. He lay back in the chair and laughed his head off.

That butter-faced old slob! Quoting religious texts at him!

But the call had served a purpose. Somehow it put the scene with Polly in the perspective of ridicule. To think of the woman sitting in her frowsy little apartment, trembling over her dingy affairs of more than ten years ago! To think she was afraid he had bled and battled for seven years because of that!

He thought about it for a moment, then shrugged. "Well, anyway, I bet it did her good."

And now he was hungry.

He thought of having a meal sent up, just to avoid a possible rendezvous with another of Stephanson's ball-throwers but decided against it. If Stephanson was really hunting him seriously, it would not be much of a job to have something put into the food he was sent. He'd be much safer eating in a restaurant chosen at random.

Besides, a few bright lights, a little gaiety, would be really welcome. This was his first night of freedom – and he had to wash that Polly taste out of his mouth.

He checked the corridor carefully before going out. There was nothing, but the action reminded him of a tiny planet near Vega where you made exactly the same precautionary gesture every time you emerged from one of the tunnels formed by the long, parallel lines of moist, carboniferous ferns.

Because if you didn't – well, there was an enormous leech like mollusc that might be waiting there, a creature which could flip chunks of shell with prodigious force. The shell merely stunned its prey, but stunned it long enough for the leech to get in close.

And that leech could empty a man in ten minutes flat.

Once he'd been hit by a fragment of shell, and while he'd been lying there, Henck – Good old Blotto Otto! Crandall smiled. Was it possible that the two of them would look back on those hideous adventures, one day, with actual nostalgia, the kind of beery, pleasant memories that soldiers develop after even the ugliest of wars? Well, and if they did, they hadn't gone through them for the sake of fat cats like Mr. Edward Ballaskia and his sanctified dreams of evil.

Nor, when you came right down to it, for dismal little frightened trollops like Polly.

Frederick Stoddard Stephanson. Frederick Stoddard –

Somebody put an arm on his shoulder and he came to, realizing that he was halfway through the lobby.

"Nick," said a rather familiar voice.

Crandall squinted at the face at the end of the arm. That slight, pointed beard – he didn't know anyone with a beard like that, but the eyes looked so terribly familiar . . .

"Nick," said the man with the beard. "I couldn't do it."

Those eyes – of course, it was his younger brother!

"Dan!" he shouted.

"It's me all right. Here." Something clattered to the floor. Crandall looked down and saw a blaster lying on the rug, a larger and much more expensive blaster than the one he was carrying. *Why was Dan toting a blaster? Who was after Dan?*

With the thought, there came half-understanding. And there was fear – fear of the words that might come pouring out of the mouth of a brother whom he had not seen for all these years . . .

"I could have killed you from the moment you walked into the lobby," Dan was saying. "You weren't out of the sights for a second. But I want you to know, Nick, that the post-criminal sentence wasn't the reason I froze on the firing button."

"No?" Crandall asked in a breath that was exhaled slowly through a retroactive lifetime.

"I just couldn't stand adding any more guilt about you. Ever since that business with Polly – "

"With Polly. Yes, of course, with Polly." Something seemed to hang like a weight from the point of his jaw; it pulled his head down and his mouth open. "With Polly. That business with Polly."

Dan punched his fist into an open palm twice. "I knew you'd come looking for me sooner or later. I almost went crazy waiting – and I did go nearly crazy with guilt. But I never figured you'd do it this way, Nick. Seven years to wait for you to come hack!"

"That's why you never wrote to me, Dan?"

"What did I have to say? What *is* there to say? I thought I loved her, but I found out what I meant to her as soon as she was divorced. I guess I always wanted what was yours because you were my older brother, Nick. That's the only excuse I can offer and I know exactly what it's worth. Because I know what you and Polly had together, what I broke up as a kind of big practical joke. But one thing, Nick: I won't kill you and I won't defend myself. I'm too tired. I'm too guilty. You know where to find me. Anytime, Nick."

He turned and strode rapidly through the lobby, the metal spangles that were this year's high masculine fashion glittering on his calves. He didn't look back, even when he was walking past the other side of the clear plastic that enclosed the lobby.

Crandall watched him go, then said "Hm" to himself in a lonely kind of way. He reached down, retrieved the other blaster and went out to find a restaurant.

As he sat, poking around in the spiced Venusian food that wasn't one-tenth as good as he had remembered it, he kept thinking about Polly and Dan. The incidents – he could remember incidents galore, now that he had a couple of pegs on which to hang them. To think he'd never suspected – but who could suspect Polly, who could suspect Dan?

He pulled the prison discharge out of his pocket and studied it. *Having duly served a maximum penal sentence of seven years, discounted from fourteen years, Nicholas Crandall is herewith discharged in a pre-criminal status –*

– to murder his ex-wife, Polly Crandall?

– to murder his younger brother, Daniel Crandall?

Ridiculous!

But they hadn't found it so ridiculous. Both of them, so blissfully secure in their guilt, so egotistically certain that they and they alone were the objects of a hatred intense enough to endure the worst that the Galaxy had to offer in order to attain vengeance – why, they had both been so positive that their normal and already demonstrated cunning had deserted them and they had completely misread the warmth in his eyes! Either one could have switched confessions in mid-explanation. If they had only not been so preoccupied with self and had noted his astonishment in time, either or both of them could still be deceiving him!

Out of the corner of his eye, he saw that a woman was standing near his table. She had been reading his discharge over his shoulder. He leaned back and took her in while she stood and smiled at him.

She was fantastically beautiful. That is, she had everything a woman needs for great beauty – figure, facial structure, complexion, carriage, eyes, hair, all these to perfection – but she had those other final touches that, as in all kinds of art, make the difference between a merely great work and an all-time masterpiece. Those final touches included such things as sufficient wealth to create the ultimate setting in coiffure and gown, as well as the single Saturnian *paeaea* stone glowing in priceless black splendor between her breasts. Those final touches included the substantial feminine intelligence that beat in her steady eyes; and the somewhat overbred, overindulged, overspoiled quality mixed in with it was the very last piquant fillip of a positively brilliant composition in the human medium.

"May I sit with you, Mr. Crandall?" she asked in a voice of which no more could be said than that it fitted the rest of her.

Rather amused, but more exhilarated than amused, he slid over on the restaurant couch. She sat down like an empress taking her throne before the eyes of a hundred tributary kings.

Crandall knew, within approximate limits, who she was and what she wanted. She was either a reigning post-debutante from the highest social circles in the System, or a theatrical star newly arrived and still in a state of nova.

And he, as a just-discharged convict, with the power of life and death in his hands, represented a taste she had not yet been able to indulge but was determined to enjoy.

Well, in a sense it wasn't flattering, but a woman like this could only fall to the lot of an ordinary man in very exceptional circumstances; he might as well take advantage of his status. He would satisfy her whim, while she, on his first night of freedom –

"That's your discharge, isn't it?" she asked and looked at it again. There was a moistness about her upper lip as she studied it – what a strange, sense-weary patina for one so splendidly young!

"Tell me, Mr. Crandall," she asked at last, turning to him with the wet pinpoints on her lip more brilliant than ever. "You've served a pre-criminal sentence for murder. It is true, is it not, that the punishment for murder and the most brutal, degraded rape imaginable are exactly the same?"

After a long silence, Crandall called for his check and walked out of the restaurant.

He had subsided enough when he reached the hotel to stroll with care around the transparent lobby housing. No one who looked like a Stephanson trigger man was in sight, although Stephanson was a cautious gambler. One attempt having failed, he'd be unlikely to try another for some time.

But that girl! And Edward Ballaskia!

There was a message in his box. Someone had called, leaving only a number to be called back.

Now what? he wondered as he went back up to his room. Stephanson making overtures? Or some unhappy mother wanting him to murder her incurable child?

He gave the number to the set and sat down to watch the screen with a good deal of curiosity.

It flickered – a face took shape on it. Crandall barely restrained a cry of delight. He did have a friend in this city from pre-convict days. Good old dependable, plodding, realistic Irv. His old partner.

And then, just as he was about to shout an enthusiastic greeting, he locked it inside his mouth. Too many things had happened today. And there was something about the expression on Irv's face . . .

"Listen, Nick," Irv said heavily at last. "I just want to ask you one question."

"What's that, Irv?" Crandall kept himself rock-steady.

"How long have you known? When did you find out?"

Crandall ran through several possible answers in his mind, finally selecting one. "A long time now, Irv. I just wasn't in a position to do anything about it."

Irv nodded. "That's what I thought. Well, listen, I'm not going to plead with you. I know that after seven years of what you've gone through, pleading isn't going to do me any good. But, believe me or not, I didn't start dipping into the till very much until my wife got sick. My personal funds were exhausted. I couldn't borrow any more, and you were too busy with your own domestic troubles to be bothered. Then, when business started to get better, I wanted to prevent a sudden large discrepancy on the books.

"So I continued milking the business, not for hospital expenses any more and not to deceive you, Nick – really! – but just so you wouldn't find out how much I'd taken from it before. When you came to me and said you were completely discouraged and wanted out – well, there I'll admit I was a louse. I should have told you. But after all, we hadn't been doing too well as partners and I saw a chance to get the whole business in my name and on its feet, so I – I – "

"So you bought me out for three hundred and twenty credits," Crandall finished for him. "How much is the firm worth now, Irv?"

The other man averted his eyes. "Close to a million. But listen, Nick, business has been terrific this past year in the wholesale line. I didn't cheat you out of all that! Listen, Nick – "

Crandall blew a snort of grim amusement through his nostrils. "What is it, Irv?"

Irv drew out a clean tissue and wiped his forehead. "Nick," he said, leaning forward and trying hard to smile winningly. "Listen to me, Nick! You forget about it, you stop hunting me down, and I've got a proposition for you. I need a man with your technical know-how in top management. I'll give you a twenty per cent interest in the business, Nick – no, make it twenty-five per cent. Look, I'll go as high as thirty per cent–thirty-*five* per cent – "

"Do you think that would make up for those seven years?"

Irv waved trembling, conciliatory hands. "No, of course not, Nick. Nothing would. But listen, Nick. I'll make it forty-five per – "

Crandall shut him off. He sat for a while, then got up and walked around the room. He stopped and examined his blasters, the one he'd purchased earlier and the one he'd gotten from Dan. He took out his prison discharge and read it through carefully. Then he shoved it back into the tunic pocket.

He notified the switchboard that he wanted a long-distance Earthside call put through.

"Yes, sir. But there's a gentleman to see you, sir. A Mr. Otto Henck."

"Send him up. And put the call in on my screen as soon as it goes through, please, Miss."

A few moments later, Blotto Otto entered his room. He was drunk, but carried it, as he always did, remarkably well.

"What do you think, Nick? What the hell do you – "

"Sh-h-h," Crandall warned him. "My call's coming in."

The Tibetan operator said, "Go ahead, New York," and Frederick Stoddard Stephanson appeared on the screen. The man had aged more than any of the others Crandall had seen tonight. Although you never could tell with Stephanson: he always looked older when he was working out a complex deal.

Stephanson didn't say anything; he merely pursed his lips at Crandall and waited. Behind him and around him was a TV Spectacular's idea of a hunting lodge.

"All right, Freddy," Crandall said. "What I have to say won't take long. You might as well call off your dogs and stop taking chances trying to kill and/or injure me. As of this moment, I don't even have a grudge against you."

"You don't even have a grudge – " Stephanson regained his rigid self-control. "Why not?"

"Because – oh, because a lot of things. Because killing you just wouldn't be seven hellish years of satisfaction, now that I'm face to face with it. And because you didn't do any more to me than practically everybody else has done – from the cradle, for all I know. Because I've decided I'm a natural born sucker: that's just the way I'm constructed. All you did was take your kind of advantage of my kind of construction."

Stephanson leaned forward, peered intently, then relaxed and crossed his arms. "You're actually telling the truth!"

"Of course I'm telling the truth! You see these?" He held up the two blasters. "I'm getting rid of these tonight. From now on, I'll be unarmed. I don't want to have the least thing to do with weighing human life in the balance."

The other man ran an index nail under a thumb nail thoughtfully a couple of times. "I'll tell you what," he said. "If you mean what you say – and I think you do – maybe we can work out something. An arrangement, say, to pay you a bit – We'll see."

"When you don't have to?" Crandall was astonished. "But why didn't you make me an offer before this?"

"Because I don't like to be forced to do anything. Up to now, I was fighting force with more force."

Crandall considered the point. "I don't get it. But maybe that's the way you're constructed. Well, we'll see, as you said."

When he rose to face Henck, the little man was still shaking his head slowly, dazedly, intent only on his own problem. "What do you think, Nick? Elsa went on a sightseeing jaunt to the Moon last month. The line to her oxygen helmet got clogged, see, and she died of suffocation before they could do anything about it. Isn't that a *hell* of thing, Nick? One month before I finish my sentence – she couldn't wait one lousy little month! I bet she died laughing at me!"

Crandall put his arm around him. "Let's go out for a walk, Blotto Otto. We both need the exercise."

Funny how the capacity for murder affected people, he thought. There was Polly's way – and Dan's. There was old Irv bargaining frantically but still shrewdly for his life. Mr. Edward Ballaskia – and that girl in the restaurant. And there was Freddy Stephanson, the only intended-victim – and the only one who wouldn't beg.

He wouldn't beg, but he might be willing to hand out largesse. Could Crandall accept what amounted to charity from Stephanson? He shrugged. Who knew what he or anyone else could or could not do?

"What do we do now, Nick?" Blotto Otto was demanding petulantly once they got outside the hotel. "That's what I want to know – what do we do?"

"Well, I'm going to do this," Crandall told him, taking a blaster in each hand. "Just this." He threw the gleaming weapons, right hand, left hand, at the transparent window walls that ran around the luxurious lobby of the Ritz-Capricorn. They struck *thunk* and then *thunk* again. The windows crashed down in long, pointed daggers. The people in the lobby swung around with their mouths open.

A policeman ran up, his badge jingling against his metallic uniform. He seized Crandall.

"I saw you! I saw you do that! You'll get thirty days for it!"

"Hm," said Crandall. "Thirty days?" He pulled his prison discharge out of his pocket and handed it to the policeman. "I tell you what we'll do, officer – Just punch the proper number of holes in this document or tear off what seems to you a proportionately sized coupon. Either or both. Handle it any way you like."

Good Night, Sophie

LINO ALDANI

(Translated by L. K. Conrad)

Lino Aldani (1926–) is an Italian writer who is principally known for his science fiction. He is the author of a pioneering study on science fiction, *La fantascienza* (1962), the first of its kind to appear in Italy.

He began publishing SF stories in the magazine *Oltre il Cielo* in 1960, under the pseudonym of N. L. Janda. In 1963 he founded and edited, with Massimo Lo Jacono and Giulio Raiola, the magazine *Futuro,* featuring exclusively science fiction written by Italian authors. In 1964 he published his first collection, *Quarta dimensione,* and continued to sell stories to various magazines and anthologies, developing an individual style mixing traditional SF tropes and striking extrapolations with literate prose and a distinctive feel for realism. For this reason, his fiction can often be compared to that of better known Italian literary fantasists writing outside the SF genre. His situation, writing in the land of Italo Calvino and Dino Buzzati, has been analogous to the situation of, say, John Wyndham or Brian W. Aldiss publishing science fiction in the land of Aldous Huxley and George Orwell. Literary fashion seems to dictate that it matters more how and where you publish it, what class signals it gives off, than what it actually is.

Lino Aldani lived in Rome until 1968, when he decided to return to his native town. He had a variety of occupations, ranging from office worker to bartender, and later taught philosophy and mathematics in high school. He also served as mayor of his native town.

Aldani has never been a prolific writer, and only in 1977 published his first novel, *Quando le radici.* Two years later it was followed by the novella

Eclissi 2000 (included in a collection with the same title). In 1985 he published *Nel segno della luna bianca,* written in collaboration with Daniela Piegai, a skilled and enjoyable fantasy novel where his distinctive voice displays new overtones. A new collection of his short fiction appeared in 1987, *Parabole per domani.* His story "Quo Vadis Francisco?" was included in *The Penguin World Omnibus of Science Fiction* (1986), edited by Brian W. Aldiss and Sam J. Lundwall. He later developed it into his most recent novel, *La croce di ghiaccio,* published in 1989. His works have been translated worldwide and are well known in France, Germany, Russia, Japan, Spain, The Netherlands, and nearly all of Eastern Europe. He is surely the Italian SF genre writer who is best known abroad.

Grey and blue overalls were running along the street. Grey and blue, no other colors. There were no stores, no agencies, there wasn't a single soda-fountain, or a window full of toys, or even a perfume store. Once in a while, on the fronts covered with soot, incrusted with rubbish and moss, the revolving door of a shop opened. Inside was dreamland: Oneirofilm, happiness within everybody's reach, to fit everybody's pocketbook; inside was Sophie Barlow, nude, for anyone who wanted to buy her.

There were seven of them and they were closing in from all sides. He swung violently, hitting one of them in the jaw, which sent him tumbling down the green marble staircase. Another, tall and brawny, appeared below, brandishing a bludgeon. He dodged the blow by hunching quickly, then grabbed the slave by the waist, hurling him against a column of the temple. Then, while he was trying to corner a third one, a vise of iron seized his neck. He tried to free himself, but another slave tackled his legs, and still another immobilized his left arm.

He was dragged away bodily. From the depths of the enormous cavern came the rhythmical notes of the sitars and tablas, an enervating, obsessive music, full of long quavers.

They tied him naked in front of the altar. Then the slaves fled into the galleries that opened like eye-sockets of skulls in the walls of the cavern. The air was filled with the smell of resin, a strong odor of musk and nard, and aphrodisiac atmosphere emitted by the burning torches, tripods and braziers.

When the dancing virgins appeared, the music stopped for a

moment, then took up again, more intensely, accompanied by a distant choir of feminine voices.

It was an orgiastic, inebriating dance. The virgins passed by him one by one, they grazed his stomach, face and chest with their light veils and the long, soft feathers of their headdresses. Diadems and necklaces flashed in the half-light.

At the end the veils fell, slowly, one at a time. He saw the swelling of their breasts, almost felt the softness of all those limbs that were moving in front of him in a tangle of unsated desire.

Then, the long, freezing sound of a gong interrupted the dance. The music ceased. The dancers, like guilt-ridden phantoms, disappeared in the depths of the cave, and in the profound silence the priestess appeared, exceedingly beautiful, wrapped in a leopard cape. She had small bare pink feet, and between her hands clasped a long bluish knife. Her eyes, black, deep, constantly shifting, seemed to search his soul.

How long did the intolerable wait last? The knife cut his bonds with devastating slowness, her great black eyes, moist and desirous, continued to stare at him, while a jumble of words, whispering, murmuring, came to his ears in a persuasive, enticing rhythm.

She dragged him to the foot of the altar. The leopard cape slid to earth, she stretched out languidly and drew him to herself with a gesture at once sweet and imperious.

In the cavern, a conch shell of sounds and shadows, the world came and went in an ebb and flow of sighs.

Bradley turned off the machine and removed the plastic helmet. He came out of the booth, his hands and forehead damp with sweat, his breathing heavy, his pulse accelerated.

Twenty technicians, the director and the principal actress rushed to the supervisor, impatiently surrounding him. Bradley's eyes moved around, looking for an armchair.

"I want a glass of water," he said.

He stretched out gingerly on an air cushion with a long, sloping back, drying the beads of perspiration, and breathing deeply. A technician made his way through the group and handed Bradley a glass, which he emptied in one gulp.

"Well? What do you think of it?" the director asked anxiously.

Bradley waved impatiently, then shook his head. "We're not there yet, Gustafson."

Sophie Barlow lowered her eyes. Bradley touched her hand.

"It has nothing to do with you, Sophie. You were terrific. I . . . only a great actress could have created that last embrace. But the Oneirofilm itself is artificial, unharmonious, unbalanced . . ."

"What's wrong with it?" the director asked.

"Gustafson! I said the film is *unharmonious*, don't you understand?"

"I heard you. You say it's 'unharmonious,' unbalanced. Okay, the music is Indian, four hundred years old, and the costumes are from central Africa. But the consumer isn't going to notice such subtleties, what interests him is – "

Gustafson! The customer is always right, never forget that. Anyway, this has nothing to do with music or costumes. The problem is something else: this Oneirofilm would rattle even a bull's nerves!"

Gustafson frowned.

"Give me the script," said Bradley, "and call the aesthetic technician."

He rifled back and forth through the pages, muttering unintelligibly, as if to reconnect the ideas.

"All right," he said at last, closing the bundle of pages suddenly. "The film starts with a long canoe trip, the protagonist is alone in a hostile, strange world, there's a struggle with the river's crocodiles, and the canoe capsizes. Then we have a trek through the jungle, rather tiring, a hand-to-hand fight with the natives. The protagonist is shut up in a hut, but during the night the chieftain's daughter Aloa comes in, and provides him with directions to the temple. Then there's the embrace with Aloa in the moonlight. Speaking of which, where's Moa Mohagry?"

The technician and the director moved apart, and Moa Mohagry, a very tall Somalian woman with sculpturesque curves, stepped forward.

"You were great, Moa, but we're going to have to do the scene over again."

"Again?" Moa exclaimed. "I could do the scene over a hundred times, but I doubt it would get any better. I really gave it all I had, Bradley . . ."

"That's exactly what Gustafson's mistake was. In this Oneirofilm the major scene is the last one, when the priestess seduces the protagonist. All the other scenes are going to have to be toned down – they should serve as atmosphere and preparation. You can't make an Oneirofilm composed of nothing but major scenes."

He turned to the aesthetic technician.

"What's the sensitivity index in the median sampling?"

"In Aloa's scene?"

"Yes, in Aloa's scene."

"84.5."

"And in the scene of the last embrace?"

"Just under 97."

Bradley shook his head.

"Theoretically it would be okay, but in practice it's all wrong. This morning I screened the scenes in the first part, one at a time. They're perfect. But the film doesn't end on the riverbank when Aloa gives herself to the protagonist. There are other, rather tiring episodes: the ones I just screened, then another trek through the jungle, and the fight with the slaves in the temple. By the time the consumer gets to this point in the film, he's exhausted, his sensory receptivity is down to a minimum. The virgins' erotic dance only partly solves the problem. I saw the film in two takes, and so I was able to appreciate the last embrace with Sophie in all its stylistic perfection. But, please, let's not mix up absolute index with relative index. The crucial thing is relative index. I'm positive that if we distributed the film the way it's put together now, the total receptivity index would fall by at least forty points, in spite of Sophie's performance."

"Bradley!" the director implored. "Now you're exaggerating."

"I'm not exaggerating," the supervisor insisted in a polemical tone. "I repeat, the last scene is a masterpiece, but the consumer gets there tired and already satisfied, in such a condition that even the most luscious fruit would taste insipid to him. Gustafson, you can't expect Sophie to accomplish miracles. The human nervous system has limits and laws."

"Then what should we do?"

"Listen to me, Gustafson. I was a director for twenty-five years, and for six years I've been a supervisor. I think I've had enough experience to give you some advice. If you leave this Oneirofilm the way it is, I won't pass it. I can't. Beyond not pleasing the public, I would risk undermining the career of an actress like Sophie Barlow. Pay attention to me, dilute all the scenes except the last, cut the embrace with Aloa, reduce it to a mere scuffle."

Moa Mohagry started angrily. Bradley took her wrist and forced her to sit on the arm of his chair.

"Listen to me, Moa. Don't think that I want to take away the right moment for you to make a big hit. You have talent, I know it. The riverbank episode shows true zeal and temperament, there's an innocent primitive passion there that would not fail to fascinate the consumer. You were fantastic, Moa. But I can't ruin a film that's cost millions, you understand, don't you? I'm going to suggest to the production committee a couple of films that will star you, Moa. There are millions and millions of consumers who go mad for Oneirofilms in a primitive setting. You'll make a big hit, too, I promise you. But not right now, it's not the right moment . . ."

Bradley got up. He felt faint, his legs weak and tired.

"Please, Gustafson. Also tone down the slaves' fight episode. Too much movement, too much violence. The waste of energy is enormous . . ."

He went tottering off, surrounded by technicians.

"Where's Sophie?" he asked as he got to the back of the room. Sophie Barlow smiled at him.

"Come in my office," he said. "I have to talk to you."

"All right, I'm not saying anything new, they're old words, stale, you must have heard them a hundred times at school and during your training course. But it would benefit you to give them some thought."

Bradley was walking back and fourth in the room, slowly, his fingers laced together behind his back. Sophie Barlow was slouched in an armchair. From time to time she stretched out a leg and stared at the toe of her shoe.

Bradley stopped for a moment in front of her.

"What's the matter with you, Sophie? Are you having a crisis?"

The woman made a nervous, awkward gesture. "Having a crisis? Me?"

"Yes. That's why I called you into the office. You know, I don't want to read you the riot act. I simply want to remind you of the fundamental precepts of our system. I'm not young any more, Sophie. There are things I can spot right off, at the first sign. Sophie! you're running after a chimera!"

Sophie Barlow squinted and then opened her eyes wide as a cat's.

"A chimera? What's a chimera, Bradley?"

"I told you, I can spot some things right off. You're having a crisis, Sophie. I wouldn't be surprised if it had something to do with the propaganda that those pigs at the Anti-Dream League put out by the truckload to undermine our social order."

Sophie seemed not to pick up the insinuation. She said:

"Was Moa's performance really that good?"

Bradley passed a hand behind his neck. "Absolutely. Mohagry will make it big, I'm convinced of it . . ."

"Better than mine?"

Bradley snorted. "That's a meaningless question."

"I made myself clear. I want to know which of us you liked better, me or Moa."

"And I repeat, your question is idiotic, lacks common sense, and just goes to confirm my suspicion – in fact, my conviction – that you're going through a crisis. You'll get over it, Sophie. All actresses go through this phase sooner or later. It seems to be a necessary stage . . ."

"I would like to know just one thing, Bradley. Something that's never said in the schools, something nobody ever talks about. *Before*. What was there before? Was everybody really unhappy?"

Bradley took up pacing around the armchair.

"Before, there was chaos."

"Bradley! I want to know if they were really unhappy."

The man stretched out his arms disconsolately.

"I don't know, Sophie. I didn't exist at the time, I wasn't born yet. One thing is sure: if the system has asserted itself, it means that objective conditions have allowed it to do so. I would like you to be aware of one very simple fact: technology has permitted the realization of all our desires, even the most secret ones. Technology, progress, the perfection of instruments and the exact knowledge of our own minds, of our own egos . . . all of that is real, tangible. Hence even our dreams are real. Sophie, don't forget that only in very rare cases is the Oneirofilm an instrument of comfort or compensation. Almost always it is an end in itself, and when just now I had you, I enjoyed your body, your words, and your odors amid a play of exotic emotions."

"Yes, but it's always artificial . . ."

"Okay, but I wasn't aware of it. And then, even the meaning of words evolves. You use the word *artificial* in the pejorative sense it had two centuries ago. But not today, today an artificial product is no longer a surrogate, Sophie. A fluorescent lamp, correctly adjusted, gives better light than the sun. This is true of the Oneirofilm as well."

Sophie Barlow looked at her fingernails.

"When did it begin, Bradley?"

"What?"

"The system."

"Eighty-five years it's been now, as you should know."

"I do, but I mean the *dreams*. When did men begin to prefer them to reality?"

Bradley squeezed his nose, as if to collect his thoughts.

"Cinematography began to develop at the beginning of the twentieth century. At first it was a question of two-dimensional images moving on a white screen. Then, sound, the panoramic screen, color photography were introduced. The consumers gathered by the hundreds in special projection halls to watch and listen, but they never *felt* the film, at most they experienced a latent participation through an effort of fantasy. Obviously the film was a surrogate, a real and proper artifice for titillating the erotic and adventurous taste of the public. However, movie-making then represented a very powerful instrument of psycho-social transformation. Women of that period felt the need of imitating actresses in their gestures, vocal inflections, dress. This was no less true of men. Life was lived according to the movies. First the economy was conditioned by it: the enormous demand for consumer goods – clothes, cars, comfortable housing – was of course due to real exigencies of nature, but also and above all to the ruthless, indefatigable advertising that harassed and seduced the consumer every minute of the day. Even then, men longed for the dream, were obsessed by it, day and night, but they were far from achieving it."

"They were unhappy, right?"

"I repeat, I don't know. I'm only trying to illustrate for you the stages of the process. Toward the middle of the twentieth century the standard woman, the standard situation was already in existence. It's true that there were directors and producers in those days that tried to produce cultural films, ideological movies, to communicate ideas and elevate the masses. But the phenomenon lasted only a short time. In 1956 scientists discovered the pleasure centers in the brain, and through experimentation revealed that electric stimulation of a certain part of the cortex produces an intense, voluptuous reaction in the subject. It was twenty years before the benefits of this discovery were made available to the public. The projection of the first three-dimensional movie with partial spectator participation signalled the death of the intellectual film. Now the public could experience odors and emotions; they could already partly identify with what was happening on the screen. The entire economy underwent an unprecedented transformation. The human race was starved for pleasure, luxury and power, and only asked to be satisfied at the cost of a few pennies."

"And the Oneirofilm?"

"The Oneirofilm came out, fully perfected, only a few years later. There's no reality that surpasses dreams, and the public became convinced of this very quickly. When participation is total, any competition from nature is ridiculous, any rebellion useless. If the product is perfect, the consumer is happy and the society is stable. That's the system, Sophie. And certainly your temporary crises are not likely to change it, not even the melodramatic chatter of the Naturists, unscrupulous people who go around collecting funds for the triumph of an idea that is unbalanced to start with, but for their own personal profit. If you want a good laugh – last week Herman Wolfried, one of the leaders of the Anti-Dream League, appeared in the offices of the Norfolk Company. And do you want to know why? He wanted a private Oneirofilm, five famous actresses in a mind-blowing orgy. Norfolk has accepted the commission and Wolfried is paying for it through the nose, so much the worse for him."

Sophie Barlow jumped up.

"You're lying, Bradley! You're lying on purpose, shamelessly."

"I have proof, Sophie. The Anti-Dream League is an organization out to dupe simpletons, incurable hypochondriacs and passéists. Perhaps there is some remnant of religious sentiment behind it, but at the center of it is only greed."

Sophie was on the verge of tears. Bradley moved toward her solicitously and put his hands on her shoulders in a tender, protective gesture.

"Don't think about it any more, Sophie."

He guided her over to the desk, opened the safe, and got out a small, flat, rectangular box.

"Here," said Bradley.

"What is it?"

"A present."

"For me?"

"Yes, actually it was to give you this that I called you into the office. You've made twenty Oneirofilms for our production company, an inspiring goal, as it were. The firm is honoring you with a small recognition of your worth . . ."

Sophie started to unwrap the present.

"Leave it," Bradley said. "You can open it at home. Run along now, I have a lot to do."

There was a line of helitaxis just outside the building. Sophie got into the first one, took a magazine from the side pocket of the vehicle, lit a cigarette and, flattered, contemplated her own face on the front cover. The helitaxi rose softly, steering for the center of the city.

Her lips were half-open in an attitude of offering, the color, the contrast between light and shadow, the expression ambiguous . . . Each detail seemed knowingly graded.

Sophie looked at herself as if in a mirror. At one time the job of acting had presented various negative aspects. When she made a love scene, there was a flesh and blood "partner," and she had to embrace him, tolerate the physical contact, kisses, words breathed straight into her face. The camera photographed the scene which the spectators then later saw on the screen. Now it was different. There was "Adam," the mannequin packed with electronic devices having two minute cameras conveniently placed in his eyes. "Adam" was a wonder of receptivity: if the actress caressed him, the receptivity valve registered the sensation of the caress and fixed it, together with the visual image, on the reel of Oneirofilm. Thus the consumer who would later use that reel would perceive the caress in all its sensory fidelity. The spectator was no longer passive but the protagonist.

Naturally, there were Oneirofilms for men and Oneirofilms for women. And they were not interchangeable: if a male consumer, plagued by morbid curiosity, inserted in his reception helmet a reel meant for female consumption, he would get an atrocious headache, and also risk short-circuiting the delicate wiring of the apparatus.

Sophie told the pilot to stop. The helitaxi had gone barely a dozen blocks, but Sophie decided to proceed on foot.

Grey and blue overalls were running along the street. Grey and blue, no other colors. There were no stores, no agencies, there wasn't a single soda-fountain, or a window full of toys, or even a perfume store. Once in a while, on the fronts covered with soot, incrusted with rubbish and moss, the revolving door of a shop opened. Inside, on the smooth glass counters, there was the *dream*, happiness for everybody, for all pocketbooks, and it was Sophie herself, nude, for anybody who wanted to have her.

They marched on. And Sophie Barlow marched along with them, an army of hallucinated people, people who worked three hours a day, prey to the spasms that the silence of their own shells yearned for: a room, an Amplex and a helmet. And reel after reel of Oneirofilms, millions of dreams of love, power and fame.

In the middle of the square, on a large platform draped in green, the fat man was gesticulating emphatically.

"Citizens!"

His voice raised itself as loud and clear as a dream speech, when the dreamer has the whole world singing hosannas at his feet.

"Citizens! An ancient philosopher once said that virtue is a habit. I am not here to ask the impossible of you. I would be a fool if I expected to renounce it immediately and completely. For years we have been slaves and succubuses, prisoners in the labyrinth of dreams, for years we have been groping in the dense darkness of uncommunicativeness and isolation. Citizens, I invite you to be free. Freedom is virtue, and virtue is a habit. We have cheated nature too long, we must rush to make amends, before we arrive at a total and definite death of the soul . . ."

How many times had she listened to speeches like that? The propaganda of the Anti-Dream League was sickening, it had always produced in her a profound sense of irritation. Lately, however, she had surprised and bewildered herself. Perhaps because she was an actress, when the orators in the squares spoke of sin, perdition, when they incited the crowds of consumers to abandon the "dream," she took the accusation as if it had been personally aimed at her; she felt a responsibility for the whole system. Perhaps behind the orators' emphatic tone there actually was some truth. Perhaps they hadn't told her everything at school. Maybe Bradley was wrong.

On the platform the fat man ranted and raved, pounding his fist on the wood of the lectern, red in the face, congested. Not a soul was listening to him.

When the veiled girl came out of a small side door, there were some in the crowd who stopped for a second. From the loudspeakers issued the sound of ancient oriental music. The girl began to take off her veils, dancing. She was pretty, very young, and made syncopated, light, eurhythmic gestures.

"An amateur," Sophie said to herself. "A would-be actress . . ."

When she was standing naked in the center of the platform, even the few men who had stopped to wait moved on. One or two of them laughed, and shook their heads, disappointed.

The Anti-Dream League girls stopped the passers-by, they approached the men, thrusting out their breasts in an absurd, pathetic offer.

Sophie lengthened her stride. But someone stopped her, grabbing her arm. It was a tall, dark young man, who stared at her with steady black eyes.

"What do you want?"

"To make you a proposition."

"Speak up."

"Come with me, tonight."

Sophie burst out laughing.

"With you! What for? What would I get out of it?"

The young man smiled faintly, patiently, a smile tinged with security and superiority. Clearly he was accustomed to this sort of refusal.

"Nothing," he admitted unperturbed. "But our duty is to – "

"Cut it out. We'd spend the night insulting each other, in a pitiful attempt to achieve 'natural harmony' . . . Dear boy, your friend up there on the platform is spewing forth a pile of nonsense."

"It's not nonsense," the young man retorted. "Virtue is a habit. I could – "

"No, you couldn't. You couldn't because you don't want me, and you don't want me because I'm real, true, living, human, because I would be a surrogate, a substitute for a reel of Oneirofilm which you could buy for a few pennies. And you? What could you offer me? Silly presumptuous young ass!"

"Wait! Listen to me, I beg of you – "

"Good-bye," Sophie cut him short. And continued her walk.

The words she aimed at the young man had been too harsh. It had been a uselessly hostile reaction; she might have rejected his proposition neither more nor less vehemently than the other passers-by did, with some grace, or better, with a self-sufficient smile. In the last analysis, what right did she have to insult him, perhaps to hurt his feelings? He was acting in good faith. But what about the leaders? Bradley had assured her a number of times that the directors of the Anti-Dream League were a band of swine. What if Bradley had been lying to her all along?

The suspicion had now been plaguing her for several weeks. All those speeches in the squares, the manifestos on the walks, the propagandistic pamphlets, the public proposition to experiment in natural relations with the League's activists . . . Was it possible that the whole thing was a lie? Perhaps there was some truth in what the orators and lecturers maintained, maybe the world was rotten to the core, and only a few enlightened men had eyes to see the horror and to assess such decadence.

Man as an island: they had all been reduced to this. On one side the producing class, a class that kept power and to which she herself belonged in her capacity of actress; on the other, the prostrate, blind army of consumers, men and women avid for solitude and darkness, silkworms coiled up in the silken filaments of their own dreams, pale bloodless larvae poisoned by inaction.

Sophie had been born in the glass. So had everybody else, for that matter. She did not know her mother. Millions of women, once a month, went to the Bank of Life; millions of men achieved orgasm by means of the Dream and donated semen to the Bank, which sorted it carefully and used it according to rigorous criteria. Marriage was an archaic institution. Sophie had been the child of a dream, of an unknown, anonymous man who in a dream had possessed an actress. Every man over forty could be her father, every woman between the age of forty and eighty her mother.

When she was younger, this thought had disturbed her greatly, then bit by bit she had got used to it. But lately all the doubts and anxieties of her adolescence had reared up again, vultures that patiently circled above, waiting for one of her moments of weakness. Who was that young man who had stopped her on the street? A champion of superior humanity, or a fool?

Certainly, if he had said to her, "I recognize you, Sophie Barlow. I recognize you in spite of your standard suit and your dark glasses." Or if he had said, "You're my favorite star, you're the obsession of all my days . . ." Or even if he'd said, "I want to get to know you, whoever you are, just as you really are . . ."

Instead, that lout had talked about duty. He had asked her to spend the night with him, but only to pay obeisance to the presumptuous new morality: Virtue is a habit. A habit, a routine of natural relations. Love one another, ladies and gentlemen, come together in self-denial! Each of your acts of love will contribute to the defeat and destruction of an unjust system. Unite yourselves, come together in reality, the sublime joy of the senses will not delay in manifesting itself! An exultation of sounds and lights will fill your souls, will glorify your bodies! And our children will once again be formed in the warmth of the womb, not in the cold glass of a test tube. – Wasn't this what the fat man on the platform had been preaching?

She went into a crowded store and made her way over to the sales counter, where hundreds and hundreds of Oneirofilms were neatly displayed, packed in elegant plastic boxes. She loved to read the descriptions printed on the covers, to listen to the conversations that the shoppers sometimes had with each other, or the zealous advice that the salesmen whispered in the ears of undecided customers.

She read a few titles.

Singapore: Eurasian singer (Milena Chung Lin) flees with the Spectator. Adventure in the underworld of this eastern port. Period, mid twentieth century. Night of love on a sampan.

The Battle: In the role of a heroic officer, the Spectator infiltrates an enemy encampment and sabotages its munitions dump. A last battle, bloody, victorious.

Ecstasy: The private jet of a Persian princess (masterful performance by Sophie Barlow) crashes in the Grand Canyon. Princess and Pilot (the Spectator) spend the night in a cave.

Descriptions in greater detail were to be found inside the boxes.

There was no danger that an exact knowledge of the contents on the part of the consumer would lower its desirability index. Mental projection inside the Amplex was accompanied by catatonic stupor in which the memory of each independent episode never connected with the next to form a whole. One could not know, experiencing the first episode, what would happen in the second and following episodes. Even if plot descriptions were learned by heart, even if one saw the same film twenty times, the conscious ego, the everyday ego was sacrificed to the urges provoked by the reel: one ceased to be oneself in order to assume the personality, the mannerisms, the voice, the impulses suggested by the film.

A salesman sidled up to her solicitously.

"May I help you to choose a gift?"

Sophie suddenly noticed that among the mob of buyers there were no other women. This was the men's department. She moved off toward the opposite counter, mingling with women of all ages, lingering before the enormous photographs of the most popular actors.

Outer Space Belongs to Us: Commander of a spaceship (Alex Morrison) falls in love with the lady doctor on board (the Spectator), the rocket changes course to discharge the crew on one of Jupiter's moons, and the Commander heads off with his lover. Trans-galactic crossing.

Tortuga: Period, mid seventeenth century. Gallant pirate (Manuel Alvarez) abducts noblewoman (the Spectator). Jealousy and duels. Love and sea voyages under a fiery sky.

"What's it like?" asked a tall girl, her buxom body suffocating in a pair of overalls too small for her.

"Fascinating," her companion asserted. "I bought four more copies of it right away.

The other girl looked skeptical. She stretched her neck over the counter, stood on the tips of her toes to read the descriptions on the farthestmost boxes. She said something in a low voice, and her companion answered in a whisper. Sophie moved off. She spent a few minutes in the "classics" section, giving a fleeting glance to the back of the shop where men and women crowded together to buy the so-called "convenience" Oneirofilms.

When she had been younger, at school, they had told her that in former times men considered taboo anything that had to do with sex. It was highly improper to write or talk about the many aspects of love life. No woman would ever have described her desires and her sexual fantasies to a stranger. There were pornographic publications and photographs, many of which were illegal. People who bought them did it on the sly and always with a feeling of guilt or embarrassment, even when they had been passed by the Censor. But with the advent of the "system" the primitive custom of sexual modesty had become obsolete. Modesty existed, if at all, in some kinds of dreams, in "convenience" films made for the over-fifty set, where the consumer seduced or raped a teary, red-faced, trembling young girl. But in real life it had disappeared, or at least verbal modesty had. Without a shadow of embarrassment or discomfort, anybody could ask for an erotic film, the same as any other film about war or adventure.

But what about real and proper modesty? Among the many who crowded round the counters to buy the luxury in a box, who would have had the courage to disrobe in the middle of the mob? Only those activists of the Anti-Dream League, who were completely unselfconscious when they propositioned people, but perhaps not quite so unselfconscious when faced with performing what they themselves considered a weighty duty. The truth was, for nearly a century men and women had lived in a state of almost complete chastity. Solitude, the measured penumbra inside the narrow walls of their habitations, the armchairs with built-in Amplex: humanity had no desire for anything else. Faced with the greater attractions of dreams, the ambition to own a comfortable house, elegant clothes, a helicar, and other amenities had simply gone by the boards. Why beat one's brains out collecting real objects when, with an Oneirofilm that cost but a few pennies, one could live like a nabob for an hour, near stupendous women, admired, respected, served hand and foot?

Eight billion human beings vegetated inside squalid beehives, isolated in mean little holes, nourished by vitamin concentrates and soybean meal. And they felt no desire to consume anything real. After the bottom fell out of the market, the industries producing consumer goods had been abandoned all at once by financiers, who transferred their funds to companies producing Oneirofilms, the only merchandise for which there was any real demand.

She looked up toward the shining chart, and was disgusted at herself. The numbers spoke clearly. The sales chart was most eloquent. Her own Oneirofilms were the ones most in demand, more than everybody else's put together.

Sophie left the store. She walked homeward, her head bent, her step slow and listless. She didn't know how to judge that crowd of men who moved all around her, without recognizing her. Were they her slaves, or was she theirs?

The videophone rang: a streak of light in an abyss of black velvet, a peal from lofty cathedral spires in a sleepy, gray dawn.

Sophie stretched out a hand toward the pulsator-button.

A red snake zig-zagged onto the screen, lingered, seemed to explode; finally it resolved itself into Bradley's image.

"What do you want?" Sophie whined, her voice slurred with sleep. "For God's sake, what time is it?"

"It's noon. Wake up, my girl. You have to go to San Francisco."

"To San Francisco? What for? Are you out of your mind?"

"We have a co-production contract with Norfolk, Sophie. It was set for next Monday, but time presses. They need you now."

"But I'm still in bed, I'm deathly tired. I'll leave tomorrow, Bradley."

"Get dressed," the supervisor barked. "A Norfolk jet will be waiting for you at the West airport. Don't waste time."

Sophie was fuming. This extra work wasn't scheduled. What she wanted to do was spend the rest of the day in bed, resting.

She struggled out from under the covers, her eyes still shut, and sluggishly, halfheartedly undressed in the bathroom. The metallic jet of the cold shower made her shiver. She dried herself, dressed hurriedly, and left the house on the run.

She knew the methods of those types at Norfolk. They were worse than Bradley, real nitpickers. Always ready to find fault even with the scenes that had come off well.

In eight minutes, the helitaxi deposited her at the entrance to the airport. She entered by the door that led to the runway for private aircraft, and looked round for the Norfolk jet.

The pilot emerged from an outbuilding and walked over to meet her with a bouncy step.

"Sophie Barlow?"

He was tall, with light blond hair and a bronze complexion, a face that looked as if it had been baked in an oven.

"I'm Mirko Glikorich, from the Norfolk Company."

Sophie said nothing. The pilot did not think her worth a glance, and spoke staring at an indefinite point somewhere out in the airfield, two cold, aggressive eyes of a fine gray color like anthracite. He took Sophie's suitcase and marched off toward the main runway, where the Norfolk jet was being prepared for takeoff. Sophie had a hard time keeping up with him.

"Hey!" she exclaimed, balking like a thoroughbred. "I'm not a runner. Couldn't you walk a little slower?"

The pilot kept moving, without so much as turning around.

"We're late," he said curtly. "We have to be in San Francisco in three hours."

She was breathless by the time they reached the aircraft.

"Do you mind if I sit in front with you?" asked Sophie.

The pilot shrugged his shoulders. He helped her up, settled himself into the cockpit, and waited for the signal from the control tower.

Sophie looked around, full of curiosity, a bit intimidated by all the dials and switches on the instrument panel. The pilot whistled softly, impatient. Sophie groped around in the pocket of her seat and pulled out a dozen magazines. They were all at least several weeks old, some from the year before, dog-eared. Her face was on the cover of each of them. There was also an Oneirofilm catalogue folded open to the page that listed the films starring Sophie.

"Are these your things?"

The pilot didn't answer, but looked stiffly ahead. The takeoff had been gentle as a feather, and Sophie hadn't felt it at all. She glanced out the window and barely stifled an "Oh!" of surprise. A sea of houses extended itself beneath them; like a downy eyelid, the gray shell of the countryside opened up before them.

"Are these yours?" Sophie insisted.

The pilot turned his head slightly, an imperceptible movement, a lightning glance. Then he stiffened again.

"Yes," he said through his teeth.

She tried to hide the intimate gratification that always pervaded her when she met one of her ardent fans.

"What did you say your name was?"

"Glikorich," the pilot growled. "Mirko Glikorich."

"That's a Russian name, isn't it?"

"Yugoslav."

She watched him for a while. His lips were narrow and taut, his profile straight and sharp . . . Mirko looked as if he had been chiseled in rock, mute, motionless. Sophie grew impatient.

"Can I ask you a question?"

"Speak."

"Before – at the airport. You came to meet me and asked me if I was Sophie Barlow. Why? You know me, don't you? These magazines and the catalogue. I'll bet you're a fan of mine. Why did you pretend not to recognize me?"

"I didn't pretend. It's different, seeing you in person. In the end I recognized you because I knew you were supposed to turn up at that entrance at the airport. But in the middle of the crowd, no; you could have passed me without my noticing."

Sophie lit a cigarette. Maybe the pilot was right: in the crowd nobody would notice her, even without her dark glasses. She felt a kind of dull anger toward the man beside her. But she kept making an effort to talk to him. Mirko proved to be dense as a jungle, impenetrable, diffident.

"Why don't you turn on the automatic pilot?" Sophie asked. "I'm bored, Mirko. Say something to me."

The pilot remained impassive. He blinked once or twice, and stuck out his chin.

Sophie caught his arm. "Mirko! Pay attention to me! Turn on the automatic pilot and have a cigarette with me."

"I prefer to leave it on manual."

Sophie lit another cigarette, then another, using the butt of the second. She leafed through a magazine, worrying the pages in a fit of uncontrollable nervousness. She started to sing to herself, tapping her foot against the rubber lining of the cockpit. She snorted, fidgeting, and finally pretended to feel nauseated.

Mirko felt around inside the pocket of his flying suit and handed her a tablet.

Sophie was furious.

"Idiot!" she cried. "I won't stay here a moment longer. I'm going back in the cabin."

The little living room behind the cockpit was attractive. There was a couch, a stowable berth, a little table and a bar.

She poured herself a drink, a tall glass of brandy, which she gulped down at once. She poured herself another immediately, and the edges of objects began to vibrate in a bluish, inviting fog. She lowered herself to the couch, thinking of Mirko, a consumer like all the rest, an imbecile. She couldn't wait to get to San Francisco, make the film, and fly back to New York.

Now she sipped the brandy with less gusto. As she set the glass on the table, she began to feel groggy.

Suddenly, the arm of the couch was shoved against her, and an abyss seemed to open beneath, as when an elevator begins to move. She watched the glass start to slide along the tabletop, spill on the rug . . . Then, a pain in her shoulder, her forehead knocked against something. . . Fog. Red and blue globes. Roaring of motors gone wild.

"Mirko!" she cried, raising herself. The door to the cockpit seemed bolted shut. She squeezed the hostile handle and, lurching, tried to pull the door open. An emptiness inside her chest, a moment of balance, then the absurd feeling of weightlessness. She saw Mirko's back, his hands tense on the throttle, the clouds racing towards them like dream vapors.

Now Mirko was talking. In fact, he was shouting, but she wasn't aware of it. She pressed herself against the back of her seat, clenched her teeth and braced herself for the crash.

The aircraft plummeted like a corkscrew.

When she opened her eyes next, she saw a white cloud in the middle of the sky. A vulture circled far up. She was lying stretched out on her back, and something moist and fresh was pressed against her brow. She raised an arm, touched her face, temples, and removed the handkerchief soaked with water. Then she rolled over on her side.

Mirko was on his feet, over by the wrecked fuselage. Behind him, a cyclopean wall of red rock rose over the landscape.

"What happened?" she asked weakly.

The pilot stretched out his arms. "I don't know," he said, shaking his head. "I can't understand it. All of a sudden the controls weren't responding, the craft lost altitude, and then we were in a tailspin. I managed to regain control by a miracle, but it was too late. Look at the skid we took before we banged up against this rock!"

Sophie pulled herself up, rubbing her bruised shoulder.

"Do you have any idea where we are?"

Mirko lowered his eyes.

"This is the Grand Canyon," he said. "We're in one of the side chasms. This is one of the most inaccessible areas, but the Bright Angel Trail shouldn't be too far away .

Sophie's eyes widened. "The Grand Canyon?"

For a moment she was speechless. Then she burst out laughing.

"The Grand Canyon!" she repeated. "That's very funny! In fact it's unbelievable."

"What's unbelievable?"

"Don't play dumb, Mirko. The engine failure, the forced landing, here, right in the middle of the Grand Canyon . . . Just like the film I made last year, *Ecstasy*. You do remember it, don't you?"

Suddenly a suspicion crossed her mind.

"Tell me something," she said, frowning. "You didn't by any chance do it on purpose, did you? I mean, there are an awful lot of coincidences here. You're a real pilot, and I may not be a Persian princess but on the other hand I am Sophie Barlow. You wanted to get marooned out here with me, didn't you? You planned it to happen just like the film."

Mirko puffed up indignantly. He turned his back on her and went over to the aircraft. Shifting aside the twisted pieces of fuselage, he managed to crawl into the cabin. He tossed out a pile of equipment, two blankets, two back-packs, a plastic canteen, a tin of synthetic food, a flashlight. He emerged from the wreck with the bottle of brandy in one hand and a heavy piece of equipment in the other.

"Let's go," he said. "Carry as much of this as you can."

"Go where?"

"Surely you don't want to rot out here among the rocks. We have to get to the main canyon. Phantom Ranch must be more than fifty miles east of here, but there's always some stupid sentimental tourist who will come west to take a picture of the pretty view."

"Did you try radioing?"

"The radio's broken. Get a move on. Take what you need and let's get out of here."

He moved fast, his stride long and springy. He had tucked the brandy bottle into his hip pocket, and he marched along stooping slightly under the burden of his pack, in which he had placed a battery and the heavy electronic device.

Sophie stumbled along behind him, carrying the food and water containers.

Half an hour later, they came to a halt. Sophie was out of breath, her eyes were pleading. Mirko stared straight ahead. It was clear that the woman was a hindrance to him, the classical ball and chain which he could not get rid of.

"Walk slower, Mirko."

The man looked at the sky, which was filling up with menacing clouds.

"Let's go," he said. "In a couple of hours it's going to be pitch black."

When they reached the main canyon, they could hardly see anything. Mirko pointed up at a place in the rocky wall, red and brown as a piece of burning paper.

"The cave," he said reverently.

"The cave," Sophie repeated. "Just like in the film. Everything is just like in the film, Mirko."

He helped her up the cliff, and lowered his pack to the floor of the black hole that opened into the rock.

She watched him as he clambered down the sandstone and granite crags, rooting out the dried-up shrubs, making big bundles of them and dragging them up to the cave entrance. "It'll be cold in a while," he said. "We'll have to start a fire."

He lit the flashlight and inspected the cave. It was about fifteen yards deep, and bent at right angles in the middle. He set the bundle of kindling right in the elbow of the cave, and lit the fire with savage delight.

They ate in silence, in the dark and glowing cave, under an enormous fluttering bat's wing.

"I opened your pack," Sophie said. "While you were down gathering kindling. I saw what you have inside there. An Amplex! What did you need to bring that along for?"

"It's worth 120 coupons," Mirko said. "For an actress like you, that's a pittance. But it takes me three months to earn that much, you see?"

He picked up the metal box and the reel case.

"Well?" Sophie asked, curious. "What are you up to now?"

"I'm going to the rear of the cave. I have a right to my privacy, don't I?"

"Yes, but what do you need the Amplex for? What are you up to, Mirko?" The man snorted. When Sophie grabbed the reel case, he didn't put up a fight. Passive, he let the woman go through his reels at her leisure, let her read the descriptions printed on the plastic boxes.

"But these are all my films, Mirko! My heavens, you have every single one of them! *Blue Skies, Seduction, Adventure in Ceylon.* There's even a matrix, the matrix for *Ecstasy.* Is that your favorite Oneirofilm, Mirko?"

Mirko lowered his eyes without answering. Sophie closed the reel box. A matrix was a luxury relatively few people could permit themselves. The ordinary Oneirofilm, once viewed, was useless, because the Amplex demagnetized the tape as it ran through. But a matrix lasted forever, it was practically indestructible. For that reason, it cost a small fortune.

"When did you buy it?" Sophie asked.

The man shrugged, annoyed. "Oh, quit it," he snapped. "You're too curious. What do you want me to say? Your films sell millions of copies to millions and millions of consumers. I'm just one of them. I bought a matrix of *Ecstasy.* So what? What's so strange about that? There was something about it that I liked. I – "

"Go on," Sophie urged, squeezing his arm.

"A day doesn't pass that I don't watch it," the pilot said tartly. "So now why don't you leave me alone, go to sleep, because in a little while it will be daylight and we have to cover quite a few miles. I'm going to the back of the cave."

"With the Amplex?"

"Yes, for God's sake. What's it to you? I want to enjoy my film in peace."

Sophie gulped. A sudden feeling of frustration passed through her, as if all desire to live had left her. This is impossible, she thought. This can't be happening to me. What do I want, anyway, from this man who has a thousand reasons not to care a hoot about me?

She felt a desire to hurt him, to heap abuse on his head, to slap his face. But the image of Mirko embracing her broke through her inhibitions and spread through her mind.

"I'm here," she was surprised to hear herself say in a seductive tone. Mirko wheeled round.

"What did you say?"

"I said, I'm here, Mirko. Tonight you don't need that reel."

"I don't need it?"

"No. You can have me, just like in the dream. Even better than in the dream . . ."

Mirko started to snicker. "It's not the same thing," he said. "And don't be ridiculous with this Anti-Dream League propaganda of yours. Who are you trying to kid, anyway?"

"I'll say it again: Mirko, you can have *me*."

"And I still say it's not the same thing."

"Mirko!" the woman pleaded, beside herself. "You need me, every day you run through that matrix, and you dream, dream, you keep on dreaming of this cave, the firelight, my kisses, this body of mine which I've just offered you. This is exactly like the film, you stupid fool. What are you waiting for? I can do everything that's in that film, even more, and it will be for real . . ."

For a moment Mirko wavered, then he shook his head. He turned and moved off toward the back of the cave.

"Mirko!" she cried, exasperated. "I am Sophie Barlow! Sophie Barlow, don't you understand?"

She pulled down the zipper of her overalls. Her shoulders shrugged out of the cloth shell, and she quickly pulled off the suit and threw it on the ground.

"Look at me!" she shouted. And as he turned around, she uncovered her breasts.

The fire burned brightly, red and green tongues lapping upward, emitting a penetrating odor of the primeval jungle. She watched the man's hands clench into fists, his lips trembling, as if in a long, wearisome struggle.

Mirko hesitated a moment longer, then threw the matrix in the fire and ran toward her.

First the blue light came and then the red. Then blue again. When the reel came to an end, the set turned off automatically.

Sophie lifted off the Amplex helmet. Her temples were perspiring, her heart pounding in spasms. All her extremities were trembling, particularly her hands. She couldn't keep them still. Never in her life had she lived a "dream" with such intensity, an Oneirofilm that forced her to be herself. She must thank Bradley right way.

She rang him up on the videophone. But faced with the image of the supervisor, the words stuck in her throat; she stammered, truly moved. Finally she started to cry.

Bradley waited patiently.

"A little present, Sophie. Just a trinket. When an actress reaches the peak of her career she deserves far greater rewards. And you will have them, Sophie. You will have all the recognition that's due you. Because the system is perfect. There's no going back."

"Yes, Bradley. I – "

"It will go away, Sophie. It happens to all actresses sooner or later. The last obstacle to overcome is always vanity. Even you felt that a man ought to prefer you to a dream. You fell into the most dangerous of all heresies, but we caught it in time and rushed to correct it. With a little gift. That matrix will help you to get over this crisis."

"Yes, Bradley. Please thank everybody for me, the machinist, the technicians, the director, everybody who was involved in making this Oneirofllm. Above all, thank the actor who played the pilot."

"He's a new fellow. A real live wire, no?"

"Well, thank him for me. I had some beautiful moments. And thank you too, Bradley. I can imagine how much time and money this film cost you. It's perfect. I'll keep it in the slot of honor in my Oneirofilm collection."

"Nonsense, Sophie. You belong to the ruling class. You can allow yourself a personal Oneirofilm from time to time. We have always helped each other out, haven't we? – But there's one thing I want you to bear in mind."

"What's that, Bradley?"

"That matrix. That's more than a gift. It's meant to be a warning."

"Okay, Bradley. I get your point."

"Don't forget it. Nothing is better than dreaming. And only in dreams can you deceive yourself to the contrary. I'm sure that after five or six viewings you will get the point and toss that matrix in the wastebasket."

She nodded, in tears.

"I'll see you tomorrow at nine in the screening room."

"Yes, Bradley, tomorrow at nine in the screening room. Good night, Bradley."

"Good night, Sophie."

Fire Watch

CONNIE WILLIS

Connie Willis (1945–) began publishing SF stories in the 1970s and became a leading writer in the genre in the late 1980s and early 1990s, following several short fiction awards and the publication of her first collection (*Fire Watch,* 1985) and novel (*Lincoln's Dreams,* 1987). Her humorous science fiction is clever and sophisticated, the work of a frantic garrulous monologuist (she is popular as a humorous speaker at SF events), but her most significant work to date appears to be in the mode of "Fire Watch," concerned with history. Her most ambitious novel to date, *Doomsday Book* (1992), a winner of the Hugo Award for best novel, is a sequel to this story.

Time travel is one of her characteristic literary devices, but her stories cover a broad range of moods and subjects. *The Encyclopedia* of Science *Fiction* says, "In the best of her stories, and in her novels, a steely felicity of mind and style appears effortlessly married to a copious empathy."

This story uses a standard SF idea, the use of time travel to preserve or retrieve the treasures of the past, in a new way. Willis writes science fiction in the tradition of the 1950s, of Mildred Clingerman, Judith Merril, and Margaret St. Clair, with character foregrounded and technology and the standard tropes of science fiction in the background.

> *History hath triumphed over time, which besides*
> *it nothing but eternity hath triumphed over.*
>   *– Sir Walter Raleigh*

September 20 – Of course the first thing I looked for was the fire watch stone. And of course it wasn't there yet. It wasn't dedicated until 1951, accompanying speech by the Very Reverend Dean Walter Matthews, and this is only 1940. I knew that. I went to see the fire watch stone only yesterday, with some kind of misplaced notion that seeing the scene of the crime would somehow help. It didn't.

The only things that would have helped were a crash course in London during the Blitz and a little more time. I had not gotten either.

"Traveling in time is not like taking the tube, Mr. Bartholomew," the esteemed Dunworthy had said, blinking at me through those antique spectacles of his. "Either you report on the twentieth or you don't go at all."

"But I'm not ready," I'd said. "Look, it took me four years to get ready to travel with St. Paul. *St. Paul.* Not St. Paul's. You can't expect me to get ready for London in the Blitz in two days."

"Yes," Dunworthy had said. "We can." End of conversation.

"Two days!" I had shouted at my roommate Kivrin. "All because some computer adds an *'s.* And the esteemed Dunworthy doesn't even bat an eye when I tell him. 'Time travel is not like taking the tube, young man,' he says. 'I'd suggest you get ready. You're leaving day after tomorrow.' The man's a total incompetent."

"No," she said. "He isn't. He's the best there is. He wrote the book on St. Paul's. Maybe you should listen to what he says."

I had expected Kivrin to be at least a little sympathetic. She had been practically hysterical when she got her practicum changed from fifteenth- to fourteenth-century England, and how did either century qualify as a practicum? Even counting infectious diseases they couldn't have been more than a five. The Blitz is an eight, and St. Paul's itself is, with my luck, a ten.

"You think I should go see Dunworthy again?" I said.

"Yes."

"And then what? I've got two days. I don't know the money, the language, the history. Nothing."

"He's a good man," Kivrin said. "I think you'd better listen to him while you can." Good old Kivrin. Always the sympathetic ear.

The good man was responsible for my standing just inside the propped-open west doors, gawking like the country boy I was supposed to be, looking for a stone that wasn't there. Thanks to the good man, I was about as unprepared for my practicum as it was possible for him to make me.

I couldn't see more than a few feet into the church. I could see a candle gleaming feebly a long way off and a closer blur of white moving toward me. A verger, or possibly the Very Reverend Dean himself. I pulled out the letter from my clergyman uncle in Wales that was supposed to gain me access to the dean, and patted my back pocket to make sure I hadn't lost the microfiche *Oxford English Dictionary, Revised, with Historical Supplements,* I'd smuggled out of the Bodleian. I couldn't pull it out in the middle of the conversation, but with luck I could muddle through the first encounter by context and look up the words I didn't know later.

"Are you from the ayarpee?" he said. He was no older than I am, a head shorter and much thinner. Almost ascetic looking. He reminded me of Kivrin. He was not wearing white, but clutching it to his chest. In other circumstances I would have thought it was a pillow. In other circumstances I would know what was being said to me, but there had been no time to unlearn sub-Mediterranean Latin and Jewish law and learn Cockney and air raid procedures. Two days, and the esteemed Dunworthy, who wanted to talk about the sacred burdens of the historian instead of telling me what the ayarpee was.

"Are you?" he demanded again.

I considered whipping out the *OED* after all on the grounds that Wales was a foreign country, but I didn't think they had microfilm in 1940. Ayarpee. It could be anything, including a nickname for the fire watch, in which case the impulse to say no was not safe at all. "No." I said.

He lunged suddenly toward and past me and peered out the open doors. "Damn," he said, coming back to me. "Where are they then? Bunch of lazy bourgeois tarts!" And so much for getting by on context.

He looked at me closely, suspiciously, as if he thought I was only pretending not to be with the ayarpee. "The church is closed," he said finally.

I held up the envelope and said, "My name's Bartholomew. Is Dean Matthews in?"

He looked out the door a moment longer as if he expected the lazy bourgeois tarts at any moment and intended to attack them with the white bundle; then he turned and said, as if he were guiding a tour, "This way, please," and took off into the gloom.

He led me to the right and down the south aisle of the nave. Thank God I had memorized the floor plan or at that moment, heading into total darkness, led by a raving verger, the whole bizarre metaphor of my situation would have been enough to send me out the west doors and back to St. John's Wood. It helped a little to know where I was. We should have been passing number twenty-six: Hunt's painting of "The Light of the World" – Jesus with his lantern – but it was too dark to see it. We could have used the lantern ourselves.

He stopped abruptly ahead of me, still raving. "We weren't asking for the bloody savoy, just a few cots. Nelson's better off than we are – at least he's got a pillow provided." He brandished the white bundle like a torch in the darkness. It was a pillow after all. "We asked for them over a fortnight ago, and here we still are, sleeping on the bleeding generals from Trafalgar because those bitches want to play tea and crumpets with the tommies at victoria and the hell with us!"

He didn't seem to expect me to answer his outburst, which was good, because I had understood perhaps one key word in three. He stomped on ahead, moving out of sight of the one pathetic altar candle and stopping again at a black hole. Number twenty-five: stairs to the Whispering Gallery, the Dome, the library (not open to the public). Up the stairs, down a hall, stop again at a medieval door and knock. "I've got to go wait for them," he said. "If I'm not there they'll likely take them over to the Abbey. Tell the Dean to ring them up again, will you?" and he took off down the stone steps, still holding his pillow like a shield against him.

He had knocked, but the door was at least a foot of solid oak, and it was obvious the Very Reverend Dean had not heard. I was going to have to knock again. Yes, well, and the man holding the pinpoint had to let go of it, too, but even knowing it will all be over in a moment and you won't feel a thing doesn't make it any easier to say, "Now!" So I stood in front of the door, cursing the history department and the esteemed Dunworthy and the computer that had made the mistake and brought me here to this dark door with only a letter from a fictitious uncle that I trusted no more than I trusted the rest of them.

Even the old reliable Bodleian had let me down. The batch of research stuff I cross-ordered through Balliol and the main terminal is probably sitting in my room right now, a century out of reach. And Kivrin, who had already done her practicum and should have been bursting with advice, walked around as silent as a saint until I begged her to help me.

"Did you go to see Dunworthy?" she said.

"Yes. You want to know what priceless bit of information he had for me? 'Silence and humility are the sacred burdens of the historian.' He also told me I would love St. Paul's. Golden gems from the Master. Unfortunately, what I need to know are the times and places of the bombs so one doesn't fall on me." I flopped down on the bed. "Any suggestions?"

"How good are you at memory retrieval?" she said.

I sat up. "I'm pretty good. You think I should assimilate?"

"There isn't time for that," she said. "I think you should put everything you can directly into long-term."

"You mean endorphins?" I said.

The biggest problem with using memory-assistance drugs to put information into your long-term memory is that it never sits, even for a microsecond, in your short-term memory, and that makes retrieval complicated, not to mention unnerving. It gives you the most unsettling sense of déjà vu to suddenly know something you're positive you've never seen or heard before.

The main problem, though, is not eerie sensations but retrieval. Nobody knows exactly how the brain gets what it wants out of storage, but short-term is definitely involved. That brief, sometimes microscopic, time information spends in short-term is apparently used for something besides tip-of-the-tongue availability. The whole complex sort-and-file process of retrieval is apparently centered in short-term, and without it, and without the help of the drugs that put it there or artificial substitutes, information can be impossible to retrieve. I'd used endorphins for examinations and never had any difficulty with retrieval, and it looked like it was the only way to store all the information I needed in anything approaching the time I had left, but it also meant that I would *never* have known any of the things I needed to know, even for long enough to have forgotten them. If and when I could retrieve the information, I would know it. Till then I was as ignorant of it as if it were not stored in some cobwebbed corner of my mind at all.

"You can retrieve without artificials, can't you?" Kivrin said, looking skeptical.

"I guess I'll have to."

"Under stress? Without sleep? Low body endorphin levels?" What exactly had her practicum been? She had never said a word about it, and undergraduates are not supposed to ask. Stress factors in the Middle Ages? I thought everybody slept through them.

"I hope so," I said. "Anyway, I'm willing to try this idea if you think it will help."

She looked at me with that martyred expression and said, "Nothing will help." Thank you, St. Kivrin of Balliol.

But I tried it anyway. It was better than sitting in Dunworthy's rooms having him blink at me through his historically accurate eyeglasses and tell me I was going to love St. Paul's. When my Bodleian requests didn't come, I overloaded my credit and bought out Blackwell's. Tapes on World War II, Celtic literature, history of mass transit, tourist guidebooks, everything I could think of. Then I rented a high-speed recorder and shot up. When I came out of it, I was so panicked by the feeling of not knowing any more than I had when I started that I took the tube to London and raced up Ludgate Hill to see if the fire watch stone would trigger any memories. It didn't.

"Your endorphin levels aren't back to normal yet," I told myself and tried to relax, but that was impossible with the prospect of the practicum looming up before me. And those are real bullets, kid. Just because you're a history major doing his practicum doesn't mean you can't get killed. I read history books all the way home on the tube and right up until Dunworthy's flunkies came to take me to St. John's Wood this morning.

Then I jammed the microfiche *OED* in my back pocket and went off feeling as if I would have to survive by my native wit and hoping I could get hold of artificials in 1940. Surely I could get through the first day without mishap, I thought, and now here I was, stopped cold by almost the first word that was spoken to me.

Well, not quite. In spite of Kivrin's advice that I not put anything in short-term, I'd memorized the British money, a map of the tube system, a map of my own Oxford. It had gotten me this far. Surely I would be able to deal with the Dean.

Just as I had almost gotten up the courage to knock, he opened the door, and as with the pinpoint, it really was over quickly and without pain. I handed him my letter and he shook my hand and said something understandable like, "Glad to have another man, Bartholomew." He looked strained and tired and as if he might collapse if I told him the Blitz had just started. I know, I know: Keep your mouth shut. The sacred silence, etc.

He said, "We'll get Langby to show you round, shall we?" I assumed that was my Verger of the Pillow, and I was right. He met us at the foot of the stairs, puffing a little but jubilant.

"The cots came," he said to Dean Matthews. "You'd have thought they were doing us a favor. All high heels and hoity-toity. 'You made us miss our tea, luv,' one of them said to me. 'Yes, well, and a good thing, too,' I said. 'You look as if you could stand to lose a stone or two.'"

Even Dean Matthews looked as though he did not completely understand him. He said, "Did you set them up in the crypt?" and then introduced us. "Mr. Bartholomew's just got in from Wales," he said. "He's come to join our volunteers." Volunteers, not fire watch.

Langby showed me round, pointing out various dimnesses in the general gloom and then dragged me down to see the ten folding canvas cots set up among the tombs in the crypt, also in passing, Lord Nelson's black marble sarcophagus. He told me I don't have to stand a watch the first night and suggested I go to bed, since sleep is the most precious commodity in the raids. I could well believe it. He was clutching that silly pillow to his breast like his beloved.

"Do you hear the sirens down here?" I asked, wondering if he buried his head in it.

He looked round at the low stone ceilings. "Some do, some don't. Brinton has to have his Horlick's. Bence-Jones would sleep if the roof fell in on him. I have to have a pillow. The important thing is to get your eight in no matter what. If you don't, you turn into one of the walking dead. And then you get killed."

On that cheering note he went off to post the watches for tonight, leaving his pillow on one of the cots with orders for me to let nobody touch it. So here I sit, waiting for my first air raid siren and trying to get all this down before I turn into one of the walking or non-walking dead.

I've used the stolen *OED* to decipher a little Langby. Middling success. A tart is either a pastry or a prostitute. (I assume the latter, although I was wrong about the pillow.) Bourgeois is a catchall term for all the faults of the middle class. A Tommy's a soldier. Ayarpee I could not find under any spelling and I had nearly given up when something in long-term about the use of acronyms and abbreviations in wartime popped forward (bless you, St. Kivrin) and I realized it must be an abbreviation. ARP. Air Raid Precautions. Of course. Where else would you get the bleeding cots from?

September 21 – Now that I'm past the first shock of being here, I realize that the history department neglected to tell me what I'm supposed to do in the three-odd months of this practicum. They handed me this journal, the letter from my uncle, and ten pounds in pre-war money and sent me packing into the past. The ten pounds (already depleted by train and tube fares) is supposed to last me until the end of December and get me back to St. John's Wood for pickup when the second letter calling me back to Wales to sick uncle's bedside comes.

Till then I live here in the crypt with Nelson, who, Langby tells me, is pickled in alcohol inside his coffin. If we take a direct hit, will he burn like a torch or simply trickle out in a decaying stream onto the crypt floor, I wonder. Board is provided by a gas ring, over which are cooked wretched tea and indescribable kippers. To pay for all this luxury I am to stand on the roofs of St. Paul's and put out incendiaries.

I must also accomplish the purpose of this practicum, whatever it may be. Right now the only purpose I care about is staying alive until the second letter from uncle arrives and I can go home.

I am doing make-work until Langby has time to "show me the ropes." I've cleaned the skillet they cook the foul little fishes in, stacked wooden folding chairs at the altar end of the crypt (flat instead of standing because they tend to collapse like bombs in the middle of the night), and tried to sleep.

I am apparently not one of the lucky ones who can sleep through the raids. I spent most of the night wondering what St. Paul's risk rating is. Practica have to be at least a six. Last night I was convinced this was a ten, with the crypt as ground zero, and that I might as well have applied for Denver.

The most interesting thing that's happened so far is that I've seen a cat. I am fascinated, but trying not to appear so, since they seem commonplace here.

September 22 – Still in the crypt. Langby comes dashing through periodically cursing various government agencies (all abbreviated) and promising to take me up on the roofs. In the meantime I've run out of make-work and taught myself to work a stirrup pump. Kivrin was overly concerned about my memory retrieval abilities. I have not had any trouble so far. Quite the opposite. I called up firefighting information and got the whole manual with pictures, including instructions on the use of the stirrup pump. If the kippers set Lord Nelson on fire, I shall be a hero.

Excitement last night. The sirens went early and some of the chars who clean offices in the City sheltered in the crypt with us. One of them woke me out of a sound sleep, going like an air raid siren. Seems she'd seen a mouse. We had to go whacking at tombs and under the cots with a rubber boot to persuade her it was gone. Obviously what the history department had in mind: murdering mice.

September 24 – Langby took me on rounds. Into the choir, where I had to learn the stirrup pump all over again, assigned rubber boots and a tin helmet. Langby says Commander Allen is getting us asbestos firemen's coats, but hasn't yet, so it's my own wool coat and muffler and very cold on the roofs even in September. It feels like November and looks it, too, bleak and cheerless with no sun. Up to the dome and onto the roofs, which should be flat but in fact are littered with towers, pinnacles, gutters, statues, all designed expressly to catch and hold incendiaries out of reach. Shown how to smother an incendiary with sand before it burns through the roof and sets the church on fire. Shown the ropes (literally) lying in a heap at the base of the dome in case somebody has to go up one of the west towers or over the top of the dome. Back inside and down to the Whispering Gallery.

Langby kept up a running commentary through the whole tour, part practical instruction, part church history. Before we went up into the Gallery he dragged me over to the south door to tell me how Christopher Wren stood in the smoking rubble of Old St. Paul's and asked a workman to bring him a stone from the graveyard to mark the cornerstone. On the stone was written in Latin, "I shall rise again," and Wren was so impressed by the irony that he had the word inscribed above the door. Langby looked as smug as if he had not told me a story every first-year history student knows, but I suppose without the impact of the fire watch stone, the other is just a nice story.

Langby raced me up the steps and onto the narrow balcony circling the Whispering Gallery. He was already halfway round to the other side, shouting dimensions and acoustics at me. He stopped facing the wall opposite and said softly, "You can hear me whispering because of the shape of the dome. The sound waves are reinforced around the perimeter of the dome. It sounds like the very crack of doom up here during a raid. The dome is one hundred and seven feet across. It is eighty feet above the nave.

I looked down. The railing went out from under me and the black-and-white marble floor came up with dizzying speed. I hung onto something in front of me and dropped to my knees, staggered and sick at heart. The sun had come out, and all of St. Paul's seemed drenched in gold. Even the carved wood of the choir, the white stone pillars, the leaden pipes of the organ, all of it golden, golden.

Langby was beside me, trying to pull me free. "Bartholomew," he shouted, "what's wrong? For God's sake, man."

I knew I must tell him that if I let go, St. Paul's and all the past would fall in on me, and that I must not let that happen because I was an historian. I said something, but it was not what I intended because Langby merely tightened his grip. He hauled me violently free of the railing and back onto the stairway, then let me collapse limply on the steps and stood back from me, not speaking.

"I don't know what happened in there," I said. "I've never been afraid of heights before."

"You're shaking," he said sharply. "You'd better lie down." He led me back to the crypt.

September 25 – Memory retrieval: ARP manual. Symptoms of bombing victims. Stage one – shock; stupefaction; unawareness of injuries; words may not make sense except to victim. Stage two – shivering; nausea; injuries, losses felt; return to reality. Stage three – talkativeness that cannot be controlled; desire to explain shock behavior to rescuers.

Langby must surely recognize the symptoms, but how does he account for the fact there was no bomb? I can hardly explain my shock behavior to him, and it isn't just the sacred silence of the historian that stops me.

He has not said anything, in fact assigned me my first watches for tomorrow night as if nothing had happened, and he seems no more preoccupied than anyone else. Everyone I've met so far is jittery (one thing I had in short-term was how calm everyone was during the raids) and the raids have not come near us since I got here. They've been mostly over the East End and the docks.

There was a reference tonight to a UXB, and I have been thinking about the Dean's manner and the church being closed when I'm almost sure I remember reading it was open through the entire Blitz. As soon as I get a chance, I'll try to retrieve the events of September. As to retrieving anything else, I don't see how I can hope to remember the right information until I know what it is I am supposed to do here, if anything.

There are no guidelines for historians, and no restrictions either. I could tell everyone I'm from the future if I thought they would believe me. I could murder Hitler if I could get to Germany. Or could I? Time paradox talk abounds in the history department, and the graduate students back from their practica don't say a word one way or the other. Is there a tough, immutable past? Or is there a new past every day and do we, the historians, make it? And what are the consequences of what we do, if there are consequences? And how do we dare do anything without knowing them? Must we interfere boldly, hoping we do not bring about all our downfalls? Or must we do nothing at all, not interfere, stand by and watch St. Paul's burn to the ground if need be so that we don't change the future?

All those are fine questions for a late-night study session. They do not matter here. I could no more let St. Paul's burn down than I could kill Hitler. No, that is not true. I found that out yesterday in the Whispering Gallery. I could kill Hitler if I caught him setting fire to St. Paul's.

September 26 – I met a young woman today. Dean Matthews has opened the church, so the watch have been doing duties as chars and people have started coming in again. The young woman reminded me of Kivrin, though Kivrin is a good deal taller and would never frizz her hair like that. She looked as if she had been crying. Kivrin has looked like that since she got back from her practicum. The Middle Ages were too much for her. I wonder how she would have coped with this. By pouring out her fears to the local priest, no doubt, as I sincerely hoped her look-alike was not going to do.

"May I help you?" I said, not wanting in the least to help. "I'm a volunteer."

She looked distressed. "You're not paid?" she said, and wiped at her reddened nose with a handkerchief. "I read about St. Paul's and the fire watch and all, and I thought perhaps there's a position there for me. In the canteen, like, or something. A paying position." There were tears in her red-rimmed eyes.

"I'm afraid we don't have a canteen," I said as kindly as I could, considering how impatient Kivrin always makes me, "and it's not actually a real shelter. Some of the watch sleep in the crypt. I'm afraid we're all volunteers, though."

"That won't do, then," she said. She dabbed at her eyes with the handkerchief. "I love St. Paul's, but I can't take on volunteer work, not with my little brother Tom back from the country." I was not reading this situation properly. For all the outward signs of distress she sounded quite cheerful and no closer to tears than when she had come in. "I've got to get us a proper place to stay. With Tom back, we can't go on sleeping in the tubes."

A sudden feeling of dread, the kind of sharp pain you get sometimes from involuntary retrieval, went over me. "The tubes?" I said, trying to get at the memory.

"Mable Arch, usually," she went on. "My brother Tom saves us a place early and I go . . ." She stopped, held the handkerchief close to her nose, and exploded into it. "I'm sorry," she said, "this awful cold!"

Red nose, watering eyes, sneezing. Respiratory infection. It was a wonder I hadn't told her not to cry. It's only by luck that I haven't made some unforgivable mistake so far, and this is not because I can't get at the long-term memory. I don't have half the information I need even stored: cats and colds and the way St. Paul's looks in full sun. It's only a matter of time before I am stopped cold by something I do not know. Nevertheless, I am going to try for retrieval tonight after I come off watch. At least I can find out whether and when something is going to fall on me.

I have seen the cat once or twice. He is coal-black with a white patch on his throat that looks as if it were painted on for the blackout.

September 27 – I have just come down from the roofs. I am still shaking.

Early in the raid the bombing was mostly over the East End. The view was incredible. Searchlights everywhere, the sky pink from the fires and reflecting in the Thames, the exploding shells sparkling like fireworks. There was a constant, deafening thunder broken by the occasional droning of the planes high overhead, then the repeating stutter of the ack-ack guns.

About midnight the bombs began falling quite near with a horrible sound like a train running over me. It took every bit of will I had to keep from flinging myself flat on the roof, but Langby was watching. I didn't want to give him the satisfaction of watching a repeat performance of my behavior in the dome. I kept my head up and my sand bucket firmly in hand and felt quite proud of myself.

The bombs stopped roaring past about three, and there was a lull of about half an hour, and then a clatter like hail on the roofs. Everybody except Langby dived for shovels and stirrup pumps. He was watching me. And I was watching the incendiary.

It had fallen only a few meters from me, behind the clock tower. It was much smaller than I had imagined, only about thirty centimeters long. It was sputtering violently, throwing greenish-white fire almost to where I was standing. In a minute it would simmer down into a molten mass and begin to burn through the roof. Flames and the frantic shouts of firemen, and then the white rubble stretching for miles, and nothing, nothing left, not even the fire watch stone.

It was the Whispering Gallery all over again. I felt that I had said something, and when I looked at Langby's face he was smiling crookedly.

"St. Paul's will burn down," I said. "There won't be anything left."

"Yes," Langby said. "That's the idea, isn't it? Burn St. Paul's to the ground? Isn't that the plan?"

"Whose plan?" I said stupidly.

"Hitler's, of course," Langby said. "Who did you think I meant?" and, almost casually, picked up his stirrup pump.

The page of the ARP manual flashed suddenly before me. I poured the bucket of sand around the still sputtering bomb, snatched up another bucket and dumped that on top of it. Black smoke billowed up in such a cloud that I could hardly find my shovel. I felt for the smothered bomb with the tip of it and scooped it into the empty bucket, then shoveled the sand in on top of it. Tears were streaming down my face from the acrid smoke. I turned to wipe them on my sleeve and saw Langby.

He had not made a move to help me. He smiled. "It's not a bad plan, actually. But of course we won't let it happen. That's what the fire watch is here for. To see that it doesn't happen. Right, Bartholomew?"

I know now what the purpose of my practicum is. I must stop Langby from burning down St. Paul's.

September 28 – I try to tell myself I was mistaken about Langby last night, that I misunderstood what he said. Why would he want to burn down St. Paul's unless he is a Nazi spy? How can a Nazi spy have gotten on the fire watch? I think about my faked letter of introduction and shudder.

How can I find out? If I set him some test, some fatal thing that only a loyal Englishman in 1940 would know, I fear I am the one who would be caught out. I *must* get my retrieval working properly.

Until then, I shall watch Langby. For the time being at least that should be easy. Langby has just posted the watches for the next two weeks. We stand every one together.

September 30 – I know what happened in September. Langby told me.

Last night in the choir, putting on our coats and boots, he said, "They've already tried once, you know."

I had no idea what he meant. I felt as helpless as that first day when he asked me if I was from the ayarpee.

"The plan to destroy St. Paul's. They've already tried once. The tenth of September. A high explosive bomb. But of course you didn't know about that. You were in Wales."

I was not even listening. The minute he had said "high explosive bomb," I had remembered it all. It had burrowed in under the road and lodged on the foundations. The bomb squad had tried to defuse it, but there was a leaking gas main. They decided to evacuate St.

Paul's, but Dean Matthews refused to leave, and they got it out after all and exploded it in Barking Marshes. Instant and complete retrieval.

"The bomb squad saved her that time," Langby was saying. "It seems there's always somebody about."

"Yes," I said, "there is," and walked away from him.

October 1 – I thought last night's retrieval of the events of September tenth meant some sort of breakthrough, but I have been lying here on my cot most of the night trying for Nazi spies in St. Paul's and getting nothing. Do I have to know exactly what I'm looking for before I can remember it? What good does that do me?

Maybe Langby is not a Nazi spy. Then what is he? An arsonist? A madman? The crypt is hardly conducive to thought, being not at all as silent as a tomb. The chars talk most of the night and the sound of the bombs is muffled, which somehow makes it worse. I find myself straining to hear them. When I did get to sleep this morning, I dreamed about one of the tube shelters being hit, broken mains, drowning people.

October 4 – I tried to catch the cat today. I had some idea of persuading it to dispatch the mouse that has been terrifying the chars. I also wanted to see one up close. I took the water bucket I had used with the stirrup pump last night to put out some burning shrapnel from one of the antiaircraft guns. It still had a bit of water in it, but not enough to drown the cat, and my plan was to clamp the bucket over him, reach under, and pick him up, then carry him down to the crypt and point him at the mouse. I did not even come close to him.

I swung the bucket, and as I did so, perhaps an inch of water splashed out. I thought I remembered that the cat was a domesticated animal, but I must have been wrong about that. The cat's wide complacent face pulled back into a skull-like mask that was absolutely terrifying, vicious claws extended from what I had thought were harmless paws, and the cat let out a sound to top the chars.

In my surprise I dropped the bucket and it rolled against one of the pillars. The cat disappeared. Behind me, Langby said, "That's no way to catch a cat."

"Obviously," I said, and bent to retrieve the bucket.

"Cats hate water," he said, still in that expressionless voice.

"Oh," I said, and started in front of him to take the bucket back to the choir. "I didn't know that."

"Everybody knows it. Even the stupid Welsh."

October 8 – We have been standing double watches for a week – bomber's moon. Langby didn't show up on the roofs, so I went looking for him in the church. I found him standing by the west doors talking to an old man. The man had a newspaper tucked under his arm and he handed it to Langby, but Langby gave it back to him. When the man saw me, he ducked out. Langby said, "Tourist. Wanted to know where the Windmill Theater is. Read in the paper the girls are starkers."

I know I looked as if I didn't believe him because he said, "You look rotten, old man. Not getting enough sleep, are you? I'll get somebody to take the first watch for you tonight."

"No," I said coldly. "I'll stand my own watch. I like being on the roofs," and added silently, where I can watch you.

He shrugged and said, "I suppose it's better than being down in the crypt. At least on the roofs you can hear the one that gets you."

October 10 – I thought the double watches might be good for me, take my mind off my inability to retrieve. The watched-pot idea. Actually, it sometimes works. A few hours of thinking about something else, or a good night's sleep, and the fact pops forward without any prompting, without any artificials.

The good night's sleep is out of the question. Not only do the chars talk constantly, but the cat has moved into the crypt and sidles up to everyone, making siren noises and begging for kippers. I am moving my cot out of the transept and over by Nelson before I go on watch. He may be pickled, but he keeps his mouth shut.

October 11 – I dreamed Trafalgar, ships' guns and smoke and falling plaster and Langby shouting my name. My first waking thought was that the folding chairs had gone off. I could not see for all the smoke.

"I'm coming," I said, limping toward Langby and pulling on my boots. There was a heap of plaster and tangled folding chairs in the transept. Langby was digging in it. "Bartholomew!" he shouted, flinging a chunk of plaster aside. "Bartholomew!"

I still had the idea it was smoke. I ran back for the stirrup pump and then knelt beside him and began pulling on a splintered chair back. It resisted, and it came to me suddenly. There is a body under here. I will reach for a piece of the ceiling and find it is a hand. I leaned back on my heels, determined not to be sick, then went at the pile again.

Langby was going far too fast, jabbing with a chair leg. I grabbed his hand to stop him, and he struggled against me as if I were a piece of rubble to be thrown aside. He picked up a large flat square of plaster, and under it was the floor. I turned and looked behind me. Both chars huddled in the recess by the altar. "Who are you looking for?" I said, keeping hold of Langby's arm.

"Bartholomew," he said, and swept the rubble aside, his hands bleeding through the coating of smoky dust.

"I'm here," I said. "I'm all right." I choked on the white dust. "I moved my cot out of the transept."

He turned sharply to the chars and then said quite calmly, "What's under here?"

"Only the gas ring," one of them said timidly from the shadowed recess, "and Mrs. Galbraith's pocketbook." He dug through the mess until he had found them both. The gas ring was leaking at a merry rate, though the flame had gone out.

"You've saved St. Paul's and me after all," I said, standing there in my underwear and boots, holding the useless stirrup pump. "We might all have been asphyxiated."

He stood up. "I shouldn't have saved you," he said.

Stage one: shock, stupefaction, unawareness of injuries, words may not make sense except to victim. He would not know his hand was bleeding yet. He would not remember what he had said. He had said he shouldn't have saved my life.

"I shouldn't have saved you," he repeated. "I have my duty to think of."

"You're bleeding," I said sharply. "You'd better lie down." I sounded just like Langby in the gallery.

October 13 – It was a high explosive bomb. It blew a hole in the Choir, and some of the marble statuary is broken, but the ceiling of the crypt did not collapse, which is what I thought at first. It only jarred some plaster loose.

I do not think Langby has any idea what he said. That should give me some sort of advantage, now that I am sure where the danger lies, now that I am sure it will not come crashing down from some other direction. But what good is all this knowing, when I do not know what he will do? Or when?

Surely I have the facts of yesterday's bomb in long-term, but even falling plaster did not jar them loose this time. I am not even trying for retrieval, now. I lie in the darkness waiting for the roof to fall in on me. And remembering how Langby saved my life.

October 15 – The girl came in again today. She still has the cold, but she has gotten her paying position. It was a joy to see her. She was wearing a smart uniform and open-toed shoes, and her hair was in an elaborate frizz around her face. We are still cleaning up the mess from the bomb, and Langby was out with Allen getting wood to board up the Choir, so I let the girl chatter at me while I swept. The dust made her sneeze, but at least this time I knew what she was doing.

She told me her name is Enola and that she's working for the WVS, running one of the mobile canteens that are sent to the fires. She came, of all things, to thank me for the job. She said that after she told the WVS that there was no proper shelter with a canteen for St. Paul's, they gave her a run in the City. "So I'll just pop in when I'm close and let you know how I'm making out, won't I just?"

She and her brother Tom are still sleeping in the tubes. I asked her if that was safe and she said probably not, but at least down there you couldn't hear the one that got you and that was a blessing.

October 18 – I am so tired I can hardly write this. Nine incendiaries tonight and a land mine that looked as though it was going to catch on the dome till the wind drifted its parachute away from the church. I put out two of the incendiaries. I have done that at least twenty times since I got here and helped with dozens of others, and still it is not enough. One incendiary, one moment of not watching Langby, could undo it all.

I know that is partly why I feel so tired. I wear myself out every night trying to do my job and watch Langby, making sure none of the incendiaries falls without my seeing it. Then I go back to the crypt and wear myself out trying to retrieve something, anything, about spies, fires, St. Paul's in the fall of 1940, anything. It haunts me that I am not doing enough, but I do not know what else to do. Without the retrieval, I am as helpless as these poor people here, with no idea what will happen tomorrow.

If I have to, I will go on doing this till I am called home. He cannot burn down St. Paul's so long as I am here to put out the incendiaries. "I have my duty," Langby said in the crypt.

And I have mine.

October 21 – It's been nearly two weeks since the blast and I just now realized we haven't seen the cat since. He wasn't in the mess in the crypt. Even after Langby and I were sure there was no one in there, we sifted through the stuff twice more. He could have been in the Choir, though.

Old Bence-Jones says not to worry. "He's all right," he said. "The jerries could bomb London right down to the ground and the cats would waltz out to greet them. You know why? They don't love anybody. That's what gets half of us killed. Old lady out in Stepney got killed the other night trying to save her cat. Bloody cat was in the Anderson."

"Then where is he?"

"Someplace safe, you can bet on that. If he's not around St. Paul's, it means we're for it. That old saw about the rats deserting a sinking ship, that's a mistake, that is. It's cats, not rats."

October 25 – Langby's tourist showed up again. He cannot still be looking for the Windmill Theatre. He had a newspaper under his arm again today, and he asked for Langby, but Langby was across town with Allen, trying to get the asbestos firemen's coats. I saw the name of the paper. It was *The Worker*. A Nazi newspaper?

November 2 – I've been up on the roofs for a week straight, helping some incompetent workmen patch the hole the bomb made. They're doing a terrible job. There's still a great gap on one side a man could fall into, but they insist it'll be all right because, after all, you wouldn't fall clear through but only as far as the ceiling, and "the fall can't kill you." They don't seem to understand it's a perfect hiding place for an incendiary.

And that is all Langby needs. He does not even have to set a fire to destroy St. Paul's. All he needs to do is let one burn uncaught until it is too late.

I could not get anywhere with the workmen. I went down into the church to complain to Matthews, and saw Langby and his tourist behind a pillar, close to one of the windows. Langby was holding a newspaper and talking to the man. When I came down from the library an hour later, they were still there. So is the gap. Matthews says we'll put planks across it and hope for the best.

November 5 – I have given up trying to retrieve. I am so far behind on my sleep I can't even retrieve information on a newspaper whose name I already know. Double watches the permanent thing now. Our chars have abandoned us altogether (like the cat), so the crypt is quiet, but I cannot sleep.

If I do manage to doze off, I dream. Yesterday I dreamed Kivrin was on the roofs, dressed like a saint. "What was the secret of your practicum?" I said. "What were you supposed to find out?"

She wiped her nose with a handkerchief and said, "Two things. One, that silence and humility are the sacred burdens of the historian. Two" – she stopped and sneezed into the handkerchief – "don't sleep in the tubes."

My only hope is to get hold of an artificial and induce a trance. That's a problem. I'm positive it's too early for chemical endorphins and probably hallucinogens. Alcohol is definitely available, but I need something more concentrated than ale, the only alcohol I know by name. I do not dare ask the watch. Langby is suspicious enough of me already. It's back to the *OED*, to look up a word I don't know.

November 11 – The cat's back. Langby was out with Allen again, still trying for the asbestos coats, so I thought it was safe to leave St. Paul's. I went to the grocer's for supplies, and hopefully an artificial. It was late, and the sirens sounded before I had even gotten to Cheapside, but the raids do not usually start until after dark. It took awhile to get all the groceries and to get up my courage to ask whether he had any alcohol – he told me to go to a pub – and when I came out of the shop, it was as if I had pitched suddenly into a hole.

I had no idea where St. Paul's lay, or the street, or the shop I had just come from. I stood on what was no longer the sidewalk, clutching my brown-paper parcel of kippers and bread with a hand I could not have seen if I held it up before my face. I reached up to wrap my muffler closer about my neck and prayed for my eyes to adjust, but there was no reduced light to adjust to. I would have been glad of the moon, for all St. Paul's watch cursed it and called it a fifth columnist. Or a bus, with its shuttered headlights giving just enough light to orient myself by. Or a searchlight. Or the kickback flare of an ack-ack gun. Anything.

Just then I did see a bus, two narrow yellow slits a long way off. I started toward it and nearly pitched off the curb. Which meant the bus was sideways in the street, which meant it was not a bus. A cat meowed, quite near, and rubbed against my leg. I looked down into the yellow lights I had thought belonged to the bus. His eyes were picking up light from somewhere, though I would have sworn there was not a light for miles, and reflecting it flatly up at me.

"A warden'll get you for those lights, old tom," I said, and then as a plane droned overhead, "Or a jerry."

The world exploded suddenly into light, the searchlights and a glow along the Thames seeming to happen almost simultaneously, lighting my way home.

"Come to fetch me, did you, old tom?" I said gaily. "Where've you been? Knew we were out of kippers, didn't you? I call that loyalty." I talked to him all the way home and gave him half a tin of the kippers for saving my life. Bence-Jones said he smelled the milk at the grocer's.

November 13 – I dreamed I was lost in the blackout. I could not see my hands in front of my face, and Dunworthy came and shone a pocket torch at me, but I could only see where I had come from and not where I was going.

"What good is that to them?" I said. "They need a light to show them where they're going."

"Even the light from the Thames? Even the light from the fires and the ack-ack guns?" Dunworthy said.

"Yes. Anything is better than this awful darkness." So he came closer to give me the pocket torch. It was not a pocket torch, after all, but Christ's lantern from the Hunt picture in the south nave. I shone it on the curb before me so I could find my way home, but it shone instead on the fire watch stone and I hastily put the light out.

November 20 – I tried to talk to Langby today. "I've seen you talking to the old gentleman," I said. It sounded like an accusation. I meant it to. I wanted him to think it was and stop whatever he was planning.

"Reading," he said. "Not talking." He was putting things in order in the choir, piling up sandbags.

"I've seen you reading then," I said belligerently, and he dropped a sandbag and straightened.

"What of it?" he said. "It's a free country. I can read to an old man if I want, same as you can talk to that little WVS tart."

"What do you read?" I said.

"Whatever he wants. He's an old man. He used to come home from his job, have a bit of brandy and listen to his wife read the papers to him. She got killed in one of the raids. Now I read to him. I don't see what business it is of yours."

It sounded true. It didn't have the careful casualness of a lie, and I almost believed him, except that I had heard the tone of truth from him before. In the crypt. After the bomb.

"I thought he was a tourist looking for the Windmill," I said.

He looked blank only a second, and then he said, "Oh, yes, that. He came in with the paper and asked me to tell him where it was. I looked it up to find the address. Clever, that. I didn't guess he couldn't read it for himself." But it was enough. I knew that he was lying.

He heaved a sandbag almost at my feet. "Of course you wouldn't understand a thing like that, would you? A simple act of human kindness?"

"No," I said coldly. "I wouldn't."

None of this proves anything. He gave away nothing, except perhaps the name of an artificial, and I can hardly go to Dean Matthews and accuse Langby of reading aloud.

I waited till he had finished in the choir and gone down to the crypt. Then I lugged one of the sandbags up to the roof and over to the chasm. The planking has held so far, but everyone walks gingerly around it, as if it were a grave. I cut the sandbag open and spilled the loose sand into the bottom. If it has occurred to Langby that this is the perfect spot for an incendiary, perhaps the sand will smother it.

November 21 – I gave Enola some of "uncle's" money today and asked her to get me the brandy. She was more reluctant than I thought she'd be, so there must be societal complications I am not aware of, but she agreed.

I don't know what she came for. She started to tell me about her brother and some prank he'd pulled in the tubes that got him in trouble with the guard, but after I asked her about the brandy, she left without finishing the story.

November 25 – Enola came today, but without bringing the brandy. She is going to Bath for the holidays to see her aunt. At least she will be away from the raids for a while. I will not have to worry about her. She finished the story of her brother and told me she hopes to persuade this aunt to take Tom for the duration of the Blitz but is not at all sure the aunt will be willing.

Young Tom is apparently not so much an engaging scapegrace as a near criminal. He has been caught twice picking pockets in the Bank tube shelter, and they have had to go back to Marble Arch. I comforted her as best I could, told her all boys were bad at one time or another. What I really wanted to say was that she needn't worry at all, that young Tom strikes me as a true survivor type, like my own tom, like Langby, totally unconcerned with anybody but himself, well-equipped to survive the Blitz and rise to prominence in the future.

Then I asked her whether she had gotten the brandy.

She looked down at her open-toed shoes and muttered unhappily, "I thought you'd forgotten all about that."

I made up some story about the watch taking turns buying a bottle, and she seemed less unhappy, but I am not convinced she will not use this trip to Bath as an excuse to do nothing. I will have to leave St. Paul's and buy it myself, and I don't dare leave Langby alone in the church. I made her promise to bring the brandy today before she leaves. But she is still not back, and the sirens have already gone.

November 26 – No Enola, and she said their train left at noon. I suppose I should be grateful that at least she is safely out of London. Maybe in Bath she will be able to get over her cold.

Tonight one of the ARP girls breezed in to borrow half our cots and tell us about a mess over in the East End where a surface shelter was hit. Four dead, twelve wounded. "At least it wasn't one of the tube shelters!" she said. "Then you'd see a real mess, wouldn't you?"

November 30 – I dreamed I took the cat to St. John's Wood.

"Is this a rescue mission?" Dunworthy said.

"No, sir," I said proudly. "I know what I was supposed to find in my practicum. The perfect survivor. Tough and resourceful and selfish. This is the only one I could find. I had to kill Langby, you know, to keep him from burning down St. Paul's. Enola's brother has gone to Bath, and the others will never make it. Enola wears open-toed shoes in the winter and sleeps in the tubes and puts her hair up on metal pins so it will curl. She cannot possibly survive the Blitz."

Dunworthy said, "Perhaps you should have rescued her instead. What did you say her name was?"

"Kivrin," I said, and woke up cold and shivering.

December 5 – I dreamed Langby had the pinpoint bomb. He carried it under his arm like a brown-paper parcel, coming out of St. Paul's Station and around Ludgate Hill to the west doors.

"This is not fair," I said, barring his way with my arm. "There is no fire watch on duty."

He clutched the bomb to his chest like a pillow. "That is your fault," he said, and before I could get to my stirrup pump and bucket, he tossed it in the door.

The pinpoint was not even invented until the end of the twentieth century, and it was another ten years before the dispossessed communists got hold of it and turned it into something that could be carried under your arm. A parcel that could blow a quarter mile of the City into oblivion. Thank God that is one dream that cannot come true.

It was a sunlit morning in the dream, and this morning when I came off watch the sun was shining for the first time in weeks. I went down to the crypt and then came up again, making the rounds of the roofs twice more, then the steps and the grounds and all the treacherous alleyways between where an incendiary could be missed. I felt better after that, but when I got to sleep I dreamed again, this time of fire and Langby watching it, smiling.

December 15 – I found the cat this morning. Heavy raids last night, but most of them over toward Canning Town and nothing on the roofs to speak of. Nevertheless the cat was quite dead. I found him lying on the steps this morning when I made my own, private rounds. Concussion. There was not a mark on him anywhere except the white blackout patch on his throat, but when I picked him up, he was all jelly under the skin.

I could not think what to do with him. I thought for one mad moment of asking Matthews if I could bury him in the crypt. Honorable death in war or something. Trafalgar, Waterloo, London, died in battle. I ended by wrapping him in my muffler and taking him down Ludgate Hill to a building that had been bombed out and burying him in the rubble. It will do no good. The rubble will be no protection from dogs or rats, and I shall never get another muffler. I have gone through nearly all of uncle's money.

I should not be sitting here. I haven't checked the alleyways or the rest of the steps, and there might be a dud or a delayed incendiary or something that I missed.

When I came here, I thought of myself as the noble rescuer, the savior of the past. I am not doing very well at the job. At least Enola is out of it. I wish there were some way I could send St. Paul's to Bath for safekeeping. There were hardly any raids last night. Bence-Jones said cats can survive anything. What if he was coming to get me, to show me the way home? All the bombs were over Canning Town.

December 16 – Enola has been back a week. Seeing her, standing on the west steps where I found the cat, sleeping in Marble Arch and not safe at all, was more than I could absorb. "I thought you were in Bath," I said stupidly.

"My aunt said she'd take Tom but not me as well. She's got a houseful of evacuation children, and what a noisy lot. Where is your muffler?" she said. "It's dreadful cold up here on the hill."

"I . . ." I said, unable to answer, "I lost it."

"You'll never get another one," she said. "They're going to start

rationing clothes. And wool, too. You'll never get another one like
that."

"I know," I said, blinking at her.

"Good things just thrown away," she said. "It's absolutely criminal,
that's what it is."

I don't think I said anything to that, just turned and walked away
with my head down, looking for bombs and dead animals.

December 20 – Langby isn't a Nazi. He's a communist. I can hardly
write this. A communist.

One of the chars found *The Worker* wedged behind a pillar and
brought it down to the crypt as we were coming off the first watch.

"Bloody communists," Bence-Jones said. "Helping Hitler, they are.
Talking against the king, stirring up trouble in the shelters. Traitors,
that's what they are."

"They love England same as you," the char said.

"They don't love nobody but themselves, bloody selfish lot. I
wouldn't be surprised to hear they were ringing Hitler up on the telephone," Bence-Jones said. " 'Ello, Adolf, here's where to drop the
bombs."

The kettle on the gas ring whistled. The char stood up and poured
the hot water into a chipped teapot, then sat back down. "Just because
they speak their minds don't mean they'd burn down old St. Paul's,
does it now?"

"Of course not," Langby said, coming down the stairs. He sat down
and pulled off his boots, stretching his feet in their wool socks. "Who
wouldn't burn down St. Paul's?"

"The communists," Bence-Jones said, looking straight at him, and I
wondered if he suspected Langby too.

Langby never batted an eye. "I wouldn't worry about them if I were
you," he said. "It's the jerries that are doing their bloody best to burn
her down tonight. Six incendiaries so far, and one almost went into
that great hole over the choir." He held out his cup to the char, and
she poured him a cup of tea.

I wanted to kill him, smashing him to dust and rubble on the floor
of the crypt while Bence-Jones and the char looked on in helpless
surprise, shouting warnings to them and the rest of the watch. "Do you
know what the communists did?" I wanted to shout. "Do you? We
have to stop him." I even stood up and started toward him as he sat
with his feet stretched out before him and his asbestos coat still over his
shoulders.

And then the thought of the Gallery drenched in gold, the communist coming out of the tube station with the package so casually under his arm, made me sick with the same staggering vertigo of guilt and helplessness, and I sat back down on the edge of my cot and tried to think what to do.

They do not realize the danger. Even Bence-Jones, for all his talk of traitors, thinks they are capable only of talking against the king. They do not know, cannot know, what the communists will become. Stalin is an ally. Communists mean Russia. They have never heard of Karinsky or the New Russia or any of the things that will make "communist" into a synonym for "monster." They will never know it. By the time the communists become what they became, there will be no fire watch. Only I know what it means to hear the name "communist" uttered here, so carelessly, in St. Paul's.

A communist. I should have known. I should have known.

December 22 – Double watches again. I have not had any sleep and I am getting very unsteady on my feet. I nearly pitched into the chasm this morning, only saved myself by dropping to my knees. My endorphin levels are fluctuating wildly, and I know I must get some sleep soon or I will become one of Langby's walking dead, but I am afraid to leave him alone on the roofs, alone in the church with his communist party leader, alone anywhere. I have taken to watching him when he sleeps.

If I could just get hold of an artificial, I think I could induce a trance, in spite of my poor condition. But I cannot even go out to a pub. Langby is on the roofs constantly, waiting for his chance. When Enola comes again I must convince her to get the brandy for me. There are only a few days left.

December 28 – Enola came this morning while I was on the west porch, picking up the Christmas tree. It has been knocked over three nights running by concussion. I righted the tree and was bending down to pick up the scattered tinsel when Enola appeared suddenly out of the fog like some cheerful saint. She stooped quickly and kissed me on the cheek. Then she straightened up, her nose red from her perennial cold, and handed me a box wrapped in colored paper.

"Merry Christmas," she said. "Go on then, open it. It's a gift."

My reflexes are almost totally gone. I knew the box was far too shallow for a bottle of brandy. Nevertheless, I believed she had remembered, had brought me my salvation. "You darling," I said, and tore it open.

It was a muffler. Gray wool. I stared at it for fully half a minute without realizing what it was. "Where's the brandy?" I said.

She looked shocked. Her nose got redder and her eyes started to blur. "You need this more. You haven't any clothing coupons and you have to be outside all the time. It's been so dreadful cold."

"I *needed* the brandy," I said angrily.

"I was only trying to be kind," she started, and I cut her off.

"Kind?" I said. "I asked you for brandy. I don't recall ever saying I needed a muffler." I shoved it back at her and began untangling a string of colored lights that had shattered when the tree fell.

She got that same holy martyr look Kivrin is so wonderful at. "I worry about you all the time up here," she said in a rush. "They're *trying* for St. Paul's, you know. And it's so close to the river. I didn't think you should be drinking. I – it's a crime when they're trying so hard to kill us all that you won't take care of yourself. It's like you're in it with them. I worry someday I'll come up to St. Paul's and you won't be here."

"Well, and what exactly am I supposed to do with a muffler? Hold it over my head when they drop the bombs?"

She turned and ran, disappearing into the gray fog before she had gone down two steps. I started after her, still holding the string of broken lights, tripped over it, and fell almost all the way to the bottom of the steps.

Langby picked me up. "You're off watches," he said grimly.

"You can't do that," I said.

"Oh, yes, I can. I don't want any walking dead on the roofs with me."

I let him lead me down here to the crypt, make me a cup of tea, put me to bed, all very solicitous. No indication that this is what he has been waiting for. I will lie here till the sirens go. Once I am on the roofs he will not be able to send me back without seeming suspicious. Do you know what he said before he left, asbestos coat and rubber boots, the dedicated fire watcher? "I want you to get some sleep." As if I could sleep with Langby on the roofs. I would be burned alive.

December 30 – The sirens woke me, and old Bence-Jones said, "That should have done you some good. You've slept the clock round."

"What day is it?" I said, going for my boots.

"The twenty-ninth," he said, and as I dived for the door, "No need to hurry. They're late tonight. Maybe they won't come at all. That'd be a blessing, that would. The tide's out."

I stopped by the door to the stairs, holding on to the cool stone. "Is St. Paul's all right?"

"She's still standing," he said. "Have a bad dream?"

"Yes," I said, remembering the bad dreams of all the past weeks – the dead cat in my arms in St. John's Wood, Langby with his parcel and his *Worker* under his arm, the fire watch stone garishly lit by Christ's lantern. Then I remembered I had not dreamed at all. I had slept the kind of sleep I had prayed for, the kind of sleep that would help me remember.

Then I remembered. Not St. Paul's, burned to the ground by the communists. A headline from the dailies. "Marble Arch hit. Eighteen killed by blast." The date was not clear except for the year. 1940. There were exactly two more days left in 1940. I grabbed my coat and muffler and ran up the stairs and across the marble floor.

"Where the hell do you think you're going?" Langby shouted to me. I couldn't see him.

"I have to save Enola," I said, and my voice echoed in the dark sanctuary. "They're going to bomb Marble Arch."

"You can't leave now," he shouted after me, standing where the fire watch stone would be. "The tide's out. You dirty – "

I didn't hear the rest of it. I had already flung myself down the steps and into a taxi. It took almost all the money I had, the money I had so carefully hoarded for the trip back to St. John's Wood. Shelling started while we were still in Oxford Street, and the driver refused to go any farther. He let me out into pitch blackness, and I saw I would never make it in time.

Blast. Enola crumpled on the stairway down to the tube, her open-toed shoes still on her feet, not a mark on her. And when I try to lift her, jelly under the skin. I would have to wrap her in the muffler she gave me, because I was too late. I had gone back a hundred years to be too late to save her.

I ran the last blocks, guided by the gun emplacement that had to be in Hyde Park, and skidded down the steps into Marble Arch. The woman in the ticket booth took my last shilling for a ticket to St. Paul's Station. I stuck it in my pocket and raced toward the stairs.

"No running," she said placidly. "To your left, please." The door to the right was blocked off by wooden barricades, the metal gates beyond pulled to and chained. The board with names on it for the stations was x-ed with tape, and a new sign that read ALL TRAINS was nailed to the barricade, pointing left.

Enola was not on the stopped escalators or sitting against the wall in the hallway. I came to the first stairway and could not get through. A family had set out, just where I wanted to step, a communal tea of

bread and butter, a little pot of jam sealed with waxed paper, and a
kettle on a ring like the one Langby and I had rescued out of the
rubble, all of it spread on a cloth embroidered at the corners with
flowers. I stood staring down at the layered tea, spread like a waterfall
down the steps.

"I – Marble Arch – " I said. Another twenty killed by flying tiles.
"You shouldn't be here."

"We've as much right as anyone," the man said belligerently, "and
who are you to tell us to move on?"

A woman lifting saucers out of a cardboard box looked up at me,
frightened. The kettle began to whistle.

"It's you that should move on," the man said. "Go on then." He
stood off to one side so I could pass. I edged past the embroidered cloth
apologetically.

"I'm sorry," I said. "I'm looking for someone. On the platform."

"You'll never find her in there, mate," the man said, thumbing in
that direction. I hurried past him, nearly stepping on the tea cloth, and
rounded the corner into hell.

It was not hell. Shopgirls folded coats and leaned back against them,
cheerful or sullen or disagreeable, but certainly not damned. Two boys
scuffled for a shilling and lost it on the tracks. They bent over the edge,
debating whether to go after it, and the station guard yelled to them to
back away. A train rumbled through, full of people. A mosquito landed
on the guard's hand and he reached out to slap it and missed. The boys
laughed. And behind and before them, stretching in all directions
down the deadly tile curves of the tunnel like casualties, backed into
the entranceways and onto the stairs, were people. Hundreds and
hundreds of people.

I stumbled back onto the stairs, knocking over a teacup. It spilled
like a flood across the cloth.

"I told you, mate," the man said cheerfully. "It's hell in there, ain't
it? And worse below."

"Hell," I said. "Yes." I would never find her. I would never save her.
I looked at the woman mopping up the tea, and it came to me that I
could not save her either. Enola or the cat or any of them, lost here in
the endless stairways and cul-de-sacs of time. They were already dead
a hundred years, past saving. The past is beyond saving. Surely that
was the lesson the history department sent me all this way to learn.
Well, fine, I've learned it. Can I go home now?

Of course not, dear boy. You have foolishly spent all your money on
taxicabs and brandy, and tonight is the night the Germans burn the

City. (Now it is too late, I remember it all. Twenty-eight incendiaries on the roofs.) Langby must have his chance, and you must learn the hardest lesson of all and the one you should have known from the beginning. You cannot save St. Paul's.

I went back out onto the platform and stood behind the yellow line until a train pulled up. I took my ticket out and held it in my hand all the way to St. Paul's Station. When I got there, smoke billowed toward me like an easy spray of water. I could not see St. Paul's.

"The tide's out," a woman said in a voice devoid of hope, and I went down in a snake pit of limp cloth hoses. My hands came up covered with rank-smelling mud, and I understood finally (and too late) the significance of the tide. There was no water to fight the fires.

A policeman barred my way and I stood helplessly before him with no idea what to say. "No civilians allowed here," he said. "St. Paul's is for it." The smoke billowed like a thundercloud, alive with sparks, and the dome rose golden above it.

"I'm fire watch," I said, and his arm fell away, and then I was on the roofs.

My endorphin levels must have been going up and down like an air raid siren. I do not have any short-term from then on, just moments that do not fit together: the people in the church when we brought Langby down, huddled in a corner playing cards, the whirlwind of burning scraps of wood in the dome, the ambulance driver who wore open-toed shoes like Enola and smeared salve on my burned hands. And in the center, the one clear moment when I went after Langby on a rope and saved his life.

I stood by the dome, blinking against the smoke. The City was on fire and it seemed as if St. Paul's would ignite from the heat, would crumble from the noise alone. Bence-Jones was by the northwest tower, hitting at an incendiary with a spade. Langby was too close to the patched place where the bomb had gone through, looking toward me. An incendiary clattered behind him. I turned to grab a shovel, and when I turned back, he was gone.

"Langby!" I shouted, and could not hear my own voice. He had fallen into the chasm and nobody saw him or the incendiary. Except me. I do not remember how I got across the roof. I think I called for a rope. I got a rope. I tied it around my waist, gave the ends of it into the hands of the fire watch, and went over the side. The fires lit the walls of the hole almost all the way to the bottom. Below me I could see a pile of whitish rubble. He's under there, I thought, and jumped free of the wall. The space was so narrow there was nowhere to throw the rubble. I was afraid I would inadvertently stone him, and I tried to toss the pieces of planking and plaster over my shoulder, but there was barely room to turn. For one awful moment I thought he might not be there at all, that the pieces of splintered wood would brush away to reveal empty pavement, as they had in the crypt.

I was numbed by the indignity of crawling over him. If he was dead I did not think I could bear the shame of stepping on his helpless body. Then his hand came up like a ghost's and grabbed my ankle, and within seconds I had whirled and had his head free.

He was the ghastly white that no longer frightens me. "I put the bomb out," he said. I stared at him, so overwhelmed with relief I could not speak. For one hysterical moment I thought I would even laugh, I was so glad to see him. I finally realized what it was I was supposed to say.

"Are you all right?" I said.

"Yes," he said, and tried to raise himself on one elbow. "So much the worse for you.

He could not get up. He grunted with pain when he tried to shift his weight to his right side and lay back, the uneven rubble crunching sickeningly under him. I tried to lift him gently so I could see where he was hurt. He must have fallen on something.

"It's no use," he said, breathing hard. "I put it out."

I spared him a startled glance, afraid that he was delirious and went back to rolling him onto his side.

"I know you were counting on this one," he went on, not resisting me at all. "It was bound to happen sooner or later with all these roofs. Only I went after it. What'll you tell your friends?"

His asbestos coat was torn down the back in a long gash. Under it his back was charred and smoking. He had fallen on the incendiary. "Oh, my God," I said, trying frantically to see how badly he was burned without touching him. I had no way of knowing how deep the burns went, but they seemed to extend only in the narrow space where the coat had torn. I tried to pull the bomb out from under him, but the casing was as hot as a stove. It was not melting, though. My sand and Langby's body had smothered it. I had no idea if it would start up again when it was exposed to the air. I looked around, a little wildly, for the bucket and stirrup pump Langby must have dropped when he fell.

"Looking for a weapon?" Langby said, so clearly it was hard to believe he was hurt at all. "Why not just leave me here? A bit of overexposure and I'd be done for by morning. Or would you rather do your dirty work in private?"

I stood up and yelled to the men on the roof above us. One of them shone a pocket torch down at us, but its light didn't reach.

"Is he dead?" somebody shouted down to me.

"Send for an ambulance," I said. "He's been burned."

I helped Langby up, trying to support his back without touching the burn. He staggered a little and then leaned against the wall, watching me as I tried to bury the incendiary, using a piece of the planking as a scoop. The rope came down and I tied Langby to it. He had not spoken since I helped him up. He let me tie the rope around his waist, still looking steadily at me. "I should have let you smother in the crypt," he said.

He stood leaning easily, almost relaxed against the wooden supports, his hands holding him up. I put his hands on the slack rope and wrapped it once around them for the grip I knew he didn't have. "I've been onto you since that day in the Gallery. I knew you weren't afraid of heights. You came down here without any fear of heights when you thought I'd ruined your precious plans. What was it? An attack of conscience? Kneeling there like a baby, whining, 'What have we done? What have we done?' You made me sick. But you know what gave you away first? The cat. Everybody knows cats hate water. Everybody but a dirty Nazi spy."

There was a tug on the rope. "Come ahead," I said, and the rope tautened.

"That WVS tart? Was she a spy, too? Supposed to meet you in Marble Arch? Telling me it was going to be bombed. You're a rotten spy, Bartholomew. Your friends already blew it up in September. It's open again."

The rope jerked suddenly and began to lift Langby. He twisted his hands to get a better grip. His right shoulder scraped the wall. I put up my hands and pushed him gently so that his left side was to the wall. "You're making a big mistake, you know," he said. "You should have killed me. I'll tell."

I stood in the darkness, waiting for the rope. Langby was unconscious when be reached the roof. I walked past the fire watch to the dome and down to the crypt.

This morning the letter from my uncle came and with it a five-pound note.

December 31 – Two of Dunworthy's flunkies met me in St. John's Wood to tell me I was late for my exams. I did not even protest. I shuffled obediently after them without even considering how unfair it was to

give an exam to one of the walking dead. I had not slept in – how long?
Since yesterday when I went to find Enola. I had not slept in a
hundred years.

Dunworthy was in the Examination Buildings, blinking at me. One
of the flunkies handed me a test paper and the other one called time.
I turned the paper over and left an oily smudge from the ointment on
my burns. I stared uncomprehendingly at them. I had grabbed at the
incendiary when I turned Langby over, but these burns were on the
backs of my hands. The answer came to me suddenly in Langby's
unyielding voice. "They're rope burns, you fool. Don't they teach you
Nazi spies the proper way to come up a rope?"

I looked down at the test. It read, "Number of incendiaries that fell
on St. Paul's Number——of land mines——Number of high
explosive bombs——Method most commonly used for extinguishing
incendiaries——land mines——high explosive bombs——Number of
volunteers on first watch——second watch——Casualties——
Fatalities——" The questions made no sense. There was only a short
space, long enough for the writing of a number, after any of the
questions. Method most commonly used for extinguishing incendiaries. How would I ever fit what I knew into that narrow space? Where
were the questions about Enola and Langby and the cat?

I went up to Dunworthy's desk. "St. Paul's almost burned down last
night," I said. "What kind of questions are these?"

"You should be answering questions, Mr. Bartholomew, not asking
them."

"There aren't any questions about the people," I said. The outer
casing of my anger began to melt.

"Of course there are," Dunworthy said, flipping to the second page
of the test. "Number of casualties, 1940. Blast, shrapnel, other."

"Other?" I said. At any moment the roof would collapse on me in a
shower of plaster dust and fury. "Other? Langby put out a fire with his
own body. Enola has a cold that keeps getting worse. The cat . . ." I
snatched the paper back from him and scrawled "one cat" in the
narrow space next to "blast." "Don't you care about them at all?"

"They're important from a statistical point of view," he said, "but as
individuals they are hardly relevant to the course of history."

My reflexes were shot. It was amazing to me that Dunworthy's were
almost as slow. I grazed the side of his jaw and knocked his glasses off.
"Of course they're relevant!" I shouted. "They *are* the history, not all
these bloody numbers!"

The reflexes of the flunkies were very fast. They did not let me start another swing at him before they had me by both arms and were hauling me out of the room.

"They're back there in the past with nobody to save them. They can't see their hands in front of their faces and there are bombs falling down on them and you tell me they aren't important? You call that being an historian?"

The flunkies dragged me out the door and down the hall. "Langby saved St. Paul's. How much more important can a person get? You're no historian! You're nothing but a – " I wanted to call him a terrible name, but the only curses I could summon up were Langby's. "You're nothing but a dirty Nazi spy!" I bellowed. "You're nothing but a lazy bourgeois tart!"

They dumped me on my hands and knees outside the door and slammed it in my face. "I wouldn't be an historian if you paid me!" I shouted, and went to see the fire watch stone.

December 31 – I am having to write this in bits and pieces. My hands are in pretty bad shape, and Dunworthy's boys didn't help matters much. Kivrin comes in periodically, wearing her St. Joan look, and smears so much salve on my hands that I can't hold a pencil.

St. Paul's Station is not there, of course, so I got out at Holborn and walked, thinking about my last meeting with Dean Matthews on the morning after the burning of the city. This morning.

"I understand you saved Langby's life," he said. "I also understand that between you, you saved St. Paul's last night."

I showed him the letter from my uncle and he stared at it as if he could not think what it was. "Nothing stays saved forever," he said, and for a terrible moment I thought he was going to tell me Langby had died. "We shall have to keep on saving St. Paul's until Hitler decides to bomb something else."

The raids on London are almost over, I wanted to tell him. He'll start bombing the countryside in a matter of weeks. Canterbury, Bath, aiming always at the cathedrals. You and St. Paul's will both outlast the war and live to dedicate the fire watch stone.

"I am hopeful, though," he said. "I think the worst is over."

"Yes, sir." I thought of the stone, its letters still readable after all this time. No, sir, the worst is not over.

I managed to keep my bearings almost to the top of Ludgate Hill. Then I lost my way completely, wandering about like a man in a graveyard. I had not remembered that the rubble looked so much like the white plaster dust Langby had tried to dig me out of. I could not find the stone anywhere. In the end I nearly fell over it, jumping back as if I had stepped on a body.

It is all that's left. Hiroshima is supposed to have had a handful of untouched trees at ground zero. Denver the capitol steps. Neither of them says, "Remember men and women of St. Paul's Watch who by the grace of God saved this cathedral." The grace of God.

Part of the stone is sheared off. Historians argue there was another line that said, "for all time," but I do not believe that, not if Dean Matthews had anything to do with it. And none of the watch it was dedicated to would have believed it for a minute. We saved St. Paul's every time we put out an incendiary, and only until the next one fell. Keeping watch on the danger spots, putting out the little fires with sand and stirrup pumps, the big ones with our bodies, in order to keep the whole vast complex structure from burning down. Which sounds to me like a course description for History Practicum 401. What a fine time to discover what historians are for when I have tossed my chance for being one out the windows as easily as they tossed the pinpoint bomb in! No, sir, the worst is not over.

There are flash burns on the stone, where legend says the Dean of St. Paul's was kneeling when the bomb went off. Totally apocryphal, of course, since the front door is hardly an appropriate place for prayers. It is more likely the shadow of a tourist who wandered in to ask the whereabouts of the Windmill Theatre, or the imprint of a girl bringing a volunteer his muffler. Or a cat.

Nothing is saved forever, Dean Matthews, and I knew that when I walked in the west doors that first day, blinking into the gloom, but it is pretty bad nevertheless. Standing here knee-deep in rubble out of which I will not be able to dig any folding chairs or friends, knowing that Langby died thinking I was a Nazi spy, knowing that Enola came one day and I wasn't there. It's pretty bad.

But it is not as bad as it could be. They are both dead, and Dean Matthews too, but they died without knowing what I knew all along, what sent me to my knees in the Whispering Gallery, sick with grief and guilt: that in the end none of us saved St. Paul's. And Langby cannot turn to me, stunned and sick at heart, and say, "Who did this? Your friends the Nazis?" And I would have to say, "No, the communists." That would be the worst.

I have come back to the room and let Kivrin smear more salve on my hands. She wants me to get some sleep. I know I should pack and get gone. It will be humiliating to have them come and throw me out, but I do not have the strength to fight her. She looks so much like Enola.

January 1 – I have apparently slept not only through the night, but through the morning mail drop as well. When I woke up just now, I found Kivrin sitting on the end of the bed holding an envelope. "Your grades came," she said.

I put my arm over my eyes. "They can be marvellously efficient when they want to, can't they?"

"Yes," Kivrin said.

"Well, let's see it," I said, sitting up. "How long do I have before they come and throw me out?"

She handed the flimsy computer envelope to me. I tore it along the perforation. "Wait," she said. "Before you open it, I want to say something." She put her hand gently on my burns. "You're wrong about the history department. They're very good."

It was not exactly what I expected her to say. "Good is not the word I'd use to describe Dunworthy," I said and yanked the inside slip free.

Kivrin's look did not change, not even when I sat there with the printout on my knees where she could surely see it.

"Well," I said.

The slip was hand-signed by the esteemed Dunworthy. I have taken a first. With honors.

January 2 – Two things came in the mail today. One was Kivrin's assignment. The history department thinks of everything – even to keeping her here long enough to nursemaid me, even to coming up with a prefabricated trial by fire to send their history majors through.

I think I wanted to believe that was what they had done, Enola and Langby only hired actors, the cat a clever android with its clockwork innards taken out for the final effect, not so much because I wanted to believe Dunworthy was not good at all, but because then I would not have this nagging pain at not knowing what had happened to them.

"You said your practicum was England in 1400?" I said, watching her as suspiciously as I had watched Langby.

"1349," she said, and her face went slack with memory. "The plague year."

"My God," I said. "How could they do that? The plague's a ten."

"I have a natural immunity," she said, and looked at her hands.

Because I could not think of anything to say, I opened the other piece of mail. It was a report on Enola. Computer-printed, facts and dates and statistics, all the numbers the history department so dearly loves, but it told me what I thought I would have to go without knowing: that she had gotten over her cold and survived the Blitz.

Young Tom had been killed in the Baedaker raids on Bath, but Enola had lived until 2006, the year before they blew up St. Paul's.

I don't know whether I believe the report or not, but it does not matter. It is, like Langby's reading aloud to the old man, a simple act of human kindness. They think of everything.

Not quite. They did not tell me what happened to Langby. But I find as I write this that I already know: I saved his life. It does not seem to matter that he might have died in hospital next day, and I find, in spite of all the hard lessons the history department has tried to teach me, I do not quite believe this one: that nothing is saved forever. It seems to me that perhaps Langby is.

January 3 – I went to see Dunworthy today. I don't know what I intended to say – some pompous drivel about my willingness to serve in the fire watch of history, standing guard against the falling incendiaries of the human heart, silent and saintly.

But he blinked at me nearsightedly across his desk, and it seemed to me that he was blinking at that last bright image of St. Paul's in sunlight before it was gone forever and that he knew better than anyone that the past cannot he saved, and I said instead, "I'm sorry that I broke your glasses, sir."

"How did you like St. Paul's?" he said, and like my first meeting with Enola, I felt I must be somehow reading the signals all wrong, that he was not feeling loss, but something quite different.

"I loved it, sir," I said.

"Yes," he said. "So do I."

Dean Matthews is wrong. I have fought with memory my whole practicum only to find that it is not the enemy at all, and being an historian is not some saintly burden after all. Because Dunworthy is not blinking against the fatal sunlight of the last morning, but into the gloom of that first afternoon, looking in the great west doors of St. Paul's at what is, like Langby, like all of it, every moment, in us, saved forever.

Goat Song

POUL ANDERSON

Poul Anderson (1926–2001) has written over sixty novels and published over forty collections of short stories in his long and influential career in science fiction. James Blish called Anderson "the enduring explosion" because of the high quality of his continuing literary production. Distinguished as a fantasy writer *(The Broken Sword* [1954] was his first adult novel) and a mystery writer (his first mystery, *Perish By the Sword* [1959], won the Cock Robin prize), he is nevertheless principally one of the heroic figures of hard science fiction. While a devotee of the hard science approach of Hal Clement, he is given to making his stories vehicles for philosophical and social commentary, in the manner of Heinlein.

Anderson has always defended the traditions of military honor in his fiction, and devoted much of his effort to adventure plots. But he has also turned out a number of colorful, powerful SF stories and novels, from *Brain Wave* (1954) to *The Boat of a Million Years* (1989), that are generally perceived as his major works – the most famous is probably *Tau Zero* (1970). These are marked by astronomical and physical speculation and large-scale Stapledonian vistas of time and space. Even in his swashbuckling adventure stories, Anderson is famous for beginning with calculations of the elements of the orbit of the world to be his setting, and allowing the physics, chemistry, and biology to follow logically, thus generating the parameters in which human beings would have to live and survive.

He is also interested in mythology and often uses myth in his fiction, as in this story. "Goat Song," from the 1970s, is one of his many Hugo Award-winning stories, hard science fiction with an overlay of mythic fantasy.

Three women: one is dead; one is alive; One is both and neither, and will never live and never die, being immortal in SUM.

On a hill above that valley through which runs the highroad, I await Her passage. Frost came early this year, and the grasses have paled. Otherwise the slope is begrown with blackberry bushes that have been harvested by men and birds, leaving only briars, and with certain apple trees. They are very old, those trees, survivors of an orchard raised by generations which none but SUM now remembers (I can see a few fragments of wall thrusting above the brambles) scattered crazily over the hillside and as crazily gnarled. A little fruit remains on them. Chill across my skin, a gust shakes loose an apple. I hear it knock on the earth, another stroke of some eternal clock. The shrubs whisper to the wind.

Elsewhere the ridges around me are wooded, afire with scarlets and brasses and bronzes. The sky is huge, the westering sun wanbright. The valley is filling with a deeper blue, a haze whose slight smokiness touches my nostrils. This is Indian summer, the funeral pyre of the year.

There have been other seasons. There have been other lifetimes, before mine and hers; and in those days they had words to sing with. We still allow ourselves music, though, and I have spent much time planting melodies around my rediscovered words. *"In the greenest growth of the May-time – "* I unsling the harp on my back, and tune it afresh, and sing it to her, straight into autumn and the waning day.

> *" – You came, and the sun came after,*
> *And the green grew golden above:*
> *And the flag-flowers lightened with laughter,*
> *And the meadowsweet shook with love."*

A footfall stirs the grasses, quite gently, and the woman says, trying to chuckle, "Why, thank you."

Once, so soon after my one's death that I was still dazed by it, I stood in the home that had been ours. This was on the hundred and first floor of a most desirable building. After dark the city flamed for us, blinked, glittered, flung immense sheets of radiance forth like banners. Nothing but SUM could have controlled the firefly dance of a million aircars among the towers: or, for that matter, have maintained the entire city, from nuclear powerplants through automated factories, physical and economic distribution networks, sanitation, repair, services, education, culture, order, everything as one immune immortal organism. We had gloried in belonging to this as well as to each other.

But that night I told the kitchen to throw the dinner it had made for me down the waste chute, and ground under my heel the chemical consolations which the medicine cabinet extended to me, and kicked the cleaner as it picked up the mess, and ordered the lights not to go on, anywhere in our suite. I stood by the vieWall, looking out across megalopolis, and it was tawdry. In my hands I had a little clay figure she had fashioned herself. I turned it over and over and over.

But I had forgotten to forbid the door to admit visitors. It recognized this woman and opened for her. She had come with the kindly intention of teasing me out of a mood that seemed to her unnatural. I heard her enter, and looked around through the gloom. She had almost the same height as my girl did, and her hair chanced to be bound in a way that my girl often favored, and the figurine dropped from my grasp and shattered, because for an instant I thought she was my girl. Since then I have been hard put not to hate Thrakia.

This evening, even without so much sundown light, I would not make that mistake. Nothing but the silvery bracelet about her left wrist bespeaks the past we share. She is in wildcountry garb: boots, kilt of true fur and belt of true leather, knife at hip and rifle slung on shoulder. Her locks are matted and snarled, her skin brown from weeks of weather; scratches and smudges show beneath the fantastic zigzags she has painted in many colors on herself. She wears a necklace of bird skulls.

Now that one who is dead was, in her own way, more a child of trees and horizons than Thrakia's followers. She was so much at home in the open that she had no need to put off clothes or cleanliness, reason or gentleness, when we sickened of the cities and went forth beyond them. From this trait I got many of the names I bestowed on her, such as Wood's Colt or Fallow Hind or, from my prowlings among ancient books, Dryad and Elven. (She liked me to choose her names, and this pleasure had no end, because she was inexhaustible.)

I let my harpstring ring into silence. Turning about, I say to Thrakia, "I wasn't singing for you. Not for anyone. Leave me alone."

She draws a breath. The wind ruffles her hair and brings me an odor of her: not female sweetness, but fear. She clenches her fists and says, "You're crazy."

"Wherever did you find a meaningful word like that?" I gibe; for my own pain and – to be truthful – my own fear must strike out at something, and here she stands. "Aren't you content any longer with 'untranquil' or 'disequilibrated'?"

"I got it from you," she says defiantly, "you and your damned archaic songs. There's another word, 'damned.' And how it suits you! When are you going to stop this morbidity?"

"And commit myself to a clinic and have my brain laundered nice and sanitary? Not soon, darling." I use *that* last word aforethought, but she cannot know what scorn and sadness are in it for me, who know that once it could also have been a name for my girl. The official grammar and pronunciation of language is as frozen as every other aspect of our civilization, thanks to electronic recording and neuronic teaching; but meanings shift and glide about like subtle serpents. (O adder that stung my Foalfoot!)

I shrug and say in my driest, most city-technological voice, "Actually, I'm the practical, nonmorbid one. Instead of running away from my emotions – via drugs, or neuroadjustment, or playing at savagery like you, for that matter – I'm about to implement a concrete plan for getting back the person who made me happy."

"By disturbing Her on Her way home?"

"Anyone has the right to petition the dark Queen while she's abroad on earth."

"But this is past the proper time – "

"No law's involved, just custom. People are afraid to meet Her outside a crowd, a town, bright flat lights. They won't admit it, but they are. So I came here precisely not to be part of a queue. I don't want to speak into a recorder for subsequent computer analysis of my words. How could I be sure She was listening? I want to meet Her as myself, a unique being, and look in Her eyes while I make my prayer."

Thrakia chokes a little. "She'll be angry."

"Is She able to be angry, anymore?"

"I . . . I don't know. What you mean to ask for is so impossible, though. So absurd. That SUM should give you back your girl. You know It never makes exceptions."

"Isn't She Herself an exception?"

"That's different. You're being silly. SUM has to have a, well, a direct human liaison. Emotional and cultural feedback, as well as statistics. How else can It govern rationally? And She must have been chosen out of the whole world. Your girl, what was she? Nobody!"

"To me, she was everybody."

"You – " Thrakia catches her lip in her teeth. One hand reaches out and closes on my bare forearm, a hard hot touch, the grimy fingernails biting. When I make no response, she lets go and stares at the ground.

A V of outbound geese passes overhead. Their cries come shrill through the wind, which is loudening in the forest.

"Well," she says, "you are special. You always were. You went to space and came back, with the Great Captain. You're maybe the only man alive who understands about the ancients. And your singing, yes, you don't really entertain, your songs trouble people and can't be forgotten. So maybe She will listen to you. But SUM won't. It can't give special resurrections. Once that was done, a single time, wouldn't it have to be done for everybody? The dead would overrun the living."

"Not necessarily," I say. "In any event, I mean to try."

"Why can't you wait for the promised time? Surely, then, SUM will re-create you two in the same generation."

"I'd have to live out this life, at least, without her," I say, looking away also, down to the highroad which shines through shadow like death's snake, the length of the valley. "Besides, how do you know there ever will be any resurrections? We have only a promise. No, less than that. An announced policy."

She gasps, steps back, raises her hands as if to fend me off. Her soul bracelet casts light into my eyes. I recognize an embryo exorcism. She lacks ritual; every "superstition" was patiently scrubbed out of our metal-and-energy world, long ago. But if she has no word for it, no concept, nevertheless she recoils from blasphemy.

So I say, wearily, not wanting an argument, wanting only to wait here alone: "Never mind. There could be some natural catastrophe, like a giant asteroid striking, that wiped out the system before conditions had become right for resurrections to commence."

"That's impossible," she says, almost frantic. "The homeostats, the repair functions – "

"All right, call it a vanishingly unlikely theoretical contingency. Let's declare that I'm so selfish I want Swallow Wing back now, in this life of mine, and don't give a curse whether that'll be fair to the rest of you."

You won't care either, anyway, I think. None of you. You don't grieve. It is your own precious private consciousnesses that you wish to preserve; no one else is close enough to you to matter very much. Would you believe me if I told you I am quite prepared to offer SUM my own death in exchange for It releasing Blossom-in-the-Sun?

I don't speak that thought, which would be cruel, nor repeat what is crueller: my fear that SUM lies, that the dead never will be disgorged. For (I am not the All-Controller, I think not with vacuum and negative energy levels but with ordinary begotten molecules; yet I can reason somewhat dispassionately, being disillusioned) consider –

The object of the game is to maintain a society stable, just, and sane. This requires satisfaction not only of somatic, but of symbolic and instinctual needs. Thus children must be allowed to come into being. The minimum number per generation is equal to the maximum: that number which will maintain a constant population.

It is also desirable to remove the fear of death from men. Hence the promise: At such time as it is socially feasible, SUM will begin to refashion us, with our complete memories but in the pride of our youth. This can be done over and over, life after life across the millennia. So death is, indeed, a sleep.

– *in that sleep of death, what dreams may come* – No. I myself dare not dwell on this. I ask merely, privately: Just when and how does SUM expect conditions (in a stabilized society, mind you) to have become so different from today's that the reborn can, in their millions, safely be welcomed back?

I see no reason why SUM should not lie to us. We, too, are objects in the world that It manipulates.

"We've quarreled about this before, Thrakia," I sigh. "Often. Why do you bother?"

"I wish I knew," she answers low. Half to herself, she goes on: "Of course I want to copulate with you. You must be good, the way that girl used to follow you about with her eyes, and smile when she touched your hand, and – But you can't be better than everyone else. That's unreasonable. There are only so many possible ways. So why do I care if you wrap yourself up in silence and go off alone? Is it that that makes you a challenge?"

"You think too much," I say. "Even here. You're a pretend primitive. You visit wildcountry to 'slake inborn atavistic impulses' . . . but you can't dismantle that computer inside yourself and simply feel, simply be."

She bristles. I touched a nerve there. Looking past her, along the ridge of fiery maple and sumac, brassy elm and great dun oak, I see others emerge from beneath the trees. Women exclusively, her followers, as unkempt as she; one has a brace of ducks lashed to her waist, and their blood has trickled down her thigh and dried black. For this movement, this unadmitted mystique has become Thrakia's by now: that not only men should forsake the easy routine and the easy pleasure of the cities, and become again, for a few weeks each year, the carnivores who begot our species; women too should seek out starkness, the better to appreciate civilization when they return.

I feel a moment's unease. We are in no park, with laid-out trails and campground services. We are in wildcountry. Not many men come here, ever, and still fewer women; for the region is, literally, beyond the law. No deed done here is punishable. We are told that this helps consolidate society, as the most violent among us may thus vent their passions. But I have spent much time in wildcountry since my Morning Star went out – myself in quest of nothing but solitude – and I have watched what happens through eyes that have also read anthropology and history. Institutions are developing; ceremonies, tribalisms, acts of blood and cruelty and acts elsewhere called unnatural are becoming more elaborate and more expected every year. Then the practitioners go home to their cities and honestly believe they have been enjoying fresh air, exercise, and good tension-releasing fun.

Let her get angry enough and Thrakia can call knives to her aid.

Wherefore I make myself lay both hands on her shoulders, and meet the tormented gaze, and say most gently, "I'm sorry. I know you mean well. You're afraid She will be annoyed and bring misfortune on your people."

Thrakia gulps. "No," she whispers. "That wouldn't be logical. But I'm afraid of what might happen to you. And then – " Suddenly she throws herself against me. I feel arms, breasts, belly press through my tunic, and smell meadows in her hair and musk in her mouth. "You'd be gone!" she wails. "Then who'd sing to us?"

"Why, the planet's crawling with entertainers," I stammer.

"You're more than that," she says. "So much more. I don't like what you sing, not really – and what you've sung since that stupid girl died, oh, meaningless, horrible! – but, I don't know why, I *want* you to trouble me."

Awkward, I pat her back. The sun now stands very little above the treetops. Its rays slant interminably through the booming, frosting air. I shiver in my tunic and buskins and wonder what to do.

A sound rescues me. It comes from one end of the valley below us, where further view is blocked off by two cliffs; it thunders deep in our ears and rolls through the earth into our bones. We have heard that sound in the cities, and been glad to have walls and lights and multitudes around us. Now we are alone with it, the noise of Her chariot.

The women shriek, I hear them faintly across wind and rumble and my own pulse, and they vanish into the woods. They will seek their camp, dress warmly, build enormous fires; presently they will eat their ecstatics, and rumors are uneasy about what they do after that.

Thrakia seizes my left wrist, above the soul bracelet, and hauls.

"Harper, come with me!" she pleads. I break loose from her and stride down the hill toward the road. A scream follows me for a moment.

Light still dwells in the sky and on the ridges, but as I descend into that narrow valley I enter dusk, and it thickens. Indistinct bramble-bushes whicker where I brush them, and claw back at me. I feel the occasional scratch on my legs, the tug as my garment is snagged, the chill that I breathe, but dimly. My perceived-outer-reality is over-powered by the rushing of Her chariot and my blood. My inner-universe is fear, yes, but exaltation too, a drunkenness which sharpens instead of dulling the senses, a psychedelia which opens the reasoning mind as well as the emotions; I have gone beyond myself, I am embodied purpose. Not out of need for comfort, but to voice what Is, I return to words whose speaker rests centuries dust, and lend them my own music. I sing:

> " – Cold is my heart, and the world's golden,
> And one peak tipped with light;
> And the air lies still about the hill
> With the first fear of night;
>
> "Till mystery down the soundless valley
> Thunders, and dark is here;
> And the wind blows, and the light goes,
> And the night is full of fear.
>
> "And I know one night, on some far height,
> In a tongue I never knew,
> I yet shall hear the tidings clear
> From them that were friends of you.
>
> "They'll call the news from hill to hill,
> Dark and uncomforted,
> Earth and sky and the winds; and I
> Shall know that you are dead. – "

But I have reached the valley floor, and She has come in sight.

Her chariot is unlit, for radar eyes and inertial guides need no lamps, nor sun nor stars. Wheel-less, the steel tear rides on its own roar and thrust of air. The pace is not great, far less than any of our mortals' vehicles are wont to take. Men say the Dark Queen rides thus slowly in order that She may perceive with Her own senses and so be the better prepared to counsel SUM. But now Her annual round is finished; She is homeward bound; until spring She will dwell with It Which is our lord. Why does She not hasten tonight?

Because Death has never a need of haste? I wonder. And as I step into the middle of the road, certain lines from the yet more ancient past rise tremendous within me, and I strike my harp and chant them louder than the approaching car:

> *"I that in heill was and gladness*
> *Am trublit now with great sickness*
> *And feblit with infirmitie: –*
> Timor mortis conturbat me."

The car detects me and howls a warning. I hold my ground. The car could swing around, the road is wide and in any event a smooth surface is not absolutely necessary. But I hope, I believe that She will be aware of an obstacle in Her path, and tune in Her various amplifiers, and find me abnormal enough to stop for. Who, in SUM's world – who, even among the explorers that It has sent beyond in Its unappeasable hunger for data – would stand in a cold wildcountry dusk and shout while his harp snarls

> *"Our pleasance here is all vain glory,*
> *This fals world is but transitory,*
> *The flesh is bruckle, the Feynd is slee: –*
> Timor mortis conturbat me.*
>
> *"The state of man does change and vary,*
> *Now sound, now sick, now blyth, now sary,*
> *No dansand mirry, now like to die: –*
> Timor mortis conturbat me.*
>
> *"No state in Erd here standis sicker;*
> *As with the wynd wavis the wicker*
> *So wannis this world's vanitie: –*
> Timor mortis conturbat me. – ?"*

The car draws alongside and sinks to the ground. I let my strings die away into the wind. The sky overhead and in the west is gray-purple; eastward it is quite dark and a few early stars peer forth. Here, down in the valley, shadows are heavy and I cannot see very well.

The canopy slides back. She stands erect in the chariot, thus looming over me. Her robe and cloak are black, fluttering like restless wings; beneath the cowl Her face is a white blur. I have seen it before, under full light, and in how many thousands of pictures; but at this hour I cannot call it back to my mind, not entirely. I list sharp-sculptured profile and pale lips, sable hair and long green eyes, but these are nothing more than words.

"What are you doing?" She has a lovely low voice; but is it, as oh, how rarely since SUM took Her to Itself, is it the least shaken? "What is that you were singing?"

My answer comes so strong that my skull resonates; for I am borne higher and higher on my tide. "Lady of Ours, I have a petition."

"Why did you not bring it before Me when I walked among men? Tonight I am homebound. You must wait till I ride forth with the new year."

"Lady of Ours, neither You nor I would wish living ears to hear what I have to say."

She regards me for a long while. Do I indeed sense fear also in Her? (Surely not of me. Her chariot is armed and armored, and would react with machine speed to protect Her should I offer violence. And should I somehow, incredibly, kill Her, or wound Her beyond chemosurgical repair, She of all beings has no need to doubt death. The ordinary bracelet cries with quite sufficient radio loudness to be heard by more than one thanatic station, when we die; and in that shielding the soul can scarcely be damaged before the Winged Heels arrive to bear it off to SUM. Surely the Dark Queen's circlet can call still further, and is still better insulated, than any mortal's. And She will most absolutely be recreated. She has been, again and again; death and rebirth every seven years keep Her eternally young in the service of SUM. I have never been able to find out when She was first born.)

Fear, perhaps, of what I have sung and what I might speak?

At last She says – I can scarcely hear through the gusts and creak-ings in the trees – "Give me the Ring, then."

The dwarf robot which stands by Her throne when She sits among men appears beside Her and extends the massive dull-silver circle to me. I place my left arm within, so that my soul is enclosed. The tablet on the upper surface of the Ring, which looks so much like a jewel, slants away from me; I cannot read what flashes onto the bezel. But the faint glow picks Her features out of murk as She bends to look.

Of course, I tell myself, the actual soul is not scanned. That would take too long. Probably the bracelet which contains the soul has an identification code built in. The Ring sends this to an appropriate part of SUM, Which instantly sends back what is recorded under that code. I hope there is nothing more to it. SUM has not seen fit to tell us.

"What do you call yourself at the moment?" She asks.

A current of bitterness crosses my tide. "Lady of Ours, why should You care? Is not my real name the number I got when I was allowed to be born?"

Calm descends once more upon Her. "If I am to evaluate properly what you say, I must know more about you than these few official data. Name indicates mood."

I too feel unshaken again, my tide running so strong and smooth that I might not know I was moving did I not see time recede behind me. "Lady of Ours, I cannot give You a fair answer. In this past year I have not troubled with names, or with much of anything else. But some people who knew me from earlier days call me Harper."

"What do you do besides make that sinister music?"

"These days, nothing, Lady of Ours. I've money to live out my life, if I eat sparingly and keep no home. Often I am fed and housed for the sake of my songs."

"What you sang is unlike anything I have heard since – " Anew, briefly, that robot serenity is shaken. "Since before the world was stabilized. You should not wake dead symbols, Harper. They walk through men's dreams."

"Is that bad?"

"Yes. The dreams become nightmares. Remember: Mankind, every man who ever lived, was insane before SUM brought order, reason, and peace."

"Well, then," I say, "I will cease and desist if I may have my own dead wakened for me."

She stiffens. The tablet goes out. I withdraw my arm and the Ring is stored away by Her servant. So again She is faceless, beneath flickering stars, here at the bottom of this shadowed valley. Her voice falls cold as the air: "No one can be brought back to life before Resurrection Time is ripe."

I do not say, "What about You?" for that would be vicious. What did She think, how did She weep, when SUM chose Her of all the young on earth? What does She endure in Her centuries? I dare not imagine.

Instead, I smite my harp and sing, quietly this time:

> *"Strew on her roses, roses,*
> *And never a spray of yew.*
> *In quiet she reposes:*
> *Ah! Would that I did too."*

The Dark Queen cries, "What are you doing? Are you really insane?" I go straight to the last stanza.

> *"Her cabin'd, ample Spirit*
> *It flutter'd and fail'd for breath.*
> *To-night it doth inherit*
> *The vasty hall of Death."*

I know why my songs strike so hard: because they bear dreads and passions that no one is used to – that most of us hardly know could exist – in SUM's ordered universe. But I had not the courage to hope She would be as torn by them as I see. Has She not lived with more darkness and terror than the ancients themselves could conceive? She calls, "Who has died?"

"She had many names, Lady of Ours," I say. "None was beautiful enough. I can tell You her number, though."

"Your daughter? I . . . sometimes I am asked if a dead child cannot be brought back. Not often, anymore, when they go so soon to the crèche. But sometimes. I tell the mother she may have a new one; but if ever We started re-creating dead infants, at what age level could We stop?"

"No, this was my woman."

"Impossible!" Her tone seeks to be not unkindly but is, instead, well-nigh frantic. "You will have no trouble finding others. You are handsome, and your psyche is, is, is extraordinary. It burns like Lucifer."

"Do You remember the name Lucifer, Lady of Ours?" I pounce. "Then You are old indeed. So old that You must also remember how a man might desire only one woman, but her above the whole world and heaven."

She tries to defend Herself with a jeer: "Was that mutual, Harper? I know more of mankind than you do, and surely I am the last chaste woman in existence."

"Now that she is gone, Lady, yes, perhaps You are. But we – Do you know how she died? We had gone to a wildcountry area. A man saw her, alone, while I was off hunting gem rocks to make her a necklace. He approached her. She refused him. He threatened force. She fled.

This was desert land, viper land, and she was barefoot. One of them bit her. I did not find her till hours later. By then the poison and the unshaded sun – She died quite soon after she told me what had happened and that she loved me. I could not get her body to chemo-surgery in time for normal revival procedures. I had to let them cremate her and take her soul away to SUM."

"What right have you to demand her back, when no one else can be given their own?"

"The right that I love her, and she loves me. We are more necessary to each other than sun or moon. I do not think You could find another two people of whom this is so, Lady. And is not everyone entitled to claim what is necessary to his life? How else can society be kept whole?"

"You are being fantastic," She says thinly. "Let me go."

"No, Lady, I am speaking sober truth. But poor plain words won't serve me. I sing to You because then maybe You will understand." And I strike my harp anew; but it is more to her than Her that I sing.

> *"If I had thought thou couldst have died,*
> *I might not weep for thee:*
> *But I forgot, when by thy side,*
> *That thou couldst mortal be:*

> *"It never through my mind had past*
> *The time would e'er be o'er,*
> *And I on thee should look my last,*
> *And though shouldst smile no more!"*

"I cannot – ." She falters. "I do not know – any such feelings – so strong – existed any longer."

"Now You do, Lady of Ours. And is that not an important datum for SUM?"

"Yes. If true." Abruptly She leans toward me. I see Her shudder in the murk, under the flapping cloak, and hear Her jaws clatter with cold. "I cannot linger here. But ride with Me. Sing to Me. I think I can bear it."

So much have I scarcely expected. But my destiny is upon me. I mount into the chariot. The canopy slides shut and we proceed.

The main cabin encloses us. Behind its rear door must be facilities for Her living on earth; this is a big vehicle. But here is little except curved panels. They are true wood of different comely grains: so She also needs

periodic escape from our machine existence, does She? Furnishing is
scant and austere. The only sound is our passage, muffled to a murmur
for us; and, because their photo-multipliers are not activated, the scan-
ners show nothing outside but night. We huddle close to a glower, hands
extended toward its fieriness. Our shoulders brush, our bare arms, Her
skin is soft and Her hair falls loose over the thrown-back cowl, smelling of
the summer which is dead. What, is She still human?

After a timeless time, She says, not yet looking at me: "The thing
you sang, there on the highroad as I came near – I do not remember
it. Not even from the years before I became what I am."

"It is older than SUM," I answer, "and its truth will outlive It."

"Truth?" I see Her tense Herself. "Sing Me the rest."

My fingers are no longer too numb to call forth chords.

> " – Unto the Death gois all Estatis,
> Princis, Prelattis, and Potestatis,
> Baith rich and poor of all degree: –
> Timor mortis conturbat me.

> "He takis the knichtis in to the field
> Enarmit under helm and scheild;
> Victor he is at all mellie: –
> Timor mortis conturbat me.

> "That strong unmerciful tyrand
> Takis, on the motheris breast sowkand,
> The babe full of benignitie: –
> Timor mortis conturbat me.

> "He takis the campion in the stour,
> The captain closit in the tour,
> The ladie in bour full of bewtie: – "

(There I must stop a moment.)

> "Timor mortis conturbat me.

> "He sparis no lord for his piscence,
> Na clerk for his intelligence:
> His awful straik may no man flee: –
> Timor mortis conturbat me.

She breaks me off; clapping hands to ears and half shrieking, "No!"

I, grown unmerciful, pursue Her: "You understand now, do You not? You are not eternal either. SUM isn't. Not Earth, not sun, not stars. We hid from the truth. Every one of us. I too, until I lost the one thing which made everything make sense. Then I had nothing left to lose, and could look with clear eyes. And what I saw was Death."

"Get out! Let Me alone!"

"I will not let the whole world alone, Queen, until I get her back. Give me her again, and I'll believe in SUM again. I'll praise It till men dance for joy to hear Its name."

She challenges me with wildcat eyes. "Do you think such matters to It?"

"Well," I shrug, "songs could be useful. They could help achieve the great objective sooner. Whatever that is. 'Optimization of total human activity' – wasn't that the program? I don't know if it still is. SUM has been adding to Itself so long. I doubt if You Yourself understand Its purpose, Lady of Ours."

"Don't speak as if It were alive," She says harshly. "It is a computer-effector complex. Nothing more."

"Are You certain?"

"I – yes. It thinks, more widely and deeply than any human ever did or could; but It is not alive, not aware, It has no consciousness. That is one reason why It decided It needed Me."

"Be that as it may, Lady," I tell Her, "the ultimate result, whatever It finally does with us, lies far in the future. At present I care about that; I worry; I resent our loss of self-determination. But that's because only such abstractions are left to me. Give me back my Lightfoot, and she, not the distant future, will be my concern. I'll be grateful, honestly grateful, and You Two will know it from the songs I then choose to sing. Which, as I said, might be helpful to It."

"You are unbelievably insolent," She says without force.

"No, Lady, just desperate," I say.

The ghost of a smile touches Her lips. She leans back, eyes hooded, and murmurs, "Well, I'll take you there. What happens then, you realize, lies outside My power. My observations, My recommendations, are nothing but a few items to take into account, among billions. However . . . we have a long way to travel this night. Give me what data you think will help you, Harper."

I do not finish the Lament. Nor do I dwell in any other fashion on grief. Instead, as the hours pass, I call upon those who dealt with the joy (not the fun, not the short delirium, but the joy) that man and woman might once have of each other.

Knowing where we are bound, I too need such comfort.

And the night deepens, and the leagues fall behind us, and finally we are beyond habitation, beyond wildcountry, in the land where life never comes. By crooked moon and waning starlight I see the plain of concrete and iron, the missiles and energy projectors crouched like beasts, the robot aircraft wheeling aloft: and the lines, the relay towers, the scuttling beetle-shaped carriers, that whole transcendent nerve-blood-sinew by which SUM knows and orders the world. For all the flitting about, for all the forces which seethe, here is altogether still. The wind itself seems to have frozen to death. Hoarfrost is gray on the steel shapes. Ahead of us, tiered and mountainous, begins to appear the castle of SUM.

She Who rides with me does not give sign of noticing that my songs have died in my throat. What humanness She showed is departing; Her face is cold and shut, Her voice bears a ring of metal. She looks straight ahead. But She does speak to me for a little while yet:

"Do you understand what is going to happen? For the next half year I will be linked with SUM, integral, another component of It. I suppose you will see Me, but that will merely be My flesh. What speaks to you will be SUM."

"I know." The words must be forced forth. My coming this far is more triumph than any man in creation before me has won; and I am here to do battle for my Dancer-on-Moonglades; but nonetheless my heart shakes me, and is loud in my skull, and my sweat stinks.

I manage, though, to add: "You *will* be a part of It, Lady of Ours. That gives me hope."

For an instant She turns to me, and lays Her hand across mine, and something makes Her again so young and untaken that I almost forget the girl who died; and she whispers, "If you knew how I hope!"

The instant is gone, and I am alone among machines.

We must stop before the castle gate. The wall looms sheer above, so high and high that it seems to be toppling upon me against the westward march of the stars, so black and black that it does not only drink down every light, it radiates blindness. Challenge and response quiver on electronic bands I cannot sense. The outer-guardian parts of It have perceived a mortal aboard this craft. A missile launcher swings about to aim its three serpents at me. But the Dark Queen answers – She does not trouble to be peremptory – and the castle opens its jaws for us.

We descend. Once, I think, we cross a river. I hear a rushing and hollow echoing and see droplets glitter where they are cast onto the viewports and outlined against dark. They vanish at once: liquid hydrogen, perhaps, to keep certain parts near absolute zero?

Much later we stop and the canopy slides back. I rise with Her. We are in a room, or cavern, of which I can see nothing, for there is no light except a dull bluish phosphorescence which streams from every solid object, also from Her flesh and mine. But I judge the chamber is enormous, for a sound of great machines at work comes very remotely, as if heard through dream, while our own voices are swallowed up by distance. Air is pumped through, neither warm nor cold, totally without odor, a dead wind.

We descend to the floor. She stands before me, hands crossed on breast, eyes half shut beneath the cowl and not looking at me nor away from me. "Do what you are told, Harper," She says in a voice that has never an overtone, "precisely as you are told." She turns and departs at an even pace. I watch Her go until I can no longer tell Her luminosity from the formless swirlings within my own eyeballs.

A claw plucks my tunic. I look down and am surprised to see that the dwarf robot has been waiting for me this whole time. How long a time that was, I cannot tell.

Its squat form leads me in another direction. Weariness crawls upward through me, my feet stumble, my lips tingle, lids are weighted and muscles have each their separate aches. Now and then I feel a jag of fear, but dully. When the robot indicates *Lie down here*, I am grateful.

The box fits me well. I let various wires be attached to me, various needles be injected which lead into tubes. I pay little attention to the machines which cluster and murmur around me. The robot goes away. I sink into blessed darkness.

I wake renewed in body. A kind of shell seems to have grown between my forebrain and the old animal parts. Far away I can feel the horror and hear the screaming and thrashing of my instincts; but awareness is chill, calm, logical. I have also a feeling that I slept for weeks, months, while leaves blew loose and snow fell on the upper world. But this may be wrong, and in no case does it matter. I am about to be judged by SUM.

The little faceless robot leads me off, through murmurous black corridors where the dead wind blows. I unsling my harp and clutch it to me, my sole friend and weapon. So the tranquility of the reasoning mind which has been decreed for me cannot be absolute. I decide that It simply does not want to be bothered by anguish. (No; wrong;

nothing so humanlike; It has no desires; beneath that power to reason is nullity.)

At length a wall opens for us and we enter a room where She sits enthroned. The self-radiation of metal and flesh is not apparent here, for light is provided, a featureless white radiance with no apparent source. White, too, is the muted sound of the machines which encompass Her throne. White are Her robe and face. I look away from the multitudinous unwinking scanner eyes, into Hers, but She does not appear to recognize me. Does She even see me? SUM has reached out with invisible fingers of electromagnetic induction and taken Her back into Itself. I do not tremble or sweat – I cannot – but I square my shoulders, strike one plangent chord, and wait for It to speak.

It does, from some invisible place. I recognize the voice It has chosen to use: my own. The overtones, the inflections are true, normal, what I myself would use in talking as one reasonable man to another. Why not? In computing what to do about me, and in programming Itself accordingly, SUM must have used so many billion bits of information that adequate accent is a negligible sub-problem.

No . . . there I am mistaken again . . . SUM does not do things on the basis that It might as well do them as not. This talk with myself is intended to have some effect on me. I do not know what.

"Well," It says pleasantly, "you made quite a journey, didn't you? I'm glad. Welcome."

My instincts bare teeth to hear those words of humanity used by the unfeeling unalive. My logical mind considers replying with an ironic "Thank you," decides against it, and holds me silent.

"You see," SUM continues after a moment that whirrs, "you are unique. Pardon Me if I speak a little bluntly. Your sexual monomania is just one aspect of a generally atavistic, superstition-oriented personality. And yet, unlike the ordinary misfit, you're both strong and realistic enough to cope with the world. This chance to meet you, to analyze you while you rested, has opened new insights for Me on human psychophysiology. Which may lead to improved techniques for governing it and its evolution."

"That being so," I reply, "give me my reward."

"Now look here," SUM says in a mild tone, "you if anyone should know I'm not omnipotent. I was built originally to help govern a civilization grown too complex. Gradually, as My program of self-expansion progressed, I took over more and more decision-making functions. They were *given* to Me. People were happy to be relieved of responsibility, and they could see for themselves how much better I was running things than any mortal could. But to this day, My authority depends on a substantial consensus. If I started playing favorites, as by re-creating your girl, well, I'd have troubles."

"The consensus depends more on awe than on reason," I say. "You haven't abolished the gods, You've simply absorbed them into Yourself. If You choose to pass a miracle for me, your prophet singer – and I will be Your prophet if You do this – why, that strengthens the faith of the rest."

"So you think. But your opinions aren't based on any exact data. The historical and anthropological records from the past before Me are unquantitative. I've already phased them out of the curriculum. Eventually, when the culture's ready for such a move, I'll order them destroyed. They're *too* misleading. Look what they've done to you."

I grin into the scanner eyes. "Instead," I say, "people will be encouraged to think that before the world was, was SUM. All right. I don't care, as long as I get my girl back. Pass me a miracle, SUM, and I'll guarantee You a good payment."

"But I have no miracles. Not in your sense. You know how the soul works. The metal bracelet encloses a pseudovirus, a set of giant protein molecules with taps directly to the bloodstream and nervous system. They record the chromosome pattern, the synapse flash, the permanent changes, everything. At the owner's death, the bracelet is dissected out. The Winged Heels bring it here, and the information contained is transferred to one of My memory banks. I can use such a record to guide the growing of a new body in the vats: a young body, on which the former habits and recollections are imprinted. But you don't understand the complexity of the process, Harper. It takes Me weeks, every seven years, and every available biochemical facility, to re-create My human liaison. And the process isn't perfect, either. The pattern is affected by storage. You might say that this body and brain you see before you remembers each death. And those are short deaths. A longer one – man, use your sense. Imagine."

I can; and the shield between reason and feeling begins to crack. I had sung, of my darling dead,

> "No motion has she now, no force;
> She neither hears nor sees;
> Roll'd round in earth's diurnal course,
> With rocks, and stones, and trees."

Peace, at least. But if the memory-storage is not permanent but circulating; if, within those gloomy caverns of tubes and wire and outerspace cold, some remnant of her psyche must flit and flicker, alone, unremembering, aware of nothing but having lost life – No!

I smite the harp and shout so the room rings: "Give her back! Or I'll kill you!"

SUM finds it expedient to chuckle; and, horribly, the smile is reflected for a moment on the Dark Queen's lips, though otherwise She never stirs. "And how do you propose to do that?" It asks me.

It knows, I know, what I have in mind, so I counter: "How do You propose to stop me?"

"No need. You'll be considered a nuisance. Finally someone will decide you ought to have psychiatric treatment. They'll query My diagnostic outlet. I'll recommend certain excisions."

"On the other hand, since You've sifted my mind by now, and since You know how I've affected people with my songs – even the Lady yonder, even Her – wouldn't you rather have me working for You? With words like, '*O taste, and see, how gracious the Lord is; blessed is the man that trusteth in him. O fear the Lord, ye that are his saints; for they that fear him lack nothing.*' I can make You into God."

"In a sense, I already am God."

"And in another sense not. Not yet." I can endure no more. "Why are we arguing? You made Your decision before I woke. Tell me and let me go!"

With an odd carefulness, SUM responds: "I'm still studying you. No harm in admitting to you, My knowledge of the human psyche is as yet imperfect. Certain areas won't yield to computation. I don't know precisely what you'd do, Harper. If to that uncertainty I added a potentially dangerous precedent – "

"Kill me, then." Let my ghost wander forever with hers, down in Your cryogenic dreams.

"No, that's also inexpedient. You've made yourself too conspicuous and controversial. Too many people know by now that you went off with the Lady." Is it possible that, behind steel and energy, a nonexistent hand brushes across a shadow face in puzzlement? My heartbeat is thick in the silence.

Suddenly It shakes me with decision: "The calculated probabilities do favor your keeping your promises and making yourself useful. Therefore I shall grant your request. However – "

I am on my knees. My forehead knocks on the floor until blood runs into my eyes. I hear through storm winds:

" – testing must continue. Your faith in Me is not absolute; in fact, you're very skeptical of what you call My goodness. Without additional proof of your willingness to trust Me, I can't let you have the kind of importance which your getting your dead back from Me would give you. Do you understand?"

The question does not sound rhetorical. "Yes," I sob.

"Well, then," says my civilized, almost amiable voice, "I computed that you'd react much as you have done, and prepared for the likelihood. Your woman's body was re-created while you lay under study. The data which make personality are now being fed back into her neurones. She'll be ready to leave this place by the time you do.

"I repeat, though, there has to be a testing. The procedure is also necessary for its effect on you. If you're to be My prophet, you'll have to work pretty closely with Me; you'll have to undergo a great deal of reconditioning; this night we begin the process. Are you willing?"

"Yes, yes, yes, what must I do?"

"Only this: Follow the robot out. At some point, she, your woman, will join you. She'll be conditioned to walk so quietly you can't hear her. Don't look back. Not once, until you're in the upper world. A single glance behind you will be an act of rebellion against Me, and a datum indicating you can't really be trusted . . . and that ends everything. Do you understand?"

"Is that all?" I cry. "Nothing more?"

"It will prove more difficult than you think," SUM tells me. My voice fades, as if into illimitable distances: "Farewell, worshipper."

The robot raises me to my feet, I stretch out my arms to the Dark Queen. Half blinded with tears, I nonetheless see that She does not see me. "Goodbye," I mumble, and let the robot lead me away.

Our walking is long through those mirk miles. At first I am in too much of a turmoil, and later too stunned, to know where or how we are bound. But later still, slowly, I become aware of my flesh and clothes and the robot's alloy, glimmering blue in blackness. Sounds and smells are muffled; rarely does another machine pass by, unheeding of us. (What work does SUM have for them?) I am so careful not to look behind me that my neck grows stiff.

Though it is not prohibited, is it, to lift my harp past my shoulder, in the course of strumming a few melodies to keep up my courage, and see if perchance a following illumination is reflected in this polished wood?

Nothing. Well, her second birth must take time – O SUM, be careful of her! – and then she must be led through many tunnels, no doubt, before she makes rendezvous with my back. Be patient, Harper.

Sing. Welcome her home. No, these hollow spaces swallow all music; and she is as yet in that trance of death from which only the sun and my kiss can wake her; if, indeed, she has joined me yet. I listen for other footfalls than my own.

Surely we haven't much farther to go. I ask the robot, but of course I get no reply. Make an estimate. I know about how fast the chariot traveled coming down . . . The trouble is, time does not exist here. I have no day, no stars, no clock but my heartbeat, and I have lost the count of that. Nevertheless, we must come to the end soon. What purpose would be served by walking me through this labyrinth till I die?

Well, if I am totally exhausted at the outer gate, I won't make undue trouble when I find no Rose-in-Hand behind me.

No, now that's ridiculous. If SUM didn't want to heed my plea, It need merely say so. I have no power to inflict physical damage on Its parts.

Of course, It might have plans for me. It did speak of reconditioning. A series of shocks, culminating in that last one, could make me ready for whatever kind of gelding It intends to do.

Or It might have changed Its mind. Why now? It was quite frank about an uncertainty factor in the human psyche. It may have reevaluated the probabilities and decided: better not to serve my desire.

Or It may have tried, and failed. It admitted the recording process is imperfect. I must not expect quite the Gladness I knew; she will always be a little haunted. At best. But suppose the tank spawned a body with no awareness behind the eyes? Or a monster? Suppose, at this instant, I am being followed by a half-rotten corpse?

No! Stop that! SUM would know, and take corrective measures. Would It? *Can It?*

I comprehend how this passage through night, where I never look to see what follows me, how this is an act of submission and confession. I am saying, with my whole existent being, that SUM is all-powerful, all-wise, all-good. To SUM I offer the love I came to win back. Oh, It looked more deeply into me than ever I did myself.

But I shall not fail.

Will SUM, though? If there has indeed been some grisly error . . . let me not find it out under the sky. Let her, my only, not. For what then shall we do? Could I lead her here again, knock on the iron gate, and cry, "Master, You have given me a thing unfit to exist. Destroy it and start over." – ? For what might the wrongness be? Something so subtle, so pervasive, that it does not show in any way save my slow, resisted discovery that I embrace a zombie? Doesn't it make better sense to look – make certain while she is yet drowsy with death – use the whole power of SUM to correct what may be awry?

No, SUM wants me to believe that It makes no mistakes. I agreed to that price. And to much else . . . I don't know how much else, I am daunted to imagine, but that word "recondition" is ugly . . . Does not my woman have some rights in the matter too? Shall we not at least ask her if she wants to be the wife of a prophet; shall we not, hand in hand, ask SUM what the price of her life is to her?

Was that a footfall? Almost, I whirl about. I check myself and stand shaking; names of hers break from my lips. The robot urges me on.

Imagination. It wasn't her step. I am alone. I will always be alone.

The halls wind upward. Or so I think; I have grown too weary for much kinesthetic sense. We cross the sounding river and I am bitten to the bone by the cold which blows upward around the bridge, and I may not turn about to offer the naked newborn woman my garment. I lurch through endless chambers where machines do meaningless things. She hasn't seen them before. Into what nightmare has she risen; and why don't I, who wept into her dying sense that I loved her, why don't I look at her, why don't I speak?

Well, I could talk to her. I could assure the puzzled mute dead that I have come to lead her back into sunlight. Could I not? I ask the robot. It does not reply. I cannot remember if I may speak to her. If indeed I was ever told. I stumble forward.

I crash into a wall and fall bruised. The robot's claw closes on my shoulder. Another arm gestures. I see a passageway, very long and narrow, through the stone. I will have to crawl through. At the end, at the end, the door is swinging wide. The dear real dusk of Earth pours through into this darkness. I am blinded and deafened.

Do I hear her cry out? Was that the final testing; or was my own sick, shaken mind betraying me; is there a destiny which, like SUM with us, makes tools of suns and SUM? I don't know. I know only that I turned, and there she stood. Her hair flowed long, loose, past the remembered face from which the trance was just departing, on which the knowing and the love of me had just awakened – flowed down over the body that reached forth arms, that took one step to meet me and was halted.

The great grim robot at her own back takes her to it. I think it sends lightning through her brain. She falls. It bears her away.

My guide ignores my screaming. Irresistible, it thrusts me out through the tunnel. The door clangs in my face. I stand before the wall which is like a mountain. Dry snow hisses across concrete. The sky is bloody with dawn; stars still gleam in the west, and arc lights are scattered over the twilit plain of the machines.

Presently I go dumb. I become almost calm. What is there left to have feelings about? The door is iron, the wall is stone fused into one basaltic mass. I walk some distance off into the wind, turn around, lower my head, and charge. Let my brains be smeared across Its gate; the pattern will be my hieroglyphic for hatred.

I am seized from behind. The force that stops me must needs be bruisingly great. Released, I crumple to the ground before a machine with talons and wings. My voice from it says, "Not here. I'll carry you to a safe place."

"What more can You do to me?" I croak.

"Release you. You won't be restrained or molested on any orders of Mine."

"Why not?"

"Obviously you're going to appoint yourself My enemy forever. This is an unprecedented situation, a valuable chance to collect data."

"You tell me this, You warn me, deliberately?"

"Of course. My computation is that these words will have the effect of provoking your utmost effort."

"You won't give her again? You don't want my love?"

"Not under the circumstances. Too uncontrollable. But your hatred should, as I say, be a useful experimental tool."

"I'll destroy You," I say.

It does not deign to speak further. Its machine picks me up and flies off with me. I am left on the fringes of a small town farther south. Then I go insane.

I do not much know what happens during that winter, nor care. The blizzards are too loud in my head. I walk the ways of Earth, among lordly towers, under neatly groomed trees, into careful gardens, over bland, bland campuses. I am unwashed, uncombed, unbarbered; my tatters flap about me and my bones are near thrusting through the skin; folk do not like to meet these eyes sunken so far into this skull, and perhaps for that reason they give me to eat. I sing to them.

> *"From the hag and hungry goblin*
> *That into rags would rend ye*
> *And the spirit that stan' by the naked man*
> *In the Book of Moons defend ye!*

That of your five sound senses
You never be forsaken
Nor travel from yourselves with Tom
Abroad to beg your bacon."

Such things perturb them, do not belong in their chrome-edged universe. So I am often driven away with curses, and sometimes I must flee those who would arrest me and scrub my brain smooth. An alley is a good hiding place, if I can find one in the oldest part of a city; I crouch there and yowl with the cats. A forest is also good. My pursuers dislike to enter any place where any wildness lingers.

But some feel otherwise. They have visited parklands, preserves, actual wildcountry. Their purpose was overconscious-measured, planned savagery, and a clock to tell them when they must go home – but at least they are not afraid of silences and unlighted nights. As spring returns, certain among them begin to follow me. They are merely curious, at first. But slowly, month by month, especially among the younger ones, my madness begins to call to something in them.

"With an host of furious fancies
Whereof I am commander
With a burning spear, and a horse of air,
To the wilderness I wander.
By a knight of ghosts and shadows
I summoned am to tourney
Ten leagues beyond the wild world's edge.
Me thinks it is no journey."

They sit at my feet and listen to me sing. They dance, crazily, to my harp. The girls bend close, tell me how I fascinate them, invite me to copulate. This I refuse, and when I tell them why they are puzzled, a little frightened maybe, but often they strive to understand.

For my rationality is renewed with the hawthorn blossoms. I bathe, have my hair and beard shorn, find clean raiment, and take care to eat what my body needs. Less and less do I rave before anyone who will listen; more and more do I seek solitude, quietness, under the vast wheel of the stars, and think.

What is man? Why is man? We have buried such questions; we have sworn they are dead – that they never really existed, being devoid of empirical meaning – and we have dreaded that they might raise the stones we heaped on them, rise and walk the world again of nights.

Alone, I summon them to me. They cannot hurt their fellow dead, among whom I now number myself.

I sing to her who is gone. The young people hear and wonder. Sometimes they weep.

> *"Fear no more the heat o' the sun,*
> *Nor the furious winter's rages;*
> *Thou thy worldly task hast done,*
> *Home art gone, and ta'en thy wages:*
> *Golden lads and girls all must*
> *As chimney-sweepers, come to dust."*

"But this is not so!" they protest. "We will die and sleep a while, and then we will live forever in SUM."

I answer as gently as may be: "No. Remember I went there. So I know you are wrong. And even if you were right, it would not be right that you should be right."

"What?"

"Don't you see, it is not right that a thing should be the lord of man. It is not right that we should huddle through our whole lives in fear of finally losing them. You are not parts in a machine, and you have better ends than helping the machine run smoothly."

I dismiss them and stride off, solitary again, into a canyon where a river clangs, or onto some gaunt mountain peak. No revelation is given me. I climb and creep toward the truth.

Which is that SUM must be destroyed, not in revenge, not in hate, not in fear, simply because the human spirit cannot exist in the same reality as It.

But what, then, is our proper reality? And how shall we attain it?

I return with my songs to the lowlands. Word about me has gone widely. They are a large crowd who follow me down the highroad until it has changed into a street.

"The Dark Queen will soon come to these parts," they tell me. "Abide till She does. Let Her answer those questions you put to us, which make us sleep so badly."

"Let me retire to prepare myself," I say. I go up a long flight of steps. The people watch from below, dumb with awe, till I vanish. Such few as were in the building depart. I walk down vaulted halls, through hushed high-ceilinged rooms full of tables, among shelves made massive by books. Sunlight slants dusty through the windows.

The half memory has plagued me of late: once before, I know not when, this year of mine also took place. Perhaps in this library I can find the tale that – casually, I suppose, in my abnormal childhood – I read. For man is older than SUM: wiser, I swear; his myths hold more truth than Its mathematics. I spend three days and most of three nights in my search. There is scant sound but the rustling of leaves between my hands. Folk place offerings of food and drink at the door. They tell themselves they do so out of pity, or curiosity, or to avoid the nuisance of having me die in an unconventional fashion. But I know better.

At the end of the three days I am little further along. I have too much material; I keep going off on sidetracks of beauty and fascination. (Which SUM means to eliminate.) My Education was like everyone else's, science, rationality, good sane adjustment. (SUM writes our curricula, and the teaching machines have direct connections to It.) Well, I can make some of my lopsided training work for me. My reading has given me sufficient clues to prepare a search program. I sit down before an information retrieval console and run my fingers across its keys. They make a clattery music.

Electron beams are swift hounds. Within seconds the screen lights up with words, and I read who I am.

It is fortunate that I am a fast reader. Before I can press the Clear button, the unreeling words are wiped out. For an instant the screen quivers with formlessness, then appears

I HAD NOT CORRELATED THESE DATA WITH THE FACTS
CONCERNING YOU. THIS INTRODUCES A NEW AND INDETERMINATE
QUANTITY INTO THE COMPUTATIONS.

The nirvana which has come upon me (yes, I found that word among the old books, and how portentous it is) is not passiveness, it is a tide more full and strong than that which bore me down to the Dark Queen those ages apast in wildcountry. I say, as coolly as may be, "An interesting coincidence. If it is a coincidence." Surely sonic receptors are emplaced hereabouts.

EITHER THAT, OR A CERTAIN NECESSARY CONSEQUENCE
OF THE LOGIC OF EVENTS.

The vision dawning within me is so blinding bright that I cannot refrain from answering, "Or a destiny, SUM?"

MEANINGLESS. MEANINGLESS. MEANINGLESS.

"Now why did You repeat Yourself in that way? Once would have sufficed. Thrice, though, makes an incantation. Are You by any chance hoping Your words will make me stop existing?"

I DO NOT HOPE. YOU ARE AN EXPERIMENT. IF I COMPUTE
A SIGNIFICANT PROBABILITY OF YOUR CAUSING SERIOUS
DISTURBANCE, I WILL HAVE YOU TERMINATED.

I smile. "SUM," I say, "I am going to terminate You." I lean over and switch off the screen. I walk out into the evening.

Not everything is clear to me yet, that I must say and do. But enough is that I can start preaching at once to those who have been waiting for me. As I talk, others come down the street, and hear, and stay to listen. Soon they number in the hundreds.

I have no immense new truth to offer them: nothing that I have not said before, although piecemeal and unsystematically; nothing they have not felt themselves, in the innermost darkness of their beings. Today, however, knowing who I am and therefore why I am, I can put these things in words. Speaking quietly, now and then drawing on some forgotten song to show my meaning, I tell them how sick and starved their lives are; how they have made themselves slaves; how the enslavement is not even to a conscious mind, but to an insensate inanimate thing which their own ancestors began; how that thing is not the centrum of existence, but a few scraps of metal and bleats of energy, a few sad stupid patterns, adrift in unbounded space-time. Put not your faith in SUM, I tell them. SUM is doomed, even as you and I. Seek out mystery; what else is the whole cosmos but mystery? Live bravely, die and be done, and you will be more than any machine. You may perhaps be God.

They grow tumultuous. They shout replies, some of which are animal howls. A few are for me, most are opposed. That doesn't matter. I have reached into them, my music is being played on their nervestrings, and this is my entire purpose.

The sun goes down behind the buildings. Dusk gathers. The city remains unilluminated. I soon realize why. She is coming, the Dark Queen Whom they wanted me to debate with. From afar we hear Her chariot thunder. Folk wail in terror. They are not wont to do that either. They used to disguise their feelings from Her and themselves by receiving Her with grave sparse ceremony. Now they would flee if they dared. I have lifted the masks.

The chariot halts in the street. She dismounts, tall and shadowy cowled. The people make way before Her like water before a shark. She climbs the stairs to face me. I see for the least instant that Her lips are not quite firm and Her eyes abrim with tears. She whispers, too low for anyone else to hear, "Oh, Harper, I'm sorry."

"Come join me," I invite. "Help me set the world free."

"No. I cannot. I have been too long with It." She straightens. Imperium descends upon Her. Her voice rises for everyone to hear. The little television robots flit close, bat shapes in the twilight, that the whole planet may witness my defeat. "What is this freedom you rant about?" She demands.

"To feel," I say. "To venture. To wonder. To become men again."

"To become beasts, you mean. Would you demolish the machines that keep us alive?"

"Yes. We must. Once they were good and useful, but we let them grow upon us like a cancer, and now nothing but destruction and a new beginning can save us."

"Have you considered the chaos?"

"Yes. It too is necessary. We will not be men without the freedom to know suffering. In it is also enlightenment. Through it we travel beyond ourselves, beyond earth and stars, space and time, to Mystery."

"So you maintain that there is some undefined ultimate vagueness behind the measurable universe?" She smiles into the bat eyes. We have each been taught, as children, to laugh on hearing sarcasms of this kind. "Please offer me a little proof."

"No," I say. "Prove to me instead, beyond any doubt, that there is *not* something we cannot understand with words and equations. Prove to me likewise that I have no right to seek for it.

"The burden of proof is on You Two, so often have You lied to us. In the name of rationality, You resurrected myth. The better to control us! In the name of liberation, You chained our inner lives and castrated our souls. In the name of service, You bound and blinkered us. In the name of achievement, You held us to a narrower round than any swine in its pen. In the name of beneficence, You created pain, and horror, and darkness beyond darkness." I turn to the people. "I went there. I descended into the cellars. I know!"

"He found that SUM would not pander to his special wishes, at the expense of everyone else," cries the Dark Queen. Do I hear shrillness in Her voice? "Therefore he claims SUM is cruel."

"I saw my dead," I tell them. "She will not rise again. Nor yours, nor you. Not ever. SUM will not, cannot raise us. In Its house is death indeed. We must seek life and rebirth elsewhere, among the mysteries."

She laughs aloud and points to my soul bracelet, glimmering faintly in the gray-blue thickening twilight. Need She say anything?

"Will someone give me a knife and an ax?" I ask.

The crowd stirs and mumbles. I smell their fear. Streetlamps go on, as if they could scatter more than this corner of the night which is rolling upon us. I fold my arms and wait. The Dark Queen says something to me. I ignore Her.

The tools pass from hand to hand. He who brings them up the stairs comes like a flame. He kneels at my feet and lifts what I have desired. The tools are good ones, a broad-bladed hunting knife and a long double-bitted ax.

Before the world, I take the knife in my right hand and slash beneath the bracelet on my left wrist. The connections to my inner body are cut. Blood flows, impossibly brilliant under the lamps. It does not hurt; I am too exalted.

The Dark Queen shrieks. "You meant it! Harper, Harper!"

"There is no life in SUM," I say. I pull my hand through the circle and cast the bracelet down so it rings.

A voice of brass: *"Arrest that maniac for correction. He is deadly dangerous."*

The monitors who have stood on the fringes of the crowd try to push through. They are resisted. Those who seek to help them encounter fists and fingernails.

I take the ax and smash downward. The bracelet crumples. The organic material within, starved of my secretions, exposed to the night air, withers.

I raise the tools, ax in right hand, knife in bleeding left. "I seek eternity where it is to be found," I call. "Who goes with me?"

A score or better break loose from the riot, which is already calling forth weapons and claiming lives. They surround me with their bodies. Their eyes are the eyes of prophets. We make haste to seek a hiding place, for one military robot has appeared and others will not be long in coming. The tall engine strides to stand guard over Our Lady, and this is my last glimpse of Her.

My followers do not reproach me for having cost them all they were. They are mine. In me is the godhead which can do no wrong.

And the war is open, between me and SUM. My friends are few, my enemies many and mighty. I go about the world as a fugitive. But always I sing. And always I find someone who will listen, will join us, embracing pain and death with a lover.

With the Knife and the Ax I take their souls. Afterward we hold for them the ritual of rebirth. Some go thence to become outlaw missionaries; most put on facsimile bracelets and return home, to whisper my word. It makes little difference to me. I have no haste, who own eternity.

For my word is of what lies beyond time. My enemies say I call forth ancient bestialities and lunacies; that I would bring civilization down in ruin; that it matters not a madman's giggle to me whether war, famine, and pestilence will again scour the earth. With these accusations I am satisfied. The language of them shows me that here, *too*, I have reawakened anger. And that emotion belongs to us as much as any other. More than the others, maybe, in this autumn of mankind. We need a gale, to strike down SUM and everything It stands for. Afterward will come the winter of barbarism.

And after that the springtime of a new and (perhaps) more human civilization. My friends seem to believe this will come in their very lifetimes: peace, brotherhood, enlightenment, sanctity. I know otherwise. I have been in the depths. The wholeness of mankind, which I am bringing back, has its horrors.

When one day

> the Eater of the Gods returns
> the Wolf breaks his chain
> the Horsemen ride forth
> the Age ends
> the Beast is reborn

then SUM will be destroyed; and you, strong and fair, may go back to earth and rain.

I shall await you.

My aloneness is nearly ended, Daybright. Just one task remains. The god must die, that his followers may believe he is raised from the dead and lives forever. Then they will go on to conquer the world.

There are those who say I have spurned and offended them. They too, borne on the tide which I raised, have torn out their machine souls and seek in music and ecstasy to find a meaning for existence. But their creed is a savage one, which has taken them into wildcountry, where they ambush the monitors sent against them and practice cruel rites. They believe that the final reality is female. Nevertheless, messengers of theirs have approached me with the suggestion of a mystic marriage. This I refused; my wedding was long ago, and will be celebrated again when this cycle of the world has closed.

Therefore they hate me. But I have said I will come and talk to them.

I leave the road at the bottom of the valley and walk singing up the hill. Those few I let come this far with me have been told to abide my return. They shiver in the sunset; the vernal equinox is three days away. I feel no cold myself. I stride exultant among briars and twisted ancient apple trees. If my bare feet leave a little blood in the snow, that is good. The ridges around are dark with forest, which waits like the skeleton dead for leaves to be breathed across it again. The eastern sky is purple, where stands the evening star. Overhead, against blue, cruises an early flight of homebound geese. Their calls drift faintly down to me. Westward, above me and before me, smolders redness. Etched black against it are the women.

The Scarlet Plague

JACK LONDON

Jack London (1876–1916) wrote enough science fiction to fill a substantial collection. This story is one of his best (his other high point is "The Red One") and certainly his most influential. It is in the tradition of the last man on Earth story, a subgenre that extends in fiction from Cousin de Grainville's *Le Dernier Homme* (1805), through Mary Shelley's *The Last Man* (1826) and M. P. Shiel's The *Purple Cloud* (1900), to George R. Stewart's *Earth Abides* (1950) and the many British SF disaster novels of the 1950s and '60s by John Wyndham, John Christopher, J. G. Ballard, and others.

London's story introduces a notable alteration in this tradition. Earlier stories show a Romantic resurgence of nature, crumbling buildings and beautiful natural vistas. London portrays the scientifically possible descent, perhaps devolution, of civilized humans into barbarism. It is an interesting contrast to Forster's "The Machine Stops." It is also one of the ancestors of the large-scale disaster novel, so much a feature of this century.

"There was a hidden side to primitivism," says Richard Gid Powers in his introduction to London's collected science fiction, *The Science Fiction of Jack London* (1975), "and that was a hatred of civilization, an almost pathological longing for a catastrophe that would sweep away civilization and restore the pre-Adamite ceremony of innocence – a will to believe that the future would be a restoration of a past that would eclipse the obscenities of the present." London's twin themes in his science fiction are Social Darwinism and revolutionary socialism. It seems possible that London's character of the Chauffeur (the dark side of J. M. Barrie's admirable Crichton) is a partial inspiration for the Boss in H. G. Wells's *Things to Come*.

I

The way led along upon what had once been the embankment of a railroad. But no train had run upon it for many years. The forest on either side swelled up the slopes of the embankment and crested across it in a green wave of trees and bushes. The trail was as narrow as a man's body, and was no more than a wild-animal runway. Occasionally, a piece of rusty iron, showing through the forest-mould, advertised that the rail and the ties still remained. In one place, a ten-inch tree, bursting through at a connection, had lifted the end of a rail clearly into view. The tie had evidently followed the rail, held to it by the spike long enough for its bed to be filled with gravel and rotten leaves, so that now the crumbling, rotten timber thrust itself up at a curious slant. Old as the road was, it was manifest that it had been of the mono-rail type.

An old man and a boy travelled along this runway. They moved slowly, for the old man was very old, a touch of palsy made his movements tremulous, and he leaned heavily upon his staff. A rude skull-cap of goat-skin protected his head from the sun. From beneath this fell a scant fringe of stained and dirty-white hair. A visor, ingeniously made from a large leaf, shielded his eyes, and from under this he peered at the way of his feet on the trail. His beard, which should have been snow-white but which showed the same weather-wear and camp-stain as his hair, fell nearly to his waist in a great tangled mass. About his chest and shoulders hung a single, mangy garment of goat-skin. His arms and legs, withered and skinny, betokened extreme age, as well as did their sunburn and scars and scratches betoken long years of exposure to the elements.

The boy, who led the way, checking the eagerness of his muscles to the slow progress of the elder, likewise wore a single garment – a ragged-edged piece of bear-skin, with a hole in the middle through which he had thrust his head. He could not have been more than twelve years old. Tucked coquettishly over one ear was the freshly severed tail of a pig. In one hand he carried a medium-sized bow and an arrow. On his back was a quiverful of arrows. From a sheath hanging about his neck on a thong projected the battered handle of a hunting knife. He was as brown as a berry, and walked softly, with almost a catlike tread. In marked contrast with his sunburned skin were his eyes – blue, deep blue, but keen and sharp as a pair of gimlets. They seemed to bore into all about him in a way that was habitual. As he went along he smelled things, as well, his distended, quivering nostrils carrying to his brain an endless series of messages from the outside world. Also, his hearing was acute, and had been so trained that it operated automatically. Without conscious effort, he heard all the slight sounds in the apparent quiet – heard, and differentiated, and classified these sounds – whether they were of the wind rustling the leaves, of the humming of bees and gnats, of the distant rumble of the sea that drifted to him only in lulls, or of the gopher, just under his foot, shoving a pouchful of earth into the entrance of his hole.

Suddenly he became alertly tense. Sound, sight, and odor had given him a simultaneous warning. His hand went back to the old man, touching him, and the pair stood still. Ahead, at one side of the top of the embankment, arose a crackling sound, and the boy's gaze was fixed on the tops of the agitated bushes. Then a large bear, a grizzly, crashed into view, and likewise stopped abruptly, at sight of the humans. He did not like them, and growled querulously. Slowly the boy fitted the arrow to the bow, and slowly he pulled the bowstring taut. But he never removed his eyes from the bear. The old man peered from under his green leaf at the danger, and stood as quietly as the boy. For a few seconds this mutual scrutinizing went on, then, the bear betraying a growing irritability, the boy, with a movement of his head, indicated that the old man must step aside from the trail and go down the embankment. The boy followed, going backward, still holding the bow taut and ready. They waited till a crashing among the bushes from the opposite side of the embankment told them the bear had gone on. The boy grinned as he led back to the trail.

"A big un, Granser," he chuckled.

The old man shook his head.

"They get thicker every day," he complained in a thin, undependable falsetto. "Who'd have thought I'd live to see the time when a man would be afraid of his life on the way to the Cliff House. When I was a boy, Edwin, men and women and little babies used to come out here from San Francisco by tens of thousands on a nice day. And there weren't any bears then. No, sir. They used to pay money to look at them in cages, they were that rare."

"What is money, Granser?"

Before the old man could answer, the boy recollected and triumphantly shoved his hand into a pouch under his bear-skin and pulled forth a battered and tarnished silver dollar. The old man's eyes glistened, as he held the coin close to them.

"I can't see," he muttered. "You look and see if you can make out the date, Edwin."

The boy laughed.

"You're a great Granser," he cried delightedly, "always making believe them little marks mean something."

The old man manifested an accustomed chagrin as he brought the coin back again close to his own eyes.

"2012," he shrilled, and then fell to cackling grotesquely. "That was the year Morgan the Fifth was appointed President of the United States by the Board of Magnates. It must have been one of the last coins minted, for the Scarlet Death came in 2013. Lord! Lord! – think of it! Sixty years ago, and I am the only person alive to-day that lived in those times. Where did you find it, Edwin?"

The boy, who had been regarding him with the tolerant curiousness one accords to the prattlings of the feeble-minded, answered promptly.

"I got it off of Hoo-Hoo. He found it when we was herdin' goats down near San José' last spring. Hoo-Hoo said it was *money*. Ain't you hungry, Granser?"

The ancient caught his staff in a tighter grip and urged along the trail, his old eyes shining greedily.

"I hope Har-Lip's found a crab . . . or two," he mumbled. "They're good eating, crabs, mighty good eating when you've no more teeth and you've got grandsons that love their old grandsire and make a point of catching crabs for him. When I was a boy – "

But Edwin, suddenly stopped by what he saw, was drawing the bowstring on a fitted arrow. He had paused on the brink of a crevasse in the embankment. An ancient culvert had here washed out, and the stream, no longer confined, had cut a passage through the fill. On the opposite side, the end of a rail projected and overhung. It showed rustily through the creeping vines which overran it. Beyond, crouching by a bush, a rabbit looked across at him in trembling hesitancy. Fully fifty feet was the distance, but the arrow flashed true; and the trans-fixed rabbit, crying out in sudden fright and hurt, struggled painfully away into the brush. The boy himself was a flash of brown skin and flying fur as he bounded down the steep wall of the gap and up the other side. His lean muscles were springs of steel that released into graceful and efficient action. A hundred feet beyond, in a tangle of bushes, he overtook the wounded creature, knocked its head on a convenient tree-trunk, and turned it over to Granser to carry.

"Rabbit is good, very good," the ancient quavered, "but when it comes to a toothsome delicacy I prefer crab. When I was a boy – "

"Why do you say so much that ain't got no sense?" Edwin impatiently interrupted the other's threatened garrulousness.

The boy did not exactly utter these words, but something that remotely resembled them and that was more guttural and explosive and economical of qualifying phrases. His speech showed distant kinship with that of the old man, and the latter's speech was approximately an English that had gone through a bath of corrupt usage.

"What I want to know," Edwin continued, "is why you call crab 'toothsome delicacy'? Crab is crab, ain't it? No one I never heard calls it such funny things."

The old man sighed but did not answer, and they moved on in silence. The surf grew suddenly louder, as they emerged from the forest upon a stretch of sand dunes bordering the sea. A few goats were browsing among the sandy hillocks, and a skin-clad boy, aided by a wolfish-looking dog that was only faintly reminiscent of a collie, was watching them. Mingled with the roar of the surf was a continuous, deep-throated barking or bellowing, which came from a cluster of jagged rocks a hundred yards out from shore. Here huge sea-lions hauled themselves up to lie in the sun or battle with one another. In the immediate foreground arose the smoke of a fire, tended by a third savage-looking boy. Crouched near him were several wolfish dogs similar to the one that guarded the goats.

The old man accelerated his pace, sniffing eagerly as he neared the fire.

"Mussels!" he muttered ecstatically. "Mussels! And ain't that a crab, Hoo-Hoo? Ain't that a crab? My, my, you boys are good to your old grandsire."

Hoo-Hoo, who was apparently of the same age as Edwin, grinned.

"All you want, Granser. I got four."

The old man's palsied eagerness was pitiful. Sitting down in the sand as quickly as his stiff limbs would let him, he poked a large rock-mussel from out of the coals. The heat had forced its shells apart, and the meat, salmon-colored, was thoroughly cooked. Between thumb and forefinger, in trembling haste, he caught the morsel and carried it to his mouth. But it was too hot, and the next moment was violently ejected. The old man spluttered with the pain, and tears ran out of his eyes and down his cheeks.

The boys were true savages, possessing only the cruel humor of the savage. To them the incident was excruciatingly funny, and they burst into loud laughter. Hoo-Hoo danced up and down, while Edwin rolled gleefully on the ground. The boy with the goats came running to join in the fun.

"Set 'em to cool, Edwin, set 'em to cool," the old man besought, in the midst of his grief, making no attempt to wipe away the tears that still flowed from his eyes. "And cool a crab, Edwin, too. You know your grandsire likes crabs."

From the coals arose a great sizzling, which proceeded from the many mussels bursting open their shells and exuding their moisture. They were large shellfish, running from three to six inches in length. The boys raked them out with sticks and placed them on a large piece of driftwood to cool.

"When I was a boy, we did not laugh at our elders; we respected them."

The boys took no notice, and Granser continued to babble an incoherent flow of complaint and censure. But this time he was more careful, and did not burn his mouth. All began to eat, using nothing but their hands and making loud mouth-noises and lip-smackings. The third boy, who was called Hare-Lip, slyly deposited a pinch of sand on a mussel the ancient was carrying to his mouth; and when the grit of it bit into the old fellow's mucous membrane and gums, the laughter was again uproarious. He was unaware that a joke had been played on him, and spluttered and spat until Edwin, relenting, gave him a gourd of fresh water with which to wash out his mouth.

"Where's them crabs, Hoo-Hoo?" Edwin demanded. "Granser's set upon having a snack."

Again Granser's eyes burned with greediness as a large crab was handed to him. It was a shell with legs and all complete, but the meat had long since departed. With shaky fingers and babblings of anticipation, the old man broke off a leg and found it filled with emptiness.

"The crabs, Hoo-Hoo?" he wailed. "The crabs?"

"I was foolin', Granser. They ain't no crabs. I never found one."

The boys were overwhelmed with delight at sight of the tears of senile disappointment that dribbled down the old man's cheeks. Then, unnoticed, Hoo-Hoo replaced the empty shell with a fresh-cooked crab. Already dismembered, from the cracked legs the white meat sent forth a small cloud of savory steam. This attracted the old man's nostrils, and he looked down in amazement. The change of his mood to one of joy was immediate. He snuffled and muttered and mumbled, making almost a croon of delight, as he began to eat. Of this the boys took little notice, for it was an accustomed spectacle. Nor did they notice his occasional exclamations and utterances of phrases which meant nothing to them, as, for instance, when he smacked his lips and champed his gums while muttering: "Mayonnaise! Just think – mayonnaise! And it's sixty years since the last was ever made! Two generations and never a smell of it! Why, in those days it was served in every restaurant with crab."

When he could eat no more, the old man sighed, wiped his hands on his naked legs, and gazed out over the sea. With the content of a full stomach, he waxed reminiscent.

"To think of it! I've seen this beach alive with men, women, and children on a pleasant Sunday. And there weren't any bears to eat them up, either. And right up there on the cliff was a big restaurant where you could get anything you wanted to eat. Four million people lived in San Francisco then. And now, in the whole city and county there aren't forty all told. And out there on the sea were ships and ships always to be seen, going in for the Golden Gate or coming out. And airships in the air-dirigibles and flying machines. They could travel two hundred miles an hour. The mail contracts with the New York and San Francisco Limited demanded that for the minimum. There was a chap, a Frenchman, I forget his name, who succeeded in making three hundred; but the thing was risky, too risky for conservative persons. But he was on the right clew, and he would have managed it if it hadn't been for the Great Plague. When I was a boy, there were men alive who remembered the coming of the first aeroplanes, and now I have lived to see the last of them, and that sixty years ago."

The old man babbled on, unheeded by the boys, who were long accustomed to his garrulousness, and whose vocabularies, besides, lacked the greater portion of the words he used. It was noticeable that in these rambling soliloquies his English seemed to recrudesce into better construction and phraseology. But when he talked directly with the boys it lapsed, largely, into their own uncouth and simpler forms.

"But there weren't many crabs in those days," the old man wandered on. "They were fished out, and they were great delicacies. The open season was only a month long, too. And now crabs are accessible the whole year around. Think of it – catching all the crabs you want, any time you want, in the surf of the Cliff House beach!"

A sudden commotion among the goats brought the boys to their feet. The dogs about the fire rushed to join their snarling fellow who guarded the goats, while the goats themselves stampeded in the direction of their human protectors. A half dozen forms, lean and gray, glided about on the sand hillocks or faced the bristling dogs. Edwin arched an arrow that fell short. But Hare-Lip, with a sling such as David carried into battle against Goliath, hurled a stone through the air that whistled from the speed of its flight. It fell squarely among the wolves and caused them to slink away toward the dark depths of the eucalyptus forest.

The boys laughed and lay down again in the sand, while Granser sighed ponderously. He had eaten too much, and, with hands clasped on his paunch, the fingers interlaced, he resumed his maunderings.

"'The fleeting systems lapse like foam,'" he mumbled what was evidently a quotation. "That's it – foam, and fleeting. All man's toil upon the planet was just so much foam. He domesticated the service-able animals, destroyed the hostile ones, and cleared the land of its wild vegetation. And then he passed, and the flood of primordial life rolled back again, sweeping his handiwork away – the weeds and the forest inundated his fields, the beasts of prey swept over his flocks, and now there are wolves on the Cliff House beach." He was appalled by the thought. "Where four million people disported themselves, the wild wolves roam to-day, and the savage progeny of our loins, with prehistoric weapons, defend themselves against the fanged despoilers. Think of it! And all because of the Scarlet Death – "

The adjective had caught Hare-Lip's ear.

"He's always saying that," he said to Edwin. "What is *scarlet?*"

"'The scarlet of the maples can shake me like the cry of bugles going by,'" the old man quoted.

"It's red," Edwin answered the question. "And you don't know it because you come from the Chauffeur Tribe. They never did know nothing, none of them. *Scarlet* is red – I know that."

"Red is red, ain't it?" Hare-Lip grumbled. "Then what's the good of gettin' cocky and calling it scarlet?"

"Granser, what for do you always say so much what nobody knows?" he asked. "Scarlet ain't anything, but red is red. Why don't you say red, then?"

"Red is not the right word," was the reply. "The plague was scarlet. The whole face and body turned scarlet in an hour's time. Don't I know? Didn't I see enough of it? And I am telling you it was scarlet because – well, because it was scarlet. There is no other word for it."

"Red is good enough for me," Hare-Lip muttered obstinately. "My dad calls red red, and he ought to know. He says everybody died of the Red Death."

"Your dad is a common fellow, descended from a common fellow," Granser retorted heatedly. "Don't I know the beginnings of the Chauffeurs? Your grand-sire was a chauffeur, a servant, and without education. He worked for other persons. But your grandmother was of good stock, only the children did not take after her. Don't I remember when I first met them, catching fish at Lake Temescal?"

"What is *education?*" Edwin asked.

"Calling red scarlet," Hare-Lip sneered, then returned to the attack on Granser. "My dad told me, an' he got it from his dad afore he croaked, that your wife was a Santa Rosan, an' that she was sure no account. He said she was a *hash-slinger* before the Red Death, though I don't know what a *hash-slinger* is. You can tell me, Edwin."

But Edwin shook his head in token of ignorance.

"It is true, she was a waitress," Granser acknowledged. "But she was a good woman, and your mother was her daughter. Women were very scarce in the days after the Plague. She was the only wife I could find, even if she was a *hash-slinger,* as your father calls it. But it is not nice to talk about our progenitors that way."

"Dad says that the wife of the first Chauffeur was a *lady* – "

"What's a *lady?*" Hoo-Hoo demanded.

"A *lady's* a Chauffeur squaw," was the quick reply of Hare-Lip.

"The first Chauffeur was Bill, a common fellow, as I said before," the old man expounded; "but his wife was a lady, a great lady. Before the Scarlet Death she was the wife of Van Worden. He was President of the Board of Industrial Magnates, and was one of the dozen men who ruled America. He was worth one billion, eight hundred millions of dollars – coins like you have there in your pouch, Edwin. And then came the Scarlet Death, and his wife became the wife of Bill, the first Chauffeur. He used to beat her, too. I have seen it myself."

Hoo-Hoo, lying on his stomach and idly digging his toes in the sand, cried out and investigated, first, his toe-nail, and next, the small hole he had dug. The other two boys joined him, excavating the sand rapidly with their hands till there lay three skeletons exposed. Two were of adults, the third being that of a part-grown child. The old man budged along on the ground and peered at the find.

"Plague victims," he announced. "That's the way they died everywhere in the last days. This must have been a family, running away from the contagion and perishing here on the Cliff House beach. They – what are you doing, Edwin?"

This question was asked in sudden dismay, as Edwin, using the back of his hunting knife, began to knock out the teeth from the jaws of one of the skulls.

"Going to string 'em," was the response.

The three boys were now hard at it; and quite a knocking and hammering arose, in which Granser babbled on unnoticed.

"You are true savages. Already has begun the custom of wearing human teeth. In another generation you will be perforating your noses and ears and wearing ornaments of bone and shell. I know. The human race is doomed to sink back farther and farther into the primitive night ere again it begins its bloody climb upward to civilization. When we increase and feel the lack of room, we will proceed to kill one another. And then I suppose you will wear human scalp-locks at your waist, as well – as you, Edwin, who are the gentlest of my grandsons, have already begun with that vile pigtail. Throw it away, Edwin, boy; throw it away."

"What a gabble the old geezer makes," Hare-Lip remarked, when, the teeth all extracted, they began an attempt at equal division.

They were very quick and abrupt in their actions, and their speech, in moments of hot discussion over the allotment of the choicer teeth, was truly a gabble. They spoke in monosyllables and short jerky sentences that was more a gibberish than a language. And yet, through it ran hints of grammatical construction, and appeared vestiges of the conjugation of some superior culture. Even the speech of Granser was so corrupt that were it put down literally it would be almost so much nonsense to the reader. This, however, was when he talked with the boys. When he got into the full swing of babbling to himself, it slowly purged itself into pure English. The sentences grew longer and were enunciated with a rhythm and ease that was reminiscent of the lecture platform.

"Tell us about the Red Death, Granser," Hare-Lip demanded, when the teeth affair had been satisfactorily concluded.

"The Scarlet Death," Edwin corrected.

"An' don't work all that funny lingo on us," Hare-Lip went on. "Talk sensible, Granser, like a Santa Rosan ought to talk. Other Santa Rosans don't talk like you."

II

The old man showed pleasure in being thus called upon. He cleared his throat and began.

"Twenty or thirty years ago my story was in great demand. But in these days nobody seems interested – "

"There you go!" Hare-Lip cried hotly. "Cut out the funny stuff and talk sensible. What's *interested?* You talk like a baby that don't know how."

"Let him alone," Edwin urged, "or he'll get mad and won't talk at all. Skip the funny places. We'll catch on to some of what he tells us."

"Let her go, Granser," Hoo-Hoo encouraged; for the old man was already maundering about the disrespect for elders and the reversion to cruelty of all humans that fell from high culture to primitive conditions.

The tale began.

"There were very many people in the world in those days. San Francisco alone held four millions – "

"What is millions?" Edwin interrupted.

Granser looked at him kindly.

"I know you cannot count beyond ten, so I will tell you. Hold up your two hands. On both of them you have altogether ten fingers and thumbs. Very well. I now take this grain of sand – you hold it, Hoo-Hoo." He dropped the grain of sand into the lad's palm and went on. "Now that grain of sand stands for the ten fingers of Edwin. I add another grain. That's ten more fingers. And I add another, and another, and another, until I have added as many grains as Edwin has fingers and thumbs. That makes what I call one hundred. Remember that word – one hundred. Now I put this pebble in Hare-Lip's hand. It stands for ten grains of sand, or ten tens of fingers, or one hundred fingers. I put in ten pebbles. They stand for a thousand fingers. I take a mussel-shell, and it stands for ten pebbles, or one hundred grains of sand, or one thousand fingers . . ."

And so on, laboriously, and with much reiteration, he strove to build up in their minds a crude conception of numbers. As the quantities increased, he had the boys holding different magnitudes in each of their hands. For still higher sums, he laid the symbols on the log of driftwood; and for symbols he was hard put, being compelled to use the teeth from the skulls for millions, and the crab-shells for billions. It was here that he stopped, for the boys were showing signs of becoming tired.

"There were four million people in San Francisco – four teeth."

The boys' eyes ranged along from the teeth and from hand to hand, down through the pebbles and sand-grains to Edwin's fingers. And back again they ranged along the ascending series in the effort to grasp such inconceivable numbers.

"That was a lot of folks, Granser," Edwin at last hazarded.

"Like sand on the beach here, like sand on the beach, each grain of sand a man, or woman, or child. Yes, my boy, all those people lived right here in San Francisco. And at one time or another all those people came out on this very beach – more people than there are grains of sand. More – more – more. And San Francisco was a noble city. And across the bay, where we camped last year, even more people lived, clear from Point Richmond, on the level ground and on the hills, all the way around to San Leandro – one great city of seven million people. – Seven teeth . . . there, that's it, seven millions."

Again the boys' eyes ranged up and down from Edwin's fingers to the teeth on the log.

"The world was full of people. The census of 2010 gave eight billions for the whole world – eight crab-shells, yes, eight billions. It was not like to-day. Mankind knew a great deal more about getting food. And the more food there was, the more people there were. In the year 1800, there were one hundred and seventy millions in Europe alone. One hundred years later – a grain of sand, Hoo-Hoo – one hundred years later, at 1900, there were five hundred millions in Europe – five grains of sand, Hoo-Hoo, and this one tooth. This shows how easy was the getting of food, and how men increased. And in the year 2000, there were fifteen hundred millions in Europe. And it was the same all over the rest of the world. Eight crab-shells there, yes, eight billion people were alive on the earth when the Scarlet Death began.

"I was a young man when the Plague came – twenty-seven years old – and I lived on the other side of San Francisco Bay, in Berkeley. You remember those great stone houses, Edwin, when we came down the hills from Contra Costa? That was where I lived, in those stone houses. I was a professor of English literature."

Much of this was over the heads of the boys, but they strove to comprehend dimly this tale of the past.

"What was them stone houses for?" Hare-Lip queried.

"You remember when your dad taught you to swim?" The boy nodded. "Well, in the University of California – that is the name we had for the houses – we taught young men and women how to think, just as I have taught you now, by sand and pebbles and shells, to know how many people lived in those days. There was very much to teach. The young men and women we taught were called students. We had large rooms in which we taught. I talked to them, forty or fifty at a time, just as I am talking to you now. I told them about the books other men had written before their time, and even, some-times, in their time – "

"Was that all you did? – just talk, talk, talk?" Hoo-Hoo demanded. "Who hunted your meat for you? and milked the goats? and caught the fish?"

"A sensible question, Hoo-Hoo, a sensible question. As I have told you, in those days food-getting was easy. We were very wise. A few men got the food for many men. The other men did other things. As you say, I talked. I talked all the time, and for this food was given me – much food, fine food, beautiful food, food that I have not tasted in sixty years and shall never taste again. I sometimes think the most wonderful achievement of our tremendous civilization was food – its inconceivable abundance, its infinite variety, its marvellous delicacy. O my grandsons, life was life in those days, when we had such wonderful things to eat."

This was beyond the boys, and they let it slip by, words and thoughts, as a mere senile wandering in the narrative.

"Our food-getters were called *freemen*. This was a joke. We of the ruling classes owned all the land, all the machines, everything. These food-getters were our slaves. We took almost all the food they got, and left them a little so that they might eat, and work, and get us more food – "

"I'd have gone into the forest and got food for myself," Hare-Lip announced; "and if any man tried to take it away from me, I'd have killed him."

The old man laughed.

"Did I not tell you that we of the ruling class owned all the land, all the forest, everything? Any food-getter who would not get food for us, him we punished or compelled to starve to death. And very few did that. They preferred to get food for us, and make clothes for us, and prepare and administer to us a thousand – a mussel-shell, Hoo-Hoo – a thousand satisfactions and delights. And I was Professor Smith in those days – Professor James Howard Smith. And my lecture courses were very popular – that is, very many of the young men and women liked to hear me talk about the books other men had written.

"And I was very happy, and I had beautiful things to eat. And my hands were soft, because I did no work with them, and my body was clean all over and dressed in the softest garments – " He surveyed his mangy goat-skin with disgust. "We did not wear such things in those days. Even the slaves had better garments. And we were most clean. We washed our faces and hands often every day. You boys never wash unless you fall into the water or go in swimming."

"Neither do you, Granser," Hoo-Hoo retorted.

"I know, I know. I am a filthy old man. But times have changed. Nobody washes these days, and there are no conveniences. It is sixty years since I have seen a piece of soap. You do not know what soap is, and I shall not tell you, for I am telling the story of the Scarlet Death.

You know what sickness is. We called it a disease. Very many of the diseases came from what we called germs. Remember that word – germs. A germ is a very small thing. It is like a woodtick, such as you find on the dogs in the spring of the year when they run in the forest. Only the germ is very small. It is so small that you cannot see it – "

Hoo-Hoo began to laugh.

"You're a queer un, Granser, talking about things you can't see. If you can't see 'em, how do you know they are? That's what I want to know. How do you know anything you can't see?"

"A good question, a very good question, Hoo-Hoo. But we did see – some of them. We had what we called microscopes and ultramicroscopes, and we put them to our eyes and looked through them, so that we saw things larger than they really were, and many things we could not see without the microscopes at all. Our best ultramicroscopes could make a germ look forty thousand times larger. A mussel-shell is a thousand fingers like Edwin's. Take forty mussel-shells, and by as many times larger was the germ when we looked at it through a microscope. And after that, we had other ways, by using what we called moving pictures, of making the forty-thousand-times germ many, many thousand times larger still. And thus we saw all these things which our eyes of themselves could not see. Take a grain of sand. Break it into ten pieces. Take one piece and break it into ten. Break one of those pieces into ten, and one of those into ten, and one of those into ten, and one of those into ten, and do it all day, and maybe, by sunset, you will have a piece as small as one of the germs."

The boys were openly incredulous. Hare-Lip sniffed and sneered and Hoo-Hoo snickered, until Edwin nudged them to be silent.

"The woodtick sucks the blood of the dog, but the germ, being so very small, goes right into the blood of the body, and there it has many children. In those days there would be as many as a billion – a crab-shell, please – as many as that crab-shell in one man's body. We called germs micro-organisms. When a few million, or a billion, of them were in a man, in all the blood of a man, he was sick. These germs were a disease. There were many different kinds of them – more different kinds than there are grains of sand on this beach. We knew only a few of the kinds. The micro-organic world was an invisible world, a world we could not see, and we knew very little about it. Yet we did know something. There was the *Bacillus anthracis;* there was the *micrococcus*; there was the *Bacterium termo*, and the *Bacterium lactis* – that's what turns the goat milk sour even to this day, Hare-Lip; and there were *Schizomycetes* without end. And there were many others . . ."

Here the old man launched into a disquisition on germs and their natures, using words and phrases of such extraordinary length and meaninglessness, that the boys grinned at one another and looked out over the deserted ocean till they forgot the old man was babbling on.

"But the Scarlet Death, Granser," Edwin at last suggested.

Granser recollected himself, and with a start tore himself away from the rostrum of the lecture-hall, where, to another-world audience, he had been expounding the latest theory, sixty years gone, of germs and germ-diseases.

"Yes, yes, Edwin; I had forgotten. Sometimes the memory of the past is very strong upon me, and I forget that I am a dirty old man, clad in goat-skin, wandering with my savage grandsons who are goatherds in the primeval wilderness. 'The fleeting systems lapse like foam,' and so lapsed our glorious, colossal civilization. I am Granser, a tired old man. I belong to the tribe of Santa Rosans. I married into that tribe. My sons and daughters married into the Chauffeurs, the Sacramentos, and the Palo-Altos. You, Hare-Lip, are of the Chauffeurs. You, Edwin, are of the Sacramentos. And you, Hoo-Hoo, are of the Palo-Altos. Your tribe takes its name from a town that was near the seat of another great institution of learning. It was called Stanford University. Yes, I remember now. It is perfectly clear. I was telling you of the Scarlet Death. Where was I in my story?"

"You was telling about germs, the things you can't see but which make men sick," Edwin prompted.

"Yes, that's where I was. A man did not notice at first when only a few of these germs got into his body. But each germ broke in half and became two germs, and they kept doing this very rapidly so that in a short time there were many millions of them in the body. Then the man was sick. He had a disease, and the disease was named after the kind of a germ that was in him. It might be measles, it might be influenza, it might be yellow fever; it might be any of thousands and thousands of kinds of diseases.

"Now this is the strange thing about these germs. There were always new ones coming to live in men's bodies. Long and long and long ago, when there were only a few men in the world, there were few diseases. But as men increased and lived closely together in great cities and civilizations, new diseases arose, new kinds of germs entered their bodies. Thus were countless millions and billions of human beings killed. And the more thickly men packed together, the more terrible were the new diseases that came to be. Long before my time, in the Middle Ages, there was the Black Plague that swept across Europe. It swept across Europe many times. There was tuberculosis, that entered into men wherever they were thickly packed. A hundred years before my time there was the bubonic plague. And in Africa was the sleeping sickness. The bacteriologists fought all these sicknesses and destroyed them, just as you boys fight the wolves away from your goats, or squash the mosquitoes that light on you. The bacteriologists – "

"But, Granser, what is a what-you-call-it?" Edwin interrupted.

"You, Edwin, are a goatherd. Your task is to watch the goats. You know a great deal about goats. A bacteriologist watches germs. That's his task, and he knows a great deal about them. So, as I was saying, the bacteriologists fought with the germs and destroyed them – sometimes. There was leprosy, a horrible disease. A hundred years before I was born, the bacteriologists discovered the germ of leprosy. They knew all about it. They made pictures of it. I have seen those pictures. But they never found a way to kill it. But in 1984, there was the Pantoblast Plague, a disease that broke out in a country called Brazil and that killed millions of people. But the bacteriologists found it out, and found the way to kill it, so that the Pantoblast Plague went no farther. They made what they called a serum, which they put into a man's body and which killed the pantoblast germs without killing the man. And in 1910, there was Pellagra, and also the hookworm. These were easily killed by the bacteriologists. But in 1947 there arose a new disease that had never been seen before. It got into the bodies of babies of only ten months old or less, and it made them unable to move their hands and feet, or to eat, or anything; and the bacteriologists were eleven years in discovering how to kill that particular germ and save the babies.

"In spite of all these diseases, and of all the new ones that continued to arise, there were more and more men in the world. This was because it was easy to get food. The easier it was to get food, the more men there were; the more men there were, the more thickly were they packed together on the earth; and the more thickly they were packed, the more new kinds of germs became diseases. There were warnings. Soldervetzsky, as early as 1929, told the bacteriologists that they had no guaranty against some new disease, a thousand times more deadly than any they knew, arising and killing by the hundreds of millions and even by the billion. You see, the micro-organic world remained a mystery to the end. They knew there was such a world, and that from time to time armies of new germs emerged from it to kill men. And that was all they knew about it. For all they knew, in that invisible micro-organic world there might be as many different kinds of germs as there are grains of sand on this beach. And also, in that same invisible world it might well be that new kinds of germs came to be. It might be there that life originated – the 'abysmal fecundity,' Soldervetzsky called it, applying the words of other men who had written before him . . ."

It was at this point that Hare-Lip rose to his feet, an expression of huge contempt on his face.

"Granser," he announced, "you make me sick with your gabble. Why don't you tell about the Red Death? If you ain't going to, say so, an' we'll start back for camp."

The old man looked at him and silently began to cry. The weak tears of age rolled down his cheeks, and all the feebleness of his eighty-seven years showed in his grief-stricken countenance.

"Sit down," Edwin counselled soothingly. "Granser's all right. He's just gettin' to the Scarlet Death, ain't you, Granser? He's just goin' to tell us about it right now. Sit down, Hare-Lip. Go ahead, Granser."

III

The old man wiped the tears away on his grimy knuckles and took up the tale in a tremulous, piping voice that soon strengthened as he got the swing of the narrative.

"It was in the summer of 2013 that the Plague came. I was twenty-seven years old, and well do I remember it. Wireless despatches – "

Hare-Lip spat loudly his disgust, and Granser hastened to make amends.

"We talked through the air in those days, thousands and thousands of miles. And the word came of a strange disease that had broken out in New York. There were seventeen millions of people living then in that noblest city of America. Nobody thought anything about the news. It was only a small thing. There had been only a few deaths. It seemed, though, that they had died very quickly, and that one of the first signs of the disease was the turning red of the face and all the body. Within twenty-four hours came the report of the first case in Chicago. And on the same day, it was made public that London, the greatest city in the world, next to Chicago, had been secretly fighting the plague for two weeks and censoring the news despatches – that is, not permitting the word to go forth to the rest of the world that London had the plague.

"It looked serious, but we in California, like everywhere else, were not alarmed. We were sure that the bacteriologists would find a way to overcome this new germ, just as they had overcome other germs in the past. But the trouble was the astonishing quickness with which this germ destroyed human beings, and the fact that it inevitably killed any human body it entered. No one ever recovered. There was the old Asiatic cholera, when you might eat dinner with a well man in the evening, and the next morning, if you got up early enough, you would see him being hauled by your window in the death-cart. But this new plague was quicker than that – much quicker. From the moment of the first signs of it, a man would be dead in an hour. Some lasted for several hours. Many died within ten or fifteen minutes of the appearance of the first signs.

"The heart began to beat faster and the heat of the body to increase. Then came the scarlet rash, spreading like wildfire over the face and body. Most persons never noticed the increase in heat and heart-beat, and the first they knew was when the scarlet rash came out. Usually, they had convulsions at the time of the appearance of the rash. But these convulsions did not last long and were not very severe. If one lived through them, he became perfectly quiet, and only did he feel a numbness swiftly creeping up his body from the feet. The heels became numb first, then the legs, and hips, and when the numbness reached as high as his heart he died. They did not rave or sleep. Their minds always remained cool and calm up to the moment their heart numbed and stopped. And another strange thing was the rapidity of decomposition. No sooner was a person dead than the body seemed to fall to pieces, to fly apart, to melt away even as you looked at it. That was one of the reasons the plague spread so rapidly. All the billions of germs in a corpse were so immediately released.

"And it was because of all this that the bacteriologists had so little chance in fighting the germs. They were killed in their laboratories even as they studied the germ of the Scarlet Death. They were heroes. As fast as they perished, others stepped forth and took their places. It was in London that they first isolated it. The news was telegraphed everywhere. Trask was the name of the man who succeeded in this, but within thirty hours he was dead. Then came the struggle in all the laboratories to find something that would kill the plague germs. All drugs failed. You see, the problem was to get a drug, or serum, that would kill the germs in the body and not kill the body. They tried to fight it with other germs, to put into the body of a sick man germs that were the enemies of the plague germs – "

"And you can't see these germ-things, Granser," Hare-Lip objected, "and here you gabble, gabble, gabble about them as if they was anything, when they're nothing at all. Anything you can't see, ain't, that's what. Fighting things that ain't with things that ain't! They must have been all fools in them days. That's why they croaked. I ain't goin' to believe in such rot, I tell you that."

Granser promptly began to weep, while Edwin hotly took up his defence.

"Look here, Hare-Lip, you believe in lots of things you can't see."

Hare-Lip shook his head.

"You believe in dead men walking about. You never seen one dead man walk about."

"I tell you I seen 'em, last winter, when I was wolf-hunting with Dad."

"Well, you always spit when you cross running water," Edwin challenged.

"That's to keep off bad luck," was Hare-Lip's defence.

"You believe in bad luck?"

"Sure."

"An' you ain't never seen bad luck," Edwin concluded triumphantly. "You're just as bad as Granser and his germs. You believe in what you don't see. Go on, Granser."

Hare-Lip, crushed by this metaphysical defeat, remained silent, and the old man went on. Often and often, though this narrative must not be clogged by the details, was Granser's tale interrupted while the boys squabbled among themselves. Also, among themselves they kept up a constant, low-voiced exchange of explanation and conjecture, as they strove to follow the old man into his unknown and vanished world.

"The Scarlet Death broke out in San Francisco. The first death came on a Monday morning. By Thursday they were dying like flies in Oakland and San Francisco. They died everywhere – in their beds, at their work, walking along the street. It was on Tuesday that I saw my first death – Miss Collbran, one of my students, sitting right there before my eyes, in my lecture-room. I noticed her face while I was talking. It had suddenly turned scarlet. I ceased speaking and could only look at her, for the first fear of the plague was already on all of us and we knew that it had come. The young women screamed and ran out of the room. So did the young men run out, all but two. Miss Collbran's convulsions were very mild and lasted less than a minute. One of the young men fetched her a glass of water. She drank only a little of it, and cried out:

"'My feet! All sensation has left them.'

"After a minute she said, 'I have no feet. I am unaware that I have any feet. And my knees are cold. I can scarcely feel that I have knees.

"She lay on the floor, a bundle of notebooks under her head. And we could do nothing. The coldness and the numbness crept up past her hips to her heart, and when it reached her heart she was dead. In fifteen minutes, by the clock – I timed it – she was dead, there, in my own classroom, dead. And she was a very beautiful, strong, healthy young woman. And from the first sign of the plague to her death only fifteen minutes elapsed. That will show you how swift was the Scarlet Death.

"Yet in those few minutes I remained with the dying woman in my classroom, the alarm had spread over the university; and the students, by thousands, all of them, had deserted the lecture-room and laboratories. When I emerged, on my way to make report to the President of the Faculty, I found the university deserted. Across the campus were several stragglers hurrying for their homes. Two of them were running.

"President Hoag, I found in his office, all alone, looking very old and very gray, with a multitude of wrinkles in his face that I had never seen before. At the sight of me, he pulled himself to his feet and tottered away to the inner office, banging the door after him and locking it. You see, he knew I had been exposed, and he was afraid. He shouted to me through the door to go away. I shall never forget my feelings as I walked down the silent corridors and out across that deserted campus. I was not afraid. I had been exposed, and I looked upon myself as already dead. It was not that, but a feeling of awful depression that impressed me. Everything had stopped. It was like the end of the world to me – my world. I had been born within sight and sound of the university. It had been my predestined career. My father had been a professor there before me, and his father before him. For a century and a half had this university, like a splendid machine, been running steadily on. And now, in an instant, it had stopped. It was like seeing the sacred flame die down on some thrice-sacred altar. I was shocked, unutterably shocked.

"When I arrived home, my housekeeper screamed as I entered, and fled away. And when I rang, I found the housemaid had likewise fled. I investigated. In the kitchen I found the cook on the point of departure. But she screamed, too, and in her haste dropped a suitcase of her personal belongings and ran out of the house and across the grounds, still screaming. I can hear her scream to this day. You see, we did not act in this way when ordinary diseases smote us. We were always calm over such things, and sent for the doctors and nurses who knew just what to do. But this was different. It struck so suddenly, and killed so swiftly, and never missed a stroke. When the scarlet rash appeared on a person's face, that person was marked by death. There was never a known case of a recovery.

"I was alone in my big house. As I have told you often before, in those days we could talk with one another over wires or through the air. The telephone bell rang, and I found my brother talking to me. He told me that he was not coming home for fear of catching the plague from me, and that he had taken our two sisters to stop at Professor Bacon's home. He advised me to remain where I was, and wait to find out whether or not I had caught the plague.

"To all of this I agreed, staying in my house and for the first time in my life attempting to cook. And the plague did not come out on me. By means of the telephone I could talk with whomsoever I pleased and get the news. Also, there were the newspapers, and I ordered all of them to be thrown up to my door so that I could know what was happening with the rest of the world.

"New York City and Chicago were in chaos. And what happened with them was happening in all the large cities. A third of the New York police were dead. Their chief was also dead, likewise the mayor. All law and order had ceased. The bodies were lying in the streets unburied. All railroads and vessels carrying food and such things into the great city had ceased running, and mobs of the hungry poor were pillaging the stores and warehouses. Murder and robbery and drunkenness were everywhere. Already the people had fled from the city by millions – at first the rich, in their private motor cars and dirigibles, and then the great mass of the population, on foot, carrying the plague with them, themselves starving and pillaging the farmers and all the towns and villages on the way.

"The man who sent this news, the wireless operator, was alone with his instrument on the top of a lofty building. The people remaining in the city – he estimated them at several hundred thousand – had gone mad from fear and drink, and on all sides of him great fires were raging. He was a hero, that man who staid by his post – an obscure newspaperman, most likely.

"For twenty-four hours, he said, no transatlantic airships had arrived, and no more messages were coming from England. He did state, though, that a message from Berlin – that's in Germany – announced that Hoffmeyer, a bacteriologist of the Metchnikoff School, had discovered the serum for the plague. That was the last word, to this day, that we of America ever received from Europe. If Hoffmeyer discovered the serum, it was too late, or otherwise, long ere this, explorers from Europe would have come looking for us. We can only conclude that what happened in America happened in Europe, and that, at the best, some several score may have survived the Scarlet Death on that whole continent.

"For one day longer the despatches continued to come from New York. Then they, too, ceased. The man who had sent them, perched in his lofty building, had either died of the plague or been consumed in the great conflagrations he had described as raging around him. And what had occurred in New York had been duplicated in all the other cities. It was the same in San Francisco, and Oakland, and Berkeley. By Thursday the people were dying so rapidly that their corpses could not be handled, and dead bodies lay everywhere. Thursday night the panic outrush for the country began. Imagine, my grandsons, people, thicker than the salmon-run you have seen on the Sacramento River, pouring out of the cities by millions, madly over the country, in vain attempt to escape the ubiquitous death. You see, they carried the germs with them. Even the airships of the rich, fleeing for mountain and desert fastnesses, carried the germs.

"Hundreds of these airships escaped to Hawaii, and not only did they bring the plague with them, but they found the plague already there before them. This we learned, by the despatches, until all order in San Francisco vanished, and there were no operators left at their posts to receive or send. It was amazing, astounding, this loss of communication with the world. It was exactly as if the world had ceased, been blotted out. For sixty years that world has no longer existed for me. I know there must be such places as New York, Europe, Asia, and Africa; but not one word has been heard of them – not in sixty years. With the coming of the Scarlet Death the world fell apart, absolutely, irretrievably. Ten thousand years of culture and civilization passed in the twinkling of an eye, 'lapsed like foam.'

"I was telling about the airships of the rich. They carried the plague with them and no matter where they fled, they died. I never encountered but one survivor of any of them – Mungerson. He was afterwards a Santa Rosan, and he married my eldest daughter. He came into the tribe eight years after the plague. He was then nineteen years old, and he was compelled to wait twelve years more before he could marry. You see, there were no unmarried women, and some of the older daughters of the Santa Rosans were already bespoken. So he was forced to wait until my Mary had grown to sixteen years. It was his son, Gimp-Leg, who was killed last year by the mountain lion.

"Mungerson was eleven years old at the time of the plague. His father was one of the Industrial Magnates, a very wealthy, powerful man. It was on his airship, the *Condor*, that they were fleeing, with all the family, for the wilds of British Columbia, which is far to the north of here. But there was some accident, and they were wrecked near Mount Shasta. You have heard of that mountain. It is far to the north. The plague broke out amongst them, and this boy of eleven was the only survivor. For eight years he was alone, wandering over a deserted land and looking vainly for his own kind. And at last, travelling south, he picked up with us, the Santa Rosans.

"But I am ahead of my story. When the great exodus from the cities around San Francisco Bay began, and while the telephones were still working, I talked with my brother. I told him this flight from the cities was insanity, that there were no symptoms of the plague in me, and that the thing for us to do was to isolate ourselves and our relatives in some safe place. We decided on the Chemistry Building, at the university, and we planned to lay in a supply of provisions, and by force of arms to prevent any other persons from forcing their presence upon us after we had retired to our refuge.

"All this being arranged, my brother begged me to stay in my own house for at least twenty-four hours more, on the chance of the plague developing in me. To this I agreed, and he promised to come for me next day. We talked on over the details of the provisioning and the defending of the Chemistry Building until the telephone died. It died in the midst of our conversation. That evening there were no electric lights, and I was alone in my house in the darkness. No more newspapers were being printed, so I had no knowledge of what was taking place outside. I heard sounds of rioting and of pistol shots, and from my windows I could see the glare of the sky of some conflagration in the direction of Oakland. It was a night of terror. I did not sleep a wink. A man – why and how I do not know – was killed on the sidewalk in front of the house. I heard the rapid reports of an automatic pistol, and a few minutes later the wounded wretch crawled up to my door, moaning and crying out for help. Arming myself with two automatics, I went to him. By the light of a match I ascertained that while he was dying of the bullet wounds, at the same time the plague was on him. I fled indoors, whence I heard him moan and cry out for half an hour longer.

"In the morning, my brother came to me. I had gathered into a handbag what things of value I purposed taking, but when I saw his face I knew that he would never accompany me to the Chemistry Building. The plague was on him. He intended shaking my hand, but I went back hurriedly before him.

"'Look at yourself in the mirror,' I commanded.

"He did so, and at sight of his scarlet face, the color deepening as he looked at it, he sank down nervelessly in a chair.

"'My God!' he said. 'I've got it. Don't come near me. I am a dead man.'

"'Then the convulsions seized him. He was two hours in dying, and he was conscious to the last, complaining about the coldness and loss of sensation in his feet, his calves, his thighs, until at last it was his heart and he was dead.

"That was the way the Scarlet Death slew. I caught up my handbag and fled. The sights in the streets were terrible. One stumbled on bodies everywhere. Some were not yet dead. And even as you looked, you saw men sink down with the death fastened upon them. There were numerous fires burning in Berkeley, while Oakland and San Francisco were apparently being swept by vast conflagrations. The smoke of the burning filled the heavens, so that the midday was as a gloomy twilight, and, in the shifts of wind, sometimes the sun shone through dimly, a dull red orb. Truly, my grandsons, it was like the last days of the end of the world.

"There were numerous stalled motor cars, showing that the gasoline and the engine supplies of the garages had given out. I remember one such car. A man and a woman lay back dead in the seats, and on the pavement near it were two more women and a child. Strange and terrible sights there were on every hand.

"People slipped by silently, furtively, like ghosts – white-faced women carrying infants in their arms; fathers leading children by the hand; singly, and in couples, and in families – all fleeing out of the city of death. Some carried supplies of food, others blankets and valuables, and there were many who carried nothing.

"There was a grocery store – a place where food was sold. The man to whom it belonged – I knew him well – a quiet, sober, but stupid and obstinate fellow, was defending it. The windows and doors had been broken in, but he, inside, hiding behind a counter, was discharging his pistol at a number of men on the sidewalk who were breaking in. In the entrance were several bodies – of men, I decided, whom he had killed earlier in the day. Even as I looked on from a distance, I saw one of the robbers break the windows of the adjoining store, a place where shoes were sold, and deliberately set fire to it. I did not go to the groceryman's assistance. The time for such acts had already passed. Civilization was crumbling, and it was each for himself."

IV

"I went away hastily, down a cross-street, and at the first corner I saw another tragedy. Two men of the working class had caught a man and a woman with two children, and were robbing them. I knew the man by sight, though I had never been introduced to him. He was a poet whose verses I had long admired. Yet I did not go to his help, for at the moment I came upon the scene there was a pistol shot, and I saw him sinking to the ground. The woman screamed, and she was felled with a fist-blow by one of the brutes. I cried out threateningly, whereupon they discharged their pistols at me and I ran away around the corner. Here I was blocked by an advancing conflagration. The buildings on both sides were burning, and the street was filled with smoke and flame. From somewhere in that murk came a woman's voice calling shrilly for help. But I did not go to her. A man's heart turned to iron amid such scenes, and one heard all too many appeals for help.

"Returning to the corner, I found the two robbers were gone. The poet and his wife lay dead on the pavement. It was a shocking sight. The two children had vanished – whither I could not tell. And I knew, now, why it was that the fleeing persons I encountered slipped along so furtively and with such white faces. In the midst of our civilization, down in our slums and labor-ghettos, we had bred a race of barbarians, of savages; and now, in the time of our calamity, they turned upon us like the wild beasts they were and destroyed us. And they destroyed themselves as well. They inflamed themselves with strong drink and committed a thousand atrocities, quarreling and killing one another in the general madness. One group of workingmen I saw, of the better sort, who had banded together, and, with their women and children in their midst, the sick and aged in litters and being carried, and with a number of horses pulling a truck-load of provisions, they were fighting their way out of the city. They made a fine spectacle as they came down the street through the drifting smoke, though they nearly shot me when I first appeared in their path. As they went by, one of their leaders shouted out to me in apologetic explanation. He said they were killing the robbers and looters on sight, and that they had thus banded together as the only means by which to escape the prowlers.

"It was here that I saw for the first time what I was soon to see so often. One of the marching men had suddenly shown the unmistakable mark of the plague. Immediately those about him drew away, and he, without a remonstrance, stepped out of his place to let them pass on. A woman, most probably his wife, attempted to follow him. She was leading a little boy by the hand. But the husband commanded her sternly to go on, while others laid hands on her and restrained her from following him. This I saw, and I saw the man also, with his scarlet blaze of face, step into a doorway on the opposite side of the street. I heard the report of his pistol, and saw him sink lifeless to the ground.

"After being turned aside twice again by advancing fires, I succeeded in getting through to the university. On the edge of the campus I came upon a party of university folk who were going in the direction of the Chemistry Building. They were all family men, and their families were with them, including the nurses and the servants.

"Professor Badminton greeted me, and I had difficulty in recognizing him. Somewhere he had gone through flames, and his beard was singed off. About his head was a bloody bandage, and his clothes were filthy. He told me he had been cruelly beaten by prowlers, and that his brother had been killed the previous night, in the defence of their dwelling.

"Midway across the campus, he pointed suddenly to Mrs. Swinton's face. The unmistakable scarlet was there. Immediately all the other women set up a screaming and began to run away from her. Her two children were with a nurse, and these also ran with the women. But her husband, Doctor Swinton, remained with her.

"'Go on, Smith,' he told me. 'Keep an eye on the children. As for me, I shall stay with my wife. I know she is as already dead, but I can't leave her. Afterwards, if I escape, I shall come to the Chemistry Building, and do you watch for me and let me in.'

"I left him bending over his wife and soothing her last moments, while I ran to overtake the party. We were the last to be admitted to the Chemistry Building. After that, with our automatic rifles we maintained our isolation. By our plans, we had arranged for a company of sixty to be in this refuge. Instead, every one of the number originally planned had added relatives and friends and whole families until there were over four hundred souls. But the Chemistry Building was large, and, standing by itself, was in no danger of being burned by the great fires that raged everywhere in the city.

"A large quantity of provisions had been gathered, and a food committee took charge of it, issuing rations daily to the various families and groups that arranged themselves into messes. A number of committees were appointed, and we developed a very efficient organization. I was on the committee of defence, though for the first day no prowlers came near. We could see them in the distance, however, and by the smoke of their fires knew that several camps of them were occupying the far edge of the campus. Drunkenness was rife, and often we heard them singing ribald songs or insanely shouting. While the world crashed to ruin about them and all the air was filled with the smoke of its burning, these low creatures gave rein to their bestiality and fought and drank and died. And after all, what did it matter? Everybody died anyway, the good and the bad, the efficients and the weaklings, those that loved to live and those that scorned to live. They passed. Everything passed.

"When twenty-four hours had gone by and no signs of the plague were apparent, we congratulated ourselves and set about digging a well. You have seen the great iron pipes which in those days carried water to all the city-dwellers. We feared that the fires in the city would burst the pipes and empty the reservoirs. So we tore up the cement floor of the central court of the Chemistry Building and dug a well. There were many young men, undergraduates, with us, and we worked night and day on the well. And our fears were confirmed. Three hours before we reached water, the pipes went dry.

"A second twenty-four hours passed, and still the plague did not appear among us. We thought we were saved. But we did not know what I afterwards decided to be true, namely, that the period of the incubation of the plague germs in a human's body was a matter of a number of days. It slew so swiftly when once it manifested itself, that we were led to believe that the period of incubation was equally swift. So, when two days had left us unscathed, we were elated with the idea that we were free of the contagion.

"But the third day disillusioned us. I can never forget the night preceding it. I had charge of the night guards from eight to twelve, and from the roof of the building I watched the passing of all man's glorious works. So terrible were the local conflagrations that all the sky was lighted up. One could read the finest print in the red glare. All the world seemed wrapped in flames. San Francisco spouted smoke and fire from a score of vast conflagrations that were like so many active volcanoes. Oakland, San Leandro, Haywards – all were burning; and to the northward, clear to Point Richmond, other fires were at work. It was an awe-inspiring spectacle. Civilization, my grandsons, civilization was passing in a sheet of flame and a breath of death. At ten o'clock that night, the great powder magazines at Point Pinole exploded in rapid succession. So terrific were the concussions that the strong building rocked as in an earthquake, while every pane of glass was broken. It was then that I left the roof and went down the long corridors, from room to room, quieting the alarmed women and telling them what had happened.

"An hour later, at a window on the ground floor, I heard pandemonium break out in the camps of the prowlers. There were cries and screams, and shots from many pistols. As we afterward conjectured, this fight had been precipitated by an attempt on the part of those that were well to drive out those that were sick. At any rate, a number of the plague-stricken prowlers escaped across the campus and drifted against our doors. We warned them back, but they cursed us and discharged a fusillade from their pistols. Professor Merryweather, at one of the windows, was instantly killed, the bullet striking him squarely between the eyes. We opened fire in turn, and all the prowlers fled away with the exception of three. One was a woman. The plague was on them and they were reckless. Like foul fiends, there in the red glare from the skies, with faces blazing, they continued to curse us and fire at us. One of the men I shot with my own hand. After that the other man and the woman, still cursing us, lay down under our windows, where we were compelled to watch them die of the plague.

"The situation was critical. The explosions of the powder magazines had broken all the windows of the Chemistry Building, so that we were exposed to the germs from the corpses. The sanitary committee was called upon to act, and it responded nobly. Two men were required to go out and remove the corpses, and this meant the probable sacrifice of their own lives, for, having performed the task, they were not to be permitted to re-enter the building. One of the professors, who was a bachelor, and one of the undergraduates volunteered. They bade good-bye to us and went forth. They were heroes. They gave up their lives that four hundred others might live. After they had performed their work, they stood for a moment, at a distance, looking at us wistfully. Then they waved their hands in farewell and went away slowly across the campus toward the burning city.

"And yet it was all useless. The next morning the first one of us was smitten with the plague – a little nurse-girl in the family of Professor Stout. It was no time for weak-kneed, sentimental policies. On the chance that she might be the only one, we thrust her forth from the building and commanded her to be gone. She went away slowly across the campus, wringing her hands and crying pitifully. We felt like brutes, but what were we to do? There were four hundred of us, and individuals had to be sacrificed.

"In one of the laboratories three families had domiciled themselves, and that afternoon we found among them no less than four corpses and seven cases of the plague in all its different stages.

"Then it was that the horror began. Leaving the dead lie, we forced the living ones to segregate themselves in another room. The plague began to break out among the rest of us, and as fast as the symptoms appeared, we sent the stricken ones to these segregated rooms. We compelled them to walk there by themselves, so as to avoid laying hands on them. It was heartrending. But still the plague raged among us, and room after room was filled with the dead and dying. And so we who were yet clean retreated to the next floor and to the next, before this sea of the dead, that, room by room and floor by floor, inundated the building.

"The place became a charnel house, and in the middle of the night the survivors fled forth, taking nothing with them except arms and ammunition and a heavy store of tinned foods. We camped on the opposite side of the campus from the prowlers, and, while some stood guard, others of us volunteered to scout into the city in quest of horses, motor cars, carts, and wagons, or anything that would carry our provisions and enable us to emulate the banded working-men I had seen fighting their way out to the open country.

"I was one of these scouts; and Doctor Hoyle, remembering that his motor car had been left behind in his home garage, told me to look for it. We scouted in pairs, and Dombey, a young undergraduate, accompanied me. We had to cross half a mile of the residence portion of the city to get to Doctor Hoyle's home. Here the buildings stood apart, in the midst of trees and grassy lawns, and here the fires had played freaks, burning whole blocks, skipping blocks and often skipping a single house in a block. And here, too, the prowlers were still at their work. We carried our automatic pistols openly in our hands, and looked desperate enough, forsooth, to keep them from attacking us. But at Doctor Hoyle's house the thing happened. Untouched by fire, even as we came to it the smoke of flames burst forth.

"The miscreant who had set fire to it staggered down the steps and out along the driveway. Sticking out of his coat pockets were bottles of whiskey, and he was very drunk. My first impulse was to shoot him, and I have never ceased regretting that I did not. Staggering and maundering to himself, with bloodshot eyes, and a raw and bleeding slash down one side of his bewhiskered face, he was altogether the most nauseating specimen of degradation and filth I had ever encountered. I did not shoot him, and he leaned against a tree on the lawn to let us go by. It was the most absolute, wanton act. Just as we were opposite him, he suddenly drew a pistol and shot Dombey through the head. The next instant I shot him. But it was too late. Dombey expired without a groan, immediately. I doubt if he even knew what had happened to him.

"Leaving the two corpses, I hurried on past the burning house to the garage, and there found Doctor Hoyle's motor car. The tanks were filled with gasoline, and it was ready for use. And it was in this car that I threaded the streets of the ruined city and came back to the survivors on the campus. The other scouts returned, but none had been so fortunate. Professor Fairmead had found a Shetland pony, but the poor creature, tied in a stable and abandoned for days, was so weak from want of food and water that it could carry no burden at all. Some of the men were for turning it loose, but I insisted that we should lead it along with us, so that, if we got out of food, we would have it to eat.

"There were forty-seven of us when we started, many being women and children. The President of the Faculty, an old man to begin with, and now hopelessly broken by the awful happenings of the past week, rode in the motor car with several young children and the aged mother of Professor Fairmead. Wathope, a young professor of English, who had a grievous bullet-wound in his leg, drove the car. The rest of us walked, Professor Fairmead leading the pony.

"It was what should have been a bright summer day, but the smoke from the burning world filled the sky, through which the sun shone murkily, a dull and lifeless orb, blood-red and ominous. But we had grown accustomed to that blood-red sun. With the smoke it was different. It bit into our nostrils and eyes, and there was not one of us whose eyes were not bloodshot. We directed our course to the southeast through the endless miles of suburban residences, travelling along where the first swells of low hills rose from the flat of the central city. It was by this way, only, that we could expect to gain the country.

"Our progress was painfully slow. The women and children could not walk fast. They did not dream of walking, my grandsons, in the way all people walk to-day. In truth, none of us knew how to walk. It was not until after the plague that I learned really to walk. So it was that the pace of the slowest was the pace of all, for we dared not separate on account of the prowlers. There were not so many now of these human beasts of prey. The plague had already well diminished their numbers, but enough still lived to be a constant menace to us. Many of the beautiful residences were untouched by fire, yet smoking ruins were everywhere. The prowlers, too, seemed to have got over their insensate desire to burn, and it was more rarely that we saw houses freshly on fire.

"Several of us scouted among the private garages in search of motor cars and gasoline. But in this we were unsuccessful. The first great flights from the cities had swept all such utilities away. Calgan, a fine young man, was lost in this work. He was shot by prowlers while crossing a lawn. Yet this was our only casualty, though, once, a drunken brute deliberately opened fire on all of us. Luckily, he fired wildly, and we shot him before he had done any hurt.

"At Fruitvale, still in the heart of the magnificent residence section of the city, the plague again smote us. Professor Fairmead was the victim. Making signs to us that his mother was not to know, he turned aside into the grounds of a beautiful mansion. He sat down forlornly on the steps of the front veranda, and I, having lingered, waved him a last farewell. That night, several miles beyond Fruitvale and still in the city, we made camp. And that night we shifted camp twice to get away from our dead. In the morning there were thirty of us. I shall never forget the President of the Faculty. During the morning's march his wife, who was walking, betrayed the fatal symptoms, and when she drew aside to let us go on, he insisted on leaving the motor car and remaining with her. There was quite a discussion about this, but in the end we gave in. It was just as well, for we knew not which ones of us, if any, might ultimately escape.

"That night, the second of our march, we camped beyond Haywards in the first stretches of country. And in the morning there were eleven of us that lived. Also, during the night, Wathope, the professor with the wounded leg, deserted us in the motor car. He took with him his sister and his mother and most of our tinned provisions. It was that day, in the afternoon, while resting by the wayside, that I saw the last airship I shall ever see. The smoke was much thinner here in the country, and I first sighted the ship drifting and veering helplessly at an elevation of two thousand feet. What had happened I could not conjecture, but even as we looked we saw her bow dip down lower and lower. Then the bulkheads of the various gas-chambers must have burst, for, quite perpendicular, she fell like a plummet to the earth. And from that day to this I have not seen another airship. Often and often, during the next few years, I scanned the sky for them, hoping against hope that somewhere in the world civilization had survived. But it was not to be. What happened with us in California must have happened with everybody everywhere.

"Another day, and at Niles there were three of us. Beyond Niles, in the middle of the highway, we found Wathope. The motor car had broken down, and there, on the rugs which they had spread on the ground, lay the bodies of his sister, his mother, and himself.

"Wearied by the unusual exercise of continual walking, that night I slept heavily. In the morning I was alone in the world. Canfield and Parsons, my last companions, were dead of the plague. Of the four hundred that sought shelter in the Chemistry Building, and of the forty-seven that began the march, I alone remained – I and the Shetland pony. Why this should be so there is no explaining. I did not catch the plague, that is all. I was immune. I was merely the one lucky man in a million – just as every survivor was one in a million, or, rather, in several millions, for the proportion was at least that."

V

"For two days I sheltered in a pleasant grove where there had been no deaths. In those two days, while badly depressed and believing that my turn would come at any moment, nevertheless I rested and recuperated. So did the pony. And on the third day, putting what small store of tinned provisions I possessed on the pony's back, I started on across a very lonely land. Not a live man, woman, or child, did I encounter, though the dead were everywhere. Food, however, was abundant. The land then was not as it is now. It was all cleared of trees and brush, and it was cultivated. The food for millions of mouths was growing, ripening, and going to waste. From the fields and orchards I gathered vegetables, fruits, and berries. Around the deserted farmhouses I got eggs and caught chickens. And frequently I found supplies of tinned provisions in the store-rooms.

"A strange thing was what was taking place with all the domestic animals. Everywhere they were going wild and preying on one another. The chickens and ducks were the first to be destroyed, while the pigs were the first to go wild, followed by the cats. Nor were the dogs long in adapting themselves to the changed conditions. There was a veritable plague of dogs. They devoured the corpses, barked and howled during the nights, and in the daytime slunk about in the distance. As the time went by, I noticed a change in their behavior. At first they were apart from one another, very suspicious and very prone to fight. But after a not very long while they began to come together and run in packs. The dog, you see, always was a social animal, and this was true before ever he came to be domesticated by man. In the last days of the world before the plague, there were many many very different kinds of dogs – dogs without hair and dogs with warm fur, dogs so small that they would make scarcely a mouthful for other dogs that were as large as mountain lions. Well, all the small dogs, and the weak types, were killed by their fellows. Also, the very large ones were not adapted for the wild life and bred out. As a result, the many different kinds of dogs disappeared, and there remained, running in packs, the medium-sized wolfish dogs that you know to-day."

"But the cáts don't run in packs, Granser," Hoo-Hoo objected.

"The cat was never a social animal. As one writer in the nineteenth century said, the cat walks by himself. He always walked by himself, from before the time he was tamed by man, down through the long ages of domestication, to today when once more he is wild.

"The horses also went wild, and all the fine breeds we had degenerated into the small mustang horse you know to-day. The cows likewise went wild, as did the pigeons and the sheep. And that a few of the chickens survived you know yourself. But the wild chicken of to-day is quite a different thing from the chickens we had in those days.

"But I must go on with my story. I travelled through a deserted land. As the time went by I began to yearn more and more for human beings. But I never found one, and I grew lonelier and lonelier. I crossed Livermore Valley and the mountains between it and the great valley of the San Joaquin. You have never seen that valley, but it is very large and it is the home of the wild horse. There are great droves there, thousands and tens of thousands. I revisited it thirty years after, so I know. You think there are lots of wild horses down here in the coast valleys, but they are as nothing compared with those of the San Joaquin. Strange to say, the cows, when they went wild, went back into the lower mountains. Evidently they were better able to protect themselves there.

"In the country districts the ghouls and prowlers had been less in evidence, for I found many villages and towns untouched by fire. But they were filled by the pestilential dead, and I passed by without exploring them. It was near Lathrop that, out of my loneliness, I picked up a pair of collie dogs that were so newly free that they were urgently willing to return to their allegiance to man. These collies accompanied me for many years, and the strains of them are in those very dogs there that you boys have to-day. But in sixty years the collie strain has worked out. These brutes are more like domesticated wolves than anything else."

Hare-Lip rose to his feet, glanced to see that the goats were safe, and looked at the sun's position in the afternoon sky, advertising impatience at the prolixity of the old man's tale. Urged to hurry by Edwin, Granser went on.

"There is little more to tell. With my two dogs and my pony, and riding a horse I had managed to capture, I crossed the San Joaquin and went on to a wonderful valley in the Sierras called Yosemite. In the great hotel there I found a prodigious supply of tinned provisions. The pasture was abundant, as was the game, and the river that ran through the valley was full of trout. I remained there three years in an utter loneliness that none but a man who has once been highly civilized can understand. Then I could stand it no more. I felt that I was going crazy. Like the dog, I was a social animal and I needed my kind. I reasoned that since I had survived the plague, there was a possibility that others had survived. Also, I reasoned that after three years the plague germs must all be gone and the land be clean again.

"With my horse and dogs and pony, I set out. Again I crossed the San Joaquin Valley, the mountains beyond, and came down into Livermore Valley. The change in those three years was amazing. All the land had been splendidly tilled, and now I could scarcely recognize it, such was the sea of rank vegetation that had overrun the agricultural handiwork of man. You see, the wheat, the vegetables, and orchard trees had always been cared for and nursed by man, so that they were soft and tender. The weeds and wild bushes and such things, on the contrary, had always been fought by man, so that they were tough and resistant. As a result, when the hand of man was removed, the wild vegetation smothered and destroyed practically all the domesticated vegetation. The coyotes were greatly increased, and it was at this time that I first encountered wolves, straying in twos and threes and small packs down from the regions where they had always persisted.

"It was at Lake Temescal, not far from the one-time city of Oakland, that I came upon the first live human beings. Oh, my grandsons, how can I describe to you my emotion, when, astride my horse and dropping down the hillside to the lake, I saw the smoke of a campfire rising through the trees. Almost did my heart stop beating. I felt that I was going crazy. Then I heard the cry of a babe – a human babe. And dogs barked, and my dogs answered. I did not know but what I was the one human alive in the whole world. It could not be true that here were others – smoke, and the cry of a babe.

"Emerging on the lake, there, before my eyes, not a hundred yards away, I saw a man, a large man. He was standing on an outjutting rock and fishing. I was overcome. I stopped my horse. I tried to call out but could not. I waved my hand. It seemed to me that the man looked at me, but he did not appear to wave. Then I laid my head on my arms there in the saddle. I was afraid to look again, for I knew it was an hallucination, and I knew that if I looked the man would be gone. And so precious was the hallucination, that I wanted it to persist yet a little while. I knew, too, that as long as I did not look it would persist.

"Thus I remained, until I heard my dogs snarling, and a man's voice. What do you think the voice said? I will tell you. It said: *'Where in hell did you come from?'*

"Those were the words, the exact words. That was what your other grandfather said to me, Hare-Lip, when he greeted me there on the shore of Lake Temescal fifty-seven years ago. And they were the most ineffable words I have ever heard. I opened my eyes, and there he stood before me, a large, dark, hairy man, heavy-jawed, slant-browed, fierce-eyed. How I got off my horse I do not know. But it seemed that the next I knew I was clasping his hand with both of mine and crying. I would have embraced him, but he was ever a narrow-minded, suspicious man, and he drew away from me. Yet did I cling to his hand and cry."

Granser's voice faltered and broke at the recollection, and the weak tears streamed down his cheeks while the boys looked on and giggled.

"Yet did I cry," he continued, "and desire to embrace him, though the Chauffeur was a brute, a perfect brute – the most abhorrent man I have ever known. His name was . . . strange, how I have forgotten his name. Everybody called him Chauffeur – it was the name of his occupation, and it stuck. That is how, to this day, the tribe he founded is called the Chauffeur Tribe.

"He was a violent, unjust man. Why the plague germs spared him I can never understand. It would seem, in spite of our old metaphysical notions about absolute justice, that there is no justice in the universe. Why did he live? – an iniquitous, moral monster, a blot on the face of nature, a cruel, relentless, bestial cheat as well. All he could talk about was motor cars, machinery, gasoline, and garages – and especially, and with huge delight, of his mean pilferings and sordid swindlings of the persons who had employed him in the days before the coming of the plague. And yet he was spared, while hundreds of millions, yea, billions, of better men were destroyed.

"I went on with him to his camp, and there I saw her, Vesta, the one woman. It was glorious and . . . pitiful. There she was, Vesta Van Warden, the young wife of John Van Warden, clad in rags, with marred and scarred and toil-calloused hands, bending over the campfire and doing scullion work – she, Vesta, who had been born to the purple of the greatest baronage of wealth the world has ever known. John Van Warden, her husband, worth one billion, eight hundred millions and President of the Board of Industrial Magnates, had been the ruler of America. Also, sitting on the International Board of Control, he had been one of the seven men who ruled the world. And she herself had come of equally noble stock. Her father, Philip Saxon, had been President of the Board of Industrial Magnates up to the time of his death. This office was in process of becoming hereditary, and had Philip Saxon had a son that son would have succeeded him. But his only child was Vesta, the perfect flower of generations of the highest culture this planet has ever produced. It was not until the engagement between Vesta and Van Warden took place, that Saxon indicated the latter as his successor. It was, I am sure, a political marriage. I have reason to believe that Vesta never really loved her husband in the mad passionate way of which the poets used to sing. It was more like the marriages that obtained among crowned heads in the days before they were displaced by the Magnates.

"And there she was, boiling fish-chowder in a soot-covered pot, her glorious eyes inflamed by the acrid smoke of the open fire. Hers was a sad story. She was the one survivor in a million, as I had been, as the Chauffeur had been. On a crowning eminence of the Alameda Hills, overlooking San Francisco Bay, Van Warden had built a vast summer palace. It was surrounded by a park of a thousand acres. When the plague broke out, Van Warden sent her there. Armed guards patrolled the boundaries of the park, and nothing entered in the way of provisions or even mail matter that was not first fumigated. And yet did the plague enter, killing the guards at their posts, the servants at their tasks, sweeping away the whole army of retainers – or, at least, all of them who did not flee to die elsewhere. So it was that Vesta found herself the sole living person in the palace that had become a charnel house.

"Now the Chauffeur had been one of the servants that ran away. Returning, two months afterward, he discovered Vesta in a little summer pavilion where there had been no deaths and where she had established herself. He was a brute. She was afraid, and she ran away and hid among the trees. That night, on foot, she fled into the mountains – she, whose tender feet and delicate body had never known the bruise of stones nor the scratch of briars. He followed, and that night he caught her. He struck her. Do you understand? He beat her with those terrible fists of his and made her his slave. It was she who had to gather the firewood, build the fires, cook, and do all the degrading camp-labor – she, who had never performed a menial act in her life. These things he compelled her to do, while he, a proper savage, elected to lie around camp and look on. He did nothing, absolutely nothing, except on occasion to hunt meat or catch fish."

"Good for Chauffeur," Hare-Lip commented in an undertone to the other boys. "I remember him before he died. He was a corker. But he did things, and he made things go. You know, Dad married his daughter, an' you ought to see the way he knocked the spots outa Dad. The Chauffeur was a son-of-a-gun. He made us kids stand around. Even when he was croakin', he reached out for me, once, an' laid my head open with that long stick he kept always beside him."

Hare-Lip rubbed his bullet head reminiscently, and the boys returned to the old man, who was maundering ecstatically about Vesta, the squaw of the founder of the Chauffeur Tribe.

"And so I say to you that you cannot understand the awfulness of the situation. The Chauffeur was a servant, understand, a servant. And he cringed, with bowed head, to such as she. She was a lord of life, both by birth and by marriage. The destinies of millions, such as he, she carried in the hollow of her pink-white hand. And, in the days before the plague, the slightest contact with such as he would have been pollution. Oh, I have seen it. Once, I remember, there was Mrs. Goldwin, wife of one of the great magnates. It was on a landing stage, just as she was embarking in her private dirigible, that she dropped her parasol. A servant picked it up and made the mistake of handing it to her – to her, one of the greatest royal ladies of the land! She shrank back, as though he were a leper, and indicated her secretary to receive it. Also, she ordered her secretary to ascertain the creature's name and to see that he was immediately discharged from service. And such a woman was Vesta Van Warden. And her the Chauffeur beat and made his slave.

" – Bill – that was it; Bill, the Chauffeur. That was his name. He was a wretched, primitive man, wholly devoid of the finer instincts and chivalrous promptings of a cultured soul. No, there is no absolute justice, for to him fell that wonder of womanhood, Vesta Van Warden. The grievousness of this you will never understand, my grandsons; for you are yourselves primitive little savages, unaware of aught else but savagery. Why should Vesta not have been mine? I was a man of culture and refinement, a professor in a great university. Even so, in the time before the plague, such was her exalted position, she would not have deigned to know that I existed. Mark, then, the abysmal degradation to which she fell at the hands of the Chauffeur. Nothing less than the destruction of all mankind had made it possible that I should know her, look in her eyes, converse with her, touch her hand – ay, and love her and know that her feelings toward me were very kindly. I have reason to believe that she, even she, would have loved me, there being no other man in the world except the Chauffeur. Why, when it destroyed eight billions of souls, did not the plague destroy just one more man, and that man the Chauffeur?

"Once, when the Chauffeur was away fishing, she begged me to kill him. With tears in her eyes she begged me to kill him. But he was a strong and violent man, and I was afraid. Afterwards, I talked with him. I offered him my horse, my pony, my dogs, all that I possessed, if he would give Vesta to me. And he grinned in my face and shook his head. He was very insulting. He said that in the old days he had been a servant, had been dirt under the feet of men like me and of women like Vesta, and that now he had the greatest lady in the land to be servant to him and cook his food and nurse his brats. 'You had your day before the plague,' he said; 'but this is my day, and a damned good day it is. I wouldn't trade back to the old times for anything.' Such words he spoke, but they are not his words. He was a vulgar, low-minded man, and vile oaths fell continually from his lips.

"Also, he told me that if he caught me making eyes at his woman he'd wring my neck and give her a beating as well. What was I to do? I was afraid. He was a brute. That first night, when I discovered the camp, Vesta and I had great talk about the things of our vanished world. We talked of art, and books, and poetry; and the Chauffeur listened and grinned and sneered. He was bored and angered by our way of speech which he did not comprehend, and finally he spoke up and said: 'And this is Vesta Van Warden, one-time wife of Van Warden the Magnate – a high and stuck-up beauty, who is now my squaw. Eh, Professor Smith, times is changed, times is changed. Here, you, woman, take off my moccasins, and lively about it. I want Professor Smith to see how well I have you trained.'

"I saw her clench her teeth, and the flame of revolt rise in her face. He drew back his gnarled fist to strike, and I was afraid, and sick at heart. I could do nothing to prevail against him. So I got up to go, and not be witness to such indignity. But the Chauffeur laughed and threatened me with a beating if I did not stay and behold. And I sat there, perforce, by the campfire on the shore of Lake Temescal, and saw Vesta, Vesta Van Warden, kneel and remove the moccasins of that grinning, hairy, apelike human brute.

" – Oh, you do not understand, my grandsons. You have never known anything else, and you do not understand.

"'Halter-broke and bridle-wise,' the Chauffeur gloated, while she performed that dreadful, menial task. 'A trifle balky at times, Professor, a trifle balky; but a clout alongside the jaw makes her as meek and gentle as a lamb.'

"And another time he said: 'We've got to start all over and replenish the earth and multiply. You're handicapped, Professor. You ain't got no wife, and we're up against a regular Garden-of-Eden proposition. But I ain't proud. I'll tell you what, Professor.' He pointed at their little infant, barely a year old. 'There's your wife, though you'll have to wait till she grows up. It's rich, ain't it? We're all equals here, and I'm the biggest toad in the splash. But I ain't stuck up – not I. I do you the honor, Professor Smith, the very great honor of betrothing to you my and Vesta Van Warden's daughter. Ain't it cussed bad that Van Warden ain't here to see?'"

VI

"I lived three weeks of infinite torment there in the Chauffeur's camp. And then, one day, tiring of me, or of what to him was my bad effect on Vesta, he told me that the year before, wandering through the Contra Costa Hills to the Straits of Carquinez, across the Straits he had seen a smoke. This meant that there were still other human beings, and that for three weeks he had kept this inestimably precious information from me. I departed at once, with my dogs and horses, and journeyed across the Contra Costa Hills to the Straits. I saw no smoke on the other side, but at Port Costa discovered a small steel barge on which I was able to embark my animals. Old canvas which I found served me for a sail, and a southerly breeze fanned me across the Straits and up to the ruins of Vallejo. Here, on the outskirts of the city, I found evidences of a recently occupied camp. Many clam-shells showed me why these humans had come to the shores of the Bay. This was the Santa Rosa Tribe, and I followed its track along the old railroad right of way across the salt marshes to Sonoma Valley. Here, at the old brickyard at Glen Ellen, I came upon the camp. There were eighteen souls all told. Two were old men, one of whom was Jones, a banker. The other was Harrison, a retired pawnbroker, who had taken for wife the matron of the State Hospital for the Insane at Napa. Of all the persons of the city of Napa, and of all the other towns and villages in that rich and populous valley, she had been the only survivor. Next, there were the three young men – Cardiff and Hale, who had been farmers, and Wainwright, a common day-laborer. All three had found wives. To Hale, a crude, illiterate farmer, had fallen Isadore, the greatest prize, next to Vesta, of the women who came through the plague. She was one of the world's most noted singers, and the plague had caught her at San Francisco. She has talked with me for hours at a time, telling me of her adventures, until, at last, rescued by Hale in the Mendocino Forest Reserve, there had remained nothing for her to do but become his wife. But Hale was a good fellow, in spite of his illiteracy. He had a keen sense of justice and right-dealing, and she was far happier with him than was Vesta with the Chauffeur.

"The wives of Cardiff and Wainwright were ordinary women, accustomed to toil with strong constitutions – just the type for the wild new life which they were compelled to live. In addition were two adult idiots from the feeble-minded home at Eldredge, and five or six young children and infants born after the formation of the Santa Rosa Tribe. Also, there was Bertha. She was a good woman, Hare-Lip, in spite of the sneers of your father. Her I took for wife. She was the mother of your father, Edwin, and of yours, Hoo-Hoo. And it was our daughter, Vera, who married your father, Hare-Lip-your father, Sandow, who was the oldest son of Vesta Van Warden and the Chauffeur.

"And so it was that I became the nineteenth member of the Santa Rosa Tribe. There were only two outsiders added after me. One was Mungerson, descended from the Magnates, who wandered alone in the wilds of Northern California for eight years before he came south and joined us. He it was who waited twelve years more before he married my daughter, Mary. The other was Johnson, the man who founded the Utah Tribe. That was where he came from, Utah, a country that lies very far away from here, across the great deserts, to the east. It was not until twenty-seven years after the plague that Johnson reached California. In all that Utah region he reported but three survivors, himself one, and all men. For many years these three men lived and hunted together, until, at last, desperate, fearing that with them the human race would perish utterly from the planet, they headed westward on the possibility of finding women survivors in California. Johnson alone came through the great desert, where his two companions died. He was forty-six years old when he joined us, and he married the fourth daughter of Isadore and Hale, and his eldest son married your aunt, Hare-Lip, who was the third daughter of Vesta and the Chauffeur. Johnson was a strong man, with a will of his own.

And it was because of this that he seceded from the Santa Rosans and formed the Utah Tribe at San José'. It is a small tribe – there are only nine in it – but, though he is dead, such was his influence and the strength of his breed, that it will grow into a strong tribe and play a leading part in the recivilization of the planet.

"There are only two other tribes that we know of – the Los Angelitos and the Carmelitos. The latter started from one man and woman. He was called Lopez, and he was descended from the ancient Mexicans and was very black. He was a cowherd in the ranges beyond Carmel, and his wife was a maidservant in the great Del Monte Hotel. It was seven years before we first got in touch with the Los Angelitos. They have a good country down there, but it is too warm. I estimate the present population of the world at between three hundred and fifty and four hundred – provided, of course, that there are no scattered little tribes elsewhere in the world. If there be such, we have not heard from them. Since Johnson crossed the desert from Utah, no word nor sign has come from the East or anywhere else. The great world which I knew in my boyhood and early manhood is gone. It has ceased to be. I am the last man who was alive in the days of the plague and who knows the wonders of that far-off time. We, who mastered the planet – its earth, and sea, and sky – and who were as very gods, now live in primitive savagery along the water courses of this California country.

"But we are increasing rapidly – your sister, Hare-Lip, already has four children. We are increasing rapidly and making ready for a new climb toward civilization. In time, pressure of population will compel us to spread out, and a hundred generations from now we may expect our descendants to start across the Sierras, oozing slowly along, generation by generation, over the great continent to the colonization of the East – a new Aryan drift around the world.

"But it will be slow, very slow; we have so far to climb. We fell so hopelessly far. If only one physicist or one chemist had survived! But it was not to be, and we have forgotten everything. The Chauffeur started working in iron. He made the forge which we use to this day. But he was a lazy man, and when he died he took with him all he knew of metals and machinery. What was I to know of such things? I was a classical scholar, not a chemist. The other men who survived were not educated. Only two things did the Chauffeur accomplish – the brewing of strong drink and the growing of tobacco. It was while he was drunk, once, that he killed Vesta. I firmly believe that he killed Vesta in a fit of drunken cruelty though he always maintained that she fell into the lake and was drowned.

"And, my grandsons, let me warn you against the medicine-men. They call themselves *doctors*, travestying what was once a noble profession, but in reality they are medicine-men, devil-devil men, and they make for superstition and darkness. They are cheats and liars. But so debased and degraded are we, that we believe their lies. They, too, will increase in numbers as we increase, and they will strive to rule us. Yet are they liars and charlatans. Look at young Cross-Eyes, posing as a doctor, selling charms against sickness, giving good hunting, exchanging promises of fair weather for good meat and skins, sending the death-stick, performing a thousand abominations. Yet I say to you, that when he says he can do these things, he lies. I, Professor Smith, Professor James Howard Smith, say that he lies. I have told him so to his teeth. Why has he not sent me the death-stick? Because he knows that with me it is without avail. But you, Hare-Lip, so deeply are you sunk in black superstition that did you awake this night and find the death-stick beside you, you would surely die. And you would die, not because of any virtues in the stick, but because you are a savage with the dark and clouded mind of a savage.

"The doctors must be destroyed, and all that was lost must be discovered over again. Wherefore, earnestly, I repeat unto you certain things which you must remember and tell to your children after you. You must tell them that when water is made hot by fire, there resides in it a wonderful thing called steam, which is stronger than ten thousand men and which can do all man's work for him. There are other very useful things. In the lightning flash resides a similarly strong servant of man, which was of old his slave and which some day will be his slave again.

"Quite a different thing is the alphabet. It is what enables me to know the meaning of fine markings, whereas you boys know only rude picture-writing. In that dry cave on Telegraph Hill, where you see me often go when the tribe is down by the sea, I have stored many books. In them is great wisdom. Also, with them, I have placed a key to the alphabet, so that one who knows picture-writing may also know print. Some day men will read again; and then, if no accident has befallen my cave, they will know that Professor James Howard Smith once lived and saved for them the knowledge of the ancients.

"There is another little device that men inevitably will rediscover. It is called gunpowder. It was what enabled us to kill surely and at long distances. Certain things which are found in the ground, when combined in the right proportions, will make this gunpowder. What these things are, I have forgotten, or else I never knew. But I wish I did know. Then would I make powder, and then would I certainly kill Cross-Eyes and rid the land of superstition – "

"After I am man-grown I am going to give Cross-Eyes all the goats, and meat, and skins I can get, so that he'll teach me to be a doctor," Hoo-Hoo asserted. "And when I know, I'll make everybody else sit up and take notice. They'll get down in the dirt to me, you bet."

The old man nodded his head solemnly, and murmured:

"Strange it is to hear the vestiges and remnants of the complicated Aryan speech falling from the lips of a filthy little skin-clad savage. All the world is topsy-turvy. And it has been topsy-turvy ever since the plague."

"You won't make me sit up," Hare-Lip boasted to the would-be medicine-man. "If I paid you for a sending of the death-stick and it didn't work, I'd bust in your head – understand, you Hoo-Hoo, you?"

"I'm going to get Granser to remember this here gunpowder stuff," Edwin said softly, "and then I'll have you all on the run. You, Hare-Lip, will do my fighting for me and get my meat for me, and you, Hoo-Hoo, will send the death-stick for me and make everybody afraid. And if I catch Hare-Lip trying to bust your head, Hoo-Hoo, I'll fix him with that same gunpowder. Granser ain't such a fool as you think, and I'm going to listen to him and some day I'll be boss over the whole bunch of you."

The old man shook his head sadly, and said:

"The gunpowder will come. Nothing can stop it – the same old story over and over. Man will increase, and men will fight. The gunpowder will enable men to kill millions of men, and in this way only, by fire and blood, will a new civilization, in some remote day, be evolved. And of what profit will it be? Just as the old civilization passed, so will the new. It may take fifty thousand years to build, but it will pass. All things pass. Only remain cosmic force and matter, ever in flux, ever acting and reacting and realizing the eternal types – the priest, the soldier, and the king. Out of the mouths of babes comes the wisdom of all the ages. Some will fight, some will rule, some will pray; and all the rest will toil and suffer sore while on their bleeding carcasses is reared again, and yet again, without end, the amazing beauty and surpassing wonder of the civilized state. It were just as well that I destroyed those cave-stored books – whether they remain or perish, all their old truths will be discovered, their old lies lived and handed down. What is the profit – "

Hare-Lip leaped to his feet, giving a quick glance at the pasturing goats and the afternoon sun.

"Gee!" he muttered to Edwin. "The old geezer gets more long-winded every day. Let's pull for camp."

While the other two, aided by the dogs, assembled the goats and started them for the trail through the forest, Edwin stayed by the old man and guided him in the same direction. When they reached the old right of way, Edwin stopped suddenly and looked back. Hare-Lip and Hoo-Hoo and the dogs and the goats passed on. Edwin was looking at a small herd of wild horses which had come down on the hard sand. There were at least twenty of them, young colts and yearlings and mares, led by a beautiful stallion which stood in the foam at the edge of the surf, with arched neck and bright wild eyes, sniffing the salt air from off the sea.

"What is it?" Granser queried.

"Horses," was the answer. "First time I ever seen 'em on the beach. It's the mountain lions getting thicker and thicker and driving 'em down."

The low sun shot red shafts of light, fan-shaped, up from a cloud-tumbled horizon. And close at hand, in the white waste of shore-washed waters, the sealions, bellowing their old primeval chant, hauled up out of the sea on the black rocks and fought and loved.

"Come on, Granser," Edwin prompted.

And old man and boy, skin-clad and barbaric, turned and went along the right of way into the forest in the wake of the goats.

"Repent Harlequin!" Said the Ticktockman

HARLAN ELLISON

Harlan Ellison (1934–) is the author of nearly a thousand short stories, essays, screenplays, and novels. Starting out as a teenager writing science fiction, by his early twenties he was widely published. His fame grew, and in the 1960s Ellison flowered into one of the leading, and cutting-edge, writers of *speculative fiction* – the term in fashion in the 1960s for science fiction with literary ambition and without central dependence on science. He won many awards in that decade and the next, and edited two hugely influential anthologies of original fiction, *Dangerous Visions* and *Again, Dangerous Visions* – and collected stories for a third, *The Last Dangerous Visions,* that remains to date, legendary and unpublished. *The Essential Ellison: a Thirty-five Year Retrospective* (1987) is a generous sampling of his short fiction.

Ellison is a powerful public figure in the SF field. In recent years he has cut back on his convention appearances, but in the 1990s he has his own show on The Sci-Fi Channel on cable television. He is a man of boundless energy and ambition, passionate, outspoken, peripatetic. In the words of Pogo artist Walt Kelly, he never retreats, though sometimes he advances backwards.

This story is one of the award-winning works upon which his literary reputation was built in the 1960s. It is perhaps reminiscent of Kurt Vonnegut, Jr.'s "Harrison Bergeron," and certainly grows out of the whole tradition of revolt against social and political repression in literature. Its central character is the cocky young rebel artist whom Ellison represented to SF in the 1960s, Harlan the Harlequin.

There are always those who ask, what is it all about? For those who
need to ask, for those who need points sharply made, who need to
know "where it's at," this:

*The mass of men serve the state thus, not as men mainly, but as machines, with their
bodies. They are the standing army, and the militia, jailors, constables, posse comi-
tatus, etc. In most cases there is no free exercise whatever of the judgment or of the
moral sense; but they put themselves on a level with wood and earth and stones; and
wooden men can perhaps be manufactured that will serve the purposes as well. Such
command no more respect than men of straw or a lump of dirt. They have the same
sort of worth only as horses and dogs. Yet such as these even are commonly esteemed
good citizens. Others – as most legislators, politicians, lawyers, ministers, and
office-holders – serve the state chiefly with their heads; and, as they rarely make any
moral distinctions, they are as likely to serve the Devil, without intending it, as God.
A very few, as heroes, patriots, martyrs, reformers in the great sense, and men, serve
the state with their consciences also, and so necessarily resist it for the most part; and
they are commonly treated as enemies by it.*

> – *Henry David Thoreau,*
> *"Civil Disobedience"*

That is the heart of it. Now begin in the middle, and later learn the
beginning; the end will take care of itself.

But because it was the very world it was, the very world they had
allowed it to *become*, for months his activities did not come to the
alarmed attention of The Ones Who Keep the Machine Functioning
Smoothly, the ones who poured the very best butter over the cams and
mainsprings of the culture. Not until it had become obvious that
somehow, someway, he had become a notoriety, a celebrity, perhaps
even a hero for (what Officialdom inescapably tagged) "an emotionally
disturbed segment of the populace," did they turn it over to the
Ticktockman and his legal machinery. But by then, because it was the
very world it was, and they had no way to predict he would happen –
possibly a strain of disease long-defunct, now, suddenly, reborn in a
system where immunity had been forgotten, had lapsed – he had been
allowed to become too real. Now he had form and substance.

   He had become a *personality*, something they had filtered out of the
system many decades ago. But there it was, and there *he* was, a very
definitely imposing personality. In certain circles – middle-class circles
– it was thought disgusting. Vulgar ostentation. Anarchistic. Shameful.
In others, there was only sniggering, those strata where thought is

subjugated to form and ritual, niceties, proprieties. But down below, ah, down below, where the people always needed their saints and sinners, their bread and circuses, their heroes and villains, he was considered a Bolivar; a Napoleon; a Robin Hood; a Dick Bong (Ace of Aces); a Jesus; a Jomo Kenyatta.

And at the top – where, like socially attuned Shipwreck Kellys, even tremor and vibration threatens to dislodge the wealthy, powerful, and titled from their flagpoles – he was considered a menace; a heretic; a rebel; a disgrace; a peril. He was known down the line, to the very heartmeat core, but the important reactions were high above and far below. At the very top, at the very bottom.

So his file was turned over, along with his time-card and his cardio-plate, to the office of the Ticktockman.

The Ticktockman: very much over six feet tall, often silent, a soft purring man when things went timewise. The Ticktockman.

Even in the cubicles of the hierarchy, where fear was generated, seldom suffered, he was called the Ticktockman. But no one called him that to his mask.

You don't call a man a hated name, not when that man, behind his mask, is capable of revoking the minutes, the hours, the days and nights, the years of your life. He was called the Master Timekeeper to his mask. It was safer that way.

"This is *what* he is," said the Ticktockman with genuine softness, "but not *who* he is? This time-card I'm holding in my left hand has a name on it, but it is the name of *what* he is, not *who* he is. This cardio-plate here in my right hand is also named, but not whom named, merely what named. Before I can exercise proper revocation, I have to know who this what is."

To his staff, all the ferrets, all the loggers, all the finks, all the commex, even the mineez, he said, "Who is this Harlequin?"

He was not purring smoothly. Timewise, it was jangle.

However, it *was* the longest speech they had ever heard him utter at one time, the staff, the ferrets, the loggers, the finks, the commex, but not the mineez, who usually weren't around to know, in any case. But even they scurried to find out.

Who is the Harlequin?

High above the third level of the city, he crouched on the humming aluminum-frame platform of the air-boat (foof! air-boat, indeed! swizzleskid is what it was, with a tow-rack jerry-rigged) and stared down at the neat Mondrian arrangement of the buildings.

Somewhere nearby, he could hear the metronomic left-right-left of the 2.47 p.m. shift, entering the Timkin roller-bearing plant in their sneakers. A minute later, precisely, he heard the softer right-left-right of the 5.00 a.m. formation, going home.

An elfish grin spread across his tanned features, and his dimples appeared for a moment. Then, scratching at his thatch of auburn hair, he shrugged within his money, as though girding himself for what came next, and threw the joystick forward, and bent into the wind as the air-boat dropped. He skimmed over a slidewalk, purposely dropping a few feet to crease the tassels of the ladies of fashion, and – inserting thumbs in large ears – he stuck out his tongue, rolled his eyes and went wugga-wugga-wugga. It was a minor diversion. One pedestrian skittered and tumbled, sending parcels everywhichway, another wet herself, a third skittered slantwise and the walk was stopped automatically by the servitors till she could be resuscitated. It was a minor diversion.

Then he swirled away on a vagrant breeze, and was gone. Hi-ho.

As he rounded the cornice of the Time-Motion Study Building, he saw the shift, just boarding the slidewalk. With practiced motion and an absolute conservation of movement, they sidestepped up onto the slowstrip and (in a chorus line reminiscent of a Busby Berkeley film of the antediluvian 1930s) advanced across the strips ostrich-walking till they were lined up on the expresstrip.

Once more, in anticipation, the elfin grin spread, and there was a tooth missing back there on the left side. He dipped, skimmed, and swooped over them; and then, scrunching about on the air-boat, he released the holding pins that fastened shut the ends of the homemade pouring troughs that kept his cargo from dumping prematurely. And as he pulled the trough-pins, the air-boat slid over the factory workers and one hundred and fifty thousand dollars' worth of jelly beans cascaded down on the expresstrip.

Jelly beans! Millions and billions of purples and yellows and greens and licorice and grape and raspberry and mint and round and smooth and crunchy outside and soft-mealy inside and sugary and bouncing jouncing tumbling clittering clattering skittering fell on the heads and shoulders and hard-hats and carapaces of the Timkin workers, tinkling on the slidewalk and bouncing away and rolling about underfoot and filling the sky on their way down with all the colors of joy and child-hood and holidays, coming down in a steady rain, a solid wash, a torrent of color and sweetness out of the sky from above, and entering a universe of sanity and metronomic order with quite-mad coocoo newness. Jelly beans!

The shift workers howled and laughed and were pelted, and broke ranks, and the jelly beans managed to work their way into the mechanism of the slidewalks after which there was a hideous scraping as the sound of a million fingernails rasped down a quarter of a million blackboards, followed by a coughing and a sputtering, and then the slidewalks all stopped and everyone was dumped thisawayandthataway in a jackstraw tumble, and still laughing and popping little jelly bean eggs of childish color into their mouths. It was a holiday, and a jollity, an absolute insanity, a giggle. But . . .

The shift was delayed seven minutes.

They did not get home for seven minutes.

The master schedule was thrown off by seven minutes.

Quotas were delayed by inoperative slidewalks for seven minutes.

He had tapped the first domino in the line, and one after another, like chik chik chik, the others had fallen.

The System had been seven minutes' worth of disrupted. It was a tiny matter, one hardly worthy of note, but in a society where the single driving force was order and unity and promptness and clocklike precision and attention to the clock, reverence of the gods of the passage of time, it was a disaster of major importance.

So he was ordered to appear before the Ticktockman. It was broadcast across every channel of the communications web. He was ordered to be *there* at 7.00 p.m. dammit on time. And they waited, and they waited, but he didn't show up till almost ten-thirty, at which time he merely sang a little song about moonlight in a place no one had ever heard of, called Vermont, and vanished again. But they had all been waiting since seven, and it wrecked *hell* with their schedules. So the question remained: Who is the Harlequin?

But the *unasked* question (more important of the two) was: how did we get *into* this position, where a laughing, irresponsible japer of jabberwocky and jive could disrupt our entire economic and cultural life with a hundred and fifty thousand dollars' worth of jelly beans . . .

Jelly for God's sake beans! This is madness! Where did he get the money to buy a hundred and fifty thousand dollars' worth of jelly beans? (They knew it would have cost that much, because they had a team of Situation Analysts pulled off another assignment, and rushed to the slidewalk scene to sweep up and count the candies, and produce findings, which disrupted *their* schedules and threw their entire branch at least a day behind.) Jelly beans! Jelly . . . *beans?* Now wait a second – a second accounted for – no one has manufactured jelly beans for over a hundred years. Where did he get jelly beans?

That's another good question. More than likely it will never be answered to your complete satisfaction. But then, how many questions ever are?

The middle you know. Here is the beginning. How it starts:

A desk pad. Day for day, and turn each day, 9.00 – open the mail. 9.45 – appointment with planning commission board. 10.30 – discuss installation progress charts with J.L. 11.45 – pray for rain. 12.00 – lunch. *And so it goes.*

"I'm sorry, Miss Grant, but the time for interviews was set at 2.30, and it's almost five now. I'm sorry you're late, but those are the rules. You'll have to wait till next year to submit application for this college again." *And so it goes.*

The 10.10 local stops at Cresthaven, Galesville, Tonawanda Junction, Selby and Farnhurst, but not at Indiana City, Lucasville and Colton, except on Sunday. The 10.35 express stops at Galesville, Selby and Indiana City, except on Sundays & Holidays, at which time it stops at . . . *And so it goes.*

"I couldn't wait, Fred. I had to be at Pierre Cartain's by 3.00, and you said you'd meet me under the clock in the terminal at 2.45, and you weren't there, so I had to go on. You're always late, Fred. If you'd been there, we could have sewed it up together, but as it was, well I took the order alone . . ." *And so it goes.*

Dear Mr. and Mrs. Atterley: in reference to your son Gerold's constant tardiness, I am afraid we will have to suspend him from school unless some more reliable method can be instituted guaranteeing he will arrive at his classes on time. Granted he is an exemplary student, and his marks are high, his constant flouting of the schedules of this school makes it impractical to maintain him in a system where the other children seem capable of getting where they are supposed to be on time. *And so it goes.*

YOU CANNOT VOTE UNLESS YOU APPEAR AT 8.45 a.m.

"I don't care if the script is good, I need it Thursday!"

CHECK-OUT TIME IS 2.00 p.m.

"You got here late. The job's taken. Sorry."

YOUR SALARY HAS BEEN DOCKED FOR TWENTY MINUTES TIME LOST

"God, what time is it, I've gotta run!"

And so it goes. And so it goes. And so it goes. And so it goes goes goes goes goes tick tock tick tock tick tock and one day we no longer let time serve us, we serve time and we are slaves of the schedule, worshippers of the sun's passing, bound into a life predicted on restrictions because the system will not function if we don't keep the schedule tight.

Until it becomes more than a minor inconvenience to be late. It becomes a sin. Then a crime. Then a crime punishable by this:

EFFECTIVE 15 JULY 2389, 12.00.00 midnight, the office of the Master Timekeeper will require all citizens to submit their time-cards and cardioplates for processing. In accordance with Statute 555-7-SGH-999 governing the revocation of time per capita, all cardioplates will be keyed to the individual holder and –

What they had done was devise a method of curtailing the amount of life a person could have. If he was ten minutes late, he lost ten minutes of his life. An hour was proportionately worth more revocation. If someone was consistently tardy, he might find himself, on a Sunday night, receiving a communique from the Master Timekeeper that his time had run out, and he would be "turned off" at high noon on Monday, please straighten your affairs, sir.

And so, by this simple scientific expedient (utilizing a scientific process held dearly secret by the Ticktockman's office) the System was maintained. It was the only expedient thing to do. It was, after all, patriotic. The schedules had to be met. After all, there *was* a war on!

But wasn't there always?

"Now that is really disgusting," the Harlequin said, when pretty Alice showed him the wanted poster. "Disgusting and *highly* improbable. After all, this isn't the days of desperadoes. A *wanted* poster!"

"You know," Alice noted, "you speak with a great deal of inflection."

"I'm sorry," said the Harlequin, humbly.

"No need to be sorry. You're always saying, 'I'm sorry.' You have such massive guilt, Everett, it's really very sad."

"I'm sorry," he repeated, then pursed his lips so the dimples appeared momentarily. He hadn't wanted to say that at all. "I have to go out again. I have to do something."

Alice slammed her coffee-bulb down on the counter. "Oh for God's *sake*, Everett, can't you stay home just *one* night! Must you always be out in that ghastly clown suit, running around *annoying* people?"

"I'm – " He stopped, and clapped the jester's hat onto his auburn thatch with a tiny tingling of bells. He rose, rinsed out his coffee-bulb at the tap, and put it into the drier for a moment. "I have to go."

She didn't answer. The faxbox was purring, and she pulled a sheet out, read it, threw it toward him on the counter. "It's about you. Of course. You're ridiculous."

He read it quickly. It said the Ticktockman was trying to locate him. He didn't care, he was going out to be late again. At the door, dredging for an exit line, he hurled back petulantly, "Well, *you* speak with inflection, *too!*"

Alice rolled her pretty eyes heavenward. "You're ridiculous." The Harlequin stalked out, slamming the door, which sighed shut softly, and locked itself.

There was a gentle knock, and Alice got up with an exhalation of exasperated breath, and opened the door. He stood there. "I'll be back about ten-thirty, okay?"

She pulled a rueful face. "Why do you tell me that? Why? You *know* you'll be late! You *know* it! You're *always* late, so why do you tell me these dumb things?" She closed the door.

On the other side, the Harlequin nodded to himself. *She's right. She's always right. I'll be late. I'm always late. Why do I tell her these dumb things?*

He shrugged again, and went off to be late once more.

He had fired off the firecracker rockets that said: I will attend the 115th annual International Medical Association Invocation at 8.00 p.m. precisely. I do hope you will all be able to join me.

The words had burned in the sky, and of course the authorities were there, lying in wait for him. They assumed, naturally, that he would be late. He arrived twenty minutes early, while they were setting up the spiderwebs to trap and hold him, and blowing a large bullhorn, he frightened and unnerved them so, their own moisturized encirclement webs sucked closed, and they were hauled up, kicking and shrieking, high above the amphitheater's floor. The Harlequin laughed and laughed, and apologized profusely. The physicians, gathered in solemn conclave, roared with laughter, and accepted the Harlequin's apologies with exaggerated bowing and posturing, and a merry time was had by all, who thought the Harlequin was a regular foofaraw in fancy pants; all, that is, but the authorities, who had been sent out by the office of the Ticktockman, who hung there like so much dockside cargo, hauled up above the floor of the amphitheater in a most unseemly fashion.

(In another part of the same city where the Harlequin carried on his "activities," totally unrelated in every way to what concerns here, save that it illustrates the Ticktockman's power and import, a man named Marshall Delahanty received his turn-off notice from the

Ticktockman's office. His wife received the notification from the grey-suited minee who delivered it, with the traditional "look of sorrow" plastered hideously across his face. She knew what it was, even without unsealing it. It was a billet-doux of immediate recognition to everyone these days. She gasped, and held it as though it were a glass slide tinged with botulism, and prayed it was not for her. Let it be for Marsh, she thought, brutally, realistically, or one of the kids, but not for me, please dear God, not for me. And then she opened it, and it *was* for Marsh, and she was at one and the same time horrified and relieved. The next trooper in the line had caught the bullet. "Marshall," she screamed, "Marshall! Termination, Marshall ohmigod, Marshall, whattl we do, whattl we do, Marshall omigodmarshall . . ." and in their home that night was the sound of tearing paper and fear, and the stink of madness went up the flue and there was nothing, absolutely nothing they could do about it.)

(But Marshall Delahanty tried to run. And early the next day, when turn-off time came, he was deep in the forest two hundred miles away, and the office of the Ticktockman blanked his cardioplate, and Marshall Delahanty keeled over, running, and his heart stopped, and the blood dried up on its way to his brain, and he was dead that's all. One light went out on his sector map in the office of the Master Timekeeper, while notification was entered for fax reproduction, and Georgette Delahanty's name was entered on the dole roles till she could remarry. Which is the end of the footnote, and all the point that need be made, except don't laugh, because that is what would happen to the Harlequin if ever the Ticktockman found out his real name. It isn't funny.)

The shopping level of the city was thronged with the Thursday-colors of the buyers. Women in canary yellow chitons and men in pseudo-Tyrolean outfits that were jade and leather and fit very tightly, save for the balloon pants.

When the Harlequin appeared on the still-being-constructed shell of new Efficiency Shopping Center, his bullhorn to his elfishly laughing lips, everyone pointed and stared, and he berated them:

"Why let them order you about? Why let them tell you to hurry and scurry like ants or maggots? Take your time! Saunter a while! Enjoy the sunshine, enjoy the breeze, let life carry you at your own pace! Don't be slaves of time, it's a helluva way to die, slowly, by degrees . . . down with the Ticktockman!"

Who's the nut? most of the shoppers wanted to know. Who's the nut oh wow I'm gonna be late. I gotta run . . .

And the construction gang on the Shopping Center received an urgent order from the office of the Master Timekeeper that the dangerous criminal known as the Harlequin was atop their spire, and their aid was urgently needed in apprehending him. The work crew said no, they would lose time on their construction schedule, but the Ticktockman managed to pull the proper threads of governmental webbing, and they were told to cease work and catch that nitwit up there on the spire with the bullhorn. So a dozen and more burly workers began climbing into their construction platforms, releasing the a-grav plates, and rising toward the Harlequin.

After the debacle (in which, through the Harlequin's attention to personal safety, no one was seriously injured), the workers tried to reassemble, and assault him again, but it was too late. He had vanished. It had attracted quite a crowd, however, and the shopping cycle was thrown off by hours, simply hours. The purchasing needs of the system were therefore falling behind, and so measures were taken to accelerate the cycle for the rest of the day, but it got bogged down and speeded up and they sold too many float-valves and not nearly enough wegglers, which meant that the popli ratio was off, which made it necessary to rush cases and cases of spoiling Smash-O to stores that usually needed a case only every three or four hours. The shipments were bollixed, the trans-shipments were misrouted, and in the end, even the swizzleskid industries felt it.

"Don't come back till you have him!" the Ticktockman said, very quietly, very sincerely, extremely dangerously.

They used dogs. They used probes. They used cardioplate crossoffs. They used teepers. They used bribery. They used stiktytes. They used intimidation. They used torment. They used torture. They used finks. They used cops. They used search&seizure. They used fallaron. They used betterment incentive. They used fingerprints. They used Bertillon. They used cunning. They used guile. They used treachery. They used Raoul Mitgong, but he didn't help much. They used applied physics. They used techniques of criminology.

And what the hell: they caught him.

After all, his name was Everett C. Marm, and he wasn't much to begin with, except a man who had no sense of time.

"Repent, Harlequin!" said the Ticktockman.

"Get stuffed!" the Harlequin replied, sneering.

"You've been late a total of sixty-three years, five months, three weeks, two days, twelve hours, forty-one minutes, fifty-nine seconds, point oh three six one one one microseconds. You've used up everything you can, and more. I'm going to turn you off."

"Scare someone else. I'd rather be dead than live in a dumb world with a bogeyman like you."

"It's my job."

"You're full of it. You're a tyrant. You have no right to order people around and kill them if they show up late."

"You can't adjust. You can't fit in."

"Unstrap me, and I'll fit my fist into your mouth."

"You're a non-conformist."

"That didn't used to be a felony."

"It is now. Live in the world around you."

"I hate it. It's a terrible world."

"Not everyone thinks so. Most people enjoy order."

"I don't, and most of the people I know don't."

"That's not true. How do you think we caught you?"

"I'm not interested."

"A girl named pretty Alice told us who you were."

"That's a lie."

"It's true. You unnerve her. She wants to belong, she wants to conform, I'm going to turn you off."

"Then do it already, and stop arguing with me."

"I'm not going to turn you off."

"You're an idiot!"

"Repent, Harlequin!" said the Ticktockman.

"Get stuffed."

So they sent him to Coventry. And in Coventry they worked him over. It was just like what they did to Winston Smith in 1984, which was a book none of them knew about, but the techniques are really quite ancient, and so they did it to Everett C. Marm, and one day quite a long time later, the Harlequin appeared on the communications web, appearing elfish and dimpled and bright-eyed, and not at all brainwashed, and he said he had been wrong, that it was a good, a very good thing indeed, to belong, and be right on time hip-ho and away we go, and everyone stared up at him on the public screens that covered an entire city block, and they said to themselves, well, you see, he was just a nut after all, and if that's the way the system is run, then let's do it that way, because it doesn't pay to fight city hall, or in this case, the Ticktockman. So Everett C. Marm was destroyed, which was a loss, because of what Thoreau said earlier, but you can't make an omelet without breaking a few eggs, and in every revolution, a few die who shouldn't, but they have to, because that's the way it happens, and if you make only a little change, then it seems to be worthwhile. Or, to make the point lucidly:

"Uh, excuse me, sir, I, uh, don't know how to uh, to uh, tell you this, but you were three minutes late. The schedule is a little, uh, bit off."

He grinned sheepishly.

"That's ridiculous!" murmured the Ticktockman behind his mask. "Check your watch." And then he went into his office, going mrmee, mrmee, mrmee, mrmee.

1967
25th Convention
New York

Blood's a Rover

CHAD OLIVER

Chad Oliver (1928–93) was the man who brought the science of anthropology into the arena of sciences used in science fiction. In his novel *Shadows in the Sun* (1954) and in the stories collected in *Another Kind* (1955) and *The Edge of Forever* (1971), Oliver introduced and popularized the concepts of his discipline. "Our field's most fascinating and comprehensive collection of anthropological science fiction," said Damon Knight in 1956, and praised him for his "ability to touch the human heart of the problem."

Until the 1950s, when Oliver entered the field and experienced his most productive decade as a writer of SF, there was a great deal of prejudice against the "soft" or life sciences, especially against the areas of psychology, the social sciences, and economics. They were second class sciences because they were not mathematically predictive, not reliable, therefore not real knowledge, so the argument went. Real science fiction, before Oliver, could use them only by making them into predictive sciences in the future (see, for instance, Katherine MacLean's "The Snowball Effect" [1952]). Oliver's easy, pleasant exposition of anthropological ideas and attitudes in his fiction throughout the 1950s paved the way for later writers such as Ursula K. Le Guin and Michael Bishop to write sophisticated anthropological science fiction in the following decades. Oliver himself continued to write novels in and out of the SF genre in the 1960s, '70s, and '80s while a professor of anthropology at the University of Texas in Austin, but no notable short fiction.

Oliver tends to focus on motivations and values, rather than violence or action, in his fiction. "I was strongly influenced by writers outside the science fiction field, notably Hemingway and Steinbeck," he said. As in this story, he usually rewards a connection to the natural world.

————————————

> *Clay lies still, but blood's a rover;*
> *Breath's a ware that will not keep.*
> *Up, lad: when the journey's over*
> *There'll be time enough to sleep.*
> — *A. E. Housman*

Night sifted through the city like flakes of soft black snow drifting down from the stars It whispered along the tree-lined canyons between the clean shafts of white buildings and pressed darkly against windows filled with warm light. Conan Lang watched the illumination in his office increase subtly in adjusting to the growing darkness outside and then looked again at the directive he held in his hand.

It still read the same way.

"Another day, another world," he said aloud. And then, paraphrasing: "The worlds are too much with us – "

Conan Lang fired up his pipe and puffed carefully on it to get it going properly. Then he concentrated on blowing neat cloudy smoke rings that wobbled across the room and impaled themselves on the nose of the three-dimensional portrait of the President. It wasn't that he had anything against President Austin, he assured himself. It was simply that Austin represented that nebulous being, Authority, and at the moment it happened that Authority was singularly unwelcome in the office of Conan Lang.

He looked back at the directive. The wording was friendly and informal enough, but the meaning was clear:

> Headquarters, Gal. Administration.
> Office of Admiral Nelson White,
> Commander, Process Planning Division.
> 15 April, 2701. Confidential.

One Agent Conan Lang
Applied Process Corps
G.A. Department Seven
Conan:

We got another directive from the Buzzard yesterday. Seems that the powers that be have decided that a change in Sirius Ten is in order – a shift from Four to Five. You're it. Make a prelim check and report to me at your convenience. Cheer up – maybe you'll get another bag of medals out of it.

Nelson

Conan Lang left the directive on his desk and got to his feet. He walked over to the window and looked out at the lights sprinkled over the city. There weren't many. Most people were long ago home in the country, sitting around the living room, playing with the kids. He puffed slowly on his pipe.

Another bag of medals. Nelson wasn't kidding anybody – wasn't even trying to, really. He knew how Conan felt because he felt the same way. They all did, sooner or later. It was fascinating at first, even fun, this tampering with the lives of other people. But the novelty wore off in a hurry – shriveled like flesh in acid under a million eyes of hate, a million talks with your soul at three in the morning, a million shattered lives. Sure, it was necessary. You could always tell yourself that; that was the charm, the magic word that was supposed to make everything fine and dandy. Necessary – but for *you,* not for them. Or perhaps for them too, in the long run.

Conan Lang returned to his desk and flipped on the intercom. "I want out," he said. "The Administration Library, Division of Extraterrestrial Anthropology. I'd like to speak to Bailey if he's there."

He had to wait thirty seconds.

"Bailey here," the intercom said.

"This is Lang. What've you got on Sirius Ten?"

"Just like that, huh? Hang on a second."

There was a short silence. Conan Lang smoked his pipe slowly and smiled as he visualized Bailey punching enough buttons to control a space fleet.

"Let's see," Bailey's voice came through the speaker. "We've got a good bit. There's McAllister's *Kinship Systems of Sirius Ten;* Jenkins' – that's B. J. Jenkins, the one who worked with Holden – *Sirius Ten Social Organization;* Bartheim's *Economic Life of Sirius Ten*; Robert Patterson's *Basic Personality Types of the Sirius Group; Preliminary and Supplementary Ethnological Surveys of the Galactic Advance Fleet* – the works."

Conan Lang sighed. "O.K.," he said. "Shoot them out to my place, will you?"

"Check – be there before you are. One thing more, Cone."

"Yes?"

"Been reading a splendid eight-volume historical novel of the

Twentieth Century. Hot stuff, I'll tell you. You want mc to send it along in case you run out of reading material?"

"Very funny. See you around."

"So long."

Conan Lang switched off the intercom and destroyed the directive. He tapped out his pipe in the waster and left the office, locking the door behind him. The empty hallway was sterile and impersonal. It seemed dead at night, somehow, and it was difficult to believe that living, breathing human beings walked through it all day long. It was like a tunnel to nowhere. He had the odd feeling that there was nothing around it at all, just space and less than space – no building, no air, no city. Just a white antiseptic tunnel to nowhere.

He shook off the feeling and caught the lift to the roof. The cool night air was crisp and clean and there was a whisper of a breeze out of the north. A half moon hung in the night, framed by stars. He looked up at it and wondered how Johnny was getting along up there, and whether perhaps Johnny was even then looking down on Earth.

Conan Lang climbed into his bullet and set the controls. The little ship rose vertically on her copter blades for two thousand feet, hovered a moment over the silent city, and then flashed off on her jets into the west.

Conan Lang sat back in his cushioned seat, looking at the stars, trying not to think, letting the ship carry him home.

Conan Lang relaxed in his armchair, his eyes closed, an icy bourbon and soda in his hand. The books he had requested – neat, white, uniform microfilm blow-ups from the Administration Library – were stacked neatly on the floor by his side, waiting. Waiting, he thought, sipping his drink. They were always waiting. No matter how much a man knew, there was always more – waiting.

The room closed in around him. He could feel it – warm, friendly, personal. It was a good room. It was a room filled with life, his life and Kit's. It was almost as if he could see the room better with his eyes closed, for then he saw the past as well as the present. There was the silver and black tapestry on the wall, given to him by old Maharani so long ago, on a world so far away that the very light given off by its sun when he was there had yet to reach the Earth as the twinkle of a star in the night sky. There were his books, there were Kit's paintings. There was the smudge – the current one – on the carpet where Rob had tracked dirt into the house before supper.

He opened his eyes and looked at his wife.

"I must be getting old, Kit," he said. "Right at the moment, it all looks pretty pointless."

Kit raised her eyebrows and said nothing.

"We tear around over the galaxy like a bunch of kids playing Spacemen and Pirates," he said, downing his drink. "Push here, pull there, shove here, reverse there. It's like some kind of half-wit game where one side doesn't even know it's playing, or on which side of the field. Sometimes – "

"Want another drink?" Kit asked softly.

"Yes. Kit – "

"I know," she said, touching his shoulder with her hand. "Go ahead and talk; you'll feel better. We go through this every time there's a new one, remember? I know you don't really mean things the way you say them, and I know why you say them that way anyhow." She kissed him lightly on the forehead and her lips were cool and patient. "I understand."

Conan Lang watched her leave the room with his empty glass. "Yes," he whispered to himself. "Yes, I guess you do."

It *was* necessary, of course. Terribly, urgently necessary. But it got to you sometimes. All those people out there, living their lives, laughing and crying, raising children. It hurt you to think about them. And it wasn't necessary for them, not for him, not for Kit. Or was it? You couldn't tell; there was always a chance. But if only they could just forget it all, just live, there was so much to enjoy –

Kit handed him a fresh bourbon and soda, icy and with just a trace of lemon in it the way he liked it, and then curled up again on the couch, smiling at him.

"I'm sorry, angel," he said. "You must get pretty sick of hearing the same sad song over and over again."

"Not when you sing it, Cone."

"It's just that sometimes I chuck my mind out the nearest window and wonder why – "

There was a thump and a bang from the rear of the house. Conan Lang tasted his drink. That meant Rob was home. He listened, waiting. There was the hollow crack – that was the bat going into the corner. There was the heavy thud – that was the fielder's glove.

"That's why," Kit said.

Conan Lang nodded and picked up the first book off the floor.

Three days later, Conan Lang went up the white steps, presented his credentials, and walked into the Buzzard's Cage. The place made him nervous. Irritated with himself, he paused deliberately and lit his pipe before going on. The Cage seemed cold, inhuman. And the Buzzard –

He shouldn't feel that way, he told himself, again offering his identification before entering the lift to the Nest. Intellectually, he understood cybernetics; there was nothing supernatural about it. The Cage was just a machine, for all its powers, even if the Buzzard did sometimes seem more – or perhaps less – than a man. Still, the place gave him the creeps. A vast thinking machine, filling a huge building, a brain beside which his own was as nothing. Of course, men had built it. Men made guns, too, but the knowledge was scant comfort when you looked into a metallic muzzle and someone pulled the trigger.

"Lang," he said to himself, "you're headed for the giggle ward."

He smiled then, knowing it wasn't so. Imagination was a prime requisite for his job, and he just had more than his share. It got in the way sometimes, but it was a part of him and that was that.

Conan Lang waded through a battery of attendants and security personnel and finally reached the Nest. He opened the door and stepped into the small, dark room. There, behind the desk where he always was, perched the Buzzard.

"Hello, Dr. Gottleib," said Conan Lang.

The man behind the desk eyed him silently. His name was Fritz Gottleib, but he had been tagged the Buzzard long ago. No one used the name to his face, and it was impossible to tell whether or not the name amused him. He spoke but seldom, and his appearance, even after you got used to it, was startling. Fritz Gottleib was squat and completely bald. He always dressed in black and his heavy eyebrows were like horizontal splashes of ink against the whiteness of his face. The Buzzard analogy, thought Conan Lang, was more than understandable; it was inevitable. The man sat high in his tower, in his Nest of controls, brooding over a machine that perhaps he alone fully understood. Alone. He always seemed alone, no matter how many people surrounded him. His was a life apart, a life whose vital force pulsed in the shifting lights of the tubes of a great machine.

"Dr. Lang," he acknowledged, unmoving, his voice sibilant, almost a hiss.

Conan Lang puffed on his pipe and dropped into the chair across from Gottleib. He had dealt with the Buzzard before and most of the shock had worn off. You could get used to anything, he supposed. Man was a very adaptable animal.

"The smoke doesn't bother you, I hope?"

Gottleib did not comment. He simply stared at him, his dark eyes unblinking. Like looking at a piece of meat, thought Conan Lang.

"Well," he said, trying again, "I guess you know what I'm here for."

"You waste words," Fritz Gottleib hissed.

"I hadn't realized they were in short supply," Lang replied, smiling. The Buzzard was irritating, but he could see the justice in the man's remark. It *was* curious the number of useless things that were said all the time – useless, at any rate, from a purely communicative point of view. It would have been sheerly incredible for Gottleib – who after all had been checking his results in the computer – *not* to have known the nature of his mission.

"O.K.," said Lang, "what's the verdict?"

Fritz Gottleib fingered a square card in his surprisingly long-fingered hands, seeming to hover over it like a bird of prey.

"It checks out," he said sibilantly, his voice low and hard to hear. "Your plan will achieve the desired transfer in Sirius Ten, and the transfer integrates positively with the Plan."

"Anything else? Anything I should know?"

"We should all know many more things than we do, Dr. Lang."

"Um-m-m. But that was all the machine said with respect to my proposed plan of operations?"

"That was all."

Conan Lang sat back, watching Gottleib. A strange man. But he commanded respect.

"I'd like to get hold of that baby sometime," he said easily. "I've got a question or two of my own."

"Sometimes it is best not to know the answers to one's questions, Dr. Lang."

"No. But I'd like to have a shot at it all the same. Don't tell the security boys I said that; they'd string me up by the toes."

"Perhaps one day, Dr. Lang. When you are old like me."

Conan Lang stood up, cupping his pipe in his hand. "I guess that's all," he said.

"Yes," said Fritz Gottleib.

"See you around."

No answer. Cold shadows seemed to fill the room.

Conan Lang turned and left the way he had come. Behind him, drilling into his back, he could feel the eyes of Fritz Gottleib following him, cold and deep like the frozen waters of an arctic sea.

The ship stood on Earth but she was not of Earth. She was poised, a mighty lance of silver, a creature of the deeps. She waited, impatient, while Conan Lang slowly walked across the vast duralloy tarmac of Space One, Admiral White at his side. The sun was bright in a clean blue sky. It touched the ship with lambent flame and warmed Conan Lang's shoulders under his uniform. A slight puff of breeze rustled across the spaceport, pushing along a stray scrap of white paper ahead of it.

"Here we go again," said Conan Lang.

"That's what you get for being good," the admiral said with a smile. "You get good enough and you'll get my job – which ought to be a grim enough prospect even for you. If you're smart, you'll botch this job six ways from Sunday and then we'll have to give you a rest."

"Yeah – play a little joke, strictly for laughs, and give 'em an atom bomb or two to stick on the ends of their hatchets. Or take 'em back to the caves. There are plenty of delicious possibilities."

The two men walked on, toward the silver ship.

"Everything's set, I suppose?" asked Conan Lang.

"Yep. Your staff is already on board and the stuff is loaded."

"Any further instructions?"

"No – you know your business or you wouldn't be going. Just try to make it as quick as you can, Cone. They're getting warm over at Research on that integration-acceleration principle for correlating data – it's going to be big and I'll want you around when it breaks."

Conan Lang grinned. "What happens if I just up and disappear one day, Nels? Does the galaxy moan and lie down and quit?"

"Search me," said Admiral Nelson White. "But don't take any more risks than you absolutely have to. Don't get the idea that you're indispensable, either. It's just that it's tiresome to break in new men."

"I'll try to stay alive if you're positive that's what you want."

They approached the ship. Kit and Rob were waiting. The admiral touched his cap and moved on, leaving Conan Lang alone with his family. Kit was lovely – she always was, Conan Lang thought. He couldn't imagine a life without her.

"Bye, darlin'," he whispered, taking her in his arms. "One of these days I'm coming back and I'm never going to leave you again."

"This is till then," Kit said softly and kissed him for keeps.

Much later, Conan Lang released her and shook hands with his son. "So long, old-timer," he said.

"Hurry back, Dad," Rob said, trying not to cry.

Conan Lang turned and joined Admiral White at the star cruiser. He did not look back.

"Good luck, Cone," the admiral said, patting him on the back. "I'll keep the medals warm and a light in the cabin window."

"OK, Nels," said Conan Lang.

He swung aboard the great ship and stepped into the lift. There was a muted hum of machinery as the car whispered up through the pneumatic tube, up into the hollowness of the ship. Already it seemed to Conan Lang that he had left Earth far behind him. The endless loneliness of the star trails rode up with him in the humming lift.

The ship rested, quiescent, on Earth. Ahead of her, calling to her, the stars flamed coldly in an infinite sea of night.

II

Conan Lang walked down the long white corridor to the afterhold, his footsteps muffled and almost inaudible in the murmur of the atomics. It *would* be a long white corridor, he thought to himself. Wherever man went, there went the long white corridors – offices, hospitals, command posts. It was almost as if he had spent half a lifetime walking through long white corridors, and now here was yet another one – cold and antiseptic, hanging in space eight light-years from Earth.

"Halt."

"Lang here," he told the Fleetman. "Kindly point that thing the other way."

"Identification, please."

Lang sighed and handed it over. The man should know him by now; after all, the ship was on his mission, and he was hardly a subversive character. Still, orders were orders – a principle that covered a multitude of sins. And they couldn't afford to take chances, not *any* chances.

"All right, sir," the Fleetman said, returning the identification. "Sorry to bother you."

"Forget it," said Conan Lang. "Keep your eyes peeled for space pirates."

The guard smiled. "Who'd want to steal space, sir?" he asked. "It's free and I reckon there's enough to go around."

"Your inning," acknowledged Conan Lang, moving into the afterhold. The kid was already there.

"Hello, sir," said Andrew Irvin.

"Hi, Andy – and cut the 'sir,' what do you say? You make me feel like I should be extinct or embalmed or something."

The kid smiled almost shyly. Conan Lang had half expected to find him there in the hold; Andy was always poking around, asking questions, trying to learn. His quick brown eyes and alert carriage reminded Conan of a young hunting dog, frisking through the brush, perpetually on the verge of flushing the grandfather of all jack rabbits.

"It doesn't seem possible, does it?" asked the kid.

Conan Lang raised his eyebrows.

"All this, I mean," Andy Irvin said, gesturing at the neat brown sacks stacked row upon row in the brightly lighted hold. "To think that a couple of sacks of that stuff can remold a planet, change the lives of millions of people – "

"It's not just the sacks, Andy. It took man a good many hundreds of thousands of years to learn what to *do* with those sacks."

"Yes, sir," the kid said, hanging on every word.

"No 'sir,' remember? I'm not giving you a lecture, and you don't have to look attentive. I'm sure that elementary anthropology isn't *too* dumbfounding to a guy who took honors at the Academy."

"Well – "

"Never mind." Conan Lang eyed him speculatively. The kid reminded him, almost too much, of someone else – a kid named Conan Lang who had started out on a great adventure himself too many years ago. "I . . . um-m-m . . . guess you know you're going to work with me on Ten."

Andy looked like Conan had just handed him a harem on a silver platter. "No, sir," he said. "I didn't know. Thank you, sir."

"The name is Conan."

"Yes, sir."

"Hellfire," said Conan Lang. How did you go about telling a kid that you were happy to have someone around with stars in his eyes again? Without sounding like a fool? The answer was simple – you didn't.

"I can't wait," Andy said. "To really do something at last – it's a great feeling. I hope I'll do OK."

"It won't be long now, Andy. Twenty-four hours from now you and I go to work. The buggy ride is about over."

The two men fell silent then, looking at the neat brown rows of sacks, feeling the star ship tremble slightly under them with the thunder of her great atomics.

It was night on Sirius Ten – a hot, humid night with a single moon hanging like frozen fire in the darkness. A small patrol craft from the cruiser floated motionless in the night sky, her batteries pouring down a protective screen around the newly cleared field. Conan Lang wiped the sweat from his forehead and washed his hands off in the clean river water that gurgled through the trench at his feet.

"That about does it, Andy," he said wearily. "Toss 'em a Four signal."

Andy Irvin turned the rheostat on his small control board to Four and flipped the switch. They waited, listening to the faint murmur of the night breeze off the river. There was no change, nothing that they could see, but they could almost feel the intense radiation pounding into the field from the patrol ship, seeping into the ground, accelerating by thousands of times the growth factor in the seeds.

"That's got it," said Conan Lang. "Give 'em release."

Andy shot the patrol craft the release signal and shut off his control board. The little ship seemed to hover uncertainly. There was a humming sound and a spot of intense white light in the sky. That was all. The ship was gone and they were alone.

"It's been a long night, kid," yawned Conan Lang. "We'd better get some sack time – we're liable to need it before morning."

"You go ahead," Andy Irvin said. "I'm not sleepy; the sunrise here ought to be something."

"Yeah," said Conan Lang. "The sunrise ought to be something."

He walked across the field and entered a structure that closely resembled a native hut in appearance but was actually quite, quite different. Too tired even to undress, he piled into bed with his clothes on and rested quietly in the darkness.

The strange, haunting, familiar-with-a-difference sounds of an alien world whispered around the hut on the soft, moist breeze from the sluggish river. Far away, an animal screamed hoarsely in the clogging brush. Conan Lang kept his eyes closed and tried not to think, but his mind ignored him. It went right on working, asking questions, demanding answers, bringing up into the light many memories that were good and some that were better forgotten.

"Kit," he said, very softly.

Tired as he was, he knew there would be no sleep for him that night.

The sunrise was a glory. The blue-white inferno of Sirius hung in the treetops across the field and then climbed into the morning sky, her white dwarf companion a smaller sun by her side. The low cumulus clouds were edged with flame – fiery red, pale blue, cool green. The fresh morning winds washed the field with air and already the young plants were out of the ground, thirsty for the sun. The chuckling water in the trenches sparkled in the light.

With the morning, the natives came.

"They're all around us," Conan Lang said quietly.

"I can't see them," whispered Andy Irvin, looking at the brush.

"They're there."

"Do you . . . expect trouble, sir?"

"Not yet, assuming we've got this deal figured right. They're more afraid of us than we are of them."

"What if we *don't* have it figured right?"

Conan Lang smiled. "Three guesses," he said.

The kid managed a wry grin. He was taking it well, Lang thought. He remembered how he'd felt the first time. It didn't really hit you until that first day, and then it upped and kicked you in the teeth. Quite suddenly, it was all a very different proposition from the manuals and the viewers and the classrooms of the Academy. *Just you, all alone,* the alien breeze sighed in your ear. *You're all alone in the middle of nowhere,* the wind whispered through the trees. *Our eyes are watching you, our world is pressing you back, waiting. What do you know of us really? What good is your knowledge now?*

"What next?" Andy asked.

"Just tend the field, kid. And try to act like a ghost. You're an ancestor of those people watching us from the brush, remember. If we've got this figured wrong – if those survey reports were haywire somewhere, or if someone's been through here who didn't belong – you should have a little warning at least. They don't use blowguns or anything – just spears, and they'd prefer a hatchet. If there's trouble, you hightail it back to the hut *at once* and man the projector. That's all."

"I'm not so sure I care to be an ancestor," Andy Irvin muttered, picking up his hoe. "Not yet, anyhow." He moved off along a water trench, checking on the plants.

Conan Lang picked up his own hoe and set to work. He could feel the natives watching him, wondering, whispering to themselves. But he was careful not to look around him. He kept his head down and dug at the plants with his hoe, clearing the water channels. The plants were growing with astonishing rapidity, thanks to the dose of radiation. They should be mature in a week. And then –

The sun blazed down on his treated skin and the sweat rolled off his body in tiny rivulets. The field was strangely silent around him; there was only the gurgle of the water and the soft sigh of the humid breeze. His hoe chopped and slushed at the mud and his back was tired from bending over so long. It was too still, unnaturally still.

Behind that brush, back in the trees – a thousand eyes.

He did not look around. Step by step, he moved down the trench, under the hellish sun, working with his hoe.

The fire-burned days and the still, hushed nights alternated rapidly. On the morning of the third day, Andy Irvin found what they had been waiting for.

In the far corner of the field, placed on a rude wood platform about four feet high, there were three objects. There was a five-foot-square bark mat, neatly woven. There was a small animal that closely resembled a terrestrial pig, face down, its throat neatly slashed. And there was a child. It was a female baby, evidently not over a week old. It had been strangled to death.

"It's . . . different . . . when you see it for yourself," Andy said quietly, visibly shaken.

"You'll get used to it," said Conan Lang, his voice purposely flat and matter-of-fact. "Get the pig and the mat – and stop looking like a prohibitionist who just found a jug of joy water in the freezer. This is old stuff to ancestors."

"Old stuff," repeated Andy without conviction.

They carried the contents of the platform back to their hut and Conan Lang wrapped the body of the child in a cloth.

"We'll bury her tonight after dark," he said. "The pig we eat. It won't do any harm to sit on the mat where they can see us while we're eating it, either."

"Well," Andy muttered. "Glad to see you're not going to eat the baby, too."

"You never can tell," smiled Conan Lang. "We anthropologists are all crazy, or hadn't you heard?"

"I've heard," agreed Andy Irvin, getting his nerves under control again. "Where's the hot sauce?"

Conan Lang stepped back outside and picked up his hoe. The blazing double sun had already produced shimmering heat waves that danced like live things in the still air over the green field. The kid was going to be all right. He'd known it all along, of course – but you could never be *sure* of a man until you worked with him under field conditions. And a misfit, an unstable personality, was anything but a joke on an alien planet where unknowable forces hung in the balance.

"Let's see if I've got this thing figured straight," Andy said, puffing away on one of Conan's pipes. "The natives are afraid of us, and still they feel that they must make us an offering because we, as their supposed ancestors, control their lives. So they pick a system of dumb barter rather than sending out the usual contact man to ferret out kinship connections."

"You're OK so far," Conan Lang said. "I guess you've studied about the dumb barter systems used on Earth in the old days; it was used whenever trade took place between groups of markedly unequal strength, such as the African pygmies and trading vessels from the west. There's a fear factor involved."

"Yes, sir."

"Forget the 'sir.' I didn't mean to lecture. I think I'll start calling you Junior."

"Sorry. The bark mat is a unit in a reciprocal trade system and the pig is a sacred animal – I get that part of it. But the baby – that's terrible, Conan. After all, we caused that death in a way – "

"Afraid not," Conan Lang corrected him. "These people practice infanticide; it's part of their religion. If the preliminary reports were correct – and they've checked out so far – they kill all the female children born on the last three days of alternate months. There's an economic reason, too – not enough food to go around, and that's a pretty effective method of birth control. The baby would have been killed regardless – we had nothing to do with it."

"Still – "

"I know. But maybe she was the lucky one after all."

"I don't quite follow you there."

"Skip it – you'll find out soon enough."

"What are you going to leave them tonight?"

"Not sure yet," Conan Lang said. "We'll have to integrate with their value system, of course. We brought some mats, and I guess a good steel knife won't hurt things any. We'll worry about that later. Come on, farmer – back to work."

Andy Irvin picked up his hoe and followed Conan Lang into the field. The clear water bubbled softly as it flowed through the trenches. The growing plants sent their roots thirstily into the ground and the fresh green shoots stretched up like tentacles into the humid air of Sirius Ten.

That night, under the great yellow moon that swam far away and lonesome among the stars, they placed exchange gifts of their own on the platform. Next morning, the invisible traders had replaced them with four mats and another dead pig.

"No babies, anyhow," Andy Irvin said, puffing industriously on one of Conan's pipes. They had decided that cigarettes, as an unfamiliar cultural trait to the natives, were out. Now, with Andy taking with unholy enthusiasm to pipe smoking, Conan Lang was threatened with a shortage of tobacco. He watched the smoke from the kid's pipe with something less than ecstasy.

"We can have smoked ham," he observed.

"It was your idea," Andy grinned.

"Call me 'sir.'"

Andy laughed, relaxed now, and picked up the pig. Conan gathered up the somewhat cumbersome mats and followed him back into the hut. The hot, close sun was already burning his shoulders. The plants were green and healthy-looking, and the air was a trifle fresher in the growing field.

"Now what?" Andy asked, standing outside the hut and letting the faint breeze cool him off as best it could.

"I figure we're about ready for an overt contact," Conan Lang said. "Everything has checked out beautifully so far, and the natives don't seem to be suspicious or hostile. We might as well get the ball rolling."

"The green branch, isn't it?"

"That's right."

They still did not get a glimpse of the natives throughout the steaming day, and that night they placed a single mat on the platform. On top of the mat they put a slim branch of green leaves, twisted around back on itself and tied loosely to form a circle. The green branch was by no means a universal symbol of peace, but, in this particular form, it chanced to be so on Sirius Ten. Conan Lang smiled a little. Man had found many curious things among the stars, and most of them were of just this unsensational but very useful sort.

By dawn, the mat and the circle branch were gone and the natives had left them nothing in return.

"Today's the day," Conan Lang said, rubbing the sleep out of his eyes. "They'll either give us the works or accept our offer. Nothing to do now but wait."

They picked up their hoes and went back into the field. Waiting can be the most difficult of all things, and the long, hot morning passed without incident. The two men ate their lunch in silence, thankful for the odorless injection that kept the swarming insects away from them. Late in the afternoon when the long blue shadows of evening were already touching the green plants and the clean, flowing water, the natives came.

There were five of them and they appeared to be unarmed. One man walked slightly in advance of the others, a circular branch of green leaves in his hand. Conan Lang waited for them, with Andy standing by at his side. It was moments like this, he thought, that made you suddenly realize that you were all alone and a long, long way from friends. The natives came on steadily. Conan felt a surge of admiration for the young man who led them. From his point of view, he was walking into a situation filled with the terror of the supernatural, which was a very real part of his life. His steps did not falter. He would, Conan supposed, be the eldest son of the most powerful chief.

The natives stopped when they were three paces away. Their leader extended the circular green branch. "We would serve you, fathers from the mountains," the native said in his own tongue.

Conan Lang stepped forward and received the branch. "We are brothers," he replied in the same language, "and we would be your friends."

The native smiled, his teeth very white. "I am Ren," he said. "I am your brother."

Conan Lang kept his face expressionless, but deep within him a dark regret and sadness coursed like ice through his veins.

It had begun again.

III

For many days, Conan Lang listened to the Oripesh natives preparing for the feast. Their small village, only a quarter of a mile from the field, was alive with excitement. The women prepared great piles of the staple ricefruit and broiled river fish in great green leaves on hot coals. The men chanted and danced interminably, cleansing the village by ritual for the coming visitation, while the children, forgotten for once, played on the banks of the river. On the appointed day, Conan Lang walked into the village with Andy Irvin at his side.

It was a crude village, necessarily so because of its transient nature. But it was not dirty. The natives watched the two men with awe, but they did not seem unfriendly. The supernatural was for them always just on the other side of the hill, hidden in the night, and now it was among them, in the open. That was all. And what, after all, thought Conan Lang, could have seemed more supernatural to them than a silver ship that dropped out of the stars? What was supernatural depended on one's point of view – and on how much one happened to know about what was *natural*.

The box he carried was heavy, and it took both arms to handle it. He watched Andy puffing at his side and smiled.

"Stick with it, kid," he said, walking steadily through the watching natives. "You may earn your pay yet."

Andy muttered something under his breath and blinked to get the sweat out of his eyes.

When they reached the clearing in the center of the village, they stopped and put their boxes down. Ren, the eldest son of the chief Ra Renne, approached them at once and offered them a drink from a large wooden bowl. Conan drank and passed the container on to Andy, who grinned broadly and took a long swallow of the warm fluid. It was sweet, although not too sweet, and it burned pleasantly on the way down. It was, Conan decided instantly, a great improvement over some native fermented horrors he had been subjected to in times past.

The natives gathered around them in a great circle. There must have been nearly five hundred of them – far more than the small village could accommodate for any length of time.

"We're celebrities," Conan Lang whispered out of the side of his mouth as he waited to be presented ceremonially to the chiefs.

"You want my autograph?" hissed Andy, his face just a trifle flushed from the drink he had taken. "I make a real fine X."

The feast followed a pattern familiar to Conan Lang. They were presented ceremonially to the tribe, having identified themselves as ancestors of four generations ago, thus making themselves kin to virtually all the tribe with their complicated lineage system, and also making refutation impossible since no one remembered that far back. They were seated with the chiefs, and ate the ritual feast rapidly. The food was good, and Conan Lang was interested in getting a good taste of the ricefruit plant, which was the basic food staple of the Oripesh.

After the eating came the drinking, and after the drinking the dancing. The Oripesh were not a musical people, and they had no drums. The men and the women danced apart from one another, each one doing an individual dance – which he owned, just as the men from Earth owned material property – to his own rhythm pattern. Conan Lang and Andy Irvin contented themselves with watching, not trusting themselves to improvise an authentic dance. They were aware that their conduct was at variance with the somewhat impulsive conduct usually attributed to ancestors in native folklore, but that was a chance they had to take. Conan was very conscious of one old chief who watched him closely with narrowed eyes.

Conan ignored him, enjoying the dancers. The Oripesh seemed to be a happy people, although short on material wealth. Conan Lang almost envied them as they danced – envied them for their simple lives and envied them their ability to enjoy it, an ability that civilized man had left by the wayside in his climb up the ladder. Climb – or descent? Conan Lang sometimes wondered.

Ren came over, his color high with the excitement of the dance. Great fires were burning now, and Conan noticed with surprise that it was night.

"That is Loe," Ren said, pointing. "My *am-ren*, my bride-to-be." His voice was filled with pride.

Conan Lang followed his gesture and saw the girl. Her name was a native word roughly translatable as *fawn*, and she was well named. Loe was a slim, very shy girl of really striking beauty. She danced with diffidence, looking into Ren's eyes. The two were obviously, almost painfully, in love – love being a part of the culture of the Oripesh. It was difficult to realize, sometimes, even after years of personal experience, that there were whole worlds of basically humanoid peoples where the very concept of romantic love did not exist. Conan Lang smiled. Loe was, if anything, a trifle too beautiful for his taste. Dancing there, with the yellow moon in her hair, moving gracefully with the leaping shadows from the crackling fires, she was ethereal, a fantasy, like a painting of a woman from another, unattainable century.

"We would give gifts to the chiefs," Conan Lang said finally. "Your Loe – she is very beautiful."

Ren smiled, quickly grateful, and summoned the chiefs. Conan Lang rose to greet them, signaling to Andy to break open the boxes. The chiefs watched intently. Conan Lang did not speak. He waited until Andy had opened both boxes and then pointed to them.

"They are yours, my brothers," he said.

The natives pressed forward. A chief picked the first object out of the box and stared at it in disbelief. The shadows flickered eerily and the night wind sighed through the village. He held the object up to the light and there was a gasp of astonishment.

The object was a ricefruit – a ricefruit the likes of which had never before been seen on Sirius Ten. It was round, fully a foot in diameter, and of a lush, ripe consistency. It made the potato-sized ricefruits of the Oripesh seem puny by comparison.

It was then that Conan Lang exploded his bombshell.

"We have come back to show you, our brothers, how to grow the great ricefruit," he said. "You can grow them over and over again, *in the same field*. You will never have to move your village again."

The natives stared at him in wonder, moving back a little in fear.

"It cannot be done," a chief whispered. "The ricefruit devours the land – every year we must move or perish."

"That is over now, Conan Lang said. "We have come to show you the way."

The dancing had stopped. The natives waited, nervous, suddenly uncertain. The yellow moon watched through the trees. As though someone had flipped a switch, sound disappeared. There was silence. The great ricefruit was magic. They looked at the two men as though seeing them for the first time. This was not the way of the past, not the way of the ancestors. This was something completely *new* and they found themselves lost, without precedent for action. Ren alone smiled at them, and even he had fear in his eyes.

Conan Lang waited tensely. He must make no move; this was the crisis point. Andy stood at his side, very still, hardly breathing.

A native walked solemnly into the silence, carrying a young pig under his arm. Conan Lang watched him narrowly. The man was obviously a shaman, a witch doctor, and his trembling body and too-bright eyes were all too clear an indication of why he had been chosen for his role in the society.

With a swiftness of motion that was numbing, the shaman slit the pig's throat with a stone knife. At once he cut the body open. The blood stained his body with crimson. His long, thin hands poked into the entrails. He looked up, his eyes wild.

"They are not ancestors," he screamed, his voice high like an hysterical woman's. They have come to do us evil!"

The very air was taut with tension.

"No," Conan Lang said loudly, keeping his voice clear and confident. "The *barath-tui*, the shaman, has been bewitched by sorcerers! Take care that you do not offend our ancestors!"

Conan Lang stood very still, fighting to keep the alarm off his face. He and Andy were helpless here, and he knew it. They were without weapons of any sort – the native loincloth being a poor place to conceal firearms. There was nothing they could do – they had miscalculated, moved too swiftly, and now they were paying the price.

"We are your brothers," he said into the ominous silence. "We are your fathers and your father's fathers. There are others who watch."

The flames leaped and danced in the stillness. An old man stepped forward. It was the chief that Conan had noticed watching him before.

"You say you are our brothers who have taken the long journey," the old chief said. "That is good. We would see you walk through the fire."

The wind sighed in the trees. Without a moment's hesitation, Conan Lang turned and walked swiftly toward the flames that crackled and hissed in the great stone fire pits.

There was nothing else in all the world except the flickering tongues of orange flame that licked nearer and nearer to his face. He saw the red, pulsing coals waiting beneath the twisted black branches in the fire and he closed his eyes. The heat singed his eyebrows and he could feel his hair shrivel and start to burn.

Conan Lang kept moving, and moved fast. He twisted a rigid clamp on his mind and refused to feel pain. He wrenched his mind out of his body, thinking as he had been trained to think, until it was as if his mind floated a thing apart, free in the air, looking down upon the body of Conan Lang walking through hell.

He knew that one of the attributes of the Oripesh ancestor gods was that they could walk through flame without injury – a fairly common myth pattern. He had known it before he left Earth. He should have been prepared, he knew that. But man was not perfect, which would have been a dangerous flaw had it not been his most valuable characteristic.

He saw that his legs were black and blistered and he smelled the suffocating smell of burning flesh. The smoke was in his head, in his lungs, everywhere, choking him. Some of the pain was coming through –

He was out. He felt Andy's hands beating out the rivulets of flame that clung to his body and he forced the clean, pure air of night into his sick lungs. The pain, the pain –

"Stick with it, Cone," Andy whispered in his ear. "Stick with it."

Conan Lang managed to open his eyes and stared blankly into a hot-red haze. The haze cleared and he was faintly surprised to find that he could still see. The natives were awestruck with fear – they had angered their gods and death was in the air. Conan Lang knew that the shaman who had denounced him would quite probably be dead of fear before the night was over – if he did not die before then of some less subtle malady. He had endangered the tribe without reason, and he would pay with his life.

Conan Lang kept his face expressionless. Inside, he was on fire. Water, he had to have water, cold water –

Ren came to him, his eyes filled with pain. "I am sorry, my brother," he whispered. "For my people, I am sorry."

"It is all right, Ren," Conan Lang heard his voice say steadily. "I am, of course, unharmed."

Conan Lang touched Andy's arm and moved across to the chiefs. He felt Andy standing behind him, ready to catch him, just in case. He could feel nothing in his feet – quite suddenly, he was convinced that he was standing on the charred stumps of his legs and he fought to keep from looking down to make sure he still had feet.

"You have doubted your brothers who have come far to help their people," he said quietly, looking directly into the eyes of the old chief who had sent him into the flames. "We are disappointed in our people – there are sorcerers at work among you, and they must be destroyed. We leave you now. If you anger your brothers again, the Oripesh shall cease to be."

He did not wait for an answer but turned and started away from the clearing, back through the village. Andy was at his side. Conan Lang set his teeth and moved at a steady pace. He must have no help until they were beyond the village; the natives must not suspect –

He walked on. The great yellow moon was high in the night sky, and there was the face of Loe with stars in her hair. The moon shuddered and burst into flame and he heard himself laughing. He bit his lips until the blood came and kept going, into the darkness, into nothing. The pain clawed at his body.

They were through the village. Something snapped in Conan Lang – the steel clamp that had carried him through a nightmare parted with a clean *ping*. There was emptiness, space. Conan Lang collapsed. He felt Andy's arm around him, holding him up.

"You'll have to carry me, kid," he whispered. "I can't walk at all."

Andy Irvin picked him up in his arms and set out through the night.

"It should have been me," he said in bitter self-reproach. "It should have been me."

Conan Lang closed his eyes and, at last, nothing mattered anymore, and there was only darkness.

A week later, Conan Lang stood in the dawn of Sirius Ten, watching the great double sun lift above the horizon and chase the shadows from the green field that they had carved out of the wilderness. He was still a very sick man, but Andy had pulled him through as best he could and now the star cruiser was coming in to pick him up and leave a replacement with the kid.

The fresh leaves of the ricefruit plants were shoulder high and the water in the irrigation trenches chuckled cleanly, waiting for the full fury of the sun. The tenuous, almost hesitant breeze crawled through the still air.

Conan Lang watched the green plants silently. The words of the dead *barathtui*, the shaman, echoed in his brain. *They are not ancestors*, the man had screamed. *They have come to do us evil!*

They have come to do us evil . . .

How could he have known – with only a pig and a stone knife? A crazy shaman working the discredited magic of divination – and he had been *right*. Coincidence? Yes, of course. There was no other way to look at it, no other *sane* way. Conan Lang smiled weakly. He remembered reading about the Snake Dance of the Hopi, long ago back on Earth. The Snake Dance had been a rain-making ceremonial, and invariably when the very early anthropologists had attended the dance they had gotten drenched on the way home. It was only coincidence and good timing, of course, but it was difficult to tell yourself that when the rain began to pour.

"Here she comes," said Andy Irvin.

There was a splitting whistle and then a soft hum as a small patrol ship settled down toward the field on her anti-gravs. She hung there in the dawn like a little silver fish seen through the glassite walls of a great aquarium, and Conan Lang could sense what he could not see – the massive bulk of the sleek star cruiser waiting out in space.

The patrol ship came down out of the sky and hovered a few feet off the ground. A man swung down out of the outlift and waved. Conan Lang recognized him as Julio Medina, who had been lifted out of another sector of Sirius Ten to come in and replace him with Andy. The ricefruit was green and fresh in the field and it hurt Conan to leave his job unfinished. There wasn't a great deal to do now until the check, of course, and Julio was a very competent and experienced man, but there was still so much that could go wrong, so much that you could never anticipate – And he didn't want anything to happen to the kid.

"So long, Cone," Andy said, his voice very quiet. "And – thanks. I won't forget what you did."

Conan Lang leaned on Andy's arm and moved toward the ship. "I'll be back, Andy," he said, trying to keep the weight off his feet. "Hold the fort – I know it'll be in good hands."

Conan Lang shook hands with Julio and then Julio and Andy helped him into the outlift. He had time for a brief wave and a final glimpse of the green field under the fiery sun, and then he was inside the patrol ship. They had somehow rigged up a bunk for him in the cramped quarters, and he collapsed into it gratefully.

"Home, James," he whispered, trying not to think about what would happen if they could not save his legs.

Conan Lang closed his eyes and lay very still, feeling the ship pulse and surge as it carried him out into the dark sea from which he had come.

IV

The doctors saved his legs, but years were to pass before Conan Lang again set foot upon Earth. Space was vast and star cruisers comparatively few. In addition, star ships were fabulously expensive to operate – it was out of the question for a ship on a mission to make the long run from Sirius to Sol for the sake of one man. Conan Lang became the prize patient of the ship medics and he stayed with the star cruiser as it operated in the Sirius area.

A star cruiser on operations was never dull and there were books to read and reports to write. Conan Lang curbed his impatience and made the best of the situation. The local treatments applied by Andy had been effective enough so that the ship medics were able to regenerate his burned tissue, and it was only a question of time before he would be strong again.

The star cruiser worked efficiently and effectively in support of Administration units in the Sirius area, sliding through the blackness of space like some leviathan of the deep, and Conan Lang rested and made himself as useful as he could. He often went up into the control room and stood watching the visiplate that looked out upon the great emptiness of space. Somewhere, on a far shore of that mighty sea, was a tiny planet called Earth. There, the air was cool and fresh under the pines and the beauty of the world, once you got away from it and could see it in perspective, was fantastic. There were Rob and Kit, friendship and tears and laughter.

There was home.

While his body healed, Conan Lang lived on the star cruiser. There was plenty of time to think. Even for a race with a life span of almost two hundred years, the days and the weeks and the months can seem interminable. He asked himself all the old questions, examined all the old answers. Here he was, on a star ship light-years from home, his body burned, waiting to go back to Sirius Ten to change the life of a planet. What thin shreds of chance, what strange webs of history, had put him there? When you added up the life of Conan Lang, of all the

Conan Langs, what did you get? Where was Earth going, that pebble that hurled its puny challenge at the infinite?

Sometimes, it was all hard to believe.

It had all started, he supposed, with cybernetics. Of course, cybernetics itself was but the logical outgrowth of a long cultural and technological trend. For centuries, man's ally, the machine, had helped him physically in his adjustment to his environment. What more natural than that it should one day help him mentally as well? There was really nothing sinister about thinking machines, except to a certain breed of perpetually gloomy poets who were unable to realize that values were never destroyed but were simply molded into new patterns in the evolution of culture. No, thinking machines were fine and comforting – for a while.

But with the dawn of space travel, man's comfortable, complacent progress toward a vague somewhere was suddenly knocked into a cocked hat. Man's horizons exploded to the rims of the universe with the perfection of the star drive – he was no longer living *on* a world but *in* an inhabited universe. His bickerings and absurdities and wars were seen as the petty things they were – and man in a few tremendous years emerged at last from adolescence.

Science gave to men a life span of nearly two hundred active years and gave him the key to forever. But there was a catch, a fearful catch. Man, who had had all he could do to survive the conflicts of local groups of his own species, was suddenly faced with the staggering prospect of living in an inhabited *universe*. He had known, of course, about the millions and millions of stars, about the infinity of planets, about the distant galaxies that swam like island universes through the dark seas of space. But he had known about them as figures on a page, as photographs, as dots of unwinking light in a telescope. They had been curiosities, a stimulus to the imagination. Now they were vital parts of his life, factors to be reckoned with in the struggle for existence. In the universe were incredible numbers of integers to be equated in the problem of survival – and *the mind of man could not even learn them all, much less form intelligent conclusions about future actions.*

And so, inevitably, man turned again to the machine. But this time there was a difference. The machine was the only instrument capable of handling the data – and man, in a million years, could not even check its most elementary conclusions. Man fed in the facts, the machine reached the conclusions, and man acted upon them – not through choice, but simply because he had no other guide he could trust.

Men operated the machines – but the machines operated men.

The science of cybernetics expanded by leaps and bounds. Men made machines to develop new machines. The great mechanical brains grew so complex that only a few men could even pretend to understand them. Looking at them, it was virtually impossible to believe that they had been born in the minds of men.

The machines did not interfere in the everyday routine of living – man would never submit to that, and in problems which he could understand he was still the best judge of his own happiness. It was in the larger problems, the problems of man's destiny in the universe in which he found himself, that the great brains were beyond value. For the machines could integrate trends, patterns, and complexes of the known worlds and go on from there to extrapolate into the unknown. The machines could, in very general terms, predict the outcome of any given set of circumstances. They could, in a very real sense, see into the future. They could see where Earth was headed.

And Earth was headed for disaster.

The machines were infallible. They dealt not with short-term probabilities, but with long-range certainties. And they stated flatly that, given the equation of the known universe, Earth would be destroyed in a matter of centuries. There was only one thing to do – man must change the equation.

It was difficult for man, so recently Earthbound, to really *think* and *act* in terms of an inhabited universe. But the machines showed conclusively that in as yet inaccessible galaxies life had evolved that was physically and mentally hostile to that of Earth. A collision of the two life-forms would come about within a thousand years, and a life-and-death struggle was inevitable. The facts were all too plain – Earth would lose and the human race would be exterminated.

Unless the equation could be changed.

It was a question of preparing the galaxy for combat. The struggle would be a long one, and factors of reserves, replacements, different cultural approaches to common problems, planets in varying stages of development, would be important. It was like a cosmic chess game, with worlds aligning themselves on a monstrous board. In battles of galactic dimensions, the outcome would be determined by centuries of preparation before contact was even made; it was not a romantic question of heroic spaceships and iron-jawed men of action, but rather one of the cultural, psychological, technological, and individual patterns which each side could bring to bear – patterns which were the outgrowths of millennia of slow evolution and development.

Earth was ready, or would be by the time contact came. But the rest of the galaxy – or at any rate as much of it as they had managed to explore – was not, and would not be. The human race was found somewhere on most of the star systems within the galaxy, but not one of them was as far advanced as were the men from Earth. That was why Earth had never been contacted from space – indeed, it was the only possible explanation, at least in retrospect. And the other galaxies, with their totally alien and forever nonunderstandable principles, were not interested in undeveloped cultures.

The problem thus became one of accelerating the cultural evolution of Earth's sister planets by means of diffusion, in order to build them up into an effective totality to combat the coming challenge. And it had to be done in such a manner that the natives of the planets were completely unaware that they were not the masters of their own destiny, since such a concept produced cultural stagnation and introduced corrupting elements into the planetary configurations. It had often been argued that Earth herself was in such a position, being controlled by the machines, but such was not the case – their choice had been a rational one, and they could abandon the machines at any time at their own risk.

Or so, at any rate, argued the thinkers of Earth.

The long months lengthened into years and, inactive though he was, Conan Lang spent his time well. It was good to have a chance to relax and think things through; it was good for the soul to stop midway in life and take stock. Almost, it was possible to make sense out of things, and the frantic rush to nowhere lost some of its shrieking senselessness.

Conan Lang smiled without humor. That was all very well for him, but what about the natives whose lives they were uprooting? Of course, they were human beings, too, and stood to lose as much as anyone in the long run – but they did not understand the problem, *could* not understand it. The plain truth was that they were being used – used for their own benefit as well as that of others, but used nonetheless.

It was true that primitive life was no bed of roses – it was not as if, Conan Lang assured himself, the men from Earth were slithering, serpent-like, into an idyllic Garden of Eden. All they were doing was accelerating the normal rate of change for a given planet. But this caused far-reaching changes in the culture as it existed – it threw some people to the dogs and elevated others to commanding positions. This was perhaps no more than was done by life itself, and possibly with better reason, but you couldn't tell yourself that when you had to face the eyes of a man who had gone from ruler to slave because of what you had done.

The real difficulty was that you couldn't *see* the threat. It was there all right – a menace besides which all the conflicts of the human race were as nothing. But it had always been difficult for men to work before the last possible moment, to prepare rather than just sit back and hope for the best. That man was working now as he had never worked before, in the face of an unseen threat from out of the stars, even to save his own existence, was a monument to his hard-won maturity. It would have been so easy, so pleasant, just to take it easy and enjoy a safe and comfortable life – and beyond question it would have meant the end of the human race.

Of one thing, Conan Lang was sure – whenever man stopped trying, stopped working and dreaming and reaching for impossible heights, whenever he settled back in complacency, on that day he shrunk to atrophied insignificance.

Sirius Ten bad been a relatively easy project because of the planet-wide nature of its culture. Sirius Ten had only one huge land mass, and one great sea. The natives all shared basically the same life pattern, built around the cultivation of dry ricefruit, and the teams of the Applied Process Corps were faced with only one major problem rather than hundreds of them as was more often the case. It was true that certain peoples who lived on the shores of the sea, together with one island group, had a variant culture based on fishing, but these were insignificant numerically and could for practical purposes be ignored.

The dry ricefruit was grown by a cutting and burning method, under which a field gave a good yield only once before the land was exhausted and the people had to move on. Under these conditions, individual ownership of land never developed, and there were no inequalities of wealth to speak of. The joint families worked different fields every year, and since there was no market for a surplus there was no effort made to cultivate more land than was really needed.

The Oripesh natives of Sirius Ten had a well-developed cult of ancestor worship, thinking of their dead as always watching over them and guiding their steps. Since whatever the ancestors did automatically had the sanction of tradition behind it, it was through them that the Corps had decided to work – it being simply a question of palming off

Corps Agents as ancestors come back from their dwelling place in the mountains to help their people. With careful preparations and experienced men, this had not proved overly difficult – but there were always miscalculations, accidents. Men were not like chemicals, and they did not always react as they were supposed to react. There was always an individual variable to be considered. That was why if a Corps Agent lived long enough to retire you knew both that he knew his stuff and that he had had more than his share of plain old-fashioned luck.

Sirius Ten had to be shifted from Stage Four to Stage Five. This was a staggering change in economics, social structure, and technology – one that had taken men on Earth many centuries to accomplish. The men of the Applied Process Corps had to do it in a matter of a few years. And so they set out, armed with a variety of ricefruit that grew well in marshy land and a sound knowledge of irrigation.

With such a lever they could move a world.

It was three years to the day when Conan Lang returned to Sirius Ten. The patrol ship came in on her anti-gravs and he waited eagerly for the outlift shaft to open. His heart was pounding in his chest and his lips were dry – it was almost like coming home again.

He swung his newly strong body into the outlift and came out of it in the green field he had planted so long ago. He took a deep breath of the familiar humid air and grinned broadly at the hot, burning sun over his head. It *was* good to be back – back at a place like so many other places he had known, places that were as close to a home as any he could ever have without Kit. The breeze whispered softly through the green ricefruit and he waved at Julio who came running across the field to meet him. These were, he knew, his kind of people – and he had missed Andy all these years.

"Hey there, Julio!" he laughed, shaking Medina's hand. "How goes it?" "Pretty good, Conan," Julio said quietly. "Pretty good."

"The kid – how's the kid?"

"Andy is dead," said Julio Medina.

Conan Lang stood stock-still while an iron fist smacked into his stomach with cold, monotonous precision. Andy dead. It could not be, *could not be.* There had been no word, nothing. He clenched his fists. It couldn't be true.

But it was. He knew that with ice cold certainty.

"It just happened the other day, Conan," Julio said. "He was a fine boy."

Conan Lang couldn't speak. *The whole planet,* his mind tortured him. *The whole stinking planet isn't worth Andy's life.*

"It was an accident," Julio said, his voice carefully matter-of-fact. "Warfare has sprung up between the rival villages like we figured. Andy was out after information and he got between them – he was hit by mistake with a spear. He never had a chance, but he managed to walk away and get back here before he died. The Oripesh don't suspect that he wasn't a god and could die just like anyone else. He saved the rest of us by coming back here – that's something."

"Yeah," Conan Lang said bitterly, "that's something."

"I buried him here in the field," Julio Medina went on. "I thought he'd like that. He . . . said good-bye to you, Conan."

It had been a long time since Conan Lang had had tears in his eyes. He turned without a word and walked away, across the green field and into the hut where he could be alone.

V

From that time on, by unspoken mutual consent, the two men never again mentioned the kid's name. They gave him the best possible write-up in their reports, and that was all that they could ever do for Andy Irvin.

"I think we've about done it here, Conan," Julio told him. "I'd like to have you make your own check and see if you come up with the same stuff I did. There's a lull in the raiding right now – the natives are worried because that spear hit an ancestor by mistake and they're pretty well occupied with rituals designed to make us feel better about the whole thing. You shouldn't have any trouble, and that ought to about wind things up."

Conan Lang nodded. "It'll be good to get home again, eh Julio?"

"Yes, you know that – and for you it should be for keeps."

Conan Lang raised his eyebrows.

"It's no secret that you're due to be kicked upstairs," Julio said. "I rather think this is your last field job."

"Well, it's a nice theory anyhow."

"You remember all us old men out here in the stars, the slave labor of the Process Corps. Bring us all home, Conan, and we'll sit around in the shade and drink cold wine and fish and tell lies to each other."

"Consider it done," said Conan Lang. "And I'll give you all some more medals."

"I've got medals."

"Can't have too many medals, Julio. They're good for what ails you."

"They're not good for what ails *me*," said Julio Medina.

Conan Lang smiled and fired up his pipe. *The kid*, his mind whispered. *The kid liked that pipe.* He thrust the thought from his mind. A man had to take death in his stride out here, he told himself. Even when it was a kid who reminded you of yourself a million years ago –

A million years ago.

"I'll start in tomorrow," Conan Lang said, puffing on his pipe. "Do you know Ren, Julio?"

"The chief's son? Yes."

"How did he come out?"

"Not well, Conan. He lost his woman, Loe, to one of the men we made wealthy; he has not been the same since."

"We're great people, Julio."

"Yes."

Conan Lang was silent then and the two men stood together in the warm evening air, watching the great double sun float slowly down below the horizon as the long black shadows came marching up from the far edge of the world.

Next morning, Conan Lang was off with the dawn on his final check. He pretty well knew what he would find – Julio Medina was an experienced hand and his information was reliable. But it was always a shock when you saw it for yourself. You never got used to it. To think that such a tiny, seemingly insignificant thing could change a planet beyond recognition. A ricefruit –

It was already hot when he passed the native fields. Their ricefruit plants were tall and healthy, and their irrigation channels well constructed. He shook his head and walked on to the native village.

Where the open, crude, friendly village had stood there was a great log wall. In front of the wall was a series of deep and ugly-looking moats. Behind the wall, he could see the tops of sturdy wooden buildings, a far cry from the huts of only a few short years ago. Conan Lang made no attempt at concealment but walked openly up to the moats and crossed them on a log bridge. He stopped outside the closed gate.

"You will remember me who walked through the flames," he said loudly in the Oripesh tongue. "You will open the gate for your brother as he would visit you."

For a moment nothing happened, and then the gate swung open. Conan Lang entered the village.

The native guard eyed him with suspicion, but he kept his distance. Conan Lang noticed that he had a bow by the log wall. There was nothing like constant warfare for the production of new weapons, he reflected. Civilization was bringing its blessings to the Oripesh with leaps and bounds.

Conan Lang walked through the village unmolested, taking rapid mental notes. He saw storehouses for ricefruit and observed slaves being marched off to work in the fields. The houses in the village were strong and comfortable, but there was a tense air in the village, a feeling of strain. Conan Lang approached a native and stopped him.

"Brother," he said, "I would see your chiefs. Where are they?"

The native looked at him warily. "The Oripesh have no chiefs," he said. "Our king is in council."

Conan Lang nodded, a sick feeling inside him. "It is well," he said. "Ren – I would see him."

The native jerked his thumb contemptuously toward the back of the village. "He is there," he said. "Outside."

Conan Lang moved through the village, watching, missing nothing. He went all the way through and came out through the back wall. There, the old-style native huts baked in squalor under the blazing sun. There was no log wall around them, although they were inside the moat system. A pig rooted around for garbage between the huts.

"Slums," Conan Lang said to himself.

He walked among the huts, ignoring the fearful, suspicious eyes of the natives. He found Ren preparing to go out into the fields. The chief's son was thin. He looked tired and his eyes were dull. He saw Conan and said nothing.

"Hello, Ren," said Conan Lang.

The native just looked at him.

Conan Lang tried to think of something to say. He knew what had happened – the chiefs and their sons had been so busy with ritual work for the tribe that they had lagged behind in the cultivation of the new ricefruit. They had stuck to the old ways too long and their people had passed them by.

"I can help you, my brother," Conan Lang said softly. "It is not too late."

Ren said nothing.

"I will help you with a field of your own," said Conan Lang. "Will you let me help you?"

The native looked at him and there was naked hate in his eyes. "You said you were my friend," he said. Without another word, he turned and left. He did not look back.

Conan Lang wiped the sweat from his forehead and went on with his work. The sensitive part of his mind retreated back into a dark, insulated corner and he let his training take over. He moved along, asking questions, watching, taking mental notes.

A little thing, he thought. A new kind of plant.

A week later, Conan Lang had completed his check. He sat by the evening cook fire with Julio, smoking his pipe, watching the shadows in the field.

"Well, we did a good job," he said. "It's awful."

"It would have come without us," Julio reminded him. "It does no good to brood about it. It is tough, sometimes, but it is a small price to pay for survival."

"Yes," said Conan Lang. "Sure."

"Your results check out with mine?"

"Mostly. It's the same old story, Julio."

Conan Lang puffed slowly on his pipe, reconstructing what had happened. The new ricefruit had made it valuable for a family to hang on to one piece of land that could be used over and over again. But only a limited amount of the land could be used, because of natural factors like the presence or absence of available water. The families that had not taken the plunge right away were virtually excluded, and the society was divided into the landed and the landless. The landless gradually had to move farther and farther from the main village to find land upon which to grow the older type of ricefruit – sometimes their fields were so far away that they could not make the round trip in a single day. And they could not get too far away and start over, because of the tribal warfare that had broken out between villages now that valuable stores of ricefruit were there for the taking. The old joint family co-operation broke down, and slaves became economically feasible.

Now that the village need not be periodically moved, it too became valuable and so was strongly fortified for defense. One old chief, grown powerful with fields of the staple ricefruit, set himself up as a king and the other chiefs went to work in his fields.

Of course, Sirius Ten was still in transition. While the old patterns were being destroyed, new ones, less obvious to the untrained eye, were taking their place. Disintegration and reintegration marched hand in hand, but it would be tough on the natives for a while. Process Corps techniques had speeded up the action almost beyond belief, but from here on in the Oripesh were on their own. They would go on and on in their individual development – although no two peoples ever went through exactly the same stages at the same time, it was possible to predict a general planet-wide trend. The Oripesh would one day learn to write, since they already had a crude pictographic system for ritual use. When the contact finally came from the hostile stars in the future, what histories would they have written? Who would they remember, what would they forget? Would there be any twisted legend or myth left that recalled the long-ago time when the gods had come out of the mountains to change the lives of their people?

That was the way to look at it. Conan Lang tapped out his pipe on a rock. Just look at it like a problem, a textbook example. Forget about the people, the individuals you could not help, the lives you had made and the lives you had destroyed. Turn off that part of your mind and think in terms of the long-range good.

Or try to.

"We're all through here, Julio," Conan Lang said. "We can head for home now."

"Yes," said Julio Medina. "It has been a long time."

The two men sat silently in the darkness, each thinking his own thoughts, watching the yellow moon sail through silver stars.

After the patrol ship had been signaled, there was nothing to do but wait until their pickup could be coordinated with the time schedules of the other Corps men and the operational schedule of the star cruiser. Conan Lang busied himself with his reports while Julio sprawled in the shade and devised intricate and impossible card games with a battered deck that was old enough to be in itself of anthropological interest.

Conan Lang was playing a game, too. He played it with his mind and he was a somewhat unwilling participant. His mind had played the game before and he was tired of it, but there was nothing he could do about it. There wasn't any button that would turn his mind off, and while it was on it played games.

It was engaged in putting two and two together.

This was not in itself uncommon, although it was not as widespread as some people fondly imagined it to be. But Conan Lang played the game where others did not even see one, much less a set of twos with a relationship between them. There is nothing so hard to see as what is termed obvious after the fact. Conan Lang's mind had played with the obvious all his life; it would not let well enough alone. He didn't like it, there were times when he would have preferred to junk it all and go fishing without a thought in his head, but he was stuck with it. When his mind wanted to play the game, it played and that was that.

While he waited for the patrol ship, his mind was playing with a set of factors. There was the history of Earth, taken as a vast overall sequence. There were thinking machines, atomic power, and the field techniques of the Process Corps. There was the fact that Earth had no record of ever having been contacted by another world – they had always done the contacting themselves. There was the new principle that Admiral White had spoken to him about, the integration – acceleration factor for correlating data. There was the incredible, explosive energy of man that had hurled him light-years into space. There was his defiant heart that could tackle the prodigious job of reshaping a galaxy when the chips were down.

Conan Lang put two and two together, and he did not get four. He got five.

He didn't know the answers yet, but he knew enough to formulate the right questions. From past experience, he knew that that was the toughest part of the game. Incorrect answers were usually the products of off-center questions. Once you had the right question, the rest was a matter of time.

The patrol ship came for them finally, and Conan Lang and Julio Medina walked across the soil of Sirius Ten for the last time. They crossed the field where the green plants grew, and neither tried to say what was in his heart. Three had come and only two could leave. Andy Irvin had lived and worked and dreamed only to fall on an alien planet light-years away from earth that could have been his. He was part of the price that was exacted for survival – and he was also a kid with stars in his eyes who had gotten a rotten, senseless break.

After the patrol ship had gone, the green leaves of the ricefruit plants stretched hungrily up toward the flaming sun. The clean water chuckled along the irrigation trenches, feeding the roots in the field. Softly, as though sad with all the memories it carried, the lonesome breeze whispered through the empty hut that had housed the men from Earth.

VI

Through the trackless depths of interstellar space the star cruiser rode on the power from her atomics. The hum that filled the ship was a good sound, and she seemed to quiver with pride and impatience. It did make a difference which way you were going in space, and the ship was going home.

Conan Lang paced through the long white corridors and walked around the afterhold where the brown sacks of ricefruit had been. He read in the library and joked with the medics who had salvaged his burned body. And, always ahead of him, swimming in the great emptiness of space, were the faces of Kit and of his son, waiting for him, calling him home again.

Rob must have grown a lot, he thought. Soon, he wouldn't be a boy any longer – he would be a man, taking his place in the world. Conan remembered his son's voice from a thousand quiet talks in the cool air of evening, his quick, eager eyes –

Like Andy's.

"Dad, when I grow up can I be like you? Can I be an Agent and ride on the ships to other worlds and have a uniform and everything?"

What could you tell your son now that you had lived so long and were supposed to know so much? That life in the Process Corps filled a man with things that were perhaps better unknown? That the star trails were cold and lonely? That there were easier, more comfortable lives? All that was true; all the men who rode the ships knew it. But they knew, too, that for them this was the only life worth living.

The time passed slowly. Conan Lang was impatient to see his family again, anxious to get home. But his mind gave him no rest. There were things he had to know, things he *would* know before he went home to stay.

Conan Lang had the right questions now. He had the right questions, and he knew where the answers were hidden.

Fritz Gottleib.

The star cruiser had hardly touched Earth again at Space One before Conan Lang was outside on the duralloy tarmac. Since the movements of the star ships were at all times top-secret matters, there was no one at the port to greet him and for once Conan was glad to have a few extra hours to himself. Admiral White wouldn't expect him to check in until tomorrow anyway, and before he saw Kit he wanted to get things straight once and for all.

The friendly sun of Earth warmed him gently as he hurried across the tarmac and the air felt cool and fresh. He helped himself to an official bullet, rose into the blue sky, and jetted eastward over the city. His brain was seething and he felt cold sweat in the palms of his hands. What was it that Gottleib had said to him on that long-ago day?

"Sometimes it is best not to know the answers to one's questions, Dr. Lang."

Well, he was going to know the answers anyhow. All of them. He landed the bullet in the space adjoining the cybernetics building and hurried inside, flashing his identification as he went. He stopped at a switchboard and showed his priority credentials.

"Call the Nest, please," he told the operator. "Tell Dr. Gottleib that Conan Lang is down here and would like to see him."

The operator nodded and spoke into the intercom. There was a moment's delay, and then he took his earphones off and smiled at Conan Lang.

"Go right on up, Dr. Lang," the operator said. "Dr. Gottleib is expecting you.

Conan Lang controlled his astonishment and went up the lift and down the long white corridors. *Expecting* him? But that was impossible. No one even knew the star cruiser was coming back, much less that he was coming here to the Nest. Impossible –

All around him in the great building he felt the gigantic mechanical brain with its millions of circuits and flashing tubes. The brain crowded him, pressed him down until he felt tiny and insignificant. It hummed and buzzed through the great shielded walls.

Laughing at him.

Conan Lang pushed past the attendants and security men and opened the door of the Nest. He moved into the small, dark room and paused to allow his eyes to become accustomed to the dim light. The room was silent. Gradually, the shadow behind the desk took form and he found himself looking into the arctic eyes of Fritz Gottleib.

"Dr. Lang," he hissed softly. "Welcome to the Buzzard's Nest."

The man had not changed; he was timeless, eternal. He was still dressed in black and it might have been minutes ago instead of years when Conan Lang had last seen him. His black eyebrows slashed across his white face and his long-fingered hands were bent slightly like claws upon his desk.

"How did you know I was coming here?" Now that he was face-to-face with Gottleib, Conan Lang felt suddenly uncertain, unsure of himself.

"I know many things, Dr. Lang," Fritz Gottleib said sibilantly. "Had I cared to, I could have told you ten years ago the exact date, within a day or so, upon which we would have this meeting. I could even have told you what you would say when you came through the door, and what you are going to say five minutes from now."

Conan Lang just stared at him, feeling like an absurd little child who had presumed to wrestle a gorilla. His mind recoiled from the strange man before him and he knew at last that he knew nothing.

"I do not waste words, Dr. Lang," Gottleib said, his eyes cold and unmoving in his head. "You will remember that when we last met you said you wanted to ask some questions of the machine. Do you remember what I said, Dr. Lang?"

Conan Lang thought back across the years. *"Perhaps one day, Dr. Lang,"* Gottleib had said. *"When you are old like me."*

"Yes," said Conan Lang. "Yes, I remember."

"You were not ready then," Dr. Gottleib said, his white face ghostly in the dim light. "You could not even have framed the right questions, at least not all of them."

Conan Lang was silent. How much *did* Gottleib know? Was there anything he *didn't* know?

"You are old enough now," said Fritz Gottleib.

He turned a switch and the surface of his desk glowed with dull red light. His face, reflected in the flamelike glow, was unearthly. His cold eyes looked out of hell. He rose to his feet, seeming to loom larger than life, filling the room. Moving without a sound, he left the room, and the door clicked shut behind him.

Conan Lang was alone in the red room. His heart hammered in his throat and his lips were dry. He clenched his fists and swallowed hard. Alone –

Alone with the great machine.

Conan Lang steadied himself. Purposefully, he made himself go through the prosaic, regular motions of lighting up his pipe. The tobacco was healthily full-bodied and fragrant and it helped to relax him. He smoked slowly, taking his time.

The red glow from the desk filled the room with the color of unreality. Crimson shadows seemed to crouch in the corners with an impossible life of their own. But was anything impossible, here? Conan Lang felt the pulse of the great machine around him and wondered.

Trying to shake off a persistent feeling of dreamlike unreality,

Conan Lang moved around and sat down behind Gottleib's desk. The red panel was a maze of switches which were used to integrate it with technical panels in other sections of the building. In the center of the panel was a keyboard on an open circuit to the machine and set into the desk was a clear square like a very fine telescreen. Conan Lang noticed that there was nothing on Gottleib's desk that was not directly connected with the machine – no curios, no pictures, no paperweights, not a single one of the many odds and ends most men picked up for their desks during a long lifetime. The whole room was frightening in its very impersonality, as though every human emotion had been beaten out of it long ago and the room had been insulated against its return.

The machines never slept and the circuits were open. Conan Lang had only to ask and any question that could be answered would be answered. The red glow in the room reminded him of the fire and he shuddered a little in spite of himself. Had that really been over three years ago? How much had he learned in those three years when he had seen the Oripesh change before his eyes and had had time for once to really think his life through? How much did he still have to learn?

Conan Lang took a long pull on his pipe and set the desk panel for manual type questioning and visual screen reception. He hesitated a moment, almost afraid of the machine at his disposal. He didn't *want* to know, he suddenly realized. It wasn't like that. It was rather that he *had* to know.

Framing his words carefully, Conan Lang typed out the question that had been haunting him for years:

IS THE EARTH ITSELF THE SUBJECT OF PROCESS MANIPULATION?

He waited nervously, sure of the answer, but fearful of it nevertheless. There was a faint, all but inaudible, hum from the machine and Conan Lang could almost feel the circuits closing in the great walls around him. The air was filled with tension. There was a brief click and one word etched itself blackly on the clear screen:

YES.

Conan Lang leaned forward, sure of himself now, and typed out another question:

HOW LONG HAS THE EARTH BEEN MANIPULATED AND HAS THIS CONTROL BEEN FOR GOOD OR EVIL?

The machine hummed and answered at once:

THE EARTH HAS BEEN GUIDED SINCE EARTH YEAR NINE-

TEEN HUNDRED A.D. *THE SECOND PART OF YOUR QUESTION IS MEANINGLESS.*

Conan Lang hesitated, staggered in spite of himself by the information he was getting. Then he typed rapidly:

WITH REFERENCE TO GOOD, EQUATE SURVIVAL OF THE HUMAN RACE.

The screen clouded, cleared, and the words formed:

THE CONTROL HAS BEEN FOR GOOD.

Conan Lang's breathing was shallow now. He typed tensely:

HAS THIS CONTROL COME FROM WITHIN THIS GALAXY? IF SO, WHERE? IS THERE USUALLY AN AGENT OTHER THAN EARTH'S IN CHARGE OF THIS MACHINE?

The hum of the machine filled the bloodred room and the screen framed the answers:

THE CONTROL HAS COME FROM WITHIN THE GALAXY. THE SOURCE IS A WORLD KNOWN AS RERMA, CIRCLING A STAR ON THE EDGE OF THE GALAXY WHICH IS UNKNOWN TO EARTH. THE MAN KNOWN AS GOTTLEIB IS A RERMAN AGENT.

Conan Lang's pipe had been forgotten and gone out. He put it down and licked his dry lips. So far so good. But the one prime, all-important question had not yet been asked. He asked it:

IF THE PLAN IS FOLLOWED, WHAT WILL BE THE FINAL OUTCOME WITH RESPECT TO RERMA AND THE EARTH?

The machine hummed again in the red glow and the answer came swiftly, with a glorious, mute tragedy untold between its naked lines:

RERMA WILL BE DESTROYED. THE EARTH WILL SURVIVE IF THE PLAN IS CAREFULLY FOLLOWED.

Conan Lang felt tears in his eyes and he was unashamed. With time forgotten now, he leaned forward, asking questions, reading replies, as the terrible, wonderful story unfolded.

Far out on the edge of the galaxy, the ancient planet of Rerma circled her yellow sun. Life had evolved early on Rerma – had evolved early and developed fast. While the other humanoid peoples of the galaxy were living in caves, the Rerma were building a great civilization. When Earth forged its first metal sword, the Rerma split the atom.

Rerma was a world of science – true science. Science had eliminated war and turned the planet into a paradise. Literature and the arts flourished hand in hand with scientific progress, and scientists worked surrounded by cool gardens in which graceful fountains splashed and chuckled in the sun. Every man was free to develop himself as an individual and no man bent his head to any other man.

The Rerma were the human race in full flower.

But the Rerma were few, and they were not a warlike people. It was not that they would not fight in an emergency, but simply that they could not possibly win an extended encounter. Their minds didn't work that way. The Rerma had evolved to a point where they were too specialized, too well-adjusted to their environment.

And their environment changed.

It was only a question of time until the Rerma asked the right questions of their thinking machines and came up with the knowledge that their world, situated on the edge of the galaxy, was directly in the path of a coming cultural collision between two star systems. The Rerma fed in the data over and over again, and each time the great machines came up with the same answer.

Rerma would be destroyed.

It was too late for the equation to be changed with respect to Rerma – she had gone too far and was unfortunately located. But for the rest of the human race, scattered on the far-flung worlds that marched along the star trails, there was a chance. There was time for the equation to be changed for them – if only someone could be found to change it! For the Rerma had the knowledge, but they had neither the manpower nor the driving, defiant spirit to do the job themselves. They were capable of making heroic decisions and sticking by them, but the task of remolding a star system was not for them. That was a job for a young race, a proud and unconquerable race. That was a job for the men of Earth.

The ships of the Rerma found Earth in the earth year 1900. They knew that in order for their plan to succeed the Rerma must stand and fight on that distant day when galaxies collided, for their power was not negligible despite their lack of know-how for a long-range combat. They must stand and fight and be destroyed – the plan, the equation, was that finely balanced. Earth was the only other planet they found that was sufficiently advanced to work with, and it was imperative that Earth should not know that she was being manipulated. She must not suspect that her plans were not her own, for a young race with its pride wounded is a dubious ally and an ineffective fighting mechanism.

The Rerma set to work – willing even to die for a future they had already lived. The scientists of Rerma came secretly to Earth, and behind them, light-years away, their crystal fountains still sparkled sadly in the sun.

Rerma would be destroyed – but humanity would not die.

Conan Lang sat alone in the red room, talking to a machine. It was all clear enough, even obvious, once you knew the facts. Either there were no advanced races in the galaxy, which would account for Earth having no record of any contact – or else the Earth *had* been contacted secretly, been manipulated by the very techniques that she herself was later to use on undeveloped worlds.

He looked back on history. Such profound and important changes as the Neolithic food revolution and the steam engine had been produced by Earth alone, making her the most advanced planet in the galaxy except for the Rerma. Earth had a tradition of technological skill behind her, and she was young and pliable. The Rerma came – and the so-called world wars had followed. Why? Not to avenge the honor of insulted royalty, not because of fanatics, not because of conflicting creeds – but in a very real sense to save the world. The world wars had been fought to produce atomic power.

After 1900, the development of Earth had snowballed in a fantastic manner. The atom was liberated and man flashed upward to other planets of the solar system. Just as Conan Lang himself had worked through the ancestor gods of the Oripesh to bring about sweeping changes on Sirius Ten, the Rerma had worked through one of the gods of the Earthmen – the machine.

Cybernetics.

Man swept out to the stars, and the great thinking machines inevitably confronted them with the menace from beyond that drew nearer with each passing year. Young and proud, the men of Earth accepted the most astounding challenge ever hurled – they set out to reshape a galaxy to give their children and their children's children a chance for life.

And always, behind the scenes, beneath the headlines, were the ancient Rerma. They subtly directed and hinted and helped. With a selflessness unmatched in the universe, these representatives of a human race that had matured too far prepared Earth for galactic leadership – and themselves for death on the edge of the galaxy. They had unified Earth and pushed and prodded her along the road to survival.

When the Rerma could have fled and purchased extra time for themselves, they chose instead – these peace-loving people – to fight for another chance for man.

* * *

Conan Lang looked up, startled, to find the black figure of Fritz Gottleib standing by his side. He looked old, very old, in the bloodred light and Conan Lang looked at him with new understanding. Gottleib's impatience with others and the vast, empty loneliness in those strange eyes – all that was meaningful now. What a life that man had led on Earth, Conan Lang thought with wonder. Alone, wanting friendship and understanding – and having always to discourage close personal contacts, having always to fight his lonely battle alone in a sterile little room, knowing that the very men he had dedicated his life to help laughed behind his back and compared him to a bird of prey.

"I've been a fool, sir," Conan Lang said, getting to his feet. "We've all been fools."

Fritz Gottleib sat down again behind his desk and turned the machine off. The red glow vanished and they were left in the semi-darkness.

"Not fools, Dr. Lang," he said. "It was necessary for you to feel as you did. The feelings of one old man – what are they worth in this game we are playing? We must set our sights high, Dr. Lang."

Conan Lang waited in the shadows, thinking, watching the man who sat across from him as though seeing him for the first time. His mind was still groping, trying to assimilate all he had learned. It was a lot to swallow in a few short hours, even when you were prepared for it beforehand by guesswork and conjecture. There were still questions, of course, many questions. He knew that he still had much to learn.

"Why me?" Conan Lang asked finally. "Why have I been told all this? Am I the only one who knows?"

Fritz Gottleib shook his head, his face ghost-white in the darkened room. "There are others who know," he said sibilantly. "Your superior officer, Nelson White, has known for years of course. You were told because you have been selected to take over his command when he retires. If you are willing, you will work very closely with him here on Earth for the next five years, and then you will be in charge."

"Will I . . . leave Earth again?"

"Not for a long time, Dr. Lang. The integration-acceleration principle will keep you busy – we are in effect lifting Earth another stage and the results will be far-reaching. But you will be home, Dr. Lang – home with your family and your people.

"That is all, Dr. Lang," Gottleib hissed.

Conan Lang hesitated. "I'll do my level best," he said finally. "Good-bye, sir . . . I'll see you again."

Conan Lang put out his hand to the man he had called the Buzzard and Gottleib shook it with a firm, powerful grip.

"Good-bye, Conan," Fritz Gottleib said softly.

Conan Lang turned and walked from the dark room, leaving the man from Rerma sitting alone in the shadows of the Nest.

The little bullet rose vertically on her copter blades through the evening sky, hovered a moment in the cool air under the frosty stars, and then flashed off on her jets into the west. Conan Lang set the controls and leaned back in the seat, at peace with himself at last. There *was* meaning to it all, there was a purpose – and Andy and all the others like him on the far trails had not sacrificed their lives for nothing.

Conan Lang breathed the clean air of Earth and smiled happily. Ahead of him, waiting for him, were Kit and Rob, and he would never have to leave them again. He opened the lateral ports and let the wind hurl itself at his face.

Sail the Tide of Mourning

RICHARD A. LUPOFF

Richard A. Lupoff (1935–) is an editor, critic, historian of popular culture, and writer – the author of twenty SF and fantasy novels and more than a hundred short stories. The extraordinary scope of his career encompasses novels and stories in every sub-genre of science fiction and fantasy, as well as a series of mystery novels. Notable works include *Sword of the Demon* (1977), a fantastic novel based on Japanese mythology: *Space War Blues* (1978), his experimental SF novel of race war in space, of which "Sail the Tide of Mourning" became a segment; and *Lovecraft's Book* (1985), a fiction adventure featuring H. P. Lovecraft, detective. Indeed, one of the hallmarks of his career is that no two Lupoff works are alike. The result is, as *The Encyclopedia of Science Fiction* says, "it is at times difficult, in spite of his clear and abundant intelligence, to identify a unique Richard A. Lupoff voice."

This story has resonances with the work of Cordwainer Smith, interesting echoes that give some evidence of the inner conversations among texts that are the very nature of a literary genre. The link between mysteries of the psyche and space travel is an enduring one in genre science fiction.

Nurundere, captain, ordered his lighter to be hauled from the storage deck of *Djanggawul* and fitted for use of Jiritzu. Sky heroes bent their efforts, sweat glistening on black skin, dirt of labor staining white duck trousers and grip-soled shoes.

Much thought was given to their work and the reasons for it

although little was said of the matter. The people of Yurakosi were not
given greatly to speech: a taciturnity, self-containment, was part of the
heritage of their race, from the days of their desert isolation in the
heartland of Australia, O'Earth.

They alone of the scattered children of Sol carried the gene that let
them sail the membrane ships. They alone carried in their skin the
pigment that filtered out the deadly radiation of the tracks between the
stars, that permitted them to clamber up masts and through rigging as
had their ancestors on the pacific waters of O'Earth centuries before,
while spacemen of other breeds clumped and heaved about in their
massive vacuum armor.

The brilliant light of the multiple star Yirrkalla wheeled overhead;
Djanggawul had completed her great tack and pointed her figureheaded
prow toward home, toward Yurakosi, bearing the melancholy tale of
her voyage to N'Jaja and N'Ala and the death of a passenger, Ham
Tamdje of N'Jaja, at the hands of the sky hero Jiritzu.

Djanggawul bore yet the scars of the attempt by surner meat to seize
control of the membrane ship and force from her crew the secret of
their ability to live unsuited in space. At N'Ala she had shuttled the
surviving surners to the orbiting Port Corley, along with the bodies of
those killed in the mutiny.

And now, passing the great tack at Yirrkalla, *Djanggawul* heeled
beneath the titanic solar wind that would fill all sails that bellied out
from the rows of masts on her three flat decks. With each moment the
ship gained momentum. Under the careful piloting of her first officer
Uraroju she would sail to Yurakosi on this momentum and on the
force of the interstellar winds she encountered on her great arcing
course. There would be no need to start her auxiliary engines, to anni-
hilate any of the precious rod of collapsed matter that hung suspended
through the long axis of *Djanggawul,* where it provided the artificial
gravity for the ship.

Sky heroes swarmed the storage deck of the ship, readying
Nurundere's lighter for Jiritzu. They fitted the tiny ship with food
concentrate, tested her recyclers, tried her hinged mast fittings, and
clamped the masts to the hull of the lighter in anticipation of her cata-
pulting from the deck of *Djanggawul.*

When the lighter was fully prepared, the sky hero Baime went to
Djanggawul's bridge to inform Nurundere and Uraroju. Others in the
work party hauled the lighter from its place in the storage deck, refixed
the now vacant moorings that had held the lighter, and worked the
tiny ship through a great cargo hatch onto the main deck of *Djanggawul.*

High above the deck Jiritzu stood balanced lightly on a spar near the top of a mainmast. He was dressed like any sky hero of the crew of *Djanggawul,* in white trousers and canvas shoes, black knitted cap and turtleneck sweater, the costume declared by Yurakosi tradition to have been the costume of the sky heroes' ancestors on O'Earth.

A tiny radio had been implanted behind one ear, and strapped to his thigh was a close-air generator. The oxygen-rich mixture that it slowly emitted clung to Jiritzu, providing him with the air he needed for breath, insulating him from the extreme temperatures of space, providing an invisible pressure suit that protected him from the vacuum all around.

He watched the cargo hatch roll slowly back onto the deck beneath him, the one of *Djanggawul*'s three identical outer decks most easily accessible from the lighter's storage place, and watched his fellow sky heroes haul the lighter onto the deck. He kept his radio turned off, and by tacit agreement no man or woman of *Djanggawul*'s crew, not even Jiritzu's kunapi half Dua, approached the mast he had climbed or made any sign of knowing of his presence.

Nurundere himself strode from the bridge of his ship to inspect the lighter, now standing empty on the deck. Jiritzu could tell him easily, not merely by his distinctive cap of white with its wide black band, but by his pale skin, the protective pigmentation of the Yurakosi almost totally faded now, whited out by the passing years and long exposure to the radiation of the naked stars.

Soon Nurundere would have to return to Yurakosi himself, give himself over to the life of a ground squirmer, crawl with the small children and the old men and women of Yurakosi, the only inhabitants of the planet whose able sons and daughters were desperately needed to sail the membrane ships between the stars.

Not so Jiritzu.

Again and again his mind flashed to the terrible scene inside the passenger tank of *Djanggawul,* the moments when the surner meat, the passengers whose payments financed the flights of the membrane ships and filled the coffers of the sky heroes' home planet, had shown firearms – an act unknown on the peaceful, neutral ships – and had briefly imprisoned much of the crew.

Again Jiritzu relived the horror of finding his betrothed, Miralaidj, daughter of Wuluwaid and Bunbulama, dead at the hand of Ham Tamdje.

Again Jiritzu relived the pleasure, the terrible pleasure of killing Ham Tamdje himself, with his bare hands. At the thought he felt sweat burst from his face and hands. His legs, where a bullet fired by Ham Tamdje had torn the flesh, throbbed with pain.

He closed his eyes tightly, turned his face from the deck below him to the blackness above, reopened his eyes.

Above him gleamed the constellation Yirrkalla, beneath which *Djanggawul* had made her great tack. The colored stars formed the facial features of the Rainbow Serpent: the pale, yellow-green eyes, the angry white nostrils, the bloodred venomous fangs. And beyond Yirrkalla, fading, fading across the immensity of the heavens, the body of the Rainbow Serpent himself, writhing and curving across the void that separated galaxies.

A drop of sweat fell from Jiritzu's forehead, rolled to the edge of one eye where it stung like a tiny insect, then rolled on, enlarged by a tear.

He looked downward, saw that the work on the deck was completed, the lighter ready for his use. With heavy heart he lowered himself slowly to the deck of *Djanggawul,* avoiding the acrobatic tumbles that had been his great joy since his earliest days on the membrane ships.

He walked slowly across the deck of the great ship, halted before the captain's lighter. A party of sky heroes had assembled at the lighter. Jiritzu examined their faces, found in them a mixture of sadness at the loss of a friend and fellow and resignation at what they knew would follow.

Nurundere was there himself. The captain of *Djanggawul* opened his arms, facing directly toward Jiritzu. He moved his lips in speech, but Jiritzu left his implanted radio turned off. The meaning of Nurundere was clear without words.

Jiritzu came to his captain. They embraced. Jiritzu felt the strong arms of the older man clasp about his shoulders. Then he was released, stepped back.

Beside Nurundere stood Uraroju, first officer of *Djanggawul.* Some junior officer, then, had been left upon the bridge. Uraroju was a younger person than Nurundere, her protective pigmentation still strong, barely beginning to white out; she would have many years before her as a sky hero, would surely become captain of *Djanggawul* with Nurundere's retirement to Yurakosi.

They embraced, Jiritzu for a moment closing his eyes, permitting himself to pretend that Uraroju was his own mother, that he was visiting his old people in their town of Kaitjouga on Yurakosi. The warmth of Uraroju, the feel of her womanhood, comforted Jiritzu. Then they released each other, and he turned to other men and women he would never again see, men and women who must return to Yurakosi with the tale of the tragic things that had transpired between Port Upatoi and Yirrkalla on the outward leg of their sail, and with the tale of the end of Jiritzu.

Watilun he embraced, Watilun the machinist and hero of the battle against the mutineers.

Baime he embraced, a common sailor, Jiritzu's messmate.

Kutjara he embraced, Kutjara with whom he had often swarmed the lines of *Djanggawul*.

Only Dua, kunapi half to Jiritzu of the aranda, spoke in their parting embrace. Radios mute, Dua spoke in the moments when his close-air envelope and that of Jiritzu were merged, when common speech could be carried without electronic aid.

"Bidjiwara is not here," Dua said. None but Jiritzu could hear this. "The loss of her aranda half Miralaidj is too great for little Bidjiwara to bear. The loss of yourself, Jiritzu, is too great for Bidjiwara. She remains below, weeping alone.

"I too have wept for you, my aranda half, but I could not remain below. I could not forego our parting time."

He kissed Jiritzu on the cheek, his lips brushing the *marajin*, the swirling scarifications born by all kunapi and aranda, whose meaning he, Dua alone of all Jiritzu's shipmates, understood.

Jiritzu clasped both Dua's hands in his own, saying nothing. Then he turned away and went to inspect the lighter given him by Nurundere. He found all in order, climbed upon the deck of the tiny membrane craft, signaled to the sky heroes on *Djanggawul*'s deck.

Watilun himself operated the catapult.

Jiritzu found himself cast from *Djanggawul*, forward and upward from her deck, the distance between the great membrane ship and tiny lighter growing with each moment. He sighed only once, then turned to the task of sailing his new ship.

Above him lay the writhing length of the Rainbow Serpent. By conference with Nurundere and Uraroju over many days it had been settled that Jiritzu would not return with *Djanggawul* to Yurakosi. His act in killing Ham Tamdje was understood. There was no question of trial, no accusation, or even suggestion of crime.

But the tradition of the sky-hero peoples held sacred any passenger on the membrane ships.

Death of meat, membrane-ship passengers, ground squirmers traveling between the stars in the tanks of sky-hero craft instead of sealed in the bellies of massive conventional spacecraft, was almost unknown. There was the half-legendary story of Elyun El-Kumarbis, traveler from the pan-semite empire of O'Earth sailing aboard *Makarata* to Al-ghoul Phi, who had passed as a sky hero and died of space radiation, his body later launched into deep space at his dying request.

And there was the new tragedy of Ham Tamdje and his killer Jiritzu, who could never again be permitted to ride the membrane ships as a sky hero.

Beneath Jiritzu and the lighter, *Djanggawul* dwindled, her great membrane ships bellied out with starwinds, her golden skin reflecting the multicolored lights of the Yirrkalla constellation.

And above Jiritzu, Yirrkalla itself, the serpent face, leering and glowing its brightness.

He erected the masts of the lighter, fixed their bases on the three equilaterally mounted decks of the lighter, climbed each mast in turn, rotating gimbaled spars into position and locking them perpendicular to the masts. The sails, the fine, almost monomolecular membranes that would catch the starwinds and carry the lighter onward, he left furled for the time being.

From the top of a mast he pushed himself gently, parallel with the deck of the lighter. He floated softly to the deck, landing with bent knees to absorb the light impact of his lean frame on the lighter's deck.

He opened the hatch and crawled into the cramped interior of the lighter to check the instruments and supplies he knew were there – the compact rations, the lighter's multiradiational telescope that he would bring with him to the deck and mount for use, the lighter's miniature guidance computer.

Instead, before even switching on the cabin light, he saw two brief reflections of the colored illumination of Yirrkalla – what he knew must be two eyes.

He flicked on his implanted radio and demanded to know the identity of the stowaway.

"Don't be angry, Jiritzu," her voice quivered, "I had to come along."

"Bidjiwara!" he cried.

She launched herself across the cabin, crossing it in an easy, gliding trajectory. She caught his hand in her two, brought it to her face, pressed his palm to the *marajin*, the graceful scarifications on her cheek.

"Don't be angry with me," she repeated.

He felt himself slump to the deck of the cabin, sitting with his back to the bulkhead, the hatchway leading to the outer deck overhead, light pouring in. He shook himself, turned to look into the face of

Bidjiwara, young Bidjiwara, she who was barely entering womanhood, whose voyage on *Djanggawul* was her first as a sky hero, her first offplanet, her first away from Yurakosi.

"Angry? Angry?" Jiritzu repeated stupidly. "No, Bidjiwara, my – my dear Bidjiwara." He brought his face close to hers, felt as she cupped his cheeks in the palms of her hands.

He shook his head. "I couldn't be angry with you. But do you understand? Do you know where this little ship is bound?"

Suddenly he pulled away from her grasp, sprang back to the deck of the lighter, sighted back in the direction of *Djanggawul*. Could he see her as a distant speck? Was that the great membrane ship – or a faint, remote star?

His radio was still on. He stood on the lighter's deck, shouted after *Djanggawul* and her crew. "Dua! Nurundere! Uraroju!"

There was no answer, only a faint, random crackling in his skull, the signals of cosmic radio emanations broadcast by colliding clouds of interstellar gas.

He dropped back through the hatch, into the cabin of the lighter.

He reached for Bidjiwara, took her extended hand, drew her with him back onto the deck of the lighter.

"You know why I am here," he said, half in question, half assertion.

She nodded, spoke softly a word in confirmation.

Still, he said, "I will die. I am here to die."

She made no answer, stood with her face to his sweater, her hands resting lightly against his shoulders. He looked down at her, saw how thin her body was, the contours of womanhood but barely emergent from the skinny, sticklike figure of the boisterous child his dead Miralaidj had loved as a little sister.

Jiritzu felt tears in his eyes.

"I could not go back to Yurakosi," he said. "I am a young man, my skin still fine and black, protecting me from the poison of the stars. I could not become a squirmer, alone in a world of children and ancients.

"I would have thrown myself with all my strength from the top of *Djanggawul's* highest mast. I would have escaped the ship, fallen forever through space like the corpse of El-Kumarbis.

"Nurundere said no." Jiritzu stopped, looked down at Bidjiwara, at her glossy, midnight hair spilling from beneath her knitted cap, her black, rounded forehead. For a moment he bent and pressed his cheek against the top of her head, then raised his eyes again to the Rainbow Serpent and spoke.

"Nurundere gave me his own ship, his captain's lighter. 'Take the lighter, Jiritzu,' he said. 'I can unload at Port Bralku with the others, by shuttle. I need no glorious captain's barge. Sail on forever,' Nurundere said, 'a better fate than the one awaiting me.'

"You understand, Bidjiwara? I mean to sail the Rainbow Serpent, the tide that flows between the galaxies. I will sail as long as the rations aboard last. I will die on this little ship, my soul will return to the Dreamtime, my body will continue onward, borne by the Rainbow Serpent.

"I will never become a ground crawler. I will never return to Yurakosi. No world will know my tread – ever."

Bidjiwara turned her face, raising her eyes from Jiritzu's ribbed sweater to look directly into his eyes.

"Very well, Jiritzu. I will sail the Rainbow Serpent with you. Where else was there for me to go?"

Jiritzu laughed bitterly. "You are a child. You should have remained aboard *Djanggawul.* You had many years before you as a sky hero. Look at your skin," he said, raising her hand to hold it before them both. No power lights were burning on the little ship, but the colors of Yirrkalla glowed white, green-yellow, bloodred.

"Black, Bidjiwara, black with the precious shield that only our people claim."

"And your own?" she responded.

"My own pigment – yes, I too would have had many more years to play at sky hero. But I killed Ham Tamdje. I broke the sacred trust. I could sail the great membrane ships no longer."

He dropped her hand and walked a few paces away. He stood, his back half-turned to her, and his words were carried to her by the tiny radios implanted in both their skulls.

"And Miralaidj," he almost whispered, "Miralaidj – in the Dreamtime. And her father Wuluwaid in the Dreamtime. No."

He turned and looked upward through naked spars to the glowing stars of Yirrkalla and the Rainbow Serpent. "We should set to work rigging sails," he said.

"I *will* stay with you then," she said. "You will not send me away, send me back."

"Dua knew you were hidden?"

She nodded yes.

"My closest friend, my half, kunapi to my aranda. Dua told me a lie."

"I begged him, Jiritzu."

For a moment he almost glared at her, anger filling his face. "Why do you wish to die?"

She shook her head. "I wish to be with you."

"You will die with me."

"I will return to the Dreamtime with you."

"You believe the old stories."

She shrugged. "We should set to work rigging sails." And scurried away, flung open lockers, drew out furled sheets of nearly monomolecular membrane, scampered up a mast and began fixing the sail to spars.

Jiritzu stood on the deck, watching. Then he crossed to another of the lighter's three equilateral decks and followed the example of Bidjiwara.

He worked until he had completed the rigging of the masts of the deck, then crossed again, to the third of the lighter's decks, opened a locker, drew membrane and clambered to the top of a mast. There he clung, knees gripping the vertical shaft, arms flung over the topmost spar, rigging the sail.

He completed the work, looked across to the farthermost mast, near the stern of the lighter. The Rainbow Serpent drew a gleaming polychromatic backdrop. The mast was silhouetted against the Serpent, and standing on the highest spar, one hand outstretched clinging to the mast, the other arm and leg extended parallel to the spar, was Bidjiwara.

Her envelope of close air shimmered with refraction of the colors of Yirrkalla. Jiritzu clung to the rigging where he had worked, struck still and silent by the beauty of the child. He wondered why she did not see him, then gradually realized, aided by the misty sidereal light of the region, that she stood with her back to him, her face raised to the great tide that flowed between the galaxies, her mind wholly unconcerned with her surroundings and unaware of his presence.

Jiritzu lowered himself silently through the spars and rigging of the lighter, through a hatchway and into the tiny cabin of the lighter. There he prepared a light meal and set it aside, lay down to rest and waited for the return of Bidjiwara.

He may have dozed and seen into the Dreamtime, for he saw the figures of Miralaidj and her father Wuluwaid floating in a vague jumble of shapes and slow, wavering movement. He opened his eyes and saw Bidjiwara lower herself through the hatchway into the cabin, white rope-soled shoes first, white duck trousers clinging close to her long skinny legs and narrow hips, then her black ribbed sweater.

"Our ship has no name," she said.

He pondered for a moment, shrugged, said, "Does it need one?"

"It would be – somehow I think we would be more with our people," Bidjiwara replied.

"Well, if you wish. What shall we make her name?"

"You have no choice?"

"None."

"We will truly sail on the great tide? On the Rainbow Serpent?"

"We are already."

"Then I would call our ship after the sacred fish. Let it bear us to the Dreamtime."

"Baramundi."

"Yes."

"As you wish."

She came and sat by him, her hands folded in her lap. She sat silently.

"Food is ready," he said.

She looked at the tiny table that served in the lighter as work space, desk, and dining table. Jiritzu saw her smile, wondered at the mixture in her face of little child and wise woman. She looked somehow as he thought the Great Mother must look, if only he believed in the Great Mother.

Bidjiwara crossed the small distance and brought two thin slices of hot biscuit. She held them both to Jiritzu. He took one, pressed the other back upon her.

Silently they ate the biscuit.

Afterward she said, "Jiritzu, is there more to do now?"

He said, "We should check our position." He undogged the ship's telescope and carried it to the deck of *Baramundi*.

Bidjiwara helped him to mount it on the gimbaled base that stood waiting for it. Jiritzu sighted on the brightest star in Yirrkalla for reference – it was a gleaming crimson star that marked the end of a fang in the serpent face, that Yurakosi tradition called Blood of Hero.

On the barrel of the telescope where control squares were mounted he tapped all of the radiational senors into life, to cycle through filters and permit the eyepiece to observe the Rainbow Serpent by turns under optical, radio, x-ray, gamma radiation.

He put his eye to the eyepiece and watched the Serpent as it seemed to move with life, its regions responding to the cycling sensitivity of the telescope.

He drew away and Bidjiwara put her eye to the telescope, standing transfixed for minutes until at last she too drew away and turned to Jiritzu.

"The Serpent truly lives," she said. "Is it – a real creature?"

Jiritzu shook his head. "The tides of the galaxies draw each other. The Serpent is a flow of matter. Stars, dust, gas. To ride with it would mean a journey of billions of years to reach the next of its kind. To sail the starwinds that fill the Rainbow Serpent, we will reach marvelous speed. As long as we can sail our craft, we can tack from wind to wind.

"And once we have gone to the Dreamtime, *Baramundi* will float on, on the tide, along the Rainbow Serpent. Someday she may beach on some distant shore."

He looked at Bidjiwara, smiled, repeated his statement.

Bidjiwara replied, "And if she does not?"

"Then she may be destroyed in some way, or simply – drift forever. Forever."

Jiritzu saw the girl stretch and yawn. She crossed the cabin and drew him down alongside the bulkhead, nestled up to him and went to sleep.

He lay with her in his arms, wondering at her trust, watching the play of sidereal light that reflected through the hatchway and illuminated her face dimly.

He extended one finger and gently, gently traced the *maraiin* on her cheek, wondering at its meaning. He pressed his face to her head again, pulled away her knitted cap and let her hair tumble loose, feeling its softness with his own face, smelling the odor of her hair.

He too slept.

They awoke together, stirring and stretching and looked into each other's face and laughed. They used the lighter's sanitary gear and nibbled a little breakfast and went on deck. Together they checked *Baramundi*'s rigging, took sightings with her multiradiational telescope, and fed information into her little computer.

The computer offered course settings in tiny, glowing display lights and Jiritzu and Bidjiwara reset *Baramundi*'s sails.

They sat on deck, bathed in the perpetual twilight of the Rainbow Serpent's softly glowing colors.

They spoke of their childhoods on Yurakosi, of their old people, their skins whited out by years of sailing the membrane ships, retired to the home planet to raise the children while all the race's vigorous adults crewed the great ships, sailed between the stars carrying freight and occasional passengers sealed inside their hulls, laughing at the clumsy craft and clumsy crews of all others than the aranda and the kunapi.

They climbed through the rigging of *Baramundi*, shinnying up masts lightly, balancing on spars, occasionally falling – or leaping – from the ship's heights, to drop gently, gently back onto her deck.

They ate and drank the smallest amounts they could of the lighter's provisions, tacitly stretching the supplies as far as they could be stretched, carefully recycling to add still more to the time they could continue.

They lay on *Baramundi*'s deck sometimes, when the rest time they had agreed upon came, Bidjiwara nestling against the taller Jiritzu, falling asleep as untroubledly as a young child, Jiritzu wondering over and over at this girl who had come to die with him, who asked few questions, who lived each hour as if it were the beginning of a long and joyous life rather than the final act of a tragedy.

Jiritzu felt very old.

He was nearly twenty by the ancient, arbitrary scale of age carried to the star worlds from O'Earth, the scale of the seasons and the years in old Arnhem Land in the great desert of their ancestral home. Six years older than Bidjiwara, he had traveled the star routes for five, had sailed the membrane ships across tens of billions of miles in that time.

And Bidjiwara asked little of him. They were more playmates than – than anything else, he thought.

"Tell me of El-Kumarbis," she said one day, perched high on a spar above *Baramundi*'s deck.

"You know all about him," Jiritzu replied.

"Where is he now?"

Jiritzu shrugged, exasperated. "Somewhere beyond Al-ghoul, no one knows where. He was buried in space."

"What if we find his body?" Bidjiwara shivered.

"Impossible."

"Why?"

"In infinite space? What chance that two objects moving at random will collide?"

"No?"

He shook his head.

"Could the computer find him?"

He shrugged. "If we knew exactly when he was buried, and where, and his trajectory and speed and momentum . . . No, it's still impossible."

"Dinnertime," she said. "You wait here, I'll fix it."

She came back with the customary biscuits and a jar filled with dark fluid. Jiritzù took the jar, held it high against the ambient light – they seldom used any of *Baramundi*'s power lights.

"Wine," Bidjiwara said.

He looked amazed.

"I found a few capsules in the ship's supplies. You just put one in some water."

They ate and drank. The wine was warm, its flavor soft. They sprawled on the deck of *Baramundi* after the biscuits were gone, passing the jar back and forth, slowly drinking the wine.

When it was gone Bidjiwara nestled against Jiritzu; for once, instead of sleeping she lay looking into his face, holding her hands to the sides of his head.

She said his name softly, then flicked off her radio and pressed her lips close to his neck so their air envelopes were one, the sound carried directly from her lips to his ear, and whispered his name again.

"Bidjiwara," he said, "you never answered why you came on board *Baramundi.*"

"To be with you, Jiritzu," she said.

"Yes, but why? Why come to die with me?"

"Tall Jiritzu," she said, "strong Jiritzu. You saw me aboard *Djanggawul,* you were kind to me but as you are kind to children. Men never know, only women know love."

He laughed, not cruelly. "You're only – "

"A woman," she said.

"And you want – ?"

Now she laughed at him. "You man, you mighty man. You don't understand that all men are the children of women."

She drew away from him, slid her black ribbed sweater over her head and dropped it to the deck. He put his hands onto her naked back, trembling, then slowly slid them around her, touching her little, half-developed breasts, fondling her soft nipples with his hands.

She buried her forehead in the side of his neck, whispered against his throat, "For this, Jiritzu, I came aboard *Baramundi* for this."

He ran his thumbs down her breastbone, to her navel, to her white duck trousers, and peeled them down, and took her.

And the next day they were nearly out of biscuit and they went on half rations to make their supplies last longer.

They played children's games, shouting and chasing each other up and down the lighter's masts.

They leaped and sailed from the decks, past the membrane sails, into the emptiness, then hung for a moment and fell back, gently, to *Baramundi*.

Jiritzu leaped too hard, too high, and feared that he had broken from the ship. He looked up – down – into the coils of the Rainbow Serpent. He felt himself revolving slowly, helplessly hanging in the emptiness, alone and unshielded except by the close air his generator made and the protection of the pigment he carried in his skin.

He thought to cry for help, then held back. If he was afloat, Bidjiwara could not help him. He turned slowly, facing toward *Baramundi*, her membranes bellied with stellar wind, her deck reflecting the lights of the Serpent; he could not see Bidjiwara.

He turned slowly, facing toward the Rainbow Serpent, feeling as if he could fall forever into its colored bands, its long coils stretching no lesser distance than the span between galaxies.

He turned slowly, revolving on the axis of his own body, feeling no motion himself but watching the stars and the Serpent and *Baramundi* the sacred fish revolve slowly around him, wheeling, wheeling, when his out-flung arm struck an object as hard and cold as the ultimate ice of a dead-star world.

He recoiled, spun involuntarily, stared.

It was – yes.

He looked back toward *Baramundi*, revolved using his own limbs as counterweights, placed himself between the corpse and the lighter, and pressed gently with the soles of his rope-soled shoes against the hard, frigid corpse.

Slowly he drifted back toward *Baramundi* – and, wheeling again as he drifted, saw the corpse drifting away, upward or downward into the lights of the Rainbow Serpent.

As he approached *Baramundi* he pondered whether or not to tell Bidjiwara of his find. Finally he told her – the incredible happenstance had occurred.

Later they crept to the farthermost deck for their loving, then back into the tiny cabin to sleep.

And soon *Baramundi*'s supplies were exhausted, and still Jiritzu and Bidjiwara continued. Their water remained, and a few of the capsules. They had wine from time to time. They gave less effort to running the ship, ceased to play in the rigging, ceased to leap.

The wound in Jiritzu's leg resumed its throbbing intermittently. He would rub it, or Bidjiwara would rub it for him, and the pain would ease.

They made love, it seemed, with increasing frequency. The sensations of their couplings seemed to increase as lack of nourishment drew their bodies ever tighter, ever more acutely into awareness of each other.

They lay together most of the time, seldom dressing fully.

They drank water only, their wine capsules exhausted.

They slept increasingly.

In *Baramundi*'s cabin Jiritzu fed telescopic data into the lighter's computer, read the responses displayed on its little illuminated screen. After the acclimatization of his eyes to none but sidereal light, even the miniature display lights were dazzling: his eyes pulsed with after-images for minutes following the exercise.

It was difficult to climb from the cabin back onto the deck.

Bidjiwara waited for him there, barefoot, sitting on the deck with her wrists clasped around her knees, wearing only her white trousers and black knitted cap. She smiled a welcome to him, asked a question wordlessly.

"Here," he said with a shrug. "Here is where we are. As we have been. Riding the Rainbow Serpent. Riding the tide. Sailing the starwinds."

He felt dizzy for a moment, reached out with one hand to steady himself against the telescope mount, then sank to a squat beside Bidjiwara.

She put her arms around him and he lay on the deck, his head in her lap. He looked up into her face. She was Bidjiwara the lovely child, Miralaidj her aranda half, she was Jiritzu's own mother on Yurakosi, the Great Mother.

He opened and closed his eyes, unable to tell which woman this was.

He reached and traced the *maraiin* on her cheek.

She nodded, began speaking softly, telling him the meaning of the scarifications.

When she had finished he took her hand, held it against his chest, and slowly told her the meaning of his own *maraiin*. He spoke with closed eyes, opened them when he felt a drop of wetness, saw her weeping softly, drew her face down to his own to kiss.

She lay down beside him and they embraced gently, then both slept.

After that they paid less attention to *Baramundi*'s needs. Jiritzu and Bidjiwara grew weaker. They slept more, confined their activity to occasional short walks on *Baramundi*'s decks. Both of them grew thinner, lighter. Their growing weakness seemed almost to be offset by the decreasing demands of the ship's artificial gravity.

They lay on deck for hours, watching the glow of the Rainbow Serpent. They were far beyond the Serpent's head now, the stars of Yirrkalla clustered now into a meaningless sparkler jumble far, far astern of *Baramundi*.

Jiritzu was awake, had taken a sparse sip of their little remaining water, left Bidjiwara to doze where she lay, her hair a mourning wreath circling her emaciated features. Jiritzu made his way unsteadily to the prow of *Baramundi*, bracing himself against masts and small stanchions as he walked.

He sighted through the ship's telescope, enjoying in a faint, detached manner the endless, kaleidoscopic changes of the Rainbow Serpent's multiradiational forms. At length he turned away from the scope and looked back toward Bidjiwara. He could not tell if she was breathing. He could not tell for a certainty who she was.

He returned to the telescope, tapped its power squares to cause it to superimpose its multiple images rather than run them in sequence. He gazed, rapt, at the Serpent for a time, then swung the scope overhead, sweeping back and forth across the sky above *Baramundi*.

He settled on a black speck that floated silhouetted against the glow of the Serpent. For a while he watched it grow larger.

He turned from the telescope back to the deck of the lighter. Bidjiwara had wakened and risen; she was walking slowly, slowly toward him.

In the glow of the Rainbow Serpent her emaciation was transformed to a fine perception that etched every line, every muscle beneath her skin. She wore sweater and trousers; Jiritzu could see her high breasts, the ribbed sweater conforming to their sharp grace, her nipples standing as points of reference for the beauty of her torso.

Her white trousers managed to retain their fit despite her starvation; Jiritzu discerned the lines of her thighs, the pubic swell over her crotch.

Her face, always thin, seemed all vertical planes now, forehead and temple, nostril and cheek. The ridges of her brows, the lines of her mouth were as if drawn on her face.

Her eyes seemed to have gained an intense brightness.

As she crossed the deck to Jiritzu she gained in strength and steadiness. She held her hands toward him, smiling, and he felt his own strength returning to him. He took the steps needed to come to her, reached and took her two hands, clasped them in his. They embraced, calling each other's name.

The dark figure of Elyun El-Kumarbis dropped onto the deck of *Baramundi*. He strode to Jiritzu and Bidjiwara.

"Lovers!" he said. "Sky heroes!"

They turned to him, arms still around each other. Each extended a hand to him, felt his: cold, cold.

"All my years," the O'Earther said, "I wanted no thing but to sail a membrane ship. To be a sky hero."

"Yes," Jiritzu said, "you are known to all sky heroes, Elyun El-Kumarbis. Your fame spans the galaxy."

"And where do you sail, sky heroes?"

"We sail the tide, we sail the Rainbow Serpent."

"Aboard your ship?"

"*Baramundi* has brought us this far, but no farther. It is fit now for us to return to the Dreamtime."

Elyun El-Kumarbis nodded. "May I – may I greet you as brother and sister sky heroes?" he asked.

"Yes," answered Jiritzu.

"Yes," answered Bidjiwara.

Elyun El-Kumarbis kissed them each on the cheek, on the *maraiin* scarifications of each. And his kiss was cold, cold.

Full of strength Jiritzu and Bidjiwara sprang to the spars of *Baramundi*'s highest mast, scrambled up lines to the topmost spar of the lighter.

They looked back at Elyun El-Kumarbis, who stood wondering beside the ship's telescope.

They took each other's hands, dropped into place on the topmost spar, and together sprang with the full strength of their sky heroes' legs, toughened and muscled by years of training in the rigging of membrane ships.

They flew up from the spar, up from *Baramundi* the sacred fish, and, looking back, saw the fish flip his tail once in farewell.

They peered ahead of themselves, into the Rainbow Serpent, saw it writhe toward the far galaxies, heard its hissing voice urging, welcoming them.

They laughed loudly, loudly, feeling strength, warmth, and joy. They plunged on and on, skimming the tide of the Rainbow Serpent, feeling the strength of the aranda, of all Yurakosi, of all sky heroes, mighty in their blood.

They threw their arms around each other, laughing for joy, and sped to the Rainbow Serpent, to the galaxies beyond the galaxies, to the Dreamtime forever.

Great Work of Time

JOHN CROWLEY

John Crowley (1942–) is the author of the classic fantasy novel *Little, Big* (1981), a monument of the genre and his masterpiece to date, and several SF novels, including the highly regarded *Engine Summer* (1979). He is currently teaching at Yale University and in 1987 embarked on a multi-volume work of the fantastic which began with *Aegypt* and continued with *Love and Sleep* (1994). He is among the most complex and literate of writers to emerge from the contemporary genre. Based upon his recent works, one might usefully consider him a postmodern writer somewhat in the vein of Thomas Pynchon, who sometimes writes in genre. His writing adds substance to critic Brian McHale's contention that contemporary science fiction is the "paraliterary shadow" of postmodernism.

He has written only a dozen or so short stories in the fantastic mode, and of them only a few are genre science fiction. This long piece is his best SF story to date. It was first published in his original collection of four stories, *Novelty* (1989). It is another SF story about time, in the same tradition as Jeschke's "The King and the Dollmaker." The idea that reality is somehow malleable, that a different future, even a different present, might result from some perhaps quite minor change in the past, has become a staple of science fiction since the 1930s. Here it is richly explored.

I: THE SINGLE EXCURSION OF CASPAR LAST

If what I am to set down is a chronicle, then it must differ from any other chronicle whatever, for it begins, not in one time or place, but everywhere at once – or perhaps *everywhen* is the better word. It might be begun at any point along the infinite, infinitely broken coastline of time.

It might even begin within the forest in the sea: huge trees like American redwoods, with their roots in the black benthos, and their leaves moving slowly in the blue currents overhead. There it might end as well.

It might begin in 1893 – or in 1983. Yes: it might be as well to begin with Last, in an American sort of voice (for we are all Americans now, aren't we?). Yes, Last shall be first: pale, fattish Caspar Last, on excursion in the springtime of 1983 to a far, far part of the Empire.

The tropical heat clothed Caspar Last like a suit as he disembarked from the plane. It was nearly as claustrophobic as the hours he had spent in the middle seat of a three-across; economy-class pew between two other cut-rate, one-week-excursion, plane-fare-and-hotel-room holiday-makers in monstrous good spirits. Like them, Caspar had taken the excursion because it was the cheapest possible way to get to and from this equatorial backwater. Unlike them, he hadn't come to soak up sun and molasses-dark rum. He didn't intend to spend all his time at the beach, or even within the twentieth century.

It had come down, in the end, to a matter of money. Caspar Last had never had money, though he certainly hadn't lacked the means to make it; with any application he could have made good money as a consultant to any of a dozen research firms, but that would have required a certain subjection of his time and thought to others, and Caspar was incapable of that. It's often said that genius can live in happy disregard of material circumstances, dress in rags, not notice its nourishment, and serve only its own abstract imperatives. This was Caspar's case, except that he wasn't happy about it: he was bothered, bitter, and rageful at his poverty. Fame he cared nothing for, success was meaningless except when defined as the solution to abstract problems. A great fortune would have been burdensome and useless. All he wanted was a nice bit of change.

He had decided, therefore, to use his "time machine" once only, before it and the principles that animated it were destroyed, for good he hoped. (Caspar always thought of his "time machine" thus, with scare-quotes around it, since it was not really a machine, and Caspar did not believe in time.) He would use it, he decided, to make money. Somehow.

The one brief annihilation of "time" that Caspar intended to allow himself was in no sense a test run. He knew that his "machine" would function as predicted. If he hadn't needed the money, he wouldn't use it at all. As far as he was concerned, the principles once discovered, the task was completed; like a completed jigsaw puzzle, it had no further interest; there was really nothing to do with it except gloat over it briefly and then sweep all the pieces randomly back into the box.

It was a mark of Caspar's odd genius that figuring out a scheme with which to make money out of the past (which was the only "direction" his "machine" would take him) proved almost as hard, given the limitations of his process, as arriving at the process itself.

He had gone through all the standard wish fulfillments and rejected them. He couldn't, armed with today's race results, return to yesterday and hit the daily double. For one thing it would take a couple of thousand in betting money to make it worth it, and Caspar didn't have a couple of thousand. More importantly, Caspar had calculated the results of his present self appearing at any point within the compass of his own biological existence, and those results made him shudder.

Similar difficulties attended any scheme that involved using money to make money. If he returned to 1940 and bought, say, two hundred shares of IBM for next to nothing: in the first place there would be the difficulty of leaving those shares somehow in escrow for his unborn self; there would be the problem of the alteration this growing fortune would have on the linear life he had actually lived; and where was he to acquire the five hundred dollars or whatever was needed in the currency of 1940? The same problem obtained if he wanted to return to 1623 and pick up a First Folio of Shakespeare, or to 1460 and a Gutenberg Bible: the cost of the currency he would need rose in relation to the antiquity, thus the rarity and value, of the object to be bought with it. There was also the problem of walking into a bookseller's and plunking down a First Folio he had just happened to stumble on while cleaning out the attic. In any case, Caspar doubted that anything as large as a book could be successfully transported "through time." He'd be lucky if he could go and return in his clothes.

Outside the airport, Caspar boarded a bus with his fellow excursionists, already hard at work with their cameras and index fingers as they rode through a sweltering lowland out of which concrete-block light industry was struggling to be born. The hotel in the capital was, as he expected, shoddy-American and intermittently refrigerated. He ceased to notice it, forwent the complimentary rum concoction promised with his tour, and after asking that his case be put in the hotel safe – extra charge for that, he noted bitterly – he went immediately to the Hall of Records in the government complex. The collection of old survey maps of the city and environs were more extensive than he had hoped. He spent most of that day among them searching for a blank place on the 1856 map, a place as naked as possible of buildings, brush, water, and that remained thus through the years. He discovered one, visited it by unmuffled taxi, found it suitable. It would save him from the awful inconvenience of "arriving" in the "past" and finding himself inserted into some local's wattle-and-daub wall. Next morning, then, he would be "on his way." If he had believed in time, he would have said that the whole process would take less than a day's time.

Before settling on this present plan, Caspar had toyed with the idea of bringing back from the past something immaterial: some knowledge, some secret that would allow him to make himself rich in his own present. Ships have gone down with millions in bullion: he could learn exactly where. Captain Kidd's treasure. Inca gold. Archaeological rarities buried in China. Leaving aside the obvious physical difficulties of these schemes, he couldn't be sure that their location wouldn't shift in the centuries between his glimpse of them and his "real" life span; and even if he could be certain, no one else would have much reason to believe him, and he didn't have the wherewithal to raise expeditions himself. So all that was out.

He had a more general, theoretical problem to deal with. Of course the very presence of his eidolon in the past would alter, in however inconsequential a way, the succeeding history of the world. The comical paradoxes of shooting one's own grandfather and the like neither amused nor intrigued him, and the chance he took of altering the world he lived in out of all recognition was constantly present to him. Statistically, of course, the chance of this present plan of his altering anything significantly, except his own personal fortunes, was remote to a high power. But his scruples had caused him to reject anything such as, say, discovering the Koh-i-noor diamond before its historical discoverers. No: what he needed to abstract from the past was something immensely trivial, something common, something the past wouldn't miss but that the present held in the highest regard; something that would take the briefest possible time and the least irruption of himself into the past to acquire; something he could reasonably be believed to possess through simple historical chance; and something tiny enough to survive the cross-time "journey" on his person.

It had come to him quite suddenly – all his ideas did, as though handed to him – when he learned that his great-great-grandfather had been a commercial traveler in the tropics, and that in the attic of his mother's house (which Caspar had never had the wherewithal to move out of) some old journals and papers of his still moldered. They were, when he inspected them, completely without interest. But the dates were right.

Caspar had left a wake-up call at the desk for before dawn the next morning. There was some difficulty about getting his case out of the safe, and more difficulty about getting a substantial breakfast served at that hour (Caspar expected not to eat during his excursion), but he did arrive at his chosen site before the horrendous tropical dawn broke, and after paying the taxi, he had darkness enough left in which to make his preparations and change into his costume. The costume – a linen suit, a shirt, hat, boots – had cost him twenty dollars in rental from a theatrical costumer, and he could only hope it was accurate enough not to cause alarm in 1856. The last item he took from his case was the copper coin, which had cost him quite a bit, as he needed one unworn and of the proper date. He turned it in his fingers for a moment, thinking that if, unthinkably, his calculations were wrong and he didn't survive this journey, it would make an interesting obol for Charon.

Out of the unimaginable chaos of its interminable stochastic fiction, Time thrust only one unforeseen oddity on Caspar Last as he, or something like him, appeared beneath a plantain tree in 1856: he had grown a beard almost down to his waist. It was abominably hot.

The suburbs of the city had of course vanished. The road he stood by was a muddy track down which a cart was being driven by a tiny and close-faced Indian in calico. He followed the cart, and his costume boots were caked with mud when at last he came into the center of town, trying to appear nonchalant and to remember the layout of the city as he had studied it in the maps. He wanted to speak to no one if possible, and he did manage to find the post office without affecting, however minutely, the heterogeneous crowd of blacks, Indians, and Europeans in the filthy streets. Having absolutely no sense of humor and very little imagination other than the most rigidly abstract helped to keep him strictly about his business and not to faint, as another might have, with wonder and astonishment at his translation, the first, last, and only of its kind a man would ever make.

"I would like," he said to the mulatto inside the brass and mahogany cage, "an envelope, please."

"Of course, sir."

"How long will it take for a letter mailed now to arrive locally?"

"Within the city? It would arrive in the afternoon post."

"Very good."

Caspar went to a long, ink-stained table, and with one of the steel pens provided, he addressed the envelope to Georg von Humboldt Last, Esq., Grand Hotel, City, in the approximation of an antique round hand that he had been practicing for weeks. There was a moment's doubt as he tried to figure how to fold up and seal the cumbersome envelope, but he did it, and gave this empty missive to the incurious mulatto. He slipped his precious coin across the marble to him. For the only moment of his adventure, Caspar's heart beat fast as he watched the long, slow brown fingers affix a stamp, cancel and date it with a pen-stroke, and drop it into a brass slot like a hungry mouth behind him.

It only remained to check into the Grand Hotel, explain about his luggage's being on its way up from the port, and sit silent on the hotel terrace, growing faint with heat and hunger and expectation, until the afternoon post.

The one aspect of the process Caspar had never been able to decide about was whether his eidolon's residence in the fiction of the past would consume any "time" in the fiction of the present. It did. When, at evening, with the letter held tight in his hand and pressed to his bosom, Caspar reappeared beardless beneath the plantain tree in the traffic-tormented and smoky suburb, the gaseous red sun was squatting on the horizon in the west, just as it had been in the same place in 1856.

He would have his rum drink after all, he decided.

"Mother," he said, "do you think there might be anything valuable in those papers of your great-grandfather's?"

"What papers, dear? Oh – I remember. I couldn't say. I thought once of donating them to a historical society. How do you mean, valuable?"

"Well, old stamps, for one thing."

"You're free to look, Caspar dear."

Caspar was not surprised (though he supposed the rest of the world was soon to be) that he found, among the faded, water-spotted diaries and papers, an envelope that bore a faint brown address – it had aged nicely in the next-to-no- time it had traveled "forward" with Caspar – and that had in its upper right-hand corner a one-penny magenta stamp, quite undistinguished, issued for a brief time in 1856 by the Crown Colony of British Guiana.

The asking price of the sole known example of this stamp, a

"unique," owned by a consortium of wealthy men who preferred to remain anonymous, was a million dollars. Caspar Last had not decided whether it would be more profitable for him to sell the stamp itself, or to approach the owners of the unique, who would certainly pay a large amount to have it destroyed, and thus preserve their unique's uniqueness. It did seem a shame that the only artifact man had ever succeeded in extracting from the nonexistent past should go into the fire, but Caspar didn't really care. His own bonfire – the notes and printouts, the conclusions about the nature and transversability of time and the orthogonal logic by which it was accomplished – would be only a little more painful.

The excursion was over; the only one that remained to him was the brief but, to him, all-important one of his own mortal span. He was looking forward to doing it first class.

II: AN APPOINTMENT IN KHARTOUM

It might be begun very differently, though; and it might now be begun again, in a different time and place, like one of those romances by Stevenson, where different stories only gradually reveal themselves to be parts of a whole . . .

The paradox is acute, so acute that the only possible stance for a chronicler is to ignore it altogether, and carry on. This, the Otherhood's central resignation, required a habit of mind so contrary to ordinary cause-and-effect thinking as to be, literally, unimaginable. It would only have been in the changeless precincts of the Club they had established beyond all frames of reference, when deep in leather armchairs or seated all together around the long table whereon their names were carved, that they dared reflect on it at all.

Take, for a single but not a random instance, the example of Denys Winterset, twenty-three years old, Winchester, Oriel College, younger son of a well-to-do doctor and in 1956 ending a first year as assistant district commissioner of police in Bechuanaland.

He hadn't done strikingly well in his post. Though on the surface he was exactly the sort of man who was chosen, or who chose himself, to serve the Empire in those years – a respectable second at Oxford, a cricketer more steady than showy, a reserved, sensible, presentable lad with sound principles and few beliefs – still there was an odd strain in him. Too imaginative, perhaps; given to fits of abstraction, even to what his commissioner called "tears, idle tears." Still, he was resourceful and hardworking; he hadn't disgraced himself, and he was now on his way north on the Cape-to-Cairo Railroad, to take a month's holiday in Cairo and England. His anticipation was marred somewhat by a sense that, after a year in the veldt, he would no longer fit into the comfortable old shoe of his childhood home; that he would feel as odd and exiled as he had in Africa. Home had become a dream, in Bechuanaland; if, at home, Bechuanaland became a dream, then he would have no place real at all to be at home in; he would be an exile for good.

The high veldt sped away as he was occupied with these thoughts, the rich farmlands of Southern Rhodesia. In the saloon car a young couple, very evidently on honeymoon, watched expectantly for the first glimpse of the eternal rainbow, visible miles off, that haloed Victoria Falls. Denys watched them and their excitement, feeling old and wise. Americans, doubtless: they had that shy, inoffensive air of all Americans abroad, that wondering quality as of children let out from a dark and oppressive school to play in the sun.

"There!" said the woman as the train took a bend. "Oh, look, how beautiful!"

Even over the train's sound they could hear the sound of the falls now, like distant cannon. The young man looked at his watch and smiled at Denys. "Right on time," he said, and Denys smiled too, amused to be complimented on his railroad's efficiency. The Bulawayo Bridge – longest and highest span on the Cape-to-Cairo line – leapt out over the gorge. "My God, that's something," the young man said. "Cecil Rhodes built this, right?"

"No," Denys said. "He thought of it, but never lived to see it. It would have been far easier to build it a few miles up, but Rhodes pictured the train being washed in the spray of the falls as it passed. And so it was built here."

The noise of the falls was immense now, and weirdly various, a medley of cracks, thumps, and explosions playing over the constant bass roar, which was not so much like a noise at all as it was like an eternal deep-drawn breath. And as the train chugged out across the span, aimed at Cairo thousands of miles away, passing here the place so hard-sought-for a hundred years ago – the place where the Nile had its origin – the spray *did* fall on the train just as Cecil Rhodes had imagined it, flung spindrift hissing on the locomotive, drops speckling the window they looked out of and rainbowing in the white air. The young Americans were still with wonder, and Denys, too, felt a lifting of his heart.

At Khartoum, Denys bid the honeymooners farewell: they were taking the Empire Airways flying boat from here to Gibraltar, and the Atlantic dirigible home. Denys, by now feeling quite proprietary about his Empire's transportation services, assured them that both flights would also certainly be right on time, and would be as comfortable as the sleepers they were leaving, would serve the same excellent meals with the same white napery embossed with the same royal insignia. Denys himself was driven to the Grand Hotel. His Sudan Railways sleeper to Cairo left the next morning.

After a bath in a tiled tub large enough almost to swim in, Denys changed into dinner clothes (which had been carefully laid out for him on the huge bed – for whom had these cavernous rooms been built, a race of Kitcheners?) He reserved a table for one in the grill room and went down to the bar. One thing he *must* do in London, he thought, shooting his cuffs, was to visit his tailor. Bechuanaland had sweated off his college baby fat, and the tropics seemed to have turned his satin lapels faintly green.

The bar was comfortably filled, before the dinner hour, with men of several sorts and a few women, and with the low various murmur of their talk. Some of the men wore *white* dinner jackets – businessmen and tourists, Denys supposed – and a few even wore shorts with black shoes and stockings, a style Denys found inherently funny, as though a tailor had made a frightful error and cut evening clothes to the pattern of bush clothes. He ordered a whiskey.

Rarely in African kraals or in his bungalow or his whitewashed office did Denys think about his Empire: or if he did, it was in some local, even irritated way, of Imperial trivialities or Imperial red tape, the rain-rusted engines and stacks of tropic-mildewed paperwork that, collectively, Denys and his young associates called the White Man's Burden. It seemed to require a certain remove from the immediacy of Empire before he could perceive it. Only here (beneath the fans' ticking, amid the voices naming places – Kandahar, Durban, Singapore, Penang) did the larger Empire that Denys had never seen but had lived in in thought and feeling since childhood open in his mind. How odd, how far more odd really than admirable or deplorable that the small place which was his childhood, circum-scribed and cozy-gray Westminster, chilly Trafalgar Square of the black umbrellas, London of the coal-smoked wallpaper and endless chimney pots – should have opened itself out so ceaselessly and for so long into huge hot places, subcontinents where rain never fell or never stopped, lush with vegetable growth or burdened with seas of sand or stone. Send forth the best ye breed: or at least large numbers of those ye breed. If one thought how odd it was – and if one thought then of what should have been natural empires, enormous spreads of restless real property like America or Russia turning in on themselves, making themselves into what seemed (to Denys, who had never seen them) to be very small places: then it did seem to be Destiny of a kind. Not a Destiny to be proud of, particularly, nor ashamed of either, but one whose compelling inner logic could only be marveled at.

Quite suddenly, and with poignant vividness, Denys saw himself, or rather felt himself once more to be, before his nursery fire, looking into the small glow of it, with animal crackers and cocoa for tea, listening to Nana telling tales of her brother the sergeant, and the Afghan frontier, and the now-dead king he served – listening, and feeling the Empire ranged in widening circles around him: first Harley Street, outside the window, and then Buckingham Palace, where the king lived; and the country then into which the trains went, and then the cold sea, and the Possessions, and the Commonwealth, stretching ever farther outward, worldwide: but always with his small glowing fire and his comfort and wonder at the heart of it.

So, there he is: a young man with the self-possessed air of an older, in evening clothes aged prematurely in places where evening clothes had not been made to go; thinking, if it could be called thinking, of a nursery fire; and about to be spoken to by the man next down the bar. If his feelings could be summed up and spoken, they were that, however odd, there is nothing more real, more pinioned by acts great and small, more clinker-built of time and space and filled brimful of this and that, than is the real world in which his five senses and his memories had their being; and that this was deeply satisfying.

"I beg your pardon," said the man next down the bar.

"Good evening," Denys said.

"My name is Davenant," the man said. He held out a square, blunt-fingered hand, and Denys drew himself up and shook it. "You are, I believe, Denys Winterset?"

"I am," Denys said, searching the smiling face before him and wondering from where he was known to him. It was a big, square, high-fronted head, a little like Bernard Shaw's, with ice-blue eyes of that twinkle; it was crowned far back with a neat hank of white hair, and was crossed above the broad jaw with upright white mustaches.

"You don't mind the intrusion?" the man said. "I wonder if you know whether the grub here is as good as once it was. It's been some time since I last ate a meal in Khartoum."

"The last time I did so was a year ago this week," Denys said. "It was quite good."

"Excellent," said Davenant, looking at Denys as though something about the young man amused him. "In that case, if you have no other engagement, may I ask your company?"

"I have no other engagement," Denys said; in fact he had rather been looking forward to dining alone, but deference to his superiors (of whom this man Davenant was surely in some sense one) was strong in him. "Tell me, though, how you come to know my name."

"Oh, well, there it is," Davenant said. "One has dealings with the Colonial Office. One sees a face, a name is attached to it, one files it but doesn't forget – that sort of thing. Part of one's job."

A civil servant, an inspector of some kind. Denys felt the sinking one feels on running into one's tutor in a wine bar: the evening not well begun. "They may well be crowded for dinner," he said.

"I have reserved a quiet table," said the smiling man, lifting his glass to Denys.

The grub was, in fact, superior. Sir Geoffrey Davenant was an able teller of tales, and he had many to tell. He was, apparently, no such dull thing as an inspector for the Colonial Office, though just what office he did fill Denys couldn't determine. He seemed to have been "attached to" or "had dealings with" or "gone about for" half the establishments of the Empire. He embodied, it seemed to Denys, the entire strange adventure about which Denys had been thinking when Sir Geoffrey had first spoken to him.

"So," Sir Geoffrey said, filling their glasses from a bottle of South African claret – no harm in being patriotic, he'd said, for one bottle – "so, after some months of stumbling about Central Asia and making myself useful one way or another, I was to make my way back to Sadiya. I crossed the Tibetan frontier disguised as a monk – "

"A monk?"

"Yes. Having lost all my gear in Manchuria, I could do the poverty part quite well. I had a roll of rupees, the films, and a compass hidden inside my prayer wheel. Mine didn't whiz around then with the same sanctity as the other fellows', but no matter. After adventures too ordinary to describe – avalanches and so on – I managed to reach the monastery at Rangbok, on the old road up to Everest. Rather near collapse. I was recovering a bit and thinking how to proceed when there was a runner with a telegram. From my superior at Ch'eng-tu. WARN DAVENANT MASSACRE SADIYA, it said. The Old Man then was famously closemouthed. But this was particularly unhelpful, as it did not say who had massacred whom – or why." He lifted the silver cover of a dish, and found it empty.

"This must have been a good long time ago," Denys said.

"Oh, yes," Davenant said, raising his ice-blue eyes to Denys. "A good long time ago. That was an excellent curry. Nearly as good as at Veeraswamy's, in London – which is, strangely, the best in the world. Shall we have coffee?"

Over this, and brandy and cigars, Sir Geoffrey's stories modulated into reflections. Pleasant as his company was, Denys couldn't overcome a sensation that everything Sir Geoffrey said to him was rehearsed, laid on for his entertainment, or perhaps his enlightenment, and yet with no clue in it as to why he had thus been singled out.

"It amuses me," Sir Geoffrey said, "how constant it is in human nature to think that things might have gone on differently from the way they did. In a man's own life, first of all: how he might have taken this or that very different route, except for this or that accident, this or that slight push – if he'd only known then, and so on. And then in history as well, we ruminate endlessly, if, what if, if only . . . The world seems always somehow malleable to our minds, or to our imaginations anyway.

"Strange you should say so," Denys said. "I was thinking, just before you spoke to me, about how very solid the world seems to me, how very – real. And – if you don't mind my thrusting it into your thoughts – you never did tell me how it is you come to know my name; or why it is you thought good to invite me to that excellent dinner."

"My dear boy," Davenant said, holding up his cigar as though to defend his innocence.

"I can't think it was chance."

"My dear boy," Davenant said in a different tone, "if anything is, that was not. I will explain all. You were on that train of thought. If you will have patience while it trundles by."

Denys said nothing further. He sipped his coffee, feeling a dew of sweat on his forehead.

"History," said Sir Geoffrey. "Yes. Of course the possible worlds we make don't compare to the real one we inhabit – not nearly so well furnished, or tricked out with details. And yet still somehow better. More satisfying. Perhaps the novelist is only a special case of a universal desire to reshape, to 'take this sorry scheme of things entire,' smash it into bits, and 'remold it nearer to the heart's desire' – as old Khayyám says. The egoist is continually doing it with his own life. To dream of doing it with history is no more useful a game, I suppose, but as a game, it shows more sport. There are rules. You can be more objective, if that's an appropriate world." He seemed to grow pensive for a moment. He looked at the end of his cigar. It had gone out, but he didn't relight it.

"Take this Empire," he went on, drawing himself up somewhat to say it. "One doesn't want to be mawkish, but one has served it. Extended it a bit, made it more secure; done one's bit. You and I. Nothing more natural, then, if we have worked for its extension in the future, to imagine its extension in the past. We can put our finger on the occasional bungle, the missed chance, the wrong man in the wrong place, and so on, and we think: if I had only been there, seen to it that the news went through, got the guns there in time, forced the issue at a certain moment – well. But as long as one is dreaming, why stop? A favorite instance of mine is the American civil war. We came very close, you know, to entering that war on the Confederacy's side."

"Did we."

"I think we did. Suppose we had. Suppose we had at first dabbled – sent arms – ignored Northern protests – then got deeper in; suppose the North declared war on us. It seems to me a near certainty that if we had entered the war fully, the South would have won. And I think a British presence would have mitigated the slaughter. There was a point, you know, late in that war, when a new draft call in the North was met with terrible riots. In New York several Negroes were hanged, just to show how little their cause was felt."

Denys had partly lost the thread of this story, unable to imagine himself in it. He thought of the Americans he had met on the train. "Is that so," he said.

"Once having divided the States into two nations, and having helped the South to win, we would have been in place, you see. The fate of the West had not yet been decided. With the North much diminished in power – well, I imagine that by now we, the Empire, would have recouped much of what we lost in 1780."

Denys contemplated this. "Rather stirring," he said mildly. "Rather coldblooded, too. Wouldn't it have meant condoning slavery? To say nothing of the lives lost. British, I mean."

"Condoning slavery – for a time. I've no doubt the South could have been bullied out of it. Without, perhaps, the awful results that accompanied the Northerners doing it. The eternal resentment. The backlash. The near genocide of the last hundred years. And, in my vision, there would have been a net savings in red men." He smiled. "Whatever might be said against it, the British Empire does not wipe out populations wholesale, as the Americans did in their West. I often wonder if that sin isn't what makes the Americans so gloomy now, so introverted."

Denys nodded. He believed implicitly that his Empire did not wipe out populations wholesale. "Of course," he said, "there's no telling what exactly would have been the result. If we'd interfered as you say."

"No," Sir Geoffrey said. "No doubt whatever result it *did* have would have to be reshaped as well. And the results of that reshaping reshaped, too, the whole thing subtly guided all along its way toward the result desired – after all, if we can imagine how we might want to alter the past we do inherit, so we can imagine that any past might well be liable to the same imagining; that stupidities, blunders, shortsightedness, would occur in any past we might initiate. Oh, yes, it would all have to be reshaped, with each reshaping . . ."

"The possibilities are endless," Denys said, laughing. "I'm afraid the game's beyond me. I say let the North win – since in any case we can't do the smallest thing about it."

"No," Davenant said, grown sad again, or reflective; he seemed to feel what Denys said deeply. "No, we can't. It's just – just too long ago." With great gravity he relit his cigar. Denys, at the oddness of this response, seeing Sir Geoffrey's eyes veiled, thought: *Perhaps he's mad.* He said, joining the game, "Suppose, though. Suppose Cecil Rhodes hadn't died young, as he did . . ."

Davenant's eyes caught cold fire again, and his cigar paused in midair. "Hm?" he said with interest.

"I only meant," Denys said, "that your remark about the British not wiping out peoples wholesale was perhaps not tested. If Rhodes had lived to build his empire – hadn't he already named it Rhodesia – I imagine he would have dealt fairly harshly with the natives."

"Very harshly," said Sir Geoffrey.

"Well," Denys said, "I suppose I mean that it's not always evil effects that we inherit from these past accidents."

"Not at all," said Sir Geoffrey. Denys looked away from his regard, which had grown, without losing a certain cool humor, intense. "Do you know, by the way, that remark of George Santayana – the American philosopher – about the British Empire, about young men like yourself? 'Never,' he said, 'never since the Athenians has the world been ruled by such sweet, just, boyish masters.'"

Denys, absurdly, felt himself flush with embarrassment.

"I don't ramble," Sir Geoffrey said. "My trains of thought carry odd goods, but all headed the same way. I want to tell you something, about that historical circumstance, the one you've touched on, whose effects we inherit. Evil or good I will leave you to decide.

"Cecil Rhodes died prematurely, as you say. But not before he had amassed a very great fortune, and laid firm claims to the ground where that fortune would grow far greater. And also not before he had made a will disposing of that fortune."

"I've heard stories," Denys said.

"The stories you have heard are true. Cecil Rhodes, at his death, left his entire fortune, and its increase, to found and continue a secret society which should, by whatever means possible, preserve and extend the British Empire. His entire fortune."

"I have never believed it," Denys said, momentarily feeling untethered, like a balloon: afloat.

"For good reason," Davenant said. "If such a society as I describe were brought into being, its very first task would be to disguise, cast doubt upon, and quite bury its origins. Don't you think that's so? In any case it's true what I say: the society was founded; is secret; continues to exist; is responsible, in some large degree at least, for the Empire we now know, in this year of grace 1956, IV Elizabeth II, the Empire on which the sun does not set."

The veranda where the two men sat was nearly deserted now; the night was loud with tropical noises that Denys had come to think of as silence, but the human noise of the town had nearly ceased.

"You can't know that," Denys said. "If you knew it, if you were privy to it, then you wouldn't say it. Not to me." He almost added: *Therefore you're not in possession of any secret, only a madman's certainty*.

"I *am* privy to it," Davenant said. "I am myself a member. The reason I reveal the secret to you – and you see, here we are, come to you and my odd knowledge of you, at last, as I promised – the reason I reveal it to you is because I wish to ask you to join it. To accept from me an offer of membership."

Denys said nothing. A dark waiter in white crept close, and was waved away by Sir Geoffrey.

"You are quite properly silent," Sir Geoffrey said. "Either I am mad, you think, in which case there is nothing to say; or what I am telling you is true, which likewise leaves you nothing to say. Quite proper. In your place I would be silent also. In your place I was. In any case I have no intention of pressing you for an answer now. I happen to know, by a roundabout sort of means that if I explained to you would certainly convince you I was mad, that you will seriously consider what I've said to you. Later. On your long ride to Cairo:

there will be time to think. In London. I ask nothing from you now. Only . . ."

He reached into his waistcoat pocket. Denys watched, fascinated: would he draw out some sign of power, a royal charter, some awesome seal? No: it was a small metal plate, with a strip of brown ribbon affixed to it, like a bit of recording tape. He turned it in his hands thoughtfully. "The difficulty, you see, is that in order to alter history and bring it closer to the heart's desire, it would be necessary to stand outside it altogether. Like Archimedes, who said that if he had a lever long enough, and a place to stand, he could move the world."

He passed the metal plate to Denys, who took it reluctantly.

"A place to stand, you see," Sir Geoffrey said. "A place to stand. I would like you to keep that plate about you, and not misplace it. It's in the nature of a key, though it mayn't look it; and it will let you into a very good London club, though it mayn't look it either, where I would like you to call on me. If, even out of simple curiosity, you would like to hear more of us." He extinguished his cigar. "I am going to describe the rather complicated way in which that key is to be used – I really do apologize for the hugger-mugger, but you will come to understand – and then I am going to bid you good evening. Your train is an early one? I thought so. My own departs at midnight. I possess a veritable Bradshaw's of the world's railroads in this skull. Well. No more. I will just sign this – oh, don't thank me. Dear boy: don't thank me."

When he was gone, Denys sat a long time with his cold cigar in his hand and the night around him. The amounts of wine and brandy he had been given seemed to have evaporated from him into the humid air, leaving him feeling cool, clear, and unreal. When at last he rose to go, he inserted the flimsy plate into his waistcoat pocket; and before he went to bed, to lie a long time awake, he changed it to the waistcoat pocket of the pale suit he would wear next morning.

As Sir Geoffrey suggested he would, he thought on his ride north of all that he had been told, trying to reassemble it in some more reasonable, more everyday fashion: as all day long beside the train the sempiternal Nile – camels, nomads, women washing in the barge canals, the thin line of palms screening the white desert beyond – slipped past. At evening, when at length he lowered the shade of his compartment window on the poignant blue sky pierced with stars, he thought suddenly: But how could he have known he would find me there, at the bar of the Grand, on that night of this year, at that hour of the evening, just as though we had some long-standing agreement to meet there?

If anything is chance, Davenant had said, that was not.

At the airfield at Ismailia there was a surprise: his flight home on the R101, which his father had booked months ago as a special treat for Denys, was to be that grand old airship's last scheduled flight. The oldest airship in the British fleet, commissioned in the year Denys was born, was to be – mothballed? Dry-docked? Deflated? Denys wondered just what one did with a decommissioned airship larger than Westminster Cathedral.

Before dawn it was drawn from its great hangar by a crowd of white-clothed fellahin pulling at its ropes – descendants, Denys thought, of those who had pulled ropes at the Pyramids three thousand years ago, employed now on an object almost as big but lighter than air. It isn't because it is so intensely romantic that great airships must always arrive or depart at dawn or at evening, but only that then the air is cool and most likely to be still: and yet intensely romantic it remains. Denys, standing at the broad, canted windows, watched the ground recede – magically, for there was no sound of engines, no jolt to indicate liftoff, only the waving, cheering fellahin growing smaller. The band on the tarmac played "Land of Hope and Glory." Almost invisible to watchers on the ground – because of its heat-reflective silver dome – the immense ovoid turned delicately in the wind as it arose.

"Well, it's the end of an era," a red-faced man in a checked suit said to Denys. "In ten years they'll all be gone, these big airships. The propeller chaps will have taken over; and the jet aeroplane, too, I shouldn't wonder."

"I should be sorry to see that," Denys said. "I've loved airships since I was a boy."

"Well, they're just that little bit slower," the red-faced man said sadly. "It's all hurry-up, nowadays. Faster, faster. And for what? I put it to you: for what?"

Now with further gentle pushes of its Rolls-Royce engines, the R101 altered its attitude again; passengers at the lounge windows pointed out the Suez Canal, and the ships passing; Lake Mareotis; Alexandria, like a mirage; British North Africa, as far to the left as one cared to point; and the white-fringed sea. Champagne was being called for, traditional despite the hour, and the red-faced man pressed a glass on Denys.

"The end of an era," he said again, raising his flute of champagne solemnly.

And then the cloudscape beyond the windows shifted, and all Africa had slipped into the south, or into the imaginary, for they had already begun to seem the same thing to Denys. He turned from the windows and decided – the effort to decide it seemed not so great here aloft, amid the potted palms and the wicker, with this pale champagne – that the conversation he had had down in the flat lands far away must have been imaginary as well.

III: THE TALE OF THE PRESIDENT *PRO TEM*

The universe proceeds out of what it has been and into what it will be, inexorably, unstoppably, at the rate of one second per second, one year per year, forever. At right angles to its forward progress lie the past and the future. The future, that is to say, does not lie "ahead" of the present in the stream of time, but at a right angle to it: the future of any present moment can be projected as far as you like outward from it, infinitely in fact, but when the universe has proceeded further, and a new present moment has succeeded this one, the future of this one retreats with it into the what-has-been, forever outdated. It is similar but more complicated with the past.

Now within the great process or procession that the universe makes, there can be no question of "movement," either "forward" or "back." The very idea is contradictory. Any conceivable movement is into the orthogonal futures and pasts that fluoresce from the universe as it is; and from those orthogonal futures and pasts into others, and others, and still others, never returning, always moving at right angles to the stream of time. To the traveler, therefore, who does not ever return from the futures or pasts into which he has gone, it must appear that the times he inhabits grow progressively more remote from the stream of time that generated them, the stream that has since moved on and left his futures behind. Indeed, the longer he remains in the future, the farther off the traveler gets from the moment in actuality whence he started, and the less like actuality the universe he stands in seems to him to be.

It was thoughts of this sort, only inchoate as yet and with the necessary conclusions not yet drawn, that occupied the mind of the President *pro tem* of the Otherhood as he walked the vast length of an iron and glass railway station in the capital city of an aged empire. He stopped to take a cigar case from within the black Norfolk overcoat he wore, and a cigar from the case; this he lit, and with its successive blue clouds hanging lightly about his hat and head, he walked on. There were hominids at work on the glossy engines of the empire's trains that came and went from this terminus; hominids pushing with their long strong arms the carts burdened with the goods and luggage that the trains were to carry; hominids of other sorts, gathered in groups or standing singly at the barricades, clutched their tickets, waiting to depart, some aided by or waited upon by other species – too few creatures, in all, to dispel the extraordinary impression of smoky empty hugeness that the cast-iron arches of the shed made.

The President *pro tem* was certain, or at any rate retained a distinct impression, that at his arrival some days before there were telephones available for citizens to use, in the streets, in public places such as this (he seemed to see an example in his mind, a wooden box whose bright veneer was loosening in the damp climate, a complex instrument within, of enameled steel and heavy celluloid); but if there ever had been, there were none now. Instead he went in at a door above which a yellow globe was alight, a winged foot etched upon it. He chose a telegraph form from a stack of them on a long scarred counter, and with the scratchy pen provided he dashed off a quick note to the Magus in whose apartments he had been staying, telling him that he had returned late from the country and would not be with him till evening.

This missive he handed in at the grille, paying what was asked in large coins; then he went out, up the brass-railed stairs, and into the afternoon, into the quiet and familiar city.

It was the familiarity that had been, from the beginning, the oddest thing. The President *pro tem* was a man who, in the long course of his work for the Otherhood, had become accustomed to stepping out of his London club into a world not quite the same as the world he had left to enter that club. He was used to finding himself in a London – or a Lahore or a Laos – stripped of well-known monuments, with public buildings and private ways unknown to him, and a newspaper (bought with an unfamiliar coin found in his pocket) full of names that should not have been there, or missing events that should have been. But here – where nothing, nothing at all, was as he had known it, no trace remaining of the history he had come from – here where no man should have been able to take steps, where even Caspar Last had thought it not possible to take steps – the President *pro tem* could not help but feel easy: had felt easy from the beginning. He walked up the cobbled streets, his furled umbrella over his shoulder, troubled by nothing but the weird grasp that this unknown dark city had on his heart.

The rain that had somewhat spoiled his day in the country had ceased but had left a pale, still mist over the city, a humid atmosphere that gave to views down avenues a stage-set quality, each receding rank of buildings fainter, more vaguely executed. Trees, too, huge and weeping, still and featureless as though painted on successive scrims. At the great gates, topped with garlanded urns, of a public park, the President *pro tem* looked in toward the piled and sounding waters of a fountain and the dim towers of poplar trees. And as he stood resting on his umbrella, lifting the last of the cigar to his lips, someone passed by him and entered the park.

For a moment the President *pro tem* stood unmoving, thinking what an attractive person (boy? girl?) that had been, and how the smile paid to him in passing seemed to indicate a knowledge of him, a knowledge that gave pleasure or at least amusement; then he dropped his cigar end and passed through the gates through which the figure had gone.

That had *not* been a hominid who had smiled at him. It was not a Magus and surely not one of the draconics either. Why he was sure he could not have said: for the same unsayable reason that he knew this city in this world, this park, these marble urns, these leaf-littered paths. He was sure that the person he had seen belonged to a different species from himself, and different also from the other species who lived in this world.

At the fountain where the paths crossed, he paused, looking this way and that, his heart beating hard and filled absurdly with a sense of loss. The child (had it been a child?) was gone, could not be seen that way, or that way – but then was there again suddenly, down at the end of a yew alley, loitering, not looking his way. Thinking at first to sneak up on her, or him, along the sheltering yews, the President *pro tem* took a sly step that way; then, ashamed, he thought better of it and set off down the path at an even pace, as one would approach a young horse or a tame deer. The one he walked toward took no notice of him, appeared lost in thought, eyes cast down.

Indescribably lovely, the President *pro tem* thought: and yet at the same time negligent and easeful and ordinary. Barefoot, or in light sandals of some kind, light pale clothing that seemed to be part of her, like a bird's dress – and a wristwatch, incongruous, yet not really incongruous at all: someone for whom incongruity was inconceivable. A reverence – almost a holy dread – came over the President *pro tem* as he came closer: as though he had stumbled into a sacred grove. Then the one he walked toward looked up at him, which caused the President *pro tem* to stop still as if a gun had casually been turned on him.

He was known, he understood, to this person. She, or he, stared unembarrassed at the President *pro tem,* with a gaze of the most intense and yet impersonal tenderness, of compassion and amusement and calm interest all mixed; and almost imperceptibly shook her head *no* and smiled again: and the President *pro tem* lowered his eyes, unable to meet that gaze. When he looked up again, the person was gone.

Hesitantly the President *pro tem* walked to the end of the avenue of yews and looked in all directions. No one. A kind of fear flew over him, felt in his breast like the beat of departing wings. He seemed to know, for the first time, what those encounters with gods had been like, when there had been gods; encounters he had puzzled out of the Greek in school.

Anyway he was alone now in the park: he was sure of that. At length he found his way out again into the twilight streets.

By evening he had crossed the city and was climbing the steps of a tall town house, searching in his pockets for the key given him. Beside the varnished door was a small plaque, which said that within were the offices of the Orient Aid Society; but this was not in fact the case. Inside was a tall foyer; a glass-paneled door let him into a hallway wainscoted in dark wood. A pile of gumboots and rubber overshoes in a corner, macs and umbrellas on an ebony tree. Smells of tea, done with, and dinner cooking: a stew, an apple tart, a roast fowl. The tulip-shaped gas lamps along the hall were lit.

He let himself into the library at the hall's end; velvet armchairs regarded the coal fire, and on a drum table a tray of tea things consorted with the books and the papers. The President *pro tem* went to the low shelves that ran beneath the windows and drew out one volume of an old encyclopedia, buckram-bound, with marbled fore-edges and illustrations in brownish photogravure.

The Races. For some reason the major headings and certain other words were in the orthography he knew, but not the closely printed text. His fingers ran down the columns, which were broken into numbered sections headed by the names of species and subspecies. *Hominidae,* with three subspecies. *Draconiidae,* with four: here were etchings of skulls. And lastly *Sylphidae,* with an uncertain number of subspecies. Sylphidae, the Sylphids. Fairies.

"Angels," said a voice behind him. The President *pro tem* turned to see the Magus whose guest he was, recently risen no doubt, in a voluminous dressing gown richly figured. His beard and hair were so long and fine they seemed to float on the currents of air in the room, like filaments of thistledown.

"'Angels,' is that what you call them?"

"What they would have themselves called," said the Magus. "What name they call themselves, among themselves, no one knows but they."

"I think I met with one this evening."

"Yes."

There was no photogravure to accompany the subsection on Sylphidae in the encyclopedia. "I'm sure I met with one."

"They are gathering, then."

"Not . . . not because of me?"

"Because of you."

"How, though," said the President *pro tem*, feeling again within him the sense of loss, of beating wings departing, "how, how could they have known, how . . ."

The Magus turned away from him to the fire, to the armchairs and the drum table. The President *pro tem* saw that beside one chair a glass of whiskey had been placed, and an ashtray. "Come," said the Magus. "Sit. Continue your tale. It will perhaps become clear to you: perhaps not." He sat then himself, and without looking back at the President *pro tem* he said: "Shall we go on?"

The President *pro tem* knew it was idle to dispute with his host. He did stand unmoving for the space of several heartbeats. Then he took his chair, drew the cigar case from his pocket, and considered where he had left off his tale in the dark of the morning.

"Of course," he said then, "Last knew: he knew, without admitting it to himself, as a good orthogonist must never do, that the world he had returned to from his excursion was not the world he had left. The past he had passed through on his way back was not 'behind' his present at all, but at a right angle to it; the future of that past, which he had to traverse in order to get back again, was not the same road, and 'back' was not where he got. The frame house on Maple Street which, a little sunburned, he reentered on his return was twice removed in reality from the one he had left a week before; the mother he kissed likewise.

"He knew that, for it was predicated by orthogonal logic, and orthogonal logic was in fact what Last had discovered – the trans-versability of time was only an effect of that discovery. He knew it, and despite his glee over his triumph, he kept his eye open. Sooner or later he would come upon something, something that would betray the fact that this world was not his.

"He could not have guessed it would be me."

The Magus did not look at the President *pro tem* as he was told this story; his pale gray eyes instead wandered from object to object around the great dark library but seemed to see none of them; what, the President *pro tem* wondered, did they see? He had at first supposed the race of Magi to be blind, from this habitual appearance of theirs; he now knew quite well that they were not blind, not blind at all.

"Go on," the Magus said.

"So," said the President *pro tem*, "Last returns from his excursion. A week passes uneventfully. Then one morning he hears his mother call: he has a visitor. Last, pretending annoyance at this interruption of his work (actually he was calculating various forms of compound interest on a half million dollars), comes to the door. There on the step is a figure in tweeds and a bowler hat, leaning on a furled umbrella: me.

"'Mr. Last,' I said. 'I think we have business.'

"You could see by his expression that he knew I should not have been there, should not have had business with him at all. He really ought to have refused to see me. A good deal of trouble might have been saved if he had. There was no way I could force him, after all. But he didn't refuse; after a goggle-eyed moment he brought me in, up a flight of stairs (Mama waiting anxiously at the bottom), and into his study.

"Geniuses are popularly supposed to live in an atmosphere of the greatest confusion and untidiness, but this wasn't true of Last. The study – it was his bedroom, too – was of a monkish neatness. There was no sign that he worked there, except for a computer terminal, and even it was hidden beneath a cozy that Mama had made for it and Caspar had not dared to spurn.

"He was trembling slightly, poor fellow, and had no idea of the social graces. He only turned to me – his eyeglasses were the kind that oddly diffract the eyes behind and make them unmeetable – and said, 'What do you want?'"

The President *pro tem* caressed the ashtray with the tip of his cigar. He had been offered no tea, and he felt the lack. "We engaged in some preliminary fencing," he continued. "I told him what I had come to acquire. He said he didn't know what I was talking about. I said I thought he did. He laughed and said there must be some mistake. I said, no mistake, Mr. Last. At length he grew silent, and I could see even behind those absurd goggles that he had begun to try to account for me.

"Thinking out the puzzles of orthogonal logic, you see, is not entirely unlike puzzling out moves in chess: theoretically chess can be played by patiently working out the likely consequences of each move, and the consequences of those consequences, and so on; but in fact it is not so played, certainly not by master players. Masters seem to have a more immediate apprehension of possibilities, an almost visceral understanding of the, however rigorously mathematical, logic of the board and pieces, an understanding that they can act on without being able necessarily to explain. Whatever sort of mendacious and feckless fool Caspar Last was in many ways, he was a genius in one or two, and orthogonal logic was one of them.

"'From when,' he said, 'have you come?'

"'From not far on,' I answered. He sat then, resigned, stuck in a sort of check impossible to think one's way out of, yet not mated. 'Then,' he said, 'go back the same way you came.'"

"'I cannot,' I said, 'until you explain to me how it is done.'

"'You know how,' he said, 'if you can come here to ask me.'

"'Not until you have explained it to me. Now or later.'

"'I never will,' he said.

"'You will,' I said. 'You will have done already, before I leave. Otherwise I would not be here now asking. Let us,' I said, and took a seat myself, 'let us assume these preliminaries have been gone through, for they have been of course, and move ahead to the bargaining. My firm are prepared to make you a quite generous offer.'

"That was what convinced him that he must, finally, give up to us the processes he had discovered, which he really had firmly intended to destroy forever: the fact that I had come there to ask for them. Which meant that he had already somehow, somewhen, already yielded them up to us."

The President *pro tem* paused again, and lifted his untouched whiskey. "It was the same argument," he said, "the same incontrovertible argument, that was used to convince me once, too, to do a dreadful thing."

He drank, thoughtfully, or at least (he supposed) appearing thoughtful; more and more often as he grew older it happened that in the midst of an anecdote, a relation, even one of supreme importance, he would begin to forget what it was he was telling; the terrifically improbable events would begin to seem not only improbable but fictitious, without insides, the incidents and characters as false as in any tawdry cinema story, even his own part in them unreal: as though they happened to someone made up – certainly not to him who told them. Often enough he forgot the plot.

"You see," he said, "Last exited from a universe in which travel 'through time' was, apparently, either not possible, or possible only under conditions that would allow such travel to go undetected. That was apparent from the fact that no one, so far as Last knew, up to the time of his own single excursion, had ever detected it going on. No one, from Last's own future that is, had ever come 'back' and disrupted his present, or the past of his present: never ever. Therefore, if his excursion could take place, and he could 'return,' he would have to return to a different universe: a universe where time travel *had* taken place, a universe in which once-upon-a-time a man from 1983 had managed to insert himself into a minor colony of the British Crown one hundred and twenty-seven years earlier. What he couldn't know in advance was whether the universe he 'returned' to was one where time travel was a commonplace, an everyday occurrence, something, anyway, that could deprive his excursion of the value it had; or whether it was one in which one excursion only had taken place, his own. My appearance before him convinced him that it was, or was about to become, common enough: common enough to disturb his own peace and quiet, and alter in unforeseeable ways his comfortable present.

"There was only one solution, or one dash at a solution anyway. I might, myself, be a singularity in Last's new present. It was therefore possible that if he could get rid of me, I would take his process 'away' with me into whatever future I had come out of to get it, and thereupon never be able to find my way again to his present and disturb it or him. Whatever worlds I altered, they would not be his, not his anyway who struck the bargain with me: if each of them also contained a Last, who would suffer or flourish in ways unimaginable to the Last to whom I spoke, then those eidolons would have to make terms for themselves, that's all. The quantum angle obtruded by my coming, and then the one obtruded by my returning, divorced all those Lasts from him for all eternity: that is why, though the angle itself is virtually infinitesimal, it has always to be treated as a right angle.

"Last showed me, on his computer, after our bargain was struck and he was turning over his data and plans to me. I told him I would not probably grasp the theoretical basis of the process, however well I had or would come to manage the practical paradoxes of it, but he liked to show me. He first summoned up x–y coordinates, quite ordinary, and began by showing me how some surprising results were obtained by plotting on such coordinates an imaginary number, specifically the square root of minus one. The only way to describe what happens, he said, is that the plotted figure, one unit high, one unit wide, generates a shadow square of the same measurements 'behind' itself, in space undefined by the coordinates. It was with such tricks that he had begun; the orthogons he obtained had first started him thinking about the generation of inhabitable – if also somehow imaginary – pasts.

"Then he showed me what became of the orthogons so constructed if the upright axis were set in motion. Suppose (he said) that this vertical coordinate were in fact revolving around the axle formed by the other, horizontal coordinate. If it were so revolving, like an aeroplane propeller, we could not apprehend it, edge on as it is to us, so to speak; but what would that motion do to the plots we were making? And of course it was quite simple, given the proper instructions to the computer, to find out. And his orthogons – always remaining at right angles to the original coordinates – began to turn in the prop wash of the whole system's progress at one second per second out of the what-was and into the what-has-never-yet-been; and to generate, when one had come to see them, the paradoxes of orthogonal logic: the cyclonic storm of logic in which all travelers in that medium always stand; the one in which Last and I, I bending over his shoulder hat in hand, he with fat white fingers on his keys and eyeglasses slipping down his nose, stood even as we spoke: a storm as unfeelable as Last's rotating axis was unseeable."

The President *pro tem* tossed his extinguished cigar into the fading fire and crossed his arms upon his breast, weary; weary of the tale.

"I don't yet understand," the other said. "If he had been so adamant, why would he give up his secrets to you?"

"Well," said the President *pro tem*, "there was, also, the matter of money. It came down to that, in the end. We were able to make him a very generous offer, as I said."

"But he didn't need money. He had this stamp."

"Yes. So he did. Yes. We were able to pick up the stamp, too, from him, as part of the bargain. I think we offered him a hundred pounds. Perhaps it was more."

"I thought it was invaluable."

"Well, so did he, of course. And yet he was not really as surprised as one might have expected him to be, when he discovered it was not; when it turned out that the stamp he had gone to such trouble to acquire was in fact rather a common one. I seemed to see it in his face, the expectation of what he was likely to find, as soon as I directed him to look it up in his Scott's, if he didn't believe me. And there it was in Scott's: the one-penny magenta 1856, a nice enough stamp, a stamp many collectors covet, and many also have in their albums. He had begun breathing stertorously, staring down at the page. I'm afraid he was suffering, rather, and I didn't like to observe it.

"'Come,' I said to him. 'You knew it was possible.' And he did, of course. 'Perhaps it was something you did,' I said. 'Perhaps you bought the last one of a batch, and the postmaster subsequently reordered, a thing he had not before intended to do. Perhaps . . .' But I could see him think it: there needed to be no such explanation. He needed to have made no error, nor to have influenced the moment's shape in any way by his presence. The very act of his coming and going was sufficient source of unpredictable, stochastic change: this world was not his, and minute changes from his were predicated. But *this* change, this of all possible changes . . .

"His hand had begun to shake, holding the volume of Scott's. I really wanted now to get through the business and be off, but it couldn't be hurried. I knew that, for I'd done it all before. In the end we acquired the stamp. And then destroyed it, of course."

The President *pro tem* remembered: a tiny, momentary fire.

"It's often been observed," he said, "that the cleverest scientists are often the most easily taken in by charlatans. There is a famous instance, famous in some worlds, of a scientist who was brought to believe firmly in ghosts and ectoplasm, because the medium and her manifestations passed all the tests the scientist could devise. The only thing he didn't think to test for was conscious fraud. I suppose it's because the phenomena of nature, or the entities of mathematics, however puzzling and elusive they may be, are not after all bent on fooling the observer; and so a motive that would be evident to the dullest of policemen does not occur to the genius."

"The stamp," said the Magus.

"The stamp, yes. I'm not exactly proud of this part of the story. We were convinced, though, that two *very* small wrongs could go a long way toward making a very great right. And Last, who understood me and the 'firm' I represented to be capable of handling – at least in a practical way – the awful paradoxes of orthogony, did not imagine us to be also skilled, if anything more skilled, at such things as burglary, uttering, fraud, and force. Of such contradictions is Empire made. It was easy enough for us to replace, while Last was off in the tropics, one volume of his Scott's stamp catalog with another printed by ourselves, almost identical to his but containing one difference. It was harder waiting to see, once he had looked up his stamp in our bogus volume, if he would then search out some other source to confirm what he found there. He did not."

The Magus rose slowly from his chair with the articulated dignity, the waste-less lion's motion, of his kind. He tugged the bell pull. He picked up the poker then, and stood with his hand upon the mantel, looking down into the ruby ash of the dying fire. "I would he had," he said.

The dark double doors of the library opened, and the servant entered noiselessly.

"Refresh the gentleman's glass," the Magus said without turning from the fire, "and draw the drapes."

The President *pro tem* thought that no matter how long he lived in this world he would never grow accustomed to the presence of draconics. The servant's dark hand lifted the decanter, poured an exact dram into the glass, and stoppered the bottle again; then his yellow eyes, irises slit like a cat's or a snake's, rose from that task toward the next, the drawing of the drapes. Unlike the eyes of the Magi, these draconic eyes seemed to see and weigh everything – though on a single scale, and from behind a veil of indifference.

Their kind, the President *pro tem* had learned, had been servants for uncounted ages, though the Magus his host had said that once they had been masters, and men and the other hominids their slaves. And they still had, the President *pro tem* observed, that studied reserve which upper servants had in the world from which the President *pro tem* had come, that reserve which says: Very well, I will do your bidding, better than you could do it for yourself; I will maintain the illusion of your superiority to me, as no other creature could.

With a taper he lit at the fire, he lit the lamps along the walls and masked them with glass globes. Then he drew the drapes.

"I'll ring for supper," the Magus said, and the servant stopped at the sound of his voice. "Have it sent in." The servant moved again, crossing the room on narrow naked feet. At the doorway he turned to them, but only to draw the double doors closed together as he left.

For a time the Magus stood regarding the doors the great lizard had closed. Then: "Outside the City," he said, "in the mountains, they have begun to combine. There are more stories every week. In the old forests whence they first emerged, they have begun to collect on appointed days, trying to remember – for they are not really as intelligent as they look – trying to remember what it is they have lost, and to think of gaining it again. In not too long a time we will begin to hear of massacres. Some remote place; a country house; a more than usually careless man; a deed of unfamiliar horridness. And a sign left, the first sign: a writing in blood, or something less obvious.

And like a spot symptomatic of a fatal disease, it will begin to spread."

The President *pro tem* drank, then said softly: "We didn't know, you know. We didn't understand that this would be the result." The drawing of the drapes, the lighting of the lamps, had made the old library even more familiar to the President *pro tem:* the dark varnished wood, the old tobacco smoke, the hour between tea and dinner; the draught that whispered at the window's edge, the bitter smell of the coal on the grate; the comfort of this velvet armchair's napless arms, of this whiskey. The President *pro tem* sat grasped by all this, almost unable to think of anything else. "We couldn't know."

"Last knew," the Magus said. "All false, all imaginary, all generated by the wishes and fears of others: all that I am, my head, my heart, my house. Not the world's doing, or time's, but yours." The opacity of his eyes, turned on the President *pro tem,* was fearful. "You have made me; you must unmake me."

"I'll do what I can," the President *pro tem* said. "All that I can."

"For centuries we have studied," the Magus said. "We have spent lifetimes – lifetimes much longer than yours – searching for the flaw in this world, the flaw whose existence we suspected but could not prove. I say 'centuries,' but those centuries have been illusory, have they not? We came, finally, to guess at you, down the defiles of time, working your changes, which we can but suffer.

"We only guessed at you: no more than men or beasts can we Magi remember, once the universe has become different, that it was ever other than it is now. But I think the Sylphids can feel it change: can know when the changes are wrought. Imagine the pain for them."

That was a command: and indeed the President *pro tem* could imagine it, and did. He looked down into his glass.

"That is why they are gathering. They know already of your appearance; they have expected you. The request is theirs to make, not mine: that you put this world out like a light."

He stabbed with the poker at the settling fire, and the coals gave up blue flames for a moment. The mage's eyes caught the light, and then went out.

"I long to die," he said.

IV: CHRONICLES OF THE OTHERHOOD

Once past the door, or what might be considered the door, or what Sir Geoffrey Davenant had told him was a club, Denys Winterset was greeted by the Fellow in Economic History, a gentle, academic-looking man called Platt.

"Not many of the Fellows about, just now," he said. "Most of them fossicking about on one bit of business or another. I'm always here." He smiled, a vague, self-effacing smile. "Be no good out there. But they also serve, eh?"

"Will Sir Geoffrey Davenant be here?" Denys asked him. He followed Platt through what did seem to be a gentlemen's club of the best kind: dark-paneled, smelling richly of leather upholstery and tobacco.

"Davenant, oh, yes," said Platt. "Davenant will be here. All the executive committee will get here, if they can. The President – *pro tem.*" He turned back to look at Denys over his half-glasses. "All our presidents are *pro tem.*" He led on. "There'll be dinner in the executive committee's dining room. After dinner we'll talk. You'll likely have questions." At that Denys almost laughed. He felt made of questions, most of them unputtable in any verbal form.

Platt stopped in the middle of the library. A lone Fellow in a corner by a green-shaded lamp was hidden by the *Times* held up before him. There was a fire burning placidly in the oak-framed fireplace; above it, a large and smoke-dimmed painting: a portrait of a chubby, placid man in a hard collar, thinning, blond hair, eyes somehow vacant. Platt, seeing Deny's look, said: "Cecil Rhodes."

Beneath the portrait, carved into the mantelpiece, were words; Denys took a step closer to read them:

> *To Ruin the Great Work of Time*
> *& Cast the Kingdoms old*
> *Into another mould.*

"Marvell," Platt said. "That poem about Cromwell. Don't know who chose it. It's right, though. I look at it often, working here. Now. It's down that corridor, if you want to wash your hands. Would you care for a drink? We have some time to kill. Ah, Davenant."

"Hullo, Denys," said Sir Geoffrey, who had lowered his *Times*. "I'm glad you've come."

"I think we all are," said Platt, taking Denys's elbow in a gentle, almost tender grasp. "Glad you've come."

He had almost not come. If it had been merely an address, a telephone number he'd been given, he might well not have; but the metal card with its brown strip was like a string tied round his finger, making it impossible to forget he had been invited. Don't lose it, Davenant had said. So it lay in his waistcoat pocket; he touched it whenever he reached for matches there; he tried shifting it to other pockets, but wherever it was on his person he felt it. In the end he decided to use it, as much to get rid of its importunity as for any other reason – so he told himself. On a wet afternoon he went to the place Davenant had told him of, the Orient Aid Society, and found it as described, a sooty French-Gothic building, one of those private houses turned to public use, with a discreet brass plaque by the door indicating that within some sort of business is done, one can't imagine what; and inside the double doors, in the vestibule, three telephone boxes, looking identical, the first of which had the nearly invisible slit by the door. His heart for some reason beat slow and hard as he inserted the card within this slot – it was immediately snatched away, like a ticket on the Underground – and entered the box and closed the door behind him.

Though nothing moved, he felt as though he had stepped onto a moving footpath, or onto one of those trick floors in a fun house that slide beneath one's feet. He was going somewhere. The sensation was awful. Beginning to panic, he tried to get out, not knowing whether that might be dangerous, but the door would not open, and its glass could not be seen out of either. It had been transparent from outside but was somehow opaque from within. He shook the door handle fiercely. At that moment the nonmobile motion reversed itself sickeningly, and the door opened. Denys stepped out, not into the vestibule of the Orient Aid Society, but into the foyer of a club. A dim, old-fashioned foyer, with faded Turkey carpet on the stairs, and an aged porter to greet him; a desk, behind which pigeonholes held members' mail; a stand of umbrellas. It was reassuring, almost absurdly so, the "then I woke up" of a silly ghost story. But Denys didn't feel reassured, or exactly awake either.

"Evening, sir."

"Good evening."

"Still raining, sir? Take your things?"

"Thank you."

A member was coming toward him down the long corridor: Platt. "Sir?"

Denys turned back to the porter. "Your key, sir," the man said, and gave him back the metal plate with the strip of brown ribbon on it.

"Like a lift," Davenant told him as they sipped whiskey in the bar. "Alarming, somewhat, I admit; but imagine using a lift for the first time, not knowing what its function was. Closed inside a box; sensation of movement; the doors open, and you are somewhere else. Might seem odd. Well, this is the same. Only you're not somewhere else: not exactly."

"Hm," Denys said.

"Don't dismiss it, Sir Geoffrey," said Platt. "It *is* mighty odd." He said to Denys: "The paradox is acute: it is. Completely contrary to the usual cause-and-effect thinking we all do, can't stop doing really, no matter how hard we try to adopt other habits of mind. Strictly speaking it is unthinkable: unimaginable. And yet there it is."

"Yes," Davenant said. "To ignore, without ever forgetting, the heart of the matter: that's the trick. I've met monks, Japanese, Tibetan, who know the techniques. They can be learned."

"We speak of the larger paradox," Platt said to Denys. "The door you came in by being only a small instance. The great instance being, of course, the Otherhood's existence at all: we here now sitting and talking of it."

But Denys was not talking of it. He had nothing to say. To be told that in entering the telephone box in the Orient Aid Society he had effectively exited from time and entered a precinct outside it, revolving between the actual and the hypothetical, not quite existent despite the solidity of its parquet floor and the truthful bite of its whiskey; to be told that in these changeless and atemporal halls there gathered a society – "not quite a brotherhood," Davenant said; "that would be mawkish, and untrue of these chaps; we call it an Otherhood" – of men and women who by some means could insert themselves into the stream of the past, and with their foreknowledge alter it, and thus alter the future of that past, the future in which they themselves had their original being; that in effect the world Denys had come from, the world he knew, the year 1956, the whole course of things, the very cast and flavor of his memories, were dependent on the Fellows of this Society, and might change at any moment, though if they did he would know nothing of it; and that he was being asked to join them in their work – he heard the words, spoken to him with a frightening casualness; he felt his mind fill with the notions, though not able to do anything that might be called thinking about them; and he had nothing to say.

"You can see," Sir Geoffrey said, looking not at Denys but into his whiskey, "why I didn't explain all this to you in Khartoum. The words don't come easily. Here, in the Club, outside all frames of reference, it's possible to explain. To describe, anyway. I suppose if we hadn't a place like this, we should all go mad."

"I wonder," said Platt, "whether we haven't, despite it." He looked at no one. "Gone mad, I mean."

For a moment no one spoke further. The barman glanced at them, to see if their silence required anything of him. Then Platt spoke again. "Of course there are restrictions," he said. "The chap who discovered it was possible to change one's place in time, an American, thought he had proved that it was only possible to displace oneself into the past. In a sense, he was correct . . ."

"In a sense," Sir Geoffrey said. "Not quite correct. The possibilities are larger than he supposed. Or rather will suppose, all this from your viewpoint is still to happen – which widens the possibilities right there, you see, one man's future being as it were another man's past. (You'll get used to it, dear boy, shall we have another of these?) The past, as it happens, is the only sphere of time we have any interest in; the only sphere in which we can do good. So you see there are natural limits: the time at which this process was made workable is the forward limit; and the rear limit we have made the time of the founding of the Otherhood itself. By Cecil Rhodes's will, in 1893."

"Be pointless, you see, for the Fellows to go back before the Society existed," said Platt. "You can see that."

"One further restriction," said Sir Geoffrey. "A house rule, so to speak. We forbid a man to return to a time he has already visited, at least in the same part of the world. There is the danger – a moment's thought will show you I'm right – of bumping into oneself on a previous, or successive, mission. Unnerving, let me tell you. Unnerving completely. The trick is hard enough to master as it is."

Denys found voice. "Why?" he said. "And why me?"

"Why," said Sir Geoffrey, "is spelled out in our founding charter: to preserve and extend the British Empire in all parts of the world, and to strengthen it against all dangers. Next, to keep peace in the world, insofar as this is compatible with the first; our experience has been that it usually is the same thing. And lastly to keep fellowship among ourselves, this also subject to the first, though any conflict is unimaginable, I should hope, bickering aside."

"The Society was founded to be secret," Platt said. "Rhodes liked that idea – a sort of Jesuits of the Empire. In fact there was no real need for secrecy, not until – well, not until the Society became the Otherhood. This jaunting about in other people's histories would not be understood. So secrecy is important. Good thing on the whole that Rhodes insisted on it. And for sure he wouldn't have been displeased at the Society's scope. He wanted the world for England.

And more. 'The moon, too,' he used to say. 'I often think of the moon.'"

"Few know of us even now," Sir Geoffrey said. "The Foreign Office, sometimes. The PM. Depending on the nature of H.M. Government at any moment, we explain more, or less. Never the part about time. That is for us alone to know. Though some have guessed a little, over the years. It's not even so much that we wish to act in secret – that was just Rhodes's silly fantasy – but well, it's just damned difficult to explain, don't you see?"

"And the Queen knows of us," Platt said. "Of course."

"I flew back with her, from Africa, that day," Davenant said. "After her father had died. I happened to be among the party. I told her a little then. Didn't want to intrude on her grief, but – it seemed the moment. In the air, over Africa. I explained more later. Plucky girl," he added. "Plucky." He drew his watch out. "And as for the second part of your question – why you? – I shall ask you to reserve that one, for a moment. We'll dine upstairs . . . Good heavens, look at the time."

Platt swallowed his drink hastily. "I remember Lord Cromer's words to us when I was a schoolboy at Leys," he said. " 'Love your country,' he said, 'tell the truth, and don't dawdle.'"

"Words to live by," Sir Geoffrey said, examining the bar chit doubtfully and fumbling for a pen.

The drapes were drawn in the executive dining room; the members of the executive committee were just taking their seats around a long mahogany table, scarred around its edge with what seemed to be initials and dates. The members were of all ages; some sunburned, some pale, some in evening clothes of a cut unfamiliar to Denys; among them were two Indians and a Chinaman. When they were all seated, Denys beside Platt, there were several seats empty. A tall woman with severe gray hair but eyes somehow kind took the head of the table.

"The President *pro tem*," she said as she sat, "is not returned, apparently, from his mission. I'll preside, if there are no objections."

"Oh, balls," said a broad-faced man with the tan of a cinema actor. "Don't give yourself airs, Huntington. Will we really need any presiding?"

"Might be a swearing-in," Huntington said mildly, pressing the bell beside her and not glancing at Denys. "In any case, best to keep up the forms. First order of business – the soup."

It was a mulligatawny, saffrony and various; it was followed by a whiting, and that by a baron of claret-colored beef. Through the clashings of silverware and crystal Denys listened to the table's talk, little enough of which he could understand: only now and then he felt – as though he were coming horribly in two – the import of the Fellows' conversation: that history was malleable, time a fiction; that nothing was necessarily as he supposed it must be. How could they bear that knowledge? How could he?

"Mr. Deng Fa-shen, there," Platt said quietly to him, "is our physicist. Orthogonal physics – as opposed to orthogonal logic – is his invention. What makes this club possible. The mechanics of it. Don't ask me to explain."

Deng Fa-shen was a fine-boned, parchment-colored man with gentle fox's eyes. Denys looked from him to the two Indians in silk. Platt said, as though reading Denys's thought: "The most disagreeable thing about old Rhodes and the Empire of his day was its racialism, of course. Absolutely unworkable, too. Nothing more impossible to sustain than a world order based on some race's supposed inherent superiority." He smiled. "It isn't the only part of Rhodes's scheme that's proved unworkable."

The informal talk began to assemble itself, with small nudges from the woman at the head of the table (who did her presiding with no pomp and few words), around a single date: 1914. Denys knew something of this date, though several of the place names spoken of (the Somme, Jutland, Gallipoli – wherever that was) meant nothing to him. Somehow, in some possible universe, 1914 had changed everything; the Fellows seemed intent on changing 1914, drawing its teeth, teeth that Denys had not known it had – or might still have once had: he felt again the sensation of coming in two, and sipped wine.

"Jutland," a Fellow was saying. "All that's needed is a bit more knowledge, a bit more jump on events. Instead of a foolish stalemate, it could be a solid victory. Then, blockade; war over in six months . . .

"Who's our man in the Admiralty now? Carteret, isn't it? Can he – "

"Carteret," said the bronze-faced man, "was killed the last time around at Jutland." There was a silence; some of the Fellows seemed to be aware of this, and some taken by surprise. "Shows the foolishness of that kind of thinking," the man said. "Things have simply gone too far by then. That's my opinion."

Other options were put forward. That moment in what the Fellows called the Original Situation was searched for into which a small intrusion might be made, like a surgical incision, the smallest possible intrusion that would have the proper effect; then the succeeding Situation was searched, and the Situation following that, the Fellows feeling with enormous patience and care into the workings of the past and its possibilities, like a blind man weaving. At length a decision seemed to be made, without fuss or a vote taken, about this place Gallipoli, and a Turkish soldier named Mustapha Kemal, who would be apprehended and sequestered in a quick action that took or would take place there; the sun-bronzed man would see, or had seen, to it; and the talk, after a reflective moment, turned again to anecdote and speculation.

Denys listened to the stories, of desert treks and dangerous negotiations, men going into the wilderness of a past catastrophe with a precious load of penicillin or of knowledge, to save one man's life or end another's; to intercept one trivial telegram, get one bit of news through, deflect one column of troops – removing one card from the ever-building possible future of some past moment and seeing the whole of it collapse silently, unknowably, even as another was building, just as fragile but happier: he looked into the faces of the Fellows, knowing that no ruthless stratagem was beyond them, and yet knowing also that they were men of honor, with a great world's peace and benefit in their trust, though the world couldn't know it; and he felt an odd but deep thrill of privilege to be here now, wherever that was – the same sense of privilege that, as a boy, he had expected to feel (and as a man had laughed at himself for expecting to feel) upon being admitted to the ranks of those who – selflessly, though not without reward – had been chosen or had chosen themselves to serve the Empire. "The difference you make makes all the difference," his headmasterish commissioner was fond of telling Denys and his fellows; and it was a joke among them that, in their form-filling, their execution of tedious and sometimes absurd directives, they were following in the footsteps of Gordon and Milner, Warren Hastings and Raffles of Singapore. And yet – Denys perceived it with a kind of inward stillness, as though his heart flowed instead of beating – a difference *could* be made. Had been made. Went on being made, in many times and places, without fuss, without glory, with rewards for others that those others could not recognize or even imagine. He crossed his knife and fork on his plate and sat back slowly.

"This 1914 business has its tricksome aspects," Platt said to him. "Speaking in large terms, not enough can really be done within our time frames. The Situation that issues in war was firmly established well before: in the founding of the German Empire under Prussian leadership. Bismarck. There's the man to get to, or to his financiers, most of whom were Jewish – little did they know, and all that. Even

Sedan is too late, and not enough seems to be able to be made, or unmade, out of the Dreyfus affair, though that does fall within our provenance. No," he said. "It's all just too long ago. If only . . . Well, no use speculating, is there? Make the best of it, and shorten the war; make it less catastrophic at any rate, a short, sharp shaking-out-above all, win it quickly. We must do the best we can."

He seemed unreconciled.

Denys said: "But I don't understand. I mean, of course I wouldn't expect to understand it as you do, but . . . well, you *did* do all that. I mean we studied 1914 in school – the guns of August and all that, the 1915 peace, the Monaco Conference. What I mean is . . ." He became conscious that the Fellows had turned their attention to him. No one else spoke. "What I mean to say is that *I* know you solved the problem, and how you solved it, in a general way; and I don't see why it remains to be solved. I don't see why you're worried." He laughed in embarrassment, looking around at the faces that looked at him.

"You're right," said Sir Geoffrey, "that you don't understand." He said it smiling, and the others were, if not smiling, patient and not censorious. "The logic of it is orthogonal. I can present you with an even more paradoxical instance. In fact I intend to present you with it; it's the reason you're here."

"The point to remember," the woman called Huntington said (as though to the whole table, but obviously for Denys's instruction), "is that here – in the Club – nothing has yet happened except the Original Situation. All is still to do: all that we have done, all still to do."

"Precisely," said Geoffrey. "All still to do." He took from his waistcoat pocket an eyeglass, polished it with his napkin, and inserted it between cheek and eyebrow. "You had a question, in the bar. You asked *why me,* meaning, I suppose, why is it you should be nominated to this Fellowship, why you and not another."

"Yes," said Denys. He wanted to go on, list what he knew of his inadequacies, but kept silent.

"Let me, before answering your question, ask you this," said Sir Geoffrey. "Supposing that you were chosen by good and sufficient standards – supposing that a list had been gone over carefully, and your name was weighed; supposing that a sort of competitive examination has been passed by you – would you then accept the nomination?"

"I – " said Denys. All eyes were on him, yet they were not somehow expectant; they awaited an answer they knew. Denys seemed to know it, too. He swallowed. "I hope I should," he said.

"Very well," Sir Geoffrey said softly. "Very well." He took a breath. "Then I shall tell you that you have in fact been chosen by good and sufficient standards. Chosen, moreover, for a specific mission, a mission of the greatest importance; a mission on which the very existence of the Otherhood depends. No need to feel flattered; I'm sure you're a brave lad, and all that, but the criteria were not entirely your sterling qualities, whatever they should later turn out to be.

"To explain what I mean, I must further acquaint you with what the oldest, or rather earliest, of the Fellows call the Original Situation.

"You recall our conversation in Khartoum. I told you no lie then; it is the case, in that very pleasant world we talked in, that good year 1956, fourth of a happy reign, on that wide veranda overlooking a world at peace – it is the case, I say, in that world and in most possible worlds like it, that Cecil Rhodes died young, and left the entire immense fortune he had won in the Scramble for the founding of a secret society, a society dedicated to the extension of that Empire which had his entire loyalty. The then Government's extreme confusion over this bequest, their eventual forming of a society – not without some embarrassment and doubt – a society from which this present Otherhood descends; still working toward the same ends, though the British Empire is not now what Rhodes thought it to be, nor the world either in which it has its hegemony – well, one of the Fellows is working up or will work up that story, insofar as it can be told, and it is, as I say, a true one.

"But there is a situation in which it is not true. In that situation which we call Original – the spine of time from which all other possibilities fluoresce – Cecil Rhodes, it appears, changed his mind."

Sir Geoffrey paused to light a cigar. The port was passed him. A cloud of smoke issued from his mouth. "Changed his mind, you see," he said, dispersing the smoke with a wave. "He did not die young, he lived on. His character mellowed, perhaps, as the years fell away; his fortune certainly diminished. It may be that Africa disappointed him, finally; his scheme to take over Tanganyika and join the Cape-to-Cairo with a single All-Red railroad line had ended in failure . . ."

Denys opened his mouth to speak; he had only a week before taken that line. He shut his mouth again.

"Whatever it was," Sir Geoffrey said, "he changed his mind. His last will left his fortune – what was left of it – to his old university, a scholarship fund to allow Americans and others of good character to study in England. No secret society. No Otherhood."

There was a deep silence at the table. No one had altered his casual position, yet there was a stillness of utter attention. Someone poured for Denys, and the liquid rattle of port into his glass was loud.

"Thus the paradox," Sir Geoffrey said. "For it is only the persuasions of the Otherhood that alter this Original Situation. The Otherhood must reach its fingers into the past, once we have learned how to do so; we must send our agents down along the defiles of time and intercept our own grandfather there, at the very moment when he is about to turn away from the work of generating us.

"And persuade him not to, you see; cause him – cause him not to turn away from that work of generation. Yes, cause him not to turn away. And thus ensure our own eventual existence."

Sir Geoffrey pushed back his chair and rose. He turned toward the sideboard, then back again to Denys. "Did I hear you say 'That's madness'?" he asked.

"No," Denys said.

"Oh," Sir Geoffrey said. "I thought you spoke. Or thought I remembered you speaking." He turned again to the sideboard, and returned again to the table with his cigar clenched in his teeth and a small box in his hands. He put this on the table. "You do follow me thus far," he said, his hands on the box and his eyes regarding Denys from under their curling brows.

"Follow you?"

"The man had to die," Sir Geoffrey said. He unlatched the box. "It was his moment. The moment you will find in any biography of him you pick up. Young, or anyway not old; at the height of his triumphs. It would have been downhill for him from there anyway."

"How," Denys asked, and something in his throat intruded on the question; it was a moment before he could complete it: "How did he die?"

"Oh, various ways," Sir Geoffrey said. "In the most useful version, he was shot to death by a young man he'd invited up to his house at Cape Town. Shot twice, in the heart, with a Webley .38-caliber revolver." He took from the box this weapon, and placed it with its handle toward Denys.

"That's madness," Denys said. His hands lay along the arms of his chair, drawing back from the gun. "You can't mean to say you went back and *shot* him, you . . ."

"Not we, dear boy," Sir Geoffrey said. "We, generally, yes; but specifically, not we. You."

"No."

"Oh, you won't be alone – not initially, at least. I can explain why it must be you and not another; I can expound the really quite dreadful paradox of it further, if you think it would help, though it seems to me best if, for now, you simply take our word for it."

Denys felt the corners of his mouth draw down, involuntarily, tightly; his lower lip wanted to tremble. It was a sign he remembered from early childhood: what had usually followed it was a fit of truculent weeping. That could not follow, here, now: and yet he dared not allow himself to speak, for fear he would be unable. For some time, then, no one spoke.

At the head of the table Huntington pushed her empty glass away.

"Mr. Winterset," she said gently. "I wonder if I might put in a word. Sit down, Davenant, will you, just for a moment, and stop looming over us. With your permission, Mr. Winterset – Denys – I should like to describe to you a little more broadly that condition of the world we call the Original Situation."

She regarded Denys with her sad eyes, then closed her fingers together before her. She began to speak, in a low voice which more than once Denys had to lean forward to catch. She told about Rhodes's last sad bad days; she told of Rhodes's chum, the despicable Dr. Jameson, and his infamous raid and the provocations that led to war with the Boers; of the shame of that war, the British defeats and the British atrocities, the brutal intransigence of both sides. She told how in those same years the European powers who confronted each other in Africa were also at work stockpiling arms and building mechanized armies of a size unheard of in the history of the world, to be finally let loose upon one another in August of 1914, unprepared for what was to become of them; armies officered by men who still lived in the previous century, but armed with weapons more dreadful than they could imagine. The machine gun: no one seemed to understand that the machine gun had changed war forever, and though the junior officers and Other Ranks soon learned it, the commanders never did. At the First Battle of the Somme wave after wave of British soldiers were sent against German machine guns, to be mown down like grain. There were a quarter of a million casualties in that battle. And yet the generals went on ordering massed attacks against machine guns for the four long years of the war.

"But they knew," Denys could not help saying. "They did know. Machine guns had been used against massed native armies for years, all over the Empire. In Afghanistan. In the Sudan. Africa. They knew."

"Yes," Huntington said. "They knew. And yet, in the Original

Situation, they paid no attention. They went blindly on and made their dreadful mistakes. Why? How could they be so stupid, those generals and statesmen who in the world you knew behaved so wisely and so well? For one reason only: they lacked the help and knowledge of a group of men and women who had seen all those mistakes made, who could act in secret on what they knew, and who had the ear and the confidence of one of the governments – not the least stupid of them, either, mind you. And with all our help it was still a close-run thing."

"Damned close-run," Platt put in. "Still hangs in the balance, in fact."

"Let me go on," Huntington said.

She went on: long hands folded before her, eyes now cast down, she told how at the end a million men, a whole generation, lay dead on the European battlefield, among them men whom Denys might think the modern world could not have been made without. A grotesque tyranny calling itself Socialist had been imposed on a war-weakened Russian empire. Only the intervention of a fully mobilized United States had finally broken the awful deadlock – thereby altering the further history of the world unrecognizably. She told how the vindictive settlement inflicted on a ruined Germany (so unlike the wise dispositions of the Monaco Conference, which had simply reestablished the old pre-Bismarck patchwork of German states and principedoms) had rankled in the German spirit; how a madman had arisen and, almost unbelievably, had ridden a wave of resentment and anti-Jewish hysteria to dictatorship.

"Yes," Denys said. *"That* we didn't escape, did we? I remember that, or almost remember it; it was just before I can remember anything. Anti-Jewish riots all over Germany."

"Yes," said Huntington softly.

"Yes. Terrible. These nice funny Germans, all lederhosen and cuckoo clocks, and suddenly they show a terrible dark side. Thousands of Jews, some of them very highly placed, had to leave Germany. They lost everything. Synagogues attacked, professors fired. Even Einstein, I think, had to leave Germany for a time."

Huntington let him speak. When Denys fell silent, unable to remember more and feeling the eyes of the Fellows on him, Huntington began again. But the things she began to tell of now simply could not have happened, Denys thought; no, they were part of a monstrous, foul dream, atrocities on a scale only a psychopath could conceive, and only the total resources of a strong and perverted science achieve. When Einstein came again into the tale, and the world

Huntington described drifted ignorantly and inexorably into an icy and permanent stalemate that could be broken only by the end of civilization, perhaps of life itself, Denys found a loathsome surfeit rising in his throat; he covered his face, he would hear no more.

"So you see," Huntington said, "why we think it possible that the life – nearly over, in any case – of one egotistical, racialist adventurer is worth the chance to alter that situation." She raised her eyes to Denys. "I don't say you need agree. There *is* a sticky moral question, and I don't mean to brush it aside. I only say you see how we might think so."

Denys nodded slowly. He reached out and put his hand on the pistol that had been placed before him. He lifted his eyes and met those of Sir Geoffrey Davenant, which still smiled, though his mouth and his mustaches were grave.

What they were all telling him was that he could help create a better world than the original, which Huntington had described; but that was not how Denys perceived it. What Denys perceived was that reality – reality, the world he had come from, reality sun-shot and whole – was somehow under threat from a disgusting nightmare of death, ignorance, and torture, which could invade and replace it forever unless he acted. He did not think himself capable of interfering with the world to make it better; but to defend the world he knew, the world that with all its shortcomings was life and sustenance and sense and cleanly wakefulness – yes, that he could do. Would do, with all his strength.

Which is why, of course, it was he who had been chosen to do it. He saw that in Davenant's eyes.

And of course, if he refused, he could not then be brought here to be asked. If it was now possible for him to be asked to do this by the Otherhood, then he must have already consented, and done it. That, too, was in Davenant's silence. Denys looked down. His hand was on the Webley; and beside it, carved by a penknife into the surface of the table, almost obscured by later waxings, were the neat initials D.W.

"I always remember what Lord Milner said," Platt spoke into his ear. *"Everyone can help."*

V: THE TEARS OF THE PRESIDENT *PRO TEM*

"I remember," the President *pro tem* of the Otherhood said, "the light: a very clear, very pure, very cool light that seemed somehow potent but reserved, as though it could do terrible blinding things, and give an unbearable heat, if it chose – well, I'm not quite sure what I mean."

There was a midnight fug in the air of the library where the President *pro tem* retold his tale. The Magus to whom he told it did not look at him; his pale gray eyes moved from object to object around the room in the aimless idiot wandering that had at first caused the President *pro tem* to believe him blind.

"The mountain was called Table Mountain – a sort of high mesa. What a place that was then – I think the most beautiful in the Empire, and young then, but not raw; a peninsula simply made to put a city on, and a city being put there, beneath the mountain: and this piercing light.

"Our party put up at the Mount Nelson Hotel, perhaps a little grand for the travelers in electroplating equipment we were pretending to be, but the incognito wasn't really important, it was chiefly to explain the presence of the Last equipment among the luggage.

"A few days were spent in reconnaissance. But you see – this is continually the impossible thing to explain – in a sense those of the party who knew the outcome were only going through the motions of conferring, mapping their victim's movements, choosing a suitable moment and all that: for they knew the story; there was only one way for it to happen, if it was to happen at all. If it was *not* to happen, then no one could predict what was to happen instead; but so long as our party was there, and preparing it, it would evidently have to happen – or would have to have had to have happened."

The President *pro tem* suddenly missed his old friend Davenant, Davenant the witty and deep, who never bumbled over his tenses, never got himself stuck in a sentence such as that one; Davenant lost now with the others in the interstices of imaginary pasthood – or rather about to be lost, in the near future, if the President *pro tem* assented to what was asked of him. "It was rather jolly," he said, "like a game rather, striving to bring about a result that you were sure had already been brought about; an old ritual, if you like, to which not much importance needed to be attached, so long as it was all done correctly . . ."

"I think," said the Magus, "you need not explain these feelings that you then had."

"Sorry," said the President *pro tem*. "The house was called Groote Schuur – that was the old Dutch name, which he'd revived, for a big granary that had stood on the property; the English had called it the Grange. It was built on the lower slopes of Devil's Peak, with a view up to the mountains, and out to sea as well. He'd only recently seen the need for a house – all his life in Africa he'd more or less pigged it in rented rooms, or stayed in his club or a hotel or even a tent pitched outside town. For a long time he roomed with Dr. Jameson, sleeping on a little truckle bed hardly big enough for his body. But now that he'd become Prime Minister, he felt it was time for something more substantial.

"It seemed to me that it would have been easier to take him out in the bush – the *bundas;* as the Matabele say. Hire a party of natives – wait till all are asleep – ambush. He often went out into the wilds with almost no protection. There was no question of honor involved – I mean, the man had to die, one way or the other, and the more explainably or accidentally the better. But I was quite wrong – I was myself, still young – and had to be put right: the one time that way was tried, the assassination initiated a punitive war against the native populations that lasted for twenty years, which ended only with the virtual extermination of the Matabele and Mashona peoples. Dreadful.

"No, it had to be the house; moreover, it had to be within a very brief span of time – a time when we knew he was there, when we knew where his will was, and *which* will it was – he made eight or nine in his lifetime – and when we knew, also, what assets were in his hands. Business and ownership were fluid things in those days; his partners were quick and subtle men; his sudden death might lose us all that we were intending to acquire by it in the way of a campaign chest, so to speak.

"So it had to be the house, in this week of this year, on this night. In fact orthogonal logic dictated it. Davenant was quite calmly sure of that. After all, that was the night when it had happened: and for sure we ought not to miss it."

That was an attempt at the sort of remark Davenant might make, and the President *pro tem* smiled at the Magus, who remained unmoved. The President *pro tem* thought it impossible that beings as wise as he knew the one before him to be, no matter how grave, could altogether lack any sense of humor. For himself, he had often thought that if he did not find funny the iron laws of orthogony he would go mad; but his jokes apparently amused only himself.

"It was not a question of getting to his house, or into it; he practically kept open house the year round, and his grounds could be walked upon by anyone. The gatekeepers were only instructed to warn walkers about the animals they might come across – he had brought in dozens of species, and he allowed all but the genuinely dangerous to roam at will. Wildebeest. Zebras. Impala. And 'human beings,' as he always called them, roamed at will, too; there were always some about. At dinner he had visitors from all over Africa, and from England and Europe as well; his bedrooms were often full. I think he hated to be alone. All of which provided a fine setting, you see, for a sensational – and insoluble – murder mystery: if only the man could be got alone, and escape made good then through these crowds of hangers-on.

"Our plan depended on a known proclivity of his, or rather two proclivities. The first was a taste he had for the company of a certain sort of a young man. He liked having them around him and could become very attached to them. There was never a breath of scandal in this – well, there was talk, but only talk. His 'angels,' people called them: good-looking, resourceful if not particularly bright, good all-rounders with a rough sense of fun – practical jokes, horseplay – but completely devoted and ready for anything he might ask them to do. He had a fair crowd of these fellows up at Groote Schuur just then. Harry Curry, his private secretary. Johnny Grimmer, a trooper who was never afraid to give him orders – like a madman's keeper, some people said, scolding him and brushing dust from his shoulders; he never objected. Bob Coryndon, another trooper. They'd all just taken on a butler for themselves, a sergeant in the Inniskillings: good-looking chap, twenty-three years old. Oddly, they had all been just that age when he'd taken an interest in them: twenty-three. Whether that was chance or his conscious choice we didn't know.

"The other proclivity was his quickness in decision-making. And this often involved the young men. The first expedition into Matabeleland had been headed up by a chap he'd met at his club one morning at breakfast just as the column was preparing for departure. Took to the chap instantly: liked his looks, liked his address. Gave him the job on the spot.

"That had worked out very well, of course – his choices often did. The pioneer column had penetrated into the heart of the *bundas,* the flag was flying over a settlement they called Fort Salisbury, and the whole of Matabeleland was in the process of being added to the Empire. Up at Groote Schuur they were kicking around possible names for the new country: Rhodia, perhaps, or Rhodesland, even Cecilia. It was that night that they settled on Rhodesia."

The President *pro tem* felt a moment's shame. There had been, when it came down to it, no doubt in his mind that what they had done had been the right thing to do: and in any case it had all happened a long time ago, more than a century ago in fact. It was not what was done, or that it had been done, only the moment of its doing, that was hard to relate: it was the picture in his mind, of an old man (though he was only forty-eight, he looked far older) sitting in the lamplight reading *The Boy's Own Paper*, as absorbed and as innocent in his absorption as a boy himself; and the vulnerable shine on his balding crown; and the tender and indifferent night: it was all that which raised a lump in the throat of the President *pro tem* and caused him to pause, and roll the tip of his cigar in the ashtray, and clear his throat before continuing.

"And so," he said, "we baited our hook. Rhodes's British South Africa Company was expanding, in the wake of the Fort Salisbury success. He was on the lookout for young men of the right sort. We presented him with one: good-looking lad, public school, cricketer; just twenty-three years old. He was the bait. The mole. The Judas."

And the bait had been taken, of course. The arrangement's having been keyed so nicely to the man's nature, a nature able to be studied from the vantage point of several decades on, it could hardly have failed. That the trick seemed so fragile, even foolish, something itself out of *The Boy's Own Paper* or a story by Henley, only increased the likelihood of its striking just the right note here: the colored fanatic, Rhodes leaving his hotel after luncheon to return to Parliament, the thug stepping out of the black noon shadows with a knife just as Rhodes mounts his carriage steps – then the young man, handily by with a stout walking stick (a gift of his father upon his departure for Africa) – the knife deflected, the would-be assassin slinking off, the great man's gratitude. You must have some reward. Not a bit, sir, anyone would have done the same; just lucky I was nearby. Come to dinner at any rate – my house on the hill – anyone can direct you. Allow me to introduce myself; my name is . . .

No need, sir, everyone knows Cecil Rhodes.

And your name is . . .

The clean hand put frankly forward, the tanned, open, boyish face smiling. My name is Denys Winterset.

"So then you see," the President *pro tem* said, "the road was open. The road up to Groote Schuur. The road that branches, in effect, to lead here: to us here now speaking of it."

"And how many times since then," the Magus said, "has the world branched? How many times has it been bent double, and broken? A thousand times, ten thousand? Each time growing smaller, having to be packed into lesser space, curling into itself like a snail's shell; growing ever weaker as the changes multiply, and more liable to failure of its fabric: how many times?"

The President *pro tem* answered nothing.

"You understand, then," the Magus said to him, "what you will be asked: to find the crossroads that leads this way and to turn the world from it."

"Yes."

"And how will you reply?"

The President *pro tem* had no better answer for this question, and he gave none. He had begun to feel at once heavy as lead and disembodied. He arose from his armchair, with some effort, and crossed the worn Turkish carpet to the tall window.

"You must leave my house now," the Magus said, rising from his chair. "There is much for me to do this night, if this world is to pass out of existence."

"Where shall I go?"

"They will find you. I think in not too long a time." Without looking back he left the room.

The President *pro tem* pushed aside the heavy drape the draconic had drawn. *Where shall I go?* He looked out the window into the square outside, deserted at this late and rainy hour. It was an irregular square, the intersection of three streets, filled with rain-wet cobbles as though with shiny eggs. It was old; it had been the view out these windows for two centuries at the least; there was nothing about it to suggest that it had not been the intersection of three streets for a good many more centuries than that.

And yet it had not been there at all only a few decades earlier, when the President *pro tem* had last walked the city outside the Orient Aid Society. Then the city had been London; it was no more. These three streets, these cobbles, had not been there in 1983; nor in 1893 either. Yet there they were, somewhere early in the twenty-first century; there they had been, too, for time out of mind, familiar no doubt to any dweller in this part of town, familiar for that matter to the President *pro tem* who looked out at them. In each of two lamp-lit cafe's on two corners of the square, a man in a soft cap held a glass and looked out into the night, unsurprised, at home.

Someone had broken the rules: there simply was no other explanation.

There had been, of course, no way for anyone, not Deng Fa-shen, not Davenant, not the President *pro tem* himself, to guess what the President *pro tem* might come upon on this, the first expedition the Otherhood was making into the future: not only did the future not exist (Deng Fa-shen was quite clear about that), but, as Davenant reminded him, the Otherhood itself, supposing the continued existence of the Otherhood, would no doubt go busily on changing things in the past far and near – shifting the ground therefore of the future the President *pro tem* was headed for. Deng Fa-shen was satisfied that that future, the ultimate future, sum of all intermediate revisions, was the only one that could be plumbed, if any could; and that was the only one the Otherhood would want to glimpse: to learn how they would do, or would come to have done; to find out, as George V whispered on his death-bed, "How is the Empire."

("Only that isn't what he said," Davenant was fond of telling. "That's what he was, understandably, reported to have said, and what the Queen and the nurses convinced themselves they heard. But he was a bit dazed there at the end, poor good old man. What he said was not 'How is the Empire,' but 'What's at the Empire,' a popular cinema. I happened," he always added gravely, "to have been with him.")

The first question had been how far "forward" the Otherhood should press; those members who thought the whole scheme insane, as Platt did, voted for next Wednesday, and bring back the Derby winners please. Deng Fa-shen was not certain the thrust could be entirely calculated: the imaginary futures of imaginary pasts were not, he thought, likely to be under the control of even the most penetrating orthogonal engineering. Sometime in the first decades of the next century was at length agreed upon, a time just beyond the voyager's own mortal span – for the house rule seemed, no one could say quite why, to apply in both directions – and for as brief a stay as was consistent with learning what was up.

The second question – who was to be the voyager – the President *pro tem* had answered by fiat, assuming an executive privilege he just at that moment claimed to exist, and cutting off further debate. (Why exactly did he insist? I'm not certain why, except that it was not out of a sense of adventure, or of fun or curiosity: whatever of those qualities he may once have had had been much worn away in his rise to the Presidency *pro tem* of the Otherhood. A sense of duty may have been part of it. It may have been to forestall the others, out of a funny sort of premonition. Duty, and premonition: of what, though? Of what?)

"It'll be quite different from any of our imaginings, you know," Davenant said, who for some reason had not vigorously contested the President's decision. "The future of all possible pasts. I envy you, I do. I should rather like to see it for myself."

Quite different from any of our imaginings: very well. The President *pro tem* had braced himself for strangeness. What he had not expected was familiarity. Familiarity – cozy as an old shoe – was certainly different from his imaginings.

And yet what was it he was familiar with? He had stepped out of his club in London and found himself to be, not in the empty corridors of the Orient Aid Society that he knew well, but in private quarters of some kind that he had never seen before. It reminded him, piercingly, of a place he did know, but what place he could not have said: some don's rich but musty rooms, some wealthy and learned bachelor's digs. How had it come to be?

And how had it come to be lit by gas?

One of the pleasant side effects (most of the members thought it pleasant) of the Otherhood's endless efforts in the world had been a general retardation in the rate of material progress: so much of that progress had been, on the one hand, the product of the disastrous wars that it was the Otherhood's chief study to prevent, and on the other hand, American. The British Empire moved more slowly, a great beast without predators, and naturally conservative; it clung to proven techniques and could impose them on the rest of the world by its weight. The telephone, the motor car, the flying boat, the wireless, all were slow to take root in the Empire that the Otherhood shaped. And yet surely, the President *pro tem* thought, electricity was in general use in London in 1893, before which date no member could alter the course of things. And gas lamps lit this place.

Pondering this, the President *pro tem* had entered the somber and apparently little-used dining room and seen the draconic standing in the little butler's pantry: silent as a statue (asleep, the President *pro tem* would later deduce, with lidless eyes only seeming to be open); a polishing-cloth in his claw, and the silver before him; his heavy jaws partly open, and his weight balanced on the thick stub of tail. He wore a baize apron and black sleeve garters to protect his clothes.

Quite different from our imaginings: and yet no conceivable amount of tinkering with the twentieth century, just beyond which the President *pro tem* theoretically stood, could have brought forth this butler, in wing collar and green apron, the soft gaslight ashine on his bald brown head.

So someone had broken the rules. Someone had dared to regress beyond 1893 and meddle in the farther past. That was not, in itself, impossible; Caspar Last had done it on his first and only excursion. It had only been thought impossible for the Otherhood to do it, because it would have taken them "back" before the Otherhood's putative existence, and therefore before the Otherhood could have wrested the techniques of such travel from Last's jealous grip, a power they acquired by already having it – that was what the President *pro tem* had firmly believed.

But it was not, apparently, so. Somewhen in that stretch of years that fell between his entrance into the telephone box of the Club and his exit from it into this familiar and impossible world, someone – many someones, or someone many times – had gone "back" far before Rhodes's death: had gone back far enough to initiate this house, this city, these races who were not men.

A million years? It couldn't have been less. It didn't seem possible it could be less.

And who, then? Deng Fa-shen, the delicate, brilliant Chinaman, who had thoughts and purposes he kept to himself; the only one of them who might have been able to overcome the theoretical limits? Or Platt, who was never satisfied with what was possible within what he called "the damned parameters"?

Or Davenant. Davenant, who was forever quoting Khayyám: *Ah, Love, couldst thou and I with Him conspire To take this sorry scheme of things entire; Would we not smash it into pieces, then Remold it nearer to the heart's desire . . .*

"There is," said the Magus behind him, "one other you have not thought of."

The President *pro tem* let fall the drape and turned from the window. The Magus stood in the doorway, a great ledger in his arms. His eyes did not meet the President *pro tem*'s, and yet seemed to regard him anyway, like the blind eyes of a statue.

One other . . . Yes, the President *pro tem* saw, there *was* one other who might have done this. One other, not so good at the work perhaps as others, as Davenant for example, but who nonetheless would have been, or would come to have been, in a position to take such steps. The President *pro tem* would not have credited himself with the skill, or the nerve, or the dreadnought power. But how else to account for the familiarity, the bottomless *suitability* to him of this world he had never before seen?

"Between the time of your people's decision to plumb our world," said the Magus, "and the time of your standing here within it, you must yourself have brought it into being. I see no likelier explanation."

The President *pro tem* stood still with wonder at the efforts he was apparently to prove capable of making. A million years at least: a million years. How had he known where to begin? Where had he found, would he find, the time?

"Shall I ring," the Magus said, "or will you let yourself out?"

* * *

Deng Fa-shen had always said it, and anyone who traveled in them knew it to be so: the imaginary futures and imaginary pasts of orthogony are imaginary only in the sense that imaginary numbers (which they very much resemble) are imaginary. To a man walking within one, it alone is real, no matter how strange; it is all the others, standing at angles to it, which exist only in imagination. Night-long the President *pro tem* walked the city, with a measured and unhurried step, but with a constant tremor winding round his rib cage, waiting for what would become of him, and observing the world he had made.

Of course it could not continue to exist. It should not ever have come into existence in the first place; his own sin (if it had been his) had summoned it out of nonbeing, and his repentance must expunge it. The Magus who had taken his confession (which the President *pro tem* had been unable to withhold from him) had drawn that conclusion: it must be put out, like a light. And yet how deeply the President *pro tem* wanted it to last forever; how deeply he believed it *ought* to last forever.

The numinous and inhuman angels, about whom nothing could be said, beings with no ascertainable business among the lesser races and yet beings without whom, the President *pro tem* was sure, this world could not go on functioning. They lived (endless?) lives unimaginable to men, and perhaps to Magi, too, who yet sought continually for knowledge of them: Magi, highest of the hominids, gentle and wise yet inflexible of purpose, living in simplicity and solitude (Were there females? Where? Doing what?) and yet from their shabby studies influencing, perhaps directing, the lives of mere men. The men, such as himself, clever and busy, with their inventions and their politics and their affairs. The lesser hominids, strong, sweet-natured, comic, like placid trolls. The draconics.

It was not simply a world inhabited by intelligent races of different kinds: it was a harder thing to grasp than that. The lives of the races constituted different universes of meaning, different constructions of reality; it was as though four or five different novels, novels of different kinds by different and differently limited writers, were to become interpenetrated and conflated: inside a gigantic Russian thing a stark and violent *policier,* and inside that something Dickensian, full of plot, humors, and eccentricity. Such an interlacing of mutually exclusive universes might be comical, like a sketch in *Punch;* it might be tragic, too. And it might be neither: it might simply be what is, the given against which all airy imaginings must finally be measured: reality.

Near dawn the President *pro tem* stood leaning on a parapet of worked stone that overlooked a streetcar roundabout. A car had just ended its journey there, and the conductor and the motorman descended, squat hominids in great-coats and peaked caps. With their long strong arms they began to swing the car around for its return journey. The President *pro tem* gazed down at this commonplace sight; his nose seemed to know the smell of that car's interior, his bottom to know the feel of its polished seats. But he knew also that yesterday there had not been streetcars in this city. Today they had been here for decades.

No, it was no good, the President *pro tem* knew: the fabric of this world he had made – if it had been he – was fatally weakened with irreality. It was a botched job: as though he were that god of the Gnostics who made the material world, a minor god unversed in putting time together with space. He had not worked well. And how could he have supposed it would be otherwise? What had got into him, that he had dared?

"No," said the angel who stood beside him. "You should not think that it was you."

"If not me," said the President *pro tem,* "then who?"

"Come," said the angel. She (I shall say "she") slipped a small cool hand within his hand. "Let's go over the tracks, and into the trees beyond that gate."

A hard and painful stone had formed in the throat of the President *pro tem.* The angel beside him led him like a daughter, like the daughter of old blind Oedipus. Within the precincts of the park – which apparently had its entrance or its entrances where the angels needed them to be – he was led down an avenue of yew and dim towers of poplar toward the piled and sounding waters of a fountain. They sat together on the fountain's marble lip.

"The Magus told me," the President *pro tem* began, "that you can feel the alterations that we make, back then. Is that true?"

"It's like the snap of a whip infinitely long," the angel said. "The whole length of time snapped and laid out differently: not only the length of time backward to the time of the change, but the length of the future forward. We felt ourselves, come into being, oldest of the Old Races (though the last your changes brought into existence); we saw in that moment the aeons of our past, and we guessed our future, too."

The President *pro tem* took out his pocket handkerchief and pressed it to his face. He must weep, yet no tears came.

"We love this world – this only world – just as you do," she said. "We love it, and we cannot bear to feel it sicken and fail. Better that it not have been than that it die."

"I shall do all I can," said the President *pro tem*. "I shall find who has done this – I suppose I know who it was, if it wasn't me – and dissuade him. Teach him, teach him what I've learned, make him see . . ."

"You don't yet understand," the angel said with careful kindness but at the same time glancing at her wristwatch. "There is no one to tell. There is no one who went beyond the rules."

"There must have been," said the President *pro tem*. "You, your time, it just isn't that far along from ours, from mine! To make this world, this city, these races . . ."

"Not far along in time," said the angel, "but many times removed. You know it to be 50: whenever you, your Otherhood, set out across the timelines, your passage generated random variation in the worlds you arrived in. Perhaps you didn't understand how those variations accumulate, here at the sum end of your journeyings."

"But the changes were so minute!" said the President *pro tem*. "Deng Fa-shen explained it. A molecue here and there, no more; the position of a distant star; some trivial thing, the name of a flower or a village. Too few, too small even to notice."

"They increase exponentially with every alteration – and your Otherhood has been busy since you last presided over them. Through the days random changes accumulate, tiny errors silting up like the blown sand that fills the streets of a desert city, that buries it at last."

"But why these changes?" asked the President *pro tem* desperately. "It can't have been chance that a world like this was the sum of those histories, it can't be. A world like *this* . . ."

"Chance, perhaps. Or it may be that as time grows softer the world grows more malleable by wishes. There is no reason to believe this, yet that is what we believe. You – all of you – could not have known that you were bringing this world into being; and yet this is the world you wanted."

She reached out to let the tossed foam of the fountain fall into her hand. The President *pro tem* thought of the bridge over the Zambezi, far away; the tossed foam of the Falls. It was true: this is what they had striven for: a world of perfect hierarchies, of no change forever. God, how they must have longed for it! The loneliness of continual change – no outback, no *bundas* so lonely. He had heard how men can be unsettled for days, for weeks, who have lived through earthquakes and felt the earth to be uncertain: what of his Fellows, who had felt time and space picked apart, never to be rewoven that way again, and not once but a hundred times? What of himself?

"I shall tell you what I see at the end of all your wishings," said the angel softly. "At the far end of the last changed world, after there is nothing left that can change. There is then only a forest, growing in the sea. I say 'forest' and I say 'sea,' though whether they are of the kind I know, or some other sort of thing, I cannot say. The sea is still and the forest is thick; it grows upward from the black bottom, and its topmost branches reach into the sunlight, which penetrates a little into the warm upper waters. That's all. There is nothing else anywhere forever. Your wishes have come true: the Empire is quiet. There is not, nor will there be, change anymore; never will one thing be confused again with another; higher for lower, better for lesser, master for servant. Perpetual Peace."

The President *pro tem* was weeping now, painful sobs drawn up from an interior he had long kept shut and bolted. Tears ran down his cheeks, into the corners of his mouth, under his hard collar. He knew what he must do, but not how to do it.

"The Otherhood cannot be dissuaded from this," the angel said, putting a hand on the wrist of the President *pro tem*. "For all of it, including our sitting here now, all of it – and the forest in the sea – is implicit in the very creation of the Otherhood itself."

"But then . . ."

"Then the Otherhood must be uncreated."

"I can't do that."

"You must."

"No, no, I can't." He had withdrawn from her pellucid gaze, horrified. "I mean it isn't because . . . if it must be done, it must be. But not by me."

"Why?"

"It would be against the rules given me. I don't know what the result would be. I can't imagine. I don't *want* to imagine."

"Rules?"

"The Otherhood came into being," said the President *pro tem*, "when a British adventurer, Cecil Rhodes, was shot and killed by a young man called Denys Winterset."

"Then you must return and stop that killing."

"But you don't see!" said the President *pro tem* in great distress. "The rules given the Otherhood forbid a Fellow from returning to a time and place that he formerly altered by his presence . . ."

"And . . ."

"And I am myself that same Denys Winterset."

The angel regarded the President *pro tem* – the Honorable Denys Winterset, fourteenth President *pro tem* of the Otherhood – and her translucent face registered a sweet surprise, as though the learning of something she had not known gave her pleasure. She laughed, and her laughter was not different from the plashing of the fountain by which they sat. She laughed and laughed, as the old man in his black coat and hat sat silent beside her, bewildered and afraid.

VI: THE BOY DAVID OF HYDE PARK CORNER

There are days when I seem genuinely to remember, and days when I do not remember at all: days when I remember only that sometimes I remember. There are days on which I think I recognize another like myself: someone walking smartly along the Strand or Bond Street, holding the *Times* under one arm and walking a furled umbrella with the other – a sort of military bearing, mustaches white (older than when I seem to have known him, but then so am I, of course), and cheeks permanently tanned by some faraway sun. I do not catch his eye, nor he mine, though I am tempted to stop him, to ask him . . . Later on I wonder – if I can remember to wonder – whether he, too, is making a chronicle, in his evenings, writing up the story: a story that can be told in any direction, starting from anywhere, leading on to a forest in the sea.

I won't look any longer into this chronicle I've compiled. I shall only complete it.

My name is Denys Winterset. I was born in London in 1933; I was the only son of a Harley Street physician, and my earliest memory is of coming upon my father in tears in his surgery: he had just heard the news that the R101 dirigible had crashed on its maiden flight, killing all those aboard.

We lived then above my father's offices, in a little building whose nursery I remember distinctly, though I was taken to the country with the other children of London when I was only six, and that building was knocked down by a bomb in 1940. A falling wall killed my mother; my father was on ambulance duty in the East End and was spared.

He didn't know quite what to do with me, nor I with myself; I have been torn all my life between the drive to discover what others whom I love and admire expect of me, and my discovery that then I don't want to do it, really. After coming down from the University I decided, out of a certain perversity which my father could not sympathize with, to join the Colonial Service. He could not fathom why I would want to fasten myself to an enterprise that everyone save a few antediluvian colonels and letter writers to the *Times* could see was a dead animal. And I couldn't explain. Psychoanalysis later suggested that it was quite simply because no one wanted me to do it. The explanation has since come to seem insufficient to me.

That was a strange late blooming of Empire in the decade after the war, when the Colonial Office took on factitious new life, and thousands of us went out to the Colonies. The Service became larger than it had been in years, swollen with ex-officers too accustomed to military life to do anything else, and with the innocent and the confused, like myself. I ended up a junior member of a transition team in a Central African country I shall not name, helping see to it that as much was given to the new native government as they could be persuaded to accept, in the way of a parliament, a well-disciplined army, a foreign service, a judiciary.

It was not after all very much. Those institutions that the British are sure no civilized nation can do without were, in the minds of many Africans who spoke freely to me, very like those exquisite japanned toffee-boxes from Fortnum & Mason that you used often to come across in native kraals, because the chieftains and shamans loved them so, to keep their juju in. Almost as soon as I arrived, it became evident that the commander in chief of the armed forces was impatient with the pace of things, and felt the need of no special transition to African, i.e., his own, control of the state. The most our Commission were likely to accomplish was to get the British population out without a blood-bath.

Even that would not be easy. We – we young men – were saddled with the duty of explaining to aged planters that there was no one left to defend their estates against confiscation, and that under the new constitution they hadn't a leg to stand on, and that despite how dearly their overseers and house people loved them, they ought to begin seeing what they could pack into a few small trunks. On the other hand, we were to calm the fears of merchants and diamond factors, and tell them that if they all simply dashed for it, they could easily precipitate a closing of the frontiers, with incalculable results.

There came a night when, more than usually certain that not a single Brit under my care would leave the country alive, nor deserved to either, I stood at the bar of the Planters' (just renamed the Republic) Club, drinking gin and Italian (tonic hadn't been reordered in weeks) and listening to the clacking of the fans. A fellow I knew slightly as a regular here saluted me; I nodded and returned to my thoughts. A moment later I found him next to me.

"I wonder," he said, "if I might have your ear for a moment."

The expression, in his mouth, was richly comic, or perhaps it was my exhaustion. He waited for my laughter to subside before speaking. He was called Rossie, and he'd spent a good many years in Africa, doing whatever came to hand. He was one of those Englishmen whom the sun turns not brown but only gray and greasy; his eyes were always watery, the cups of his lids red and painful to look at.

"I am," he said at last, "doing a favor for a chap who would like your help."

"I'll do what I can," I said.

"This is a chap," he said, "who has been too long in this country, and would like to leave it."

"There are many in his situation."

"Not quite."

"What is his name?" I said, taking out a memorandum book. "I'll pass it on to the Commission."

"Just the point," Rossie said. He drew closer to me. At the other end of the bar loud laughter arose from a group consisting of a newly commissioned field marshal – an immense, glossy, nearly blue-black man – and his two colonels, both British, both small and lean. They laughed when the field marshal laughed, though their laugh was not so loud, nor their teeth so large and white.

"He'll want to tell you his name himself," Rossie said. "I've only brought the message. He wants to see you, to talk to you. I said I'd tell you. That's all."

"To tell us . . ."

"Not you, all of you. *You:* you."

I drank. The warm, scented liquor was thick in my throat. "Me?"

"What he asked me to ask you," Rossie said, growing impatient, "was would you come out to his place, and see him. It isn't far. He wanted you, no one else. He said I was to insist. He said you were to come alone. He'll send a boy of his. He said tell no one."

There were many reasons why a man might want to do business with the Commission privately. I could think of none why it should be done with me alone. I agreed, with a shrug. Rossie seemed immediately to put the matter out of his mind, mopped his red face, and ordered drinks for both of us. By the time they were brought we were already discussing the Imperial groundnut scheme, which was to have kept this young republic self-sufficient, but which, it was now evident, would do no such thing.

I too put what had been asked of me out of my mind, with enough success that when on a windless and baking afternoon a native boy shook me awake from a nap, I could not imagine why.

"Who are you? What are you doing in my bungalow?"

He only stared down at me, as though it were he who could not think why I should be there before him. Questions in his own language got no response either. At length he backed out the door, clearly wanting me to follow; and so I did, with the dread one feels on remembering an unpleasant task one has contrived to neglect. I found him outside, standing beside my Land-Rover, ready to get aboard.

"All right," I said. "Very well." I got into the driver's seat. "Point the way."

It was a small spread of tobacco and a few dusty cattle an hour's drive from town, a low bungalow looking beaten in the ocher heat. He gave no greeting as I alighted from the Land-Rover but stood in the shadows of the porch unmoving: as though he had stood so a long time. He went back into the house as I approached, and when I went in, he was standing against the netting of the window, the light behind him. That seemed a conscious choice. He was smiling, I could tell: a strange and eager smile.

"I've waited a long time for you," he said. "I don't mind saying."

"I came as quickly as I could," I said.

"There was no way for me to know, you see," he said, "whether you'd come at all."

"Your boy was quite insistent," I said. "And Mr. Rossie – "

"I meant: to Africa." His voice was light, soft, and dry. "There being so much less reason for it, now. I've wondered often. In fact I don't think a day has passed this year when I haven't wondered." Keeping his back to the sunward windows, he moved to sit on the edge of a creaking wicker sofa. "You'll want a drink," he said.

"No." The place was filled with the detritus of an African bachelor farmer's digs: empty paraffin tins, bottles, tools, hanks of rope and motor parts. He put a hand behind him without looking and put it on the bottle he was no doubt accustomed to find there. "I tried to think reasonably about it," he said, pouring a drink. "As time went on, and things began to sour here, I came to be more and more certain that no lad with any pluck would throw himself away down here. And yet I couldn't know. Whether there might not be some impulse, I don't know, traveling to you from – elsewhere . . . I even thought of writing to you. Though whether to convince you to come or to dissuade you I'd no idea."

I sat, too. A cool sweat had gathered on my neck and the backs of my hands.

"Then," he said, "when I heard you'd come – well, I was afraid, frankly. I didn't know what to think." He dusted a fly from the rim of his glass, which he had not tasted. "You see," he said, "this was against the rules given me. That I – that I and – that you and I should meet."

Perhaps he's mad, I thought, and even as I thought it I felt intensely the experience called *déjà vu,* an experience I have always hated, hated like the nightmare. I steeled myself to respond coolly and took out my memorandum book and pencil. "I'm afraid you've rather lost me," I said – briskly I hoped. "Perhaps we'd better start with your name."

"Oh," he said, smiling again his mirthless smile, "not the hardest question first, please."

Without having, so far as I knew, the slightest reason for it, I began to feel intensely sorry for this odd dried jerky of a man, whose eyes alone seemed quick and shy. "All right," I said, "nationality, then. You are a British subject."

"Well, yes."

"Proof?" He answered nothing. "Passport?" No. "Army card? Birth certificate? Papers of any kind?" No. "Any connections in Britain? Relatives? Someone who could vouch for you, take you in?"

"No," he said. "None who could. None but you. It will have to be you."

"Now hold hard," I said.

"I don't know why I must," he said, rising suddenly and turning away to the window. "But I must. I must go back. I imagine dying here, being buried here, and my whole soul retreats in horror. I must go back. Even though I fear that, too."

He turned from the window, and in the sharp side light of the late afternoon his face was clearly the face of someone I knew. "Tell me," he said. "Mother and father. Your mother and father. They're alive?"

"No," I said. "Both dead."

"Very well," he said, "very well"; but it did not seem to be very well with him. "I'll tell you my story, then."

"I think you'd best do that."

"It's a long one."

"No matter." I had begun to feel myself transported, like a Sinbad, into somewhere that it were best I listen, and keep my counsel: and yet the first words of this specter's tale made that impossible.

"My name," he said, "is Denys Winterset."

I have come to believe, having had many years in which to think about it, that it must be as he said, that an impulse from somewhere else (he meant: some previous present, some earlier version of these circumstances) must press upon such a life as mine. That I chose the Colonial Service, that I came to Africa – and not just to Africa, but to that country: well, *if anything is chance, that was not* – as I understand Sir Geoffrey Davenant to have once said.

In that long afternoon, there where I perhaps could not have helped arriving eventually, I sat and perspired, listening – though it was for a long time very nearly impossible to hear what was said to me: an appointment in Khartoum some months from now, and some decades past; a club, outside all frames of reference; the Last equipment. It was quite like listening to the unfollowable logic of a madman, as meaningless as the roar of the insects outside. I only began to hear when this aged man, older than my grandfather, told me of something that he – that I – that he and I – had once done in boyhood, something secret, trivial really and yet so shameful that even now I will not write it down; something that only Denys Winterset could know.

"There now," he said, eyes cast down. "There now, you must believe me. You *will* listen. The world has not been as you thought it to be, any more than it was as I thought it to be, when I was as you are now. I shall tell you why: and we will hope that mine is the last story that need be told."

And so it was that I heard how he had gone up the road to Groote Schuur, that evening in 1893 (a young man then of course, only twenty-three), with the Webley revolver in his breast pocket as heavy as his heart, nearly sick with wonder and apprehension. The tropical suit he had been made to wear was monstrously hot, complete with full waistcoat and hard collar; the topee they insisted he use was as weighty as a crown. As he came in sight of the house, he could hear the awesome cries from the lion house, where the cats were evidently being given their dinner.

The big house appeared raw and unfinished to him, the trees yet ungrown and the great masses of scentless flowers – hydrangea, bougainvillaea, canna – that had smothered the place when last he had seen it, some decades later, just beginning to spread.

"Rhodes himself met me at the door – actually he happened to be going out for his afternoon ride – and welcomed me," he said. "I think the most striking thing about Cecil Rhodes, and it hasn't been noticed much, was his utter lack of airs. He was the least self-conscious man I have ever known; he did many things for effect, but he was himself entirely single: as whole as an egg, as the old French used to say.

"'The house is yours,' he said to me. 'Use it as you like. We don't dress for dinner, as a rule; too many of the guests would be taken short, you see. Now some of the fellows are playing croquet in the Great Hall. Pay them no mind.'

"I remember little of that evening. I wandered the house; the great skins of animals, the heavy beams of teak, the brass chandeliers. I looked into the library, full of the specially transcribed and bound classics that Rhodes had ordered by the yard from Hatchard's: all the authorities that Gibbon had consulted in writing the *Decline and Fall*. All of them: that had been Rhodes's order.

"Dinner was a long and casual affair, entirely male – Rhodes had not even any female servants in the house. There was much toasting and hilarity about the successful march into Matabeleland, and the foundation of a fort, which news had only come that week; but Rhodes seemed quiet at the table's head, even melancholy: many of his closest comrades were gone with the expeditionary column, and he seemed to miss them. I do remember that at one point the conversation turned to America. Rhodes contended – no one disputed him – that if we (he meant the Empire, of course) had not lost America, the peace of the world could have been secured forever. 'Forever,' he said. 'Perpetual Peace.' And his pale opaque eyes were moist.

"How I comported myself at table – how I joined the talk, how I kept up conversations on topics quite unfamiliar to me – none of that do I recall. It helped that I was supposed to have been only recently arrived in Africa: though one of Rhodes's band of merry men looked suspiciously at my sun-browned hands when I said so.

"As soon as I could after dinner, I escaped from the fearsome horse-play that began to develop among those left awake. I pleaded a touch of sun and was shown to my room. I took off the hateful collar and tie (not without difficulty) and lay on the bed otherwise fully clothed, alert and horribly alone. Perhaps you can imagine my thoughts."

"No," I said. "I don't think I can."

"No. Well. No matter. I must have slept at last; it seemed to be after midnight when I opened my eyes and saw Rhodes standing in the doorway, a candlestick in his hand.

" 'Asleep?' he asked softly.

" 'No,' I answered. 'Awake."

" 'Can't sleep either,' he said. 'Never do, much.' He ventured another step into the room. 'You ought to come out, see the sky,' he said. 'Quite spectacular. As long as you're up.'

"I rose and followed him. He was without his coat and collar; I noticed he wore carpet slippers. One button of his wide braces was undone; I had the urge to button it for him. Pale starlight fell in blocks across the black and white tiles of the hall, and the huge heads of beasts were mobile in the candlelight as we passed. I murmured something about the grandness of his house.

"'I told my architect,' Rhodes answered. 'I said I wanted the big and simple – the barbaric, if you like.' The candle flame danced before him. 'Simple. The truth is always simple.'

"The chessboard tiles of the hall continued out through the wide doors onto the veranda – the *stoep* as the old Dutch called it. At the frontier of the *stoep* great pillars divided the night into panels filled with clustered stars, thick and near as vine blossoms. From far off came a long cry as of pain: a lion, awake.

"Rhodes leaned on the parapet, looking into the mystery of the sloping lawns beyond the *stoep*. 'That's good news, about the chaps up in Matabeleland,' he said a little wistfully.

"'Yes.'

"'Pray God they'll all be safe.'

"'Yes.'

"'*Zambesia*,' he said after a moment. "What d'you think of that?'

"'I beg your pardon?'

"'As a name. For this country we'll be building. *Beyond the Zambesi*, you see.'

"'It's a fine name.'

"He fell silent a time. A pale, powdery light filled the sky: false dawn. 'They shall say, in London,' he said, '"Rhodes has taken for the Empire a country larger than Europe, at not a sixpence of cost to us, and we shall have that, and Rhodes shall have six feet by four feet."'

"He said this without bitterness, and turned from the parapet to face me. The Webley was pointed toward him. I had rested my (trembling) right hand on my left forearm, held up before me.

"'Why, what on earth,' he said.

"'Look,' I said.

"Drawing his look slowly away from me, he turned again. Out in the lawn, seeming in that illusory light to be but a long leap away, a male lion stood unmoving.

"'The pistol won't stop him,' I said, 'but it will deflect him. If you will go calmly through the door behind me, I'll follow.'

"Rhodes backed away from the rail, and without haste or panic turned and walked past me into the house. The lion, ochre in the blue night, regarded him with a lion's expression, at once aloof and concerned, and returned his look to me. I thought I smelled him. Then I saw movement in the young trees beyond. I thought for a moment that my lion must be an illusion, or a dream, for he took no notice of these sounds – the crush of a twig, a soft voice – but at length he did turn his eyes from me to them. I could see the dim figure of a game-keeper in a wide-awake hat, carrying a rifle, and Negroes with nets and poles: they were closing in carefully on the escapee. I stood for a moment longer, still poised to shoot, and then beat my own retreat into the house.

"Lights were being lit down the halls, voices calling: a lion does not appear on the lawn every night. Rhodes stood looking, not out the window, but at me. With deep embarrassment I clumsily pocketed the Webley (*I* knew what it had been given to me for, after all, even if he did not), and only then did I meet Rhodes's eyes.

"I shall never forget their expression, those pale eyes: a kind of exalted wonder, almost a species of adoration.

"'That's twice now in one day,' he said, 'that you have kept me from harm. You must have been sent, that's all. I really believe you have been sent.'

"I stood before him staring, with a horror dawning in my heart such as, God willing, I shall never feel again. I knew, you see, what it meant that I had let slip the moment: that now I could not go back the way I had come. The world had opened for an instant, and I and my companions had gone down through it to this time and place; and now it had closed over me again, a seamless whole. I had no one and nothing; no Last equipment awaited me at the Mount Nelson Hotel; the Otherhood could not rescue me, for I had canceled it. I was entirely alone.

"Rhodes, of course, knew nothing of this. He crossed the hall to where I stood with slow steps, almost reverently. He embraced me, a sudden great bear hug. And do you know what he did then?"

"What did he do?"

"He took me by the shoulders and held me at arm's length, and he insisted that I stay there with him. In effect, he offered me a job. For life, if I wanted it."

"What did you do?"

"I took it." He had finished his drink, and poured more. "I took it. You see, I simply had no place else to go."

Afternoon was late in the bungalow where we sat together, day hurried away with this tale. "I think," I said, "I shall have that drink now, if it's no trouble."

He rose and found a glass; he wiped the husk of a bug from it and filled it from his bottle. "It has always astonished me," he said, "how the mind, you know, can construct with lightning speed a reasonable, if quite mistaken, story to account for an essentially unreasonable event: I have had more than one occasion to observe this process.

"I was sure, instantly sure, that a lion which had escaped from Rhodes's lion house had appeared on the lawn at Groote Schuur just at the moment when I tried, but could not bring myself, to murder Cecil Rhodes. I can still see that cat in the pale light of predawn. And yet I cannot know if that is what happened, or if it is only what my mind has substituted for what did happen, which cannot be thought about.

"I am satisfied in my own mind – having had a lifetime to ponder it – that it cannot be possible for one to meet oneself on a trip into the past or future: that is a lie, invented by the Otherhood to forestall its own extinction, which was, however, inevitable.

"But I dream, sometimes, that I am lying on the bed at Groote Schuur, and a man enters – it is not Rhodes, but a man in a black coat and a bowler hat, into whose face I look as into a rotted mirror, who tells me impossible things.

"And I know that in fact there was no lion house at Groote Schuur. Rhodes wanted one, and it was planned, but it was never built."

In the summer of that year Rhodes – alive, alive-oh – went on expedition up into Pondoland, seeking concessions from an intransigent chief named Sicgau. Denys Winterset – this one, telling me the tale – went with him.

"Rhodes took Sicgau out into a field of mealies where he had had us set up a Maxim gun. Rhodes and the chief stood in the sun for a moment, and then Rhodes gave a signal; we fired the Maxim for a few seconds and mowed down much of the field. The chief stood unmoving for a long moment after the silence returned. Rhodes said to him softly: 'You see, this is what will happen to you and all your warriors if you give us any further trouble.'

"As a stratagem, that seemed to me both sporting and thrifty. It worked, too. But we were later to use the Maxims against men and not mealies. Rhodes knew that the Matabele had finally to be suppressed, or the work of building a white state north of the Zambezi would be hopeless. A way was found to intervene in a quarrel the Matabele were having with the Mashona, and in not too long we were at war with the Matabele. They were terribly, terribly brave; they were, after all, the first eleven in those parts, and they believed with reason that no one could withstand their leaf-bladed spears. I remember how they would come against the Maxims, and be mown down like the mealies, and fall back, and muster for another attack. Your heart sank; you prayed they would go away, but they would not. They came on again, to be cut down again. These puzzled, bewildered faces: I cannot forget them.

"And Christ, such drivel was written in the papers then, about the heroic stand of a few beleaguered South African police against so many battle-crazed natives! The only one who saw the truth was the author of that silly poem – Belloc, was it? You know – 'Whatever happens, we have got/The Maxim gun, and they have not.' It was as simple as that. The truth, Rhodes said, is always simple."

He took out a large pocket-handkerchief and mopped his face and his eyes; no doubt it was hot, but it seemed to me that he wept. Tears, idle tears.

"I met Dr. Jameson during the Matabele campaign," he continued. "Leander Starr Jameson. I think I have never met a man – and I have met many wicked and twisted ones – whom I have loathed so completely and so instantly. I had hardly heard of him, of course; he was already dead and unknown in this year as it had occurred in my former past, the only version of these events I knew. Jameson was a great lover of the Maxim; he took several along on the raid he made into the Transvaal in 1896, the raid that would eventually lead to war with the Boers, destroy Rhodes's credit, and begin the end of Empire: so I have come to see it. The fool.

"I took no part in that war, thank God. I went north to help put the railroad through: Cape-to-Cairo." He smiled, seemed almost about to laugh, but did not; only mopped his face again. It was as though I were interrogating him, and he were telling me all this under the threat of the rubber truncheon or the rack. I wanted him to stop, frankly; only I dared say nothing.

"I made up for a lack of engineering expertise by my very uncertain knowledge of where and how, one day, the road would run. The telegraph had already reached Uganda; next stop was Wadi Halfa. The rails would not go through so easily. I became a sort of scout, leading the advance parties, dealing with the chieftains. The Maxim went with me, of course. I learned the weapon well."

Here there came another silence, another inward struggle to continue. I was left to picture what he did not say: *That which I did I should not have done; that which I should have done I did not do.*

"Rhodes gave five thousand pounds to the Liberal party to persuade them not to abandon Egypt: for there his railroad must be hooked to the sea. But then of course came the end of the whole scheme in German Tanganyika: no Cape-to-Cairo road. Germany was growing great in the world; the Germans wanted to have an Empire of their own. It finished Rhodes.

"By that time I was a railroad expert. The nonexistent Uganda Railroad was happy to acquire my services: I had a reputation, among the blacks, you see . . . I think there was a death for every mile of that road as it went through the jungle to the coast: rinderpest, fever, Nanda raids. We would now and then hang a captured Nanda warrior from the telegraph poles, to discourage the others. By the time the rails reached Mombasa, I was an old man; and Cecil Rhodes was dead."

He died of his old heart condition, the condition that had brought him out to Africa in the first place. He couldn't breathe in the awful heat of that summer of 1902, the worst anyone could remember; he wandered from room to room at Groote Schuur, trying to catch his breath. He lay in the darkened drawing room and could not breathe. They took him down to his cottage by the sea, and put ice between the ceiling and the iron roof to cool it; all afternoon the punkahs spooned the air. Then, suddenly, he decided to go to England. April was there: April showers. A cold spring: it seemed that could heal him. So a cabin was fitted out for him aboard a P&O liner, with electric fans and refrigerating pipes and oxygen tanks.

He died on the day he was to sail. He was buried at that place on the Matopos, the place he had chosen himself; buried facing north.

"He wanted the heroes of the Matabele campaign to be buried there with him. I could be one, if I chose; only I think my name would not be found among the register of those who fought. I think my name does not appear at all in history: not in the books of the Uganda Railroad, not in the register of the Mount Nelson Hotel for 1893. I have never had the courage to look."

I could not understand this, though it sent a cold shudder between my shoulder blades. The Original Situation, he explained, could not be returned to; but it could be restored, as those events that the Otherhood brought about were one by one come upon in time, and then not brought about. And as the Original Situation was second by second restored, the whole of his adventure in the past was continually worn away into nonbeing, and a new future replaced his old past ahead of him.

"You must imagine how it has been for me," he said, his voice now a whisper from exertion and grief. "To everyone else it seemed only that time went on – history – the march of events. But to me it has been otherwise. It has been the reverse of the nightmare from which you wake in a sweat of relief to find that the awful disaster has not occurred, the fatal step was not taken: for I have seen the real world gradually replaced by this other, nightmare world, which everyone else assumes is real, until nothing in past or present is as I knew it to be; until I am like the servant in Job: *I only am escaped to tell thee.*"

March 8, 1983

I awoke again this morning from the dream of the forest in the sea: a dream without people or events in it, or anything whatever except the gigantic dendrites, vast masses of pale leaves, and the tideless waters, light and sunshot toward the surface, darkening to impenetrability down below. It seemed there were schools of fish, or flocks of birds, in the leaves, something that faintly disturbed them, now and then; otherwise, stillness.

No matter that orthogonal logic refutes it, I cannot help believing that my present succeeds in time the other presents and futures that have gone into making it. I believe that as I grow older I come to incorporate the experiences I have had as an older man in pasts (and futures) now obsolete: as though in absolute time I continually catch up with myself in the imaginary times that fluoresce from it, gathering dreamlike memories of the lives I have lived therein. Somewhere God (I have come to believe in God; there was simply no existing otherwise) is keeping these universes in a row, and sees to it that they happen in succession, the most recently generated one last – and so felt to be last, no matter where along it I stand.

I remember, being now well past the age that he was then, the Uganda Railroad, the Nanda arrows, all the death.

I remember the shabby library and the coal fire, the encyclopedia in another orthography; the servant at the double doors.

I think that in the end, should I live long enough, I shall remember nothing but the forest in the sea. That is the terminus: complete strangeness that is at the same time utterly changeless; what cannot be becoming all that has ever been.

I took him out myself, in the end, abandoning my commission to do so, for there was no way that he could have crossed the border by himself, without papers, a nonexistent man. And it was just at that moment, as we motored up through the Sudan past Wadi Halfa, that the Anglo-French expeditionary force took Port Said. The Suez incident, that last hopeless spasm of Empire, was taking its inevitable course. Inevitable: I have not used the word before.

When we reached the Canal, the Israelis had already occupied the east bank. The airport at Ismailia was a shambles, the greater part of the Egyptian Air Force shot up, planes scattered in twisted attitudes like dead birds after a storm. We could find no plane to take us. *He* had gone desperately broody, wide-eyed and speechless, useless for anything. I felt as though in a dream where one is somehow saddled with an idiot brother one had not had before.

And yet it was only the confusion and mess that made my task possible at all, I suppose. There were so many semiofficial and unofficial British scurrying or loafing around Port Said when we entered the city that our passage was unremarked. We went through the smoke and dust of that famously squalid port like two ghosts – two ghosts progressing through a ghost city at the retreating edge of a ghost of empire. And the crunch of broken glass continually underfoot.

We went out on an old oiler attached to the retreating invasion fleet, which had been ordered home having accomplished nothing except, I suppose, the end of the British Empire in Africa. He stood on the oiler's boat deck and watched the city grow smaller and said nothing. But once he laughed, his dry, light laugh: it made me think of the noise that Homer says the dead make. I asked the reason.

"I was remembering the last time I went out of Africa," he said. "On a day much like this. Very much like this. This calm weather; this sea. Nothing else the same, though. Nothing else." He turned to me smiling, and toasted me with an imaginary glass. "The end of an era," he said.

March 10

My chronicle seems to be degenerating into a diary.

I note in the *Times* this morning the sale of the single known example of the 1856 magenta British Guiana, for a sum far smaller than was supposed to be its worth. Neither the names of the consortium that sold it nor the names of the buyers were made public. I see in my mind's eye a small, momentary fire.

I see now that there is no reason why this story should come last, no matter my feeling, no matter that in Africa he hoped it would. Indeed there is no reason why it should even fall last in this chronicling, nor why the world, the sad world in which it occurs, should be described as succeeding all others – it does not, any more than it precedes them. For the sake of a narrative only, perhaps; perhaps, like God, we cannot live without narrative.

I used to see him, infrequently, in the years after we both came back from Africa: he didn't die as quickly as we both supposed he would. He used to seek me out, in part to borrow a little money – he was living on the dole and on what he brought out of Africa, which was little enough. I stood him to tea now and then and listened to his stories. He'd appear at our appointed place in a napless British Warm, ill-fitting, as his eyeglasses and National Health false teeth were also. I imagine he was terribly lonely. I know he was.

I remember the last time we met, at a Lyons teashop near the Marble Arch. I'd left the Colonial Service, of course, under a cloud, and taken a position teaching at a crammer's in Holborn until something better came along (nothing ever did; I recently inherited the headmaster's chair at the same school; little has changed there over the decades but the general coloration of the students).

"This curious fancy haunts me," he said to me on that occasion. "I picture the Fellows, all seated around the great table in the executive committee's dining room; only it is rather like Miss Havisham's, you know, in Dickens: the roast beef has long since gone foul, and the silver tarnished, and the draperies rotten; and the Fellows dead in their chairs, or mad, dust on their evening clothes, the port dried up in their glasses. Huntington. Davenant. The President *pro tem.*"

He stirred sugar in his tea (he liked it horribly sweet; so, of course, do I). "It's not true, you know, that the Club stood somehow at a nexus of possibilities, amid multiplying realities. If that were so, then what the Fellows did would be trivial or monstrous or both: generating endless new universes just to see if they could get one to their liking. No: it is we, out here, who live in but one of innumerable possible worlds. In there, they were like a man standing at the north pole, whose only view, wherever he looks, is south: they looked out upon a single encompassing reality, which it was their opportunity – no, their duty, as they saw it – to make as happy as possible, as free from the calamities they knew of as they could make it.

"Well, they were limited people, more limited than their means to work good or evil. That which they did they should not have done. And yet what they hoped for us was not despicable. The calamities they saw were real. Anyone who could would try to save us from them: as a mother would pull her child, her foolish child, from the fire. They ought to be forgiven; they ought."

I walked with him up toward Hyde Park Corner. He walked now with agonizing slowness, as I will, too, one day; it was a rainy autumn Sunday, and his pains were severe. At Hyde Park Corner he stopped entirely, and I thought perhaps he could go no farther: but then I saw that he was studying the monument that stands there. He went closer to it, to read what was written on it.

I have myself more than once stopped before this neglected monument. It is a statue of the boy David, a memorial to the Machine Gun Corps, and was put up after the First World War. Some little thought must have gone into deciding how to memorialize that arm which had changed war forever; it seemed to require a religious sentiment, a quote from the Bible, and one was found. Beneath the naked boy are written words from Kings:

> *Saul has slain his thousands*
> *But David his tens of thousands.*

He stood in the rain, in his vast coat, looking down at these words, as though reading them over and over; and the faint rain that clung to his cheeks mingled with his tears:

> *Saul has slain his thousands*
> *But David his tens of thousands.*

I never saw him again after that day, and I did not seek for him: I think it unlikely he could have been found.

AFTERWORD

Much of the impulse and many of the details of the preceding come from the second and third volumes of Jan Morris's enthralling chronicle of the rise and decline of the British Empire, *Pax Britannica* (1968) and *Farewell the Trumpets* (1978). I hope she will forgive the author the liberties he has taken, and accept his gratitude for the many hours she has allowed him to spend dawdling in a world more fantastical than any he could himself invent.

The story of Rhodes's death and many details of his character and conversation are taken from Sarah Gertrude Millin's elegant and neglected biography *Cecil Rhodes* (London, 1933).

The story of Rhodes in Pondoland, along with much else that was suggestive, comes from John Ellis's book *The Social History of the Machine Gun* (1975).

For an introduction to that book, for his convincing analysis of the possibilities and limits of what I have called orthogonal logic, and in general for his infectious enthusiasm for notions, the author's thanks to Bob Chasell (hi, Bob).

The Dimple in Draco

PHILIP LATHAM

Philip Latham is the pseudonym of Robert S. Richardson (1902–81), a distinguished astronomer who occasionally wrote articles under his own name, but published fiction between the 1940s and 1960s only under the Latham name. His stories characteristically feature astronomers, and until his later years always focused on science, especially theoretical physics embodied as fact.

From the flamboyant, apocalyptic astronomical fiction of Camille Flammarion in the late 19th century to the works of Fred Hoyle and Gregory Benford, working astronomers and astrophysicists have contributed stories of broad scope and cosmic speculation to the development of science fiction. The word "astronomical" is, after all, a synonym for very large in number or scale. Cosmology and astronomy are primary repositories of images for the SF genre, as was nature for the Romantic poets. And, of course, it is the astronomers who investigate the environments that are the literal settings of much science fiction. But it is also the teasing, ambiguous border between the physical and the metaphysical that astronomical science fiction often confronts, and that gives depth and emotional force to the cold and the distant. As in this story.

There was never any doubt when quitting time came to the Institute for Cosmological Physics, Bill Backus reflected. Promptly at 4.53 p.m. the women all started heading for the powder room, whence shortly thereafter came the sound of water in turbulence. It was one of the zero points in this uneasy world.

For the third time he reached for the telephone and for the third time hesitated. It was 4.57 now. The girl at the switchboard always got sore if you kept her after five o'clock. Oh, well, the hell with her. He needed help. He seized the phone.

"Two-seven, please."

No answer . . . no answer . . . no . . .

"MacCready," came a noncommittal voice.

"Mac, this is Bill."

"Bill! It's so good to hear your voice!"

"Listen, Mac, I've got something down here in the measuring room I think will interest you."

"So's my wife. She's probably mixing it now."

"I'd like your opinion very much. Shouldn't take ten minutes."

One . . . two . . . three . . .

"All right. See you."

A few minutes later MacCready sauntered into the measuring room, hoisted one leg over a corner of the bench that ran along the wall, and applied a match to his pipe. When the tobacco was going to his satisfaction, he folded his arms and gazed expectantly at Bill.

"Here I am. Interest me."

Bill indicated the Toepfer measuring engine beside him.

"Plate's on there. Got it last week with the prime focus spectrograph. Six-hour exposure in the second order blue. I nearly froze. Coldest night in the memory of man – "

"You don't look so good," MacCready remarked.

"Maybe that's because I don't feel so good," Bill said. He rose and began pacing the floor. "Take a look at the plate, will you, and tell me what you think."

"But your feet seem better," MacCready added encouragingly.

"Yeah, they are better. Now will you look at the plate?"

MacCready laid aside his pipe and peered into the eyepiece.

"Nice spectrum," he said. "Real sharp lines."

"But *what* lines?" Bill cried. "I've been working on those lines for three days. Can't identify a single one." He ran his fingers through his black hair. "It's driving me crazy."

"Well, d'you have to get so dramatic about it?" MacCready asked. He gave the focusing screw a touch. "What is this famous object, anyhow?"

"Well, you see, that's what I don't know."

"You don't know!" MacCready stared at him. "Do you realize how much it cost the Institute to get this plate? Do you know that we have

seventeen applications on file for time at this instrument? Applications from highly qualified individuals with no suspicion of insanity in their background. And then you take our giant eye, as the newspapers are pleased to call it, and bang away at any old – "

"Mac, shut up." Bill lit a cigarette. "I was after NGC 2146, that way-north nebula in Cepheus, I guess it is. This new night assistant was on that evening. Poor guy got all balled up. My fault as much as his. You wouldn't believe it possible, but he got set on the wrong side of the pole. Landed me over in Draco somewhere. I thought the setting looked kind of funny – "

"Couldn't you tell from your star field?"

"Well, I should, but the fields weren't so different. Anyhow – "

" – anyhow you goofed but you got *something*," MacCready finished for him. "By any chance would you have the vaguest notion what it is? Radio source? Interloper? QSG? Haro-Luyten object? Humason-Zwicky star? Have I left out anything?"

"All I know, it's got a spectrum nobody ever saw before."

"Then what are you griping about?" MacCready demanded. "That's *good*. Maybe this object's got the world's biggest red shift. You've probably dredged up some lines buried thousands of angstroms deep in the ultraviolet."

"Nope, won't suit, Mac. Remember the Houston meeting? It was agreed we're living in an exploding universe with a q-zero of 2.5. This thing's way off the beam – much too bright."

"You know what your problem is, Bill?" MacCready was suddenly serious. "You've always got to relate to somebody else. You're afraid to take your results just as they stand."

"But there must be an answer," Bill protested. "What else can it be?"

MacCready shrugged and fell to scrutinizing the plate again.

"Wouldn't surprise me if the answer's staring us right in the face," he said. "Only it's so simple we can't see it."

He moved the plate carriage a bit.

"Now you take these three big lines I see here . . . Why couldn't the one on my left be that Hell line at – what is it? – 1640? And the one in the middle – "

"Oh, my gawd, don't you think I've been all through that search list?" Bill said wearily. "None of 'em's any good. I've tried a bunch of hundred-to-one shots. They're no good either. Nothing fits."

"Too bad." MacCready frowned slightly. "Strange . . . these lines are all in absorption, aren't they?"

"Here's my list of wavelengths," Bill said, handing him a sheet of paper. "They're the means of my measures on the machine and some runs with the electronic line-profile comparator. They ought to be pretty good."

"I'm sure they are," MacCready murmured. He shot a sudden glance at Bill. "You sure you set the grating in the right order spectrum?"

"Mac, I *couldn't* make a mistake like that."

"Congratulations."

There was a long silence broken only by an occasional motor starting up in the parking lot, and the steady rumble of traffic from the boulevard nearby. MacCready was the first to speak.

"After you got this plate, did you take another exposure on a familiar object, same spectrograph – same emulsion – same everything?"

"Yes."

"All right?"

"Yes."

"It was?"

"Yes!" Bill shouted. "In France it's *oui*. In Spanish it's *si*. In Russian it's *da*."

MacCready transferred his attention from the plate to Bill's list of wavelengths.

"You know, these three big lines remind me of something," he muttered. "But I'll confess I haven't the faintest notion what it is."

Bill looked completely deflated. He began pacing the room again, clasping and unclasping his hands behind him. MacCready seemed to have forgotten his existence.

Bill tossed away his cigarette.

"Well, thanks for coming down, Mac. I'd gotten to the end of my rope. Thought perhaps you could suggest something."

There was no response. Bill paced the floor for another five minutes.

"Well, I've got to go. We're having company tonight."

"Yeah, you run along," MacCready told him. "Leaving myself in a minute . . . just want to check one thing."

Bill was nearly out the door when MacCready called suddenly, "Bill."

"Yeah?"

"Call my wife, will you? Tell her I'll be a little late."

Bill had to wait forever before he got a break in the traffic at Los

Robles. Why did he keep coming this way? he asked himself. There was no answer. You saw an opening – you took a deep breath – uttered a prayer – and if you were lucky you made it.

Turning north toward Hillhurst he saw that the signal at Cordova was going to be red, as usual. The signal was always red at Cordova. In the past five years he must have crossed Cordova going north at least two thousand times. There had been just three times by actual count when he had hit the green light. His confidence in the theory of probability had been badly shaken.

Through the tangle of varicolored lights, leering Santa Clauses, liquor advertisements, and five-pointed stars* of Bethlehem, Bill perceived a huge sign looming ahead, VILLAGE MARKET. *Click!* What was he supposed to do? What was he supposed to – Helen's grocery list, of course, Good old autohypnosis.

Within the Village Market the aisles were abustle with hausfrauen pushing metal carts, their vacant gaze reflecting the trancelike state induced by the sight of merchandise in profusion. Bill took a cart himself and went to work on Helen's grocery list, tracking down the various items by the awkward process of taking them in the order written. Occasionally when it seemed like a good idea he tossed in an extra item or two. How often he had come in for a fifty-nine-cent piece of cheese and departed laden down with a lot of junk he never originally had the slightest intention of buying. But who were we? Mere puppets moving at the bidding of the vast formless things that operate these huge pleasure domes of produce.

Helen wrote her shopping items in a code that might have baffled the best brains in Interpol. This time, however, it had been pretty clear sailing. He now had in the cart the "6 nce rd rpe toms" and the "2 pkes lmn jlo," and finally had reached the last item, "2 dz Ye Olde Eng Muffs." This sounded almost too easy. On any rational distribution system Olde English Muffins could hardly be anywhere else but in the bread section. He glanced at the Store Guide. Bread? . . . Bread? . . . Section 5. Where was he? Way over in 21 among Frozen Desserts and mouthwash. He deftly changed course and started bearing toward smaller numbers. 2 . . . 3 . . . 4 . . . 6 . . . 7. No 5! Must have missed it. Scan more carefully now . . . 3 . . . 4 . . . 6 . . . 7. Number 5 was absolutely and positively missing.

He looked around for a clerk, but there was none in sight. Neither was there any bread. He explored one aisle after another as fast as traffic permitted. There were shelves and bins loaded with pickles and

*Stars do not have points sticking out of them. Stars are spherical.

olives, wieners and knockwurst, yoghurt and horseradish. But no Olde English Muffins. Well, he couldn't spend the evening pushing a metal cart around the Village Market. He picked up a box of Bixmix and headed for Checkers' Row.

The porch lights were already burning when he turned into the driveway. That was bad. It meant that even now company was ominously near. Closing the garage door, he noticed the stars of Auriga rising over the mountains to the north. How odd Capella looked, reddened almost to the color of Mars by the smoke and haze. Auriga had always been his favorite constellation. All the constellations had a background rich in mythological lore – except Auriga. Auriga was known as "the Charioteer." But where were his chariot and horse? Nobody knew. The stars of Auriga were meaningless.

"Well, where have *you* been?" Helen demanded, as he staggered into the kitchen with his load of groceries. She was a small woman whose early blond prettiness was beginning to show signs of wear under the ceaseless battering of suburbia: the Garden Club, the Art League, WAGS,† etc., etc.

"Where do you think?" Bill growled. "Picking up the stuff you forgot."

She started sorting over the groceries. "It shouldn't have taken – *Where's the muffins?*"

"Couldn't find 'em. Got Bixmix instead."

"Why couldn't you find them?"

"Hidden too well, I guess."

"Why, they're right by the bread."

"Couldn't find the bread either."

"Did you ask a clerk?"

"Didn't see any to ask."

"But there's always – "

"It's the truth!" he cried. "What do you want me to do? Lie to you?"

"Oh, do as you like. I don't care." With a resigned air she began putting away the various items. "Now hurry and change your clothes. They'll be here any minute."

He was scarcely halfway up the stairs when she came dashing after him. "Your feet! What's happened to your feet?"

"Don't know." He shrugged. "They just didn't hurt when I got up this morning."

"What did I tell you," Helen told him triumphantly. "You wouldn't go to see Dr. Levine. He's only the best orthopedic specialist in town but of course you know more than he does. If I hadn't made an

†Women Against Smog.

appointment for you, you'd *never* have gone. Now admit it. Those arch supporters did help, didn't they?"

"If I'd worn those arch supporters one more day I wouldn't be ambulant now."

"But they must have done you *some* good." She regarded him with despair. "If it wasn't the arch supporters, what was it?"

Bill did not answer immediately. He leaned against the railing, gazing thoughtfully at some of Helen's abstract artwork on the opposite wall.

"Last night," he declared solemnly, "my feet were healed."

"Healed?"

He nodded. "What they called a miracle in the old days."

"So it was a miracle and not the arch supporters?"

"Why couldn't I be cured by a miracle?" he demanded angrily. "Other people are. People with their stomach and lungs eaten up by cancer. Suddenly they're all right. They rise from their bed and walk. They've got sworn medical testimony to prove it."

Helen hesitated uncertainly. "But you're not the miracle type."

"What's the matter with me?"

"I always supposed you had to be kind of on the saintly side."

He dismissed her objection with a wave of his hand.

"Merely a technicality." He closed his eyes for a few moments as if in meditation. "I hadn't intended to say anything about it, but for your information, I was healed by an angel who appeared in my room last night."

"So that was what I heard going on in there."

"She appeared over by the filing cabinet," Bill continued. "She was surrounded by a golden halo that illuminated the whole room. I thought I'd forgotten to turn the lights out at first." His voice dropped almost to a whisper. "She was no ordinary angel, either."

"It's so nice you got special attention."

"She had the most beautiful golden red hair." There was a faraway look in his eyes. "Her name was Edna."

"No last name?"

"Naturally I was somewhat startled at the sudden appearance of this apparition. 'What do you want?' I asked, in a voice that trembled.

"'Have no fear, William,' she replied, approaching the bed. 'I have come to heal you. Not to harm you.

"'To heal me?' I whispered.

"'Move over, William,' she said, 'so that I may touch you.'

"So I shoved over in the bed a little – "

His narrative was interrupted by the flash of headlights and the sound of a car pulling up in the driveway.

"There they are now!" Helen exclaimed. "And here I've been wasting my time talking to you about your feet and this redheaded angel."

Bill slowly mounted the stairs, his lips continuing to move inaudibly. In his room he stood for a while inspecting the place where he had recounted Edna's appearance. From the lower depths came the shriek of feminine voices raised in greeting interspersed with occasional masculine rumbles. Evidently the Nortons had picked up Bernice and Clem on the way over. Clem Tuttle was in advertising and Jim Norton was an agent for Inertia Acres, a real-estate project for the retired. Bernice Tuttle and Dottie Norton were among his favorite wives, but he found it hard to work up much enthusiasm for their husbands. It was while struggling into his shirt that it occurred to him that all the people they saw were friends of Helen's. Outside the office he had no friends.

Bill came downstairs, said hello all around, and made a quick exit to the kitchen to mix the cocktails. He put too much vodka into the martinis and had to drink a couple of glasses to provide more room for the vermouth. Back in the living room he had hoped to strike up a conversation with Bernice or Dottie, but the situation was hopeless. The girls were in ecstasy over Helen's Christmas tree, which was not a Christmas tree at all but a dead limb salvaged from the oak in the back yard. She had adorned its gnarled branches with blue and silver balls, with here and there an aerodynamically inadequate angel in flight. Since the girls were engaged, he was thrown upon the company of Jim and Clem, who were discussing the situation that had developed at Anoakia U., their old alma mater. It appeared that the quality of the faculty and student body had been steadily deteriorating since their departure in '41. Since Bill had never attended Anoakia U., and never had had much use for the place anyhow, he found the conversation less than fascinating. He sipped his cocktail, and moodily contemplated Bernice Tuttle's knees.

As if from a great distance he heard Helen calling him.

"Bill, telephone." He went into the hall, taking his glass with him. As he expected, it was Mac.

"Bill, what's your dispersion on that plate?"

"Hundred and ninety angstroms per millimeter."

"What kind of plate was it?"

"IIa-O, baked. Why?"

"Just checking, was all."

"Say, Mac, I explained to your wife it was my fault about getting home late."

"Well, as a matter of fact, I'm still at the office."

"Still at the office!" Bill went cold sober in an instant. "Mac, what do you know?"

"Nothing I want to talk about yet. But I think I'm gaining on it."

"Give me a ring – " But he had hung up.

Bill's mind was racing. Mac would never have called unless he was on to something big. A "critical" object that might settle the cosmological controversy once and for all. He gulped down the rest of his drink and casually strolled back to the living room. How petty they all were. Jim and Clem were thoroughly in agreement that autonomy was not for Anoakia U. The girls were deploring the Santa Claus situation that had developed at the various department stores around town. That Santa Claus at the Bon Marché, they must have got him from central casting! Did you get a whiff of his breath? And the way he talked to the children! Honestly, you'd have thought he was playing King Lear!

The soggy part of a Hillhurst evening came after dinner, when the guests were swollen with food, and the cocktails only a dull memory. There were two ways to endure the time till departure: (1) the men gathered at one end of the room and talked about their automobiles and their children, while the women went into a huddle at the other end and talked about their clothes and their children; or (2) somebody showed color slides of their trip to Hawaii last summer. One hostess had made a valiant attempt to break the pattern by handing out selected passages from Ovid and Chaucer to be read aloud, but some of the men had balked. But a few bold spirits still fought on. When her guests were comfortably relaxed over their coffee and liqueurs, Helen stepped to the center of the room and clapped her hands.

"Now I'm not going to let you sit around all evening," she informed them. "We're going to play a game called Three Answers. One person, called the Grand Inquisitor, asks the questions. The rest of us give the answers. We make up some sort of story and the Grand Inquisitor, by questioning us, tries to find the key to it."

This announcement was followed by a brief silence.

"Sounds like one of these fun things," Clem grunted, knocking the ashes from his cigar.

Jim raised his hand. "Mrs. Chairman, I would like to nominate my wife for Grand Inquisitor. She can beat any lie detector that was ever invented."

Dottie had a question. "How do we know what answers to give?"

"We answer as a group," Helen said. "The Grand Inquisitor can ask all the questions he likes. But we can only answer in three ways: yes, no, or maybe. I'll explain the details later. Now who'll be Grand Inquisitor?"

"I hereby nominate Bill Backus for G.I.," Clem said.

"Second the motion," Jim said promptly.

"Bill analyzes this deep space stuff all day," Clem said. "Ought to be easy for him.

"I'd *love* to be analyzed by Bill," Dottie cried.

"Well, darling, I guess you're Grand Inquisitor," Helen said. "Now go out in the kitchen and wait there till I call you."

Bill shuffled out to the kitchen, where he began picking at the remains of the turkey. From the front room came snatches of conversation and bursts of stifled laughter, but he was unable to distinguish any words. His mind kept going back to Mac at the office. It was nearly eleven. He had hoped to hear from him by this time if he knew anything exciting. Probably the whole thing had collapsed and Mac was home in bed. He had half a notion to give him a ring when he heard Helen calling him, "All right, you can come now."

Bill strode into the living room trying to assume the grim expression appropriate to a Grand Inquisitor. How to begin this crazy game? Try some questions of a general nature until he got a lead.

"Has Clem landed that brassiere account yet?"

"No," they responded in unison.

"Have Jim and Bernice run off together?"

"No."

"Was it some sort of crime?"

"Yes."

"Was the crime committed in this city?"

"Maybe."

"In this immediate area?"

"Yes."

"Was it a murder?"

"No."

"Something more ghastly?"

"Maybe."

This was tougher than he had anticipated. Why had Helen ever gotten him into this thing? How to proceed? They were gazing at him expectantly . . . gleefully . . .

"Was the person involved a man?"

"No."

"A woman?"

"No."

"An animal, then?"

"No."

No? What on earth . . . ? A suspicion began to dawn. *Was* it something on *Earth?*

"Was the victim a creature from outer space?"

"Yes!"

On the trail at last!

"Was it a creature from Mars?"

"No."

"Was it from Venus?"

"No."

"Mercury?"

"Maybe."

Not what he had expected, but keep on.

"Was it from Jupiter? Saturn? Uranus?"

"No! No! No!"

Well . . . there weren't many planets left. With elaborate casualness he inquired, "Did this creature, by any chance, come from Pluto?"

"Yes!" they shrieked.

At last!

"Is this Plutonian creature at present somewhere within the environs of this city?"

"Maybe."

"So you don't know?"

"Maybe."

Perhaps it would help if he knew more about the creature itself.

"Have you seen this creature?"

"Yes."

"Is it larger than man-size?"

"Yes."

"Is this creature affected adversely by the heat?"

"No."

A flash of inspiration.

"Is it in this house right now?"

"Maybe."

They were hedging now.

"Is it in the basement?"

"No."

"The attic?"

"No."

"The refrigerator?"

"No."

"Under the stairway?"

"Maybe."

Relentlessly he pursued the phantom creature over the house. But despite his best efforts it eluded him. He fancied he detected a hint of scorn . . . even contempt . . . in their eyes. Suddenly he recalled Mac's remark: *The answer may be staring us right in the face. Only it's so simple we can't see it.*

Go back . . . see if he had overlooked anything.

"You said this creature is also an inhabitant of Mercury?"

"Maybe."

"Then it *is* capable of withstanding a high temperature?"

"Yes."

He was groping for the next question when the telephone rang. *Mac!*

"Don't go. Be back in a minute."

It was Mac, all right.

"Well, Bill, I think I've got the answer." He sounded more relaxed. "But I'll be darned if I know what it means."

"Let me have it anyhow."

"Remember those three big lines I said reminded me of something? You naturally assumed they were ultraviolet lines Doppler-shifted into the visible. Only you couldn't identify 'em with anything in the UV. Neither could I. Wasted about two hours convincing myself of the fact."

He took about a three count.

"So, since I was all alone, I decided to play a crazy hunch. Bill, do you know what those lines are?"

"How the hell – "

"They're those three big ionized calcium lines in the infrared."

"Infrared!"

"This thing's got a velocity of about 0.6c."

"That wouldn't give so much of a redshift."

"Who said anything about a redshift? This is a violetshift. Bill, this thing is coming *our way*."

"Get out!"

"Fact!"

"Mac, you can't screw up the whole universe that easy. Why, it contradicts everything we know. Besides, three lines aren't enough. You could force an agreement . . . a pretty good agreement."

"I'm sorry, Bill, but everything else fits, too. Your line at 3929 is 7699 of potassium . . . 4494 is 8806 of magnesium . . ."

"Mac, what does it *mean*?"

"From the geometry of the situation I would say it means there's a dimple in the expanding universe in the direction of Draco."

It was so long before he spoke again that Bill began to wonder if he'd hung up.

"I'm only giving you an answer, Bill. What it means is *your* problem."

Bill found his guests in various stages of relaxation when he returned to the living room. It was hard to get his mind on Hillhurst again.

"I'm afraid it's getting late," Bernice said. "Clem and I have to be up early tomorrow. We're driving to Carmel, you know."

"Oh, don't go," Helen protested.

"It's been such a lovely evening," Dottie told her. "But really – "

"Now wait a minute," Jim boomed, coming from the bathroom. "We've got to put the Grand Inquisitor straight first."

"Sure do," Clem chuckled. "Bill would toss all night."

Jim shook his head regretfully. "Bill, old boy, I'm afraid the game was rigged."

"Rigged?" He had only been half listening.

"You see," Jim went on, "if the last letter in the last word of a question was a vowel we all answered yes. If it was a consonant we answered no. And if it was a W or Y we answered maybe." He grinned. "Get it?"

It took a while.

"So I could have gone on asking questions forever," Bill said slowly. "And you could have gone on giving me answers forever. And I'd never have known any more than in the beginning."

"Afraid that's about the size of it," Jim said. He crunched out his cigar. "Well, Dottie, go get your costly mink . . ."

Bill accompanied his guests to the door, dutifully went through the ritual of parting, and waved as they went down the driveway.

Back in the living room Helen gazed listlessly at the remains of the hors d'oeuvres and the cigarette trays. "No use cleaning up tonight, I guess." She glanced at Bill standing by the north window. "What's the matter? Aren't you coming to bed?"

"I believe I'll stay down here for a while," he told her.

"I should think you'd be anxious to see your redheaded friend."

"Perhaps I am.

Helen paused at the stairs. "You didn't exactly sparkle tonight, did you?" she remarked. "What was the matter?"

"Tired, I guess.

"Who was it called?"

"MacCready."

"What did he want?"

"Oh . . . nothing."

"Nothing! When he calls after midnight!"

"It was about a dimple in Draco."

"A dimple – "

"Object's headed toward the Earth. Everything else is rushing away. Puts a dimple in the universe out in Draco."

"Headed toward the Earth! Very fast?"

Bill shrugged. "About six-tenths c – hundred thousand miles a second."

"You mean it's going to hit us?"

"Afraid not. You see, it's quite a ways off."

"How far?"

"Oh, hell, I don't know," he said impatiently. "A billion light-years maybe."

"Well, you don't need to be so disagreeable about it. I can ask, can't I?"

"It's like Job asking the Voice out of the Whirlwind how much torque He's got."

Helen stood without speaking for several moments, then turned and went slowly up the stairs. Bill waited until he heard her door close. Then he switched out the lights and drew the curtains away from the window.

Capella was far above the haze now, shining in the stars of Auriga with a golden reddish glow, as bright as the glow of Edna's hair. Suddenly Bill had the most intense sense of identity with Auriga. How lonely he must be up there among all those gods and monsters, the only one without a story. Did the old Charioteer ever ponder the meaning of his stars? If so, what were *his* answers? Or did he bother to ask questions anymore – when the answers had no meaning?

Consider Her Ways

JOHN WYNDHAM

John Wyndham is the pseudonym of John Beynon Harris (1903–69), an important British genre SF writer of the mid-century. His early career, during which he wrote under a variety of bylines, including John Beynon, John Beynon Harris, Wyndham Parkes, and others, overlapped that of Olaf Stapledon in the 1930s and early '40s; his later career, at which point he changed to the John Wyndham byline, overlapped the advent of Arthur C. Clarke in the late 1940s.

Wyndham and Clarke and Eric Frank Russell, all British SF authors, hit their stride as mature SF writers at about the same time and were major figures in '50s science fiction. "The new Wyndham," said Damon Knight in *In Search of Wonder* (1956), "has turned out to be something remarkably like H. G. Wells – not the wise-old-owl Wells, more interested in sermon than story, but the young Wells, with that astonishing, compelling gift of pure storytelling."

Wyndham is most famous for his disaster novels *Day of the Triffids* (1951) and *The Midwich Cuckoos* (1957), both made into movies. His work ranged from pulp magazine adventure stories and serials in the 1930s to sophisticated and complex works such as this novella. His mature period began in 1950 and continued through 1961, after which he published little.

This story is arguably his best. It is a surprisingly advanced presentation of gender politics. It elicited enthusiastic comments at the time of its first publication in 1956 and shared a special Hugo Award (it was published with two other pieces, by William Golding and Mervyn Peake, in a book, *Sometime, Never,* that won a Hugo). Kingsley Amis, in a discussion of this story in *New Maps of Hell,* says, "The core of the story, occupying one third of its length, is a conversation . . . saying all that can be said for the notion that women would be better off without men and making what seem to me some fairly damaging criticisms of the contemporary female role."

There was nothing but myself.

I hung in a timeless, spaceless, forceless void that was neither light, nor dark. I had entity, but no form; awareness, but no senses; mind, but no memory. I wondered, is this – this nothingness – my soul? And it seemed that I had wondered that always, and should go on wondering it for ever . . .

But, somehow, timelessness ceased. I became aware that there was a force: that I was being moved, and that spacelessness had, therefore, ceased, too. There was nothing to show that I moved; I knew simply that I was being drawn. I felt happy because I knew there was something or someone to whom I wanted to be drawn. I had no other wish than to turn like a compass-needle and then fall through the void . . .

But I was disappointed. No smooth, swift fall followed. Instead, other forces fastened on me. I was pulled this way, and then that. I did not know how I knew it; there was no outside reference, no fixed point, no direction even; yet I could feel that I was tugged hither and thither, as though against the resistance of some inner gyroscope. It was as if one force were in command of me for a time, only to weaken and lose me to a new force. Then I would seem to slide towards some unknown point, until I was arrested, and diverted upon another course. I wafted this way and that, with the sense of awareness continually growing firmer; and I wondered whether rival forces were fighting for me, good and evil, perhaps, or life and death . . .

The sense of pulling back and forth became more definite until I was almost jerked from one course to another. Then, abruptly, the feeling of struggle finished. I had a sense of travelling faster and faster still, plunging like a wandering meteorite that had been trapped at last . . .

"All right," said a voice. "Resuscitation was a little retarded, for some reason. Better make a note of that on her card. What's the number? Oh, only her fourth time. Yes, certainly make a note. It's all right. Here she comes!"

It was a woman's voice speaking, with a slightly unfamiliar accent. The surface I was lying on shook under me. I opened my eyes, saw the

ceiling moving along above me, and let them close. Presently, another
voice, again with an unfamiliar intonation, spoke to me:

"Drink this," she said.

A hand lifted my head, and a cup was pressed against my lips. After
I had drunk the stuff I lay back with my eyes closed again. I dozed for
a little while, and came out of it feeling stronger. For some minutes I
lay looking up at the ceiling and wondering vaguely where I was. I
could not recall any ceiling that was painted just this pinkish shade of
cream. Then, suddenly, while I was still gazing up at the ceiling, I was
shocked, just as if something had hit my mind a sharp blow. I was
frighteningly aware that it was not just the pinkish ceiling that was
unfamiliar – everything was unfamiliar. Where there should have been
memories there was just a great gap. I had no idea who I was, or where
I was; I could recall nothing of how or why I came to be here . . . In a
rush of panic I tried to sit up, but a hand pressed me back, and
presently held the cup to my lips again.

"You're quite all right. Just relax," the same voice told me, reassuringly.

I wanted to ask questions, but somehow I felt immensely weary, and
everything was too much trouble. The first rush of panic subsided,
leaving me lethargic. I wondered what had happened to me – had I
been in an accident, perhaps? Was this the kind of thing that happened
when one was badly shocked? I did not know, and now for the moment
I did not care: I was being looked after. I felt so drowsy that the
questions could wait.

I suppose I dozed, and it may have been for a few minutes, or for an
hour. I know only that when I opened my eyes again I felt calmer –
more puzzled than alarmed – and I lay for a time without moving. I
had recovered enough grasp now to console myself with the thought
that if there had been an accident, at least there was no pain.

Presently I gained a little more energy, and, with it, curiosity to
know where I was. I rolled my head on the pillow to see more of the
surroundings.

A few feet away I saw a contrivance on wheels, something between
a bed and a trolley. On it, asleep, with her mouth open, was the most
enormous woman I had ever seen. I stared, wondering whether it was
some kind of cage over her to take the weight of the covers that gave
her the mountainous look, but the movement of her breathing soon
showed me that it was not. Then I looked beyond her and saw two
more trolleys, both supporting equally enormous women.

I studied the nearest one more closely, and discovered to my surprise that she was quite young – not more than twenty-two, or twenty-three, I guessed. Her face was a little plump, perhaps, but by no means over-fat; indeed, with her fresh, healthy young colouring and her short-cropped gold curls, she was quite pretty. I fell to wondering what curious disorder of the glands could cause such a degree of anomaly at her age.

Ten minutes or so passed, and there was a sound of brisk, business-like footsteps approaching. A voice inquired:

"How are you feeling now?"

I rolled my head to the other side, and found myself looking into a face almost level with my own. For a moment I thought its owner must be a child, then I saw that the features under the white cap were certainly not less than thirty years old. Without waiting for a reply she reached under the bed-clothes and took my pulse. Its rate appeared to satisfy her, for she nodded confidently.

"You'll be all right now, Mother," she told me.

I stared at her, blankly.

"The car's only just outside the door there. Do you think you can walk it?" she went on.

Bemusedly, I asked:

"What car?"

"Why, to take you home, of course," she said, with professional patience. "Come along now." And she pulled away the bedclothes.

I started to move, and looked down. What I saw there held me fixed. I lifted my arm. It was like nothing so much as a plump, white bolster with a ridiculous little hand attached at the end. I stared at it in horror. Then I heard a far-off scream as I fainted . . .

When I opened my eyes again there was a woman – a normal-sized woman – in white overalls with a stethoscope round her neck, frowning at me in perplexity. The white-capped woman I had taken for a child stood beside her, reaching only a little above her elbow.

" – I don't know, Doctor," she was saying. "She just suddenly screamed and fainted."

"What is it? What's happened to me? I know I'm not like this – I'm not, I'm not," I said, and I could hear my own voice wailing the words.

The doctor went on looking puzzled.

"What does she mean?" she asked.

"I've no idea, Doctor," said the small one. "It was quite sudden, as if she'd had some kind of shock – but I don't know why."

"Well, she's been passed and signed-off, and, anyway, she can't stay here. We need the room," said the doctor. "I'd better give her a sedative."

"But what's happened? Who am I? There's something terribly wrong. I know I'm not like this. P-please t-tell me – " I implored her, and then somehow lost myself in a stammer and a muddle.

The doctor's manner became soothing. She laid a hand gently on my shoulder.

"That's all right, Mother. There's nothing to worry about. Just take things quietly. We'll soon have you back home."

Another white-capped assistant, no taller than the first, hurried up with a syringe, and handed it to the doctor.

"No!" I protested. "I want to know where I am. Who am I? Who are you? What's happened to me?" I tried to slap the syringe out of her hand, but both the small assistants flung themselves on my arm, and held on to it while she pressed in the needle.

It was a sedative, all right. It did not put me out, but it detached me. An odd feeling: I seemed to be floating a few feet outside myself and considering me with an unnatural calmness. I was able, or felt that I was able, to evaluate matters with intelligent clarity. Evidently I was suffering from amnesia. A shock of some kind had caused me to 'lose my memory,' as it is often put. Obviously it was only a very small part of my memory that had gone – just the personal part: who I was, what I was, where I lived – all the mechanism for day-to-day getting along seemed to be intact: I'd not forgotten how to talk, or how to think, and I seemed to have quite a well-stored mind to think with.

On the other hand there was a nagging conviction that everything about me was somehow *wrong*. I *knew*, somehow, that I'd never before seen the place I was in; I *knew*, too, that there was something queer about the presence of the two small nurses; above all, I *knew*, with absolute certainty, that this massive form lying here was not mine. I could not recall what face I ought to see in a mirror, not even whether it would be dark or fair, or old or young, but there was no shadow of doubt in my mind that, whatever it was like, it had never topped such a shape as I had now.

– And there were the other enormous young women, too. Obviously, it could not be a matter of glandular disorder in all of us, or there'd not be this talk of sending me 'home,' wherever that might be . . .

I was still arguing the situation with myself in, thanks no doubt to the sedative, a most reasonable-seeming manner, though without making any progress at all, when the ceiling above my head began to move again, and I realized I was being wheeled along. Doors opened at the end of the room, and the trolley tilted a little beneath me as we went down a gentle ramp beyond.

At the foot of the ramp, an ambulance-like car, with pink coachwork polished until it gleamed, was waiting with the rear doors open. I observed interestedly that I was playing a part in a routine procedure. A team of eight diminutive attendants carried out the task of transferring me from the trolley to a sprung couch in the ambulance as if it were a kind of drill. Two of them lingered after the rest to tuck in my coverings and place another pillow behind my head. Then they got out, closing the doors behind them, and in a minute or two we started off.

It was at this point – and possibly the sedative helped in this, too – that I began to have an increasing sense of balance and a feeling that I was perceiving the situation. Probably there *had* been an accident, as I had suspected, but obviously my error, and the chief cause of my alarm, proceeded from my assumption that I was a stage further on than I actually was. I had assumed that after an interval I had recovered consciousness in these baffling circumstances, whereas the true state of affairs must clearly be that I had *not* recovered consciousness. I must be still in a suspended state, very likely with concussion, and this was a dream, or hallucination. Presently, I should wake up in conditions that would at least be sensible, if not necessarily familiar.

I wondered now that this consoling and stabilizing thought had not occurred to me before, and decided that it was the alarming sense of detailed reality that had thrown me into panic. It had been astonishingly stupid of me to be taken in to the extent of imagining that I really was a kind of Gulliver among rather over-size Lilliputians. It was quite characteristic of most dreams, too, that I should lack a clear knowledge of my identity, so we did not need to be surprised at that. The thing to do was to take an intelligent interest in all I observed: the whole thing must be chockful of symbolic content which it would be most interesting to work out later.

The discovery quite altered my attitude and I looked about me with a new attention. It struck me as odd right away that here was so much circumstantial detail, and all of it in focus – there was none of that sense of foreground in sharp relief against a muzzy, or even non-existent, background that one usually meets in a dream. Everything was presented with a most convincing, three-dimensional solidity. My own sensations, too, seemed perfectly valid. The injection, in particular, had been quite acutely authentic. The illusion of reality fascinated me into taking mental notes with some care.

The interior of the van, or ambulance, or whatever it was, was finished in the same shell-pink as the outside – except for the roof, which was powder-blue with a scatter of small silver stars. Against the front partition were mounted several cupboards, with plated handles. My couch, or stretcher, lay along the left side: on the other were two fixed seats, rather small, and upholstered in a semi-glazed material to match the colour of the rest. Two long windows on each side left little solid wall. Each of them was provided with curtains of a fine net, gathered back now in pink braid loops, and had a roller blind furled above it. Simply by turning my head on the pillow I was able to observe the passing scenery – though somewhat jerkily, for either the springing of the vehicle scarcely matched its appointments, or the road surface was bad: whichever the cause, I was glad my own couch was independently and quite comfortably sprung.

The external view did not offer a great deal of variety save in its hues. Our way was lined by buildings standing back behind some twenty yards of tidy lawn. Each block was three storeys high, about fifty yards long, and had a tiled roof of somewhat low pitch, suggesting a vaguely Italian influence. Structurally the blocks appeared identical, but each was differently coloured, with contrasting window-frames and doors, and carefully considered, uniform curtains. I could see no one behind the windows; indeed there appeared to be no one about at all except here and there a woman in overalls mowing a lawn, or tending one of the inset flowerbeds.

Further back from the road, perhaps two hundred yards away, stood larger, taller, more utilitarian-looking blocks, some of them with high, factory-type chimneys. I thought they might actually be factories of some kind, but at the distance, and because I had no more than fugitive views of them between the foreground blocks, I could not be sure.

The road itself seldom ran straight for more than a hundred yards at a stretch, and its windings made one wonder whether the buildings had not been more concerned to follow a contour line than a direction. There was little other traffic, and what there was consisted of lorries, large or small, mostly large. They were painted in one primary colour or another, with only a five-fold combination of letters and figures on their sides for further identification. In design they might have been any lorries anywhere.

We continued this uneventful progress at a modest pace for some twenty minutes, until we came to a stretch where the road was under repair. The car slowed, and the workers moved to one side, out of our way. As we crawled forward over the broken surface I was able to get a good look at them. They were all women or girls dressed in denim-like trousers, sleeveless singlets and working boots. All had their hair cut quite short, and a few wore hats. They were tall and broad-shouldered, bronzed and healthy-looking. The biceps of their arms were like a man's, and the hafts of their picks and shovels rested in the hard, strong hands of manual toilers.

They watched with concern as the car edged its way on to the rough patch, but when it drew level with them they transferred their attention, and jostled and craned to look inside at me.

They smiled widely, showing strong white teeth in their browned faces. All of them raised their right hands, making some sign to me, still smiling. Their goodwill was so evident that I smiled back. They walked along, keeping pace with the crawling car, looking at me expectantly while their smiles faded into puzzlement. They were saying something but I could not hear the words. Some of them insistently repeated the sign. Their disappointed look made it clear that I was expected to respond with more than a smile. The only way that occurred to me was to raise my own right hand in imitation of their gesture. It was at least a qualified success; their faces brightened though a rather puzzled look remained. Then the car lurched on to the made-up road again and their still somewhat troubled faces slid back as we speeded up to our former sedate pace. More dream symbols, of course – but certainly not one of the stock symbols from the book. What on earth, I wondered, could a party of friendly Amazons, equipped with navvying implements instead of bows, stand for in my subconscious? Something frustrated, I imagined. A suppressed desire to dominate? I did not seem to be getting much further along that line when we passed the last of the variegated but nevertheless monotonous blocks, and ran into open country.

The flower beds had shown me already that it was spring, and now I was able to look on healthy pastures, and neat arable fields already touched with green; there was a hazelike green smoke along the trim hedges, and some of the trees in the tidily placed spinneys were in young leaf. The sun was shining with a bright benignity upon the most precise countryside I had ever seen; only the cattle dotted about the fields introduced a slight disorder into the careful dispositions. The farmhouses themselves were part of the pattern; hollow squares of neat buildings with an acre or so of vegetable garden on one side, an orchard on another, and a rickyard on a third. There was a suggestion of a doll's landscape about it – Grandma Moses, but tidied up and rationalized. I could see no random cottages, casually sited sheds, or unplanned outgrowths from the farm buildings. And what, I asked myself, should we conclude from this rather pathological exhibition of tidiness? That I was a more uncertain person than I had supposed, one who was subconsciously yearning for simplicity and security? Well, well . . .

An open lorry which must have been travelling ahead of us turned off down a lane bordered by beautifully laid hedges, towards one of the farms. There were half a dozen young women in it, holding implements of some kind; Amazons, again. One of them, looking back, drew the attention of the rest to us. They raised their hands in the same sign that the others had made, and then waved cheerfully. I waved back.

Rather bewildering, I thought: Amazons for domination and this landscape for passive security: the two did not seem to tie up very well.

We trundled on, at our unambitious pace of twenty miles an hour or so, for what I guessed to be three-quarters of an hour, with the prospect changing very little. The country undulated gently and appeared to continue like that to the foot of a line of low blue hills many miles away. The tidy farmhouses went by with almost the regularity of milestones, though with something like twice the frequency. Occasionally there were working-parties in the fields; more rarely, one saw individuals busy about the farms, and others hoeing with tractors, but they were all too far off for me to make out any details. Presently, however, came a change.

Off to the left of the road, stretching back at right angles to it for more than a mile, appeared a row of trees. At first I thought it just a wood, but then I noticed that the trunks were evenly spaced, and the trees themselves topped and pruned until they gave more the impression of a high fence.

The end of it came to within twenty feet of the road, where it turned, and we ran along beside it for almost half a mile until the car slowed, turned to the left, and stopped in front of a pair of tall gates. There were a couple of toots on the horn.

The gates were ornamental, and possibly of wrought iron under their pink paint. The archway that they barred was stucco-covered, and painted the same colour.

Why, I inquired of myself, this prevalence of pink, which I regard as a nambypamby colour, anyway? Flesh-colour? Symbolic of an ardency for the flesh which I had insufficiently gratified? I scarcely thought so. Not pink. Surely a burning red . . . I don't think I know anyone who can be really ardent in a pink way . . .

While we waited, a feeling that there was something wrong with the gatehouse grew upon me. The structure was a single-storey building, standing against the left, inner side of the archway, and coloured to match it. The woodwork was pale blue, and there were white net curtains at the windows. The door opened, and a middle-aged woman in a white blouse-and-trouser suit came out. She was bare-headed, with a few grey locks in her short, dark hair. Seeing me, she raised her hand in the same sign the Amazons had used, though perfunctorily, and walked over to open the gates. It was only as she pushed them back to admit us that I suddenly saw how small she was – certainly not over four feet tall. And that explained what was wrong with the gatehouse: it was built entirely to her scale . . .

I went on staring at her and her little house as we passed. Well, what about that? Mythology is rich in gnomes and 'little people', and they are fairly pervasive of dreams, too. Somebody, I was sure, must have decided that they are a standard symbol of something, but for the moment I could not recall what it was. Would it be repressed philo-progenitiveness, or was that too unsubtle? I stowed that away, too, for later contemplation and brought my attention back to the surroundings.

We were on our way, unhurriedly, along something more like a drive than a road, with surroundings that suggested a compromise between a public garden and a municipal housing estate. There were wide lawns of an unblemished velvet green, set here and there with flower beds, delicate groups of silver birch, and occasional larger, single trees. Among them stood pink, three-storey blocks, dotted about, seemingly to no particular plan.

A couple of the Amazon-types in singlets and trousers of a faded rust-red were engaged in planting-out a bed close beside the drive, and we had to pause while they dragged their handcart full of tulips onto the grass to let us pass. They gave me the usual salute and amiable grin as we went by.

A moment later I had a feeling that something had gone wrong with my sight, but as we passed one block we came in sight of another. It was white instead of pink, but otherwise exactly similar to the rest – except that it was scaled down by at least one-third . . .

I blinked at it and stared hard, but it continued to seem just the same size.

A little further on, a grotesquely huge woman in pink draperies was walking slowly and heavily across a lawn. She was accompanied by three of the small, white-suited women looking, in contrast, like

children, or very animated dolls: one was involuntarily reminded of
tugs fussing round a liner.

I began to feel swamped: the proliferation and combination of
symbols was getting well out of my class.

The car forked to the right, and presently we drew up before a flight
of steps leading to one of the pink buildings – a normal-sized building,
but still not free from oddity, for the steps were divided by a central
balustrade; those to the left of it were normal, those to right, smaller
and more numerous.

Three toots on the horn announced our arrival. In about ten
seconds half a dozen small women appeared in the doorway and came
running down the right-hand side of the steps. A door slammed as the
driver got out and went to meet them. When she came into my range
of view I saw that she was one of the little ones, too, but not in white
as the rest were; she wore a shining pink suit like a livery that exactly
matched the car.

They had a word together before they came round to open the door
behind me, then a voice said brightly:

"Welcome, Mother Orchis. Welcome home."

The couch or stretcher slid back on runners, and between them they
lowered it to the ground. One young woman whose blouse was badged
with a pink St. Andrew's cross on the left breast leaned over me. She
inquired considerately:

"Do you think you can walk, Mother?"

It did not seem the moment to inquire into the form of address. I
was obviously the only possible target for the question.

"Walk?" I repeated. "Of course I can walk." And I sat up, with
about eight hands assisting me.

'Of course' had been an overstatement. I realized that by the time I
had been heaved to my feet. Even with all the help that was going on
around me it was an exertion which brought on heavy breathing. I
looked down at the monstrous form that billowed under my pink
draperies, with a sick revulsion and a feeling that, whatever this
particular mass of symbolism disguised, it was likely to prove a
distasteful revelation later on. I tried a step. 'Walk' was scarcely the
word for my progress. It felt like, and must have looked like, a slow
series of forward surges. The women, at little more than my elbow
height, fluttered about me like a flock of anxious hens. Once started, I
was determined to go on, and I progressed with a kind of wave-motion,
first across a few yards of gravel, and then, with ponderous delibera-
tion, up the left-hand side of the steps.

There was a perceptible sense of relief and triumph all round as I reached the summit. We paused there a few moments for me to regain my breath, then we moved on into the building. A corridor led straight ahead, with three or four closed doors on each side; at the end it branched right and left. We took the left arm, and, at the end of it, I came face to face, for the first time since the hallucination had set in, with a mirror.

It took every volt of my resolution not to panic again at what I saw in it. The first few seconds of my stare were spent in fighting down a leaping hysteria.

In front of me stood an outrageous travesty, an elephantine female form, looking the more huge for its pink swathings. Mercifully, they covered everything but the head and hands, but these exposures were themselves another kind of shock, for the hands, though soft and dimpled and looking utterly out of proportion, were not uncomely, and the head and face were those of a girl.

She was pretty, too. She could not have been more than twenty-one, if that. Her curling fair hair was touched with auburn lights, and cut in a kind of bob. The complexion of her face was pink and cream, her mouth was gentle, and red without any artifice. She looked back at me, and at the little women anxiously clustering round me, from a pair of blue-green eyes beneath lightly arched brows. And this delicate face, this little Fragonard, was set upon that monstrous body: no less outrageously might a blossom of freesia sprout from a turnip.

When I moved my lips, hers moved; when I bent my arm, hers bent; and yet, once I got the better of that threatening panic, she ceased to be a reflection. She was nothing like me, so she must be a stranger whom I was observing, though in a most bewildering way. My panic and revulsion gave way to sadness, an aching pity for her. I could weep for the shame of it. I did. I watched the tears brim on her lower lids; mistily, I saw them overflow.

One of the little women beside me caught hold of my hand.

"Mother Orchis, dear, what's the matter?" she asked, full of concern.

I could not tell her: I had no clear idea myself. The image in the mirror shook her head, with tears running down her cheeks. Small hands patted me here and there; small, soothing voices encouraged me onward. The next door was opened for me and, amid concerned fussing, I was led into the room beyond.

We entered a place that struck me as a cross between a boudoir and a ward. The boudoir impression was sustained by a great deal of pink

– in the carpet, coverlets, cushions, lampshades, and filmy window
curtains; the ward motif, by an array of six divans, or couches, one of
which was unoccupied.

It was a large enough room for six couches, separated by a chest, a
chair and table for each, to be arranged on each side without an effect
of crowding, and the open space in the middle was still big enough to
contain several expansive easy chairs and a central table bearing an
intricate flower-arrangement. A not displeasing scent faintly pervaded
the place, and from somewhere came the subdued sound of a string
quartette in a sentimental mood. Five of the bed-couches were already
mountainously occupied. Two of my attendant party detached themselves and hurried ahead to turn back the pink satin cover on the sixth.

Faces from all the five other beds were turned towards me. Three of
them smiling in welcome, the other two were less committal.

"Hallo, Orchis," one of them greeted me in a friendly tone. Then,
with a touch of concern, she added: "What's the matter, dear? Did you
have a bad time?"

I looked at her. She had a kindly, plumply pretty face, framed by
light brown hair as she lay back against a cushion. The face looked
about twenty-three or twenty-four years old. The rest of her was a
huge mound of pink satin. I couldn't make any reply, but I did my best
to return her smile as we passed.

Our convoy hove-to by the empty bed. After some preparation and
positioning I was helped into it by all hands, and a cushion was
arranged behind my head.

The exertion of my journey from the car had been considerable, and
I was thankful to relax. While two of the little women pulled up the
coverlet and arranged it over me, another produced a handkerchief
and dabbed gently at my cheeks. She encouraged me:

"There you are, dear. Safely home again now. You'll be quite all
right when you've rested a bit. Just try to sleep for a little."

"What's the matter with her?" inquired a forthright voice from one
of the other beds. "Did she make a mess of it?"

The little woman with the handkerchief – she was the one who wore
the St. Andrew's cross and appeared to be in charge of the operation
– turned her head sharply.

"There's no need for that tone, Mother Hazel. Of course Mother
Orchis had four beautiful babies – didn't you, dear?" she added to me.
"She's just a bit tired after the journey, that's all."

"H'mph," said the girl addressed, in an unaccommodating tone, but
she made no further comment.

A degree of fussing continued. Presently the small woman handed me a glass of something that looked like water, but had unsuspected strength. I spluttered a little at the first taste, but quickly felt the better for it. After a little more tidying and ordering, my retinue departed, leaving me propped against my cushion, with the eyes of the five other monstrous women dwelling upon me speculatively.

An awkward silence was broken by the girl who had greeted me as I came in.

"Where did they send you for your holiday, Orchis?"

"Holiday?" I asked blankly.

She and the rest stared at me in astonishment.

"I don't know what you're talking about," I told them.

They went on staring, stupidly, stolidly.

"It can't have been much of a holiday," observed one, obviously puzzled. "I'll not forget my last one. They sent me to the sea, and gave me a little car so that I could get about everywhere. Everybody was lovely to us, and there were only six Mothers there, including me. Did you go by the sea, or in the mountains?"

They were determined to be inquisitive, and one would have to make some answer sooner or later. I chose what seemed the simplest way out for the moment.

"I can't remember," I said. "I can't remember a thing. I seem to have lost my memory altogether."

That was not very sympathetically received, either.

"Oh," said the one who had been addressed as Hazel, with a degree of satisfaction. "I thought there was something. And I suppose you can't even remember for certain whether your babies were Grade One this time, Orchis?"

"Don't be stupid, Hazel," one of the others told her. "Of course they were Grade One. If they'd not been, Orchis wouldn't be back here now – she'd have been re-rated as a Class Two Mother, and sent to Whitewich." In a more kindly tone she asked me: "When did it happen, Orchis?"

"I – I don't know," I said. "I can't remember anything before this morning at the hospital. It's all gone entirely."

"Hospital!" repeated Hazel, scornfully.

"She must mean the Centre," said the other. "But do you mean to say you can't even remember us, Orchis?"

"No," I admitted, shaking my head. "I'm sorry, but everything before I came round in the Hosp – in the Centre – is all blank."

"That's queer," Hazel said, in an unsympathetic tone. "Do they know?"

One of the others took my part.

"Of course they're bound to know. I expect they don't think that remembering or not has anything to do with having Grade One babies. And why should it, anyway? But look, Orchis – "

"Why not let her rest for a bit," another cut in. "I don't suppose she's feeling too good after the Centre, and the journey, and getting in here. I never do myself. Don't take any notice of them, Orchis, dear. You just go to sleep for a bit. You'll probably find it's all quite all right when you wake up."

I accepted her suggestion gratefully. The whole thing was far too bewildering to cope with at the moment; moreover, I did feel exhausted. I thanked her for her advice, and lay back on my pillow. In so far as the closing of one's eyes can be made ostentatious, I made it so. What was more surprising was that, if one can be said to sleep within an hallucination or a dream, I slept . . .

In the moment of waking, before opening my eyes, I had a flash of hope that I should find the illusion had spent itself. Unfortunately, it had not. A hand was shaking my shoulder gently, and the first thing that I saw was the face of the little women's leader, close to mine.

In the way of nurses she said:

"There, Mother Orchis, dear. You'll be feeling a lot better after that nice sleep, won't you?"

Beyond her, two more of the small women were carrying a long-legged bed-tray towards me. They set it down so that it bridged me and was convenient to reach. I stared at the load on it. It was, with no exception, the most enormous and nourishing meal I had ever seen put before one person. The first sight of it revolted me – but then I became aware of a schism within, for it did not revolt the physical form that I occupied: that, in fact, had a watering mouth, and was eager to begin. An inner part of me marvelled in a kind of semidetachment while the rest consumed two or three fish, a whole chicken, some slices of meat, a pile of vegetables, fruit hidden under mounds of stiff cream, and more than a quart of milk, without any sense of surfeit. Occasional glances showed me that the other 'Mothers' were dealing just as thoroughly with the contents of their similar trays.

I caught one or two curious looks from them, but they were too seriously occupied to take up their inquisition again at the moment. I wondered how to fend them off later, and it occurred to me that if only I had a book or a magazine I might be able to bury myself effectively, if not very politely, in it.

When the attendants returned, I asked the badged one if she could let me have something to read. The effect of such a simple request was astonishing: the two who were removing my tray all but dropped it. The one beside me gaped for an amazed moment before she collected her wits. She looked at me, first with suspicion and then with concern.

"Not feeling quite yourself yet, dear?" she suggested.

"But I am," I protested. "I'm quite all right now."

The look of concern persisted, however.

"If I were you I'd try to sleep again," she advised.

"But I don't want to. I'd just like to read quietly," I objected.

She patted my shoulder, a little uncertainly.

"I'm afraid you've had an exhausting time, Mother. Never mind, I'm sure it'll pass quite soon."

I felt impatient. "What's wrong with wanting to read?" I demanded.

She smiled a smug, professional-nurse smile.

"There, there, dear. Just you try to rest a little more. Why, bless me, what on earth would a Mother want with knowing how to read?"

With that she tidied my coverlet, and bustled away, leaving me to the wide-eyed stares of my five companions. Hazel gave a kind of contemptuous snigger; otherwise there was no audible comment for several minutes.

I had reached a stage where the persistence of the hallucination was beginning to wear away my detachment. I could feel that under a little more pressure I should be losing my confidence and starting to doubt its unreality. I did not at all care for its calm continuity: inconsequent exaggerations and jumps, foolish perspectives, indeed, any of the usual dream characteristics would have been reassuring; but, instead, it continued to present obvious nonsense, with an alarming air of conviction and consequence. Effects, for instance, were unmistakably following causes. I began to have an uncomfortable feeling that were one to dig deep enough one might begin to find logical causes for the absurdities, too. The integration was far too good for mental comfort – even the fact that I had enjoyed my meal as if I were fully awake, and was consciously feeling the better for it, encouraged the disturbing quality of reality.

"Read!" Hazel said suddenly, with a scornful laugh. "And write, too, I suppose?"

"Well, why not?" I retorted.

They all gazed at me more attentively than ever, and then

exchanged meaningful glances among themselves. Two of them smiled at each other. I demanded irritably: "What on earth's wrong with that? Am I supposed not to be able to read or write, or something?"

One said kindly, soothingly:

"Orchis, dear. Don't you think it would be better if you were to ask to see the doctor? Just for a check-up?"

"No," I told her flatly. "There's nothing wrong with me. I'm just trying to understand. I simply ask for a book, and you all look at me as if I were mad. Why?"

After an awkward pause the same one said humouringly, and almost in the words of the little attendant:

"Orchis, dear, do try to pull yourself together. What sort of good would reading and writing be to a Mother? How could they help her to have better babies?"

"There are other things in life besides having babies," I said, shortly.

If they had been surprised before, they were thunderstruck now. Even Hazel seemed bereft of suitable comment. Their idiotic astonishment exasperated me and made me suddenly sick of the whole nonsensical business. Temporarily, I *did* forget to be the detached observer of a dream.

"Damn it," I broke out. "What is all this rubbish? Orchis! Mother Orchis! – for God's sake! Where am I? Is this some kind of lunatic asylum?"

I stared at them, angrily, loathing the sight of them, wondering if they were all in some spiteful complicity against me. Somehow I was quite convinced in my own mind that whoever, or whatever, I was, I was not a mother. I said so, forcibly, and then, to my annoyance, burst into tears.

For lack of anything else to use, I dabbed at my eyes with my sleeve. When I could see clearly again I found that four of them were looking at me with kindly concern. Hazel, however, was not.

"I said there was something queer about her," she told the others, triumphantly. "She's mad, that's what it is."

The one who had been most kindly disposed before, tried again:

"But, Orchis, *of course* you are a Mother. You're a Class One Mother – with three births registered. Twelve fine Grade One babies, dear. You *can't* have forgotten that!"

For some reason I wept again. I had a feeling that something was trying to break through the blankness in my mind; but I did not know what it was, only that it made me feel intensely miserable.

"Oh, this is cruel, cruel! Why can't I stop it? Why won't it go away and leave me?" I pleaded. "There's a horrible cruel mockery here – but I don't understand it. What's wrong with me? I'm not obsessional – I'm not – I – oh, can't somebody help me . . . ?"

I kept my eyes tight shut for a time, willing with all my mind that the whole hallucination should fade and disappear.

But it did not. When I looked again they were still there, their silly, pretty faces gaping stupidly at me across the revolting mounds of pink satin.

"I'm going to get out of this," I said.

It was a tremendous effort to raise myself to a sitting position. I was aware of the rest watching me, wide-eyed, while I made it. I struggled to get my feet round and over the side of the bed, but they were all tangled in the satin coverlet and I could not reach to free them. It was the true, desperate frustration of a dream. I heard my voice pleading: "Help me! Oh, Donald, darling, please help me . . ."

And suddenly, as if the word "Donald" had released a spring, something seemed to click in my head. The shutter in my mind opened, not entirely, but enough to let me know who I was. I understood, suddenly, where the cruelty had lain.

I looked at the others again. They were still staring half-bewildered, half-alarmed. I gave up the attempt to move, and lay back on my pillows again.

"You can't fool me anymore," I told them. "I know who I am, now."

"But, Mother Orchis – " one began.

"Stop that," I snapped at her. I seemed to have swung suddenly out of self-pity into a kind of masochistic callousness. "I am *not* a mother," I said harshly. "I am just a woman who, for a short time, had a husband, and who hoped – but only hoped – that she would have babies by him."

A pause followed that; a rather odd pause, where there should have been at least a murmur. What I had said did not seem to have registered. The faces showed no understanding; they were as uncomprehending as dolls.

Presently, the most friendly one seemed to feel an obligation to break the silence. With a little vertical crease between her brows: "What," she inquired tentatively, "what is a husband?"

I looked hard from one face to another. There was no trace of guile in any of them; nothing but puzzled speculation such as one sometimes sees in a child's eyes. I felt close to hysteria for a moment; then I took a grip on myself. Very well, then, since the hallucination would not leave me alone, I would play it at its own game, and see what came of

that. I began to explain with a kind of dead-pan, simple-word serious-
ness:

"A husband is a man whom a woman takes . . ."

Evidently, from their expressions I was not very enlightening.
However, they let me go on for three or four sentences without interruption. Then, when I paused for breath, the kindly one chipped in
with a point which she evidently felt needed clearing up:

"But what," she asked, in evident perplexity, "what is a man?"

A cool silence hung over the room after my exposition. I had an
impression I had been sent to Coventry, or semi-Coventry, by them,
but I did not bother to test it. I was too much occupied trying to force
the door of my memory further open, and finding that beyond a
certain point it would not budge.

I knew now that I was Jane. I had been Jane Summers, and had
become Jane Waterleigh when I had married Donald.

I was – had been – twenty-four when we were married: just twenty-
five when Donald was killed, six months later. And there it stopped. It
seemed like yesterday, but I couldn't tell . . .

Before that, everything was perfectly clear. My parents and friends,
my home, my schools, my training, my job, as Dr. Summers, at the
Wraychester Hospital. I could remember my first sight of Donald
when they brought him in one evening with a broken leg – and all that
followed . . .

I could remember now the face that I ought to see in a looking-glass
– and it was certainly nothing like that I had seen in the corridor
outside – it should be more oval, with a complexion looking faintly
sun-tanned; with a smaller, neater mouth; surrounded by chestnut hair
that curled naturally; with brown eyes rather wide apart and perhaps
a little grave as a rule.

I knew, too, how the rest of me should look – slender, long-legged,
with small, firm breasts – a nice body but one that I had simply taken
for granted until Donald gave me pride in it by loving it . . .

I looked down at the repulsive mound of pink satin, and shuddered.
A sense of outrage came welling up. I longed for Donald to comfort
and pet me and love me and tell me it would be all right; that I wasn't
as I was seeing myself at all, and that it *really* was a dream. At the same
time I was stricken with horror at the thought that he should ever see
me gross and obese like this. And then I remembered that Donald
would never see me again at all – never anymore – and I was wretched
and miserable, and the tears trickled down my cheeks again.

The five others just went on looking at me, wide-eyed and wondering. Half an hour passed, still in silence, then the door opened to admit a whole troop of the little women, all in white suits. I saw Hazel look at me, and then at the leader. She seemed about to speak, and then to change her mind. The little women split up, two to a couch. Standing one on each side, they stripped away the coverlet, rolled up their sleeves, and set to work at massage.

At first it was not unpleasant, and quite soothing. One lay back and relaxed. Presently, however, I liked it less: soon I found it offensive.

"Stop that!" I told the one on the right, sharply.

She paused, smiled at me amiably, though a trifle uncertainly, and then continued.

"I said stop it," I told her, pushing her away.

Her eyes met mine. They were troubled and hurt, although a professional smile still curved her mouth.

"I mean it," I added, curtly.

She continued to hesitate, and glanced across at her partner on the farther side of the bed.

"You, too," I told the other. "That'll do."

She did not even pause in her rhythm. The one on the right plucked a decision and returned. She restarted just what I had stopped. I reached out and pushed her, harder this time. There must have been a lot more muscle in that bolster of an arm than one would have supposed. The shove carried her half across the room, and she tripped and fell.

All movement in the room suddenly ceased. Everybody stared, first at her, and then at me. The pause was brief. They all set to work again. I pushed away the girl on the left, too, though more gently. The other one picked herself up. She was crying and she looked frightened, but she set her jaw doggedly and started to come back.

"You keep away from me, you little horrors," I told them threateningly.

That checked them. They stood off, and looked miserably at each other. The one with the badge of seniority fussed up.

"What's the trouble, Mother Orchis?" she inquired. I told her. She looked puzzled.

"But that's quite right," she expostulated.

"Not for me. I don't like it, and I won't have it," I replied.

She stood awkwardly, at a loss.

Hazel's voice came from the other side of the room:

"Orchis is off her head. She's been telling us the most disgusting things. She's quite mad."

The little woman turned to regard her, and then looked inquiringly at one of the others. When the girl confirmed with a nod and an expression of distaste she turned back to me, giving me a searching inspection.

"You two go and report," she told my discomfited masseuses.

They were both crying now, and they went wretchedly down the room together. The one in charge gave me another long, thoughtful look, and then followed them.

A few minutes later all the rest had packed up and gone. The six of us were alone again. It was Hazel who broke the ensuing silence.

"That was a bitchy piece of work. The poor little devils were only doing their job," she observed.

"If that's their job, I don't like it," I told her.

"So you just get them a beating, poor things. But I suppose that's the lost memory again. You wouldn't remember that a Servitor who upsets a Mother is beaten, would you?" she added sarcastically.

"Beaten?" I repeated, uneasily.

"Yes, beaten," she mimicked. "But you don't care what becomes of them, do you? I don't know what's happened to you while you were away, but whatever it was it seems to have produced a thoroughly nasty result. I never did care for you, Orchis, though the others thought I was wrong. Well, now we all know."

None of the rest offered any comment. The feeling that they shared her opinion was strong, but luckily I was spared confirmation by the opening of the door.

The senior attendant re-entered with half a dozen small myrmidons, but this time the group was dominated by a handsome woman of about thirty. Her appearance gave me immense relief. She was neither little, nor Amazonian, nor was she huge. Her present company made her look a little over-tall, perhaps, but I judged her at about five foot ten; a normal, pleasant-featured young woman with brown hair, cut somewhat short, and a pleated black skirt showing beneath white over-alls. The senior attendant was almost trotting to keep up with her longer steps, and was saying something about delusions and 'only from the Centre today, Doctor.'

The woman stopped beside my couch while the smaller women huddled together, looking at me with some misgiving. She thrust a thermometer into my mouth and held my wrist. Satisfied on both these counts, she inquired:

"Headache? Any other aches or pains?"

"No," I told her.

She regarded me carefully. I looked back at her.

"What – ?" she began.

"She's mad," Hazel put in from the other side of the room. "She says she's lost her memory and doesn't know us."

"She's been talking about horrid, disgusting things," added one of the others.

"She's got delusions. She thinks she can read and write," Hazel supplemented.

The doctor smiled at that.

"Do you?" she asked me.

"I don't see why not – but it should be easy enough to prove," I replied, brusquely.

She looked startled, a little taken aback, then she recovered her tolerant half-smile.

"All right," she said, humouring me.

She pulled a small notepad out of her pocket and offered it to me, with a pencil. The pencil felt a little odd in my hand; the fingers did not fall into place readily on it, nevertheless I wrote:

I'M ONLY TOO WELL AWARE THAT I HAVE DELUSIONS – AND
THAT YOU ARE PART OF THEM.

Hazel tittered as I handed the pad back.

The doctor's jaw did not actually drop, but her smile came right off. She looked at me very hard indeed. The rest of the room, seeing her expression, went quiet, as though I had performed some startling feat of magic. The doctor turned towards Hazel.

"What sort of things has she been telling you?" she inquired.

Hazel hesitated, then she blurted out:

"Horrible things. She's been talking about two human sexes – just as if we were like the animals. It was disgusting!"

The doctor considered a moment, then she told the senior attendant:

"Better get her along to the sick bay. I'll examine her there."

As she walked off there was a rush of little women to fetch a low trolley from the corner to the side of my couch. A dozen hands assisted me on to it, and then wheeled me briskly away.

"Now," said the doctor grimly, "let's get down to it. Who told you all this stuff about two human sexes? I want her name."

We were alone in a small room with a gold-dotted pink wallpaper.

The attendants, after transferring me from the trolley to a couch again, had taken themselves off. The doctor was sitting with a pad on her knee and a pencil at the ready. Her manner was that of an unbluffable inquisitor.

I was not feeling tactful. I told her not to be a fool.

She looked staggered, flushed with anger for a moment, and then took a hold on herself. She went on:

"After you left the Clinic you had your holiday, of course. Now, where did they send you?"

"I don't know," I replied. "All I can tell you is what I told the others – that this hallucination, or delusion, or whatever it is, started in that hospital place you call the Centre."

With resolute patience she said:

"Look here, Orchis. You were perfectly normal when you left here six weeks ago. You went to the Clinic and had your babies in the ordinary way. *But* between then and now somebody has been filling your head with all this rubbish – and teaching you to read and write, as well. Now you are going to tell me who that somebody was. I warn you you won't get away with this loss of memory nonsense with me. If you are able to remember this nauseating stuff you told the others, then you're able to remember where you got it from."

"Oh, for heaven's sake, talk sense," I told her. She flushed again.

"I can find out from the Clinic where they sent you, and I can find out from the Rest Home who were your chief associates while you were there, but I don't want to waste time following up all your contacts, so I'm asking you to save trouble by telling me now. You might just as well. We don't want to have to make you talk," she concluded, ominously.

I shook my head.

"You're on the wrong track. As far as I am concerned this whole hallucination including my connection with this Orchis, began somehow at the Centre – how it happened I can't tell you, and what happened to her before that just isn't there to be remembered."

She frowned, obviously disturbed.

"What hallucination?" she inquired, carefully.

"Why this fantastic set-up – and you, too." I waved my hand to include it all. "This revolting great body, all those little women, everything. Obviously it is all some projection of the subconscious – and the state of my subconscious is worrying me, for it's certainly no wish-fulfillment."

She went on staring at me, more worried now.

"Who on earth has been telling you about the subconscious and wish-fulfillments?" she asked uncertainly.

"I don't see why, even in an hallucination, I am expected to be an illiterate moron," I replied.

"But a Mother doesn't know anything about such things. She doesn't need to."

"Listen," I said. "I've told you, as I've told those poor grotesques in the other room, that I am not a Mother. What I am is just an unfortunate M.B. who is having some kind of nightmare."

"M.B.?" she inquired, vaguely.

"Bachelor of Medicine. I practise medicine," I told her.

She went on looking at me curiously. Her eyes wandered over my mountainous form, uncertainly.

"You are claiming to be a doctor?" she said, in an odd voice.

"Colloquially – yes," I agreed.

There was indignation mixed with bewilderment as she protested:

"But this is sheer nonsense! You were brought up and developed to be a Mother. You are a Mother. Just look at you!"

"Yes," I said, bitterly. "Just look at me!"

There was a pause.

"It seems to me," I suggested at last, "that, hallucination or not, we shan't get much further simply by going on accusing each other of talking nonsense. Suppose you explain to me what this place is, and who you think I am. It might jog my memory."

She countered that. "Suppose," she said, "that first you tell me what you can remember. It would give me more idea of what is puzzling you."

"Very well," I agreed, and launched upon a potted history of myself as far as I could recollect it – up to the time, that is to say, when Donald's aircraft crashed.

It was foolish of me to fall for that one. Of course, she had no intention of telling me anything. When she had listened to all I had to say, she went away, leaving me impotently furious.

I waited until the place quietened down. The music had been switched off. An attendant had looked in to inquire, with an air of polishing off the day's duties, whether there was anything I wanted, and presently there was nothing to be heard. I let a margin of half an hour elapse, and then struggled to get up – taking it by very easy stages this time. The greatest part of the effort was to get on to my feet from a sitting position, but I managed it at the cost of heavy breathing.

Presently I crossed to the door, and found it unfastened. I held it a little open, listening. There was no sound of movement in the corridor, so I pulled it wide open, and set out to discover what I could about the place for myself. All the doors of the rooms were shut. Putting my ear close to them I could hear regular, heavy breathing behind some, but there were no other sounds in the stillness. I kept on, turning several corners, until I recognized the front door ahead of me. I tried the latch, and found that it was neither barred nor bolted. I paused again, listening for some moments, and then pulled it open and stepped outside.

The park-like garden stretched out before me, sharp-shadowed in the moonlight. Through the trees to the right was a glint of water, to the left was a house similar to the one behind me, with not a light showing in any of its windows.

I wondered what to do. Trapped in this huge carcase, all but helpless in it, there was very little I could do, but I decided to go on and at least find out what I could while I had the chance. I went forward to the edge of the steps that I had earlier climbed from the ambulance, and started down them cautiously, holding on to the balustrade.

"Mother," said a sharp, incisive voice behind me. "What are you doing?"

I turned and saw one of the little women, her white suit gleaming in the moonlight. She was alone. I made no reply, but took another step down. I could have wept at the outrage of the heavy, ungainly body, and the caution it imposed on me.

"Come back. Come back at once," she told me.

I took no notice. She came pattering down after me and laid hold of my draperies.

"Mother," she said again, "you must come back. You'll catch cold out here."

I started to take another step, and she pulled at the draperies to hold me back. I leant forward against the pull. There was a sharp tearing sound as the material gave. I swung round and lost my balance. The last thing I saw was the rest of the flight of steps coming up to meet me . . .

As I opened my eyes a voice said:

"That's better, but it was very naughty of you, Mother Orchis, And lucky it wasn't a lot worse. Such a silly thing to do. I'm ashamed of you – really, I am."

My head was aching, and I was exasperated to find that the whole stupid business was still going on; altogether I was in no mood for reproachful drip. I told her to go to hell. Her small face goggled at me for a moment, and then became icily prim. She applied a piece of lint and plaster to the left side of my forehead, in silence, and then departed, stiffly.

Reluctantly, I had to admit to myself that she was perfectly right. What on earth had I been expecting to do – what on earth *could* I do, encumbered by this horrible mass of flesh? A great surge of loathing for it and a feeling of helpless frustration brought me to the verge of tears again. I longed for my own nice, slim body that pleased me and did what I asked of it. I remembered how Donald had once pointed to a young tree swaying in the wind, and introduced it to me as my twin sister. And only a day or two ago . . .

Then, suddenly, I made a discovery which brought me struggling to sit up. The blank part of my mind had filled up. I could remember everything . . . The effort made my head throb, so I relaxed and lay back once more, recalling it all, right up to the point where the needle was withdrawn and someone swabbed my arm . . .

But what had happened after that? Dreams and hallucinations I had expected . . . but not the sharp-focused, detailed sense of reality . . . not this state which was like a nightmare made solid . . .

What, what in heaven's name, had they done to me . . . ?

I must have fallen asleep again soon, for when I opened my eyes again there was daylight outside, and a covey of little women had arrived to attend to my toilet.

They spread their sheets dexterously and rolled me this way and that with expert technique as they cleaned me up. I suffered their industry patiently, feeling the fresher for it, and glad to discover that the headache had all but gone.

When we were almost at the end of our ablutions there came a peremptory knock, and without invitation two figures, dressed in black uniforms with silver buttons, entered. They were the Amazon type, tall, broad, well set-up, and handsome. The little women dropped everything and fled with squeaks of dismay into the far corner of the room where they cowered in a huddle.

The two gave me the familiar salute. With an odd mixture of decision and deference one of them inquired:

"You are Orchis – Mother Orchis?"

"That's what they're calling me," I admitted.

The girl hesitated, then in a tone rather more pleading than ordering she said:

"I have orders for your arrest, Mother. You will please come with us."

An excited, incredulous twittering broke out among the little women in the corner. The uniformed girl quelled them with a look.

"Get the Mother dressed and make her ready," she commanded.

The little women came out of their corner hesitantly, directing nervous, propitiatory smiles towards the pair. The second one told them briskly, though not altogether unkindly:

"Come along now. Jump to it."

They jumped.

I was almost swathed in my pink draperies again when the doctor strode in. She frowned at the two in uniform.

"What's all this? What are you doing here?" she demanded.

The leader of the two explained.

"Arrest!" exclaimed the doctor. "Arrest a Mother! I never heard such nonsense. What's the charge?"

The uniformed girl said, a little sheepishly:

"She is accused of Reactionism."

The doctor simply stared at her.

"A Reactionist Mother! What'll you people think of next? Go on, get out, both of you."

The young woman protested:

"We have our orders, Doctor."

"Rubbish. There's no authority. Have you ever heard of a Mother being arrested?"

"No, Doctor."

"Well, you aren't going to make a precedent now. Go on."

The uniformed girl hesitated unhappily, then an idea occurred to her.

"If you would let me have a signed refusal to surrender the Mother . . . ?" she suggested helpfully.

When the two had departed, quite satisfied with their piece of paper, the doctor looked at the little women gloomily.

"You can't help tattling, you Servitors, can you? Anything you happen to hear goes through the lot of you like a fire in a cornfield, and makes trouble all round. Well, if I hear anymore of this I shall know where it comes from." She turned to me. "And you, Mother Orchis, will in future please restrict yourself to yes-and-no in the hearing of these nattering little pests. I'll see you again shortly. We want to ask you some questions," she added, as she went out, leaving a subdued, industrious silence behind her.

* * *

She returned just as the tray which had held my gargantuan breakfast was being removed, and not alone. The four women who accompanied her and looked as normal as herself were followed by a number of little women lugging in chairs which they arranged beside my couch. When they had departed, the five women, all in white overalls, sat down and regarded me as if I were an exhibit. One appeared to be much the same age as the first doctor, two nearer fifty, and one sixty, or more.

"Now, Mother Orchis," said the doctor, with an air of opening the proceedings, "it is quite clear that something highly unusual has taken place. Naturally we are interested to understand just what and, if possible, why. You don't need to worry about those police this morning – it was quite improper of them to come here at all. This is simply an inquiry – a scientific inquiry – to establish what has happened."

"You can't want to understand more than I do," I replied. I looked at them, at the room about me, and finally at my massive prone figure. "I am aware that all this must be an hallucination, but what is troubling me most is that I have always supposed that any hallucination must be deficient in at least one dimension – must lack reality to some of the senses. But this does not. I have all my senses, and can use them. Nothing is insubstantial: I am trapped in flesh that is, very palpably too, too solid. The only striking deficiency, so far as I can see, is reason – even symbolic reason."

The four other women stared at me in astonishment. The doctor gave them a sort of now-perhaps-you'll-believe-me glance, and then turned to me again.

"We'll start with a few questions," she said.

"Before you begin," I put in, "I have something to add to what I told you last night. It has come back to me."

"Perhaps the knock when you fell," she suggested, looking at my piece of plaster. "What were you trying to do?"

I ignored that. "I think I'd better tell you the missing part – it might help – a bit, anyway."

"Very well," she agreed. "You told me you were – er – married, and that your – er – husband was killed soon afterwards." She glanced at the others; their blankness of expression was somehow studious. "It was the part after that that was missing," she added.

"Yes," I said. "He was a test-pilot," I explained to them. "It happened six months after we were married – only one month before his contract was due to expire.

"After that, an aunt took me away for some weeks. I don't suppose I'll ever remember that part very well – I – I wasn't noticing anything very much . . .

"But then I remember waking up one morning and suddenly seeing things differently, and telling myself that I couldn't go on like that. I knew I must have some work, something that would keep me busy.

"Dr. Hellyer, who is in charge of the Wraychester Hospital, where I was working before I married, told me he would be glad to have me with them again. I went back, and worked very hard, so that I did not have much time to think. That would be about eight months ago, now.

"Then one day Dr. Hellyer spoke about a drug that a friend of his had succeeded in synthesizing. I don't think he was really asking for volunteers, but I offered to try it out. From what he said it sounded as if the drug might have some quite important properties. It struck me as a chance to do something useful. Sooner or later, someone would try it, and as I didn't have any ties and didn't care very much what happened, anyway, I thought I might as well be the one to try it."

The spokeswoman doctor interrupted to ask:

"What was this drug?"

"It's called chuinjuatin," I told her. "Do you know it?"

She shook her head. One of the others put in:

"I've heard the name. What is it?"

"It's a narcotic," I told her. "The original form is in the leaves of a tree that grows chiefly in the South of Venezuela. The tribe of Indians who live there discovered it somehow, like others did quinine, and mescaline. And in much the same way they use it for orgies. Some of them sit and chew the leaves – they have to chew about six ounces of them – and gradually they go into a zombie-like, trance state. It lasts three or four days during which they are quite helpless and incapable of doing the simplest thing for themselves, so that other members of the tribe are appointed to look after them as if they were children, and to guard them.

"It's necessary to guard them because the Indian belief is that chuinjuatin liberates the spirit from the body, setting it free to wander anywhere in space and time, and the guardian's most important job is to see that no other wandering spirit shall slip into the body while the true owner is away. When the subjects recover they claim to have had wonderful mystical experiences. There seem to be no physical ill-effects, and no craving results from it. The mystical experiences, though, are said to be intense, and clearly remembered.

"Dr. Hellyer's friend had tested his synthesized chuinjuatin on a number of laboratory animals and worked out the dosage, and tolerances, and that kind of thing, but what he could not tell, of course, was what validity, if any, the reports of the mystical experiences had. Presumably they were the product of the drug's influence on the nervous system – but whether that effect produced a sensation of pleasure, ecstasy, awe, fear, horror, or any of a dozen more, it was impossible to tell without a human guinea-pig. So that was what I volunteered for."

I stopped. I looked at their serious, puzzled faces, at the billow of pink satin in front of me . . .

"In fact," I added, "it appears to have produced a combination of the absurd, the incomprehensible, and the grotesque."

They were earnest women, these, not to be sidetracked. They were there to disprove an anomaly – if they could.

"I *see*," said the spokeswoman with an air of preserving reasonableness, rather than meaning anything. She glanced down at a paper on which she had made a note from time to time.

"Now, can you give us the time and date at which this experiment took place?"

I could, and did, and after that the questions went on and on and on . . .

The least satisfactory part of it from my point of view was that even though my answers caused them to grow more uncertain of themselves as we went on, they did at least get them; whereas when I put a question it was usually evaded, or answered perfunctorily, as an unimportant digression.

They went on steadily, and only broke off when my next meal arrived. Then they went away, leaving me thankfully in peace – but little the wiser. I half-expected them to return, but when they did not I fell into a doze from which I was awakened by the incursion of a cluster of the little women once more. They brought a trolley with them, and in a short time were wheeling me out of the building on it – but not by the way I had arrived. This time we went down a ramp where another, or the same, pink ambulance waited at the bottom. When they had me safely loaded aboard three of them climbed in, too, to keep me company. They were chattering as they did so, and they kept it up inconsequentially, and almost incomprehensibly, for the whole hour and a half of the journey that ensued.

The countryside differed little from that I had already seen. Once we were outside the gates there were the same tidy fields and standardized farms. The occasional built-up areas were not extensive and consisted of the same types of blocks close by, and we ran on the same, not very good, road surfaces. There were groups of the Amazon types, and, more rarely, individuals, to be seen at work in the fields; the sparse traffic was lorries, large or small, and occasional buses, but with never a private car to be seen. My illusion, I reflected, was remarkably consistent in its details. Not a single group of Amazons, for instance, failed to raise its right hands in friendly, respectful greeting to the pink car.

Once, we crossed a cutting. Looking down from the bridge I thought at first that we were over the dried bed of a canal, but then I noticed a post leaning at a crazy angle among the grass and weeds: most of its attachments had fallen off, but there were enough left to identify it as a railway signal.

We passed through one concentration of identical blocks which was in size, though in no other way, quite a town, and then, two or three miles further on, ran through an ornamental gateway into a kind of park.

In one way it was not unlike the estate we had left, for everything was meticulously tended; the lawns like velvet, the flower beds vivid with spring blossoms, but it differed essentially in that the buildings were not blocks. They were houses, quite small for the most part, and varied in style, often no larger than roomy cottages. The place had a subduing effect on my small companions; for the first time they left off chattering, and gazed about them with obvious awe.

The driver stopped once to inquire the way of an overalled Amazon who was striding along with a hod on her shoulder. She directed us, and gave me a cheerful, respectful grin through the window, and presently we drew up again in front of a neat little two-storey Regency-style house.

This time there was no trolley. The little women, assisted by the driver, fussed over helping me out, and then half-supported me into the house, in a kind of buttressing formation.

Inside, I was manoeuvred with some difficulty through a door on the left, and found myself in a beautiful room, elegantly decorated and furnished in the period-style of the house. A white-haired woman in a purple silk dress was sitting in a wing-chair beside a wood fire. Both her face and her hands told of considerable age, but she looked at me from keen, lively eyes.

"Welcome, my dear," she said, in a voice which had no trace of the quaver I half-expected.

Her glance went to a chair. Then she looked at me again, and thought better of it.

"I expect you'd be more comfortable on the couch," she suggested.

I regarded the couch – a genuine Georgian piece, I thought – doubtfully.

"Will it stand it?" I wondered.

"Oh, I think so," she said, but not too certainly.

The retinue deposited me there carefully, and stood by, with anxious expressions. When it was clear that, though it creaked, it was probably going to hold, the old lady shooed them away, and rang a little silver bell. A diminutive figure, a perfect parlourmaid three foot ten in height, entered.

"The brown sherry, please, Mildred," instructed the old lady. "You'll take sherry, my dear?" she added to me.

"Y-yes – yes, thank you," I said, faintly. After a pause I added: "You will excuse me, Mrs. – er – Miss – ?"

"Oh, I should have introduced myself. My name is Laura – not Miss, or Mrs., just Laura. You, I know, are Orchis – Mother Orchis."

"So they tell me," I owned, distastefully.

We studied one another. For the first time since the hallucination had set in I saw sympathy, even pity, in someone else's eyes. I looked round the room again, noticing the perfection of details.

"This is – I'm not mad, am I?" I asked.

She shook her head slowly, but before she could reply the miniature parlourmaid returned, bearing a cut-glass decanter and glasses on a silver tray. As she poured out a glass for each of us I saw the old lady glance from her to me and back again, as though comparing us. There was a curious, uninterpretable expression on her face. I made an effort.

"Shouldn't it be madeira?" I suggested.

She looked surprised, and then smiled, and nodded appreciatively.

"I think you have accomplished the purpose of this visit in one sentence," she said.

The parlourmaid left, and we raised our glasses. The old lady sipped at hers and then placed it on an occasional table beside her.

"Nevertheless," she went on, "we had better go into it a little more. Did they tell you why they have sent you to me, my dear?"

"No." I shook my head.

"It is because I am a historian," she informed me. "Access to history is a privilege. It is not granted to many of us nowadays – and then somewhat reluctantly. Fortunately, a feeling that no branches of knowledge should be allowed to perish entirely still exists – though some of them are pursued at the cost of a certain political suspicion." She smiled deprecatingly, and then went on. "So when confirmation is required it is necessary to appeal to a specialist. Did they give you any report on their diagnosis?"

I shook my head again.

"I thought not. So like the profession, isn't it? Well, I'll tell you what they told me on the telephone from the Mother's Home, and we shall have a better idea of what we are about. I was informed that you have been interviewed by several doctors whom you have interested, puzzled – and, I suspect, distressed – very much, poor things. None of them has more than a minimum smattering of history, you see. Well, briefly, two of them are of the opinion that you are suffering from delusions of a schizophrenic nature: and three are inclined to think you are a genuine case of projected perception. It is an extremely rare condition. There are not more than three reliably documented cases, and one that is more debatable, they tell me; but of those confirmed two are associated with the drug chuinjuatin, and the third with a drug of very similar properties.

"Now, the majority of three found your answers coherent for the most part, and felt that they were authentically circumstantial. That is to say that nothing you told them conflicted directly with what they know, but, since they know so little outside their professional field, they found a great deal of the rest both hard to believe and impossible to check. Therefore, I, with my better means of checking, have been asked for my opinion."

She paused, and looked me over thoughtfully.

"I rather think," she added, "that this is going to be one of the most curiously interesting things that has happened to me in my quite long life – your glass is empty, my dear."

"Projected perception," I repeated wonderingly, as I held out my glass. "Now, if *that* were possible – "

"Oh, there's no doubt about the *possibility*. Those three cases I mentioned are fully authenticated."

"It might be that – almost," I admitted. "At least, in some ways it might be – but not in others. There is this nightmare quality. You seem perfectly normal to me, but look at me, myself – and at your little maid! There's certainly an element of delusion. I *seem* to be here, like this, and talking to you – but it can't really be so, so where am I?"

"I can understand, better than most, I think, how unreal this must seem to you. In fact, I have spent so much of my time in books that it sometimes seems unreal to me – as if I did not quite belong anywhere. Now, tell me, my dear, when were you born?"

I told her. She thought for a moment.

"H'm," she said. "George the Sixth – but you'd not remember the second big war?"

"No," I agreed.

"But you might remember the coronation of the next monarch? Whose was that?"

"Elizabeth – Elizabeth the Second. My mother took me to see the procession," I told her.

"Do you remember anything about it?"

"Not a lot really – except that it rained, nearly all day," I admitted.

We went on like that for a little while, then she smiled, reassuringly.

"Well, I don't think we need anymore to establish our point. I've heard about that coronation before – at secondhand. It must have been a wonderful scene in the Abbey." She mused a moment, and gave a little sigh. "You've been very patient with me, my dear. It is only fair that you should have your turn – but I'm afraid you must prepare yourself for some shocks."

"I think I must be inured after my last thirty-six hours – or what has appeared to be thirty-six hours," I told her.

"I doubt it," she said, looking at me seriously.

"Tell me," I asked her. "Please, explain it all – if you can."

"Your glass, my dear. Then I'll get the crux of it over." She poured for each of us, then she asked:

"What strikes you as the oddest feature of your experience, so far?"

I considered. "There's so much – "

"Might it not be that you have not seen a single man?" she suggested.

I thought back. I remembered the wondering tone of one of the Mothers asking: "What is a man?"

"That's certainly one of them," I agreed. "Where are they?"

She shook her head, watching me steadily.

"There aren't any, my dear. Not anymore. None at all."

I simply went on staring at her. Her expression was perfectly serious and sympathetic. There was no trace of guile there or deception while I struggled with the idea. At last I managed:

"But – but that's impossible! There must be some somewhere . . . You couldn't – I mean, how – ? I mean . . ." My expostulation trailed off in confusion.

She shook her head.

"I know it must seem impossible to you, Jane – may I call you Jane? But it is so. I am an old woman now, nearly eighty, and in all my long life I have never seen a man – save in old pictures and photographs.

Drink your sherry, my dear. It will do you good." She paused. "I'm afraid this upsets you."

I obeyed, too bewildered for further comment at the moment, protesting inwardly, yet not altogether disbelieving, for certainly I had not seen one man, nor sign of any. She went on quietly, giving me time to collect my wits:

"I can understand a little how you must feel. I haven't had to learn all my history entirely from books, you see. When I was a girl, sixteen or seventeen, I used to listen a lot to my grandmother. She was as old then as I am now, but her memory of her youth was still very good. I was able almost to see the places she talked about – but they were part of such a different world that it was difficult for me to understand how she felt. When she spoke about the young man she had been engaged to, tears would roll down her cheeks, even then – not just for him, of course, but for the whole world that she had known as a girl. I was sorry for her, although I could not really understand how she felt – How should I? But now that I am old, too, and have read so much, I am perhaps a little nearer to understanding her feelings, I think." She looked at me curiously. "And you, my dear. Perhaps you, too, were engaged to be married?"

"I was married – for a little time," I told her.

She contemplated that for some seconds, then:

"It must be a very strange experience to be owned," she remarked, reflectively.

"Owned?" I exclaimed, in astonishment.

"Ruled by a husband," she explained, sympathetically.

I stared at her.

"But it – it wasn't like that – it wasn't like that at all," I protested. "It was – " But there I broke off, with tears too close. To steer her away I asked:

"But what happened? What on earth happened to the men?"

"They all died," she told me. "They fell sick. Nobody could do anything for them, so they died. In little more than a year they were all gone – all but a very few."

"But surely – surely everything would collapse?"

"Oh, yes. Very largely it did. It was very bad. There was a dreadful lot of starvation. The industrial parts were the worst hit, of course. In the more backward countries and in rural areas women were able to turn to the land and till it to keep themselves and their children alive, but almost all the large organizations broke down entirely. Transport ceased very soon: petrol ran out, and no coal was being mined. It was quite a dreadful state of affairs because, although there were a great many women, and they had outnumbered the men, in fact, they had only really been important as consumers and spenders of money. So when the crisis came it turned out that scarcely any of them knew how to do any of the important things because they had nearly all been owned by men, and had to lead their lives as pets and parasites."

I started to protest, but her frail hand waved me aside.

"It wasn't their *fault* – not entirely," she explained. "They were caught up in a process, and everything conspired against their escape. It was a long process, going right back to the eleventh century, in Southern France. The Romantic conception started there as an elegant and amusing fashion for the leisured classes. Gradually, as time went on, it permeated through most levels of society but it was not until the latter part of the nineteenth century that its commercial possibilities were intelligently perceived, and not until the twentieth that it was really exploited.

"At the beginning of the twentieth century women were starting to have their chance to lead useful, creative, interesting lives. But that did not suit commerce: it needed them much more as mass-consumers than as producers – except on the most routine levels. So Romance was adopted and developed as a weapon against their further progress and to promote consumption, and it was used intensively.

"Women must never for a moment be allowed to forget their sex, and compete as equals. Everything had to have a 'feminine angle' which must be different from the masculine angle, and be dinned in without ceasing. It would have been unpopular for manufacturers actually to issue an order 'back to the kitchen,' but there were other ways. A profession without a difference, called 'housewife,' could be invented. The kitchen could be glorificd and made more expensive; it could be made to seem desirable, and it could be shown that the way to realize this heart's desire was through marriage. So the presses turned out, by the hundred thousand a week, journals which concentrated the attention of women ceaselessly and relentlessly upon selling themselves to some man in order that they might achieve some small, uneconomic unit of a home upon which money could be spent.

"Whole trades adopted the romantic approach and the glamour was spread thicker and thicker in the articles, the write-ups, and most of all in the advertisements. Romance found a place in everything that women might buy, from underclothes to motor-bicycles, from 'health' foods to kitchen stoves, from deodorants to foreign travel, until soon they were too bemused to be amused anymore.

"The air was filled with frustrated moanings. Women maundered in front of microphones yearning only to 'surrender,' and 'give themselves,' to adore and to be adored. The cinema most of all maintained the propaganda, persuading the main and important part of their audience, which was female, that nothing in life was worth achieving but dewy-eyed passivity in the strong arms of Romance. The pressure became such that the majority of young women spent all their leisure time dreaming of Romance, and the means of securing it. They were brought to a state of honestly believing that to be owned by some man and set down in a little brick box to buy all the things that the manufacturers wanted them to buy would be the highest form of bliss that life could offer."

"But – " I began to protest again. The old lady was now well launched, however, and swept on without a cheek.

"All this could not help distorting society, of course. The divorce-rate went up. Real life simply could not come near to providing the degree of romantic glamour which was being represented as every girl's proper inheritance. There was probably, in the aggregate, more disappointment, disillusion, and dissatisfaction among women than there had ever been before. Yet, with this ridiculous and ornamented ideal grained-in by unceasing propaganda, what could a conscientious idealist do but take steps to break up the short-weight marriage she had made, and seek elsewhere for the ideal which was hers, she understood, by right?

"It was a wretched state of affairs brought about by deliberately promoted dissatisfactions; a kind of rat-race with, somewhere safely out of reach, the glamourized romantic ideal always luring. Perhaps an exceptional few almost attained it, but, for all except those very few, it was a cruel, tantalizing sham on which they spent themselves, and of course their money, in vain."

This time I did get in my protest.

"But it wasn't like that. Some of what you say may be true – but that's all the superficial part. It didn't feel a bit like the way you put it. I was in it. I *know*."

She shook her head reprovingly.

"There is such a thing as being too close to make a proper evaluation. At a distance we are able to see more clearly. We can perceive it for what it was – a gross and heartless exploitation of the weaker-willed majority. Some women of education and resolution were able to withstand it, of course, but at a cost. There must always be a painful price for resisting majority pressure – even they could not always altogether escape the feeling that they might be wrong, and that the rat-racers were having the better time of it.

"You see, the great hopes for the emancipation of women with which the century had started had been outflanked. Purchasing-power had passed into the hands of the ill-educated and highly suggestible. The desire for Romance is essentially a selfish wish, and when it is encouraged to dominate every other it breaks down all corporate loyalties. The individual woman thus separated from, and yet at the same time thrust into competition with, all other women was almost defeneeless; she became the prey of organized suggestion. When it was represented to her that the lack of certain goods or amenities would be fatal to Romance she became alarmed and, thus, eminently exploitable. She could only believe what she was told, and spent a great deal of time worrying about whether she was doing all the right things to encourage Romance. Thus, she became, in a new, a subtler way, more exploited, more dependent, and less creative than she had ever been before."

"Well," I said, "this is the most curiously unrecognizable account of my world that I have ever heard – it's like something copied, but with all the proportions wrong. And as for 'less creative' – well, perhaps families were smaller, but women still went on having babies. The population was still increasing."

The old lady's eyes dwelt on me a moment.

"You are undoubtedly a thought-child of your time, in some ways," she observed. "What makes you think there is anything creative about having babies? Would you call a plant-pot creative because seeds grow in it? It is a mechanical operation – and, like most mechanical operations, is most easily performed by the least intelligent. Now, bringing up a child, educating, helping her to become a person, that is creative. But unfortunately, in the time we are speaking of, women had, in the main, been successfully conditioned into bringing up their daughters to be unintelligent consumers, like themselves."

"But," I said helplessly, "I *know* the time. It's my time. This is all distorted."

"The perspective of history must be truer," she told me again, unimpressed, and went on: "But if what happened *had* to happen, then it chose a fortunate time to happen. A hundred years earlier, even fifty years earlier, it would very likely have meant extinction. Fifty years later might easily have been too late – it might have come upon a world in which all women were profitably restricted to domesticity and consumership. Luckily, however, in the middle of the century women were still entering the professions, and by far the greatest number of professional women was to be found in medicine – which is to say that they were only really numerous in, and skilled in, the very profession which immediately became of vital importance if we were to survive at all.

"I have no medical knowledge, so I cannot give you any details of the steps they took. All I can tell you is that there was intensive research on lines which will probably be more obvious to you than they are to me.

"A species, even our species, has great will to survive, and the doctors saw to it that the will had the means of expression. Through all the hunger, and the chaos, and the other privations, babies somehow continued to be born. That had to be. Reconstruction could wait: the priority was the new generation that would help in the reconstruction, and then inherit it. So babies were born: the girl babies lived, the boy babies died. That was distressing, and wasteful, too, and so, presently, only girl babies were born – again, the means by which that could be achieved will be easier for you to understand than for me.

"It is, they tell me, not nearly so remarkable as it would appear at first sight. The locust, it seems, will continue to produce female locusts without male, or any other kind of assistance; the aphis, too, is able to go on breeding alone and in seclusion, certainly for eight generations, perhaps more. So it would be a poor thing if we, with all our knowledge and powers of research to assist us, should find ourselves inferior to the locust and the aphis in this respect, would it not?"

She paused, looking at me somewhat quizzically for my response. Perhaps she expected amazed – or possibly shocked – disbelief. If so, I disappointed her: technical achievements have ceased to arouse simple wonder since atomic physics showed how barriers fall before the pressure of a good brainsteam. One can take it that most things are possible: whether they are desirable, or worth doing, is a different matter – and one that seemed to me particularly pertinent to her question. I asked her:

"And what is it that you have achieved?"

"Survival," she said, simply.

"Materially," I agreed. "I suppose you have. But when it has cost all the rest, when love, art, poetry, excitement, and physical joy have all been sacrificed to mere continued existence, what is left but a soulless waste? What reason is there any longer for survival?"

"As to the reason, I don't know – except that survival is a desire common to all species. I am quite sure that the reason for that desire was no clearer in the twentieth century than it is now. But, for the rest, why should you assume that they are gone. Did not Sappho write poetry? And your assumption that the possession of a soul depends upon a duality of sexes surprises me: it has so often been held that the two are in some sort of conflict, has it not?"

"As a historian who must have studied men, women, and motives you should have taken my meaning better," I told her.

She shook her head, with reproof. "You are so much the conditioned product of your age, my dear. They told you, on all levels, from the works of Freud to that of the most nugatory magazines for women, that it was sex, civilized into romantic love, that made the world go round – and you believed them. But the world continues to go round for others, too – for the insects, the fish, the birds, the animals – and how much do you suppose they know of romantic love, even in their brief mating-seasons? They hoodwinked you, my dear.

"Between them they channelled your interests and ambitions along courses that were socially convenient, economically profitable, and almost harmless."

I shook my head.

"I just don't believe it. Oh, yes, you know something of my world – from the outside. But you don't understand it, or feel it."

"That's your conditioning, my dear," she told me, calmly.

Her repeated assumption irritated me. I asked:

"Suppose I were to believe what you say, what is it, then, that *does* make the world go round?"

"That's simple, my dear. It is the will to power. We have that as babies; we have it still in old age. It occurs in men and women alike. It is more fundamental, and more desirable, than sex; I tell you, you were misled – exploited, sublimated for economic convenience.

"After the disease had struck, women ceased, for the first time in history, to be an exploited class. Without male rulers to confuse and divert them they began to perceive that all true power resides in the female principle. The male had served only one brief useful purpose; for the rest of his life he was a painful and costly parasite.

"As they became aware of power, the doctors grasped it. In twenty years they were in full control. With them were the few women engineers, architects, lawyers, administrators, some teachers, and so on, but it was the doctors who held the keys of life and death. The future was in their hands and, as things began gradually to revive, they, together with the other professions, remained the dominant class and became known as the Doctorate. It assumed authority; it made the laws; it enforced them.

"There was opposition, of course. Neither the memory of the old days, nor the effect of twenty years of lawlessness, could be wiped out at once, but the doctors had the whip-hand – any woman who wanted a child had to come to them, and they saw to it that she was satisfactorily settled in a community. The roving gangs dwindled away, and gradually order was restored.

"Later on, they faced better organized opposition. There was a party which contended that the disease which had struck down the men had run its course, and the balance could, and should, be restored – they were known as Reactionists, and they became an embarrassment.

"Most of the Council of the Doctorate still had clear memories of a system which used every weakness of women, and had been no more than a more civilized culmination of their exploitation through the ages. They remembered how they themselves had only grudgingly been allowed to qualify for their careers. They were now in command: they felt no obligation to surrender their power and authority, and eventually, no doubt, their freedom to a creature whom they had proved to be biologically, and in all other ways, expendable. They refused unanimously to take a step that would lead to corporate suicide, and the Reactionists were proscribed as a subversive criminal organization.

"That, however, was just a palliative. It quickly became clear that they were attacking a symptom and neglecting the cause. The Council was driven to realize that it had an unbalanced society at its hands – a society that was capable of continuity, but was in structure, you might say, little more than the residue of a vanished form. It could not continue in that truncated shape and, as long as it tried to, disaffection would increase. Therefore, if power were to become stable, a new form suitable to the circumstances must be found.

"In deciding the shape it should take, the natural tendencies of the little-educated and uneducated woman were carefully considered – such qualities as her feeling for hierarchical principles and her disposition to respect artificial distinctions. You will no doubt recollect that in your own time any fool of a woman whose husband was ennobled or honoured at once acquired increased respect and envy from other women though she remained the same fool; and also, that any gathering or society of unoccupied women would soon become obsessionally enmeshed in the creation and preservation of social distinctions. Allied to this is the high value they usually place upon a feeling of security. Important, too, is the capacity for devoted self-sacrifice, and slavery to conscience within the canons of any local convention. We are naturally very biddable creatures. Most of us are happiest when we are being orthodox, however odd our customs may appear to an outsider; the difficulty in handling us lies chiefly in establishing the required standards of orthodoxy.

"Obviously, the broad outline of a system which was going to stand any chance of success would have to provide scope for these and other characteristic traits. It must be a scheme where the interplay of forces would preserve equilibrium and respect for authority. The details of such an organization, however, were less easy to determine.

"An extensive study of social forms and orders was undertaken, but for several years every plan put forward was rejected as in some way unsuitable. The architecture of that finally chosen was said, though I do not know with how much truth, to have been inspired by the Bible – a book at that time still unprohibited, and the source of much unrest. I am told that it ran something like: 'Go to the ant, thou sluggard; consider her ways.'

"The Council appears to have felt that this advice, suitably modified, could be expected to lead to a state of affairs which would provide most of the requisite characteristics.

"A four-class system was chosen as the basis, and strong differentiations were gradually introduced. These, now that they have become well established, greatly help to ensure stability: there is scope for ambition within one's class, but none for passing from one class to another. Thus, we have the Doctorate – the educated ruling-classes, fifty percent of whom are actually of the medical profession. The Mothers, whose title is self-explanatory. The Servitors, who are numerous and, for psychological reasons, small. The Workers, who are physically and muscularly strong, to do the heavier work. All the three lower classes respect the authority of the Doctorate. Both the employed classes revere the Mothers. The Servitors consider themselves more favoured in their tasks than the Workers; and the Workers tend to regard the puniness of the Servitors with a semi-affectionate contempt.

"So you see a balance has been struck, and though it works somewhat crudely as yet, no doubt it will improve. It seems likely, for instance, that it would be advantageous to introduce sub-divisions into the Servitor class before long, and the police are thought by some to be put at a disadvantage by having no more than a little education to distinguish them from the ordinary Worker . . ."

She went on explaining with increasing detail while the enormity of the whole process gradually grew upon me.

"Ants!" I broke in, suddenly. "The ant-nest! You've taken *that* for your model?"

She looked surprised, either at my tone, or the fact that what she was saying had taken so long to register.

"And why not?" she asked. "Surely it is one of the most enduring social patterns that nature has evolved – though of course some adaptation – "

"You're – are you telling me that only the Mothers have children?" I demanded.

"Oh, members of the Doctorate do, too, when they wish," she assured me.

"But – but."

"The Council decides the ratios," she went on to explain. "The doctors at the clinic examine the babies and allocate them suitably to the different classes. After that, of course, it is just a matter of seeing to their specialized feeding, glandular control, and proper training."

"But," I objected wildly, "what's it *for?* Where's the sense in it? What's the good of being alive, like that?"

"Well, what *is* the sense in being alive? You tell me," she suggested.

"But we're *meant* to love and be loved, to have babies we love by people we love."

"There's your conditioning again; glorifying and romanticizing primitive animalism. Surely you consider that we are superior to the animals?"

"Of course I do, but – "

"Love, you say, but what can you know of the love there can be between mother and daughter when there are no men to introduce jealousy? Do you know of any purer sentiment than the love of a girl for her little sisters?"

"But you don't understand," I protested again. "How should you understand a love that colours the whole world? How it centers in your heart and reaches out from there to pervade your whole being, how it can affect everything you are, everything you touch, everything you hear . . . It can hurt dreadfully, I know, oh, I know, but it can run like sunlight in your veins . . . It can make you a garden out of a slum; brocade out of rags; music out of speaking voice. It can show you a whole universe in someone else's eyes. Oh, you don't understand . . . you don't know . . . you can . . . Oh, Donald, darling, how can I show her what she's never even guessed at . . . ?"

There was an uncertain pause, but presently she said:

"Naturally, in your form of society it was necessary for you to be given such a conditioned reaction, but you can scarcely expect us to surrender our freedom, to connive at our own re-subjection by calling our oppressors into existence again."

"Oh, you *won't* understand. It was only the more stupid men and women who were continually at war with one another. Lots of us were complementary. We were pairs who formed units."

She smiled. "My dear, either you are surprisingly ill-informed on your own period, or else the stupidity you speak of was astonishingly dominant. Neither as myself, nor as a historian, can I consider that we should be justified in resurrecting such a state of affairs. A primitive stage of our development has now given way to a civilized era. Woman, who is the vessel of life, had the misfortune to find man necessary for a time, but now she does so no longer. Are you suggesting that such a useless and dangerous encumbrance ought to be preserved, out of sheer sentimentality? I will admit that we have lost some minor conveniences – you will have noticed, I expect, that we are less inventive mechanically, and tend to copy the patterns we have inherited; but that troubles us very little; our interests lie not in the inorganic, but in the organic and the sentient. Perhaps men could show us how to travel twice as fast, or how to fly to the moon, or how to kill more people more quickly; but it does not seem to us that such kinds of knowledge would be good payment for re-enslaving ourselves. No, our kind of world suits us better – all of us except a few Reactionists. You have seen our Servitors. They are a little timid in manner, perhaps, but are they oppressed, or sad? Don't they chatter among themselves as brightly and perkily as sparrows? And the Workers – those you called the Amazons – don't they look strong, healthy, and cheerful?"

"But you're robbing them all – robbing them of their birthright."

"You mustn't give me cant, my dear. Did not your social system conspire to rob a woman of her 'birthright' unless she married? You not only let her know it, but socially you rubbed it in: here, our Servitors and Workers do not know it, and they are not worried by a sense of inadequacy. Motherhood is the function of the Mothers, and understood as such."

I shook my head. "Nevertheless, they are being robbed.

A woman has a right to love – "

For once she was a little impatient as she cut me short.

"You keep repeating to me the propaganda of your age. The love you talk about, my dear, existed in your little sheltered part of the world by polite and profitable convention. You were scarcely ever allowed to see its other face, unglamourized by Romance. You were never openly bought and sold, like livestock; you never had to sell yourself to the first comer in order to live; you did not happen to be one of the women who through the centuries screamed in agony and suffered and died under invaders in a sacked city – nor were you ever flung into a pit of fire to be saved from them; *you* were never compelled to suttee upon you dead husband's pyre; *you* did not have to spend your whole life imprisoned in a harem; *you* were never part of the cargo of a slave-ship; *you* never retained your own life only at the pleasure of your lord and master . . .

"That is the other side – the age-long side. There is going to be no more of such things. They are finished at last. Dare you suggest that we should call them back, to suffer them all again?"

"But most of these things had already gone," I protested. "The world was getting better."

"Was it?" she said. "I wonder if the women of Berlin thought so when it fell? Was it, indeed? – or was it on the edge of a new barbarism?"

"But if you can only get rid of evil by throwing out the good, too, what is there left?"

"There is a great deal. Man was only a means to an end. We needed him in order to have babies. The rest of his vitality accounted for all the misery in the world. We are a great deal better off without him."

"So you really consider that you've improved on nature?"

"Tcha!" she said, impatient with my tone. "Civilization *is* improvement on nature. Would you want to live in a cave and have most of your babies die in infancy?"

"There are some things, some fundamental things – " I began, but she checked me, holding up her hand for silence.

Outside, the long shadows had crept across the lawns. In the evening quiet I could hear a choir of women's voices singing some little distance away. We listened for some minutes until the song was finished.

"Beautiful!" said the old lady. "Could angels themselves sing more sweetly? They sound happy enough, don't they? Our own lovely children – two of my granddaughters are there among them. They are happy, and they've reason to be happy: they're not growing up into a world where they must gamble on the goodwill of some man to keep them; they'll never need to be servile before a lord and master; they'll never stand in danger of rape and butchery, either. Listen to them!"

Another song had started and came lilting lightly to us out of the dusk.

"Why are you crying?" the old lady asked me as it ended.

"I know it's stupid – I don't really believe any of this is what it seems to be – so I suppose I'm crying for all you would have lost if it were true," I told her. "There should be lovers out there under the trees; they should be listening hand in hand to that song while they watch the moon rise. But there are no lovers now, there won't be any more . . ." I looked back at her.

"Did you ever read the lines: 'Full many a flower is born to blush unseen, and waste its sweetness on the desert air'? Can't you feel the forlornness of this world you've made? Do you *really* not understand?" I asked.

"I know you've only seen a little of us, but do *you* not begin to understand what it can be like when women are no longer forced to fight one another for the favours of men?" she countered.

We talked on while the dusk gave way to darkness and the lights of other houses started to twinkle through the trees. Her reading had been wide. It had given her even an affection for some periods of the past, but her approval of her own era was unshaken. She felt no aridity in it. Always it was my "conditioning" which prevented me from seeing that the golden age of woman had begun at last.

"You cling to too many myths," she told me. "You speak of a full life, and your instance is some unfortunate woman hugging her chains in a suburban villa. Full life, fiddlesticks! But it was convenient for the traders that she could be made to think so. A truly full life would be an exceedingly short one, in any form of society."

And so on . . .

At length, the little parlourmaid reappeared to say that my attendants were ready to leave when it should be convenient. But there was one thing I very much wanted to know before I left. I put the question to the old lady.

"Please tell me. How did it – how could it – happen?"

"Simply by accident, my dear – though it was the kind of accident that was entirely the product of its time. A piece of research which showed unexpected, secondary results, that's all."

"But how?"

"Rather curiously – almost irrelevantly, you might say. Did you ever hear of a man called Perrigan?"

"Perrigan?" I repeated. "I don't think so; it's an uncommon name."

"It became very commonly known indeed," she assured me.

"Doctor Perrigan was a biologist, and his concern was the extermination of rats – particularly the brown rat, which used to do a great deal of expensive damage.

"His approach to the problem was to find a disease which would attack them fatally. In order to produce it he took as his basis a virus infection often fatal to rabbits – or, rather, a group of virus infections that were highly selective, and also unstable since they were highly liable to mutation. Indeed, there was so much variation in the strains that when infection of rabbits in Australia was tried, it was only at the sixth attempt that it was successful; all the earlier strains died out as the rabbits developed immunity. It was tried in other places, too, though with indifferent success until a still more effective strain was started in France, and ran through the rabbit population of Europe.

"Well, taking some of these viruses as a basis, Perrigan induced new mutations by irradiation and other means, and succeeded in producing a variant that would attack rats. That was not enough, however, and he continued his work until he had a strain that had enough of its ancestral selectivity to attack only the brown rat, and with great virulence.

"In that way he settled the question of a long-standing pest, for there are no brown rats now. But something went amiss. It is still an open question whether the successful virus mutated again, or whether one of his earlier experimental viruses was accidentally liberated by escaped 'carrier' rats, but that's academic. The important thing is that somehow a strain capable of attacking human beings got loose, and that it was already widely disseminated before it was traced – also, that once it was free, it spread with devastating speed; too fast for any effective steps to be taken to check it.

"The majority of women were found to be immune; and of the ten percent or so whom it attacked over eight percent recovered. Among men, however, there was almost no immunity, and the few recoveries were only partial. A few men were preserved by the most elaborate precautions, but they could not be kept confined forever, and in the end the virus, which had a remarkable capacity for dormancy, got them, too."

Inevitably several questions of professional interest occurred to me, but for an answer she shook her head.

"I'm afraid I can't help you there. Possibly the medical people will be willing to explain," she said, but her expression was doubtful.

I maneuvered myself into a sitting position on the side of the couch.

"I see," I said. "Just an accident – yes, I suppose one could scarcely think of it happening any other way."

"Unless," she remarked, "unless one were to look upon it as divine intervention."

"Isn't that a little impious?"

"I was thinking of the Death of the Firstborn," she said, reflectively.

There did not seem to be an immediate answer to that. Instead, I asked:

"Can you honestly tell me that you never have the feeling that you are living in a dreary kind of nightmare?"

"Never," she said. "There was a nightmare – but it's over now. Listen!"

The voices of the choir, reinforced now by an orchestra, reached us distantly out of the darkened garden. No, they were not dreary: they even sounded almost exultant – but then, poor things, how were they to understand . . . ?

My attendants arrived and helped me to my feet. I thanked the old lady for her patience with me and her kindness. But she shook her head.

"My dear, it is I who am indebted to you. In a short time I have learnt more about the conditioning of women in a mixed society than all my books have been able to show me in the rest of my long life. I hope, my dear, that the doctors will find some way of enabling you to forget it and live happily here with us."

At the door I paused and turned, still helpfully shored up by my attendants.

"Laura," I said, using her name for the first time, "so many of your arguments are right – yet, over all, you're, oh, so *wrong*. Did you never read of lovers? Did you never, as a girl, sigh for a Romeo who would say: 'It is the east, and Laura is the sun!'?"

"I think not. Though I have read the play. A pretty, idealized tale – I wonder how much heartbreak it has given to how many would-be Juliets? But I would set a question against yours, my dear Jane. Did you ever see Goya's cycle of pictures called 'The Horrors of War'?"

The pink car did not return me to the 'Home'. Our destination turned out to be a more austere and hospital-like building where I was fussed into bed in a room alone. In the morning, after my massive breakfast, three new doctors visited me. Their manner was more social than professional, and we chatted amiably for half an hour. They had evidently been fully informed on my conversation with the old lady, and they were not averse to answering my questions. Indeed, they found some amusement in many of them, though I found none, for there was nothing consolingly vague in what they told me – it all sounded too disturbingly practicable, once the technique had been worked out. At the end of that time, however, their mood changed. One of them, with an air of getting down to business, said:

"You will understand that you present us with a problem. Your fellow Mothers, of course, are scarcely susceptible to Reactionist disaffection – though you have in quite a short time managed to disgust and bewilder them considerably – but on others less stable your influence might be more serious. It is not just a matter of what you may say; your difference from the rest is implicit in your whole attitude. You cannot help that, and, frankly, we do not see how you, as a woman of education, could possibly adapt yourself to the placid, unthinking acceptance that is expected of a Mother. You would quickly feel frustrated beyond endurance. Furthermore, it is clear that the conditioning you have had under your system prevents you from feeling any goodwill towards ours."

I took that straight; simply as a judgment without bias. Moreover, I could not dispute it. The prospect of spending the rest of my life in pink, scented, softmusicked illiteracy, interrupted, one gathered, only by the production of quadruplet daughters at regular intervals, would certainly have me violently unhinged in a very short time.

"And so – what?" I asked. "Can you reduce this great carcass to normal shape and size?"

She shook her head. "I imagine not – though I don't know that it has ever been attempted. But even if it were possible, you would be just as much of a misfit in the Doctorate – and far more of a liability as a Reactionist influence."

I could understand that, too.

"What, then?" I inquired.

She hesitated, then she said gently:

"The only practicable proposal we can make is that you should agree to a hypnotic treatment which will remove your memory."

As the meaning of that came home to me I had to fight off a rush of panic. After all, I told myself, they were being reasonable with me. I must do my best to respond sensibly. Nevertheless, some minutes must have passed before I answered, unsteadily.

"You are asking me to commit suicide. My mind is my memories: they are me. If I lose them I shall die, just as surely as if you were to kill my – this body."

They did not dispute that. How could they?

There is just one thing that makes my life worth living – knowing that you loved me, my sweet, sweet Donald. It is only in my memory that you live now. If you ever leave there you will die again – and forever.

"No!" I told them. "No! No!"

At intervals during the day small Servitors staggered in under the weight of my meals. In between their visits I had only my thoughts to occupy me, and they were not good company.

"Frankly," one of the doctors had put it to me, not unsympathetically, "we can see no alternative. For years after it happened the annual figures of mental breakdowns were our greatest worry. Even though the women then could keep themselves fully occupied with the tremendous amount of work that had to be done, so many of them could not adjust. And we can't even offer you work."

I knew that it was a fair warning she was giving me – and I knew that, unless the hallucination which seemed to grow more real all the time could soon be induced to dissolve, I was trapped.

During the long day and the following night I tried my hardest to get back to the objectivity I had managed earlier, but I failed. The whole dialectic was too strong for me now; my senses too consciously aware of my surroundings; the air of consequence and coherence too convincingly persistent . . .

When they had let me have twenty-four hours to think it over, the same trio visited me again.

"I think," I told them, "that I understand better now. What you are offering me is painless oblivion, in place of a breakdown followed by oblivion – and you see no other choice."

"We don't," admitted the spokeswoman, and the other two nodded. "But, of course, for the hypnosis we shall need your co-operation."

"I realize that," I told her, "and I also see now that in the circumstances it would be obstinately futile to withhold it. So I – I – yes, I'm willing to give it – but on one condition."

They looked at me questioningly.

"It is this," I explained, "that you will try one other course first. I want you to give me an injection of chuinjuatin. I want it in precisely the same strength as I had it before – I can tell you the dose.

"You see, whether this is an intense hallucination, or whether it is some kind of projection which makes it seem very similar, it must have something to do with that drug. I'm sure it must – nothing remotely like this has ever happened to me before. So, I thought that if I could repeat the condition – or, would you say, believe myself to be repeating the condition? – there may be just a chance . . . I don't know. It may be simply silly . . . but even if nothing comes of it, it can't make things worse in any way now, can it? So, if you will let me try it . . .?"

The three of them considered for some moments.

"I can see no reason why not . . ." said one.

The spokeswoman nodded.

"I shouldn't think there'll be any difficulty with authorization in the circumstances," she agreed. "If you want to try, well, it's fair to let you, but – I'd not count on it too much . . ."

In the afternoon half a dozen small servitors arrived, bustling around, making me and the room ready, with anxious industry. Presently there came one more, scarcely tall enough to see over the trolley of bottles, trays, and phials which she pushed to my bedside.

The three doctors entered together. One of the little Servitors began rolling up my sleeve. The doctor who had done most of the talking looked at me, kindly, but seriously.

"This is a sheer gamble, you know that?" she said.

"I know. But it's my only chance. I'm willing to take it."

She nodded, picked up the syringe, and charged it while the little servitor swabbed my monstrous arm. She approached the bedside, and hesitated.

"Go on," I told her. "What is there for me here, anyway?"

She nodded, and pressed in the needle . . .

Now, I have written the foregoing for a purpose. I shall deposit it with my bank, where it will remain unread unless it should be needed.

I have spoken of it to no one. The report on the effect of chuinjuatin – the one that I made to Dr. Hellyer where I described my sensation as simply one of floating in space – was false. The foregoing was my true experience.

I concealed it because after I came around, when I found that I was back in my own body in my normal world, the experience haunted me as vividly as if it had been actuality. The details were too sharp, too vivid, for me to get them out of my mind. It overhung me all the time, like a threat. It would not leave me alone . . .

I did not dare to tell Dr. Hellyer how it worried me – he would have put me under treatment. If my other friends did not take it seriously enough to recommend treatment, too, then they would have laughed over it, and amused themselves at my expense interpreting the symbolism. So I kept it to myself.

As I went over parts of it again and again in detail, I grew angry with myself for not asking the old lady for more facts, things like dates, and details that could be verified. If, for instance, the thing should, by her account, have started two or three years ago, then the whole sense of threat would fall to pieces: it would all be discredited. But it had not occurred to me to ask that crucial question . . . And then, as I went on thinking about it, I remembered that there was one, just one, piece of information that I could check, and I made inquiries. I wish now that I had not, but I felt forced to . . .

So I have discovered that:

There *is* a Dr. Perrigan, he *is* a biologist, he does work with rabbits and rats . . .

He is quite well known in his field. He has published papers on pest-control in a number of journals. It is no secret that he is evolving new strains of myxomatosis to attack rats; indeed, he has already developed a group of them and calls them mucosimorbus, though he has not yet succeeded in making them either stable or selective enough for general use . . .

But I had never heard of this man or his work until his name was mentioned by the old lady in my 'hallucination.' . . .

I have given a great deal of thought to this whole matter. What sort of experience is it that I have recorded above? If it should be a kind of pre-vision of an inevitable, predestined future, then nothing anyone could do would change it. But this does not seem to me to make sense: it is what has happened, and is happening now, that determines the future. Therefore, there must be a great number of *possible* futures, each a possible consequence of what is being done now. It seems to me that under chuinjuatin I saw *one* of those futures . . .

It was, I think, a warning of what *may* happen – unless it is prevented . . .

The whole idea is so repulsive and misconceived, it amounts to such a monstrous aberration of the normal course, that failure to heed the warning would be neglect of duty to one's kind.

I shall, therefore, on my own responsibility and without taking any other person into my confidence, do my best to ensure that such a state as I have described *cannot* come about.

Should it happen that any other person is unjustly accused of doing, or of assisting me to do, what I intend to do, this document must stand in his defence. That is why I have written it.

It is my own unaided decision that Dr. Perrigan must not be permitted to continue his work.

(Signed) JANE WATERLEIGH.

The solicitor stared at the signature for some moments; then he nodded.

"And so," he said, "she then took her car and drove over to Perrigan's – with this tragic result.

"From the little I do know of her, I'd say that she probably did her best to persuade him to give up his work – though she can scarcely have expected any success with that. It is difficult to imagine a man who would be willing to give up the work of years on account of what must sound to him like a sort of gypsy's warning. So, clearly, she went prepared to fall back on direct action, if necessary. It looks as if the police are quite right when they suppose her to have shot him deliberately; but not so right when they suppose that she burnt the place down to hide evidence of the crime. The statement makes it pretty obvious that her main intention in doing that was to wipe out Perrigan's work."

He shook his head. "Poor girl! There's a clear conviction of duty in her last page or two: the sort of simplified clarity that drives martyrs on, regardless of consequences. She has never denied that she did it. What she wouldn't tell the police is *why* she did it."

He paused again, before he added: "Anyway, thank goodness for this document. It ought at least to save her life. I should be very surprised indeed if a plea of insanity could fail, backed up by this." He tapped the pile of manuscript with his finger. "It's a lucky thing she put off her intention of taking it to her bank."

Dr. Hellyer's face was lined and worried.

"I blame myself most bitterly for the whole thing," he said. "I never ought to have let her try the damned drug in the first place, but I thought she was over the shock of her husband's death. She was trying to keep her time fully occupied, and she was anxious to volunteer. You've met her enough to know how purposeful she can be. She saw it as a chance to contribute something to medical knowledge – which it was, of course. But I ought to have been more careful, and I ought to have seen afterwards that there was something wrong. The real responsibility for this thing runs right back to me."

"H'm," said the solicitor. "Putting that forward as a main line of defence isn't going to do you a lot of good professionally, you know, Hellyer."

"Possibly not. I can look after that when we come to it. The point is that I hold a responsibility for her as a member of my staff, if for no other reason. It can't be denied that, if I had refused her offer to take part in the experiment, this would not have happened. Therefore it seems to me that we ought to be able to argue a state of temporary insanity; that the balance of her mind was disturbed by the effects of the drug which I administered. And if we can get that as a verdict it will result in detention at a mental hospital for observation and treatment – perhaps quite a short spell of treatment."

"I can't say. We can certainly put it up to counsel and see what he thinks of it."

"It's valid, too," Hellyer persisted. "People like Jane don't do murder if they are in their right minds, not unless they're really in a corner, then they do it more cleverly. Certainly they don't murder perfect strangers. Clearly, the drug caused an hallucination sufficiently vivid to confuse her to a point where she was unable to make a proper distinction between the actual and the hypothetical. She got into a state where she believed the mirage was real, and acted accordingly."

"Yes. Yes, I suppose one might put it that way," agreed the solicitor. He looked down again at the pile of paper before him. "The whole account is, of course, unreasonable," he said, "and yet it is pervaded throughout with such an air of reasonableness. I wonder . . ." He paused pensively, and went on: "This expendability of the male, Hellyer. She doesn't seem to find it so much incredible, as undesirable. That seems odd in itself to a layman who takes the natural order for granted, but would you, as a medical scientist, say it was – well, not impossible, in theory?"

Dr. Hellyer frowned.

"That's very much the kind of question one wants more notice of. It would be very rash to proclaim it *impossible*. Considering it purely as an abstract problem, I can see two or three lines of approach . . . Of course, if an utterly improbable situation were to arise calling for intensive research – research, that is, on the sort of scale they tackled the atom – well, who can tell . . . ?" He shrugged.

The solicitor nodded again.

"That's just what I was getting at," he observed. "Basically it is only just such a little way off the beam; quite near enough to possibility to be faintly disturbing. Mind you, as far as the defense is concerned, her air of thorough conviction, taken in conjunction with the near-plausibility of the thing, will probably help. But as far as I am concerned it is just that nearness that is enough to make me a trifle uneasy."

The doctor looked at him rather sharply.

"Oh, come! Really now! A hard-boiled solicitor, too! Don't tell me you're going in for fantasy-building. Anyway, if you are, you'll have to conjure up another one. If Jane, poor girl, has settled one thing, it is that there's no future in this particular fantasy. Perrigan's finished with, and all his work's gone up in smoke."

"H'm," said the solicitor again. "All the same, it would be more satisfactory if we knew of some way other than this" – he tapped the pile of papers – "some other way in which she is likely to have acquired a knowledge of Perrigan and his work. There is, as far as one knows, no other way in which he can have come into her orbit at all – unless, perhaps, she takes an interest in veterinary subjects?"

"She doesn't. I'm sure of that," Hellyer told him, shaking his head.

"Well, that, then, remains one slightly disturbing aspect. And there is another. You'll think it foolish of me, I'm sure – and no doubt time will prove you right to do so – but I have to admit I'd be feeling easier in my mind if Jane had been just a bit more thorough in her inquiries before she went into action."

"Meaning – ?" asked Dr. Hellyer, looking puzzled.

"Only that she does not seem to have found out that there is a son. But there is, you see. He appears to have taken quite a close interest in his father's work, and is determined that it shan't be wasted. In fact he has already announced that he will do his best to carry it on with the very few specimens that were saved from the fire . . .

"Laudably filial, no doubt. All the same it does disturb me a little to find that he, also, happens to be D.Sc., a biochemist; and that, very naturally, his name, too, is Perrigan . . ."

Something Ending

EDDY C. BERTIN

Eddy C. Bertin (1944–) lives in Flanders and is a leading Belgian SF and horror writer. He has published over 500 stories, over fifty in English, some Lovecraftian horror, some science fiction. He started writing at age thirteen, in Dutch, and published twenty-five books for adults between 1970 and 1986 in the Netherlands; he then switched to writing for children and young adults, and has published sixteen more books since 1986. He has in the past published poetry, translations, and 140 issues of his own *SF Guide* over eighteen years. He has written an SF future history trilogy that has not been published in English.

Most European countries have at least a few long-time science fiction writers, who have been producing fiction for decades. They are not always highly regarded internationally, but they have kept the international SF movement alive for its own sake for decades, in spite of the waves of literary fashion. Often they travel to meet other SF people at their own expense in other countries, and publish small press magazines to keep their own culture informed. Bertin is a distinguished representative of these men from the 1960s and the present. This story is a small jewel of a mood piece.

"You don't exist," was the first thing the ugly little fat man said to me as I entered the pub. He was seated on a barstool which was much too tall for someone his size, and his short stubby legs in their wrinkled trousers dangled freely without even touching the floor. He could hardly be called an attractive specimen of homo sapiens. His face looked like a sponge, with flabby cheeks and slobbering thin lips. His deep-sunken eyes were blurred by the amount of strong drinks he had had, and in these he showed an amazing appetite for variations, as indicated by the outstanding series of different empty glasses in front of him, and which he refused to let be taken away. The barman was eyeing him with open hostility and annoyance.

He looked me over once more, nodded, satisfied at his own reflection in the mirror, and repeated with more intonation: "No, you really don't exist." Satisfied with the approval of his mirror-image, he ordered another drink. There was no other place vacant, so I took the stool beside him, and since he made no gesture of buying me a drink, I ordered my own.

"You seem very certain of that," I said. Not that I cared very much what any fat drunk muttered to me, but I hate just sitting and drinking. I had been obliged to spent the evening in town, with no friends I cared to see, and no movie worth going to, either. In fact I had been preparing myself for a quiet evening at home with a good novel or maybe a rock-show on the tube, and a couple of good Napoleon brandies, when Vodier had called me on the phone, asking if I were at home that evening. This had immediately resulted in my stating that I had to rush off to an urgent press-conference in a couple of minutes, and wouldn't be home till the next day. Vodier was a nice chap, but he had the irritating habit of hanging around till the early hours of the next morning, and his conversational habits were limited to one single subject: himself. Since I knew Vodier was liable to drive over anyway, just in the vague hope that my conference had been cancelled at the last instant, there was only one thing to do: get out as fast as possible. Which I had done.

Maybe this weirdo would bring some amusement in an otherwise dreary evening, and since there seemed to be no free female companionship available in this pub, I might as well make the best of it. Ghent is a nice city to live in, but it hasn't much to offer as nightlife, compared to Brussels or Antwerp, and I didn't feel like driving another couple of miles to find another more interesting café.

The stranger shook his head pityingly, murmuring: "Poor, poor chap, so utterly convinced that he really exists, that he has real life, and what is he in fact? Phut. Nothing. Zero. A hole. A vacuum."

"Can't say I ever thought about myself that way," I said grinning. "Maybe my reasoning is a bit confused, but I feel my hands here, flesh and bone, and here a head on top of my body. *Cogito ergo sum*, I think therefore I am. More, I FEEL that I am. Seems quite logical to me."

"Bloody nonsense," he said angrily. "You only BELIEVE that you exist; there's quite a difference between believing and being. You have no real proof of your existence. You're just a dummy; you may as well believe me. Knowing the truth about oneself always makes one happier, or so I've been told."

I laughed. The funny chap had his voice remarkably under control, hut he clearly was completely stoned. You don't meet them often that way and still able to talk.

"All right, I don't exist," I grinned. "So what next?What makes you so goddamn sure anyway? If I don't exist, then why are you speaking to me?"

He looked me over with what surely must be the special look he reserved for people asking insane questions. "I am speaking to you because I want to," he said. "Because nothing exists except me and what I want. You are here because of me, you exist because I want you to exist here and now. I would have thought that was very simple to see, don't you? Oh, go to hell! One can't talk with someone of your kind. You understand nothing, accept nothing, bah."

He rose and dropped himself from his high seat of judgment. He threw some money at the barman and walked away, without saying as much as good night.

I concentrated on my drink and had two more, still thinking with amusement of the words of the funny madman. Then I drove home, got out and walked straight in the arms of a grinning Vodier, who had brought a crate of beer with him and kept me up till four o'clock in the morning.

The second time I ran into the funny-talking fat stranger was at quite a different place, at a charity ball of all things. It was one of those dry and hot evenings, which reassures you in advance that it will be raining like hell before the evening is done. The heat was unbearable in the dancing hall, and the fridge of the bar had chosen that exact evening to break down, so they had no ice cubes for the warm drinks. I decided to get a breath of fresh air on the terrace. And just guess who was standing there, his small hands on his back, staring up at the night stars? Yes, you got it right the first time. Mister You-don't-exist himself.

He looked over his shoulder as he heard my footsteps approaching and smiled amicably. He seemed sober this time.

"Hello, Mister Dummy," he said as a manner of greeting. "Made your mind up yet about whether or not you exist?"

"One day or other you're gonna get punched in the mouth if you speak to anyone like that," I said. For a moment I considered whether I should turn around and just walk away. After all he was no more than a bizarre but harmless weirdo. Still something about the fat little man intrigued me, and I decided to stay around for a couple of minutes. But he had already turned away from me and contemplated the night sky. He spoke again, this time more to himself, as if it were totally unimportant whether I listened or not.

"Nice shining stars up there," he said. "Specially the great sparkling one over there. You know, if I could stand up high enough and stretch my arms, I could just pick them right out of the sky. That specific star as well as all the other fake ones. It might convince you that I'm not crazy. And maybe then I would find out what's on the other side of that sky."

I shrugged. "Then why don't you just do that?"

He grinned. "It doesn't work," he said. "I tried it a couple of times, but they're faster than me. As soon as I stand on my toes, they just raise the sky a bit higher, out of my reach."

"So?" I asked. "First I don't exist. Now the sky is a curtain where you can pick the fake stars from. You do hold some pretty cranky ideas."

"Cranky?" He seemed shocked. "Wasn't it Shakespeare who said that the world's a stage? Or was that someone else? Not that it matters that much who said it, he or she surely had some idea about the truth of existence. But why am I bothering with you? One can't talk sense into an empty head. You're nothing, go away, shoo!"

"So, I am nothing. Well, just feel this hand. Feel the flesh, the muscles, the bones. That seems real enough to me. And you do hear me, don't you? So I can speak, too."

He smiled, all sympathy. "You got me all wrong, Mister. I am not talking about your material body. Of course that exists, just as this terrace and these stars exist for the time being. A window dummy exists, which doesn't means that he IS. The ego, the mind, the 'I' which you call 'me,' that doesn't exist. The material body you have, the streets over there, they are for real, too, but only temporary. They're make-believes, stage settings, just as the whole neighborhood. As soon as I'll be gone, they and you will stop existing. It's all here, because I am here. There must be air for me to breathe, there must be a terrace since I can't be standing here floating in empty air, and since I feel like talking to someone, you are here. If I decided to go to China now, this Europe would cease to exist the moment I left it. It would no longer be needed, since I would have left it."

This was just too much, and my laughing exploded in his face. It wasn't very polite, I admit, and it even might have been dangerous. You never know with a crazy; he didn't look aggressive, but you never know. But then, I was bigger than he, and I was certain that I could handle him if he tried to attack me. But he didn't.

"That's a good one," I said after I had stopped laughing. "Well, let me tell you that I know very well what I've been doing those last weeks, and I don't recall you being with me then or being in the neighborhood where I was."

"Artificial memories," he shrugged. "They're very good at them. They just put them inside your head so that you would be able to play your part as true-to-life as possible."

"They did, huh? And the rest of the world, all those other countries? I suppose they don't exist now since you aren't there?"

"Quite right," he said as if stating an indisputable fact. "They're just illusions, make-believes created to convince me that the world does exist. Tell me, were you ever really there? In China or Australia, in India or in Hungary?"

"Well no," I said. "I haven't been there. I wouldn't know why I should go there. But there are photographs, films, libraries . . ."

"Nonsense, it's all fake. You know only that small part of the world or even of this country in which you are, here and now. All the rest you know only by hearsay. I tell you, there is no world, no other countries, not even a real sky. It's just a stage curtain. Humanity, as such, is a dream. The only reality is my own being, and the stage they erect wherever I go. And of course all the dummies like yourself who only come into existence whenever I am near. People like you, and taxi drivers, and barkeepers, and cops, and traveling salesmen and housewives . . . people . . ."

I gasped at him. He couldn't mean that, could he? If he did . . . well, I had met quite some weirdos in my life, but this one was really too much. He was ready for the men in the white suits to come and drag him away.

"The truth hurts, doesn't it?" he asked innocently. "But don't worry about it, Mister. After a while, you'll get used to being a third-rate character in the play I'm performing."

With these words, he turned and disappeared into the crowd inside.

During the following months, somehow or other, my thoughts often returned to the crazy little fellow. Strange how some crazies manage to sound too utterly convincing and logical, even while they're talking absolute nonsense. Like when he spoke of those other faraway countries which only existed on films and photographs or just because others tell us they do exist. But, then, in the little man's mind, all those others were no more than animated showroom dummies themselves, so it hardly mattered. Must be quite a frightening stage in his own mind, I thought, a world-wide theater in which performs one fat little ugly performer.

History tends to repeat itself, as they say, and so does this story, because when I met the stranger the third time, he was stone-drunk again. It was in another bar this time, one which had chairs small enough for him to sit on with his feet on the ground, which was as well, since I doubt if he would have managed his balance otherwise. I sat down in front of him, his eyes seemed more hidden below the ridges of fat than before, and he had to look three times before recognizing me.

"Oh, yes, it's you again," he said. "My own Mister Nothing. They must think quite a lot of your character for giving you three stage acts. Have a drink with me, since you're here anyway."

He seemed preoccupied and moody. We had a drink and then another one, but he didn't brighten. He did talk, however.

"I'm scared," he said in an appropriate stage whisper. "You see, I've started doubting my own existence. Suppose, just suppose that I, too, don't really exist? What if I am no more than one of the dummies, a walking-talking-singing-drinking doll with a set of false memories? What sense would the world have then if it wasn't made for me? What if it is made and kept in existence for someone else? I couldn't bear that thought. If I was sure, I would have to hunt and kill that man or woman. But who knows? Maybe I would then cease to exist completely, as well as the rest of the world."

"That would be some problem indeed," I agreed.

"And it's not that fantastic at all," he continued. "I know, I have always known that I exist. But how can I prove it to myself? There is only one way to go about it: catch them! CATCH THEM AT IT! But how? I've tried everything possible so far. I went somewhere and suddenly changed direction. I bought a ticket to Africa and to London. But they're so fast, by the time the plane got there, they had built Africa and peopled it, complete with animals and tourists, just like in the traveler's catalogues. And when I got to London, they had already gotten it ready, except for part of the Tower, but they had their explanation ready: the Tower was being repaired just then. Everything turns out to be exactly as in the movies and pictures. They're good all right! It's almost as if they know in advance what I intend to do, or else they're just too damned fast and good at stage-building. They're smart, and they know I'm trying to catch them."

"THEY," I said. "You're always rambling about THEM. Who or what are THEY?"

"Isn't that clear yet? The builders, the owners of the stage, of course. They who hide themselves behind the sky-curtain, they who have built this world-theater and put me here in their play. You see, I think this is something like those intelligence tests they're always supposed to be doing with rats and mice and guinea pigs. They put them in a maze, and the food is at the other end of the maze. The guinea pig has to find its way through the corridors of the maze or it'll starve to death. Since the guinea pig has no gun to burn itself a straight way through the maze, it has to search, but at regular intervals they change the corridors of the maze, so the guinea pig has to adapt all the time in order to get to the food and survive. See, that's what I think I am. A rat in a maze, and they control the corridors. But I am more than a rat, I know they're THERE, and I intend to find out about them. I'm gonna burn myself through that maze in a straight line!"

"But why . . . would THEY go to all that trouble?"

"I don't know, but I have several ideas," he whispered. "Maybe all of this is just THAT: an experiment with a lower animal. A kind of reaction test. Maybe they just want to know how I'll work it all out, how fast I react to stimulations. And maybe . . . they're afraid of me. It isn't that silly, there must be a very logical reason for my being that all-important to them, to go to all that work and trouble. Maybe this is some kind of prison they've put me in, and they've taken some memories out of my mind, so I can't remember who I am or why I'm here. Maybe it's some kind of mental symbiosis: maybe they only exist because I exist, and MY being is their only reason for being. Maybe I'm a psychotic god, a lonely god, who has built a neurotic wall around himself and is now trying to get sane again. Maybe I even created THEM myself, so they could put me in their own play! As a snake eating its own tail. Maybe I am the one and only center of the universe, and therefore they – as my creations – are afraid of me."

He took a sip of his drink, and wiped his mouth with his sleeve. The drink was getting to him, his speech was becoming less clear every minute.

"But it'll be over soon now," he whispered. "I'm not that stupid, you see. I said I would burn my way through at them in a straight line, and that's what I'm gonna do. I've found the way to get them, the bastards!"

He ordered new drinks and bent lower so that I had trouble understanding his words. "I'm going to them damn stars," he whispered. "Sounds like nut talk, doesn't it? I don't look like a scientist or a spaceman, but I'm going anyway. Right through those fake stars, and then let them try to make a universe for me. I've been thinking about it for some time. I can't make a spaceship, but if I'm that important, then there must be other ways for me to get out of their maze. I've built a ship. Well, no, not exactly what you could call a spaceship. It's no more than just a hollow sphere with a chair in it. I can seal it airtight from the inside, and I'm taking oxygen tanks, food and drink. Probably I won't even need any of that, if the powers I've tapped inside my mind work out as I intend them to. Because I'm going to do it with my mind and nothing else."

He patted his head, grinning. "Yeah, ol' man, inside my head, there it is. Inside my brain, all the power I need to get at them. I've been reading up on such things as telekinesis, the transportation of matter by mental powers. Enough to lift the sphere and myself up to that damn sky, and burn through it. If there is only one really existing mind, which is mine, then that mind must possess those powers. I'm getting out of here tonight. You're the only one who knows now, and you're just another dummy, after all. Now once I'm through their sky-curtain let them try to keep up the illusion. Let them try to create real space, real stars, out there!"

"It's crazy." I said. "You need a real spaceship for that, engines, computers, technicians. It's an absurd idea!"

"Course it is," he agreed. "That's why it's genius. They'll never think of it before I get there and see for myself! You don't think I'm doing this without some preparations, do you? I've been testing my mental powers for weeks now, lifting tables, opening doors without touching them. Then other things, more heavy. Then giving them speed, always more speed! Oh, yes, I'm certain it'll work as I planned it. I just . . . FEEL it. I set my starting date for next month, so of course I'll be taking off tonight! I'll catch them all right when they're totally unprepared for me. But I thought I'd have a couple of drinks first, to test my courage. It may turn out to be a long trip if they try to create the universe when I'm coming, and I'm pretty sure they'll try. Even if I manage to drive my speed up towards the speed of light, it's still more than five light-years to the closest star, Alpha Centauri. But I may encounter them sooner than that."

When I left him, he was still drinking and muttering to himself how he'd finally get them, the bastards.

About eleven o'clock, I saw his sphere rising from the center of the city where I knew he lived. It was just a small, dark ball, which rose hesitatingly above the buildings, but then suddenly picked up speed, floating faster and faster towards the skies. It looked like a toy balloon, getting smaller and smaller, but it moved in one straight line up. He was going to burn his way through all right, just as he had said he would. He had left earlier than he had said, but I had expected that, too.

I waited till he had left the atmosphere, calculating the orbit he would follow to get away from earth and then the trajectory he would be following in the years to come, beyond the outer planets and into the void beyond, towards Alpha Centauri. I had already set the apparatus, and the projections of the outer planets and the stars would pass off satisfactorily on his eyes. There would be no errors. I still had time enough to catch up with him before he reached his destination. After all, I would have to be on the meeting committee.

"Boy, do your best," I thought. "You've wasted thirty-seven years down here: you should already be in the second-stage for a long time. Why doesn't your mind work faster, better?"

It wasn't my fault, nor my symbiont-wife's; our genes matched perfectly. Our getting a retarded child was just one of those things, it happens sometimes.

But now he HAD to succeed. He had left the nursery now, and was speeding towards the kindergarten. By then he would have figured it all out, he would have to! If he didn't he would be considered a total failure. I would be allowed no more children, and he . . . he would be erased from existence. The committee didn't lose its time with the unfit for the universe. They will be waiting for him, when he gets there, at Alpha Centauri, and I will be among them, unable to help him. He'll have to make it on his own, my son. And, though retarded, he hasn't been doing too badly after all. It was fortunate that they had at least let me work on the nursery years.

He has made a few errors and misjudgments, of course. What infant doesn't? He had drawn the wrong conclusion also when he had said that the world doesn't exist. When I do something, I do it well. There IS a real world. Now I'm beginning to tear it down.

Sundance

ROBERT SILVERBERG

Robert Silverberg (1935–) is the author of many SF novels and stories. He has published more than twenty collections of his short fiction. His most famous novels include *Dying Inside* (1972), one of the most impressive SF novels of character, and *Lord Valentine's Castle* (1980), the first of a series of popular fantasy works somewhat in the tradition of Jack Vance.

Silverberg is one of the leading conscious literary craftsmen of the genre in the last forty years. Of particular interest is his anthology *Robert Silverberg's Worlds of Wonder* (1987), which is perhaps the best single discussion, with examples, of the craft of SF writing. It includes an essay on this story that clearly lines out the conscious literary choices involved in the composition of "Sundance."

The range and breadth of Silverberg's vision, as well as his legendary facility, put him in the top rank of SF writers in the contemporary period. If there is a continuum from the pole of sentiment to the pole of artifice, Silverberg's work, when it errs, errs in the direction of artifice. In "Sundance," however, it seems to me Silverberg achieves a fine balance. It is a story of an American Indian in the future on another planet finding himself, and also a formal experiment in technique within genre boundaries.

Today you liquidated about 50,000 Eaters in Sector A, and now you are spending an uneasy night. You and Herndon flew east at dawn, with the green-gold sunrise at your backs, and sprayed the neural pellets over a thousand hectares along the Forked River. You flew on into the prairie beyond the river, where the Eaters have already been wiped out, and had lunch sprawled on that thick, soft carpet of grass where the first settlement is expected to rise. Herndon picked some juiceflowers, and you enjoyed half an hour of mild hallucinations. Then, as you headed toward the copter to begin an afternoon of further pellet spraying, he said suddenly, "Tom, how would you feel about this if it turned out that the Eaters weren't just animal pests? That they were *people*, say, with a language and rites and a history and all?"

You thought of how it had been for your own people.

"They aren't," you said.

"Suppose they were. Suppose the Eaters – "

"They aren't. Drop it."

Herndon has this streak of cruelty in him that leads him to ask such questions. He goes for the vulnerabilities; it amuses him. All night now his casual remark has echoed in your mind. Suppose the Eaters . . . supposed the Eaters . . . suppose . . . suppose . . .

You sleep for a while, and dream, and in your dreams you swim through rivers of blood.

Foolishness. A feverish fantasy. You know how important it is to exterminate the Eaters fast, before the settlers get here. They're just animals, and not even harmless animals at that; ecology-wreckers is what they are, devourers of oxygen-liberating plants, and they have to go. A few have been saved for zoological study. The rest must be destroyed. Ritual extirpation of undesirable beings, the old old story. But let's not complicate our job with moral qualms, you tell yourself. Let's not dream of rivers of blood.

The Eaters don't even *have* blood, none that could flow in rivers, anyway. What they have is, well, a kind of lymph that permeates every tissue and transmits nourishment along the interfaces. Waste products go out the same way, osmotically. In terms of process, it's structurally analogous to your own kind of circulatory system, except there's no network of blood vessels hooked to a master pump. The life-stuff just oozes through their bodies as though they were amoebas or sponges or some other low-phylum form. Yet they're definitely high-phylum in nervous system, digestive setup, limb-and-organ template, etc. Odd, you think. The thing about aliens is that they're alien, you tell yourself, not for the first time.

The beauty of their biology for you and your companions is that it lets you exterminate them so neatly.

You fly over the grazing grounds and drop the neural pellets. The

Eaters find and ingest them. Within an hour the poison has reached all sectors of the body. Life ceases; a rapid breakdown of cellular matter follows, the Eater literally falling apart molecule by molecule the instant that nutrition is cut off; the lymph-like stuff works like acid; a universal lysis occurs; flesh and even the bones, which are cartilaginous, dissolve. In two hours, a puddle on the ground. In four, nothing at all left. Considering how many millions of Eaters you've scheduled for extermination here, it's sweet of the bodies to be self-disposing. Otherwise what a charnel house this world would become!

Suppose the Eaters . . .

Damn Herndon. You almost feel like getting a memory-editing in the morning. Scrape his stupid speculations out of your head. If you dared. If you dared.

In the morning he does not dare. Memory-editing frightens him; he will try to shake free of his newfound guilt without it. The Eaters, he explains to himself, are mindless herbivores, the unfortunate victims of human expansionism, but not really deserving of passionate defense. Their extermination is not tragic; it's just too bad. If Earthmen are to have this world, the Eaters must relinquish it. There's a difference, he tells himself, between the elimination of the Plains Indians from the American prairie in the nineteenth century and the destruction of the bison on that same prairie. One feels a little wistful about the slaughter of the thundering herds; one regrets the butchering of millions of the noble brown woolly beasts, yes. But one feels outrage, not mere wistful regret, at what was done to the Sioux. There's a difference. Reserve your passions for the proper cause.

He walks from his bubble at the edge of the camp toward the center of things. The flagstone path is moist and glistening. The morning fog has not yet lifted, and every tree is bowed, the long, notched leaves heavy with droplets of water. He pauses, crouching, to observe a spider-analog spinning its asymmetrical web. As he watches, a small amphibian, delicately shaded turquoise, glides as inconspicuously as possible over the mossy ground. Not inconspicuously enough; he gently lifts the little creature and puts it on the back of his hand. The gills flutter in anguish, and the amphibian's sides quiver. Slowly, cunningly, its color changes until it matches the coppery tone of the hand. The camouflage is excellent. He lowers his hand and the amphibian scurries into a puddle. He walks on.

He is forty years old, shorter than most of the other members of the expedition, with wide shoulders, a heavy chest, dark glossy hair, a blunt, spreading nose. He is a biologist. This is his third career, for he has failed as an anthropologist and as a developer of real estate. His name is Tom Two Ribbons. He has been married twice but has had no children. His great-grandfather died of alcoholism; his grandfather was addicted to hallucinogens; his father had compulsively visited cheap memory-editing parlors. Tom Two Ribbons is conscious that he is failing a family tradition, but he has not yet found his own mode of self-destruction.

In the main building he discovers Herndon, Julia, Ellen, Schwartz, Chang, Michaelson, and Nichols. They are eating breakfast; the others are already at work. Ellen rises and comes to him and kisses him. Her short soft yellow hair tickles his cheeks. "I love you," she whispers. She has spent the night in Michaelson's bubble. "I love you," he tells her, and draws a quick vertical line of affection between her small pale breasts. He winks at Michaelson, who nods, touches the tops of two fingers to his lips, and blows them a kiss. We are all good friends here, Tom Two Ribbons thinks.

"Who drops pellets today?" he asks.

"Mike and Chang," says Julia. "Sector C."

Schwartz says, "Eleven more days and we ought to have the whole peninsula clear. Then we can move inland."

"If our pellet supply holds up," Chang points out.

Herndon says, "Did you sleep well, Tom?"

"No," says Tom. He sits down and taps out his breakfast requisition. In the west, the fog is beginning to burn off the mountains. Something throbs in the back of his neck. He has been on this world nine weeks now, and in that time it has undergone its only change of season, shading from dry weather to foggy. The mists will remain for many months. Before the plains parch again, the Eaters will be gone and the settlers will begin to arrive. His food slides down the chute and he seizes it. Ellen sits beside him. She is a little more than half his age; this is her first voyage; she is their keeper of records, but she is also skilled at editing. "You look troubled," Ellen tells him. "Can I help you?"

"No. Thank you."

"I hate it when you get gloomy."

"It's a racial trait," says Tom Two Ribbons.

"I doubt that very much."

"The truth is that maybe my personality reconstruct is wearing thin. The trauma level was so close to the surface. I'm just a walking veneer, you know."

Ellen laughs prettily. She wears only a sprayon half-wrap. Her skin looks damp; she and Michaelson have had a swim at dawn. Tom Two Ribbons is thinking of asking her to marry him, when this job is over. He has not been married since the collapse of the real estate business. The therapist suggested divorce as part of the reconstruct. He some-times wonders where Terry has gone and whom she lives with now. Ellen says, "You seem pretty stable to me, Tom."

"Thank you," he says. She is young. She does not know.

"If it's just a passing gloom I can edit it out in one quick snip."

"Thank you," he says. "No."

"I forgot. You don't like editing."

"My father – "

"Yes?"

"In fifty years he pared himself down to a thread," Tom Two Ribbons says. "He had his ancestors edited away, his whole heritage, his religion, his wife, his sons, finally his name. Then he sat and smiled all day. Thank you, no editing."

"Where are you working today?" Ellen asks.

"In the compound, running tests."

"Want company? I'm off all morning."

"Thank you, no," he says, too quickly. She looks hurt. He tries to remedy his unintended cruelty by touching her arm lightly and saying, "Maybe this afternoon, all right? I need to commune a while. Yes?"

"Yes," she says, and smiles, and shapes a kiss with her lips.

After breakfast he goes to the compound. It covers a thousand hectares east of the base; they have bordered it with neutral-field projectors at intervals of eighty meters, and this is a sufficient fence to keep the captive population of two hundred Eaters from straying. When all the others have been exterminated, this study group will remain. At the southwest corner of the compound stands a lab bubble from which the experiments are run: metabolic, psychological, physiological, ecological. A stream crosses the compound diagonally. There is a low ridge of grassy hills at its eastern edge. Five distinct corpses of tightly clustered knifeblade trees are separated by patches of dense savanna. Sheltered beneath the grass are the oxygen-plants, almost completely hidden except for the photosynthetic spikes that jut to heights of three or four meters at regular intervals, and for the lemon-colored respiratory bodies, chest high, that make the grassland sweet and dizzying with exhaled gases. Through the fields move the Eaters in a straggling herd, nibbling delicately at the respiratory bodies.

Tom Two Ribbons spies the herd beside the stream and goes

toward it. He stumbles over an oxygen-plant hidden in the grass but deftly recovers his balance and, seizing the puckered orifice of the respiratory body, inhales deeply. His despair lifts. He approaches the Eaters. They are spherical, bulky, slow-moving creatures, covered by masses of coarse orange fur. Saucer-like eyes protrude above narrow rubbery lips. Their legs are thin and scaly, like a chicken's, and their arms are short and held close to their bodies. They regard him with bland lack of curiosity. "Good morning, brothers!" is the way he greets them this time, and he wonders why.

I noticed something strange today. Perhaps I simply sniffed too much oxygen in the fields; maybe I was succumbing to a suggestion Herndon planted; or possibly it's the family masochism cropping out. But while I was observing the Eaters in the compound, it seemed to me, for the first time, that they were behaving intelligently, that they were functioning in a ritualized way.

I followed them around for three hours. During that time they uncovered half a dozen outcroppings of oxygen-plants. In each case they went through a stylized pattern of action before starting to munch. They:

Formed a straggly circle around the plants.

Looked toward the sun.

Looked toward their neighbors on left and right around the circle.

Made fuzzy neighing sounds *only* after having done the foregoing.

Looked toward the sun again.

Moved in and ate.

If this wasn't a prayer of thanksgiving, a saying of grace, then what was it? And if they're advanced enough spiritually to say grace, are we not therefore committing genocide here? Do chimpanzees say grace? Christ, we wouldn't even wipe out chimps the way we're cleaning out the Eaters! Of course, chimps don't interfere with human crops, and some kind of coexistence would be possible, whereas Eaters and human agriculturalists simply can't function on the same planet. Nevertheless, there's a moral issue here. The liquidation effort is predicated on the assumption that the intelligence level of the Eaters is about on par with that of oysters, or, at best, sheep. Our consciences stay clear because our poison is quick and painless and because the Eaters thoughtfully dissolve upon dying, sparing us the mess of incinerating millions of corpses. But if they pray – I won't say anything to the others just yet. I want more evidence – hard, objective. Films, tapes, record cubes. Then we'll see. What if I can show that we're exterminating intelligent beings? My family knows a little about genocide, after all, having been on the receiving end just a few centuries back. I doubt that I could halt what's going on here. But at the very least I could withdraw from the operation. Head back to Earth and stir up public outcries.

I hope I'm imagining this.

I'm not imagining a thing. They gather in circles; they look to the sun; they neigh and pray. They're only balls of jelly on chicken-legs, but they give thanks for their food. Those big round eyes now seem to stare accusingly at me. Our tame herd here knows what's going on: that we have descended from the stars to eradicate their kind, and that they alone will be spared. They have no way of fighting back or even of communicating their displeasure, but they *know*. And hate us. Jesus, we have killed two million of them since we got here, and in a metaphorical sense I'm stained with blood, and what will I do, what can I do?

I must move very carefully, or I'll end up drugged and edited.

I can't let myself seem like a crank, a quack, an agitator. I can't stand up and *denounce!* I have to find allies. Herndon, first. He surely is onto the truth; he's the one who nudged *me* to it, that day we dropped pellets. And I thought he was merely being vicious in his usual way!

I'll talk to him tonight.

He says, "I've been thinking about that suggestion you made. About the Eaters. Perhaps we haven't made sufficiently close psychological studies. I mean, if they really *are* intelligent – "

Herndon blinks. He is a tall man with glossy dark hair, a heavy beard, sharp cheekbones. "Who says they are, Tom?"

"You did. On the far side of the Forked River, you said – "

"It was just a speculative hypothesis. To make conversation."

"No, I think it was more than that. You really believed it."

Herndon looks troubled. "Tom, I don't know what you're trying to start, but don't start it. If I for a moment believed we were killing intelligent creatures, I'd run for an editor so fast I'd start an implosion wave."

"Why did you ask me that thing, then?" Tom Two Ribbons says.

"Idle chatter."

"Amusing yourself by kindling guilts in somebody else? You're a bastard, Herndon. I mean it."

"Well, look, Tom, if I had any idea that you'd get so worked up about a hypothetical suggestion – " Herndon shakes his head. "The

Eaters aren't intelligent beings. Obviously. Otherwise we wouldn't be under orders to liquidate them."

"Obviously," says Tom Two Ribbons.

Ellen said, "No, I don't know what Tom's up to. But I'm pretty sure he needs a rest. It's only a year and a half since his personality reconstruct, and he had a pretty bad breakdown back then."

Michaelson consulted a chart. "He's refused three times in a row to make his pellet-dropping run. Claiming he can't take time away from his research. Hell, we can fill in for him, but it's the idea that he's ducking chores that bothers me."

"What kind of research is he doing?" Nichols wanted to know.

"Not biological," said Julia. "He's with the Eaters in the compound all the time, but I don't see him making any tests on them. He just watches them."

"And talks to them," Chang observed.

"And talks, yes," Julia said.

"About what?" Nichols asked.

"Who knows?"

Everyone looked at Ellen. "You're closest to him," Michaelson said. "Can't you bring him out of it?"

"I've got to know what he's in, first," Ellen said. "He isn't saying a thing."

You know that you must be very careful, for they outnumber you, and their concern for your welfare can be deadly. Already they realize you are disturbed, and Ellen has begun to probe for the source of the disturbance. Last night you lay in her arms and she questioned you, obliquely, skillfully, and you knew what she is trying to find out. When the moons appeared she suggested that you and she stroll in the compound, among the sleeping Eaters. You declined, but she sees that you have become involved with the creatures.

You have done probing of your own – subtly, you hope. And you are aware that you can do nothing to save the Eaters. An irrevocable commitment has been made. It is 1876 all over again; these are the bison, these are the Sioux, and they must be destroyed, for the railroad is on its way. If you speak out here, your friends will calm you and pacify you and edit you, for they do not see what you see. If you return to Earth to agitate, you will be mocked and recommended for another reconstruct. You can do nothing. You can do nothing.

You cannot save, but perhaps you can record.

Go out into the prairie. Live with the Eaters; make yourself their friend; learn their ways. Set it down, a full account of their culture, so that at least that much will not be lost. You know the techniques of field anthropology. As was done for your people in the old days, do now for the Eaters.

He finds Michaelson. "Can you spare me for a few weeks?" he asks.

"Spare you, Tom? What do you mean?"

"I've got some field studies to do. I'd like to leave the base and work with Eaters in the wild."

"What's wrong with the ones in the compound?"

"It's the last chance with wild ones, Mike. I've got to go."

"Alone, or with Ellen?"

"Alone."

Michaelson nods slowly. "All right, Tom. Whatever you want. Go. I won't hold you here."

I dance in the prairie under the green-gold sun. About me the Eaters gather. I am stripped; sweat makes my skin glisten; my heart pounds. I talk to them with my feet, and they understand.

They understand.

They have a language of soft sounds. They have a god. They know love and awe and rapture. They have rites. They have names. They have a history. Of all this I am convinced.

I dance on thick grass.

How can I reach them? With my feet, with my hands, with my grunts, with my sweat. They gather by the hundreds, by the thousands, and I dance. I must not stop. They cluster about me and make their sounds. I am a conduit for strange forces. My great-grandfather should see me now! Sitting on his porch in Wyoming, the firewater in his hand, his brain rotting – see me now, old one! See the dance of Tom Two Ribbons! I talk to these strange ones with my feet under a sun that is the wrong color. I dance. I dance.

"Listen to me," I say. "I am your friend, I alone, the only one you can trust. Trust me, talk to me, teach me. Let me preserve your ways, for soon the destruction will come."

I dance, and the sun climbs, and the Eaters murmur.

There is the chief. I dance toward him, back, toward, I bow, I point to the sun, I imagine the being that lives in that ball of flame, I imitate the sounds of these people, I kneel, I rise, I dance. Tom Two Ribbons dances for you.

I summon skills my ancestors forgot. I feel the power flowing in me. As they danced in the days of the bison, I dance now, beyond the Forked River.

I dance, and now the Eaters dance too. Slowly, uncertainly, they move toward me, they shift their weight, lift leg and leg, sway about. "Yes, like that!" I cry. "Dance!"

We dance together as the sun reaches noon height.

Now their eyes are no longer accusing. I see warmth and kinship. I am their brother, their redskinned tribesman, he who dances with them. No longer do they seem clumsy to me. There is a strange ponderous grace in their movements. They dance. They dance. They caper about me. Closer, closer, closer!

We move in holy frenzy.

They sing, now, a blurred hymn of joy. They throw forth their arms, unclench their little claws. In unison they shift weight, left foot forward, right, left, right. Dance, brothers, dance, dance, dance! They press against me. Their flesh quivers; their smell is a sweet one. They gently thrust me across the field, to a part of the meadow where the grass is deep and untrampled. Still dancing, we seek the oxygen-plants, and find clumps of them beneath the grass, and they make their prayer and seize them with their awkward arms, separating the respiratory bodies from the photosynthetic spikes. The plants, in anguish, release floods of oxygen. My mind reels. I laugh and sing. The Eaters are nibbling the lemon-colored perforated globes, nibbling the stalks as well. They thrust their plants at me. It is a religious ceremony, I see. Take from us, eat with us, join with us, this is the body, this is the blood, take, eat, join. I bend forward and put a lemon-colored globe to my lips. I do not bite; I nibble, as they do, my teeth slicing away the skin of the globe. Juice spurts into my mouth while oxygen drenches my nostrils. The Eaters sing hosannas. I should be in full paint for this, paint of my forefathers, feathers too, meeting their religion in the regalia of what should have been mine. Take, eat, join. The juice of the oxygen-plant flows in my veins. I embrace my brothers. I sing, and as my voice leaves my lips it becomes an arch that glistens like new steel, and I pitch my song lower, and the arch turns to tarnished silver. The Eaters crowd close. The scent of their bodies is fiery red to me. Their soft cries are puffs of steam. The sun is very warm; its rays are tiny jagged pings of puckered sound, close to the top of my range of hearing, plink! plink! plink! The thick grass hums to me, deep and rich, and the wind hurls points of flame along the prairie. I devour another oxygen-plant, and then a third. My brothers laugh and shout. They tell me of their gods, the god of warmth, the god of food, the god of pleasure, the god of death, the god of holiness, the god of wrongness, and the others. They recite for me the names of their kings, and I hear their voices as splashes of green mold on the clean sheet of the sky. They instruct me in their holy rites. I must remember this, I tell myself, for when it is gone it will never come again. I continue to dance. They continue to dance. The color of the hills becomes rough and coarse, like abrasive gas. Take, eat, join. Dance. They are so gentle!

I hear the drone of the copter, suddenly.

It hovers far overhead. I am unable to see who flies in it. "No!" I scream. "Not here! Not these people! Listen to me! This is Tom Two Ribbons! Can't you hear me? I'm doing a field study here! You have no right — !"

My voice makes spirals of blue moss edged with red sparks. They drift upward and are scattered by the breeze.

I yell, I shout, I bellow. I dance and shake my fists. From the wings of the copter the jointed arms of the pellet-distributors unfold. The gleaming spigots extend and whirl. The neural pellets rain down into the meadow, each tracing a blazing track that lingers in the sky. The sound of the copter becomes a furry carpet stretching to the horizon, and my shrill voice is lost in it.

The Eaters drift away from me, seeking the pellets, scratching at the roots of the grass to find them. Still dancing, I leap into their midst, striking the pellets from their hands, hurling them into the stream, crushing them to powder. The Eaters growl black needles at me. They turn away and search for more pellets. The copter turns and flies off, leaving a trail of dense oily sound. My brothers are gobbling the pellets eagerly.

There is no way to prevent it.

Joy consumes them and they topple and lie still. Occasionally a limb twitches; then even this stops. They begin to dissolve. Thousands of them melt on the prairie, sinking into shapelessness, losing spherical forms, flattening, ebbing into the ground. The bonds of the molecules will no longer hold. It is the twilight of protoplasm. They perish. They vanish. For hours I walk the prairie. Now I inhale oxygen; now I eat a lemon-colored globe. Sunset begins with the ringing of leaden chimes. Black clouds make brazen trumpet calls in the east and the deepening wind is a swirl of coaly bristles. Silence comes. Night falls. I dance. I am alone.

The copter comes again, and they find you, and you do not resist as they gather you in. You are beyond bitterness. Quietly you explain what you have done and what you have learned, and why it is wrong to exterminate these people. You describe the plant you have eaten and the way it affects your senses, and as you talk of the blessed synesthesia, the texture of the wind and the sound of the clouds and the timbre of the sunlight, they nod and smile and tell you not to worry, that everything will be all right soon, and they touch something cold to your forearm, so cold that it is a whir and a buzz and the deintoxicant sinks into your vein and soon the ecstasy drains away, leaving only the exhaustion and the grief.

He says, "We never learn a thing, do we? We export all our horrors to the stars. Wipe out the Armenians, wipe out the Jews, wipe out the Tasmanians, wipe out the Indians, wipe out everyone who's in the way, and then come here and do the same damned murderous thing. You weren't with me out there. You didn't dance with them. You didn't see what a rich, complex culture the Eaters have. Let me tell you about their tribal structure. It's dense: seven levels of matrimonial relationships, to begin with, and an exogamy factor that requires – "

Softly Ellen says, "Tom, darling, nobody's going to harm the Eaters."

"And the religion," he goes on. "Nine gods, each one an aspect of *the* god. Holiness and wrongness both worshiped. They have hymns, prayers, a theology. And we, the emissaries of the god of wrongness – "

"We're not exterminating them," Michaelson says. "Won't you understand that, Tom? This is all a fantasy of yours. You've been under the influence of drugs, but now we're clearing you out. You'll be clean in a little while. You'll have perspective again."

"A fantasy?" he says bitterly. "A drug dream? I stood out in the prairie and saw you drop pellets. And I watched them die and melt away. I didn't dream that."

"How can we convince you?" Chang asks earnestly. "What will make you believe? Shall we fly over the Eater country with you and show you how many millions there are?"

"But how many millions have been destroyed?" he demands.

They insist that he is wrong. Ellen tells him again that no one has ever desired to harm the Eaters. "This is a scientific expedition, Tom. We're here to *study* them. It's a violation of all we stand for to injure intelligent lifeforms."

"You admit that they're intelligent?"

"Of course. That's never been in doubt."

"Then why drop the pellets?" he asks. "'Why slaughter them?"

"None of that has happened, Tom," Ellen says. She takes his hand between her cool palms. "Believe us. Believe us."

He says bitterly, "If you want me to believe you, why don't you do the job properly? Get out the editing machine and go to work on me. You can't simply *talk* me into rejecting the evidence of my own eyes."

"You were under drugs all the time," Michaelson says.

"I've never taken drugs! Except for what I ate in the meadow, when I danced – and that came after I had watched the massacre going on for weeks and weeks. Are you saying that it's a retroactive delusion?"

"No, Tom," Schwartz says. "You've had this delusion all along. It's part of your therapy, your reconstruct. You came here programmed with it."

"Impossible," he says.

Ellen kisses his fevered forehead. "It was done to reconcile you to mankind, you see. You had this terrible resentment of the displacement of your people in the nineteenth century. You were unable to forgive the industrial society for scattering the Sioux, and you were terribly full of hate. Your therapist thought that if you could be made to participate in an imaginary modern extermination, if you could come to see it as a necessary operation, you'd be purged of your resentment and able to take your place in society as – "

He thrusts her away. "Don't talk idiocy! If you knew the first thing about reconstruct therapy, you'd realize that no reputable therapist could be so shallow. There are no one-to-one correlations in reconstructs. No, don't touch me. Keep away. Keep away."

He will not let them persuade him that this is merely a drug-born dream. It is no fantasy, he tells himself, and it is no therapy. He rises. He goes out. They do not follow him. He takes a copter and seeks his brothers.

Again I dance. The sun is much hotter today. The Eaters are more numerous. Today I wear paint, today I wear feathers. My body shines with my sweat. They dance with me, and they have a frenzy in them that I have never seen before. We pound the trampled meadow with our feet. We clutch for the sun with our hands. We sing, we shout, we cry. We will dance until we fall.

This is no fantasy. These people are real, and they are intelligent, and they are doomed. This I know.

We dance. Despite the doom, we dance.

My great-grandfather comes and dances with us. He too is real. His nose is like a hawk's, not blunt like mine, and he wears the big head-dress, and his muscles are like cords under his brown skin. He sings, he shouts, he cries.

Others of my family join us.

We eat the oxygen-plants together. We embrace the Eaters. We know, all of us, what it is to be hunted.

The clouds make music and the wind takes on texture and the sun's warmth has color.

We dance. We dance. Our limbs know no weariness.

The sun grows and fills the whole sky, and I see no Eater now, only my own people, my father's fathers across the centuries, thousands of gleaming skins, thousands of hawk's noses, and we eat the plants, and we find sharp sticks and thrust them into our flesh, and the sweet blood flows and dries in the blaze of the sun, and we dance, and we dance, and some of us fall from weariness, and we dance, and the prairie is a sea of bobbing headdresses, an ocean of feathers, and we dance, and my heart makes thunder, and my knees become water, and the sun's fire engulfs me, and I dance, and I fall, and I dance, and I fall, and I fall, and I fall.

Again they find you and bring you back. They give you the cool snout on your arm to take the oxygen-plant drug from your veins, and then they give you something else so you will rest. You rest and you are very calm. Ellen kisses you and you stroke her soft skin, and then the others come in and they talk to you, saying soothing things, but you do not listen, for you are searching for realities. It is not an easy search. It is like falling through many trapdoors, looking for the one room whose floor is not hinged. Everything that has happened on this planet is your therapy, you tell yourself, designed to reconcile an embittered aborigine to the white man's conquest; nothing is really being exterminated here. You reject that and fall through and realize that this must be the therapy of your friends; they carry the weight of accumulated centuries of guilts and have come here to shed that load, and you are here to ease them of their burden, to draw their sins into yourself and give them forgiveness. Again you fall through, and see that the Eaters are mere animals who threaten the ecology and must be removed; the culture you imagined for them is your hallucination, kindled out of old churnings. You try to withdraw your objections to this necessary extermination, but you fall through again and discover that there is no extermination except in your mind, which is troubled and disordered by your obsession with the crime against your ancestors, and you sit up, for you wish to apologize to these friends of yours, these innocent scientists whom you have called murderers. And you fall through.

Swarm

BRUCE STERLING

Bruce Sterling (1954–) is a journalist and SF writer who was the chief polemicist behind the launch of "cyberpunk" science fiction in the 1980s. Sterling's pseudonymous presentation (as Vincent Omniveritas) of the Movement, in his small press fanzine, *Cheap Truth,* and elsewhere, particularly in *Mirrorshades: the Cyberpunk Anthology* invigorated science fiction in the 1980s. Sterling, William Gibson, Lewis Shiner, and John Shirley, the four central figures of the Movement, positioned themselves as radical reformers of hard science fiction, and attracted many followers and imitators. Sterling and Gibson, at least, became public figures far outside science fiction.

Now Sterling is a major voice of his generation, a successful revolutionary. His picture has been on the cover of *Wired.* His stories, from pure fantasy to hard science fiction, are collected in *Crystal Express* (1989) and *Globalhead: Stories* (1994). He has also published a novel in collaboration with William Gibson, *The Difference Engine* (1990).

Sterling, whose career in SF began in the mid-70s, began the major phase of his writing with his stories of the Shaper/Mech series in the early 1980s. Sterling's first novel, *Involution Ocean* (1977), was billed as "A Harlan Ellison Discovery," and is a work heavily influenced by the 1960s New Wave writers, particularly J. G. Ballard. His second novel, *The Artificial Kid* (1980), first showed serious interest in technological speculation. It escaped general notice in the early 1980s that Sterling had begun a series of stories rich in scientific speculation and technological detail set in a future solar system swarming with humanity and aliens. The first of these is "Swarm."

Then came *Schismatrix* (1985), the culmination of his "swarm" stories of the early 80s, one of the best SF novels of the decade. *Schismatrix* is in the tradition of van Vogtian SF adventure, artfully written to a literary standard far above the general run of hard science fiction, but definitely genre science fiction. The stories and the novel have recently been republished together as *Schismatrix Plus* (1996).

"Swarm" is thematically in the man versus machine tradition of SF stories of biological versus technological progress, one of the great intellectual and social conflicts of our century.

I will miss your conversation during the rest of the voyage," the alien said.

Captain-Doctor Simon Afriel folded his jeweled hands over his gold-embroidered waistcoat. "I regret it also, ensign," he said in the alien's own hissing language. "Our talks together have been very useful to me. I would have paid to learn so much, but you gave it freely."

"But that was only information," the alien said. He shrouded his bead-bright eyes behind thick nictitating membranes. "We Investors deal in energy, and precious metals. To prize and pursue mere knowledge is an immature racial trait." The alien lifted the long ribbed frill behind his pinhole-sized ears.

"No doubt you are right," Afriel said, despising him. "We humans are as children to other races, however; so a certain immaturity seems natural to us." Afriel pulled off his sunglasses to rub the bridge of his nose. The starship cabin was drenched in searing blue light, heavily ultraviolet. It was the light the Investors preferred, and they were not about to change it for one human passenger.

"You have not done badly," the alien said magnanimously. "You are the kind of race we like to do business with: young, eager, plastic, ready for a wide variety of goods and experiences. We would have contacted you much earlier, but your technology was still too feeble to afford us a profit."

"Things are different now," Afriel said. "We'll make you rich."

"Indeed," the Investor said. The frill behind his scaly head flickered rapidly, a sign of amusement. "Within two hundred years you will be wealthy enough to buy from us the secret of our starflight. Or perhaps your Mechanist faction will discover the secret through research."

Afriel was annoyed. As a member of Reshaped faction, he did not appreciate the reference to the rival Mechanists. "Don't put too much stock in mere technical expertise," he said. "Consider the aptitude for languages we Shapers have. It makes our faction a much better trading partner. To a Mechanist, all Investors look alike."

The alien hesitated. Afriel smiled. He had appealed to the alien's personal ambition with his last statement, and the hint had been taken. That was where the Mechanists always erred. They tried to treat all Investors consistently, using the same programmed routines each time. They lacked imagination.

Something would have to be done about the Mechanists, Afriel thought. Something more permanent than the small but deadly confrontations between isolated ships in the Asteroid Belt and the ice-rich Rings of Saturn. Both factions maneuvered constantly, looking for a decisive stroke, bribing away each other's best talent, practicing ambush, assassination, and industrial espionage.

Captain-Doctor Simon Afriel was a past master of these pursuits. That was why the Reshaped faction had paid the millions of kilowatts necessary to buy his passage. Afriel held doctorates in biochemistry and alien linguistics, and a master's degree in magnetic weapons engineering. He was thirty-eight years old and had been Reshaped according to the state of the art at the time of his conception. His hormonal balance had been altered slightly to compensate for long periods spent in free-fall. He had no appendix. The structure of his heart had been redesigned for greater efficiency, and his large intestine had been altered to produce the vitamins normally made by intestinal bacteria. Genetic engineering and rigorous training in childhood had given him an intelligence quotient of one hundred and eighty. He was not the brightest of the agents of the Ring Council, but he was one of the most mentally stable and the best trusted.

"It seems a shame," the alien said, "that a human of your accomplishments should have to rot for two years in this miserable, profitless outpost."

"The years won't be wasted," Afriel said.

"But why have you chosen to study the Swarm? They can teach you nothing, since they cannot speak. They have no wish to trade, having no tools or technology. They are the only spacefaring race that is essentially without intelligence.

"That alone should make them worthy of study."

"Do you seek to imitate them, then? You would make monsters of yourselves." Again the ensign hesitated. "Perhaps you could do it. It would be bad for business, however."

There came a fluting burst of alien music over the ship's speakers, then a screeching fragment of Investor language. Most of it was too high-pitched for Afriel's ears to follow.

The alien stood, his jeweled skirt brushing the tips of his clawed birdlike feet. "The Swarm's symbiote has arrived," he said.

"Thank you," Afriel said. When the ensign opened the cabin door, Afriel could smell the Swarm's representative; the creature's warm yeasty scent had spread rapidly through the starship's recycled air.

Afriel quickly checked his appearance in a pocket mirror. He touched powder to his face and straightened the round velvet hat on his shoulder-length reddish-blond hair. His earlobes glittered with red impact-rubies, thick as his thumbs' ends, mined from the Asteroid Belt. His knee-length coat and waistcoat were of gold brocade; the shirt beneath was of dazzling fineness, woven with red-gold thread. He had dressed to impress the Investors, who expected and appreciated a prosperous look from their customers. How could he impress this new alien? Smell, perhaps. He freshened his perfume.

Beside the starship's secondary airlock, the Swarm's symbiote was chittering rapidly at the ship's commander. The commander was an old and sleepy Investor, twice the size of most of her crewmen. Her massive head was encrusted in a jeweled helmet. From within the helmet her clouded eyes glittered like cameras.

The symbiote lifted on its six posterior legs and gestured feebly with its four clawed forelimbs. The ship's artificial gravity, a third again as strong as Earth's, seemed to bother it. Its rudimentary eyes, dangling on stalks, were shut tight against the glare. It must be used to darkness, Afriel thought.

The commander answered the creature in its own language. Afriel grimaced, for he had hoped that the creature spoke Investor. Now he would have to learn another language, a language designed for a being without a tongue.

After another brief interchange the commander turned to Afriel. "The symbiote is not pleased with your arrival," she told Afriel in the Investor language. "There has apparently been some disturbance here involving humans, in the recent past. However, I have prevailed upon it to admit you to the Nest. The episode has been recorded. Payment for my diplomatic services will be arranged with your faction when I return to your native star system."

"I thank Your Authority," Afriel said. "Please convey to the symbiote my best personal wishes, and the harmlessness and humility of my intentions – " He broke off short as the symbiote lunged toward him, biting him savagely in the calf of his left leg. Afriel jerked free and leaped backward in the heavy artificial gravity, going into a defensive position. The symbiote had ripped away a long shred of his pants leg; it now crouched quietly, eating it.

"It will convey your scent and composition to its nestmates," said the commander. "This is necessary. Otherwise you would be classed as an invader, and the Swarm's warrior caste would kill you at once."

Afriel relaxed quickly and pressed his hand against the puncture wound to stop the bleeding. He hoped that none of the Investors had noticed his reflexive action. It would not mesh well with his story of being a harmless researcher.

"We will reopen the airlock soon," the commander said phlegmatically, leaning back on her thick reptilian tail. The symbiote continued to munch the shred of cloth. Afriel studied the creature's neckless segmented head. It had a mouth and nostrils; it had bulbous atrophied eyes on stalks; there were hinged slats that might be radio receivers, and two parallel ridges of clumped wriggling antennae, sprouting among three chitinous plates. Their function was unknown to him.

The airlock door opened. A rush of dense, smoky aroma entered the departure cabin. It seemed to bother the half-dozen Investors, who left rapidly. "We will return in six hundred and twelve of your days, as by our agreement," the commander said.

"I thank Your Authority," Afriel said.

"Good luck," the commander said in English. Afriel smiled.

The symbiote, with a sinuous wriggle of its segmented body, crept into the airlock. Afriel followed it. The airlock door shut behind them. The creature said nothing to him but continued munching loudly. The second door opened, and the symbiote sprang through it, into a wide, round stone tunnel. It disappeared at once into the gloom.

Afriel put his sunglasses into a pocket of his jacket and pulled out a pair of infrared goggles. He strapped them to his head and stepped out of the airlock. The artificial gravity vanished, replaced by the almost imperceptible gravity of the Swarm's asteroid nest. Afriel smiled, comfortable for the first time in weeks. Most of his adult life had been spent in free-fall, in the Shapers' colonies in the Rings of Saturn.

Squatting in a dark cavity in the side of the tunnel was a disk-headed furred animal the size of an elephant. It was clearly visible in the infrared of its own body heat. Afriel could hear it breathing. It waited patiently until Afriel had launched himself past it, deeper into the tunnel. Then it took its place in the end of the tunnel, puffing itself up

with air until its swollen head securely plugged the exit into space. Its
multiple legs sank firmly into sockets in the walls.

The Investors' ship had left. Afriel remained here, inside one of the
millions of planetoids that circled the giant star Betelgeuse in a girdling
ring with almost five times the mass of Jupiter. As a source of potential
wealth it dwarfed the entire solar system, and it belonged, more or less,
to the Swarm. At least, no other race had challenged them for it within
the memory of the Investors.

Afriel peered up the corridor. It seemed deserted, and without other
bodies to cast infrared heat, he could not see very far. Kicking against
the wall, he floated hesitantly down the corridor.

He heard a human voice. "Dr. Afriel!"

"Dr. Mirny!" he called out. "This way!"

He first saw a pair of young symbiotes scuttling toward him, the tips
of their clawed feet barely touching the walls. Behind them came a
woman wearing goggles like his own. She was young, and attractive in
the trim, anonymous way of the genetically reshaped.

She screeched something at the symbiotes in their own language,
and they halted, waiting. She coasted forward, and Afriel caught her
arm, expertly stopping their momentum.

"You didn't bring any luggage?" she said anxiously.

He shook his head. "We got your warning before I was sent out. I
have only the clothes I'm wearing and a few items in my pockets."

She looked at him critically. "Is that what people are wearing in the
Rings these days? Things have changed more than I thought."

Afriel glanced at his brocaded coat and laughed. "It's a matter of
policy. The Investors are always readier to talk to a human who looks
ready to do business on a large scale. All the Shapers' representatives
dress like this these days. We've stolen a jump on the Mechanists; they
still dress in those coveralls."

He hesitated, not wanting to offend her. Galina Mirny's intelligence
was rated at almost two hundred. Men and women that bright were
sometimes flighty and unstable, likely to retreat into private fantasy
worlds or become enmeshed in strange and impenetrable webs of plotting and rationalization. High intelligence was the strategy the Shapers
had chosen in the struggle for cultural dominance, and they were
obliged to stick to it, despite its occasional disadvantages. They had
tried breeding the Superbright – those with quotients over two
hundred – but so many had defected from the Shapers' colonies that
the faction had stopped producing them.

"You wonder about my own clothing," Mirny said.

"It certainly has the appeal of novelty," Afriel said with a smile.

"It was woven from the fibers of a pupa's cocoon," she said. "My original wardrobe was eaten by a scavenger symbiote during the troubles last year. I usually go nude, bnt I didn't want to offend you by too great a show of intimacy."

Afriel shrugged. "I often go nude myself, I never had much use for clothes except for pockets. I have a few tools on my person, but most are of little importance. We're Shapers, our tools are here." He tapped his head. "If you can show me a safe place to put my clothes . . ."

She shook her head. It was impossible to see her eyes for the goggles, which made her expression hard to read. "You've made your first mistake, Doctor. There are no places of our own here. It was the same mistake the Mechanist agents made, the same one that almost killed me as well. There is no concept of privacy or property here. This is the Nest. If you seize any part of it for yourself – to store equipment, to sleep in, whatever – then you become an intruder, an enemy. The two Mechanists – a man and a woman – tried to secure an empty chamber for their computer lab. Warriors broke down their door and devoured them. Scavengers ate their equipment, glass, metal, and all."

Afriel smiled coldly. "It must have cost them a fortune to ship all that material here."

Mirny shrugged. "They're wealthier than we are. Their machines, their mining. They meant to kill me, I think. Surreptitiously, so the warriors wouldn't be upset by a show of violence. They had a computer that was learning the language of the springtails faster than I could."

"But you survived," Afriel pointed out. "And your tapes and reports – especially the early ones, when you still had most of your equipment – were of tremendous interest. The Council is behind you all the way. You've become quite a celebrity in the Rings, during your absence."

"Yes, I expected as much," she said. —

Afriel was nonplused. "If I found any deficiency in them," he said carefully, "it was in my own field, alien linguistics." He waved vaguely at the two symbiotes who accompanied her. "I assume you've made great progress in communicating with the symbiotes, since they seem to do all the talking for the Nest."

She looked at him with an unreadable expression and shrugged. "There are at least fifteen different kinds of symbiotes here. Those that accompany me are called the springtails, and they speak only for themselves. They are savages, Doctor, who received attention from the Investors only because they can still talk. They were a spacefaring race once, but they've forgotten it. They discovered the Nest and they were absorbed, they became parasites." She tapped one of them on the head. "I tamed these two because I learned to steal and beg food better than they can. They stay with me now and protect me from the larger ones. They are jealous, you know. They have only been with the Nest for perhaps ten thousand years and are still uncertain of their position. They still think, and wonder sometimes. After ten thousand years there is still a little of that left to them."

"Savages," Afriel said. "I can well believe that. One of them bit me while I was still aboard the starship. He left a lot to be desired as an ambassador."

"Yes, I warned him you were coming," said Mirny. "He didn't much like the idea, but I was able to bribe him with food . . . I hope he didn't hurt you badly."

"A scratch," Afriel said. "I assume there's no chance of infection."

"I doubt it very much. Unless you brought your own bacteria with you."

"Hardly likely," Afriel said, offended. "I have no bacteria. And I wouldn't have brought microorganisms to an alien culture anyway."

Mirny looked away. "I thought you might have some of the special genetically altered ones . . . I think we can go now. The springtail will have spread your scent by mouth-touching in the subsidiary chamber, ahead of us. It will be spread throughout the Nest in a few hours. Once it reaches the Queen, it will spread very quickly."

She jammed her feet against the hard shell of one of the young springtails and launched herself down the hall. Afriel followed her. The air was warm and he was beginning to sweat under his elaborate clothing, but his antiseptic sweat was odorless.

They exited into a vast chamber dug from the living rock. It was arched and oblong, eighty meters long and about twenty in diameter. It swarmed with members of the Nest.

There were hundreds of them. Most of them were workers, eight-legged and furred, the size of Great Danes. Here and there were members of the warrior caste, horse-sized furry monsters with heavy fanged heads the size and shape of overstuffed chairs.

A few meters away, two workers were carrying a member of the sensor caste, a being whose immense flattened head was attached to an atrophied body that was mostly lungs. The sensor had great platelike eyes, and its furred chitin sprouted long coiled antennae that twitched feebly as the workers bore it along. The workers clung to the hollowed rock of the chamber walls with hooked and suckered feet.

A paddle-limbed monster with a hairless, faceless head came sculling past them, through the warm reeking air. The front of its head was a nightmare of sharp grinding jaws and blunt armored acid spouts. "A tunneler," Mirny said. "It can take us deeper into the Nest – come with me." She launched herself toward it and took a handhold on its furry, segmented back. Afriel followed her, joined by the two immature spring-tails, who clung to the thing's hide with their forelimbs. Afriel shuddered at the warm, greasy feel of its rank, damp fur. It continued to scull through the air, its eight fringed paddle feet catching the air like wings.

"There must be thousands of them," Afriel said.

"I said a hundred thousand in my last report, but that was before I had fully explored the Nest. Even now there are long stretches I haven't seen. They must number close to a quarter of a million. This asteroid is about the size of the Mechanists' biggest base – Ceres. It still has rich veins of carbonaceous material. It's far from mined out."

Afriel closed his eyes. If he was to lose his goggles, he would have to feel his way, blind, through these teeming, twitching, wriggling thousands. "The population's still expanding, then?"

"Definitely," she said. "In fact, the colony will launch a mating swarm soon. There are three dozen male and female alates in the chambers near the Queen. Once they're launched, they'll mate and start new Nests. I'll take you to see them presently." She hesitated. "We're entering one of the fungal gardens now."

One of the young springtails quietly shifted position. Grabbing the tunneler's fur with its forelimbs, it began to gnaw on the cuff of Afriel's pants. Afriel kicked it soundly, and it jerked back, retracting its eyestalks.

When he looked up again, he saw that had entered a second chamber, much larger than the first. The walls around, overhead, and below were buried under an explosive profusion of fungus. The most common types were swollen barrel-like domes, multibranched massed thickets, and spaghetti-like tangled extrusions that moved very slightly in the faint and odorous breeze. Some of the barrels were surrounded by dim mists of exhaled spores.

"You see those caked-up piles beneath the fungus, its growth medium?" Mirny said.

"Yes."

"I'm not sure whether it is a plant form or just some kind of complex biochemical sludge," she said. "The point is that it grows in sunlight, on the outside of the asteroid. A food source that grows in naked space! Imagine what that would be worth, back in the Rings."

"There aren't words for its value," Afriel said.

"It's inedible by itself," she said. "I tried to eat a very small piece of it once. It was like trying to eat plastic."

"Have you eaten well, generally speaking?"

"Yes. Our biochemistry is quite similar to the Swarm's. The fungus itself is perfectly edible. The regurgitate is more nourishing, though. Internal fermentation in the worker hindgut adds to its nutritional value."

Afriel stared. "You grow used to it," Mirny said. "Later I'll teach you how to solicit food from the workers. It's a simple matter of reflex tapping – it's not controlled by pheromones, like most of their behavior." She brushed a long lock of clumped and dirty hair from the side of her face. "I hope the pheromonal samples I sent back were worth the cost of transportation."

"Oh, yes," said Afriel. "The chemistry of them was fascinating. We managed to synthesize most of the compounds. I was part of the research team myself." He hesitated. How far did he dare trust her? She had not been told about the experiment he and his superiors had planned. As far as Mirny knew, he was a simple, peaceful researcher, like herself. The Shapers' scientific community was suspicious of the minority involved in military work and espionage.

As an investment in the future, the Shapers had sent researchers of each of the nineteen alien races described to them by the Investors. This had cost the Shaper economy many gigawatts of precious energy and tons of rare metals and isotopes. In most cases, only two or three researchers could be sent; in seven cases, only one. For the Swarm, Galina Mirny had been chosen. She had gone peacefully, trusting in her intelligence and her good intentions to keep her alive and sane. Those who had sent her had not known whether her findings would be of any use or importance. They had only known that it was imperative that she be sent, even alone, even ill-equipped, before some other faction sent their own people and possibly discovered some technique or fact of overwhelming importance. And Dr. Mirny had indeed discovered such a situation. It had made her mission into a matter of Ring security. That was why Afriel had come.

"You synthesized the compounds?" she said. "Why?"

Afriel smiled disarmingly. "Just to prove to ourselves that we could do it, perhaps."

She shook her head. "No mind-games, Dr. Afriel, please. I came this far partly to escape from such things. Tell me the truth."

Afriel stared at her, regretting that the goggles meant he could not meet her eyes. "Very well," he said. "You should know, then, that I have been ordered by the Ring Council to carry out an experiment that may endanger both our lives."

Mirny was silent for a moment. "You're from Security, then?"

"My rank is captain."

"I knew it . . . I knew it when those two Mechanists arrived. They were so polite, and so suspicious – I think they would have killed me at once if they hadn't hoped to bribe or torture some secret out of me. They scared the life out of me, Captain Afriel . . . You scare me, too."

"We live in a frightening world, Doctor. It's a matter of faction security."

"Everything's a matter of faction security with your lot," she said. "I shouldn't take you any farther, or show you anything more. This Nest, these creatures – they're not *intelligent*, Captain. They can't think, they can't learn. They're innocent, primordially innocent. They have no knowledge of good and evil. They have no knowledge of *anything*. The last thing they need is to become pawns in a power struggle within some other race, light-years away."

The tunneler had turned into an exit from the fungal chambers and was paddling slowly along in the warm darkness. A group of creatures like gray, flattened basketballs floated by from the opposite direction. One of them settled on Afriel's sleeve, clinging with frail whiplike tentacles. Afriel brushed it gently away, and it broke loose, emitting a stream of foul reddish droplets.

"Naturally I agree with you in principle, Doctor," Afriel said smoothly. "But consider these Mechanists. Some of their extreme factions are already more than half machine. Do you expect humanitarian motives from them? They're cold, Doctor – cold and soulless creatures who can cut a living man or woman to bits and never feel their pain. Most of the other factions hate us. They call us racist supermen. Would you rather that one of these cults do what we must do, and use the results against us?"

"This is double-talk." She looked away. All around them workers laden down with fungus, their jaws full and guts stuffed with it, were spreading out into the Nest, scuttling alongside them or disappearing into branch tunnels departing in every direction, including straight up and straight down. Afriel saw a creature much like a worker, but with only six legs, scuttle past in the opposite direction, overhead. It was a parasite mimic. How long, he wondered, did it take a creature to evolve to look like that?

"It's no wonder that we've had so many defectors, back in the

Rings," she said sadly. "If humanity is so stupid as to work itself into a corner like you describe, then it's better to have nothing to do with them. Better to live alone. Better not to help the madness spread."

"That kind of talk will only get us killed," Afriel said. "We owe an allegiance to the faction that produced us."

"Tell me truly, Captain," she said. "Haven't you ever felt the urge to leave everything – everyone – all your duties and constraints, and just go somewhere to think it all out? Your whole world, and your part in it? We're trained so hard, from childhood, and so much is demanded from us. Don't you think it's made us lose sight of our goals, somehow?"

"We live in space," Afriel said flatly. "Space is an unnatural environment, and it takes an unnatural effort from unnatural people to prosper there. Our minds are our tools, and philosophy has to come second. Naturally I've felt those urges you mention. They're just another threat to guard against. I believe in an ordered society. Technology has unleashed tremendous forces that are ripping society apart. Some one faction must arise from the struggle and integrate things. We Shapers have the wisdom and restraint to do it humanely. That's why I do the work I do." He hesitated. "I don't expect to see our day of triumph. I expect to die in some brush-fire conflict, or through assassination. It's enough that I can foresee that day."

"But the arrogance of it, Captain!" she said suddenly. "The arrogance of your little life and its little sacrifice! Consider the Swarm, if you really want your humane and perfect order. Here it is! Where it's always warm and dark, and it smells good, and food is easy to get, and everything is endlessly and perfectly recycled. The only resources that are ever lost are the bodies of the mating swarms, and a little air. A Nest like this one could last unchanged for hundreds of thousands of years Hundreds . . . of thousands . . . of years. Who, or what, will remember us and our stupid faction in even a thousand years?"

Afriel shook his head. "That's not a valid comparison. There is no such long view for us. In another thousand years we'll be machines, or gods." He felt the top of his head; his velvet cap was gone. No doubt something was eating it by now.

The tunneler took them deeper into the asteroid's honeycombed free-fall maze. They saw the pupal chambers, where pallid larvae twitched in swaddled silk; the main fungal gardens; the graveyard pits, where winged workers beat ceaselessly at the soupy air, feverishly hot from the heat of decomposition. Corrosive black fungus ate the bodies of the dead into coarse black powder, carried off by blackened workers themselves three-quarters dead.

Later they left the tunneler and floated on by themselves. The woman moved with the ease of long habit; Afriel followed her, colliding bruisingly with squeaking workers. There were thousands of them, clinging to ceiling, walls, and floor, clustering and scurrying at every conceivable angle.

Later still they visited the chamber of the winged princes and princesses, an echoing round vault where creatures forty meters long hung crooked-legged in midair. Their bodies were segmented and metallic, with organic rocket nozzles on their thoraxes, where wings might have been. Folded along their sleek backs were radar antennae on long sweeping booms. They looked more like interplanetary probes under construction than anything biological. Workers fed them ceaselessly. Their bulging spiracled abdomens were full of compressed oxygen.

Mirny begged a large chunk of fungus from a passing worker, deftly tapping its antennae and provoking a reflex action. She handed most of the fungus to the two springtails, who devoured it greedily and looked expectantly for more.

Afriel tucked his legs into a free-fall lotus position and began chewing with determination on the leathery fungus. It was tough, but tasted good, like smoked meat – a delicacy he had tasted only once. The smell of smoke meant disaster in a Shaper's colony.

Mirny maintained a stony silence. "Food's no problem," Afriel said. "Where do we sleep?"

She shrugged. "Anywhere . . . there are unused niches and tunnels here and there. I suppose you'll want to see the Queen's chamber next."

"By all means."

"I'll have to get more fungus. The warriors are on guard there and have to be bribed with food."

She gathered an armful of fungus from another worker in the endless stream, and they moved on. Afriel, already totally lost, was further confused in the maze of chambers and tunnels. At last they exited into an immense lightless cavern, bright with infrared heat from the Queen's monstrous body. It was the colony's central factory. The fact that it was made of warm and pulpy flesh did not conceal its essentially industrial nature. Tons of predigested fungal pap went into the slick blind jaws at one end. The rounded billows of soft flesh digested and processed it, squirming, sucking, and undulating, with loud machine-like churnings and gurglings. Out of the other end came an endless conveyor-like blobbed stream of eggs, each one packed in a thick hormonal paste of lubrication. The workers avidly licked the eggs clean and bore them off to nurseries. Each egg was the size of a man's torso.

The process went on and on. There was no day or night here in the lightless center of the asteroid. There was no remnant of a diurnal rhythm in the genes of these creatures. The flow of production was as constant and even as the working of an automated mine.

"This is why I'm here," Afriel murmured in awe. "Just look at this, Doctor. The Mechanists have cybernetic mining machinery that is generations ahead of ours. But here – in the bowels of this nameless little world – is a genetic technology that feeds itself, maintains itself, runs itself, efficiently, endlessly, mindlessly. It's the perfect organic tool. The faction that could use these tireless workers could make itself an industrial titan. And our knowledge of biochemistry is unsurpassed. We Shapers are just the ones to do it."

"How do you propose to do that?" Mirny asked with open skepticism. "You would have to ship a fertilized queen all the way to the solar system. We could scarcely afford that, even if the Investors would let us, which they wouldn't."

"I don't need an entire Nest," Afriel said patiently. "I only need the genetic information from one egg. Our laboratories back in the Rings could clone endless numbers of workers."

"But the workers are useless without the Nest's pheromones. They need chemical cues to trigger their behavior modes."

"Exactly," Afriel said. "As it so happens, I possess those pheromones, synthesized and concentrated. What I must do now is test them. I must prove that I can use them to make the workers do what I choose. Once I've proven it's possible, I'm authorized to smuggle the genetic information necessary back to the Rings. The Investors won't approve. There are, of course, moral questions involved, and the Investors are not genetically advanced. But we can win their approval back with the profits we make. Best of all, we can beat the Mechanists at their own game."

"You've carried the pheromones here?" Mirny said. "Didn't the Investors suspect something when they found them?"

"Now it's you who has made an error," Afriel said calmly. "You assume that the Investors are infallible. You are wrong. A race without curiosity will never explore every possibility, the way we Shapers did." Afriel pulled up his pants cuff and extended his right leg. "Consider this varicose vein along my shin. Circulatory problems of this sort are common among those who spend a lot of time in free-fall. This vein, however, has been blocked artificially and treated to reduce osmosis. Within the vein are ten separate colonies of genetically altered bacteria, each one specially bred to produce a different Swarm pheromone."

He smiled. "The Investors searched me very thoroughly, including X-rays. But the vein appears normal to X-rays, and the bacteria are trapped within compartments in the vein. They are indetectable. I have a small medical kit on my person. It includes a syringe. We can use it to extract the pheromones and test them. When the tests are finished – and I feel sure they will be successful, in fact I've staked my career on it – we can empty the vein and all its compartments. The bacteria will die on contact with air. We can refill the vein with the yolk from a developing embryo. The cells may survive during the trip back, but even if they die, they can't rot inside my body. They'll never come in contact with any agent of decay. Back in the Rings, we can learn to activate and suppress different genes to produce the different castes, just as is done in nature. We'll have millions of workers, armies of warriors if need be, perhaps even organic rocketships, grown from altered alates. If this works, who do you think will remember me then, eh? Me and my arrogant little life and little sacrifice?"

She stared at him; even the bulky goggles could not hide her new respect and even fear. "You really mean to do it, then."

"I made the sacrifice of my time and energy. I expect results, Doctor."

"But it's kidnapping. You're talking about breeding a slave race."

Afriel shrugged, with contempt. "You're juggling words, Doctor. I'll cause this colony no harm. I may steal some of its workers' labor while they obey my own chemical orders, but that tiny theft won't be missed. I admit to the murder of one egg, but that is no more a crime than a human abortion. Can the theft of one strand of genetic material be called 'kidnapping'? I think not. As for the scandalous idea of a slave race – I reject it out of hand. These creatures are genetic robots. They will no more be slaves than are laser drills or cargo tankers. At the very worst, they will be our domestic animals."

Mirny considered the issue. It did not take her long. "It's true. It's not as if a common worker will be staring at the stars, pining for its freedom. They're just brainless neuters."

"Exactly, Doctor."

"They simply work. Whether they work for us or the Swarm makes no difference to them."

"I see that you've seized on the beauty of the idea."

"And if it worked," Mirny said, "if it worked, our faction would profit astronomically."

Afriel smiled genuinely, unaware of the chilling sarcasm of his expression. "And the personal profit, Doctor . . . the valuable expertise of the first to exploit the technique." He spoke gently, quietly. "Ever see a nitrogen snowfall on Titan? I think a habitat of one's own there – larger, much larger than anything possible before . . . A genuine city, Galina, a place where a man can scrap the rules and discipline that madden him . . ."

"Now it's you who are talking defection, Captain-Doctor."

Afriel was silent for a moment, then smiled with an effort. "Now you've ruined my perfect reverie," he said. "Besides, what I was describing was the well-earned retirement of a wealthy man, not some self-indulgent hermitage . . . There's a clear difference." He hesitated. "In any case, may I conclude that you're with me in this project?"

She laughed and touched his arm. There was something uncanny about the small sound of her laugh, drowned by a great organic rumble from the Queen's monstrous intestines Do you expect me to resist your arguments for two long years? Better that I give in now and save us friction."

"Yes."

"After all, you won't do any harm to the Nest. They'll never know anything has happened. And if their genetic line is successfully reproduced back home, there'll never be any reason for humanity to bother them again."

"True enough," said Afriel, though in the back of his mind he instantly thought of the fabulous wealth of Betelgeuse's asteroid system. A day would come, inevitably, when humanity would move to the stars en masse, in earnest. It would be well to know the ins and outs of every race that might become a rival.

"I'll help you as best I can," she said. There was a moment's silence. "Have you seen enough of this area?"

"Yes." They left the Queen's chamber.

"I didn't think I'd like you at first," she said candidly. "I think I like you better now. You seem to have a sense of humor that most Security people lack."

"It's not a sense of humor," Afriel said sadly. "It's a sense of irony disguised as one."

There were no days in the unending stream of hours that followed. There were only ragged periods of sleep, apart at first, later together, as they held each other in free-fall. The sexual feel of skin and body became an anchor to their common humanity, a divided, frayed humanity so many light-years away that the concept no longer had any meaning. Life in the warm and swarming tunnels was the here and now; the two of them were like germs in a bloodstream, moving ceaselessly with the pulsing ebb and flow. Hours stretched into months, and time itself grew meaningless.

The pheromonal tests were complex, but not impossibly difficult. The first of the ten pheromones was a simple grouping stimulus, causing large numbers of workers to gather as the chemical was spread from palp to palp. The workers then waited for further instructions; if none were forthcoming, they dispersed. To work effectively, the pheromones had to be given in a mix, or series, like computer commands; number one, grouping, for instance, together with the third pheromone, a transferral order, which caused the workers to empty any given chamber and move its effects to another. The ninth pheromone had the best industrial possibilities; it was a building order, causing the workers to gather tunnelers and dredgers and set them to work. Others were annoying; the tenth pheromone provoked grooming behavior, and the workers' furry palps stripped off the remaining rags of Afriel's clothing. The eighth pheromone sent the workers off to harvest material on the asteroid's surface, and in their eagerness to observe its effects the two explorers were almost trapped and swept off into space.

The two of them no longer feared the warrior caste. They knew that a dose of the sixth pheromone would send them scurrying off to defend the eggs, just as it sent the workers to tend them. Mirny and Afriel took advantage of this and secured their own chambers, dug by chemically hijacked workers and defended by a hijacked airlock guardian. They had their own fungal gardens to refresh the air, stocked with the fungus they liked best, and digested by a worker they kept drugged for their own food use. From constant stuffing and lack of exercise the worker had swollen up into its replete form and hung from one wall like a monstrous grape.

Afriel was tired. He had been without sleep recently for a long time; how long, he didn't know. His body rhythms had not adjusted as well as Mirny's, and he was prone to fits of depression and irritability that he had to repress with an effort. "The Investors will be back sometime," he said. "Sometime soon."

Mirny was indifferent. "The Investors," she said, and followed the remark with something in the language of the springtails, which he didn't catch. Despite his linguistic training, Afriel had never caught up with her in her use of the springtails' grating jargon. His training was almost a liability; the springtail language had decayed so much that it was a pidgin tongue, without rules or regularity. He knew enough to give them simple orders, and with his partial control of the warriors he had the power to back it up. The springtails were afraid of him, and the two juveniles that Mirny had tamed had developed into fat, over-grown tyrants that freely terrorized their elders. Afriel had been too busy to seriously study the springtails or the other symbiotes. There were too many practical matters at hand.

"If they come too soon, I won't be able to finish my latest study," she said in English.

Afriel pulled off his infrared goggles and knotted them tightly around his neck. "There's a limit, Galina," he said, yawning. "You can only memorize so much data without equipment. We'll just have to wait quietly until we can get back. I hope the Investors aren't shocked when they see me. I lost a fortune with those clothes."

"It's been so dull since the mating swarm was launched. If it weren't for the new growth in the alates' chamber, I'd be bored to death." She pushed greasy hair from her face with both hands. "Are you going to sleep?"

"Yes, if I can."

"You won't come with me? I keep telling you that this new growth is important. I think it's a new caste. It's definitely not an alate. It has eyes like an alate, but it's clinging to the wall."

"It's probably not a Swarm member at all, then," he said tiredly, humoring her. "It's probably a parasite, an alate mimic. Go on and see it, if you want to. I'll be here waiting for you."

He heard her leave. Without his infrareds on, the darkness was still not quite total; there was a very faint luminosity from the steaming, growing fungus in the chamber beyond. The stuffed worker replete moved slightly on the wall, rustling and gurgling. He fell asleep.

When he awoke, Mirny had not yet returned. He was not alarmed. First, he visited the original airlock tunnel, where the Investors had first left him. It was irrational – the Investors always fulfilled their contracts – but he feared that they would arrive someday, become impatient, and leave without him. The Investors would have to wait, of course. Mirny could keep them occupied in the short time it would take him to hurry to the nursery and rob a developing egg of its living cells. It was best that the egg be as fresh as possible.

Later he ate. He was munching fungus in one of the anterior chambers when Mirny's two tamed springtails found him. "What do you want?" he asked in their language.

"Food-giver no good," the larger one screeched, waving its forelegs in brainless agitation. "Not work, not sleep."

"Not move," the second one said. It added hopefully, "Eat it now?"

Afriel gave them some of his food. They ate it, seemingly more out of habit than real appetite, which alarmed him. "Take me to her," he told them.

The two springtails scurried off; he followed them easily, adroitly dodging and weaving through the crowds of workers. They led him several miles through the network, to the alates' chamber. There they stopped, confused. "Gone," the large one said.

The chamber was empty. Afriel had never seen it empty before, and it was very unusual for the Swarm to waste so much space. He felt dread. "Follow the food-giver," he said. "Follow the smell."

The springtails snuffled without much enthusiasm along one wall; they knew he had no food and were reluctant to do anything without an immediate reward. At last one of them picked up the scent, or pretended to, and followed it up across the ceiling and into the mouth of a tunnel.

It was hard for Afriel to see much in the abandoned chamber; there was not enough infrared heat. He leaped upward after the springtail.

He heard the roar of a warrior and the springtail's choked-off screech. It came flying from the tunnel's mouth, a spray of clotted fluid bursting from its ruptured head. It tumbled end over end until it hit the far wall with a flaccid crunch. It was already dead.

The second springtail fled at once, screeching with grief and terror. Afriel landed on the lip of the tunnel, sinking into a crouch as his legs soaked up momentum. He could smell the acrid stench of the warrior's anger, a pheromone so thick that even a human could scent it. Dozens of other warriors would group here within minutes, or seconds. Behind the enraged warrior he could hear workers and tunnelers shifting and cementing rock.

He might be able to control one enraged warrior, but never two, or twenty. He launched himself from the chamber wall and out an exit.

He searched for the other springtail – he felt sure he could recognize it, since it was so much bigger than the others – but he could not find it. With its keen sense of smell, it could easily avoid him if it wanted to.

Mirny did not return. Uncountable hours passed. He slept again. He returned to the alates' chamber; there were warriors on guard there, warriors that were not interested in food and brandished their immense serrated fangs when he approached. They looked ready to rip him apart; the faint reek of aggressive pheromones hung about the place like a fog. He did not see any symbiotes of any kind on the warriors' bodies. There was one species, a thing like a huge tick, that clung only to warriors, but even the ticks were gone.

He returned to his chambers to wait and think. Mirny's body was not in the garbage pits. Of course, it was possible that something else might have eaten her. Should he extract the remaining pheromone from the spaces in his vein and try to break into the alates' chamber? He suspected that Mirny, or whatever was left of her, was somewhere in the tunnel where the springtail had been killed. He had never explored that tunnel himself. There were thousands of tunnels he had never explored.

He felt paralyzed by indecision and fear. If he was quiet, if he did nothing, the Investors might arrive at any moment. He could tell the Ring Council anything he wanted about Mirny's death; if he had the genetics with him, no one would quibble. He did not love her; he respected her, but not enough to give up his life, or his faction's investment. He had not thought of the Ring Council in a long time, and the thought sobered him. He would have to explain his decision . . .

He was still in a brown study when he heard a whoosh of air as his living airlock deflated itself. Three warriors had come for him. There was no reek of anger about them. They moved slowly and carefully. He knew better than to try to resist. One of them seized him gently in its massive jaws and carried him off.

It took him to the alates' chamber and into the guarded tunnel. A new, large chamber had been excavated at the end of the tunnel. It was filled almost to bursting by a black-splattered white mass of flesh. In the center of the soft speckled mass were a mouth and two damp, shining eyes, on stalks. Long tendrils like conduits dangled, writhing, from a clumped ridge above the eyes. The tendrils ended in pink, fleshy pluglike clumps.

One of the tendrils had been thrust through Mirny's skull. Her body hung in midair, limp as wax. Her eyes were open, but blind.

Another tendril was plugged into the braincase of a mutated worker. The worker still had the pallid tinge of a larva; it was shrunken and deformed, and its mouth had the wrinkled look of a human mouth. There was a blob like a tongue in the mouth, and white ridges like human teeth. It had no eyes.

It spoke with Mirny's voice. "Captain-Doctor Afriel . . ."

"Galina . . ."

"I have no such name. You may address me as Swarm."

Afriel vomited. The central mass was an immense head. Its brain almost filled the room.

It waited politely until Afriel had finished.

"I find myself awakened again," Swarm said dreamily. "I am pleased to see that there is no major emergency to concern me. Instead it is a threat that has become almost routine." It hesitated delicately. Mirny's body moved slightly in midair; her breathing was inhumanly regular. The eyes opened and closed. "Another young race."

"What are you?"

"I am the Swarm. That is, I am one of its castes. I am a tool, an adaptation; my specialty is intelligence. I am not often needed. It is good to be needed again."

"Have you been here all along? Why didn't you greet us? We'd have dealt with you. We meant no harm."

The wet mouth on the end of the plug made laughing sounds. "Like yourself, I enjoy irony," it said. "It is a pretty trap you have found yourself in, Captain-Doctor. You meant to make the Swarm work for you and your race. You meant to breed us and study us and use us. It is an excellent plan, but one we hit upon long before your race evolved."

Stung by panic, Afriel's mind raced frantically. "You're an intelligent being," he said. "There's no reason to do us any harm. Let us talk together. We can help you."

"Yes," Swarm agreed. "You will be helpful. Your companion's memories tell me that this is one of those uncomfortable periods when galactic intelligence is rife. Intelligence is a great bother. It makes all kinds of trouble for us."

"What do you mean?"

"You are a young race and lay great stock by your own cleverness," Swarm said. "As usual, you fail to see that intelligence is not a survival trait."

Afriel wiped sweat from his face. "We've done well," he said. "We came to you, and peacefully. You didn't come to us."

"I refer to exactly that," Swarm said urbanely. "This urge to expand, to explore, to develop, is just what will make you extinct. You naively suppose that you can continue to feed your curiosity indefinitely. It is an old story, pursued by countless races before you. Within a thousand years – perhaps a little longer – your species will vanish."

"You intend to destroy us, then? I warn you it will not be an easy task – "

"Again you miss the point. Knowledge is power! Do you suppose that fragile little form of yours – your primitive legs, your ludicrous arms and hands, your tiny, scarcely wrinkled brain – can *contain* all that power? Certainly not! Already your race is flying to pieces under the impact of your own expertise. The original human form is becoming obsolete. Your own genes have been altered, and you, Captain-Doctor, are a crude experiment. In a hundred years you will be a relic. In a thousand years you will not even be a memory. Your race will go the same way as a thousand others."

"And what way is that?"

"I do not know." The thing on the end of the Swarm's arm made a chuckling sound. "They have passed beyond my ken. They have all discovered something, learned something, that has caused them to transcend my understanding. It may be that they even transcend *being*. At any rate, I cannot sense their presence anywhere. They seem to do nothing, they seem to interfere in nothing; for all intents and purposes, they seem to be dead. Vanished. They may have become gods, or ghosts. In either case, I have no wish to join them."

"So then – so then you have – "

"Intelligence is very much a two-edged sword, Captain-Doctor. It is useful only up to a point. It interferes with the business of living. Life, and intelligence, do not mix very well. They are not at all closely related, as you childishly assume."

"But you, then – you are a rational being – "

"I am a tool, as I said." The mutated device on the end of its arm made a sighing noise. "When you began your pheromonal experiments, the chemical imbalance became apparent to the Queen. It triggered certain genetic patterns within her body, and I was reborn. Chemical sabotage is a problem that can best be dealt with by intelligence. I am a brain replete, you see, specially designed to be far more intelligent than any young race. Within three days I was fully self-conscious. Within five days I had deciphered these markings on my body. They are the genetically encoded history of my race . . . within five days and two hours I recognized the problem at hand and knew what to do. I am now doing it. I am six days old."

"What is it you intend to do?"

"Your race is a very vigorous one. I expect it to be here, competing with us, within five hundred years. Perhaps much sooner. It will be necessary to make a thorough study of such a rival. I invite you to join our community on a permanent basis."

"What do you mean?"

"I invite you to become a symbiote. I have here a male and a female, whose genes are altered and therefore without defects. You make a perfect breeding pair. It will save me a great deal of trouble with cloning."

"You think I'll betray my race and deliver a slave species into your hands?"

"Your choice is simple, Captain-Doctor. Remain an intelligent, living being, or become a mindless puppet, like your partner. I have taken over all the functions of her nervous system; I can do the same to you."

"I can kill myself."

"That might be troublesome, because it would make me resort to developing a cloning technology. Technology, though I am capable of it, is painful to me. I am a genetic artifact; there are fail-safes within me that prevent me from taking over the Nest for my own uses. That would mean falling into the same trap of progress as other intelligent races. For similar reasons, my life span is limited. I will live for only a thousand years, until your race's brief flurry of energy is over and peace resumes once more."

"Only a thousand years?" Afriel laughed bitterly. "What then? You kill off my descendants, I assume, having no further use for them."

"No. We have not killed any of the fifteen other races we have taken for defensive study. It has not been necessary. Consider that small scavenger floating by your head, Captain-Doctor, that is feeding on your vomit. Five hundred million years ago its ancestors made the galaxy tremble. When they attacked us, we unleashed their own kind upon them. Of course, we altered our side, so that they were smarter, tougher, and, naturally, totally loyal to us. Our Nests were the only world they knew, and they fought with a valor and inventiveness we never could have matched. . Should your race arrive to exploit us, we will naturally do the same."

"We humans are different."

"Of course."

"A thousand years here won't change us. You will die and our descendants will take over this Nest. We'll be running things, despite you, in a few generations. The darkness won't make any difference."

"Certainly not. You don't need eyes here. You don't need anything."

"You'll allow me to stay alive? To teach them anything I want?"

"Certainly, Captain-Doctor. We are doing you a favor, in all truth. In a thousand years your descendants here will be the only remnants of the human race. We are generous with our immortality; we will take it upon ourselves to preserve you."

"You're wrong, Swarm. You're wrong about intelligence, and you're wrong about everything else. Maybe other races would crumble into parasitism, but we humans are different."

"Certainly. You'll do it, then?"

"Yes. I accept your challenge. And I will defeat you."

"Splendid. When the Investors return here, the springtails will say that they have killed you, and will tell them to never return. They will not return. The humans should be the next to arrive."

"If I don't defeat you, they will."

"Perhaps." Again it sighed. "I'm glad I don't have to absorb you. I would have missed your conversation."

Other titles available from Robinson

The Mammoth Book of Best New SF 15   Ed. Gardner Dozois   **£9.99** ☐
Now in its fifteenth fabulous year, this annual offering of the best new SF stories includes the work of established masters of the form and young talents. It embraces every aspect of the genre – soft, hard, cyberpunk, cyper noir, anthropological, military and adventure.

The Mammoth Book of Future Cops   **£6.99** ☐
Ed. Maxim Jakubowski & M. Christian
Maxim Jakubowski and M. Christian present their new collection of great future noir writing – haunting and bleak, brutal and heroic, always visionary.

The Mammoth Book of On the Road   **£6.99** ☐
Ed. Maxim Jakubowski & M. Christian
This wideranging collection features journeys along trails carved through dense jungle, or six-lane superhighways, cops and criminals barrelling down midnight boulevards, summer vacation trips gone wildly wrong, sentimental journeys bringing hope or despair, wandering wise men and post-apocolyptic road warriors.

Robinson books are available from all good bookshops or can be ordered direct from the Publisher. Just tick the title you want and fill in the form below.

TBS Direct
Colchester Road, Frating Green, Colchester, Essex CO7 7DW
Tel: +44 (0) 1206 255777
Fax: +44 (0) 1206 255914
Email: sales@tbs-ltd.co.uk

UK/BFPO customers please allow £1.00 for p&p for the first book, plus 50p for the second, plus 30p for each additional book up to a maximum charge of £3.00.

Overseas customers (inc. Ireland), please allow £2.00 for the first book, plus £1.00 for the second, plus 50p for each additional book.

Please send me the titles ticked above.

NAME (block letters)...

ADDRESS..

....

.... POSTCODE...

I enclose a cheque/PO (payable to TBS Direct) for ....

I wish to pay by Switch/Credit card

Number...

Card Expiry Date ....

Switch Issue Number ....